D0464843

A Small Circus

A Small Circus

HANS FALLADA

Translated by MICHAEL HOFMANN

With a Foreword by JENNY WILLIAMS

PENGUIN CLASSICS
an imprint of
PENGUIN BOOKS

PENGUIN CLASSICS

Published by the Penguin Group
Penguin Books Ltd, 80 Strand, London WC2R 0RL, England
Penguin Group (USA) Inc., 375 Hudson Street, New York, New York 10014, USA
Penguin Group (Canada), 90 Eglinton Avenue East, Suite 700, Toronto, Ontario,
Canada M4P 2Y3 (a division of Pearson Canada Inc.)
Penguin Ireland, 25 St Stephen's Green, Dublin 2, Ireland (a division of Penguin Books Ltd)
Penguin Group (Australia), 250 Camberwell Road, Camberwell, Victoria 3124,
Australia (a division of Pearson Australia Group Pty Ltd)
Penguin Books India Pvt Ltd, 11 Community Centre,
Panchsheel Park, New Delhi – 110 017, India
Penguin Group (NZ), 67 Apollo Drive, Rosedale, Auckland 0632, New Zealand
(a division of Pearson New Zealand Ltd)
Penguin Books (South Africa) (Pty) Ltd, 24 Sturdee Avenue,
Rosebank 2196, South Africa

Penguin Books Ltd, Registered Offices: 80 Strand, London WC2R 0RL, England

www.penguin.com

First published in German as *Bauern, Bonzen und Bomben* 1931
This translation first published 2012
1

Copyright © Aufbau-Verlagsgruppe GmbH, Berlin, 1994
Translation and editorial material copyright © Michael Hofmann, 2012
Foreword copyright © Jenny Williams, 2012
All rights reserved

The moral right of the copyright holder and the translator has been asserted

Set in Dante MT
Typeset by Palimpsest Book Production Limited,
Falkirk, Stirlingshire
Printed in Great Britain by Clays Ltd, St Ives plc

ISBN: 978–0–141–19655–8

www.greenpenguin.co.uk

Contents

Foreword

A Small Circus, first published in 1931, is one of the best fictional representations of the forces that brought the Weimar Republic to its knees and paved the way for National Socialism. It also marked the literary breakthrough of Rudolf Ditzen (1893–1947), who wrote under the name of Hans Fallada.

The events depicted in the book are based on the author's experience of the small town of Neumünster in Schleswig-Holstein where he worked on the local newspaper from November 1928 to January 1930. Here he observed at close quarters the inner workings of provincial journalism, the plight of the farmers and the machinations of the town hall. Fallada was present in Neumünster on 1 August 1929, the day of the demonstration depicted in the novel which ended in disarray and attracted nationwide media coverage, and he experienced at first hand the subsequent farmers' boycott of the town. He reported on the inquiry into the demonstration, both for the local press as well as for two national publications.

Fallada announced his intention of writing 'the story of an ailing newspaper in a provincial town' two weeks after the demonstration, and he submitted the manuscript of *A Small Circus* in September 1930. In the interim, German reparations were revised downwards for the second time since the end of the First World War. Under the Young Plan, Germany agreed to pay 120,000 million gold marks over a period of fifty-nine years, a significant reduction but still a considerable burden on the country, which was also shaken to its core by the Wall Street crash of October 1929. By the time *A Small Circus* appeared in March 1931, the first democracy in German history, which is portrayed in the novel as fatally flawed, had practically ceased to exist. The chancellor, Heinrich Brüning, no longer commanded a parliamentary majority and was reduced to ruling by a series of emergency decrees.

The economic crisis had a particularly adverse effect on the farming community of Schleswig-Holstein. These were not large landowners or tenant farmers but small, independent farmers who owned their land and whose families had been farming for generations. They concentrated on growing vegetables and on animal husbandry, borrowing money in the spring to buy young animals and selling them on later in the year. Not only did the demand for their meat, butter, milk and vegetables drop significantly as a result of the economic crisis, they were also unable to sell their animals and thus repay their debts. In addition, a succession of government austerity measures increased their tax burden significantly. The scene in Part I of the novel, which depicts the arrival of bailiffs to impound a farmer's animals, was one that became increasingly common in the course of 1928 and 1929. The farmers banded together to form the 'Landvolk', a loosely structured grouping that organized mass meetings, largely peaceful protests, as well as civil disobedience campaigns. The farmers were not political activists. Indeed their political naivety made their organization vulnerable to infiltration by agitators, such as Henning and Padberg in *A Small Circus*, whose only interest in the farmers was the potential for stirring up opposition to the democratic institutions of the Weimar Republic. The political consequences of the 'Landvolk' were plain to see in the elections of September 1930 when the National Socialists increased their vote in Schleswig-Holstein from 4 per cent to 27 per cent.

The significance of the 'small circus' in the title of the novel lies in the incident in the Prologue that introduces the theme of dishonest and corrupt practices in the newspaper world. A travelling circus refuses to advertise in the *Chronicle*, claiming, correctly, that the official circulation figures are grossly inflated and that advertising in such a 'fish-and-chip paper' makes no financial sense. The editor of the *Chronicle*, Stuff, takes his revenge by penning a damning review of a performance, which he has not seen. In the course of the novel the newspapers are not content to merely report the news, they play a central role in making it. Newspaper owners, editors and journalists are motivated by greed, self-interest and political prejudice. Gebhardt, who owns both a conservative and a liberal paper and is most anxious to keep his ownership of two competing newspapers secret, has only one goal: to make a profit.

In *A Small Circus* Fallada presents the full range of political parties in Altholm, the fictional representation of Neumünster in the novel. The Social Democrats (SPD), who were instrumental in establishing and defending the first German Republic, are in power at the town hall. Then there are the Democrats, a Left-liberal party, and the Centre, a Catholic party, both also committed to parliamentary democracy. The Reichswirtschaftspartei, representing middle-class business interests, is present too. So is the Volkspartei, a Right-wing, nationalist party, bitterly opposed to the Weimar Republic and determined to reinstate the Hohenzollern monarchy and have the Treaty of Versailles declared null and void. The Communists (KPD) are depicted as following Soviet party policy, for they identify the Social Democrats as their main enemy, which makes any coalition with the Social Democrats against National Socialism impossible. The National Socialists (NSDAP) themselves are on the rise, with their call for strong leadership, their populist, xenophobic programme and bully-boy tactics. Throughout Germany the Nazis took advantage of the economic and political turmoil between 1928 and 1930 to increase their representation in Parliament from fourteen to one hundred and seven.

All these parties are portrayed as corrupt to a greater or lesser degree and their leaders are shown to be motivated by factionalism, self-interest and self-advancement at the expense of others. The SPD apparatchik Temborius is more interested in the smooth running of the party machinery than in issues of policy or principle. Fallada was particularly well placed to comment on the SPD, for he had joined the party himself in 1928. His depiction of the SPD mayor of Altholm, Gareis, owes much to the insights he gained into the workings of the party in Neumünster. This larger-than-life character who makes every effort to promote the common good is not above stooping to dubious means to achieve his (mostly) worthy ends. Indeed, in a novel that is singularly lacking in a hero Gareis comes closest to filling this role. If the novel has a moral it is 'that you can be in a bad way, and do lots of bad things, and remain somehow decent'. The notion of 'decency' ('Anständigkeit') was central to Fallada's personal values and can be traced from its first appearance in *A Small Circus*, where it refers to the importance of maintaining a clear conscience despite doing 'lots of bad things', to *Alone in Berlin*, where it marks a refusal to compromise one's humanity in the face of fascist terror.

A Small Circus introduces the first of Fallada's many 'little men', in the person of the hapless Tredup who ekes out a miserable existence selling advertising space in a Right-wing newspaper with a dwindling circulation in a Social Democratic town. He lives in fear of losing his job and dreams of becoming an editor. As he becomes increasingly mired in the political intrigues of Altholm, Tredup gradually abandons the last vestiges of decency, and manages to return to a decent way of life only when he decides to withdraw into the private sphere. The private idyll as a response to political and economic upheaval was to play a large role in Fallada's next novel, the bestselling *Little Man, What Now?* of 1932.

A particularly striking feature of *A Small Circus* is the use of dialogue, which accounts for almost two-thirds of the novel. Fallada succeeds in not only using direct speech as a vehicle for plot development but also in providing credible and authentic voices for a very wide range of characters. This technique was associated with the New Sobriety (Neue Sachlichkeit) movement in the arts in Germany in the 1920s, which rejected the subjectivity and emotionalism of Expressionism in favour of a more realistic and 'sober' approach.

A key feature of this type of realism was the almost complete disappearance of the author's voice. Contemporary reviews of the novel reflect Fallada's success in performing this act of narrative self-effacement. The Right-wing press praised what they saw as an attack on the hated Weimar Republic, while Communist reviewers welcomed what they read as an attack on the SPD. Since then critics have been undecided whether Fallada was on the side of the farmers or the townspeople or whether he was a neutral observer. He clarified his position in a letter to his brother-in-law on 26 November 1930. Here Fallada agreed with the impression expressed by fellow author Ernst von Salomon after reading the novel that it was about 'poor Germany'. 'That was my aim,' commented Fallada, 'not the impression: poor farmers.'

Jenny Williams, 2012

Dramatis Personae

The Fourth Estate

Stuff, Hermann: editor, local-affairs reporter, film reviewer and sportswriter on the Altholm *Chronicle*.
Wenk: lanky managing editor of the *Chronicle*.
Tredup, Max: chronically hard-up 'advertising manager' of the *Chronicle*, freelance photographer and aspiring writer.
Heinze, Clara (a.k.a. 'Clarabelle' and 'Heinzelmann'): receptionist and typist on the *Chronicle*, and (towards the end of the month) freelance beauty.
Schabbelt: proprietor of the *Chronicle*, negligent husband and hobby inventor.

Heinsius: editor-in-chief of the Right-ish *News* (a Gebhardt paper), oracle, stay-at-home, nationalist and (last and least) belletrist.
Blöcker: reporter on the *News* and a friend of Stuff's.
Pinkus: reporter on the *Volkszeitung*, an SPD-supporting paper.

Gebhardt: ever-acquisitive but enduringly small, the 'little newspaper magnate of Pomerania'.
Trautmann: Gebhardt's business manager and prompter.

Padberg, Heino: writer and editor on the *Bauernschaft*, the farmers' paper (based in Stolpe).

Law and Order

Gareis: Chief Commissioner of Police (also Head of Welfare, Housing and Town Development) for Altholm, and Social Democrat (q.v. Politicians).
Frerksen, Fritz: Police Commander and Social Democrat.
Kallene: Police Superintendent and returned Social Democrat.
Bering, Katzenstein and *Hebel*: Police Inspectors.
Perduzke, Emil: long-time Deputy Inspector and surprisingly good egg.
Maak and *Hart*: Police Sergeants.
also *Maurer, Schmidt, Soldin, Meierfeld, Geier, Erdmann*, lower ranks and constables.

Colonel Senkpiel (q.v. Politicians) and *Lieutenant Wrede* (both militia).

Kalübbe and *Thiel* (q.v. Troublemakers): both bailiffs.

Greve: Prison Director.

Rural Constable Zeddies-Haselhorst.

Detective Inspector Josef Tunk: political section and provocateur (Stolpe) (q.v. Troublemakers).

The Politicians

'Fatty' or *'Red' Gareis*: the big man, Mayor of Altholm (q.v. Law and Order); prodigious walker and conciliator (q.v. Law and Order).
Stein: Gareis's (Jewish) political adviser and close friend.
Piekbusch: Gareis's secretary.
Niederdahl: man of the Right, Gareis's titular superior, the Ober-bürgermeister of Altholm; for the most part a valetudinarian and an absentee.
Town Councillor Geier, Party Secretary Nothmann, Reichstag Member Koffka: all SPD, troika of 'men in dark suits'.

Temborius: District President, quiet-lifer and ineligible bachelor ('the gelding in Stolpe').
Meier: Temborius's (Jewish) chief adviser and quondam emergency treasurer.
Colonel Senkpiel, Government Councillor Schimmel, Revenue Councillor Andersson: Temborius's kitchen cabinet.
Gehl, Klara: Temborius's housekeeper and cook.

(unnamed) the Minister, in Berlin.

The Pillars of the Community

Textil-Braun and *Emil Rag-Meisel*: local businessmen and council members.
Manzow, Franz: local businessman, council leader and ardent paedo-phile.
Revenue Councillor Berg and *Bishop Schwarz*: council members.
Medical Councillor Dr Lienau: council and Stahlhelm member.
Dr Hüppchen: accountant, teetotaller and vegetarian. An incomer.

Toleis: chauffeur and specimen.
also *Rehfelder, Besen, Gropius, Severing, Plosch, Röstel, Hempel*, etc.

The Farmers

Päplow: aggrieved owner of confiscated cattle in Gramzow (not to be confused with Agricultural Councillor Päplow, at Temborius's staged meeting in Stolpe).
Reimers, Franz: Headman of Gramzow and leading figure in the Bauernschaft movement.
Bandekow, Ernst, Count: younger brother to Count Bodo Bandekow, and farmer (Bandekow-Ausbau).
Padberg, Heino: leading figure in the Bauernschaft movement and editor of the newspaper of the same name.
Benthin, 'Cousin', 'Father' or 'Moth-Head': Altholm's only resident farmer: public-speaker and expectant father.
Banz, Albin: dirt-farmer (Stolpermünde-Abbau), paterfamilias and man with a grudge.
Kehding (Karolinenhorst): farmer and writer of letters to the press.
also *Rehder, Rohwer, Feinbube, Henke*, etc.

The Troublemakers

Henning, Georg: 'presently travelling in mineral oils and lubricants' (or is it 'milking-machines and centrifuges'?); flag-designer, flag-waver and all-round dasher.
Thiel: ex-Revenue official, gone over to the farmers' side.
'Bonkers' Gruen: Auxiliary Prison Warden; lost the balance of his mind in the course of a mock-execution by Spartacist troops in November 1918.
Matthies: sword-stealer and Moscow-line Communist.
Farmer Megger: from Meggerkoog ('near Hanover') (q.v. Detective Inspector Josef Tunk, Law and Order).
Padberg, Heino: (q.v. Fourth Estate, q.v. Farmers).
Stuff, Hermann: (q.v. Fourth Estate).
Tredup, Max: (q.v. Fourth Estate).
Gareis: (q.v. Law and Order, q.v. Politicians).
etc., etc.,

Michael Hofmann, 2012

A Small Circus

Prologue:

A Small Circus Called Monte

I

A young man is striding rapidly along the Burstah. As he walks, he darts furious sidelong looks at the shopfronts, which – here on the main street of Altholm – are rather plentiful.

The young man, who is in his mid-twenties, married and quite nice-looking, is wearing a threadbare black coat, a broad-brimmed black felt hat and black-rimmed spectacles. Factor in his pale face too, and ignore the unseemly haste, and he might be an undertaker, with a 'rest in peace' or 'the dear departed' never far from his lips.

The Burstah is Altholm's Broadway, but there's not much of it. At the end of three minutes, the young man has reached the last building on it, on the station square. He spits forcefully, and after this latest manifestation of his mood, disappears into the home of the *Pomeranian Chronicle for Altholm and Environs, news-sheet for every class*.

Behind the dispatch counter sits a bored typist, who hurriedly starts to put away her romance novel. Seeing that it's only advertising manager Tredup in front of her, she doesn't bother.

He tosses a scrap of paper on the counter. 'There! That's all there is. Give it to the setters. – Are the others inside?'

'Where else would they be?' the belle replies, naughtily answering the question with a question. 'Do they need an invoice?'

'Of course they don't need a flaming invoice. Have you ever known any of those monkeys pay for space?! It was all of nine marks. Has the owner come down?'

'The owner has been up inventing since five this morning.'

'God protect him! And his wife? Sozzled?'

'Not sure. Think so. Fritz had to go and get her a bottle of cognac at eight.'

'Then everything's as it should be. – Oh, Jesus, how I hate this place! – Are they in there?'

'You asked me that once already.'

'Oh, don't be like that, Clara, Clarabella, Clarissima. You know I saw you come out of the Grotto at half past midnight.'

'Well, if I'm to live off what he pays me – '

'I know, I know. I wonder if the boss has money.'

'No chance.'

'And what about Wenk – is there any in the cashbox?'

'The Baltic Cinema paid yesterday.'

'So I'll get my advance. He is in there, is he?'

'I think you asked –'

'– you that already. Change the reel, won't you, sweetie. Don't forget the copy.'

'My God. And what if I do.'

II

Tredup pulls back the sliding door to the editorial office, walks in, and slides it shut behind him. The lanky managing editor, Wenk, is sprawled across an armchair, fiddling with his nails. Editor Stuff is scribbling something or other.

Tredup slings his folder on to a shelf, hangs his hat and coat up by the stove, and sits down at his desk. Indifferently, seemingly unaware of the questioning glances coming his way, he pulls out a card index file and begins sorting the cards. Wenk stops trimming his nails, examines the penknife blade in the sunlight, wipes it on the sleeve of his rayon jacket, shuts his knife and looks at Tredup. Stuff carries on writing.

Nothing happens. Wenk pulls one foot off the armrest and asks benevolently: 'Well, Tredup?'

'Herr Tredup, if you don't mind!'

'Well, *Herr* Tredup?'

'I've had it with that bloody "well" of yours.'

Wenk turns to Stuff. 'He's got nothing, I tell you, Stuff. Nothing.'

Stuff shoots a look at Tredup from under his pince-nez, sucks his greying moustache through his teeth, and affirms: 'Of course he's got nothing.'

Tredup jumps up in a rage. The card index file clatters to the ground. 'What do you mean, "of course"? How dare you "of course" me! I've been round to thirty businesses. I can't make them take space, can I? Pull the advertisements out of their noses? If they won't, they won't. I'm reduced to begging them . . . And the scribbler says "of course". Ridiculous!'

'Don't get het up, Tredup. What's the point?'

'Of course I get het up about your "of course". Why don't you try collecting copy? Those monkeys. Those grocers. Those swivel-eyed idiots. "I'm not advertising for the moment" – "I'm not sure about your paper" – "Is the *Chronicle* still going? I thought it had folded long ago." – "Try again tomorrow" – It's sickening.'

Wenk murmurs from the depths of his armchair: 'I ran into the master mechanic on the *News* this morning. They're coming out with five pages of ads today.'

Stuff spits contemptuously. 'Wretched rag. Big deal. Their circulation is fifteen thousand.'

'They have fifteen thousand the way we have seven thousand.'

'Excuse me. We have an audited confirmation of seven thousand.'

'You'd better rub out the spot where the date is. It's completely black from where you've kept your thumb over it for the best part of three years.'

'I don't care about any audited confirmation. But I'd love to give the *News* a black eye.'

'You can't. The boss won't have it.'

'Of course. The boss borrows money from those Charlies, so we need to let them badmouth us.'

Wenk begins again. 'So, you've got nothing, eh, Tredup?'

'An eighth of a page from Braun. For nine marks.'

Stuff groans. 'Nine marks? We've hit rock bottom.'

'And that's it?'

'I could have got the closing-down-sale announcement from the watchmaker who's going bust, but we would have had to take payment in kind.'

'Save us. What would I do with more alarm clocks? I've got one at home, and I'm buggered if I get up for that.'

'What about the Circus Monte?'

Tredup stops his pacing back and forth. 'I told you there wasn't anything, Wenk. Now get off my case.'

'But we carried ads for Monte every year! Did you even try them, Tredup?'

'Let me tell you something, Wenk. Let me tell you something calmly and objectively. If you say anything to me ever again about "even trying" anyone, I'll clock you one –'

'But they bought space from us every year, Tredup!'

'So they did, did they . . . Well, let me tell you something, they won't be doing it this year. And I don't care what you say, and I don't care what the proprietor says, and I don't care what Stuff says, but I'm not going to that effing circus ever again.'

'What happened?'

'What happened? Impertinence happened. I was checked by those wretched gyppos. The day before yesterday they got their advance billing in the News. I slog over there, all the way out to the playground. The circus wasn't even there yet.'

'In that case, their manager must have gone round to the News to give them the copy.'

'And he gave us a miss. Exactly. Yesterday morning, I slogged out there again. They're just setting up. Where's the manager? In the countryside. Plastering cow-villages with posters. As if the farmers were in any mood for a circus just now. Expected back at one. One o'clock is when he likes to have his lunch. So I hang around for an hour. The manager, one of those nasty yellow gypsies, needs to talk to his boss. I'm to come back at six. I'm back at six. He hasn't been able to see his boss yet, why don't I come back this morning?'

'Kudos, and all the way out to the playground each time.'

'That's what I think. So this morning I get to meet the big shot, overlord of one and a half apes, a spavined nag and a moth-eaten camel. Hat in hand, salaam down to the ground.

'And that piece of shit says it's not worth his while advertising in the *Chronicle*! No one reads our fish-and-chip paper!'

'So then what did you say?'

'I wanted to smack him one. Then I thought of my family, and I exercised restraint. After all, my wife wants her housekeeping money on the first of the month.'

Stuff takes off his pince-nez and asks: 'Were those his words? "Fish-and-chip paper"?'

'As sure as I'm sitting here, Stuff.'

And Wenk puts in his tuppenceworth: 'You mustn't let him get away with it. Surely this is a case for Stuff. You should kick sand in his face.'

'I would do too. I would. But the proprietor doesn't want –'

'But it would be a great way to put the frighteners on potential advertisers. If one gets it in the chops, the rest of them will be so scared they'll buy space from sheer dread.'

'But the proprietor –!'

'Ach, never mind the proprietor. We'll all three of us go to him and say something has to be done.'

'Wouldn't I love to stick it to him,' muses Stuff.

'I've got an idea!' cries Tredup. 'You tell him you want to lay into the Socialists, and then he'll leave you Monte as a sop.'

'Not bad at all,' nods Stuff. 'There a story just doing the rounds about the police superintendent . . .'

'Well, what are we waiting for, let's go up to the lab . . .'

'Right now?'

'Of course, right now. You have to trash yesterday's gala opening.'

'All right then, let's go and see the proprietor.'

III

There was some hitch in the compositors' room. Both linotypes were abandoned, and the machine compositors were standing by the window with the job-setters and the maker-up. They were staring out at the yard. There was an unusual feeling of bated breath in the room.

Wenk inquired: 'Is it time for breakfast? What's going on?'

A little reluctantly the cluster of people by the window broke up. The maker-up, with a stricken expression on his creased face, said: 'She's lying outside.'

The other three pushed through the group in front of the window, took a look outside, and then they too didn't know what to say.

It's only a small courtyard, ringed by other buildings, paved with tiles, and with a small patch of green at the centre. Round the thin grass runs a low balustrade, one of those low wrought-iron balustrades that offer no protection. The sort of thing you trip over when it's dark.

It was broad daylight now, and she had still managed to trip over it. She lay there sprawled out on the grass as she had fallen, her black skirt rucked up, exposing black stockings and white undergarments.

'She will have been crossing the yard to get schnapps from Krüger.'

'Fritz took her a bottle at eight o'clock.'

'She's out cold.'

'No, she knows what she's doing, lying there in front of all those windows.'

'Ever since her boy drank himself to death.'

Suddenly everyone is speaking at once. They're all staring out at the black patch of shadow.

Stuff squares his shoulders, puts on his pince-nez. 'This isn't on. Come along, Tredup, we're going to bring her in.'

Wenk watches them go. He asks worriedly: 'I wonder if this is right. The proprietor can see everything from his window.'

The old maker-up hisses: 'There's something you don't understand, Herr Wenk. If he sees his wife in that condition, he's not seeing her.'

Wenk goes off after the other two. Once in the yard, he senses heads being pulled back quickly from windows, wanting not to be caught indulging their curiosity.

Tomorrow the whole town will know. All that money, and the woman's grubbing around in the dirt. Now, if *I* had that sort of money . . .

That's life, thinks the advertising manager. The usual nonsense . . . It's not the son drinking himself to death so much as the fact of everybody *knowing* he drank himself to death . . . Small town.

'Come on, madam. Let's get you sitting up.'

A ravaged face – bloodless, yellow-grey, with hanging jowls – looks stubbornly up at the sun. 'Turn the light off,' she mutters. 'Stuff, turn it out. 'S'night-time.'

'Come along, Frau Schabbelt. We'll have a grog together in the editors' room, and I'll tell some jokes.'

'Swine,' the drunk woman says. 'Do you think I want to listen to jokes?' Then, with sudden animation: 'Yes, go on, tell me jokes. He loves jokes. I can sit by his bed now, he doesn't get cross with me any more.'

And suddenly, getting up, between the two men (Wenk follows after, holding the neck of the cognac bottle disdainfully between finger and thumb), suddenly she seems to be listening to something far away. 'No more jokes please, Herr Stuff. I know my Herbert's dead. But I want to be lying on your sofa with the phone ringing, and the radio reports coming in, and the newspapers coming hot off the presses. That feels a bit like proper life to me.'

There's a sheepish and chaotic return to work in the machinists' room. No one looks up.

'Don't forget my cognac!' the woman suddenly shouts.

On the sofa she gets one more glass, and then she's asleep, mouth open, jaws relaxed, passed out.

'Who's going to stay with her?' asks Stuff. 'Someone has to stay with her.'

'Are you going to see the proprietor now?'

'If you need to ask like that, you stay. Come on, Tredup.'

They go. Wenk watches them go. Looks down at the sleeping woman, listens to the deputation set off, grips the bottle of cognac, and takes a deep pull on it.

IV

The lab is no modern laboratory of glass, bright and clean and airy, it's the grotto of an eccentric inventor drowning in gear, ideas, rubble and filth.

At a table covered with half-eroded linoleum sits a sort of gnome with white stubble, a fat, spherical creature, a red-lacquered dwarf. He has raised his weak, bulbous blue eyes to his visitors. 'You can't talk to me now. Do your stuff by yourselves.'

Stuff says: 'I'm just wanting to piss all over someone, Herr Schabbelt – with your permission.'

The dwarf holds a zinc plate up against the light, checks it anxiously. 'The autotype isn't coming out.'

'Perhaps the grid is too fine, Herr Schabbelt?'

'What do you know about it? Clear off, I said! What's Tredup doing, filthying up the air? Get out! – Maybe it is too fine. You're not stupid, you know, Stuff. You could be right. – Who do you want to piss on?'

'The Socialists.'

'No. Fifty-five per cent of our readers are workers and junior officials. Socialists? No. Even if we are on the Right ourselves.'

'It's a good story, Herr Schabbelt.'

'Well, tell it to me, then, Stuff. Wherever you can find room. But, Tredup, you've got to go, you reek of acquisition.'

'I'm happy to do something else, if that's all right by you,' grumbles Tredup.

'Rubbish! You enjoy your work. Get out!'

'We need him here. Later on, with the story.'

'All right, go and stand in the dark somewhere I can't see you. On you go, Stuff.'

'Do you know Police Superintendent Kallene? Of course you do. After the Revolution he was a Red. Social Democrat, Independent Socialist, whatever – anyway, he got his reward. The stupidest junior policeman got to be superintendent.'

'I know.'

'When he got the job, he left the Party, returned his Party book, became what he had been before, a fervent Nationalist.'

'And . . .?'

'Well, in the evenings he "superintends" the cleaners in the town hall. When the offices are deserted, Herr Schabbelt!'

'And . . .?'

'Well, there are a couple of young women among them, easy on the eye. You can imagine, when they're on their hands and knees scrubbing, you might get the odd eyeful –'

'*You* may imagine that, Stuff.'

'Well, of course, it isn't just Kallene who gets ideas.'

'Get to the point, Stuff. Who caught him?'

'The Red mayor!' cries Stuff. 'Fatty Gareis in person. They were doing it on his desk.'

'And . . .?'

'Now, Herr Schabbelt! What a question! Kallene's got his Party book back.'

'Interesting story,' says Schabbelt. 'But not for us. Maybe the KPD. Tredup can talk it up.'

'Herr Schabbelt!'

'I can't help you, Stuff. You'll have to try and fill your column with local news.'

'But if we're not allowed to shake things up! The paper's losing class. We've been called a fish-and-chip paper.'

'Who by?'

'Isn't that right, Tredup?'

Tredup takes a step forward out of the shadows and affirms: 'Bumf paper, the daily smear, swastika sell-out, shithouse squares. All under exclusion of the public.'

Stuff chimes in: 'Aunt from the cow-village. The bore on all four walls. Fart in a phone-box. Scandal sheet. The weevil. Read it and sleep.'

Tredup again: 'I swear, Herr Schabbelt. Only this morning, a potential advertiser told me –'

The proprietor has gone back to his zinc plates. 'So who is it you want to dump on?'

Both together: 'the Circus Monte.'

And Schabbelt: 'Well, if you must. To put the fear of God into the non-advertisers. And to reward you for the fine grid.'

'Thank you, Herr Schabbelt.'

'That's OK. But leave me alone for the rest of the week. I'm busy.'

'We won't bother you again. Good morning to you.'

V

Stuff is sitting at his desk looking at the still-sleeping woman. Her face has reddened slightly, ice-grey bunches of hair are plastered over her head and hanging down into her face. He thinks: The cognac bottle is almost empty. When I sent Wenk out, he reeked of drink. Now he's even stealing it from his drunk proprietress. I'll get him, see if I don't.

Facing the woman again: I'll make her a coffee, hot and strong, for her to drink when she wakes up. I'll ring for Grete.

He looks at the bell push by the door, and then at the blank paper in front of him on the desk. What good will coffee do? None at all.

He twiddles with the buttons on the radio. A voice speaks up: 'Achtung! Achtung! Achtung! This is the Social Democratic Press service.'

Ah, fuck it! I'll write my column.

He sits down, has a little think, and writes:

Last night, a small circus by the name of Monte opened its tents on our municipal playground, and gave its first performance. The turns were not outstanding in any way, in fact they were barely mediocre. After the shows that our town was privileged to witness lately from the Circus Kreno and the Circus Stern, the items on the Monte bill of fare were pretty wretched, at best good enough to please children.

He reads it back to himself. That'll do for the moment, he thinks. The trainee wanders in. 'I want this set up right away, Fritz. And tell the maker-up to set it as local lead. I'm going to the cop shop now, and then the local assizes. If there's anything to come, I'll phone. All right. – Oh, and tell Grete to make Frau Schabbelt a cup of coffee.'

The boy wanders out. Stuff looks at the sleeping woman, and then at the cognac bottle. He picks it up, and drinks it dry. He shudders.

I'll go out on the piss tonight. A proper bender, he thinks. Intoxicate myself, get far away, forget. The most swinish profession in the world: local editor of a provincial newspaper.

He looks glumly through his pince-nez and pushes off. First the police, then the assizes.

PART I

The Farmers

An Order of Attachment in the Country

At Haselhorst Station two men climb out of the train that goes from Altholm to Stolpe. Both are wearing town clothes, but are carrying raincoats over their arms and have knotty canes in their hands. One of them is dour-looking and in his forties, while his scrawny twenty-year-old companion looks round alertly in all directions. Everything seems to interest him.

They follow the main street through Haselhorst. The roofs of the farmhouses peep through the green everywhere, some reed, some thatch, some tile, some tin. Every farm is its own world, ringed with trees, and careful to turn its narrow side to the main road.

They leave Haselhorst behind them and walk along the rowan-lined avenue towards Gramzow. There are cattle standing at pasture in the meadows, red and white or black and white, idly looking round at the wanderers, slowly chewing.

'It's nice to get out of the office once in a while,' says the young man.

'There was a time I thought that as well,' replies the older one. 'Nothing but figures all the time, it's too much.'

'Figures are easier to deal with than people. More predictable.'

'Herr Kalübbe, do you really think something could happen?'

'Don't talk rot. Of course nothing's going to happen.'

The younger man reaches into his back pocket. 'At least I've got my pistol with me.'

The older man suddenly stops dead, waves his arms furiously, and his face goes purple. 'You idiot, you! You blasted idiot!'

His rage deepens. He throws his hat and coat down on the road, and the briefcase he was carrying under his raincoat.

'All right! Go on! Do your own thing! What insane stupidity! And a hothead like that . . .' He is incapable of going on.

The younger man has turned pale, whether from indignation, anger or shock. But he is at least able to master himself. 'Herr Kalübbe, please, what was it I said to annoy you like that?'

'If I so much as hear the words "At least I've got my pistol with me"! You propose to go among farmers with your pistol? I have a wife and children.'

'But this morning the revenue councillor briefed me about the use of arms.'

Kalübbe is dismissive. 'Oh, him! Sits at his desk all day. Knows nothing but paper. He should come out with me on an actual attachment one day, to Poseritz or Dülmen or, why not, Gramzow, today . . . He would soon stop giving briefings!'

Kalübbe grins sneeringly at the thought of the revenue councillor accompanying him on one of his attachment trips.

Suddenly he laughs. 'Here, let me show you something.' He pulls his pistol out of his own back pocket, aims it at his colleague.

'What are you doing? Put that away!' the younger man shouts, and jumps to the side.

Kalübbe pulls the trigger. 'You see – nothing! It's not loaded. That's what I think of your sort of protection.'

He puts his pistol away. 'And now give me yours.' He pulls the barrel back with a jerk and ejects one bullet after another. The young man picks them up in silence. 'Put them in your waistcoat pocket, and hand them back to the revenue councillor tonight. That's *my* briefing on self-defence, Thiel.'

Thiel has also picked up stick and coat and briefcase, and hands them all silently to his colleague. They walk on. Kalübbe looks across meadows that are yellow with crowfoot, or whitish-rose with cardamine. 'Don't take it amiss, Thiel. Here, shake hands, no hard feelings. – That's right. All of you cooped up in the revenue building, you've got no idea of what it means to be working out here.

'I was pleased when I became a bailiff. Not just for the per diems and travel allowances, which I can really use, with a wife and three little ones. But also for being out here, on a spring day, when everything is green and fresh. Not just stone. You respond to it.

'And now – now you're the most shameful and disgusting blot on the State.'

'Herr Kalübbe, you, who everyone praises so!'

'Yes, them indoors! If a farmer comes to see you, or if ten farmers come to see you, it's the same thing, it's a farmer in town. And if they ever get really insolent, as you term it, then there's plenty of you around. Behind the glass screen. And with a direct line to the police up on the wall.

'But here, where we're walking now, the farmer's been sat for a hundred years, for a thousand years. Here it's us that don't belong. And I'm all alone in their midst, with my briefcase and my blue cuckoo stamp. And I am the State, and if things go well, then I will take with me just an edge of their self-esteem, and the cow out of their byre, and if things are rough, why, then I make them home-less at the end of a thousand years of their occupation.'

'Can they really not pay?'

'Sometimes they can't, and sometimes they won't. And of late they really haven't wanted to. – You see, Thiel, there have always been a few rich farmers, who did really well for themselves, and they don't see why they should be reduced to gnawing on a crust. And they don't run their businesses in a rational way . . .'

'But what do we know about it? It's none of our beeswax. What do we care about the farmers? They hoe their row, we hoe ours. But what bothers me is the way I walk among them dis-honestly, like a hangman from the Middle Ages, who is despised, like a harlot with her parasol on her arm, that they all spit at, and with whom no one will sit down at a table.'

'Hold it! Stop!' calls Thiel, and he grabs his colleague by the sleeve. In the dust is a butterfly, a brown peacock butterfly, with trembling wings. Its antennae are moving gropingly in the sun-shine, in the light, the warmth.

Kalübbe pulls his foot, which was already hovering over the creature, back. Pulls it back and stands still, looking down at the living brown dust.

'Yes, there's that as well, Thiel,' he says in relief. 'God knows you're right. There's that as well. And sometimes you manage to stop your foot in mid-air. – And now I've got one thing I want to ask you.'

'What's that?' says Thiel.

'Just now you showed restraint, and I was the wild one. Maybe we'll swap roles in the course of the day. Then you must remember you will have to endure any insult, any scorn without reply – have to, you hear. A good bailiff doesn't press charges for offensive behaviour or foul and abusive language, he just collects. You must never raise your hand, even if the other guy does. There are always too many witnesses against you. In fact, there are only witnesses against you. Will you remember that? Will you promise me?'

Thiel raises his hand.

'And can you keep your promise?'

'Yes,' says Thiel.

'All right then, we're going to Farmer Päplow in Gramzow to auction off his two oxen.'

II

It's a little before eleven. It's still morning, and the two revenue workers have shaken hands on the road to Gramzow.

The Krug at Gramzow is full to the rafters. All the tables are occupied. The farmers are sitting over beer and grog, and schnapps glasses are in evidence too. But it's almost silent in the public bar, you hardly hear a word spoken. It's as though everyone was straining their ears to listen to the back.

There are more farmers sitting in the back bar, round the table with the crocheted cloth, under the walnut clock. There are seven of them round the table, and an eighth standing by the door. On the sofa with a glass of grog is a lanky fellow with a creased, angular face, cold eyes and thin lips. 'All right,' he says from his sitting position, 'you old-established farmers of Gramzow, you've heard Farmer Päplow's complaint against the decision of the tax office in Altholm. Those who support him raise your hands, those who are against him leave them down in impunity. All do as you think right, only as you think right. – And now, cast your votes.'

Seven hands go up.

The lanky, clean-shaven man gets up off the sofa. 'Open the door, Päplow, so that everyone can hear. I'll announce the decision of the farmers of Gramzow.'

The door swings open, and at the same moment the farmers outside get up. The lanky man asks a white-bearded farmer standing by the front door: 'Are the sentries posted?'

'The sentries are posted, Headman.'

The tall man asks in the direction of the bar and the little weasel of a landlord: 'And are there no womenfolk in the vicinity?'

'No womenfolk, Headman.'

'Then I, District Headman Reimers of Gramzow, announce the decision of the Farmers' League, duly arrived at by their elected representatives:

'The tax office in Altholm has ruled on the 2nd of March against Farmer Päplow, to the effect that he has to pay four hundred and sixty-three marks in back taxes from 1928.

'We have heard what Farmer Päplow has to say about this ruling. He has made it clear that the ruling is based on the average yield of farms in this area. But this average does not pertain to him, because in 1928 he suffered extraordinary losses. He lost two horses from colic. A heifer of his died while calving. He had to move his father out of his house and into the hospital at Altholm, and keep him there for over a year.

'These mitigating factors are known to the tax office, both directly through Farmer Päplow, and indirectly through me, the district headman. The tax office would agree no reduction.

'We, the farmers of Gramzow, declare the ruling of the tax office at Altholm to be null and void because it constitutes an attack on the substance of the farm. We deny the tax office and its masters, the German State, any assistance in this matter, regardless of the consequences for ourselves.

'The confiscation of two well-grazed oxen belonging to Farmer Päplow announced two weeks ago is null and void. Whoever puts in a bid for these oxen at the auction set for today is from that moment forth to be cast out by the Farmers' League. Let him be despised, no one is to come to his assistance, whether he be in financial or physical or spiritual travail. He is to be ostracized, both in Gramzow and the district of Lohstedt in the province of Pomerania, and throughout the State of Prussia, and throughout the length and breadth of the German Reich. No one is to bandy words with him, not even to give him the time of day. Our children are not to speak with his children, nor our wives with his wife. He is to live alone, and die alone. Whoever acts against one of us, acts against all of us. He is already dead.

'Have ye all heard me, farmers of Gramzow?'

'We have heard, Headman.'

'Then to action. I call the meeting closed. Withdraw the sentries.'

The door between the public bar and the back bar is closed again. District Headman Reimers sits down, wipes his brow, and takes a swallow from his glass of grog, now gone cold. Then he looks at his watch. 'Five to eleven. Time for you to be gone, Päplow, otherwise the representative of the tax office can read the protocol to you.'

'Yes, Reimers. But what will happen when they drive my oxen away?'

'They won't drive your oxen away, Päplow.'

'How will you stop them? By violence?'

'No violence. No violence against this State and its administration. I have another idea.'

'If you have another idea . . . But it has to work. I need the money for the oxen.'

'It will work. Tomorrow farmers all over the country will know how we in Gramzow deal with the tax office. Go, and don't worry.'

Farmer Päplow goes out through the back door, crosses the yard, and disappears round the corner. Seven farmers funnel out into the crowded bar.

III

There is some commotion outside the pub: the two tax officials are coming. Each of them has a red ox on a halter.

They have been to Päplow's farm. Some farmhand was there, and let them into the cow-byre, to the attached animals. The farmer and his wife were nowhere to be found, there was no one to whom to present the order to pay. So they led away the two beasts, and brought them to the Krug, to hold the auction as duly announced.

They tether the animals to the post outside the door, and walk into the pub. In the bar there was some murmuring of conversation, perhaps the odd oath, when they saw the men with the two beasts. Now there is silence. But thirty or forty farmers are staring fixedly and expressionlessly at the two officials.

'Is there a Herr Päplow from Gramzow here?' Kalübbe asks into the silence.

No reply.

Kalübbe walks down the middle of the room to the bar. Under so many hostile eyes his walk is clumsy and awkward. He knocks against a stick that is hanging over the back of a chair. It falls to the ground with a clatter. Kalübbe bends down to pick it up, hooks it over the chairback again, and mumbles, 'Excuse me.'

The farmer merely looks at him, and then stares out the window.

Kalübbe says to mine host: 'I am here as you know to hold an auction. Would you set up a table for me here?'

The host growls: 'There's no table here, nor no room for one neither.'

'You know you have to make space for me.'

'How would you want me to do that, sir? Who do I send away? Perhaps you could make some room for yourself? Sir?'

Kalübbe says emphatically: 'You know you are required –'

And the weaselly publican, quickly: 'I know. I know. But give me some advice. Not the law, but some advice I can follow.'

A commanding voice calls through the pub: 'Put up a table outside.'

Suddenly the little landlord is all action and politeness. 'A table outside the door. Of course. What a good idea. From there the animals will be in plain view too.'

The table is brought out. The host in person carries two chairs.

'And now a couple of glasses of beer for ourselves, Landlord.'

The landlord stops, his face creases with worry. He squints at the open windows, at which farmers are sitting. 'Gentlemen, please . . .'

'Two glasses of beer! What's the –?'

The landlord raises his hands imploringly. 'Gentlemen, please don't ask me . . .'

Kalübbe looks over to Thiel, who is looking at the tabletop. 'You see, Thiel!' And to the landlord: 'You *have* to give us two beers. If you don't, and I press charges, you've lost your licence.'

And the landlord, in exactly the same tone: 'And if I do, I've lost my custom. Heads I lose, and tails I lose as well.'

Kalübbe and the landlord look at each other for what seems like a long time.

'Well, let them know inside that the auction's beginning.'

The landlord half bows. 'I think one should try and be decent as long as possible.'

He goes inside. The official takes a protocol and a list of condi tions out of his briefcase and lays them out on the table in front of him. Thiel wants Kalübbe to look at him, so he says: 'I just thought of the pistol. I think I'm learning that weapons don't help.'

Kalübbe, leafing through his protocol, says drily: 'The day's not over. When you're home, you'll have learned more.'

A shadow falls across the table. A young man, dressed in black, with black horn-rims, and the strap of a camera across his shoulder, approaches them, doffing his hat. 'Morning, gentlemen, Tredup's the name, I represent the *Altholm Chronicle*. I've just come from Podejuch, taking photographs of the restored church for our pages. I was cycling by, when I saw there was an auction being held here.'

'The announcement was in your paper.'

'And those are the distrained animals? – You know, one hears

so much about trouble at attachments. Did you experience any
yourselves?'

'Herr Berg is the man to turn to for official information.'

'So you experienced no difficulties? Would you have any objec-
tions if I took pictures of the auction?'

To which Kalübbe, roughly: 'Stop bothering us. We've got no
time for you and your chit-chat.'

Tredup shrugs his shoulders loftily. 'Whatever you say. I'll
take some pictures anyway. – We all have work to do, and yours
doesn't seem to be much to your taste.'

He crosses over to the other side of the village street and starts
setting up his camera.

Kalübbe in turn shrugs his shoulders. 'He's right, basically. It's
his job, and I shouldn't have been rude to him. But I've got a bone
to pick with the *Chronicle*. They're nothing better than blackmailers. Did you happen to catch the review of the Circus Monte
there a couple of days ago?'

'I did. Yes.'

'Bare-faced extortion. The whole town knows that no one
from the *Chronicle* saw the show. The owner wanted to bring
charges against them for damaging his trade, but there's really
no point. Schabbelt has a screw loose, his wife is on the sauce, the
fellow who writes it, Stuff, has his wobbles from time to time . . .
And as for the rest of them . . .'

'My God. Who reads the *Chronicle* anyway? I'm a *News* reader
myself.'

'I wonder what the man will find to write about the auction.
Doesn't seem to be eliciting much interest from anyone.'

They look in the direction of the pub windows. It looks to
them as if the place may have somewhat emptied, even though
there are still plenty of farmers sitting there.

'Will you go over to the doorway and call out that we're about
to begin. And then ask the landlord to see me again, if you will.'

Thiel gets up and goes over to the door. Kalübbe hears him
shout something. Someone else shouts something back. There is
laughter, and then a harsh voice calls for quiet. Thiel comes back.

'What just happened?' Kalübbe asks with equanimity.

'The landlord's on his way. – Oh yes, some joker told me to go home, my mummy wants to wash behind my ears. And then a tall fellow told him to shut up.'

The landlord steps up to the table. 'Yes, gentlemen?'

'Were there any cattle-dealers here this morning?'

'Yes, there were some. Cattle-dealers.'

'Who?'

The landlord hesitates. 'I'm not sure. I don't know their names.'

'Of course you don't. And they've left?'

'Yes, they've left.'

'Thanks. That was all.' The landlord goes away, and Kalübbe says to Thiel: 'I'll give the butcher Storm a shout. I buy meat from him myself. Maybe he'll be brave and buy the animals for a nominal price. I'll give him a good deal.'

'And if he doesn't?'

'My God, then I'll call the office. Berg can decide what to do next.'

Thiel sits and looks at the sunny village street. A couple of hens are pecking for grain in horse-apples, a cat with tail erect is stalking across the nearest farmyard. It could be so lovely here, he thinks. There's everything here, but there's a bad feeling in the air. The man from the *Chronicle* seems to have accepted that the auction won't happen. He's just mooching off. He's still got his camera out, maybe he's found something better to photo-graph. – Stop your mooing, ox. I'm thirsty as well, and I'm not getting anything to drink, even though there's a well in every one of these farms. – Kalübbe is pretty hacked off, but he's putting a good face on it. Farmers are farmers. A thick skin and do your job, and don't think too much. The Middle Ages and hangmen – wonder where that comes from? He must have read about it somewhere. I play skat, and he has his family, and we both have Altholm, so what do we need farmers for? It's pretty here, even though there's something bad in the air . . .

He dozes gently in the noonday sun. The two oxen toss their heads from side to side, and switch their tails to keep off flies.

IV

Kalübbe is standing in front of the table. 'Drop off, did you? Yes, there could be a storm coming. It's a day to curdle milk. – Well, Storm isn't interested. He's afraid of being blacklisted, and then he won't be able to buy meat any more anywhere. Leave him be. My wife will change her butcher.'

'And the revenue councillor?'

'Yes, well, the revenue councillor, our Herr Berg, of course he doesn't get what's happening. He's baffled. But he says he wants to send the farmers a message. We are to drive the oxen to Hasel-horst, and put them on a train to Stettin. Pleasant prospect, eh? I've ordered up a cattle car. So I think we'd best be on our way. The sooner we get there, the sooner we'll get our glass of beer. The station pub will have to serve us.'

'All right then! Let's go. Which one will you take?'

'Leave me the one with the crooked horn. He's a bit of a fidget. If yours gets any ideas, just keep a hold of the rope, and give him one over the muzzle. That'll make him think again.'

They have untethered the beasts from the post, and are about to set off. The pub door opens, and a dozen, two dozen, three dozen farmers emerge into the open. They line up by the roadside and stand there in silence to watch the two men set off.

They drive the oxen along the village street. The beasts are placid. Kalübbe turns to Thiel and remarks: 'How do you like this running a gauntlet?'

'Well, so long as they're happy!'

'Sure they are! – Hey, what's that?'

They're at the end of the village. There's a sharp bend in the road, and the tree-lined avenue to Haselhorst is in front of them. On either side of the road, wide water-filled ditches, and some three hundred yards in front of them, an obstacle, something pale but clearly visible lying across the road.

'What is it?'

'I can't work it out. Are they building some kind of barrier?'

'It looks so bright. Fluffy, almost. Like straw. Well, we'll ignore it. Straight through.'

'What if we can't get by? The ditches are too wide to get across.'

'Well, then we'll wait. Some car or wagon is bound to pass.'

They are reasonably close now, and Thiel says, relieved: 'It's nothing. Someone's dropped a load of straw.'

'Yes, I can see.'

Then, a little closer: 'There's something fishy here. They're not picking it up. In fact, they're leading horses and wagons away!'

'Never mind! We'll get through. Just kick it aside.'

And now they are very close. There are three or four people standing by the straw, which is lying across the whole roadway. One of them bends down, and suddenly there is a flickering here, and another there. A flame dances aloft. Ten flames. A hundred. Smoke, thick white gouts of it, spews up.

The oxen throw back their heads, dig their feet in. Turn violently away.

And suddenly the wind gets into the flames, searing heat beats into their faces, they are standing in a pall of smoke.

'Go! Go! Back to the village!' yells Kalübbe, smacking his steer on the muzzle. The cartilage makes an echoey noise.

Almost side by side, pulled up by the ropes each time they stumble, they are racing to the village.

A hundred yards on, their beasts are walking more calmly. Breathlessly Kalübbe shouts: 'There's nothing for it this time, I'm going to have to write a report!'

'And what do we do now?'

'They won't let us get to Haselhorst. That's pointless. But just to show them, we'll go to Lohstedt by way of Nippmerow, Banz and Eggermühle.'

'But that's ten miles!'

'So what! Do we want to put the oxen back in Päplow's byre?'

'Absolutely not!'

'Well then!'

They are now back at the Krug. There are the farmers, staring at them.

'They've been waiting for us. Well, don't think you're going to get your beasts back. – Drive by as quickly and smoothly as possible!'

All the faces are staring at them. They are young and old, pale blond, doughy, smooth and creased, with grey or black beards, with skin tanned by autumn storms and winter rains. At Thiel and Kalübbe's approach, the farmers break up. Some step across to the other side of the village street, and now, as the two men try to pass them, they all start walking, silently and close to them, like an impromptu escort. Faces lowered or upraised, seeing nothing, sticks in their hands.

They've not finished with us, thinks Kalübbe. This isn't going to go smoothly. I wish I could get nearer to Thiel, to see that he doesn't lose his cool.

But the farmers press him too closely, and now the oxen are almost running, they have the smell of home, of Päplow's byre in their nostrils.

But Kalübbe is paying attention. Just at the moment his ox makes to turn home into the entry, he gives him a resounding thwack on the right horn, and jabs the tip of his stick into the animal's side, and the steer races blindly off, straight along the village street.

That did the trick, thinks Kalübbe in pursuit, surprised that the farmers haven't given up, but are still providing a trotting escort. And there's Thiel coming up alongside him as well. Breathless from running, he whispers to Thiel: 'Don't worry about anything. Keep the rope looped round your wrist. Don't let them steal the animal off you. It rightfully belongs to the State, and we have to get it to Lohstedt, whatever happens.'

The farmers are trotting alongside. They are distracting, and they restrict his vision. Even so! There ahead, across the middle of the road, is the pale straw again.

This time there's no stopping. We have to go through, thinks Kalübbe.

The alarmed beast is rumbling along so fast, Kalübbe can't manage to turn round. He hears the sticks of the farmers raining blows down on his ox, and he shouts, 'Look out, Thiel, we'll cut on to the pasture!'

And there is the fire already. He sees, in bizarrely sharp focus, six or eight faces, and suddenly he spots the man from the *Chronicle* as well, camera in hand, he just manages to catch a farmer lashing out at the camera with his stick . . .

Then the blaze is there, the heat, the choking smoke.

He can't see anything any more. His ox is practically pulling his hand off.

Now he's standing under a tree. He's made it, the road ahead of him is clear, he is breathing hard, through choking lungs.

He looks back. Thick clouds of yellow-white smoke roll over the pastureland. Shadows dart hither and thither.

Where is Thiel?

Then he sees the other steer racing across the grass, leaderless, tail up and head down.

He waits for fifteen minutes, thirty. He can't leave his beast, after all – it belongs to the State. Finally he stops waiting. Thiel will turn up somewhere along the way. The farmers won't hurt him.

Kalübbe takes his ox all the way to Lohstedt.

2

The Hunt for the Photograph

I

It's almost eleven at night. Stuff has just stepped out of the cinema and joined Wenk at his table in Tucher's.

'What'll you have? Just beer? No, that's not enough, I've got flies buzzing round my brain again today. – Franz, I'll have a pint of lager and a short.'

'What was the film like?'

'Load of rubbish. To have to praise something like that, just because the bastards buy space.'

'Well, and what was it?'

'Hokum. Sex. Nudity.'

'I thought you liked that?'

'Get lost, Wenk! What they call sexy these days! Why take anything off? You know it all anyway.'

Stuff drinks. First a schnapps. Then a long pull on his beer. Then another schnapps.

'That's better. I recommend it. It'll improve your mood.'

'I can't. Not allowed to. My nightwatchman gets angry if I smell of strong drink.'

'Oh, your old lady. Must be funny, always the same one. No surprises. Do you still enjoy it?'

'Wrong question. Marriage isn't a matter of enjoyment.'

'That's what I thought. And no surprises either. No, thank you. You know, that's the reason modern female fashions are such crap: you know everything in advance. Those stupid slips! Whereas before, remember baggy white camiknickers!' He loses himself in a reverie.

'Which one's your man?' Wenk butts in.

'My man? What man? Oh, you mean Kalübbe! Over there.

Two tables over. The elderly guy playing skat, putting on weight.'

'I see, so that's Kalübbe,' says Wenk, disappointed. 'I pictured him differently.'

'Pictured him differently? He's fine the way he is. The two fellows playing with him. They must make the revenue councillor very happy.'

'Who are they, then?'

'You must know the one in the grey uniform, surely? Every child knows who that is. No? That's Auxiliary Prison Warden Gruen. They call him Bonkers Gruen because he lost his mind after the privates stood him up against the wall in November 1918.'

'Why?'

'Because he was too hard on them, probably. They wanted to shoot him full of holes, and I don't think it's quite dawned on him yet that he's survived. – You should look at him when the Right wing are waving their black-white-and-red banner, he's incapable of walking past a flag. He pulls off his hat and intones: "You know we never starved under this flag." The children follow him everywhere.'

'And that kind of thing works for the government?'

'Why not? Presumably he's still capable of locking and unlocking doors.'

'All right. And the other man, then?'

'He's the train-driver Thienelt. Senior locomotive driver in the region. The directorship of the railway has been on at him for years to wear uniform. He won't do it. You know why?'

'Nope. Tell me.'

'Very simple. He won't, because then he would have to wear a cap. – You're not smart enough, Wenk. You can hold your drink, but you're not smart. – There's a newfangled eagle on the uniform, and he prefers the old-fashioned design . . .'

'So he won't wear it?'

'He won't wear it. Now they've left him in sole charge of a shunting-engine, but he thinks: I'll stick it for the remaining two years until I draw my pension. His superiors leave him alone, but it's his colleagues. Colleagues are always the worst.'

Pause. Stuff drinks plentifully.

'Maybe Kalübbe will go out and pee, so I can talk to him in private.'

'Do you think he will?'

'If I go about it the right way, he will.'

'You're taking a chance, aren't you?'

'Why? If it gets out, then it was just the drink talking.'

'Hey, Stuff, the young fellow by himself at the corner table keeps staring at you.'

'Well, if he likes what he sees. No, I've no idea who it is. Ex-officer, I'd guess. Presently travelling in mineral oils and lubricants.'

'It looks to me as though he'd like a word with you.'

'Maybe he knows me. – Cheers! Cheers!' Stuff calls out to the unknown young man right across the pub, who raises his own beer glass back.

'So you do know him?'

'No idea. He's after something. Well, let him come.'

'Funny thing, to drink to you like that.'

'What's so funny about it? Maybe he likes my potato nose. Well, I'll have another schnapps first, Kalübbe's sitting tight.'

'Say, Stuff,' Wenk begins again. 'Tredup was complaining about you today. Says you never let him earn any money.'

'Tredup can get knotted. I've not spoken to Tredup for a fortnight.'

'Because of the oxen?'

'The oxen? Does that ox think I'll run his article about the cattle auction just so he can earn his five pfennigs a line?!'

'I think he's short.'

'Listen, we're all short. Let me tell you something, Wenk, all the people who don't have enough money are useless. Tredup is as keen on money as a cat is on catnip.'

'What if his family is going hungry?'

'And that's reason enough for me to alienate everyone by running his stupid report? If I carry something that's *pro* the farmers, then look to your advertising section: Revenue Department, police, government announcements, they'll drop us just like that.'

'But he says he's written a second report *against* the farmers?'

'Well . . .? So I'm to be against the farmers now, am I? Actually, I feel a sneaking sympathy with them. Would I be sitting here otherwise, waiting for Kalübbe, who seems to be intent on keeping his flies buttoned up? – Ah, at last! Speak of the devil . . . See you later!'

And Stuff heavily pads off in pursuit of Kalübbe.

II

Stuff takes up position in the urinals beside Kalübbe, who is staring vacantly at the running water. Stuff says: 'Evening, Kalübbe!'

'Evening! Oh, it's you, Stuff. How's life treating you?'

'Shitty, as ever.'

'Why would it be any other way?'

'Well, there's a thing! Even officialdom is starting to moan!'

'Officialdom? Hardly . . .'

'I thought you were. Whereas if my Schabbelt succeeds in making gold from lettuce he'll shut the paper and I'll be out on my ear.'

'Well. You with your province-wide reputation.'

'Truer of you these days. Since that affair with the oxen –'

'Sorry, Stuff, no time. I've got to get back to my skat game –'

'Of course. – Is it true that the case is due to be heard tomorrow?'

'Could be. – Look, I'm keeping Thienelt and Gruen waiting.'

'And that *you're* supposed to identify the culprits?'

'Skat calls.'

'And that Thiel, your assistant, was summarily sacked?'

'Jesus, if you know everything, what are you doing asking? Evening, Stuff!'

'Do you want to be in on a secret, Kalübbe? You're about to be demoted. But don't breathe a word.'

Kalübbe stares at him silently. The water runs and trickles and gurgles into the conduit. The men stand facing each other.

'Me? Are you talking about me? I'm being demoted? They must have shit for brains! Leave me be with your nonsense. I brought my ox back.'

'That's the reason. You should have put them in the stall of the district headman. That way there would have been tongues wagging.'

'The revenue councillor says I did well.'

'Don't give me the revenue councillor! There's plenty brighter spoons stirring the soup than him.'

'I'm not being demoted.'

'Oh yes, you are. Listen, Kalübbe –'

Three men barge into the pissoir. Kalübbe turns to face the mirror and starts elaborately washing his hands. The three greet Stuff boisterously. He stands by the urinal, and acts all busy, while darting an eye at Kalübbe. Kalübbe who is showing no signs of urgency to leave. Stuff grins to himself.

After some time, the three men go out and leave Stuff and Kalübbe alone again.

Kalübbe says briskly: 'Now listen to me, Stuff. I've thought about it. Maybe I really will get demoted. That's the way they like to do things nowadays. The buck stops anywhere, but only with us junior employees. But that's of no interest to you, and if you breathe so much as a word about it in your bloody *Chronicle* –'

'Not one word. You're being demoted. Small earthquake in Chile. The only question is: Are you planning to take anyone else down with you?'

'Down with me? I see – depends who you mean?'

'Well, those farmers. Tomorrow is the date for the case. If you identify any of them, they'll spend months behind bars.'

'I've got no cause to want to play fair by the farmers.'

'But why be vindictive? Wouldn't you behave just like them if you were being forced off your property?'

'What they did that morning was pretty unconscionable.'

'All right, so you do the bidding of your creepy bosses. You know that revenue councillor of yours will laugh all the way to the bank if he has a few more farmers to lock up. That means another nice round of expropriations.'

'That bastard! Listen, Stuff, what do you think? He tells me on the phone that I've absolutely got to get the oxen to Haselhorst, and then he punishes me because I was only able to get mine as far as Lohstedt. What kind of behaviour is that?'

'That's the way they are nowadays!' Stuff spits into the urinal. 'Are you about to take punishment from them, and name some of the farmers at the same time?'

Kalübbe hesitates. 'It was all over in a flash. If I wasn't able to identify the farmers . . . But there's always Thiel!'

'Let me worry about him! Do you think Thiel will talk? He fell in a ditch, his ox took off, his suit was wrecked, he's bruised and battered and out of a job as of now, because he let his ox run away – do you think he's about to make any identifications? Is he as stupid as that?'

'You tell me.'

'I know what the answer is. Between ourselves: Thiel has got a new job. At a newspaper. But I'm not saying where.'

For a while the two men are silent, then Kalübbe says: 'Well, I think it all happened too quickly. I really couldn't say which farmers I saw in the Krug, and who was doing the straw fire.'

'You see, Kalübbe. And if you're ever fed up with serving orders and things, just send me a postcard . . .'

They turn to leave . . .

III

A voice speaks up behind them: 'Just one moment, gentlemen. That was very interesting.'

In the door to one of the stalls is the young man Stuff raised his glass to just a quarter of an hour back.

'Really. Extraordinarily interesting. – Yes, I was busy in there, gentlemen. I didn't want to interrupt. I think it's about the clearest case of tampering with a witness I've ever experienced personally. Charming.'

He stands in the doorway, the toilet seat behind him, quite needlessly fiddling with his braces. There are a thousand little

wrinkles playing around his eyes, and in the midst of his discom-
fiture, Stuff manages to think: A boy? That son of a bitch is a
thousand years old. Been round the block. What a piece of work.

He growls back: 'Don't get any ideas. You couldn't hear much.
Not with the water going the whole time.'

The young man reaches into his pocket and pulls out a wad of
paper. 'Excuse the material, it's toilet paper. But I do shorthand.
Your conversation struck me as worthy of being recorded.'

'You're lying. That's white paper. Don't think you can fool me.
Let's have a look at it.'

Fat Stuff grabs with extraordinary speed at the left hand of the
youth, which is holding the paper. But like a hammer his right fist
slams against Stuff's arm. Stuff tries a left into the solar plexus of
the youth, who doubles back over the toilet seat.

Stuff grunts: 'Come on, Kalübbe, we have to get hold of the
paper!'

And the youth, completely calm, now standing on top of the
loo seat: 'Very droll, gentlemen –'

The toilet door swings open, and a couple of men walk in.
The three combatants take up various casual poses. Kalübbe is
fooling with the soap dispenser. Stuff is leaning against the stall
door, apparently giving advice to the slim young fellow, who is
reaching up into the cistern: 'It must be the float.'

At last the gentlemen are finished. One tries to start a conversation with Stuff, but he cuts him off: 'Leave me alone. I want to
puke in peace!' And the gentleman vanishes.

The door is not yet closed when Stuff undertakes a lightning
attack against one of the youth's legs, grabs it, and with a roar
pulls him off the loo seat. His head in the process hits the wall
not once but several times. He's left lying in a corner, pale and
bloodied, while Stuff tries to force open the hand that is still holding the bunch of papers in its grip.

'You won't do it. It's held the odd grenade neck in its time,
Stuff –'

'I thought you knew me –' Stuff lets him go, and looks at him
appraisingly. Kalübbe, silent, still deathly pale, peers over his
shoulder.

The youth stands up and bows. 'At your service, Henning. Georg Henning. And please excuse my little joke. I'm still a little childish at times.'

'Probably right,' says Stuff. And turning to Kalübbe: 'Don't worry. He won't blab.'

'See, here's my shorthand. And now I'll consign it to the waves. We pull the flush. Never to be seen again.'

'What do you want now?' asks Stuff. 'I don't imagine you forfeited that quite without –?'

'No, no. Of course not. But some other way. Not the way you might imagine. At least not just that. There's a photograph of the straw fire and the panicking oxen.'

'Surely not!'

'There may even be two.'

'Now how could I not know that!?' exclaims Stuff in indignation.

'Wait!' interjects Kalübbe. 'Wait a minute. He's right. How could I have forgotten about that? There was someone from a newspaper, he wanted to take pictures at the auction. Later I saw him again, behind a tree, at the straw fire over towards Haselhorst. And then a third time, just when we were going through the flames . . . A farmer, a fellow with a black beard, was knocking the box out of his hands.'

'And that young man,' says Georg Henning, 'that young man is on the staff of your newspaper, Herr Stuff, and rejoices in the name of Tredup.'

Stuff stares at Henning, before turning to Kalübbe, who nods in affirmation. Stuff lowers his head, reaches into his pocket, plays with his keys. Looks round, starts playing with his watch-chain.

All of them are silent.

'I'll tell you something, gentlemen. I don't know you, Henning, but I know you well enough. I'm in the picture.

'The evening after the distraint of the cattle, Tredup comes up to me in high excitement, he wants to write a piece for me. Half a column. It turns into two columns. You must understand that Tredup doesn't draw a salary from the paper, we pay him a commission on whatever ads he sells. Whereas if he writes for us, he gets five pfennigs a line.

'I say to him: "Tredup, your piece is good, but it's rubbish. I know you're on your uppers, and you have a wife and children, but I'm not taking that piece. I'm going to personally put your piece in the furnace. This is a farmers' matter and a government matter and it's nothing to do with the town of Altholm and the readers of the Altholm *Chronicle*."'

'What did Tredup do? Was he angry?'

'No, the opposite, really. He just said whenever he had anything good I wasn't interested. And he went off. Since then he's not said a word to me, or written me a line, or helped me in any way.'

Henning asks: 'And he didn't mention that he had a picture or pictures?'

'That's just it. Not one word about it.'

'Then he's got something up his sleeve.'

'Or maybe the pictures didn't turn out?'

'He had no cause to keep quiet about that. He wouldn't even have had them developed at that stage!'

Henning says: 'Tomorrow is the court case, and by then we have to know whether there are pictures or not. You, Kalübbe, are in the clear. The train leaves at half past nine. By then you'll have heard about your statement. You, Stuff, will leave now, and we'll rendezvous at the corner of Burstah and Stolper Strasse. Tredup lives at 72 Stolper Strasse. We'll be there by half past midnight. We'll catch him asleep, and it'll be easier to pull the wool over his eyes.'

'What a tactician! – You must have fought? Sure you did.'

'Only the last six months of the war. I wasn't old enough. But I made up for it later, in the Baltic, the Ruhr, Upper Silesia, wherever there was anything going on.'

'It shows. Well, that's all for now!'

And at long last the bathroom is vacated.

IV

'There are hardly any lights left burning on the Stolper Strasse after midnight. The two men approach one another in silence, and head off together.

Stuff asks: 'What happened with Thiel's ox, by the way?'

'Caught and slaughtered.'

'Of course. Keeping it somewhere would have been too risky.'

'Of course. There are always traitors.'

They walk on in silence.

Stuff again: 'I was only at the Front for six months myself. I spent the rest of the four years behind the lines, and not by choice either. It was because I was a qualified typesetter, and they needed them.'

'The Baltic theatre was the best,' the other said pensively. 'My God! Being master in a foreign land! Not having to pay any regard to the civilian population. And the girls!'

'Come off it! Stories like that, and girls!'

'I travel,' said Georg Henning calmly, 'for a Berlin manufacturer of milking machines and centrifuges. There's not a woman that remembers me.'

'Do you not drink?'

'I never get drunk.'

'That's all right then.'

They walk on in silence.

'I don't know what your plan is,' Georg Henning begins this time, 'but I have here a genuine police ID with photograph. And a badge as well.'

He flips back the lapel of his summer coat and reveals a police badge.

'No, that won't work. Tredup will know all the local cops. And if it goes wrong, there'll be a huge fuss. That would be good for later on. I think what we use for now is money.'

'Whatever you say, comrade,' says the lad, and tips his hat. That gives Stuff a nice warm feeling inside. He walks faster, and looks enterprisingly at the low two-storey cottages.

'It's the next corner,' says Henning. 'Facing the back. We just need to climb over the fence.'

'You know what you're about.'

'I've been on his trail for the past five days. But he's cagey. Doesn't go into bars, doesn't drink, doesn't smoke, nothing with girls.'

'He's got no money.'

'Exactly. Those are the hardest cases.'

'Or maybe the easiest.'

'Not him.'

They climb quietly over a fence, cut around a barn, and the little yard, with gardens on two sides of it, is in front of them.

There's a light on in one curtained window. 'That's where he lives. Let's take a look.'

They try to look inside. 'No, nothing? Why is his light still on? Why isn't he asleep yet, it's one in the morning? – Wait a minute. You stand aside, so that he doesn't see you right away. I'm going to knock on the window.'

Stuff knocks softly.

No sooner has the sound died away than a shadow falls across the curtain, as though the man within had been waiting for the knock.

'We're not going to take him by surprise,' murmurs Stuff, and his mate pats him on the shoulder in agreement.

The curtain is pulled aside, the window opens, and a dark head asks quietly: 'Yes? Who is it?'

'It's me, Stuff. Can I talk to you, Tredup?'

'No reason why not. If it's not too humble for you inside. Come in, I'll open the door.'

The window closes, and the curtain is pushed across again.

'Do you want me to come in with you?' asks Henning.

'Of course. He's not someone you stand on ceremony with.'

The door on to the yard opens quietly. Tredup stands in the doorway. 'Come on in, Stuff. Oh, there's two of you? Well, welcome, the pair of you.'

It's not a big room that they enter from the yard. On a dresser is a shaded paraffin lamp, lighting piles of envelopes, an address book, ink and a pen. Along the walls are two beds, with shapes in them. Deep, rhythmic breathing.

'You can talk softly here. The children have a sound sleep, and my wife never hears anything that's not meant for her ears.'

'What are you doing up so late, Tredup?' Stuff gestures to the dresser. 'By the way – Herr Henning – Herr Tredup.'

'I write addresses. For a publisher in Munich. Five marks per thousand. The *Chronicle* isn't overly generous in what it pays, wouldn't you agree, Stuff?'

'I'm sorry about your article, Tredup. But I've got a better proposition here. That's why I came to you with this gentleman, who's passing through town. He's a buyer of photographs for an illustrated magazine, and he's interested in your pictures of the cattle confiscation. He would pay fifty marks for a picture.'

Tredup has listened to Stuff's faintly awkward speech with a quiet smile on his lips. 'I have no photographs of the cattle confiscation.'

'Tredup! I know for a fact you do. It's a lot of money for you!'

'And I would take it, honestly I would! I'm not choosy. Yes, I was taking pictures. But they didn't turn out. One of those bastard farmers knocked the camera out of my hands.'

'I knew that, Herr Tredup,' says Henning. 'A little birdie. But you got off some pictures before that. One. Or maybe two.'

'One.'

'Very well, one. I'll pay you for each picture, if you sell me the film and all prints, one hundred marks.'

Tredup grins. 'That's as much as twenty thousand addresses. One hundred and sixty hours of night work. But we unlucky bleeders miss out on good deals like that. The first picture is just fresh air.'

Stuff says imploringly: 'Tredup . . .!'

Tredup smiles again. 'Oh, you don't believe me. You take me for a millionaire, who scribbles addresses for the fun of it. Well, I can fix that.'

He opens a drawer in the dresser and starts ferreting around in it. 'It was a roll of film with twelve exposures. Three of the church restoration in Podejuch. Two interiors, one exterior. Two photographs of the confiscation. Here's the air shot. All smoke. Hold the film up against the light, and you'll see it really is smoke. Here's the failed shot when the farmer knocked a hundred marks out of my grip. Next is one you bought from me, Stuff: the crashed car on the road to Stettin. Six. Seven to ten: four pictures of the weekly market. Eleven and twelve: the opening of the new petrol station. Is that right?'

'My God, Tredup, as if we wouldn't take your word for it.'

'Hardly.'

'I'm sorry,' says Henning. 'I would have liked to make a deal with you. But maybe you'll sell me the three pictures of Pode-juch church. My magazine can use them. Five marks apiece. Is that all right?'

'Fine.'

'There. And now I'll leave you in peace. You need to go to bed.'

'Yes, I think I can stop for tonight. I'm dog-tired. Don't fall over anything when you go. Wait, I'll open the gate for you. Good-night, gents, and thank you.'

The two of them walk down the road.

'Do you think,' Stuff asks hesitatingly, 'that that was on the level?'

'I don't know what to think. The twelve pictures were just a little bit too handy and worked out.'

'Oh, where that's concerned, Tredup is a model of pedantry and good order. And for a hundred marks . . .'

'That's what's comforting me too. Then you can tell Kalübbe tomorrow morning that he won't have to recognize anyone.'

'Yes. Well, goodbye now, Herr Henning.'

'We'll see each other again somewhere. My hotel is this way. Goodnight.'

'Goodnight.'

Tredup has turned out the light, and lies down beside his wife. 'Let me tell you something, Elise. We have two mayors here. The Oberbürgermeister is on the Right, and has no power, and is gen-erally useless. The mayor is on the Left, and he's also the chief of police. It's him I'm going to be seeing tomorrow.'

'I expect you know what you're doing, Max,' says his wife. 'Just see that we get a little money into the house. Hans's shoes need new soles, and Grete must have two new blouses.'

'We have fifteen marks for now. But I won't be bought for fif-teen marks. Nor yet for one hundred. Five hundred is more my price.'

And with that they go to sleep.

V

Every morning at ten Tredup goes to the town hall, where he asks the office manager for public announcements to put in the advertising section of the *Chronicle*.

Today, after pushing two or three sheets of paper into his brief-case, he climbs the stairs from the ground floor to the first floor. He goes through a double door; a long white corridor with red doors lies ahead of him. He knows that somewhere hereabouts Mayor Gareis, the police chief of Altholm, is to be found.

He starts reading the names on the doors: MARKET POLICE, TRAFFIC POLICE, CRIMINAL INVESTIGATION DEPARTMENT, DEPUTY COMMISSIONER. There it is: mayor. But a red arrow points the visitor to the next door: mayor's outer office. Visitors report here.

He didn't think about there being an outer office! He will have to sit and wait there, other people will be sitting there too, one of them will recognize him, and Stuff will get to hear that Tredup, the advertising manager of the Right-wing *Chronicle*, has paid a call on the Leftist mayor.

Falteringly he turns back. He can't risk his job, and the exist-ence of the three people who depend on him.

At the top of the stairs, he changes his mind again. In the course of the night, five hundred marks have become a thou-sand. The police and public prosecutors pay out money like that pretty regularly. And a thousand marks seems to offer security, a decent living . . . maybe a little shop.

But he won't do the outer office. He will have to risk it. And with a sudden jerk he opens the door of the mayor's inner sanc-tum. But it's a double door, and he opens the inner one much more gently.

He's in luck. The mayor is alone, seated at his desk, telephon-ing. At the sound of the opening door, he turns his head to the incomer. He narrows his eyes a little in the effort to recognize him, then points him to the outer office.

Tredup pulls the door quietly shut after him, and remains where he is, leaning forward and alert.

Mayor Gareis continues to telephone.

Tredup has heard it said that the mayor is the tallest man in Altholm. But this man isn't just tall, he's huge, a colossus, an elephant. Great big limbs, quantities of flesh barely held together by his suit, a face with two chins, pendulous dewlaps, massy thick hands.

After his initial dismissive gesture, the mayor has not looked at the visitor again. He continues to talk calmly on the telephone, about the time of some meeting, not an interesting conversation.

Tredup begins to look around the room.

Suddenly he notices that the mayor is looking at him, and a painful feeling comes over him, that these clear, bright eyes – under the smooth black hair – can see everything: the unironed trousers, the dirty shoes, the poorly washed hands, the pasty complexion.

But now he can't ignore it any more: across the telephone receiver, Mayor Gareis is smiling at him. And now he's pointing him to a chair in front of the desk, he makes a hospitable gesture, and now, right in the middle of his conversation he says: 'I'll be with you in just a moment.'

Tredup sits down, the mayor puts the receiver down on its cradle, smiles once more, and asks quickly: 'Where's the fire?'

Suddenly Tredup has the sensation that he can tell this man everything, that he will understand anything that is put to him. He feels a rush of emotion, a hot, grateful enthusiasm spreads through his body. He says: 'The fire? The fire's in Gramzow, on the roads to Haselhorst and Lohstedt.'

The mayor is serious, he nods once or twice, looks pensively at a mammoth pencil his hands are toying with, and he says: 'There was a fire there.'

'And are the police interested in catching the arsonists?'

'Might be. Do you know them?'

'A friend of mine. Just might.'

'"Friend" is too ambiguous. Let's just say: an unknown party. X.'

'All right then, my friend X.'

The mayor's shoulders heave. 'Are you from Gramzow?'

'My friend? No. He's from town.'

'This town?'

'Could be.'

The mayor gets up. Tredup is alarmed. It's as though a mountain has started moving. He gets up and gets up and it still isn't all of him. From somewhere near the top, a voice intones down to Tredup, curled up in his armchair: 'I've got all the time in the world for sense, but no time to spare for nonsense. We're not playing cops and robbers here. You want something from me, presumably money. Sell me some news. Well, I'm not interested.'

Tredup wants to raise an objection. The voice overrides it. 'All right, I'm not interested. Gramzow isn't part of my constituency. The country warden in Lohstedt might be. Or perhaps Stolpe.'

The mayor sits down again. Suddenly he breaks into a smile: 'But perhaps I can help you anyway. Just stop talking nonsense. Spit it out. I've learned to be discreet over the course of my life.'

The somewhat crushed Tredup rallies. He says eagerly: 'I was there, that afternoon. I saw the whole thing: the officials, the farmers, the oxen.'

'You would be able to identify them, I expect?'

Tredup nods eagerly. 'More than that.'

'You know their names?'

'No, not the names. But . . .'

'But . . .?'

'But I took a couple of photographs, one of the fire on the road to Haselhorst, the other from the Lohstedt Road. The farmers are on them, the ones who set the fire, who scattered the straw, who are standing by, all of them . . .'

The mayor, pensively now, asks: 'I'm not up with the statements that have been brought in. But so far as I know, none of them mentions a stranger standing there taking pictures.'

Tredup thinks in a rushed way: It's not his affair? He doesn't know all the statements? And he knows . . . Something warns him, and he just says: 'I've got the pictures.'

'Not posed pictures? The difference is obvious.'

'The other side knows about them. At one o'clock this morning, I was offered five hundred marks for them.'

'That's a good price,' says the mayor. 'Maybe they're no longer worth the celluloid they're printed on. The case is up in Gramzow at the moment. If the officials recognize the farmers there, then your pictures will be worthless.'

'If . . . The party that offered me five hundred will have thought about what to do with the officials too.'

The mayor surveys his visitor long and thoughtfully. 'You've got something about you. How much are the pictures?'

'A thousand. Today.'

'And tomorrow? No, let's not play that. It's not out of the question. So you have the pictures with you?'

Tredup ducks the question: 'They can be made available any time.'

'I believe they exist. And they are clear, usable? You can recognize people's faces on them?'

'Just as I'm sitting in front of you, Mayor.'

'All right then, Herr X. Perhaps you'll wait outside for ten minutes. As I say, *I'm* not interested. But it may be that Stolpe is. So wait a little. And thanks for the moment.'

Tredup is hardly out of the door before the mayor is ringing his bell.

'Listen to me, Piekbusch. Will you pick up a few files, and cross the corridor as casually as you can. There's a young man there, black hat, trousers out at the knees, briefcase, pale, the laces on his right shoe are undone. Take a casual look at him and see if you know him. Come straight back and report to me.'

Secretary Piekbusch goes.

The mayor picks up the telephone: 'Get me the district president. Personal and urgent. While you're waiting to get him on the line, get me Commander Frerksen. And then County Judge Grumbach. – Is that you, Frerksen? – Yes, please come and see me right away. Get yourself driven. You will be taking someone to Stolpe in fifteen minutes. – Yes, right away. – Well, Piekbusch, do you know the man?'

'I've seen him before, Herr Mayor, but –'

'So you don't know him. Will you go down to the Criminal Investigation Department. Get whoever's there to step out into the corridor, go to this office or that, go to the toilet. As soon as anyone can identify him, call me. Or, no, better report in person.

'Yes, who is it? Judge Grumbach? – Yes, Judge, this is Mayor Gareis. I wanted to ask you, if possible, to delay the hearing at Gramzow by a couple of hours, if you can do such a thing. – Interesting new lead. – Local hearing is probably unnecessary. Why? Well, you'll see. – We have our sources. – I can't tell you yet, but I'm about to call Stolpe. – Yes, on my say-so. – The Revenue? Pah, what those gentlemen come up with. It's not enough to sentence anyone, maybe not even enough to mount a case. – It's either all or nothing. – Well, you'll be hearing from me. Or from the district president. – What's it to do with Temborius? He has to pay. It costs money, money and more money. – That's right, I'll leave him the bill, and will be happy with the renown. Ha, bye-bye now!'

He puts down the telephone. The secretary walks into the office.

'Piekbusch, leave me. Once someone can identify him, I said.'

'The young man has disappeared, Herr Mayor.'

'Disappeared?! You mean he's gone?' The mayor gives a start. He thinks: If some enemy of mine has played me false, then I'm really in the soup. He could have been a spy, trying to find out what the government has up its sleeve. Then I'm done for. Ach, that wasn't a spy. He will have been scared off. And, aloud: 'Go and check the toilet, Piekbusch. He's maybe just gone for a pee.'

Piekbusch turns to leave. 'Hold it! And I want to see Frerksen. What's keeping him? – Ah, Frerksen, there you are. – Now, Piekbusch, whoever's in the outer office, send them along to Stein. He can hold the fort for me. If it's very important, I can deal with it in fifteen minutes. – Now, Frerksen, sit yourself down, something's come up, it looks as though we'll at last be able to make a favourable impression on Comrade Temborius in Stolpe.'

3

The First Bomb

I

The inner sanctum of District President Temborius is a long, dark, wood-panelled room. The lights are always turned down low there. The windows decorated with coats of arms and gaudy putti are enough to tone down the brightest summer day.

This official, kept in power by the support of his party, a modicum of administrative expertise and a lot of string-pulling, is no friend of loud noises. Quiet, soothing, chiaroscuro murmur suits him better. Quietly, soothingly and murmuringly is how Comrade Temborius has steered the fortunes of his district, and quiet, discreet murmur also describes the conversation between him, his militia colonel and Revenue Councillor Andersson. Somewhere in the darkest recess a fat little adviser is minuting the remarks of the three gentlemen for subsequent filing, to the security of his boss.

'It remains regrettable,' murmurs the softly spoken provincial representative of the Minister of the Interior, 'regrettable that the lawyer was not contactable at such short notice. What happened at Gramzow was not a chance incident, but a sign of things to come.'

Colonel Senkpiel is pining for a cigar. 'We should hit them, and hit them hard.'

'If the pictures do what Gareis promises, then we will be able to nab the ringleaders at last.'

'Yes, from *one* place. The movement has long since ceased to be local.'

'That's right! So we'll see if there were emissaries from other places around.'

'Gentlemen . . .' The president begins, falters, stops. And then again, with an irked twitch of the shoulders: 'The views of the prosecution would have been extraordinarily valuable to me.'

'It's all in the open,' Revenue Councillor Andersson comforts him. 'If the identities of the guilty parties can be confirmed from the photographs, heavy penalties will be handed down.'

Temborius remains unhappy. 'But will it help? Will it deter others?'

The colonel looks at the revenue councillor, the revenue councillor looks back at the colonel.

Then they both turn their heads and stare into the corner, where the completely insignificant adviser is sitting.

First to speak is the colonel: 'Deter them? I should think so. If they get six or twelve months, it should help them think straight.'

The president raises his hand, a narrow, bony, long-fingered hand with thick veins. 'You say it will. But will it really? Gentlemen, I must confess, I see this movement as highly dangerous, extremely dangerous, potentially much more dangerous than the KPD or NSDAP. It's the worst thing that can happen: the administrative machinery grinds to a halt. I tell you, I can see the day when the countryside becomes ungovernable.'

Consternation among the gentlemen: 'Oh, President.'

'Indeed. Our district headman left much to be desired. Compliance was sluggish. Invariably there were delays. Today, these delays have turned into full-blown passive resistance. Files remain out in the villages for weeks, if not months. Written warnings are a waste of time, fines can only be collected in the context of an overall confiscation process –' He breaks off.

And starts again: 'The district already has at least two dozen headmen who fail to pass on tax demands to their community members, no, who return them to us. As unfair. Unfair, you hear! We are unable to count on their assistance during distraint procedures, see the recent example of Gramzow. And the movement is growing. Our machinery is grumbling and creaking. And that it has to be in my district . . .!'

'The minister is very appreciative of your efforts,' says Andersson.

'No, no, even the minister . . . I have the sense that Berlin is not happy with developments in the province.'

The colonel says: 'The situation will change at a stroke, the instant people switch from passive to active resistance. Gramzow was the farmers' first mistake. We will – should the pictures permit the guilty ones to be recognized – come down on them like a ton of bricks. That will cause the farmers to make more mistakes. Give me leave to send in my people, there will be incidents, and wherever there are incidents we can be sure of victory.'

'You're an optimist, Senkpiel,' remarks Temborius. 'There's nothing so uncertain as the outcome of such a process. – We should have had someone here from the prosecution.'

'Nothing so certain,' contradicts the colonel, 'so long as the pictures are good enough.'

'The pictures won't do it by themselves. The two revenue officials will have to give evidence. Can we rely on their cooperation?'

Andersson grimaces. 'You're right. You're right. I heard some bewildering news from my colleague Berg in Altholm this morning. Apparently there's a rumour going around there that Kalübbe – you remember, the doughty fellow, who got his ox as far as Lohstedt – well, that Kalübbe is being demoted. And that the other man, Thiel, who was only informally employed by us, has been sacked.'

The district president heaves his shoulders. 'Can anyone explain that to me?'

Andersson braces himself. 'Well, it's not the farmers. No question, other people must be involved. I presume . . .' – enigmatically, to the tense faces of his listeners – 'Berlin. The card has been played with great skill. My colleague Berg assures me that Kalübbe is a changed man, a broken reed, if you will. When Berg talked of promoting him, his reaction was sceptical, doubting. He simply didn't believe it.'

'Then why not promote him immediately!' calls the district president.

'Now, before the case?' objects Andersson.

'Excuse me,' says the colonel eagerly. 'I remember a case

where His Majesty promoted a man to sergeant, who had shot some members of the public who had provoked him.'

An uncomfortable silence ensues. This time, Andersson and Temborius exchange glances, while the colonel clears his throat several times, hard.

'In any case,' observes the revenue councillor coolly, 'a promotion is out of the question for the moment. Even if the official won't testify with the enthusiasm we would have liked. Much more serious, to my mind, is the fact that Thiel, the other man, has completely disappeared.'

'Disappeared? What do you mean, "disappeared"? People don't just disappear! Doesn't he have an address somewhere? Parents?'

'He lives in furnished rooms. His things are still there. The police have made discreet inquiries, but there's no sign of him.'

The colonel tries to widen the breach: 'Perhaps it's wrong to go looking for him. Shouldn't we look for the man responsible for spreading the rumour? It is just a rumour, I take it?'

'Rumour . . .' says Andersson irritably. 'Well. Of course there's been an inquiry as to whether the two men didn't exceed their rights in taking the oxen to Lohstedt instead of Haselhorst. At any rate, as things stand now, we will neither punish nor sack them.'

The colonel crows: 'As I thought! It was considered . . . You have to look for the people who leaked.'

The telephone rings.

Temborius turns round. 'Chief Adviser Meier, will you answer it? I have left instructions that I am not to be disturbed. Find out who has disregarded my instructions.'

The chief adviser goes over to the telephone. The three gentlemen stop talking. There is something in the air. They look expectantly at the adviser, who first listens, then says 'Yes', listens again, says 'No', continues to listen . . .

The district president: 'Please, Chief Adviser . . .'

Across the room, the adviser holds the receiver out to the president. He looks suddenly pale, there are drops of sweat on his brow. 'I think . . .' he whispers '. . . it seems to be serious . . . you should . . .'

Protestingly, Temborius gets to his feet. He goes to the phone, muttering to himself: 'What is it now?' The receiver in his hand: 'Yes, this is District President Temborius . . . yes, in person . . . who is it?' Out of patience: 'What is it you want?!'

A man's voice says: 'The photograph seller Tredup and Commander Frerksen have just entered the building. In five minutes the regional centre of government will be blown sky-high.'

II

Receiver in hand, the long, thin, dry, softly spoken bureaucrat suddenly shouts at the top of his voice: 'What? What?! If this is your idea of a joke, sir . . .' Then, imploringly: 'Please, tell me who you are? What's your name at least! What?'

He drops the receiver, stares at his colleagues. 'What do you say now? What on earth do you say now? The government presidium will be blown up in five minutes.'

'A hoaxer,' says the colonel, walks over to the president, and simply takes the telephone from the president's hand. 'Miss! Miss! Get me the police barracks right away! – Who am I talking to? – First Lieutenant Wrede? Er, comrade, I want all men to report immediately to Government House. I'll be looking for you in the driveway. We're under attack! – Miss, quickly call all offices: vacate the building. *Immediately.* Your colleague in the meantime should take steps to establish who just called. – You listened in, I take it? Aha. As I thought.'

He puts down the receiver. Smiles. 'There, gentlemen, four minutes. But as I say: hoaxers!'

'But that's mad!' shouts Temborius. 'Who would dare –?'

The door opens. Behind Commander Frerksen, pale and shifty-looking, in creased clothes, in walks Tredup. Frerksen gives a military salute: 'At your service, District President.'

The president winks at him. 'From Altholm? On account of the photographs?'

Frerksen nods.

The president whispers: 'This is all your mayor's fault! Gareis is responsible! You can stick your wretched pictures! I wish you would just go to –'

Andersson intervenes. 'President, if I might . . .? Forgive us . . .' Turning to the entirely bewildered visitors: 'The thing is, the building is going to be blown up in three minutes . . . We're a little agitated on account of that . . .'

The president again: 'I'm sorry, gentlemen. There are important papers, documents of State . . . I must urgently . . . Chief Adviser Meier, I authorize you to . . . Will you pay a reward to . . . gentlemen, the documents . . .'

A dark pair of double doors closes noiselessly.

The colonel says quickly: 'All right, Chief Adviser, you're in charge. Will you excuse me. I need to join my men.'

And Commander Frerksen: 'Comrade, if you'll allow. The solution of this policing task interests me . . .'

And Andersson: 'If you're in charge, then I'm *de trop*. Goodbye.'

He hurries out.

There are two men left in the huge room: Chief Adviser Meier, small, pallid, very Jewish-looking, slightly sweaty. And Tredup, scrawny, pale, untidy, unshaven.

The adviser looks at the man standing in the doorway. 'Aren't you scared?' he asks.

'I want my money,' says Tredup, unmoved. 'Here are the pictures.'

He pulls them out of his inside pocket, unwraps them, holds them out to the adviser, one in either hand.

The adviser casts a fleeting look at them, sees men, smoke, a lanky, clean-shaven, chiselled-looking farmer fanning flames.

'Very good. Put them down there. Aren't you scared?'

'First the money. – You're still here too.'

'Right. Wasn't that . . .?' He listens to a sound outside the window, whistles, people running, voices in a crowd. 'You know what, why don't you come for your money tomorrow?'

Tredup is insistent: 'No. Now.'

And the adviser, hurriedly: 'I feel we're the last people left in the building. Where do you want to get your money from?'

'What about the safe?' suggests Tredup.

And Chief Adviser Meier: 'Must we?'

'Of course. No money, no pictures.'

'Well. Let's go.'

He leads the way, small, bandy-legged, flat-footed, but at least he leads the way. The doors are open on all the corridors, a stack of files has toppled off a chair where it was put. There's a powder puff lying on the floor. The open goods lift goes spectrally up and down.

The adviser hesitates. 'No, we'll take the stairs. If the man left a bomb, it's probably in the lift shaft. – Well, that's nonsense too. If it goes off, we're done for anyway. Come on.'

On the ground floor, the iron door of the accounts office is open. They walk in. The adviser murmurs: 'This is mad.'

The great safe is gaping open. The mobile till behind the barrier opens its grating. It is littered with packets of notes.

'Well, then,' says the adviser. 'Help yourself. But please be as quick about it as you can.' Tredup looks inquiringly. 'Do you want me to –?'

Impatiently: 'Yes, go on, man! What do you take me for, some kind of hero?'

And Tredup: 'If you don't mind, I'll take it in tens.'

Chief Adviser Meier groans: 'Not that as well!'

To which Tredup: 'It doesn't notice so much when it comes to spending it.'

'True. If you ever get around to spending it.'

Tredup counts out the money, slowly and carefully. It takes a while, but eventually he gets to a thousand.

'And now let's get out of here.'

'Don't you want a receipt from me?'

'No. I want to go.'

The presidium has been sealed off by the police. The crowd has been kept back to the far ends of the market square, a long way back.

Two figures emerge on to the granite steps, and slowly, to the breathless silence of the crowd, make their way across the market square.

Colonel Senkpiel steps out to meet them, with his stopwatch upraised. 'What did I tell you, gentlemen? Twelve minutes! A childish prank!'

Chief Adviser Meier shakes hands with the advertising manager of the *Chronicle*. 'I was glad to be of assistance. If you need anything else from me, look me up.'

He spots his boss, and heads off in his direction.

Tredup makes his way through the crowd. Something occurs to him. He turns back, and after some negotiation with a constable, is allowed to pass through the security screen.

There is Chief Adviser Meier, in a group of six or eight gentlemen. Tredup lays his hand on his shoulder. 'I'm sorry to bother you, Chief Adviser, but we forgot all about the photographs. Here they are.'

And the district president, appalled: 'Chief Adviser, I sometimes don't understand you! I really have to do everything myself around here . . .'

III

A motorbike cuts down the road from Stolpe to Gramzow on a bright summer morning. Georg Henning, the milking machine and centrifuge representative from Berlin, is aboard. He's doing an even fifty, but his aim is to get there ahead of the telephone call that at any moment can be put through to the rural constabulary in Haselhorst, ordering the arrest of District Headman Reimers.

He's counting on the confusion in Stolpe, and hopes to reach Reimers in time. In such cases he has always managed to get there in time.

The road rises, falls, rises again. A bend. And again, up – down – up. Another bend. Fields. Meadows. Pastures. A few trees. A patch of woodland. Fields. A village. More open road.

Life is good, thinks Henning. I know what I'm doing.

Haselhorst!

He doesn't know which house the rural constable lives in, but he keeps his eyes peeled for the sign with the plucked vulture.

Maybe he'll see it. Everything seems quiet in the village, hardly anyone to be seen, even the railway station looks deserted.

If I encounter the constable on his bike outside Gramzow, I'll just run him over, thinks Henning. Franz Reimers has to have time to pack some belongings, get some money together, burn some papers.

Shortly afterwards: Never mind the packing. – It's essential that I get hold of Stuff tonight. – And then the *Bauernschaft*. They'll be in the editorial office till eight or nine. And then to Thiel. Well, you Stolpers, you'll be in for a nice surprise tonight!

The first buildings of Gramzow appear in front of him. As he rushes by, he looks at the hedges and ditches, to see if there are any traces of straw left out. Doesn't seem to be much. Paler grass has grown back where the straw fires scorched the earth. This is where it began. You wait, you bureaucrats, I'll show you . . .

At last, the farm. He props his motorbike against the cowshed, runs up the steps to the main house. In the dark hallway a maid squeals with surprise. 'Easy, Marie,' he calls, puts his arm round her, and gives her a kiss.

Then he knocks, and walks into the farmer's parlour.

It's no longer the pre-War parlour with mahogany furniture, pillarets and shell epergne, and the mirror cabinet. This is a farmer's room from the inflation era. Heavy, modern furniture with turbulent marbling, wide armchairs, a leather sofa, a writing desk, a bookshelf, whose central section has been made over into a gun cupboard.

The farmer is sitting at his big desk, puffing away on a post-prandial cigar. In front of him is a cup of coffee with cognac.

'Hello, Georg,' he says.

'Morning, Franz. Ah, you've got coffee. Can I get a cup as well? And if you've got anything left over from lunch . . .'

The farmer goes out and gives instructions. He brings the cup himself. 'There. Mix it up as you like.' And while Henning is mixing coffee and cognac: 'The hay harvest is looking good this year.'

'Ah, crap! The milking-machine business is looking lousy this year. – By the way, you're going to be arrested in the course of today.'

The farmer pulls on his cigar. 'The business with the oxen?'
'Yes, that.'
'So the son of a bitch on the *Chronicle* did take pictures?'
'Yes,' Henning affirms.
'We should have offered him more money.'
'I know. But he would never have sold us the pictures on the instalment plan.'
'It's always money. We'd be ten times further along if . . . bah, never mind . . .'

The farmer paces up and down, up and down. Smokes. The maid comes in, sets lunch out on the desk, goes away. Slowly, and with enjoyment, Henning begins to eat. Once he gets up to fetch some mustard from the kitchen, the maids can be heard squealing. The farmer continues to pace.

Finally, Henning is finished, he pours himself another cup of coffee, drinks it, lights himself a cigarette. 'Don't you want to pack anything, Franz?'
'No.'
'Or see about money? Or burn any papers or anything?'
'They can be here any moment?'
'Exactly.'
'Who told you anyway, and how come they aren't here yet?'
'When I left you last night, I got the sense: he does have photographs. This morning, first thing, I called Stuff, and he hadn't seen Tredup yet.'
'You shouldn't get involved with Stuff, you know.'
'I'm always careful not to tell him anything he's not supposed to know. – Then I think to myself: Who's going to be in the market for those pictures anyway? The State prosecution doesn't pay out money, they just summon witnesses. The Red Mayor Gareis isn't free to slosh money around in the way he'd like to. The Centre-Right keep an eye on him. Which leaves only the gelding in Stolpe.'
'So I go to Stolpe. Sure enough, just after twelve, they show up. You know, that snooty Frerksen who bootlicked his way from ABC school all the way to commander. And Tredup in tow. Tredup just spots me as I'm ducking round a corner.'

'You need to be careful *you're* not arrested.'

'That can wait. Tonight we're going to pull a very big job. But tomorrow I'll be out of here. – I wait five minutes, then I call Temborius. From a phone box at the post office. First they refused to put me through to him, but then I said his life was at risk, and so I got him.'

'And what did you say?'

'Well, that his snoop photographer and security detail had just arrived, and . . .'

'And?'

'And that in five minutes, the whole building was going to be blown sky-high. You should have heard the sudden gasp on the line. I could smell his pants filling.'

'And then?'

'Well, as I was starting my motorbike to go over to yours, the militia were just setting off.'

'Not bad. Not bad at all. But the newspapers will be full of it, and you know if there's one thing we farmers don't want it's a stir.'

'The newspapers? I'll eat my hat if there's so much as five lines about it in the newspapers. It'll be some attention-seeker playing a practical joke . . . Or, no, that the whole thing was just a practice run to test the emergency services . . .'

'Maybe so. But you should look after yourself, Georg, leave that stuff alone. We're on to a good thing here, we don't need the fuss.'

'You don't, true. But believe me, Franz, I don't think we can pull the thing off without drama.' And hastily, as Franz makes to interrupt him: 'It won't be anything to do with any of you. No one will know anything. I'll do the whole thing myself.'

Pause. Then: 'With a couple of others. Can't manage alone. But you won't know them.'

The farmer stands there. 'Maybe you're right. I won't ask you, and I won't get in your way. But . . .' – and here he raises his voice – 'if you're lying in the gutter, I won't lift a finger to help you. None of us will. This is about the cause, all right?'

Henning says drily: 'I've never gone to anyone for help.

Whenever anyone bested me, I took my lumps. End of subject. – When are you planning to run?'

'I'm not going to run.'

'It'll be cushy as hell. I'll put you on the passenger seat and run you up to Stolpermünde. You can spend two or three months crewing on a herring boat. At the end of that, so much will have happened that you can come back, no probs.'

'But I can't just disappear like that. The movement needs me.'

'What use are you in prison?'

'A lot of use. Maybe more use than I am outside. Let me tell you something: it won't be a hick policeman that arrests me today, it'll be the militia. Make sure the farmers know all about it. Call round the neighbouring villages, get everyone here who has legs. Tell messengers to make sure the whole district knows. Oh, Georg, imagine if they tied me up, imagine if they hauled me off in chains! Have a photographer here, and get the pictures printed in the next issue of the *Bauernschaft*!'

'You're right. This time, it will be the militia that comes for you.'

The farmer reflects. 'I'll be sitting in the room, cleaning my guns. Maybe they'll send a young lieutenant for me, someone who'll go crazy when he sees other people have weapons as well. Nowadays the entire militia is like that. They must be driven out of their minds! You have no idea how hard it is to get the farmers going. They work their jaws when they lose their livelihoods a beast at a time, but they knuckle under. It's the feudal heritage, it's in their blood. But if something like this happens, then maybe, just maybe, it'll have an effect . . .'

'You bet it'll have an effect!'

'One other thing, Georg. Have a word today with Rehder from Karolinenhorst, he's taking over from me. Have some fellows from four or five villages ride all over the area on Sunday, announcing the breach of law. Let Padberg at the *Bauernschaft* find the form of words for you. They should call a Farmers' Parliament and have a big protest meeting in Altholm. Then you should demonstrate outside the prison. I'll hear you from my cell.'

'I'll do everything you say.'

'And don't forget, they need to have a collection for me. We need money. The *Bauernschaft* should call for an emergency levy. I need the best lawyer available. It has to be made a political case.'

'I know just the man. I'll talk to people in Berlin.'

'The very best! Georg, I tell you, when they descend on me with their militia, when they cuff me and beat me up: it will be the best day of my life!'

IV

Henning only waited for Reimers's arrest. Then he rode to Altholm to talk to Stuff.

By the time he gets there, it's already dark, but he finds Stuff easily enough. Altholm has forty or fifty bars, Stuff is bound to be in one of them. He finds him in the third place he tries.

Stuff is moody and laconic. Henning tries telling him about Tredup, but nothing seems to rile Stuff today. He drinks rapidly, and Henning has the feeling Stuff is not listening properly. His only response to the events in Stolpe is to say: 'Silly buggers!' He asks impatiently: 'Is that all?'

Henning begins again. Talks about Reimers's arrest. 'I wasn't allowed to be there for it myself, I wasn't supposed to let anyone see me, but I watched from round the corner, and later on I asked people, and Frau Reimers.'

'Well, and what went off! A common-or-garden arrest! And quite right too.'

'Now hang on a minute: quite right too! Is there any danger of him attempting flight?'

'Risk of collusion.'

'When the pictures are lying there. What's left for him to collude? – But never mind.' Henning gives way. 'What's the point of us arguing about it? – A little after six they came, two detectives and a lorryload of militia. The scale of it! The government is making itself a laughing stock. All for *one* man. Well, I had done my bit. The village street was full of people. And more flocked along all the time.'

'So it wasn't just about *one* man.'

'Oh, come on! We're talking about peaceable farmers here. They might stop and look, but they're certainly not going to take part. – The militia sealed off the farmyard with a chain. The detectives went into the house, along with half a dozen militia and their commander.'

'Who was it?'

'Think of it, we were hoping it might be a lieutenant. It was Colonel Senkpiel in person. – The rest of it I know from Reimers's wife and workers. They walk into the room, there's Franz – Reimers – by the table, with a gun in his hand. There's another five guns laid out on the table. Apparently they got quite a fright. The young cops moved for their pistols, the old detectives took cover behind the stove.'

'No one likes to get shot up if they can help it.'

'It was six against one!'

'Doesn't change a thing. – And then?'

'The colonel kept his cool. He made a joke, and sat down in an armchair. Reimers turfed him out, because he said he hadn't invited him to sit down, and he demanded that everyone take off their hats and caps in his room.'

'What nonsense. Soldiers taking off their caps!'

'Precisely. – Well, the colonel started to get a bit testy, and the detectives asked to see a permit for all the guns. Reimers said: "That's with Franz."

'"Who's Franz?" they ask.

'"That's my secretary," replies Reimers.

'He's to call him. But he says he can only fetch him in person. They're not in favour of that, because they think he might do a runner, they want to get him themselves.

'So where's Franz? – In the loft. – What loft? The hayloft? – No, the loft. – Can he not call him? – If they think there's any point in trying, he can. – Well, all right, try.

'They all troop out into the yard, and then Reimers stands and yells at the loft: "Franz is to come down. The police want to see him." Well, nothing stirs. Reimers yells till he's blue in the face, he's still cradling his gun in his arms, but nothing stirs.

'"Might Franz possibly be asleep?"

'And Reimers: He has no idea whether Franz is asleep or awake.

'They want to send a man up to him. What door is it?

'"The one in front of you when you get up to the attic."

'A militiaman climbs up, and crawls around, and comes back down: there was a padlock on the door. And Reimers acts surprised, didn't they realize that you didn't leave attics unlocked just like that?

'It's beginning to dawn on them that they're being taken for a ride, and the kitchen girls, who heard the farmer call for "Franz" at the top of his voice, are peeing themselves laughing.

'They go back inside with him, and ask him right out about this Franz fellow whom he keeps under lock and key.

'"Well, my secretary, Franz."

'How come? You don't just lock people up. – Oh yes you did. Why, that was precisely why they were come, the gentlemen. – Did he keep people imprisoned here? – Imprisoned? Can you imprison a secretary, a secretaire, a piece of furniture, painted red? Whom he's called Franz ever since he can remember?

'And it's all true. Everybody knows Reimers has names for his different suits, for pieces of furniture, for his carts and bits of gear.'

'Playing silly buggers! I don't see how that's going to help the farmers!'

'You're very contrary today. But you must be enjoying it, you let me talk and talk.'

'Enjoying it? Seeing as you've sat down at my table and refuse to go away?'

'You can imagine how furious they were. Two men have to come forward and take his shotgun off him. And the rest of them have to reassemble the locks he's just taken apart and oiled. And three men have to accompany him up to the attic and look over his shoulder while he goes through the secretary, drawer by drawer. Till he remembers his licence is downstairs after all, in his desk.

'Then they tell him the gun licence no longer interests them. The weapons are being confiscated anyway. Not bad for a violation of a man's civil rights, eh?'

'If you say so,' says Stuff.

'But that's what it is. Breach of civil rights. And then they start to question him, and they want to know who drove the straw cart. And he tells them they'd better ask Orsche. They've become suspicious by now, they're not interested in Orsche, he just has to tell them what he knows. And he says: No, they're to say what they know, and he can tell them which bits are true or not. Well, they don't want that. And then they tell him that he's under arrest, and has to accompany them. And he says, "I can't right away. I first have to do my taxes. And I need to give the community chest into safe keeping."

'They're getting madder and madder all the time. The whole village is packed with people, there are cars parked on the pasture, and photographers taking pictures. And Reimers is sitting at his desk, not moving a muscle. Why doesn't he let them take care of the chest? – No, he doesn't want to do that. It's been known for money to go missing that way. Haven't they heard about funds being embezzled in the army and the militia, and munitions being flogged off, and all the other scandalous stuff?'

'Well, and . . .?'

'Well, and now you need to remember I can see it all happening before my very eyes. I wasn't there, but this is how I see it. There are the militia sentries lined up along the wall and by the door, with their rubber truncheons in their hands, and their pistol holsters unbuttoned. And the detectives are standing there, and Colonel Senkpiel, and they're foaming with anger. And if they had had him to themselves, in a private place, I tell you, they'd have broken every bone in his body. But outside there are hundreds of farmers –'

'Call it fifty.'

'Hundreds and hundreds. Not a woman among them, only men. The farmers didn't allow any women to stand out there on the street. All silent, completely silent. And a chain of thirty militiamen. And inside there's a man, just one man, and he's been making monkeys of them for the past hour, and they're helpless to do anything about it.'

'You have a vivid imagination. But the militia and detectives are used to it, they're dealing with bandits all the time.'

'They were boiling with rage. The colonel was the colour of an aubergine.

'"Come with us!"

'"Call my deputy, so that I can give the chest into his keeping!"

'"You're to come along with us! If you don't get up this minute, we'll have to use force."

'And three men stand around him, one each side, and one at his back.'

'And did he go?'

'That's when Reimers plays his trump card. He agrees to go with them, but first he wants to see the warrant for his arrest. And then it comes out that the detectives were leaving it to the colonel, and the colonel was leaving it to the detectives, and between them they haven't got the bloody red form.

'Then they start to quarrel among themselves, and the young fellows, the militiamen, are white with rage, and Reimers is sitting in his chair, hugging his knees with delight, and clapping his hands, and making "Tss! Tss!" noises to incite them against each other, and is generally dying of laughter.'

'Well, and then? Did they finally pick him up?'

'They went very quiet, and the colonel said the lack of a warrant didn't matter. The arrest is lawful, and he has to go with them.

'And he answers back that he knows the law in Germany, and he is entitled to see the warrant. And if they've messed up something, then they will have to be like ordinary civilians and do it all over again, in accordance with the proverb that says what you haven't got in your head, you have to make up for with your legs.

'And the colonel starts ranting and raving: he is to come with them. – He's not coming without a warrant. – And they instructed him two and three times, but he didn't get up. Then they grabbed hold of him, and pulled him up.

'And then he screamed – and I tell you it went through me like a knife, as I stood out there on the bend in the road – he screamed: "Woe to justice in the land of Germany!" And then they cuffed him, and led him out to the cars in chains.

'Reimers went willingly with them through the massed ranks of farmers. And no one spoke a word, but they doffed their hats when he passed. And then they took him away.'

'And what happened then? And what did you do?'

'Me? I rode here, and told you everything that happened, and get no thanks from you.'

'Thanks! You're not about thanks, you came because you want something. – But never mind that. Only one question: Wouldn't it have been smarter of you if you'd followed the militia to see if they didn't pull over in some nice secluded place and give your friend a good going-over?'

Henning has turned pale. He leans over the tables, and his face is a map of wrinkles. 'Dammit!' he swears. 'Damn me and damn my ancestors. I hope I get scabies and the big S for not having thought of that!'

'You're young,' says Stuff, suddenly turning old and wise. 'You think panache is everything. But in this business you need to work hard and think hard, and derring-do is actually crap. Everything you did today is crap. Your Reimers has something, it takes something to be as full of hate as he is, and to discipline himself and stay cool and make them lose their rag. I don't want to hear him howling tonight in his cell for not just whacking them while he had them in front of him. – No, Reimers is OK, but you've got a lot to learn.'

'But it was good that I called the president. Would Reimers have had the time to prepare himself otherwise?'

'I don't think a man like that needs much time to get ready. His hate is always on tap. – And your coming to me is crap as well. What am I supposed to do with your stories? They're farmers' stories, nothing for town people.'

'I thought,' Henning says quietly, 'I thought you might come with me to Stolpe tonight. We have a discussion with the editors of the *Bauernschaft*.'

'What do I care about the yellow journalists on the *Bauernschaft*! Altholm is an industrial town! Bring me material against the Reds, that's another matter!'

'But this is material against the Reds!'

'Bullshit! This is against the government, against the State. Do
you think my subscribers want to read about the house they're
sitting in being about to collapse? You talked to me about the Baltic and Upper Silesia, but in fact you're . . .' Stuff curbs himself.
'All right, you thought you could take advantage of me. Let me
tell you something! I'll be the one taking the advantage, if I can
ever use you for anything. And I'd be doing you a favour. And
that's all for today. I've got a lot of things to do still. If you had an
ounce of sense in your mind, I would tell you: Don't do anything
else today, this isn't a good day for you. But you're going to go on
and do more stupid things.'

Henning bows, and walks out of the bar.

Stuff watches him go sadly, quickly drinks a glass of beer and
a schnapps, and starts writing: 'Incredible humiliation for the
government. – The bomb in the presidium. – Police make arrest
without warrant.'

He writes and he writes.

This is no good for the provinces, he thinks. But Berlin will
take it. It'll earn me at least a hundred marks. Nice kid, that Henning, may he remain so. Well, I'll just phone my guff through to
the night editors.

V

That night the housekeeper of District President Temborius
doesn't get home till half past midnight. She passed the evening in the cinema, where she met friends, and spent a couple of
hours with them in the Café Koopmann.

Housekeeper Klara Gehl is a familiar and respected personality
in Stolpe. Everyone knows she used to be a humble kitchen maid.
Her efficient and tactful nature got her promoted so that she is
now managing the big household of the bachelor Temborius. And
everyone in town and country knows that the best approach to
Temborius is the unofficial one through his housekeeper: while
bureaucracy puts up one hurdle after another, Klara Gehl is still
able to tease the odd trace of humanity out of him.

She was rather indiscreet in the café. She kept having to retell the story of how the practical joke this morning took effect on the district president, how he went to bed right away, gravely ill, and took at least three Pyramidon.

'I made him sweat. He had to drink lime-blossom tea for me, and at eight o'clock I turned out the lights, and said I was going out. Otherwise he would have rung for me all evening.'

Now she's on her way home, it's half past midnight. But she's not afraid, even though her way takes her through a largely unlit street of villas. There are trees lining the road, and the gardens and in some places the road itself are almost completely dark.

A couple of hundred paces from the house, two men walk past her. One tips his hat to her, and politely and quietly says: 'Good evening, ma'am.'

She thanks him, and goes on. When she opens the garden gate she has a feeling of being watched, and she turns round to look at the street. Dimly she can make out the two forms; the men have stopped.

You're wasting your time, she thinks. When I was twenty years younger, maybe, but not any more . . .

She walks down the gravel path, and quietly sets about unlocking the door, because the president's bedroom faces on to the front. She mustn't disturb him.

Surprisingly the door is open. It wasn't locked at all. Those naughty maids, she thinks. It's time I told them off again. And Erna will have to get her marching orders, and marry her Willem. Two more weeks, and not even Temborius would remain ignorant of the biological condition of his parlourmaid.

When she cautiously turns on the light in the hallway, she has fresh cause to be displeased with her girls. Smack in the middle of the hall is a chest, a plain white margarine chest. So Mahlmann did manage to send the preserves after all! And the girls just left them standing there!

Klara tucks the box under her arm, and goes down the long passage to the kitchen, which is in the newer part of the house. She leaves the chest in the pantry, checks to see that the gas is turned off, turns off all the lights on her way back, and mounts the stairs to her bedroom.

As she draws the curtain she looks out at the street once more. Strange, the two men have come closer, she can see their darker shadows in the shadows of the trees.

Perhaps one of the girls has a new man? She is certain she doesn't know either of them, even though she didn't get a good look at them.

Then she goes back inside the room, switches on the light, and is about to pull back the covers.

At that instant it's as though a hurricane bursts into the room. She feels herself carried aloft, eyes closed, higher and higher . . .

The ceiling must come any moment, surely . . .

And now she's falling . . . There's a crack, the crack of doom. She thinks she can hear herself screaming . . .

But now she knows she is lying somewhere. It is so deathly still . . .

And now there's a trickle of powder, incessantly, in the walls, in her ears . . .

And now everything is just black. Dull, bitter black.

4

A Storm Brews

I

A man is walking along the sandy track from Dülmen to Bandekow-Ausbau. Everything about his clothing and shoes bespeaks the gentleman, but somewhere something is lacking: no maid introducing him would have taken him for a gentleman.

It's a warm day, and the man is taking his time. He dawdles along, stops now and then, and examines the tracks in the sand.

A motorbike has come this way, he thinks, that much is clear. And not come out. According to the map, there is only this one approach to the farm. Nice, godforsaken stretch of country. Ten miles to the nearest railway station.

The man stops again and looks around while he catches his breath. The country is nothing particular, a poor mix of scrubland, clumps of pine, blueberry swamp and any amount of juniper.

Actually I always thought aristocrats must live in these kind of settings. I think there is some count here too, someone so hungry he can't get to sleep at night. – I wonder what this is going to lead to.

If you're fifty-two and still a deputy inspector in spite of all your diligence, then thoughts like this may give rise to feelings of a hopeful nature. Since the Revolution, Deputy Inspector Perduzke (Altholm) has seen plenty of his colleagues promoted to inspector, commander, even superintendent. He, for all his diligence, has remained what he was.

And if I manage to solve this bomb hoax, then they'll have to promote me, even if I don't have a Party book ten times over.

He stares. Rubbish! If they behaved the way they ought to, then they would have made me inspector in the wake of the

Kapp Putsch. Shameful, the way that Red duo Gareis and Frerk-sen have strung me along.

Perduzke is a born sleuth. Hunting is his passion. Even the chance that the proferred sausage will be snatched away from him isn't enough to rob him of his enthusiasm for the chase. He is already on the case after finding that note in his in tray this morning, with just two words: 'Bombs – Bandekow.'

He didn't tell his superiors anything about this lead. If he man-ages to find anything out, he'll report straight to the government or the minister, otherwise they'll intercept his reports and claim the credit for his work. Officially-unofficially he is on the trail of some cattle-rustlers. The best sort of introduction to that so-called gentleman farmer, Bandekow!

It's July, a quiet month in the country calendar. On the fields, which have now taken over from the scrubland, there's no one to be seen. There's nothing grazing on the pastures. It's another fortnight till the rye harvest, and the hay is in.

Annoying that there's no one around. It's the girls that are usu-ally the best sources of information.

Now a car is coming up behind him, an Opel four-seater with the top down. Perduzke stands on the verge, but there's not all that much dust. The car crawls and bumps along, the sand is too loose to make a decent surface. That way the detective is able to get a good view of the four gentlemen.

The two in the back are farmers, that's for sure, though he doesn't know them. He doesn't know any of the farmers here-abouts. But in the front . . .

And now his heart starts to race a little. What a good break it was that he set off the moment he got that little anonymous note! Who would have thought of Bandekow! But there's a bad smell around Bandekow now, that's for certain.

He knows the driver well, that's Padberg, the editor of the *Bauernschaft*, the farmers' rag that loved to inveigh against the Reds. (Only it had no readers.)

And the one in the passenger seat, the young fellow, that was Thiel, regardless of how much he might try to look the other way. That was Thiel, in quest of whom the whole province had been quietly turned upside down for the past five weeks. The ox-drover from the revenue office at Altholm, disappeared only to resurface in a car with *Bauernschaft* and farmers.

Stolpe plates, notes Perduzke. We know the number. It'll be Padberg's. So they're the ones who've bought the boy! Funny, I'd never have guessed it. First they make fun of him, put him through an ordeal by fire, throw him in a ditch, and then they give him a ride in their automobile. – It didn't happen like that before the War.

He goes on his way and wonders how to go about his business.

Maybe they recognized me. Someone like that paper man, Padberg, they can always spot a detective. The half-hour till I get to the farm is plenty of time for them to hide the boy. But I'm on the trail.

He crunches on through the sand till he gets to the gates of the farm, where he is met by the legend: RESIDENCE OF COUNT BANDE-KOW. ISN'T BUYING. ISN'T SELLING. NO VISITORS.

Perduzke nods appreciatively. A nice touch! And when you hear the dogs as well, sweet-natured critters . . .

They rush up to the bars, with open mouths, drooling chops, obviously set on ripping the visitor into tiny pieces.

So this isn't the way in, Perduzke sees. The car's seen to it. But maybe the other side. He scrambles over the ditch.

II

The farm Bandekow-Ausbau is only a small offshoot of the principal seat of Bandekow. And its owner, Count Ernst Bandekow, isn't especially close to his older brother, Count Bodo Bandekow, for several reasons, not least the material ones. An old bachelor, he is squatting on the farm, feels more like a farmer, and has taken their part.

It's barely more than a farm cottage, the place where the four occupants of the car are now sitting, along with the count with his pepper-and-salt beard and the slender Henning.

The gentlemen have only just got here. The car is parked in the yard, beside the dungheap, and the dogs have been set loose. Then Count Bandekow sent the two maids and the housekeeper into the garden, and pulled out some schnapps and a Mosel.

'Now we can talk freely,' he says. 'Padberg, you start.'

'Then it's last thing first: Henning, you'll have to clear off, there's a detective on the way.'

'Bah! How would a detective find his way out here?'

'A couple of miles ago there was one of those bastards slinking along the road. I had half a mind to run him over.'

'A cattle-dealer, perhaps. There is a resemblance.'

Thiel pipes up: 'It was a detective, I can tell you. It was Perduzke from Altholm!'

'My golly!' Henning mocks him. 'Someone pour the lad a brandy. He's all white around the gills.'

'You can do whatever you want,' Thiel insists, 'I'm getting out of here.'

'Why? Do you think anyone would get past the dogs alive?'

'What if he shoots them?'

'Then I shoot him,' says the count. 'But leave all that for now. What's he doing in Bandekow, Padberg?'

'You see! What's he doing in Bandekow? That's the question. And here's the other thing. – This morning I walk into the editorial office and find my desk open. I'd left it locked. I check everything, and the only thing that's missing is the card you wrote me, Count, telling us to meet here today.'

Farmer Rehder-Karolinenhorst: 'I expect you forgot to lock it. And the card will be lying around somewhere.'

'If there's one thing I've had to get used to doing in my life, it's keeping an eye out for paper.'

'So the detectives checked at night. They're in a state about the bombs anyway.'

'Nah, they do things officially. They wreck the locks and leave everything a complete mess.'

Henning says in a bored voice: 'All right then, Padberg, why don't you tell us what you think. I'm sure you've formed a suspicion. – And anyway, cheers!'

'Yes, why don't we raise our glasses! Cheers!'

Padberg fishes a letter from his briefcase and passes it round. 'Please take a look at this letter. Don't worry so much about what it says. Some needy journalist. But look at the actual letter. What do you think?'

They all look at it, hesitant, a little perplexed, awkward.

'Well, come on, answers on a postcard!' Padberg gees them up.

'Stop showing off, Padberg,' says Henning. 'We don't have time to play Sherlock Holmes here.'

'None of you?'

'Hang on! One minute!' Thiel comes in. 'Just a question, it might be stupid. Was the letter in the setting shop?'

'Finally!' says a gratified Padberg. 'At least one of you. – No, my son, the letter wasn't in the setting shop.'

'But then a typesetter's laid his grubby mitts on it?'

'Shouldn't have done.'

'But the letter was lying in your drawer, somewhere near the top?'

'That's right, my son, along with the card that's disappeared.'

'Then,' says Thiel, breathing hard, 'then it was a typesetter that stole the card as well. The fingerprints on the letter are printer's ink.'

'If there's nothing more to it than that,' says Henning, 'I could have told you that ages ago. All printers are Reds. They belong to something called a trade union.'

'What a smart boy you are!' Padberg jeers. 'The perspicacity! Yes, they're in a printers' union. But that doesn't mean they go around stealing postcards, least of all such an unimportant card, from some gentleman saying he'd like to see me.'

The count combs his beard with his fingernails. 'It seems to me we've got more important subjects to cover. Keep it short, Herr Padberg.'

'All right. Briefly: in our printshop we have someone who with the aid of perfect night-keys steals documents to order. The fellow's a little bit dim, because first he would have thought about not leaving fingerprints, and second he would have remembered to lock the desk drawer afterwards.

'The person who commissioned the theft must be very well informed. Otherwise we wouldn't have had Perduzke along as early as this morning.'

There is a stricken silence into which Farmer Rehder slowly says: 'I know Franz Reimers would have opposed it. I opposed it. Rohwer opposed it. We three elected leaders of our movement all opposed it. And still you did it, Henning!'

'Well, I'm glad I did and all! They're all so almighty slow about everything they do!' Henning blurts unapologetically.

'We have a good cause,' Farmer Rohwer from Nippmerow. 'You plunged it into noise and stench. The country's been full of talk ever since that kitchen was blown up.'

'And you lied too,' Rehder carries on. 'It was pure chance that nothing but the kitchen went up. You were hoping for something more.'

Henning glowers at Thiel. 'There are some old women I could mention who can't shut up about anything.'

Thiel blushes and looks away.

'I don't agree with you there,' says Padberg smoothly. 'I'm a newspaper man. Newspapers are propaganda, from the first page to the last. Whether it's soap powder or politics, they're always propaganda. Propaganda is something I know something about. Your movement was good, but it was taking place in a vacuum. It made nothing happen, it had no effect. It didn't register with the government. It didn't register with the revenue office. It didn't register with the militia. To the town-dweller it was a bucket of cold spit.

'Henning has given you a propaganda coup. He made a bang. You're right, it was a big bang, one hundred per cent, big propaganda. And now there's life in the movement, people are sitting up: What are the farmers up to? Your movement is getting attention. The movement is getting respect. The movement will be able to get things done.'

'The farmers aren't in favour of that sort of thing,' says Rohwer. 'We don't like it.'

The count says: 'And you don't have to have anything to do with it. None of you was involved in it, none of you knew the least thing about it. If the worst comes to the worst,' he says, raising his voice, 'they were strangers, outsiders, mystery men.'

With a grin of approval, Padberg says: 'Yes, the usual anarcho bomb-chuckers, whom we condemn in the strongest terms.'

'We the anarcho bomb-chuckers thank you for your kind words,' says Henning, also with a grin. 'We aim to give satisfaction.'

'But what are we going to do about the police?'

'I don't have time at the moment to get myself arrested,' explains Henning, 'I have to go to the demonstration.'

'What a prospect,' mocks Padberg. 'Marching openly through the streets of Altholm. An arrest in broad daylight! No no, sonny, you're staying here.'

'I'm going. You need me.'

'What do you mean, we need you? No one is irreplaceable.'

'Come on. I'll show you something.'

'What?'

'You'll see. Come along.'

III

Henning leads the five men across the farmyard into the barn. In the chiaroscuro of the threshing floor – a ray of sunshine is just striking it – he shows off the product of several days of voluntary detention: a flag.

There's a white, rough staff, a handle as for a hayfork, very long, culminating in an upright scythe. The cloth –

Henning comments eagerly on his creation: 'I've thought very carefully about it. The cloth is black. As a sign of mourning over this Jewish republic. On it there's a white plough: symbol of our peaceable work. But also, as a sign that we may not always mean peace, a red sword. All in the colours of the old Reich flag: black, white, red.'

'What a clever boy!' says Padberg mockingly.

'What do you mean, "boy"?' asks Henning sharply. 'Isn't it

good? You say, Rehder! What do you think, Rohwer? Open your mouth, Thiel! What's your view, Count? It's based on the flag of Florian Geyer. You know,' he says to the farmers, who don't know, 'Florian Geyer, the leader of a farmers' revolt. Back in the Middle Ages.'

'Yes. Admittedly against the creation of large estates,' Padberg says mockingly. 'But all that's just so much nonsense. What are we wasting our time on?'

'Excuse me,' says Rohwer. 'The flag's good. Will you wave it, Henning?'

'No, no, not on the farm,' says the count hastily. 'Listen!' The furious barking of the dogs has come to his attention.

'It's Perduzke, see,' Thiel is peering through a crack in a door on the other side of the barn.

In the meantime, Henning has started waving his flag. It opens out, swishing and spanking. He stands there proudly. Waves it, lets it circle in the air.

Rehder is delighted. 'You have to be our flag-bearer on Monday.'

Thiel reports: 'Perduzke has crossed the ditch.'

'But I'm supposed to be arrested,' says Henning.

'I wonder if he'll be able to find the front door,' Count Bandekow observes sarcastically.

'Include that flag in your procession,' Padberg argues, 'and the police will have you broken up in five minutes flat.'

Rehder says: 'We'll put young farmers at the head. Woe betide anyone who messes with our flag.'

Rohwer: 'But the scythe will have to be blunted. Otherwise it could lead to excesses.'

Henning: 'If you like. I'll take the edge off with some metal-cutters.'

And Padberg, astonished: 'So you farmers approve of this bit of flummery?'

The count: 'I think it's very good. It'll have a great effect.'

And Thiel: 'I think it'll be terrific.'

Then Padberg again: 'Who will carry it? Seeing as Henning will be arrested.'

Rehder, energetically: 'Henning is our flag-bearer.'

Padberg, rather impatiently: 'Don't be stupid. They'll arrest Henning in the first minute. They know he offered to buy Tredup's pictures. And he was in front of the presidium when Tredup went in there with Frerksen. And will presumably have been the one who called with the bomb threat. And whoever knew about the false bomb, will have laid the real one. – Well, then?'

'I know a way I can be there,' Henning said languidly, 'and not be arrested.'

'Well? But be quick about it, otherwise you'll be arrested before we've heard it.'

'No one will come on to the farm. He's safe here,' insists the count.

'If someone . . .' Henning begins, but then he thinks again. Then slowly, directly addressing Thiel: 'Let's say you packed your bags at eight or so, and set off into the twilight. And came close to this Perduzke-Perdeuce-Perdee. And suddenly took off. And allowed yourself to be arrested. And let's say you confessed in the morning. And said your accomplice was, well, say the picture idiot on the *Chronicle*, and you stuck to your story till Monday . . .'

Everyone looks at Thiel, who hesitates: 'Well, I'm not sure, I'm getting in over my head . . . You know, I'm not sure . . . Do you want me to be the monkey who pulls your chestnuts out of the fire?'

'Let me tell you something,' Henning comes back. 'I've got a friend, fellow by the name of Gruen, who works in the penitentiary in Altholm. He's nuts, which makes him fireproof. What if he happened to leave a ladder by the prison wall? And then there are the fishermen at Stolpermünde. Depending on the wind, it's a six- or seven-hour sail to the island of Møn. And Møn is Danish territory. And the bomb is political.'

And suddenly, very quickly and fervently: 'Go on, say "yes"!'

Thiel stands there, sheepish, undecided. 'I'd really rather not . . . You see, my parents . . . And why should I get Tredup into trouble? He's just another poor bastard . . .'

Padberg says: 'Well, at any rate, there's two hours till it gets dark. We can think about it till then. Shall we go back inside and talk about the demonstration? I bet a thousand farmers will be there.'

'Three thousand.'

IV

In the mornings, at half past nine, after Stuff has completed the politics and the announcements for his newspaper, he goes on the hunt for local news.

He trots along the Burstah on his hurting flat feet, a small, puffing walrus, notes, blinking through his pince-nez, every single alteration, down to the least new commercial sign, addresses officials, is addressed by them, stops and makes notes.

Altholm has a population of forty thousand or so, and he needs three columns – at the very least two and a half – of local news, for the competition, if for nothing else. And his lines are long, because the *Chronicle* has not yet gone over to four columns per page.

When Stuff has been along the whole of the Burstah he finds himself in the marketplace, a long square at the intersection of two wide avenues, with a war memorial to 1870/1871, the post office, a public convenience and the town hall all situated on it.

By now it's ten o'clock, and already damned hot, when he sets foot in the town hall this July morning. Stuff drips. For the umpteenth time he decides he must change his socks twice a week, once isn't enough. His feet are burning with sweat. And I'm going to start washing them now too.

Stuff knocks quickly and enters the town hall guardroom through the door marked NO ENTRY. This is the room where the town soldiers go to rest up. (Altholm doesn't have militia, it has town police.) A few men are loafing on their pallets, and greet Stuff with the cry, 'Are you buying this round, mate?'

'It's youse's turn! So what's new?'

'New? How long have you got? But first . . .'

'Maurer, I bought you a beer and a short only last week. Have you any idea of the short leash Wenk keeps us on? If I put in for twenty marks a month expenses, he has a hissy fit.'

'Then you just go to Schabbelt!'

'Schabbelt? I keep hearing Schabbelt. What's Schabbelt?'

'Joker! Schabbelt is your proprietor.'

'I haven't clapped eyes on him in a month.'

'He ought to take better care of his wife. Day before yesterday she was singing on the Burstah in broad daylight. It's getting hard to ignore.'

'She's drinking herself to death, is what she is.'

'Shame about her.'

'Well, we all have to die. Maybe it's better to die of drink than to starve to death.'

'It's a point of view. – Well, so what's new?'

'Christ, man, how would we know? Ask Maak in the guard-house. He'll look it up in the incident book.'

'Isn't the Red around?'

'Commander Frerksen is closeted with His Red Excellency. The coast is clear. Perduzke's up there too. They're planning something.'

'Well, off I go! I'll see you later. We must have a drink one of these days.'

'Yes, don't you forget, man.'

'New?' growls Maak. 'Dunno. I'll go and look in the book. Oh yes, man, before I forget, they've got this training course up in Stettin. You might ask under the rubric 'Readers' Letters' why they only sent Party members. The rest of us are just about good enough to do the job, with no training and no perks, and that's it.'

'Will do. It won't change anything, but it'll cause some irrita-tion. Come on now, before the big Red man gets back.'

'Also, there was a car crash. The usual bad corner. Soldin can fill you in on the details, he's been to look. Last night there was another punch-up in the Banana Cellar, we were called out with six men. Talk to the landlord, he'll buy space to make sure you don't write anything unfavourable about his place. And someone found a pram with a baby in it. That's about the size of it –'

The door swings open. Both spin round. Commander Frerksen is standing in the doorway.

'Stuff! Stuff! I must have told you a dozen times to get your news from me, and not from the rank and file!'

'Yes, and when I come to you, you're always busy.'

'It really doesn't matter to your readers whether they get their information one day or the next.'

'I don't think you understand newspapers.'

'Anyway, please leave the guardroom right away, and don't come here again. – I'm going to report you, Maak, to the mayor.'

'I didn't tell Herr Stuff anything!'

'He said I should ask you.'

'Of course, the *Chronicle* won't disclose its sources. Your employees should try and make themselves a little more presentable –'

'Frerksen, how dare you!'

'All right! Now you're getting out of here right away.' And the commander pulls the door shut behind him.

Stuff goes into a rant: 'The swine! The conceited ass! I taught him how to play football! That stringy pen-pusher, I'd like to break his glasses for him.'

And Maak: 'There! You see. And I've lost my rubber.'

'But I'm going to get you, chum, you see if I don't. Your turn will come. No one likes you, you stuck-up piece of shit. You fell upstairs all the way to commander, and you won't let anyone forget it.'

'Mate, it's best you leave now. I'll get the comeuppance later.'

'OK, Maak, I'm going. But mark my words, we'll have him.'

Up a flight of stairs, outside the door of the Criminal Investigation Department: If he caught me hanging around here, that would really set the cat among the pigeons. – Well, who cares, I need news. – 'Morning, Messrs Detectives! What have you got to be so pleased about, Perduzke?'

Perduzke takes the beam off his face, and his 'Good Morning' sounds as tepid as his colleagues'.

Stuff pulls up a chair and reaches for a file.

A hand holds it fast.

'Hey, what's the matter with you today? You must have caught something from your boss!'

'What boss? What do you know about our boss? And which of them do you mean anyway, Gareis or Frerksen?'

'Frerksen, of course. What do I care about Gareis?'

'And what about Frerksen?'

'Well . . .' And Stuff relates.

'Typical, the big-headed idiot!'

'He should just do his job, instead of bullying people.'

'He licks the arses of the high-ups, and kicks us in ours. But I gave it to him,' says Perduzke. 'Did I tell you what happened recently, when the commission turned up, with all the big shots?'

'Yes, but you can tell it to me again. I always like to hear it.'

'Well, you remember the visiting commission from Stettin, all the big shots. The Oberbürgermeister is giving them a tour. They come in here too. I'm sitting here, writing something up. I get up, and say, "Good morning," and go back to work. The Ober is rabbiting on about something or other. I'm writing. Then the Red bandit comes over to me, and says, "Herr Perduzke, will you kindly wait outside until we're done?"

'"Commander," I say. "I'm doing my work, and I'm not bothering anyone."

'"Herr Perduzke, I hereby order you as your superior to go out on to the corridor."

'"I'm busy. My report has to go to the prosecution authorities."

'Well, Frerksen flushes purple. "Herr Oberbürgermeister! Herr Oberbürgermeister! Herr Perduzke is refusing to obey my orders!"

'"Well, Herr Frerksen, what is it he's not doing?"

'"He's supposed to go out in the corridor."

'"Leave him be, why don't you. He's not bothering anyone."'

Loud laughter: 'You give it to him!'

'He must get quite a bit of grief like that!'

'Well, Stuff, do you know why he's in a filthy mood with you today –?' Inspector Bering begins.

'Don't, Karl, you know he can't keep his mouth shut.'

And Stuff, looking through his pince-nez in astonishment: 'What's going on here? Something's the matter. There's something in the air.'

And Perduzke: 'Really, it's better that you don't know.'

'He can find out tomorrow, can't he?' says Commander Reinbrecht.

'Great, so the competition is on to it first!' protests Stuff.

'I give you my word of honour that neither Pinkus at the *Volkszeitung* nor Blöcker at the *News* will hear about it before you.'

'Well, all right. But can you really not tell me now?'

'Out of the question!' declares Perduzke.

And from the other side of the table, Hebel says: 'Another matter! You've got someone at the *Chronicle* – what was his name again? Treadle – Trepan – Tredup. What kind of character is he?'

The question is followed by silence, rather a deep silence, thinks Stuff. He reflects, blinking his eyes. Suddenly he starts laughing: 'Oh, you fools! You idiots! Now I get it. You're upset about the pictures. That it wasn't you that made the big discovery about the straw fires and the oxen, but our advertising manager. I could have told you that long ago.'

The others exchange looks. 'Well, if you know, mate – what's he like, Tredup?'

'Well,' begins Stuff willingly enough, 'so long as he's got money, he's a perfectly OK guy . . .'

V

In another hour, Stuff starts to think that his idea that it was all about the photographs was off-beam. And after two hours, over lunch, he says: 'The brothers made a monkey of me, that's for sure. Frerksen's known for weeks that the pictures are from Tredup. So why do they say he's got a bone to pick with us *today*?'

He starts to ponder. And concludes that Tredup must have done something that the police know about. I'll buy him tonight. I'll take him out on the town.

But Tredup's not in the mood, he has to work.

'What, writing out addresses? But you've got the money for the photographs. That's a lot of moolie.'

'The pictures? Leave it out, Stuff! And not a word about them tonight.'

'So, it's nine o'clock at Tucher's?'

'Nine's too late for me. It's already dark then. Let's make it eight.'

'OK, eight. Eight suits me fine. Then we can take a stroll across the red light district and look at the girls.'

Stuff forms the following plan of action: I'll get Tredup so juiced up that he starts talking, and I'll listen.

But in the afternoon Stuff gets together with Agricultural Councillor Feinbube from the Union of Jersey Cattle-Breeders, and Plosch, the syndic for the local Craftsmen's Association, and they start drinking. Stuff can't get away. He sends a boy to Tucher's with the message to Tredup to come and join them.

But Tredup doesn't come, and Stuff carries on drinking.

After a while he remembers the rendezvous, and he calls the waiter from the bar. 'What did Tredup say?'

'He refuses to come in. He's standing outside on the pavement.'

'And you didn't tell me all this time? – All right, gentlemen, we'll meet again on Monday. You'll be going to see the farmers' demonstration, I take it?'

Tredup is pacing back and forth outside, back and forth.

The Burstah and the station square are full of people at this early and mild hour of the evening. Lots of light dresses, and couples in every doorway, including, naturally, the *Chronicle*.

'There now, Tredup,' says Stuff, awkwardly taking his arm. 'There in the entrance to the *Chronicle* is the youngest of our cleaning girls, Grete Schade, and it seems she's got a new swain.'

'Whatever a man needs . . .'

'Yes, she's a good-looking girl, but she's not even fifteen . . .'

'She won't tell swain that, surely . . .'

'He knows she only left school this Easter. There's no excuse, if the trap snaps shut, he's in it.'

'That's your worry.'

'Mine? Hmm, maybe. If she's lying. You can never tell. I'll tell you the story, but you have to promise to keep quiet about it.'

'Of course.'

'Word of honour?'

'Word of honour!'

'Well, about three months ago – we still had the heating on – I come into the office straight from the bar. I couldn't see out of my eyes. Grete is just cleaning the place, and blow me if the little minx doesn't suddenly plonk herself on my lap. My Lord, the warmth! I felt, let's say, a changed man. All she had on over her chemise was a little wool dress. And the warmth of her. The bosom on her!'

'You're not about to – are you, Stuff? Or are you?'

'Well, what if I do? Who could blame me? And is it right that I get hauled off for seducing a minor, when . . .? Pissed like I was, and the curves on her. No, anyway . . .' And Stuff suddenly goes into a different mode: 'So you have to be a man, and keep yourself under control. Nothing happened, as I say. I pushed her off. – There, and now let's go into the Grotto.'

'The Grotto? I'm not sure I want to go to the Grotto. My wife wouldn't like it.'

'Does she wear the trousers, then?'

'What if she does? Any sensible man is happy to find someone to share the responsibilities with him.'

'The man always has to be in charge, though,' lectures Stuff.

'Rubbish! You try being married for ten years! You try being married for one! Always in charge! You should look around and see how you and a wife of yours get on!'

'Do you know what you are!' yells Stuff. 'You're decadent!'

'Ach, give over,' says Tredup contemptuously. 'You're like a blind man talking about colour! If you were married, you'd talk differently. Just, no one wanted you.'

'No one wanted me,' Stuff growls back crossly. 'Do you want to go out together now or not?'

'Do I want to? It was you who asked me in the first place!' They stop where they are, in the middle of the bridge, and look at each other challengingly.

On the left is the pond where the River Blosse flows, on the right the water flows quietly and clearly over the weir. It's dark here under the trees. A few gaslights drop their reflections on the tarmac road, daub trembly, glittery forms on the black surface of the pond. In the background are the bright lights over the entrance to the Grotto.

'Me ask you!' says Stuff incredulously. 'As if!' And, in a sudden fury: 'How would you like to be thrown in the water?! You rat! You traitor!'

Tredup looks at Stuff, and the empty street losing itself under the darkness of the trees. He links arms with Stuff. 'Come on, Stuff, what are you fussing about? There's the Grotto right there.'

And suddenly Stuff remembers what he wanted from the man. It was something to do with the police, or those wretched photographs. Or anything but the photographs, whatever. He can't quite recall. It'll come to him when he's sitting over a beer.

And then the door to the Grotto opens. Jazz breathes into the summer night. The sound of the water is toned down.

Stuff clings on to Tredup's arm a little tighter. 'Come on, son. It's time to down a few. I'm thirsty, aren't you?'

VI

Two hours later, the pair of them are still in the Grotto. They have both drunk valiantly, and Stuff's face is purple and puffy. Tredup looks pale, and has to be excused at frequent intervals.

Stuff, fat, hard-boiled Stuff, is still bothered by something Tredup said that pierced him to the heart, that there wasn't a woman that wanted him. That's why he's now started filling Tredup in about some of the triumphs of his past life.

'I promise you, Tredup, there's no park bench and no shrubbery where I haven't been with a girl. And the dark passage outside the town hall . . . Oh, I should tell you how I was once surprised there . . .'

And he tells the story, lingers on the details, and finally: 'Back then women were women, you know, Tredup, not half-starved sparrows the way they are today! And the white bloomers, the way they used to glow in the dark! When I think of those mauve and beige ham bags nowadays, I tell you the charm is gone.'

'What I wanted to ask you,' Tredup starts somewhere else. 'You said something about "traitor" back then. "Little traitor" is what you said. Was that about the photographs?'

'Don't get into it, Tredup, leave it out!' says Stuff, moved. 'None of us is an angel. If all the wicked things I've done were known, then I'd be in prison for years and years.'

'I'm sure you're exaggerating. – Do you really think anyone else knows about me selling the photos?'

'Exaggerating! I tell you, Tredup, in a back house on the Kleine Lastadie in Stettin there's a woman – and if she felt like talking, and knew my name. My God, there . . .'

Stuff loses his thread, and Tredup manages to get in his question: 'Do you think the farmers know about my photographs? For the past few days, someone . . .'

'The first time, I went there with Henni. Henni was so dead set against. I didn't have to marry her, and I wouldn't have to shell out any money, and she would bring up the kid by herself. Of course I go with her to see the woman. We walk in. – I'd told Henni I'd stop loving her if she didn't go ahead. "Please let me keep the kid," she begged me.

'We walk in, it's just an ordinary kitchen-diner, you know, with the woman's two grown-up sons. They walk out the minute we come in, you know, not a word. She's a little wizened woman, used to be a midwife. No need to tell her anything, she gets the picture right away. "Just lie down on the table over there!" And to me: "That'll be twenty-five marks."'

Stuff sighs gustily, and looks straight into space.

'Well, and then it's over in a jiffy. She does it with water and a syringe, it just has to be done at the right moment. Two days or twenty-four hours later, the kid arrived. No one even noticed with Henni. She lost it overnight, and the next day she was back at work. She was a parlourmaid.

'But when she told me about it, Tredup, I still dream of it at night. "I looked at it before I threw it away," she says. "It would have been a girl." I howled when she told me, Tredup, really howled.'

'Well, it was all a long time ago, I'm sure,' Tredup says blandly.

'Not that long at all,' boasts Stuff. 'And I've been three times to see her since. – And once I persuaded the girl to perjure herself too . . .

'Yes, men are swine, Tredup, we're all swine. By day we run around and do exactly the same dumb work as all the others, but at night, if we've spent long enough sitting around in bars, and there's just a little bit of sense left in our brains, then we see what swine we are: me, you, all of us.'

'Stuff,' says Tredup on a sudden impulse, pale with agitation, 'Stuff, someone keeps following me.'

'Ooh, I'm sure you're only imagining it.'

'And I think it's to do with the pictures . . .'

'What pictures? Oh, those pictures. No, that's all sorted, nothing will happen to you over that. If I were you, I wouldn't hang around here on Monday, when the farmers are holding their demonstration, but other than that, I'm sure you're in the clear.'

'No, no, that's not what I mean. And there's the bomb as well, that went off in the president's house.'

'Where's the connection with the pictures! You idiot!' laughs Stuff. 'The bomb was about taxes, and to frighten the government. And they've shut themselves and all, you can bet on it.'

'But someone's following me,' Tredup insists. 'Not back then, but in the last few days.'

'Could it be someone knows something about the money? How much did you get anyway?'

'Three hundred. – No, no one knows anything about that.'

'So that'd be five hundred, then. Did you spend much of it?'

'Just ten marks!'

'And your missus?'

'She doesn't know either. The money's not in the house.'

'Then you'd better let someone know where it is. In case something happens to you.'

'You see, you believe it too! See! No, no one's going to get to hear about that, it's buried. Even if you beat my brains out, I'm not telling you.'

'Don't blather. You're pissed. Who's going to beat your brains out?'

'Well, the guy from the magazine, for instance, who turned up with you the other night. Or the man who's following me around.'

'Who is he?'

'A short fat guy. With wiry hair. Black hair.'

Stuff suddenly has an idea. 'Hey, did you ever meet Perduzke?'

'Perduzke? No. Who's he?'

'Listen to me, Tredup,' says Stuff, leaning forward across the table. 'Have you got in some trouble lately? I mean, something big, not a little piffling thing while you're alone in the office, selling space.'

'Stuff, you're a bastard,' says Tredup. 'You're a real bastard. But for your information, I've done nothing, whether small or big.'

'You really sure?' Stuff persists with big round eyes.

'Positive. Not theft nor false witness nor abortion nor bombs nor anything else.'

'I think he's telling the truth myself,' says Stuff. 'Then Perduzke's a fool. Let him chase after you, Tredup, he can't harm you. He's after the wrong person.'

'But I'm scared, Stuff. Each time I turn round suddenly, I see someone. And worst of all is when I don't see him, then I'm sort of flinching till I see him again.'

'You're a coward! You should have been on the Front with us . . .'

But Tredup carries on: 'There's a spot on the back of my skull which I keep feeling. There, just below the crown. I'm not kidding you. I feel a sort of pressure there all the time, and I just know that one day I'm going to get whacked there with a mattock. Right there. I can feel it now. A blow from behind. And then I'll I've had my chips.'

He looks at Stuff expectantly.

'We had a corporal at the Front,' says Stuff. 'With him it began like that too –'

'I don't want you to talk,' Tredup interrupts him. 'Tell me what to do. I think I'm going to go mad.'

'The corporal,' Stuff persists, 'wound up in an asylum –'

Tredup abruptly gets up. 'G'night, Stuff. You're good for the bill, aren't you?' And he takes his hat and walks out.

VII

It's still a summer night outside, a dark, moonless summer night, with a gentle rustle of leaves. The water over the weir is still burbling, and the shining reflections of the gaslights are lying on the black surface of the pond.

Tredup leans against a tree and scrutinizes the road into town. The tarmac is still and clear in the light of the lamps, and the pavement is also empty and reasonably well lit.

But there are rows of trees on either side, and a man could be hiding, or even two, behind the stout linden trunks, who's to know? And then they leap out, and there's the spot on the back of his head . . . Once he's been hit, it won't be so bad, but the moment of expectation must be gruesome.

The best thing is to go back to the bar and call for a taxi from the station, he thinks. But no, what about Stuff? I won't be able to shake him off, and the drinking will begin again, and all the stupid talk about women . . .

Tredup steps out into the middle of the roadway and slowly starts to walk. Each time he's on the level of two trees, he looks carefully behind them before going on.

Five or six pairs of trees are already behind him, ahead of him at the end of the avenue are the lights from the market square, when suddenly from out of the deepest shadow, a small, round, bearded fellow confronts him . . . the one he saw earlier on today . . .

Tredup sees something like an outstretched hand coming for him . . . He takes a huge leap in the direction of the market square, screams, and starts to run.

Behind him he hears hurried footfall, there are two of them now. One calls: 'Stop or I shoot!'

Tredup runs for all he's worth.

A second voice calls: 'Let him go, Perduzke. We'll catch him anyway.'

Perduzke? Tredup thinks. Perduzke? Who's Perduzke? But he needs to keep running, otherwise they'll catch him, and smash him on the painful spot on the back of his skull.

He runs right across the lit-up market square, which, now, after midnight, is completely deserted, and into Probstenstrasse.

I can get home this way, he thinks. Oh, how I wish I was already back with Elise! And he runs even faster.

There seems to be only one of them following him now; Tredup is hopeful he can shake him off, because the fellow is panting rather badly. And right by here is the town park, if he can reach that, it's dark, and they won't find him.

He hangs a bend. His pursuer is at least twenty paces behind him.

Then there's the crunch of gravel underfoot. It's splendidly dark and deep night in here. Tredup hops over a piece of lawn, crashes through a bush, runs silently over some more lawn – and, while he's turning into the back end of Calvinstrasse, he sees his pursuer a long way back, waving a torch around, looking for him.

When he opens his front door a quarter of an hour later, he finds the fat man with the black beard sitting on the chair next to the dresser. A tearful Elise, bundled up in her blanket, is perched on the side of the bed. The children pop their heads out, and withdraw them again.

'Welcome home, Herr Tredup,' says the fat man. 'My colleague is still making his way here. My name is Perduzke, from the CID. Unless I'm mistaken, Herr Stuff will have mentioned my name to you in the course of today.'

'It was you who followed me from the Grotto, was it?' asks Tredup nervously.

'A colleague and I,' confirms Perduzke. 'Admittedly, you seem to have shaken him off.'

'And it's you who's been tailing me these past few days?'

'For almost forty-eight hours, since the evening of the day before yesterday.'

'Well, if I'd only known that,' says Tredup, with a deep sigh. 'Then I could have spared myself the trouble.'

'That's what you say now,' says Perduzke sounding unconvinced, 'Anyway, I'm arresting you.'

'What for?'

'What for? You tell me.'

'I don't know of any reason.'

Perduzke says grandly: 'They all like to sound as stupid as they can. But we'll talk about it in the morning. It will all look very different once you've spent the night in a cell.'

'Max,' whispers Frau Tredup. 'Max, if you've got anything on your conscience, it might be best to own up to it right away, and then the gentleman might let you stay here.'

'Think about it,' says Perduzke. 'Your wife is a sensible woman.'

'There isn't anything, Elise, don't worry. It's all nonsense. But go along to the town hall first thing tomorrow morning, and see Mayor Gareis, and tell him I've been arrested and need to talk to him.'

'Gareis? What have you got to do with our mayor?'

'All right, Elise, don't forget, and don't do it any later, and then I'll be back home tomorrow evening.'

'That's the sort of miracle not even a Red mayor can perform. Come along, Herr Tredup.'

'And tell Stuff what happened. Not Wenk. Stuff. Goodnight, Elise.'

'Goodnight, Max. Oh, Max, how will I be able to sleep . . . and the children . . . oh, Max.'

'It's nothing, Elise, nothing at all. It's even for the best, my being arrested now. I'll be able to get a proper night's kip.'

'Oh, Max . . .'

VIII

In Mayor Gareis's office the following afternoon – a bright and sunny July afternoon – four gentlemen are sitting together. Floods of joyful light come in through the large windows and illumine the amiable, sweet face of the heaviest man of Altholm, the mobile, now somewhat downcast, features of Chief Adviser Meier, representative of the government in Stolpe, the pinched, unhappy face of Militia Colonel Senkpiel, and the alert expression of Commander Frerksen.

Gareis looks even more amiable, smiles even more sweetly. 'But, my dear friends from Stolpe, why in all the world would I want to ban the farmers' demonstration?'

And Chief Adviser Meier, a little irritably: 'I've already told you several times: for fear of incidents.'

'With our farmers? It wouldn't occur to them to offer violence.'

Chief Adviser Meier says with heavy emphasis: 'The farmers' movement is more dangerous than the KPD and NSDAP combined. I quote verbatim something said by our president, isn't that so, Colonel?'

Colonel Senkpiel growls assent: 'We must have the militia here on Monday.'

Gareis smiles even more brilliantly. 'Surely not against my own wishes, Colonel?'

And Chief Adviser Meier, hurriedly: 'What I relayed to you are the wishes of the president. I need hardly say that you would be making yourself solely responsible, if you were to disregard them.'

Meier pokes in his waistcoat pocket and pulls out a piece of paper. 'With all de —' he begins, and peers short-sightedly through his pince-nez. The mayor folds his hands over his belly and leans back submissively. 'With all demonstrations, two factors are to be kept in view at all times: the mood of the demonstrators, and the mood of the rest of the population.

'In the present case, feeling in the farming community is running dangerously high. I call to mind the ox confiscation in Gramzow, the bomb in the president's villa . . .

'The danger is all the greater, as the farmers are no settled community, but something fluid and volatile. They have no written membership or leaders.

'In the case of other demonstrations, Herr Mayor, you speak to the leaders. You discuss the parameters with them, you agree an itinerary and a time and a place. You are dealing with people who take responsibility. Not here. Everyone is authorized, and no one is.

'Second factor: the mood of the population. The strongest

parties locally are the SPD and KPD. Self-evidently, neither is sympathetic to the farmers. There are a thousand potential spark-points, all unpredictable. A shout can set off a punch-up, a punch-up can be the prelude to a pitched battle.

'You have some eighty officers –'

'Seventy-eight,' Commander Frerksen chips in.

'Quite. Seventy-eight. Twenty at any given time will be on leave.'

'Twenty-one.'

'All right, Herr Frerksen. Shall we say the odd one, give or take, doesn't matter.'

Frerksen crumples.

'All right . . . I take away . . . How does it go? Commander, can you help me out . . . twenty-one from . . .'

'There would be fifty-seven men available.'

'That's it. Fifty-seven. In practical terms, fifty, because some would have to remain on traffic duty, et cetera.'

'Really only forty,' says the mayor.

'Very good, forty. Forty! Mayor, Herr Gareis, please! There are three or four or even five thousand farmers, demonstrating, in a hostile environment, in a Red town – forgive me, I'm a Party member myself! – and you want to control them with forty men from an unspecialized local force . . . It looks like insanity to me! But Herr Gareis, what do you say!'

'The short answer is I'm not about to ban the demonstration!

'First, I don't have any legal right to. Every day I sanction marches and demonstrations from every party. I can't suddenly make an exception . . .

'Second, I see no grounds for a ban. The farmers' movement may be everything you claim it is, but its members are not *aggressive*. Gramzow is a case in point. Passive resistance occurred there, and oxen were beaten, but no one had a hair of their head harmed.

'Now, I understand that the bombing in Stolpe has made people there nervous, but –'

'Nervous, Mayor . . .?'

'Well, then, not nervous. There is no evidence that that incident is connected to the farmers in any way. The first arrest made was of an employee of the Revenue Department, who claimed he wanted to get his own back on the district president, whom for some stupid reason he holds responsible for his losing his job. And the second is even less of a Bauernschaft man, as you of all people should know, Chief Adviser.'

'In my view that arrest is a mistake.'

'Then we're agreed on that count. To conclude. The Bauernschaft is not aggressive. There remains the question of the mood among our working population. The demonstration will probably take place at a time when our workers will be in their factories.

'Finally, a matter of principle. Demonstrations should be allowed to run their course. The more fuss, the more resources, the more possibilities of friction. If you bring in a couple of platoons, the instant effect is that the farmers will be made aware of their power. Forty men isn't a lot, but they're quite enough. I say: Nothing will happen.

'And I say: I'm not going to do anything either.'

The mayor makes a brisk movement. 'As I say, let them run their course. That's it. I'm done. I'm sorry it took so long. But I think it's all clear now.'

And Gareis beams round at the little circle of visitors. While he does, his hand gropes behind him. There, dangling from his desk, is the bulb of a bell-push. He presses it once, twice, three times.

Chief Adviser Meier bestirs himself: 'No, Mayor, let me say again: nothing has been made clear. Your decision is impossible. I refuse to take such a decision with me back to Stolpe. The district president has instructed me –'

The door opens, and Secretary Piekbusch appears in some agitation. 'Mayor! The Oberbürgermeister asks if you have a moment. It's very urgent.'

The mayor gets up. 'I am called away. Excuse me, gentlemen. I'll be back as soon as I can. Perhaps you could discuss things further with Frerksen. Herr Frerksen can furnish you with more information.'

And Gareis disappears.

IX

Gareis stands panting in his outer office. 'Leave them to chatter on in there, Comrade Piekbusch, it was high time I brought proceedings to a halt. Those Stolpers – a firecracker goes off, and because their little lives were briefly at risk, they want to impose a state of emergency on the whole world.'

'Political Adviser Stein has Farmer Benthin with him. I thought it as well that your visitors didn't catch sight of him.'

'Very good. You've done well.'

And Gareis crosses the corridor, swaying and puffing, to his political adviser's office.

In the corridor is a rather irresolute-looking woman, whose face seems to lighten when she sees him. The mayor, who has the whole help-seeking world in his outer office – he is also in charge of the Welfare Department – the mayor stops and asks: 'Did you want to see me, madam?'

'Oh, yes, Mayor. Yes, please. And then I was told I couldn't see you. Even though you've had my husband arrested.'

'Your husband? That's bad. Who is your husband?'

'Tredup, Your Worship, Tredup from the *Chronicle*, who came to see you over the photographs once.' Falling over herself with hurry and worry: 'Even if he's in trouble now, and not everything was right about the pictures, he is a good man deep down. It's just that we're not lucky, and that we stumble from one thing to the next. He's hard-working and he doesn't drink and he doesn't gamble, and he will go anywhere to sell space, and he addresses envelopes all evening, until deep into the night. Only, not all of it seems to help, and we have two little ones, and we're just barely treading water.'

'But surely you must be doing a little bit better now that he's got a thousand marks for the pictures?'

'A thousand marks? My Max? But, Your Worship, that can't be right, because surely I'd know about it then. We've had no money in the house these past days, not until Wenk, who's the manager of the paper, gave him an advance of ten marks.'

Gareis blinks his eyes. 'Well, maybe he hasn't got the money yet. But he certainly will. I'll, er, look into it.'

And Frau Tredup: 'Are you really sure about the thousand marks? Oh, Your Worship, if that's true! A thousand marks . . . That would mean we could buy clothes and shoes for the children, and I'm sure Max could use –'

'It's quite certain, Frau Tredup. But now your husband has been arrested?'

'Yes. Oh Lord, and I forgot all about it. It's only because I got so excited. And would you be kind enough to visit him? If you want. And if it's not an impertinence to ask you.'

'No, no, not at all. I'll go and see him. Probably some time today. And don't worry. Your husband isn't in any trouble. You'll get him back very soon.'

'Oh, thank you, Your Worship! And the thousand marks?'

'They're yours. – Well, I'll give him your best, shall I, your – Max?'

'Thank you, Your Worship! And then –'

But Gareis has already slipped into Political Adviser Stein's office, and the door is just shutting behind him.

Standing by the window is Farmer Benthin, the only farmer in Altholm, known by the name of 'Moth-Head', because some condition has eaten round 'moth-holes' in his greying blond thatch. He is puffing on an almighty stogey.

'Keep it there, Father Benthin, you puff away. Well, and how's life treating you? Your wife well? Is the boy come yet?'

'Thank'ee, Herr Mayor. All are doing well. The son and heir is still keeping us waiting. It'll be any day now.'

'Same with us here, I gather.'

'With us? How do you mean, Herr Mayor?'

'It's come to my attention that you're planning on holding a great demonstration here. Public commotion. Ten thousand farmers. Resistance against State authority. Unrest. Revolution.'

'Golly, Herr Mayor, what do you take me for? I'm a peace-loving man.'

'But what about the others? The farmers? The movement?'

'But them's all people like me, Herr Mayor.'

'But what are you after? Surely you must be after something? You wouldn't go parading on the street for nothing at all?'

'All we want is to show our support for Franz Reimers. See here, Herr Mayor, the man's in prison now, and it's all for those bloody taxes. It's difficult with taxes, Herr Mayor, believe me.'

'Oh, I know, I know, Cousin Benthin. I think it's time we put on a nice exhibition again, like the two of us did last year. That spreads a bit of cheer.'

'That were a good exhibition, Herr Mayor, there's no doubting that.'

'Well, and, er, Monday – will that be good too?'

'Golly, why wouldn't it be good? We're peaceable folk. There'll be singing, and probably some speeches. And you see, Herr Mayor, there be some young farmers among us, and some as are bitter, some are faring awful badly. Anyway, you needn't listen to what they say. There's some as always have plenty to say for themselves. But that don't mean anything will happen.'

'Let me tell you something, Benthin, the reason I've asked you to come and see me. You're an old Altholm hand, and I'm thinking you have some regard for the place, even if it's just an old industrial town these days. Cousin Benthin, we put on a fine exhibition together, and now will you look me in the eye and tell me to my face that there won't be any agitation on Monday, and no trouble, and no breakage.'

'Herr Mayor, it'll pass off quietly, if I know my farmers.'

'And you'll promise me, Cousin Benthin, that you'll come and see me on Monday morning with the leaders, so that we can talk about how and when and where you'll march?'

'I give you my word, Herr Mayor.'

'And you'll promise me by all that's holy that you'll come to me of your own accord on Monday if you notice that there's going to be a shindig? It would be a pity if it turned out that the farmers had caused trouble in Altholm.'

'I give you my word, Herr Mayor.'

'Well, then all's well, Cousin Benthin. And give my best to your wife. And let's hope your son and heir arrives safely and soon.'

'Thank you for that, Herr Mayor.'

'And you'll promise me that I can rest easy, Cousin Benthin, and without concerns?'

'As easy as I wish my son shall sleep in his cradle, Herr Mayor, as easy as my son.'

X

'I want to tell you something,' Chief Adviser Meier is saying at this precise moment, with unusual emphasis. 'It doesn't even occur to me to take that pig-headed decision from Gareis back to Stolpe with me. You know how it is, Colonel. My respected boss would tear my ears off.'

Meier gets up, the pince-nez drops from the bridge of his nose and, hanging on its ribbon, bangs against his waistcoat once or twice. 'My ears? I'd be finished, done for, if I go back to Stolpe with that decision. And I mean to tell your mayor in words of one syllable, Commander Frerksen: the demonstration must be banned!'

He stood there, his feisty face trembling, the hair hanging down into his brow.

'I too am of the view –' began the colonel.

But Meier was in the grip of some exceptional surge of energy, he saw his career under threat, he shouted: 'This isn't about views or opinions, this is about reasons of State. The demonstration must be stopped!'

'Inasmuch as I know my boss –' Frerksen begins with careful intensity.

'I know my boss too!' shouts the adviser. 'Do you think he can just cast aside the bomb episode? You brought that on us! You, Herr Frerksen, and your wonderful Comrade Gareis. Does he take himself for Mussolini, or what? "I have no doubts." Terrific, just as *my* boss –'

He breaks off, and stares into space, to begin again with renewed violence: 'You're responsible for sending us this picture man, this whole debacle began with the picture man. Without the pictures, there'd be no bomb. Temborius will never forgive! And he has connections in the ministry!'

The militia colonel clears his throat in deprecation.

The adviser, more quietly and sibilantly: 'We are among ourselves. Herr Frerksen, even if you wear the uniform, you are a civilian person. In confidence: The district president told me before I left: "I demand an exceptionally ruthless treatment of those layabouts of farmers."'

The colonel clears his throat again, louder.

And the adviser, even more urgently and sibilantly: 'We are among ourselves, Colonel. Do you want blood to flow? The farmers are insolent . . .' – then slickly – 'they thumb their noses at the State! Stopping the demonstration will avoid worse excesses. Two platoons of militia, under experienced leadership, and newly arriving demonstrators are efficiently dispersed. Commander!'

Frerksen inclines his head regretfully. 'I'm afraid I have no influence, Chief Adviser.'

'You are not *without* influence. I know exactly how things work around here! You are the man of his choice, of his trust. He has made you commander, against the wishes of the Right, against the Oberbürgermeister, against the magistracy, practically against his own comrades. He will listen to you.'

'He will only listen to himself.'

'I want you to tell him: the local force is too weak. Tell him you can't accept the responsibility. Put the pistol to his chest, go on holiday – whatever you do, stop the demonstration. Gareis needs you to carry out his commands. Deny him your assistance, and stop this crazy, treasonous demonstration.'

'It exceeds my power –'

'Who, after all, is Gareis? A chance elected representative of a chance locally elected majority. There are fresh elections due in autumn. The connections of the president –'

'Gentlemen,' says Colonel Senkpiel, who abruptly gets to his feet. 'This isn't on.'

The other two stare at him.

'Moreover, Gareis is on close personal terms with the minister.'

'We are among our own, Colonel, you need have no worries,

we are among our own. What, after all, is a mayor? Am I right, or am I right? You want to make a career, don't you, Commander? Stop this demonstration!'

'Gentlemen,' the commander begins hastily and whisperingly, and looks anxiously at the door. 'I understand your point of view, I would almost say, I share it. But your assumptions are wrong. I have neither power nor influence. If you try to convince him, Chief Adviser, I will be happy to try and back you up, as far as my job allows. That's the most I can do.'

'As far as your job allows!' The adviser sounds scathing. 'Sometimes, my dear Commander, a man has to make a choice. Sometimes he has to make a sacrifice in the interests of some greater objective.'

'Even so! Even so! My job here. I am not well liked in the town.'

Senkpiel drums his fingers on the windowpane. 'Are you nearly finished, gentlemen? None of this sounds very nice. Anyway, Gareis may be back at any moment.'

The adviser jumps up, runs agitatedly back and forth. 'And you want things to stay with this decision? Not possible! Completely out of the question! There has to –' He stops, his features brighten. 'Come closer, gentlemen. You too, Colonel, please. I have another proposal. The demonstration takes place. We allow it. How's that, gentlemen? Surprised? Yes, we permit the farmers' demonstration, we are magnanimous. But . . .

'But you, Commander Frerksen, you are in charge of the local constabulary. You oversee the demonstration. You keep an eye on things, an exceptionally sharp eye.'

Very slowly: 'And the instant you notice anything, anything offensive, provocative, anything against the State – it can be as little as a shout, perhaps, or a song – then you step in, and you break up the demonstration.'

The adviser looks round in triumph, the colonel remarks drily: 'With forty local constables? Congratulations on your assignment, Frerksen.'

The adviser smiles. 'Yes. I hadn't got around to that yet. I would think dear Herr Gareis will agree to the following little concession, seeing as I have gone so far to meet him. We keep a couple of platoons in readiness, without anyone knowing. Behind the town hall, in the Marbede School, which is handy. He'll agree to that, wouldn't you think, Herr Frerksen?'

'I don't know . . . Possibly . . . But I wonder . . .?'

'They're not there to be used, you understand. Only in an extreme emergency, Commander; he will surely agree to that!'

He turns quickly to face the returning Gareis; 'Well now, Your Worship. We've talked it all over once more. Herr Frerksen has made some valuable points: our doubts are not dispelled, but we will try to minimize them. It's true you may have an outstanding line to the farmers, ever since your wonderfully successful exhibition. Well then, the demonstration can happen, it has been sanctioned.'

'I already told one of the local farmers' leaders as much.'

Meier looks as though he'd just bitten into something unpleasant tasting. 'Well. Anyway. That's fine, then. You will just have to make the one concession to us. In case of dire emergency, we lay by a couple of platoons of militia, in the town hall courtyard, in a school.' Very quickly: 'No, no, no one will get to hear about it, the men will be brought in overnight. It's just so that you will have reinforcements to hand, in case they are required. I would even, if you'll allow me, place them under your personal command.'

The colonel grunts.

The chief adviser smiles uneasily.

'Our dear Colonel Senkpiel seems inclined to protest. But you do understand, Colonel, tricky as the case is. We're really all of one mind, isn't that right, Mayor?'

The mayor smiles. 'I am long since of one mind, namely with myself. I'm not having the militia in Altholm. Everything you say about things happening "secretly" and "unbeknown to anyone" is, if you'll pardon my saying so, Chief Adviser, so much rot. About a hundred windows face on to the town hall square, quite apart from the fact that even in Altholm people are sometimes awake at night, and might see the militia moving in.

'No, all of that is out of the question. There won't be any clashes.'

'Mayor, please, the district president –'

'The district president can't change my decision either.'

'We will issue you with an order!'

'Then I'll turn to the minister. – But, my dear Chief Adviser, what are we doing getting hot under the collar? I'll bear the responsibility on my own. That's all there is to it.'

'That's not all. It cannot and will not be settled in this way.'

'And I tell you, it's settled.'

'In that case,' cries the adviser in desperation, 'in that case, we have no alternative but to call the militia to Grünhof and Ernst-tal. Into the suburbs.'

'I can't prevent things from being done outside my district. But I'm not happy about it, because the militia will be seen there too.'

'And I predict that you will use those militia, Mayor. I prophesy –'

'No prophecies, Chief Adviser, prophets never have credit in their own country. – Another question, though, while I have you. Do you know if Tredup got his thousand marks?'

'Yes he did,' replies the adviser ill-humouredly.

'Are you quite certain?'

'I was standing there while he took it.'

'Took the money – I like that. But it's strange . . .'

'Well, Mayor, my work here is finished. I won't keep from you the fact that I'm leaving with a heavy heart. The district president will be extremely unhappy.'

'On Tuesday you'll know I was right.'

'I hope so, but I can't think so. Goodbye, Mayor.'

'Goodbye, Chief Adviser. Always a pleasure.'

The adviser and the commander shake hands. 'Goodbye, Herr Frerksen.' Sotto voce: 'We're relying on you.'

The government deputation takes its leave.

The mayor, very sharply: 'On what matter is Stolpe relying on you, if I might ask, Herr Frerksen?'

Frerksen is all aquiver. 'Oh, they were just banging on at me to stay on your case about the militia.'

Gareis takes a long look at his police commander. 'Whatever you say, Frerksen. I think the business about the militia is taken care of. No, please, don't start. But . . .' – and very sharply – 'remember it's my orders that count here.'

And then in a sudden transition, with seraphic smile: 'And if you learned anything from the episode with the photographs, surely it's about the sort of thanks you get from Stolpe. I'm only a little horse' – he moves his giant bulk – 'but at the moment I feel I'm making the running.'

XI

The province's principal prison lies some way outside Altholm. With its red-brick construction, the whitish-grey of the cement cladding, interrupted only by the monotonous rows of window bars, it makes a dispiriting sight, even on the most radiant July afternoon.

This Mayor Gareis knows, having been there often enough. When a guard answers his ring and unlocks the gatehouse door, he says curtly: 'I've come to see Director Greve. I can find my own way.'

The guard watches him go, heavily and unhurriedly stepping out of the gatehouse, crossing the yard into the sunshine. This is the place for him all right, the Red bastard, he thinks, and he slides the heavy bolts back.

Twenty square metres of lawn, two beds of geraniums and four rose bushes constitute a shy attempt at creating a park-like atmosphere, but it remains a prison yard, a chill agglomeration of granite, brick, cement and iron. To the left the remand prison, to the right the young offenders' wing, straight ahead the management block, atop which, crowned by a golden cross, is the prayer room, the prison chapel.

When he sees the flashing golden cross, Gareis is unable to keep from thrusting out his lower lip, shaking his shoulders, and mouthing a silent 'Ha!'

Loud, threatening voices, a noisy exchange of words, and his attention is drawn back from the cross to a car, a locked private vehicle, parked in front of the remand prison. Beside the car are two uniformed guards, a civilian in whom he recognizes his own Inspector Katzenstein, and a second civilian who is being loudly talked to by the other three men.

The civilian is supposed to do something, perhaps get into the car, but he stands where he is, his back pressed against the wall, his hands extended in front of him in self-defence. The guards are telling him off, patient, calmer, more in the background, is Katzenstein.

For a moment, Gareis stands there uncertainly, then he suddenly remembers who the civilian is. He crosses the yard, hurries up to the man in trouble with the law, and holds out his hand. 'Hello, Herr Reimers. I'm pleased to see you. Are you going on an outing?'

Reimers eyes him coldly, but not altogether dismissively. 'Is this a chance meeting, Mayor, or is there more to it?'

Gareis laughs. 'You get a little suspicious, don't you, if you're locked up in a cage, day in day out, all by yourself? All the people outside are in cahoots against you.'

'Would you be talking from experience there?'

'Are you asking me if I've done time? I have indeed, I have indeed. An infraction of the press laws once. But they couldn't prove anything against me, and so I ended up as Mayor of Altholm.'

'You were lucky. They've got proofs in my case.'

'But you have mitigating circumstances. It won't be so bad. And it doesn't seem you're cut out to be a mayor anyway.'

'I'm a farmer.'

'The best thing to be,' avers Gareis. 'By the way, how's the Holstein steer that won first prize at our agricultural show?'

Reimers smiles, he actually smiles. 'We showed him at the great agricultural fair in Stettin, and he won the special prize from the Chamber of Agriculture.'

'Well, then,' says Gareis. 'By the way, our running into each other really is pure chance. I'm on my way to visit someone else, though, come to think of it, he may have some connection to you. One Tredup.'

'Tredup . . .? The son of a bitch who passed on the photographs? You're on your way to see him?!'

'That's right! I'm on my way to see him. You see, he's under suspicion of having planted the bomb the night you were arrested.'

'Him . . .?! The police –'

And that's as far as Reimers gets. One of the guards has been listening to the conversation between the mayor and the prisoner with waxing anger. Now he almost explodes: 'It's forbidden to talk to prisoners without special permission. Go away!'

The mayor beams. 'Quite so. A conscientious official. Tell me, did the man over there, Katzenstein, did he show you his special permission?'

'That's none of my beeswax. He's a detective.'

'Right. And I'm that detective's superior. So . . .?'

The other guard, seeing his colleague standing dumbstruck, comes in: 'That's something else. Herr Mayor, please, that's something else, isn't it? A formality?'

'Correct. A formality. So I would like to ask you and your conscientious colleague to go along to Director Greve, and report that I am here, speaking to a remand prisoner.'

The guards exchange glances, whisper something. The lad goes out. In the meantime, the mayor has returned to the prisoner. 'What was the argument you were having about?'

In place of the prisoner, who won't say anything, Inspector Katzenstein replies: 'I've been instructed to take Herr Reimers to Stolpe, for questioning over the bomb. He refused to get in the car.'

'Questioning me over the bomb is ridiculous. They're trying to make sure I'm out of here when the farmers have their demonstration.'

'That would be my feeling too,' says Gareis sensibly. 'They'd prefer you to be somewhere else. Do you think that's such a bad idea?'

'No, they're sharp. But I'm pretty sharp too.'

'Remember,' the mayor begins slowly, 'they could always force you to go. There are a lot of them, and only one of you. You could shout, but they're used to that here. I always think it's stupid to resist when the odds are stacked against you.'

'But it's wrong just to give in, you should fight back.'

Suddenly Gareis becomes animated. 'Of course you should fight back, Herr Reimers. Fight for your farm, for the farmers, against the State if you must – that's the struggle. But one man taking on twenty in a brawl – that's just stupid.'

'I'm not going anywhere,' says the farmer stubbornly.

'Of course you are,' says Gareis mildly. 'Of course you're going. This prison,' he looks up the walls, 'houses eight hundred to a thousand inmates. On Monday, there'll be a demonstration under these windows, with bands playing, and people giving speeches and yelling – do you think I'm stupid enough to allow all that, so that eight hundred prisoners can spend the night beside themselves, wailing and raging and yelling and wishing they could get out? Just because it tickles your vanity?'

'I'm not vain.'

'In that case you're stupid. Did you really think people would come demonstrating under your windows?'

'Are you banning the demonstration?!'

'Let me tell you something, Reimers. People have come to me from all sorts of different quarters, calling on me to ban it. I'm allowing it, because I know you farmers. I'm allowing you to assemble in the market square, to march through the town, I'm allowing speeches in your auction hall, but – I'm not having any farmers standing under the walls of this prison, I promise you!'

'They won't allow you to keep them away! They'll come whatever you say.'

'They won't. On Monday morning I'll have word put out that you're no longer here. It doesn't greatly matter to me whether you are here then or not.'

'That's mean!'

'Mean to you, maybe, but it's a kindness to the other seven hundred and ninety-nine. Be sensible, man – fight, slap me in the face, I'm just another one of those officials you hate. I'll hit you back, and I'll fight you. But don't be a fool, don't be a numbskull.'

Gareis stands there a moment longer, as though thinking about something. Then he doffs his hat, surprisingly shakes hands with the farmer, says: 'Good day to you, Herr Reimers,' and goes off in the direction of a man who a few moments before had emerged with the warden and stopped a little way off to listen.

The farmer watches him go, then he turns his eyes heavenward, and then looks at the faces nearest him.

'Well, let's go,' he says, and he gets into the car.

XII

Prison Director Greve and Mayor Gareis shake hands with a sort of cool intimacy.

The director says with a smile, 'Wherever you show up, Mayor, bristles are soothed, and the rough is smoothed over. You've certainly done me a great favour, I would not have liked to use force on the man.'

'How is he getting on?'

'What to say after just a few days! All these people are a problem. Whichever way you treat them, they become martyrs. In the end, I don't treat them.'

'But he's not intractable?'

'No – not yet.'

'What will you do with him once he's been sentenced? Have him glue paper bags? Weave mats? Knot nets?'

The director hesitates. 'I don't know yet. You've covered most of the options.'

'But you have some prisoners doing gardening, do you not?'

'Yes, I do, my dear fellow, but there are rules. The only prisoners who are eligible for gardening duty are those who have already got through six months with good conduct. Gardening work is a reward.'

'I'd be tempted to make an exception, no?'

'Not me. Thank you for your views, though, Herr Gareis. Early on in this job you might make exceptions, but you soon get out of the habit. Not only because no one resents them so much as the other prisoners, but the wardens are also unhappy about them, they are the first to complain. Especially people from your Party, Mayor.'

'Yes, I'm sure. There are always some zealots. But that reminds me . . .'

The gentlemen stop walking. Gareis dips his hand into his jacket pocket and fishes out a piece of paper, a letter as it transpires.

'Some eager beaver left that on my desk, anonymously of course, and it comes from your establishment, Director.'

The director opens the letter. It's written on the prison letter-form complete with cell number and sender. The sender is none other than remand prisoner Franz Reimers. It is a not-unimportant document, in fact it is a letter of keen interest to the director. From prison, Reimers is giving a certain Georg instructions for the demonstration due to take place on Monday. 'Cameras. Collections. Don't allow yourself to be intimidated. Cold contempt. We must gain power, this government is impossible.'

'Hmm,' says the director. 'An interesting letter. Still more interesting would be to know how it came to land up on your desk.'

'It seems to be an original,' says the mayor. 'Which means it never reached the person for whom it was intended. It would be up to you, Director, to find out where in your establishment it disappeared.'

'There's no censor's mark on it. It never got as far as the Clerical Department, therefore. Either a warden confiscated it, or another prisoner stole it. Those are the possibilities. Perhaps it would be easier to establish who left it on your desk.'

'It came in the post. In an ordinary envelope, addressed personally to me. This morning.'

'And the envelope? Did you happen to bring it?'

'No. It was typed. Nothing to be gleaned from it.'

A pause ensues.

'Anyway, I'll have to look into the matter. It's yet another fine piece of skulduggery. I tell you, this place, full of people, is a veritable hell of lies, envy, betrayal, licentiousness and resentment. Here,' he says, with a mournful smile, 'is where we improve human nature.'

'And you will deliver the letter to the intended recipient?'

'Of course. Seeing as it came into my hands intact.'

'There remains the possibility that the thief took a copy.'

'What would he do with it? Is there much point in that? The addressee is one Georg Henning of Bandekow-Ausbau. Wholly unknown to me.'

'Probably a farmer,' hazards the mayor.

'Certainly a farmer. Well, I owe you a second round of thanks.'

'You can make it up to me very quickly, Herr Greve. I would

like to speak for a few minutes to one Tredup who was brought into remand last night.'

The director pulls a face. 'You know I am not authorized to do that, Mayor. Remand prisoners can be seen only with express permission of investigating magistrates.'

'It's a matter of excess of zeal on the part of one of my detectives. A mistake that can be cleared up in a sentence or two. And in human terms it's an unfortunate case. The detainee's wife and two young children are consumed with anxiety.'

The director: 'Why don't you apply to the investigating magistrate?'

'It wasn't in my authority to urge Reimers to get in the car. It wasn't in my authority to give you this letter back.'

'I know. I know. I'm very grateful to you too.'

'That's a word. But you are no man of fine phrases . . .'

'No. But you have no idea of the way that stupid bomb has ruffled feathers all the way to Berlin and beyond. I've had to vacate all the cells around Tredup's. He has a sentry standing underneath his window.'

'I'd have nothing against your witnessing the conversation, Director.'

'No. Not even then. My mind is made up. It's not possible. No.'

'Well, then, I'll have to forgo the pleasure. Poor Tredup, he will spend an uncomfortable few days. – Well, it remains then for me to say goodbye, Director.'

'Goodbye, Mayor. – As I say, I'm sorry. – Wait, I'll walk you to the gate.'

'I don't want to put you to the trouble.'

'No trouble, Mayor.'

XIII

Back in his office, the mayor sits down at his desk for a moment to think. He props his head in his hands, and doesn't move. The whole building is deathly still, office hours are long over. He thinks and thinks.

There are things he wants, and things that get in his way. He replays the scenes to himself: the exchange with Reimers, then Greve arriving on the scene. Greve has a solid bourgeois background. He has made his own way up. If you've come up in the world, you can't afford to be too sensitive to dirt.

The mayor goes to a built-in cupboard, lets water run into a basin. He lets it run for a long time. The noise does him good. It lulls his thoughts, he no longer needs to think. Then he drinks a glass of water, and after that he paces back and forth, back and forth, and thinks some more.

He never unconditionally believed the proposition that the end justifies the means, today he is close to thinking it can never be true. Whatever, he's too old to be changed. What's worse: he no longer wants to be.

He goes to the telephone and picks up the receiver.

And then he puts it down again and goes back to pacing, for a long, long while.

The sky outside is becoming a sheer green, and the birds have ceased their noise in the treetops.

Then he picks up the receiver and asks for a connection. 'This is the mayor speaking. – Is Pinkus there, from the *Volkszeitung*? – No? – But he's expected? – Very well. Would you let him know he can print the letter tomorrow after all. On the front page. – The letter. – Yes. – Just say "the letter", he'll know what I mean. – And if he could come and see me at home, tonight. – I'd like to discuss the presentation.'

The mayor puts down the receiver.

It's grown quite dark in his office.

5

The Bolt of Lightning in the Cloud

I

It was Sunday, and now it's Monday, even in Altholm. The sun rose at four fourteen, the sky is pale blue. It promises to be a lovely day, even in Altholm.

For Stuff, Monday is a bad day, not just this one, but every Monday. It always gets later than he thinks on Sunday, and his heart can't really take the drinking any more. Even so, it's only just past six in the morning when he shuffles down the Burstah, first to the station to buy the Stettin papers, from which with the help of his 'Solingen assistant' he puts together the sports section of the *Chronicle*: a cut-and-paste job.

I hope there's not too much happening, he thinks, as he unlocks the door to the *Chronicle* offices, and takes one last look back down the Burstah. The street is almost deserted, it looks so pitiful in the fresh light of morning. The posters on the shops look old and bled of colour. As if we'd all forgotten to die, thinks Stuff.

Police Sergeant Maak comes by from the station guardroom, where he's probably been on night duty. Stuff gives him a wave. Maybe he'll be good for one or two overnight stories, a juicy local column.

But Maak has nothing to report. Everything peaceful. Maybe the town hall guard-post?

'I'll be along there at ten o'clock. Bloody headache! What'll happen today with the farmers?'

'Nothing much. Maybe there won't even be a demonstration. They took Reimers to Stolpe on Friday.'

'Are you sure? What's your source? Who moved him? Your pig of a superior?'

'Oh yes, I'm sure. Katzenstein took him there in person in his own car. And the mayor visited the prison on Friday, I happen to know.'

'A good start to the week. Just when you think at last there's a bit of life in the old place, the mayors get out and chase the ne'er-do-wells somewhere else. Well, it'll be enough for a local item.'

'Yes, but I never told you anything.'

'No, of course not. I know. Morning.'

Maak dawdles off down the street. The traffic posts are not yet manned, the only vehicles on the road are a couple of milk carts. He is feeling wonderfully tired, and is looking forward firstly to his bed, and secondly to his morning coffee with fresh rolls and honey beforehand, and thirdly to catching the children before they go to school.

Stuff gets a fright when he walks into the office and finds a white-haired, shiny red dwarf sitting there: his proprietor.

'Good morning, Herr Schabbelt.'

'Rubbish. What's going on with Tredup?'

'He's in the slammer. He's charged with having set off the bomb in the president's house.'

'Rubbish. And what's going on with the farmers?'

'Nothing. They secretly transferred their leader to Stolpe on Friday.'

'Listen, they want to stop giving us the magistrates' announcements. They wrote to say it wasn't worth their while, and they had to economize.'

'Who signed it?'

'Gareis.'

'Is that certain?'

'We might be able to appeal the decision. Go round and see him this morning, and tell him we'll be good. Maybe he'll let us keep the announcements.'

'Couldn't Wenk do that?'

'No, he bloody couldn't. That's not a man, that's a pissed hatstand.'

'I'm not keen to go, Herr Schabbelt.'

'I don't like having to sell this shit either, and I've still got to do it.'

'What shit, excuse me?'

'Well, this shit here!' The gnome smites the desk with fury. 'All this shit, editorial, print, the works!'

'Herr Schabbelt!'

'I know. I know. There are bonds, and the bastards cancelled my loans, it's a conspiracy.'

'Who's the buyer?'

'It could be Meier from Berlin or Schulze from Stettin or Müller from Pforzheim.'

'A front?'

'Of course it's a front, on behalf of that intriguing shit Gebhardt, who owns the *News*, and reeks of money.'

'Oh, Herr Schabbelt!'

'I know, Stuff. It hurts being gobbled up by the competition, I know. You'll have to crawl to them while you still can, so they keep you on. That's why I thought I'd let you know. Morning.'

'Christ, what a week . . .' says Stuff, and stares into space.

The sergeant is in for a surprise as well, when he turns up at the station to clock off.

Superintendent Kallene is there to greet him. 'You can't go home today. State of readiness. Get a couple of hours' kip next door in the guardroom if you can. The new roster will be given out at nine.'

He runs into more irked colleagues in the guardroom.

'What's it all about? Fucking outrage.'

'Why do you think? It's the Commies planning to march on the Labour Exchange.'

'It never. It's the farmers.'

'It's not the farmers, that's for sure. Gareis sent Reimers off to Stolpe in person.'

'Who's responsible for this crap?'

'I was going to dig potatoes in my allotment.'

'I've got my wife waiting for me with coffee.'

'Who else is responsible but that pathetic Frerksen? The bastard is always plotting something.'

'He won't even visit his parents any more, that's how snooty the scholarship boy has got. Because his father was a rag-and-bone man once.'

'Not exactly. He used to hawk buttons and braces round the villages.'

'How's a man going to get some sleep with all this chit-chat? Can you keep it down?'

'You'll fall asleep soon enough when you see your old lady.'

'Ssh! Enough!'

'Quiet!'

'You shut up yourself!'

'Quiet!!!'

II

Commander Frerksen gets up. It's a little after seven. His wife has put out his aftershave already. Sunday's grey suit is back in the wardrobe, and the uniform is folded over a chair.

He is feeling sullen and irritable. He looks out into the sunshine furiously. When the children make a noise in the next room, he swears and hurls a shoe against the door.

Then he slowly starts to get dressed.

His wife walks in.

'Why did you put out the uniform for me? I want my suit.'

'But –'

'How many more times do I have to tell you, I want my suit!'

It's put out for him.

Frerksen starts shaving. He mutters to himself: 'I've half a mind to call in sick.'

'Sick? Are you sick?'

'Why would I be sick? Rubbish. I said I'd half a mind to call in sick.'

'What's got into you today? Are you upset about something, Fritz?'

Frerksen throws down his razor and screams: 'Don't ask! Don't ask me any questions! Go back to the kitchen!' Frau Frerksen goes out without another word.

The birds are rowing in the trees, and now here comes a wretched bastard motorcyclist with a clattering exhaust. Too bad

I can't make out the number. I'd have liked to sting him. – God, if only I was on holiday!

Not a word is spoken at table. The little boy and girl, warned by their mother, sit there in silence, not looking up from their plates. The mother butters rolls and lays them on her husband's plate. He eats absent-mindedly, his gaze directed out of the window, with a deep vertical frown line down his forehead.

The wife's shy voice: 'Would you like more coffee?'

'What's that? Yes, give me some more. – And I think I want the uniform after all.'

The woman gets up to do it right away.

'No. It can wait. After.' – A pause. – 'By the way, today's going to be awful.'

'Awful . . .?'

'Yes, awful! I'm caught between two fires.'

'Fritz . . . can you talk to me about . . .?'

'The mayor wants one thing, and the president wants the opposite. Whatever I do will be wrong.'

'But don't we owe everything to the mayor?'

'Jesus Christ, that goddamned female tripe! That horrible syrupy gush with everything! Yes, go on, let's have tears as well. Instead of a helpmate –' Then, abruptly: 'What are you sitting around for, you wretches! Get lost! Go to school!' When they're by themselves: 'I'm sorry, Anna, please forgive me! My nerves are shot. And today, when the farmers come in . . . Perhaps I'll have to use my sabre or pistol . . . The government is putting such pressure on me. I had nightmares about it. I'm not cut out for that kind of thing. No, I know you're right. I'm going to do what Gareis wants. I've got no choice.'

III

The room of the district president is as cool and dimly lit as ever. There is no world outside these dark, book-lined shelves, these thick, sound-proofing carpets, this black-brown oak furniture.

Chief Adviser Meier has just chased off the cleaning women, and here comes Temborius, and it's not yet eight in the morning.

'What's keeping Tunk?'

'He'll be along any minute. It's not eight yet.'

'It is. My watch says eight. – What's the overnight intelligence say?'

'Assemblies in every district. Lots of young farmers dressed in mourning, issuing a call to attend the Parliament in Altholm.'

'This right of assembly for traitors is madness. I need to talk to the minister about it.'

Meier bows.

'Well, go on! Anything else? Hasn't the appearance of the letter in the *Volkszeitung* had any effect?'

'The farmers don't read the *Volkszeitung*. And if they do, they say it's all a pack of lies.'

'Where did it come from anyway?'

'From Gareis.'

'From Gareis? Not possible!'

'I know it from Pinkus. Gareis took him the letter in person.'

'Can you make any sense of that? He allows the demonstration, and then tries to stir up feeling against it?'

'Maybe he is feeling a bit uneasy. Taking steps to keep it manageable.'

'Uneasy? The fellow's a swine, I say! Seventeen wardens of every political stripe don't worry me as much as one Gareis, who's even in my Party. He's the farmers' friend!'

Detective Inspector Tunk is announced.

'Have him come in. – You're late, Tunk. It's five past eight.'

'The presidium clock hasn't struck the hour yet.'

'It's five past eight.'

The presidium clock strikes.

'Chief Adviser, will you tell the janitor to set the clock accurately. It's an incitement to inefficiency and sloth. Yes, right now . . . Inspector, have you been told what your task is?'

'At your orders, sir. I have been told to take the nine o'clock train to Altholm, and observe the farmers.'

'Observe . . .! You're to mingle with them. Meet their leaders. Learn their names. Make a note of what they say in their speeches. All of that. All of that. You can always discreetly go out to jot something down. You join in the demonstration. Go to the hall. Remember the speeches and speakers. Most important, whatever happens in front of the prison.'

The detective inspector bows.

'But all that is secondary. Of crucial importance . . . are you familiar with the views of Mayor Gareis?'

'Yes, sir.'

'Gareis is of the view that the farmers are not involved in anything seditious; my view is – they are. I've offered to put some militia at his disposal, he's declined them. As of ten a.m., two platoons will be in Grünhof.'

'Yes, sir.'

'You are an experienced policeman, Herr Tunk. You've worked in the political section for many years.'

The detective looks expectantly at his boss.

'You have judgement. You can tell when a situation becomes dangerous. The State, listen carefully here, the State must not experience a humiliation. Detective inspector, I want you to be responsible for the militia not standing idly by in Grünhof, should the situation become dangerous.'

'Yes, sir.'

'Have you *fully* taken my meaning?'

'I've *fully* taken your meaning, District President.'

'You are not to liaise with Commander Frerksen or with anyone else in Altholm. You are there as my personal observer. – Well, Chief Adviser, is the clock right now?'

'Yes, District President.'

And the district president, smiling amiably: 'Don't you think, Chief Adviser, that our detective inspector looks every inch a farmer in his green loden with his top-boots and the chamois brush on his hat? How much are a dozen eggs, farmer?'

And the three gentlemen laugh heartily.

IV

In Bandekow-Ausbau everyone is up early this morning. They are sitting at the open window facing on to the garden, a small, almost frivolous farm garden with yew tree, berry-patch, gladioli and Cross of Jerusalem. In the middle is a sort of shelf, covered with thatch, with about twenty woven beehives on it. The bees teem in and out of the window, drawn by the fragrant smell of stewed apples and sugar-beets.

'The bees are flying high,' says Farmer Rohwer. 'That means a fine day.'

'Don't bet on it,' says Henning. 'That's all we need, on top of this botched demonstration.'

And Rohwer: 'If the bees are flying high, what is there to bet on?'

'Are we talking about the weather,' asks a clearly nervous Padberg, 'or taking a decision on whether Henning is coming with us or not?'

Rohwer: 'I say he's coming.'

And Rehder: 'He comes.'

And Henning: 'Of course. I'm going to carry the flag.'

And Count Bandekow: 'Who else could possibly?'

'I seem to be outvoted,' says Padberg. 'Well, I'll go on anyway. What you're proposing is stupid. Bound to be stupid. If there's a punch-up, if there's blood, we'll lose the support of the farmers. You remember the effect on them of that one ill-judged bomb.'

'There's a chance there may be a punch-up –' begins Count Bandekow.

'You see!' crows Padberg. 'Will you pass the eggs, Rehder?'

'– not,' the count finishes his sentence, 'because we have Henning as flag-bearer, but because the government is nervous. I've listened around: there's no suspicion of Henning, because they've arrested Thiel and Tredup.'

'You believe that?'

'I know it. Our dear damned government would like the bomb *not* to be from the farmers, because then Germany might wake up. It's some bunch of chancers, can't be anything else. There-fore, so long as Henning is with us, he stays beyond suspicion.'

'Why should there be blood?' asks Farmer Rohwer from Nipp-merow. 'We're not out to break heads.'

'That's just it,' affirms the count. 'We're not breaking any heads. So why should the others break ours?'

Henning says: 'Listen, there won't be any fisticuffs. Fat old Gareis is far too comfortable. Old Father Benthin in Altholm has told me that Gareis is afraid of just one thing, that something could happen.'

'I don't see how you can speak for three thousand farmers!' mocks Padberg. 'Three quarrelsome individuals, and there'll be blood.'

'That's right. We'll call them to order,' says Rehder.

'Oh, really. You're children. You've just got no idea of all the unforeseen things that could happen.'

'Oh, stop your gloom-mongering, Padberg.'

'All right. Whatever you say. Whatever you say. I'm not say-ing anything else. I just want you to promise me, Henning, that you're not taking a weapon, and that you won't defend yourself.'

'What do you mean, "no weapon"? Am I to hold out my face and let them punch me?'

'Exactly that.'

'I'd rather eat a broomstick.'

'This time I agree with Padberg,' says the count. 'If you have a weapon, give it here, Henning.'

'I wouldn't dream of it.'

'I want your word. Otherwise you're staying here.'

'You're all cowards,' says Henning. 'I'll do it and I'll not do it.'

'We want obedience here,' says the count.

'Why would you want that? I thought we had no chiefs?'

'In the name of the Bauernschaft, I demand your weapon,' says Rehder.

Henning sticks his hands in his pockets and doesn't say any-thing.

'What would you be wanting with a pistol, anyway?' says Farmer Rohwer. 'The banner's big and heavy as it is. Are you proposing to throw it down and start banging away?'

'That's right,' remarks the count. 'A flag-bearer stands and falls by his flag. A weapon would be useless to you.'

'Well, then,' says Henning, and chucks his pistol on the table, 'there you are. But I promise you, if anyone touches me, I'll skewer him on the flagpole.'

'Which is why I wanted your word.'

'There's absolutely no question of my giving it to you.'

'Leave him be. He'll have both hands full with his flag.'

They leave. The countryside is quiet and peaceful.

'Not much traffic.'

'Most will be coming by train.'

'How many farmers can afford to keep a car these days?'

'Oh, plenty. But they're afraid of the drive home when they're plastered.'

The four men laugh, only Henning is still sullen. But then, as they come through Grünhof, it's his turn to be electrified. 'Did you see that? Militia! Four lorryloads!' And leaning back in triumph: 'There you are, then! They're going to make mincemeat of us!'

The others are excited as well, but in the end the count says: 'Why is the militia in Grünhof and not in Altholm? Tactical reserve. Just in case. Thank God we've taken your pistol off you. And now I do after all want you to promise me that you won't get violent.'

V

Mayor Gareis is in his office, in festive mood. He is going on holiday tomorrow, going on a cruise to Rügen.

Today . . .: 'The demonstration is fizzing out. I just spoke to Feinbube, the agricultural councillor, and he's in despair that Reimers has been taken away.'

'But the farmers don't know that,' Frerksen objects.

'They'll get to hear about it soon enough. The *Volkszeitung* and the *News* are both carrying the story.'

'Shame it's not in the *Chronicle*, which is the earliest to come out, and the one the farmers read, if they read any of them.'

'I'll have a word with Stuff. I think I'll be able to pull him round too.'

'Stuff is a dangerous individual.'

'Pah, you just don't like him because he's laid into you in print the odd time.'

Frerksen gestures.

'All right. Never mind. I don't care for him myself. His feelings always run away with him. Anyway, I think we'll be able to harness him. Especially now. Well, we can save that for later. – Did you hear when Benthin and his leaders plan on coming?'

'No. Not a word.'

'I'm here until one o'clock. In the afternoon I'll be at home, but only in a real emergency.'

'Very well, Your Worship.'

'I want the police to keep a discreet eye on the bars and pubs. If anything looks dangerous, I want them to report straight away.'

'Oh, Herr Gareis, there's no relying on most of them, I'm afraid. They are just as far Right as most of the farmers.'

'Well, I think they'll do their job. – I want the demonstrators to be protected under all circumstances, got that, Frerksen? Under all circumstances.'

'Yes, Mayor.'

'Disposition of forces as discussed previously. Police to stay in the background, in a monitoring function. And I want no demonstrators assembling outside the prison.'

'Yes – but how? My numbers –'

'No police. We'll do it like this: take six or eight people from Altholm, civilians, low profile. Put two or three in prison-warden uniforms, and have them happen to stroll out of the prison gates. Then they can tell the farmers as they're gathering that Reimers isn't there. A couple more can be let go as if they were prisoners, and they all tell the same story. New faces all the time, never the same people twice, I want no suspicion among the farmers.'

'We'd need Greve's agreement for that.'

'That's right. I want you to call him in half an hour, and tell him about the idea. The suggestion is to have come from you. I've been on holiday since Saturday. OK?'

'Not quite.'

'Do you want reasons why? Well, think of a certain letter that appeared in the *Volkszeitung*. Better?'

Frerksen smiles a little awkwardly. 'Ye-es, a little.'

'A little is good. So you half understand? – What's the matter, Piekbusch?'

'Lieutenant Wrede of the militia is outside.'

'Wrede . . .? Ah, yes, good old Temborius. I tell you, Frerksen, he'll have his militia in Grünhof by now and will be busy yanking on the chain back in Stolpe.'

The militia lieutenant walks in.

'Ah, my dear Lieutenant Wrede, what gives us the pleasure?'

'I first have to report to you that two platoons are at your disposal in Grünhof, Mayor.'

'I hope it won't be too boring for them there.'

'Further, I have some secret orders for you. To be opened only in the event that you call on the militia.'

'Thank you, Lieutenant. Will you come for the billet-doux this evening?'

'You mean, if it's not been opened?'

'It'll be here. Just so you know. I'll tell Piekbusch as well. I'm going on holiday this afternoon. That's how rattled I am by this demonstration.'

Wrede bows and smiles.

'Well, I'll see you next when I'm back, I suppose. – What is it now, Piekbusch?'

'Herr Stuff from the *Chronicle* is here to see you, Mayor.'

'Stuff? Perfect timing. You'd best leave by this door, Frerksen. I don't want Stuff's mood to be spoiled by the sight of you.'

VI

'Well, Herr Stuff, what's happened that the *Chronicle*'s readers simply have to know about, and that can only be learned from me?'

Stuff says stroppily: 'I've just seen your Herr Frerksen. Perhaps you could find time to tell the gentleman to treat the press a little better. Blöcker on the *News* says the same thing. When we want to learn something, it's never the moment, he waves us away. Next time the police administration needs us for something, we won't be anywhere to be found.'

'You find Frerksen arrogant? I've never found that myself. He's always been assiduous and friendly.'

'Yes. To you.'

'No, not just to me. But I understand that people in Altholm can't forget that someone who leaves school at fourteen can become a police officer. They still think of his father, who must have been a town parks gardener.'

'A pedlar.'

'You see. It's not forgotten.'

'Other people have become better things, and that's fine. Frerksen isn't fine, because he doesn't have the moral or technical attributes to become a police officer.'

'He has performed all his designated tasks outstandingly well.'

'We can all drive on a flat, straight road. Wait till things get a little bumpy. If the farmers' demonstration today goes off badly –'

'There's not going to be a farmers' demonstration today. Reimers is no longer being held in the Central Prison, I can tell you in confidence. I am on holiday as of this afternoon.'

'And who will stand in for you?'

'Frerksen!'

'Well. In confidence or not, I can tell you, Mayor, that there will be a demonstration here, even if you've taken care to have the leader shipped off somewhere else.'

'It was Katzenstein who managed the transport. Just by the by. And will the *Chronicle* be carrying the story this lunchtime that Reimers is no longer here, and that the demonstration has lost its *raison d'être*?'

'At any rate, Reimers is in prison. It doesn't really matter where, Altholm or Stolpe – but that people can demonstrate against it, that matters. That's a defensible position too.'

'What use to you are the farmers? They don't read you. While I'm on the point, how can you sympathize with bombers?'

'Everything's possible. But for now it's not been proven that the farmers were the bombers.'

The mayor says quickly and intently: 'Herr Stuff, why are you my enemy?'

And Stuff, caught out: 'I'm not your enemy.'

'You are. You always have been. I've always respected you as a human being, even though our political views diverged. Don't be unjust. Tell me what you have against me.'

'Newspapermen aren't concerned with justice. I have nothing against you.'

'Then I'm relieved.'

The mayor leans back.

'You have to see clearly. I had the sense you were convinced from the start that I was opposed to the farmers' demonstration. I am in favour of it, not because it's a farmers' demonstration, but because it's a demonstration, and I believe in equal rights for all.'

'It's possible to be for something officially, and unofficially against it. The removal of Reimers . . .'

'Happened on the orders of the Justice Department, and was done by Katzenstein. If I stopped to talk to Reimers, that was purely to spare him the use of force.'

'And the letter in the *Volkszeitung*?'

'What do I know about the *Volkszeitung*? Incidentally, that letter should give you pause too. For the leaders of the Bauernschaft, everything comes down to money, apparently.'

'The letter's a fake.'

'Hardly. The declaration in the *Bauernschaft* newspaper was just to cover their embarrassment.'

'It seems we see everything differently,' says Stuff. 'There's not one detail we agree on.'

And the mayor: 'We can differ on matters of fact, if we agree on the human side. Do I have your assurance that you have no personal animus against me?'

'None at all.'

'All right! And what will the position of the *Chronicle* be this lunchtime?'

'I can't say as yet. I'll have to talk to Herr Schabbelt first.'

To Schabbelt?! But you are the *Chronicle*, Herr Stuff!'

'You're wrong about that, Mayor. But irrespective of that, I'm still surprised you seem to attach so much importance to us. A paper that the town administration will no longer use to make its announcements in, because it's too unimportant!'

'That's not the reason! Good God, that's not the reason! We have to make economies. The city fathers, well, you know . . . Save. Save. Save. It's a few thousand marks, after all. And the *Chronicle* just happens to be the smallest of the town's newspapers. I'm sorry, but I can't help it.'

'Our print run is seven thousand one hundred and sixty. The *Volkszeitung* only distributes five thousand copies in Altholm.'

'That can't be right, Herr Stuff. That can't be right. Five thousand? Nine thousand!'

'I would suggest you stand out on the Burstah one day at half past eleven, Mayor, and count the number of bales that the Stettin car drops off at the *Volkszeitung* offices for distribution. I say: five thousand, including propaganda flyers.'

'You must be mistaken, Herr Stuff, I have dependable information. Whereas how can I check up on the seven thousand you claim for the *Chronicle*?'

'By allowing me to show you an audited confirmation from Notary Pepper that agrees that number on the basis of our books and subscribers' list.'

'That confirmation exists, Herr Stuff?'

'I can let you see it.'

'That won't be necessary. Your word is good enough for me. So the *Chronicle* has a distribution of seven thousand plus?'

'Seven thousand one hundred and sixty.'

'Good. Give me that in writing and you'll continue to receive public announcements from the municipality.' And, with emphasis: 'Of course, that's always assuming that the municipal government is not directly attacked by the *Chronicle*. Our mouthpiece may not simultaneously be our enemy.'

'We can't possibly give you a blank cheque for your policies in advance.'

'My dear Herr Stuff! We understand each other. Objective criticism is always valuable.' Smiling: 'And what's your take on today's farmers' demonstration?'

And Stuff, also smiling: 'I've already told Feinbube that I think it'll fail.'

The mayor, purring: 'You see, there are points of agreement between us. Here's to a fruitful collaboration, Herr Stuff!'

'Let's hope so. Morning to you, Herr Mayor.'

VII

Herr Gebhardt, the little newspaper magnate of Pomerania, as his friends – he has none – call him, is in his office at nine, as he is every day. His business manager, Trautmann, is standing by, because the most important thing every day is to report on the amount of space taken out, and the sum realized from its sale.

'You know,' Gebhardt likes to say, 'I read my newspapers from back to front. I don't really care what the headlines are. It's the advertisements that matter.'

Today is Monday, a bad day, barely two pages of advertising, they will have to pad it out. 'Let's put in the half-page of Persil too. If we have to fill . . .'

Trautmann disagrees: 'No, if we're reduced to padding, then take something that the advertiser won't see. Otherwise we'll wreck our price structure. Let's take Ford, they don't have a representative in town.'

The boss agrees. 'By the way, Herr Trautmann, the *Chronicle* is in the bag. The sale is done. Schabbelt signed on the dotted line last night.'

'What conditions?'

'We made absolutely no concessions. Why should we, when he's in such trouble? He's lucky we let him hang on to his flat.'

'Anyway, it wouldn't have been possible to put him out on the street, the Housing Department would have got involved.'

'Quite. So what will we do now? Send for Stuff?'

'I don't think so. Let him come and see us if he wants.'

'But we are keeping him, aren't we?' asks the boss.

'Of course we're keeping him. No one has so many connections here. And the man can write.'

'What sort of wage should we pay him?' asks the boss anxiously.

'When I last heard he was on five hundred.'

'Five hundred! Are you crazy! The *Chronicle* would never bear five hundred!'

'No. Or rather, it might be able to bear it, but we wouldn't be interested in paying it. Three hundred and fifty, plus twenty in expenses, to sweeten the pill.'

'What if he doesn't agree?'

'What else will he do? He's pushing fifty, and he'll never leave Altholm.'

'At any rate, it'll have to be done in such a way that people don't notice that we now own the *Chronicle*. Otherwise circulation will suffer.'

'Quite. But we'll have to let Heinsius and Blöcker into the secret.'

'Do you think? Will you do it, or shall I?'

'You, of course! Funny question. You're the owner.'

'All right then, Herr Trautmann, will you give them a call. – Please.'

'OK. I'll send them along.'

Heinsius, the editor of the biggest paper in Altholm, a big bald man in a rayon jacket, comes running in first, with a sheaf of proofs still in his hand.

'Morning, Herr Gebhardt! Sleep well? Sleep well? We're going with a local lead on the 25th anniversary of the Glaziers' Guild . . . I've come up with a few well-chosen words myself, for the community's interest . . . If you'd like to hear them, if you have a moment . . .'

'Not just now. What's happening with the farmers' demonstration?'

'The farmers!' Heinsius is contempt itself. 'The farmers won't demonstrate. Now that Reimers is in Stolpe. You do know that Reimers is in Stolpe?'

'Yes. But the mayor went away on holiday this morning, for three days, so I hear . . .'

'So . . .?'

'Could it be there's something in the offing? Is he trying to keep his head below the parapet?'

'Do you think so, Herr Gebhardt? I'll make some inquiries. And if he is – why, then I'll write something with some satirical bite. We here won't let Oberbürgermeister Niederdahl forget that he didn't invite you to the celebration dinner for the opening of the orphanage . . .'

'Couldn't he just have forgotten?'

'He didn't forget! I've heard it said . . . No, I'd better not say, it's too upsetting . . .'

'Oh, what is it now! No, please, tell me right now. I can't stomach these insinuations. Spit it out.'

'He is supposed to have said, and I know this from an excellent source, that even if Gebhardt buys a hundred newspapers, he will remain a little man trying to look big.'

'That . . . why! Who did he say that to?'

'Of course I gave my word never to divulge the name, but for you I'll make an exception.'

And the newspaper magnate, tormented: 'Well, say it!'

'Councillor Meisel.'

'Right. I'll make a note of that. The arrogance of those academics! – Herr Heinsius, we're getting into a more and more difficult situation. After all the snubs I've received at the hands of Niederdahl, we can't possibly support his political platform. We can't go with the Socialist Gareis, otherwise we stand to lose our advertisers, the entrepreneurial classes, and we can't represent business, because most of our subscribers are workers. What on earth can we do?'

His editor comforts him: 'We'll pick our way through. On a case-by-case basis. Just leave it to me. I've got good instincts. I don't offend people. And as for the little dig at Niederdahl today – I'll see why he's gone away. If it's to duck his responsibilities, then he'll be in for a shock!'

'Check with Stuff. He always knows everything.'

'With Stuff . . .? Anyway, he doesn't at all know everything.'

'Oh yes he does. Stuff.'

'You mean Stuff on the *Chronicle?*'

'Yes.'

'But, Herr Gebhardt!'

'Herr Stuff is my employee, as of today.'

'Your . . .? So that means you own . . .?'

'The *Chronicle* passed into my ownership last night.'

The proofs flutter gently to the ground. Heinsius raises his arms and his permanently red-rimmed eyes to the heavens. 'Herr Gebhardt! Herr Gebhardt! That it should be vouchsafed to me to experience this moment! The rivalry is over! Stuff – our stable-mate! Herr Gebhardt! Oh, thank you! Thank you! Our employee Stuff . . .'

He shakes his boss's hand again and again.

'But it's to remain a secret, Herr Heinsius. I don't want the public to hear about it. It might harm the sales of the *Chronicle*, which of course is to stay strongly Right-wing.'

'A secret? That's a shame. Still, I'll be able to give instructions to Stuff. We'll have the use of his material and research. He comes out two hours ahead of us. I'll cut and paste him religiously from now on. And we can send him on ahead. Our pit canary . . .'

Heinsius is in a whirl of delight. He is in the world of dreams. 'I'll make Stuff pay for flogging off two hundred copies of my novel *German Blood and German Need* for fifty pfennigs apiece at the last Michaelmas market.'

Gebhardt clears his throat. 'Let's not get emotional here. You're colleagues now, and your sole interest is the flourishing of the business.'

'Your business, of course, Herr Gebhardt. I am being entirely unemotional here. You will see what a renaissance the *News* will experience.'

'Will you give Blöcker the information too, confidentially. Why hasn't he come, by the way? He doesn't come as often as he ought. I like to see my editors on a daily basis.'

'I don't know. He had someone with him. Anyway. You know

he shouldn't go out so much at night, Herr Gebhardt, to his glee club. An editor shouldn't have a private life.'

'Blöcker's bound to be seeing Stuff some time today. I want him to have him come here at eight o'clock. Stuff will know why. He's to use the back entrance, so that no one sees him.'

'Very good, Herr Gebhardt.'

'And I want you to hold over the dig at the Ober. We'll wait for confirmation of the renewal of the municipal contracts first.'

'I'll find out about that.'

'Good. And bring Trautmann back.'

Trautmann comes in. The boss, to him coming in: 'Listen, Trautmann, you got me into the newspaper business. You've advised me from day one. That gabby old woman Heinsius just told me that the Ober said I would remain a little man, never mind how big I wanted to be. How can we fix the Ober?'

'We'll get him. But who is he supposed to have said it to? You can't believe everything Heinsius says.'

VIII

When Stuff emerges from the town hall on to the marketplace at half past eleven, there isn't the usual meagre morning presence of isolated pedestrians and one or two cars cutting through Altholm on their way from Stettin to Stolpe, or Stolpe to Stettin.

Everywhere there are groups of people, and their clothes, their thoughtful, somehow rather ponderous gestures – as though their bones were unusually heavy – their way of talking loudly and slowly, identified them as farmers, even if Stuff couldn't have named many of them.

But he doesn't feel like addressing any of them, he's tired and fed up, all the vows of eternal friendship with that fat schmoozer Gareis disgust him. He's longing for a dark nook at Auntie Lieschen's, for beer and schnapps, for oblivion.

As he trots along, Stuff thinks: I will show up when the farmers have their demonstration. You never can tell. It's due to go off at three, that's another four hours. There's time for a couple of drinks, maybe. And now I'll just take in the stills at the Baltic Cinema so that I can cobble together my eighteeen lines on the new feature.

In front of the stills vitrine there's a back that looks familiar. 'Blöcker, what are you doing here, you old bugger? Didn't you make it to the flicker either last night?'

The friendly foes crewing the *News* and the *Chronicle* shake hands.

Newspapers may be enemies, newspaper owners may want to spit at one another, editors may hate each other: the friendship between local reporters is indestructible. They swap titbits, they steal from each other, they give each other a leg-up: 'Will you go to the assizes for me?' – 'Give me your arson in Juliusruh.'

'Have you been to the police yet, mate? What's new?'

'A break-in in an allotment hut. A punch-up at Krüger's. A drunk found wandering round the back of the general store with a bloody head. Ach, I'll give it to you later. How's about you?'

'Two-car collision on the Stolpe Road.'

'Any dead?'

'Nah.'

'Damn. Injured?'

'Two, badly.'

'Local?'

'Nah, from Stettin.'

'Well, it's no good to me, then. But you can let me have it any-way.'

'It'll make ten lines, I would think.'

'Five is the most I can have. – What are you going to do about the farmers today?'

The man from the *News* blinks. 'Farmers? Not interested. That's a damp squib.'

'I'm inclined to agree. There's five hundred of them here, at the most.'

'I'd say three.'

'Could be. I'm not going to be there at three,' announces Stuff.

'At three? You're crazy. Three is when I have my nap.'

'See! Me too.'

And Blöcker: 'So what about it? Shall we have a jar? I'm buying.'

'You're buying? In the morning? Are you unwell?'

'Listen, it's warm, and I'm thirsty.'

'Funny. But then today's a funny day. Well, you'll tell me what-ever it is.'

'No, I don't want to go in there. It's all full of farmers now. We'll go to Krüger's wine bar. It's cool and quiet, and he can fill us in about the punch-up.'

They walk on in silence, Blöcker is wondering how to break it to Stuff that Gebhardt wants to see him.

'Well, Cousin Benthin, who're you looking for?' Stuff calls out to the moth-eaten farmer.

'G'day, Stuff. You wouldn't have seen Rohwer from Nipp-merow, would you?'

'I've no idea. The whole place is full of farmers. Do you have a message for him if I see him?'

'I promised the mayor that me and some of the leaders would go round and talk to him. But now I can't find him anywhere.'

'The mayor? Why would you farmers go and talk to a Red?'

'Gareis isn't so bad, even if he is a Red. Now I must go and find Rohwer.'

'Well, I'll tell him you're looking for him, Cousin Benthin.'

'Thanks, Stuff. You should catch the speeches this afternoon. There's some bad news in them for Revenue and State.'

'I'll save the front page!' mocks Stuff. 'Gah, you farmers! Now come along, Blöcker.'

They step into Krüger's.

IX

There is a farm called Stolpermünde-Abbau, five miles from the fishing village of Stolpermünde. The road, which is a rough, sandy track, winds across the dunes and over brackish meadows that are more reeds and horse-tails than grass. Gulls live there, and wild rabbits. There's nothing exists more remote and aban-doned than Stolpermünde-Abbau.

Nor is it properly speaking a farm, it's more a sort of croft with forty or fifty acres of very poor soil. Of the little bit of corn and oats that grow, most goes to the rabbits. The farmer and his family live on potatoes.

There are no farmhands or maids. Farmer Banz and his wife and nine children do all the work themselves. When his wife goes into Stolpermünde four or five times a year with the children, she complains that they are so small. 'It's the hard labour from an early age, and the fact they never get enough to eat.'

The farmer is big and broad, his wife is big and scraggy, but the children are broad and knobbly dwarves, silent dwarves with frightening hands.

Sometimes the farmer has a horse, and sometimes he hasn't. Then wife and children are put before plough, harrow and potato drill. That still happens.

The children hardly ever go to school. Where's the child that can walk ten miles to school? But once, a year and a half ago, an enforcement official made it out to Stolpermünde-Abbau: since then there hasn't been a horse even some of the time. Back then the farmer disappeared for a few months, the confiscation hadn't gone smoothly, and so he was given a few months to cool down in prison.

When he returned, he put a sign up on the wall that read: 'In Winter 1927, this farm was criminally robbed by militia and fiscal officials in the service of the German Republic.'

A ridiculous sign, it hung there, no one saw it, who ever would have seen it?

The next big event was a car recently making it all the way out to the Abbau farm, at night. The wife and children slept through it, but they saw the tyre marks on the sand track the following day. Were they people who were after something, well, it was the father who dealt with them. Come to think of it, the father has been away from the farm a lot of late, at night.

Since that time, the barn has been padlocked. If that's the farmer's way, no one asks why. Ask a lot of questions, you get plenty of answers.

'I need straw for the cow,' says the farmer's wife to the farmer one morning.

'Make me up some sandwiches,' says the farmer, and leaves the kitchen.

After a while, he comes back. 'Where's my sandwiches? Is that all? I need food for the whole day.'

'The cow's going to calve today,' says the farmer's wife.

'The cow's not going to calve today,' says Farmer Banz.

'Unlock the barn. I'll fetch the straw myself.'

'If I find Franz nosing around the barn one more time,' says the farmer furiously, 'I'll smash his head open.'

The farmer goes back outside, and hammers the scythe straight. After a while the farmer's wife stands herself in the way of the anvil. 'What do you think you're doing, padlocking up the barn?'

'You're to cut clover for the sow later,' says the farmer, and hones the edge.

'You'll carry on for so long till they carry you back to the house dead.'

'I'm not sure that's a loss. If there's ten of you starving, it's easier than eleven.'

'What have you got in the barn?' asks the wife angrily.

'Nothing that will bite you.'

'I'll break the door down with the axe.'

'Anyone who sets foot in that barn is dead. Then the farm and all who live on it are gone.'

'I don't want you going back to prison, Banz.'

'Do you remember in the Bible, where it says "honour and obey", wife?'

'You have to obey the law as well.'

'That law is not the same as God's Law.'

'What will I do by myself here when you're dead?'

The farmer looks up, runs his tough thumb once more along the edge. 'A cartload of clover for the sow, no more than that. And in the feed-chest there's a sack of wheat. Mix up her feed for one day. It's possible I'll not be back till tomorrow morning.'

'I want to know where you're going.'

'Now come with me.'

The farmer walks on ahead, his wife follows at a distance of

two paces. He walks between house and barn, along the seam of
the field, between the rye and potatoes. The children are weed-
ing the potato field.

The farmer counts them: 'Nine.'

When they get to the edge of the wood: 'Look behind and
check that none have come after you.'

'Nine,' says the farmer's wife.

They walk on. The ground is glib with pine needles, the sound
of the sea gets louder. Under an old fir, the farmer stops.

'If I don't come back, and they've arrested me, someone will
come and tell you. Then you just live as before. You don't allow
strangers on to the farm. Whatever is in the barn will be collected by the man who brings you the news.'

'Yes.'

'If I don't come back at all, then you're to move away from
here, and go and live in the city. You can sew or serve in a house,
and the children can work as well. What's lying here in the rabbit hole is not for you to spend. Not until you're in the city. And
slowly, so no one suspects anything. There's nine hundred and
ninety marks, all in tens.'

'Where did you get such money from?' asks the wife.

'I found it,' says the farmer. 'It's wrapped up in oilcloth. The
rabbits brought it to light.'

'You found it, Banz . . .?'

'It is as I say. Someone hid it here, perhaps for an emergency.
It's to stay here. It's for an emergency. Only if you're in dire need
do you touch it.'

'I don't want money, I want you,' says the wife.

'And keep an eye on Franz. See that he doesn't go in the barn
– Franz is nosy.'

'He won't go in the barn.'

'Go back right away, in case he gets ideas. I'm going to head off
down the beach.'

'Are you going now?'

Farmer Banz disappears between the tree trunks, in the direction of the white dunes.

His wife watches him go. Two minutes. She makes a move, a step.

Then she turns round and walks slowly back to the Stolpermünde-Abbau farm.

X

Cousin Benthin has found Rohwer. He was standing by the bar at Auntie Lieschen's, making cow's eyes at the barmaid. He thinks all the things Benthin discussed with Gareis are nonsense.

'Let me tell you, Benthin, what are we doing with the Socialist? Are we to do his job for him, or what? We're allowed to demonstrate, it's covered by law. And the way he deals with demonstration, that's his job, that's what he's paid for.'

'You've got a point,' nods Cousin Benthin.

'Come to him with the leaders?' asks Rohwer. 'I'll tell you something else, Benthin, which of us is a leader? Is it you or me or the young fellow with the school cap from agricultural college?'

'You,' says Benthin quickly.

'Nonsense. Why me? Has anyone elected me?'

'No. You're not elected.'

'Or has anyone appointed me, then? Maybe Red Gareis? Or the paper pusher in Stolpe?'

'Nor that neither.'

'We're no political party, Benthin, let me say, we're no organization. And much less do we have any leaders.'

'But when I shook hands with him, and promised to go and see him with the leaders? Do me the kindness, Rohwer, it'll only be ten minutes.'

'What did you promise him?'

'That I'd go and see him with the leaders.'

'What if there's no leaders . . .?'

Benthin looks at him uneasily.

'Then you can't go and see him with the leaders, that's surely obvious. And you haven't broken your word neither.'

'But what if he's looking for me?'

'We'll think of something. What if he doesn't find you? You

stay here at Auntie Lieschen's in the dark, behind the bar. – Young Farmer!'

'Yes, Farmer?'

'Go round the bars will you and leave word that if the police are looking for Cousin Benthin from Altholm, they're to say: He's just popped next door. You got that?'

'I'll do that, Farmer,' and with that the young farmer leaves.

At the table by the door are a couple of men in plain half-town suits and no collars, maybe master craftsmen or something of that sort.

'Did you hear that?' Perduzke asks Inspector Bering.

'I didn't hear anything,' he replies, 'I'm just here for the beer.'

'They're wanting to make mugs of us.'

'Leave them be. Then we'll make monkeys of Fatty Gareis and Frerksen, when we give in our claim for expenses, and haven't heard anything.'

'You're right,' says Perduzke. 'A pestilence on that pig Frerksen. Auntie Lieschen, will you bring us two more pints?'

The men go on drinking.

The door swings open, and in stalks Commander Frerksen in full fig. His fair hair pokes out at odd angles under his cap, his face is flushed, his eyes peer out angrily behind his spectacles. His glance brushes his two detectives, and burrows into the knot of farmers, surrounded by a nimbus of pipe and cigarette smoke; he opens his mouth to speak, shuts it again. Finally he calls out: 'Is Farmer Benthin from Altholm here by any chance?'

A sort of silence descends, the farmers turn towards the policeman and stare at him. No one replies.

'I asked,' Frerksen repeats, 'whether Farmer Benthin from Altholm is here?'

More silence.

Then a very high voice cries: 'There's no Benthin here.'

And another growls slowly: 'Cousin Benthin's slipped up in the Banana Cellar.'

'I've just come from there!' Frerksen replies angrily.

'Then he must be in the Red Cupboard!'

'Nah, he's at Tucher's!'

'You mean Krüger's!'

'He's here at Auntie Lieschen's!'

'He's with his sweetheart in the Grotto!'

'His old lady's just given birth to twins!'

'Quiet!' roars a voice. There is silence.

Frerksen cranes his neck and looks into the tangle of people. He has turned pale. Then he turns on his heel and stalks out.

Bering says into the buzz of renewed conversation: 'Jesus, Perduzke, this time we've really done it. We shouldn't have made our boss go through that.'

'What are you saying! We're here on a secret assignment to observe. How can we possibly get up and talk to a uniformed copper?'

'Did you see how pale he went? The farmers have taken a scunner to the police.'

At the bar, Rohwer says to the agitated Benthin: 'That was very good, Cousin Benthin, you did that very well.'

'That was mean of them,' pouts Cousin Benthin. 'Frerksen's a good Altholmer too.'

'That's because you're used to the blue soldier's uniform. Us from the country, who are proper farmers, it makes us see red when we see the blue.'

'The fellows should leave my wife out of it! My boy is mine!'

'We know, Cousin Benthin. You've got a good wife. And now come with us to Tucher's. We've got a leaders' meeting.'

'Leaders' meeting?'

'Well, that's what they call it. They're not proper leaders. So come along!'

XI

Rohwer and Benthin walk slowly and silently along, their heavy arms dangling down clumsily at their sides.

'You must own a stick,' says Rohwer.

'No, actually I –' begins Benthin.

'I'm not sure what I've done now,' Rohwer carries on, 'did I take mine with me this morning or not? Then it must be hanging in a bar somewhere. But which one?'

'I didn't bring one, because –'

'A farmer without a cane is like a girl without a brain. Let's go into Zemlin the umbrella-makers, and buy us each a stick.'

'We're not permitted to carry sticks on the march.'

'Really? The things you come out with. Who says we can't?'

'The administration. The police. Sticks on the march are forbidden.'

'But not for farmers, surely? If a worker takes a stick, it means he wants to beat someone up. If a farmer has a stick, it's because he needs the feeling of carrying something in his hand. Come in with me.'

'I'm not buying one.'

'Suit yourself. You go on ahead to Tucher's.'

And Rohwer walks into the shop.

Benthin wanders up and down outside. He looks at the farmers walking past: almost all of them are carrying sticks. We're not allowed to, he thinks. But what if everyone does it? It doesn't feel right, walking empty-handed.

He wants to buy one too.

'Why there you are, Herr Benthin,' says a voice behind him, and Commander Frerksen holds out his hand.

Benthin has an almighty shock. 'Er, yes, here I am . . . I was just . . .'

'With your wife? With the baby?'

'No. Not. No, I was . . .'

'Now, Herr Benthin, why didn't you go up and see the mayor in the town hall?'

'Because there are no leaders.'

'No leaders?'

'No. None. Reimers has been locked up.'

'So Reimers is your leader?'

'No, no, I didn't say that, Officer. Reimers isn't our leader either. We don't have one.'

'But you just said . . .'

Cousin Benthin is very agitated. 'You mustn't try and set a trap for me, Officer. That's not fair. Trapping don't count.'

'No one wants to trap you. I'm just asking. Who's set the time and place?'

'I don't know.'

'You're just all setting out when you feel like it? On impulse? A few of you now, and a few more later?'

'But we have the Stahlhelm band from Stettin,' says Benthin, offended. 'And then we've got a banner, and when the banner is unfurled, that's the signal to go.'

'So you've got a banner too?'

'A fine, proud banner. The Altholmers will stare.'

'Then your flag-bearer will be your leader? Who is he?'

'I don't know. Don't ask me that, Officer, I don't know anything. You've brought me along to the town hall, but I'm nothing, and I have nothing to tell you about the farmers.'

'Too right you don't,' says Farmer Rohwer, standing right next to him.

'Perhaps you do, then?' suggests Frerksen. 'What's your name?'

'You can ask me that when the cock's laid eggs. I didn't ask you your name either.'

'Weren't you standing by the bar a moment ago, when I asked if anyone had seen Herr Benthin?'

'I don't turn my head when a copper shouts something. I look the other way, and I might walk the other way too. – Come on, Cousin Benthin, let's be having you.'

Farmer Rohwer walks slowly off. Frerksen forces a smile. 'Excitable people, your new friends, Herr Benthin. They're no friends of ours.'

'They're farmers. They don't mean it that way. And they're not too fond of a uniform.'

'But I haven't done anything to hurt them!'

'You?! All uniforms have hurt us. The whole State hurts us. Earlier, we used to have a living off the land, now . . . I'd like to know how you'd feel if someone turns up in uniform and takes the cows out of your byre.'

'I've never yet taken anyone's cow away.'

'No, but you asked what his name was on the public street, and that's something no decent person does.'

'I didn't mean it like that. Everybody's so excitable today.'

'You're excitable, Officer.'

'Me? Not a bit of it. I'm going on holiday tomorrow, I'm not thinking about anything except my trip.'

'That's not how you seem to me, Officer.'

'But that's how I am. – Now, Herr Benthin, we're a couple of old Altholm hands, and we don't either of us want anything to happen to the dear old place, do we?'

'No, we don't.'

'Well then, Cousin Benthin, come, let's you and me shake on doing all we can to make things pass off safely.'

'I can promise you that all right. We farmers aren't going to make any trouble.'

'And if you happen to hear anything about things not passing off safely, Herr Benthin, and there are some people who do want trouble, then please come and see me. Then we'll take care of it quietly, so that it doesn't get any worse.'

'I'll shake on that too – If I can find you.'

'Well now,' says Commander Frerksen, drawing a deep breath of relief, 'now we've given each other our promises as citizens of Altholm, let's aim to keep them. For the sake of the old place.'

'That's right, Officer. And now don't you go running around in the sun, because that doesn't agree with you. Better to sit down and drink a cool beer in the shade somewhere. My God, man, you're running with sweat!'

'All the best then, Herr Benthin!'

'Goodbye, sir!'

XII

It's the quiet hour after lunch in the central prison in Altholm. The iron walkways along the vast five-storey wells in the four wings of the prison are all deserted. The sergeant is sitting in his glass box writing, not raising his eyes. At this hour there is nothing to look out for in all the passages you can see from his eyrie. The prison is asleep.

From the guardroom at Station C4 a guard comes striding softly along. He stops briefly at the rail of his walkway, looks down the well in the direction of the sergeant. Nothing stirs.

He stands there, grimly resolved that even if the sergeant should look up, he will go into Cell 357. Auxiliary Prison Warden Gruen walks another ten steps, stops outside the door of 357. He cuts a lamentable figure, a herring with the rosy face of an infant, pale blue prominent Basedow eyes, a much-too-blond little chin beard, and his skull as bald as an egg. The sergeant bawls him out about his ratty uniform every day, with split shoes, and string for laces, only partly disguised by boot blacking.

There he stands, auxiliary warden in the services of the Prussian Minister of Justice, recipient of one hundred and eighty five marks a month, on which he has to feed himself, his wife and three children, temporary overlord of Station C4, comprising forty inmates. Among them is the remand prisoner Tredup, whom Gruen takes to be a bomber. He has been removed from the remand prison into the penal wing, so as to cut him off from the outside world completely.

Gruen has a last look down at the glass box with his enemy, the fat sergeant. He is feeling a little confused, he doesn't yet know what he wants to do, but he has seen what's going on at the gate. Even if they think he's a little bonkers, he knows they're putting one over on the farmers, there's some sort of Red plot, like there was then, when they stood him against the wall.

He very quietly slides back the bolt on # 357. Then he peers through the spyhole: the prisoner's lying on his bed asleep. Gruen nods to himself and laughs. He turns the key, once, twice. Then he opens the door.

Now he can no longer see the sergeant, but if he hears three raps of a key on the iron rail, he'll know that he's been seen unlocking the cell door in spite of the ban on doing so.

All quiet. It's as though the building were calmly breathing and sleeping. Gruen laughs again, enters the cell and quietly pulls the door shut after him.

Outside the prison there's been a lively coming and going all morning. Yes, Feinbube, and Rehder and Rohwer, and Benthin and Bandekow have passed on the word in the bars: Reimers is no longer in Altholm, the demonstration outside the prison is off.

But there are farmers who are curious, who want to see the building where their leader was languishing before. And then there was a farmer from other parts, from around Hanover way, with top-boots and a chamois tuft on his hat, a delegate and confederate, someone who was clued in to the details of the farmers' organization, who whispered behind his hand: It's all a lie, Reimers is still in Altholm, and they're keeping him locked up like a dog.

A few of the farmers just rang the bell and demanded to speak to Reimers. Others stood on the street and stared across to where the grey cement front of the prison rose up behind the tall red perimeter wall, a smooth, sheer and cheerless wall, punctuated only by the monotonous barred windows.

They discussed which of those hundreds of holes might have their Franz locked behind it. Then the prison gate creaked open, and an official came out with his pot of coffee under his arm, at the end of his shift, or a pale, half-starved prisoner with a cardboard box on a string, containing all his worldly goods.

Right now there's another group of farmers looking silently up at the grey wall. It all looks so dead, impossible to imagine there's any life going on behind it at all, behind each hole a man who misses his freedom.

The great locks in the gate crack open, the farmers look to see a man come out, a big raw-boned man in corduroy clothes and greased boots. He exchanges a few words with the sergeant who escorts him out. Then the gate closes, and the man stands there with his brown cardboard box on a string, and looks out at the wide square basking there in the hot sun of a July afternoon.

He wedges his box under his arm, takes a few steps, looks round, and notices the farmers. He hesitates briefly again, and then makes straight for them.

'G'day to youse farmers,' he says, and doffs his cap, 'any of youse be needing a hand on your farm?'

The farmers look at him in silence.

'Don't think,' says the big raw-boned fellow, 'that I don't know what work is. I've mowed the vetch on Count Bandekow's estate, and I pick up my couple of hunnerdweight like a feather.'

The farmers don't say anything.

'Don't think I'm a thief either,' says the man, 'that would be a mistake. I don't steal. It was over a little girl. She were willing. But because some other people happened along, she started to screech. And then she pretty well had to stick to her story that I forced her.'

'You must,' asks Farmer Banz, 'have spent a long while in the slammer?'

'Quite a bit,' says the man. 'Nine months. Now, how about it, don't any of you want a strong man to help bring in the rye?'

'You must know everyone in there?' asks Farmer Banz again.

The man laughs uproariously. 'Everyone? You've got a strange notion. I don't even know everyone on my station.'

'I don t know about such things,' says the farmer in confusion. 'But would you know one Franz Reimers?'

'Reimers?' asks the man. 'Hang on a minute. There was so many. He wasn't in for long, was he?'

'Isn't he there any more, then?'

'Now I've got him. Big tall fellow, clean-shaven, hair starting to grey?'

The farmers nod eagerly.

'He did something, something to do with taxes, he told me once during association. Was there oxen involved, or something?'

The farmers nod eagerly. 'That's the man,' says Banz.

'But listen to me, friends. He's gone. He's no longer there. He's in Stolpe.'

'Are you sure about that?' Banz asks after a lengthy silence.

'If I tell you,' rebuts the tall fellow. 'He was in the cell beside mine, only a week ago. Then he was moved to Stolpe.'

'Did he tell you he was going to Stolpe?' asks Banz again.

'"They want to question me in Stolpe," he told me, "because

there was a big bang there. Even though I was already locked up in here," he said, "when it went off.'"

The farmers look at one another, at the big man, at the bare, grey cement walls.

At that moment there's a sound from above. One of the windows has been pushed open. Something white appears: a hand, clasping the bars. Something white, bigger, round and white: in the corner, pressed against the wall, a face.

The farmers see it clearly, from below: a hole opens in the white form, a small black hole, and it starts screaming down to them: 'Help me, farmers! They're killing me! Help, farmers!'

The farmers take a sudden step towards the red perimeter wall, then they take a look at the big man – the voice above still screaming for help – the big man, who is staring in astonishment.

'What's that, then?' yells Banz. 'You robber, I ask you, explain that!'

'That's not him. That can't be Reimers. Reimers went away from here in a car!'

'Yes, it is Reimers!'

'Who else can it be?!'

'That's our Franz!'

'You liar!'

And Banz suddenly: 'You spy! You robber! Just you wait, I'll . . .'

The voice from on high screams and cries: 'Help me, farmers, help! I did it for you! Help me! Help!'

And suddenly it's as though the building fizzed up, the dead building. In all the window openings the glass is pushed aside, everywhere white hands, white round faces with black mouth holes, a hellish yelling: 'Help us, farmers! Help us, farmers!'

Mixed in with it a bell ringing frantically, whistles, shouts, alarms.

The big fellow gathers himself, runs away from Banz's hands to the prison gate, bangs on it. Two or three farmers chase him, hold him terrified, raise their fists against him.

Two are staring at the wall, at the inmates yelling, and at the white spot that was the first to cry.

'Quickly, run into town. Everyone has to come out here!'

And Banz: 'Everyone come! It's terrible what they're doing here!'
'Everyone has to come here! Everyone!'
And, while running along: 'Was that actually Franz?'
'Who can tell at that distance! I expect it was, though.'
They run into town.

XIII

Tucher's is the bar in Altholm with the most space. Hundreds of farmers are sitting there, standing around, drinking, smoking, or leaning patiently on the walls.

A dense group rings Henning and Bandekow, who are in the process of assembling the banner that had been taken apart for the drive. Henning is working with a pair of pliers; not looking up, he tightens the nuts that are holding a tin sleeve round the shaft. Attached to it is the scythe.

'There. That should do it.'

'It still looks a bit wobbly to me,' opines Bandekow.

'Because I forgot the screwdriver. But it'll hold.'

'Excuse me,' a voice pipes up, 'excuse me, I want to introduce myself: I'm Farmer Megger from Hanover district. Near Stade. Meggerkoog.'

In front of Henning is a squat little man in top-boots, green loden suit, and a chamois brush on his hat.

Henning is on the point of introducing himself, when he gets a nudge in the back. 'What's this all about,then?'

He turns. Behind him is Padberg, giving him a meaningful look, and with his mouth forming the word: 'Stoolie!'

Henning smiles. 'Have you got the screwdriver by chance? Would you tell Friedrich . . . Oh right, yes, sorry, the scythe isn't fixed properly.'

'That's a nice flag you've got there . . .' says the farmer from around Hanover, with a friendly smile.

'Yes? You reckon? Yes, flag,' says Henning seriously.

'An unusual flag. A symbolic flag. Would you explain it to me? We Hanoverian farmers are anxious to help.'

'Yes? The best way I can explain it is if I show it. – Make room, you farmers!'

Space is created around Henning. He raises the flag aloft, swings it with one hand, catches it in the other. The cloth unfolds with a loud crash: the white plough, the red sword – gules on sable – on black background.

'Get in line! Get in line!' call many voices. 'We're on our way! Get in line!'

6

The Storm Breaks

I

The farmers come streaming out of the pubs and bars. The marketplace is full of them, some are running around, but others are already forming into a mass, a column, behind a line of eight abreast outside the entrance to Tucher's pub.

They form up behind. Villages stick together, for the most part the order takes care of itself; Padberg, hustling back and forth, hardly has to say a word.

Curious onlookers stop and watch on the pavements, not in numbers, but all those who in a factory town of forty thousand inhabitants are out and about on a hot and cloudless July afternoon: unemployed, children, women, a few business people. All the windows facing the marketplace are thrown open, maids crowd into one to watch, in the next one along there are ladies. They exchange impressions and observations.

'Look! Here comes a flag!'

'Ooh, isn't it black!'

'It's like a pirate flag!'

They all crane their necks.

'You can't do that, Henning,' says Padberg, 'the scythe is loose. If it falls off, someone could get hurt, and we'll look silly.'

'Herr Haas,' says Henning to the landlord of Tucher's, 'what's keeping Friedrich with his bloody screwdriver? I can't tighten the nuts any more with these pliers.'

'He's coming, he's coming. Just wait in the corridor. I've got the French wrench.'

Henning and his flag take themselves off.

'He's worried about his black rag,' says an unemployed man.

'Well, not everything can be as red as the rag you follow around.'

'Better than your black-red-and-shite banner!'

'If you –!'

'Quiet, gentlemen,' says Perduzke, pushing through the bodies. 'Why get het up? It's warm enough as it is!'

All laugh.

In the meantime, Henning is tinkering with his flag.

'Say, Padberg, what happened with the music?'

Padberg grunts. 'I've forgotten all about it! The fellows will be sitting with Chairman Besen by the pond, drinking like fish, if I know anything.'

'Send a young farmer round.'

'Sure. – Hey, you! Will you run and tell the music master of the Stahlhelm band to come right away with his men? He's sitting with Besen at his pond. You know it? Hurry!'

The young farmer scoots off.

'The snoop, you know, he just wanted to have your name.'

'The second you nudged me, and I saw your dirty face, I knew the score.'

'He almost got the flag in his face.'

'That's what I meant to happen. – There, that'll hold. I can run through ten policemen with it.'

'You shouldn't think shit like that.'

'I don't. It thinks itself.'

'Well, we've got your word, remember.'

'You have. More's the pity. I won't raise my hand in anger.'

They walk out on to the market square again. The column has become endless, farmers are backed up on to the Stolpe Road.

'Ah, doesn't it do you good to see a sight like that.'

'Three thousand! And how many more still in the bars and pubs along the Burstah!'

'We'll take them with us when we move off. – You know you were right, Henning, without a flag it wouldn't have been anything!'

'It gives the whole thing a bit of atmosphere!'

They both look up at the flag, which is unfurling in the mild summer breeze. The plough seems to move across the black earth, while the red sword hangs motionless above.

'Let's go now, can't we?' suggests Henning.

'Why? What about the band!'

'People are getting impatient.'

'Nonsense. Farmers don't get impatient.'

A whole troop of town police push their way through the people on the pavement, led by a uniformed officer with thick epaulettes and a moustache. The men have the straps of their shako helmets under their chins.

'Is that all for us?' asks Henning.

'Wait and see! I've no idea what they want. We're peaceable folk.'

'Of course.'

But the town police have already moved on. All of them looked up at the flag, their officer passed some remark, and the people near him grinned.

'You see,' says Henning, referring to the flag.

'You never can tell,' says Padberg drily. 'Grzesinski's a deep one.'

II

A man comes striding across the market square in blue uniform, a pair of spectacles on the bridge of his nose, his service cap somewhat pushed back, revealing a hank of reddish-blond hair.

Commander Frerksen is on his way to his office after lunch. He is calm and resolved to follow the instructions of his mayor, to allow the farmers to demonstrate, and to go off on holiday the next day.

He sees the gathering of people, the onlookers. He stops.

It is an extraordinary mass of people, an army, he never thought there would be so many.

He sees the flag. Slowly, blinking his near-sighted eyes, he comes nearer. It's a sinister-looking black drape. Something red on it, and something white. Slowly the flag flutters in the breeze, never quite opening out to its full extent, staying half folded.

The commander stops on the edge of the pavement. He looks

across at the flag, at the young man holding it, an older man with spectacles standing next to him.

He looks up at the windows crammed with people. Altholm has its big event, its sensation. Someone in the crowd behind him mutters – and he has the feeling it is meant for him – 'A pirate flag like that, they shouldn't stand for it!'

And another voice, equally aware of being listened to, opines: 'It's always the workers that cops it!'

Suddenly his heart begins to beat violently. He can feel himself sweating.

Shame, he thinks, if I'd slept for five minutes longer, the march would be up and away already.

He looks back in the direction of the town hall, with its red gables. I could have been sitting there. Shame. And he thinks of another office, dark, with bullseye panes and heavy oak furniture. Your Gareis is responsible for all this – wasn't that what he said?

That or words to that effect.

Henning and Padberg are standing on the roadway, ten yards off.

'Who's that twat?' asks Padberg.

'That's the police supremo of Altholm. A prize jerk.'

'He looks it.'

'He wants something from us.'

'Well, we don't want anything from him.'

The commander slowly covers the ten yards to them. However slow his walk, his voice still sounds breathless as he says to them: 'Gentlemen, this flag . . . you can't have that.'

And Henning, rudely: 'Can't have what?'

The commander: 'Please understand . . . Would you take the flag back to the bar?'

Frerksen speaks slowly, endeavouring to articulate each word.

'The flag's part of the march. The flag stays,' Padberg says roughly.

The commander reaches out his hand to the flag.

Henning with both hands lifts it away from his chest.

One, two, three times.

The nearest farmers move their left legs, and set them down again, take the first step. The column is off and away.

Frerksen sees the distance widen between his hand and the flagstaff. He feels people barging into him, pushing him away. Big, shut faces approach him, shoulders knock into him.

If only, he thinks in his breathless way, if only I had . . .

He finds himself on the roadway.

'Why didn't you call us?' Sergeant Maurer, patrolling about under the trees with his colleague Schmidt, asks reproachfully.

'Yes, of course,' says the commander, and gazes at the flag, which is another ten yards further off.

'Move! At the double!' he suddenly yells. 'We have to get that flag.'

III

The column hasn't advanced more than twenty yards or so when Frerksen and his two men start to run. The farmers stare in mystification at the running policemen. Only the first eight or ten of them saw the incident, and they will hardly have understood what was at issue, so softly did the commander speak.

While running, Frerksen holds the grip of his sabre, so that it doesn't get caught up in his legs. His uniform bothers him. He has the feeling that everyone is staring at him because he's running down the middle of the road: the farmers, the townspeople on the pavement, the burghers of Altholm looking down from their windows. He has the feeling he's looking particularly pale, and while running he tries to feel his face (it's flushed), it's cold to the touch. Suddenly he remembers that the whole town hates him, and that the only reason he's there is because Gareis keeps supporting him.

How can Gareis have gone off on holiday! How can he be lounging around in his flat! If he saw me like this, surely he would come and help me.

Still running, he tries to think how Gareis would tackle the problem: would he be running like this, for a start? That fat pig, sitting around at home. He would chat them up, he would schmooze them and soft-soap them . . . I don't schmooze. I don't like it . . .

Behind his boss runs Sergeant Maurer. What a load of nonsense! he thinks. Frerksen always messes things up. Where are all the others? Is it going to be left to the three of us to . . .? Schmidt is off the pace too. Well, it doesn't matter. Those stubborn so-and-sos. We'll collar their flag.

And Sergeant Schmidt, fat and sweating fantastically, miles behind. Of course me, of course I have to run. All the rest of the guys are loafing on the Burstah, only I'm running to catch my death. Longbones Maurer can do it with his ten stone, but not me at double that. I must do something about my weight. Maybe a lemon diet . . .

Suddenly Frerksen has broken through to the front of the march. Not looking round, he charges up to Henning, grips the flagstaff, cries in a breathless voice: 'I hereby confiscate your flag! Do you hear me, I'm confiscating your flag!'

Henning barely listens to him, he grips the flag in front of his chest with both hands.

'The flag is ours!'

The little group at the head make to halt, but the procession is on the move, and they keep going. The next rows want to see what the commotion is about, the flag is waving, everything overflows, a crush through which Sergeant Maurer can barely force his way. He reaches instinctively for the flagpole that Frerksen is holding, the flag sways violently, tips, falls. The scythe jangles on the paving stones.

Frerksen gets a shove in the back, half turns round, two burning eyes glower at him, two fists are raised, a voice threatens him: 'Get your dirty paws off our flag!'

Another jolt. A blow. Many blows on his shoulder. There is Maurer, he is yanking at the flag, which Henning just still has a hold of. Frerksen stumbles over someone's outstretched leg. Maurer is lying on the ground, the flagpole still in his hands, still with Henning and three or four farmers holding on to it too. Half the flag seems to cover him.

What's keeping Schmidt? What's keeping the regular police? This is going wrong, thinks Frerksen. Blows keep landing on him.

He backs hard into the men besetting him, finds he can breathe at last, takes the opportunity to unsheathe his sabre . . .

A hand clasps his arm, he looks into the livid face of the man who chased him away from the flag-bearer a moment ago. Padberg orders him: 'Put that thing away, man!'

They tussle for it. Frerksen tries to free his arm, to deliver a blow. All these faces, so hate-filled, and up in the windows, those others full of curiosity. The man twists his wrist, the bones crack: the sabre jangles on the ground. He briefly sees it shining underfoot, then a boot treads on it, a leg obscures it from vision.

Frerksen manages to free his hand. He reaches into his holster. Over there stands a flushed-looking Maurer. 'Draw side arms!' shrieks Frerksen with breaking voice. 'Out of my way!'

Somehow a road opens in front of him, he stumbles along, half blind behind his slipping, fogged-up glasses, wheezing with exertion. Now he's on the opposite pavement, people let him pass. Their faces look abashed when they look at him . . .

He leans against a wall . . .

Maurer joins him. 'That didn't work. There's not enough of us.'

'Where's Schmidt?' pants the commander.

'Someone got hold of him some time ago at the back. Here he comes now. Ah, he and Perduzke have arrested someone, they're taking him back to the station.'

Above the procession the flag, the black, fluttering flag, now reappears. The scythe is bent, but still the flag waves. And the procession wends its way.

IV

'Let me go!' shouts Farmer Rohwer excitedly. 'You must let me go! You struck me, and I want to bring a complaint against you with your authorities.'

'You need to calm down first,' says Perduzke mildly. 'Drink a glass of water back at the station.'

'I don't want your effing water. You have no right to detain me.'

'Did you see how he almost broke my arm on the lamp post?' says fat Schmidt to Perduzke. 'Boy, this isn't the first punch-up you've been involved in, is it?'

'Do you think I'll stand by while you beat me up? If you hit me, I hit back!'

'I had to,' wheezes the fat sergeant, endlessly sweating, 'I had to call out "make way" several times. If you don't move aside, then you'll get a taste of my truncheon.'

'How can I move, if everything's chock-a-block? Were you able to move?'

'If a policeman calls out "make way",' observes Schmidt sagely, 'then you have to step aside. How you do it is up to you.'

'The next time I visit your damned Altholm, I'll have eyes in my arse, so that I can see you coming,' growls the furious Rohwer.

'Cool it,' says Perduzke calmly. 'When we get to the station, we'll write it all down, and that'll clear our heads.'

'Look at that,' one farmer says to another in the demonstration. 'They're arresting a Communist.'

'The Red bastards won't allow us our flag.'

'Did you see, it disappeared for a moment. But now it's back up and flying.'

'The demo has police protection.'

'There's not much to protect! I'd like to see those Soviets tangling with us!'

Through the mass of people, little Pinkus from the *Volkszeitung* eagerly makes his way.

'Tell me, Comrade Erdmann, what happened a moment ago? I just missed it.'

'I'm not rightly sure. There was some carry-on with Frerksen and the flag-bearer. Then there was some pushing and shoving, and a few blows. I don't know what happened after. Look, there he is, leaning against the wall. Ask him.'

Pinkus pushes his way through the crowd of onlookers.

Against the wall, almost unnoticed in a corner, stands Frerksen, still panting, his empty scabbard in his hand.

'What happened just now, Frerksen? Did I miss something?'

'You, Pinkus? I'm confiscating the flag. It's a provocation, a flag is not permitted.'

'But they've taken the flag with them.'

'I'm still confiscating it. Where are the reserves? I've sent Maurer for reserves.'

'Where are the rest of your men?'

'On the Burstah.'

'Wait, I'll send a cyclist. – And I'd have thought if you want to get hold of the flag, you should be at the head of the column. – What happened to your sabre?'

Frerksen stands there. He has unbuckled his belt and is staring at his empty scabbard.

'Where's your sabre?'

'They took my sabre off me, the bastards! – Wait, send the cyclist.'

Frerksen looks around. He doesn't altogether know what to do, but he must first get rid of the empty, laughable scabbard, symbol of a disgrace for the whole town.

He stands in a shop doorway. Cautiously he tries the door and looks inside. The shop appears to be empty. Knitwear, wool, the *tricoteuses* of the French Revolution, Frerksen thinks mechanically.

With a sudden jerk, he tosses the empty scabbard into the empty shop, he hears it jingle as it lands on the floor. He closes the door and sighs with relief.

Then he gets going. He trots along beside the march, past indifferent, curious, familiar faces. The quiet, settled official is jogging through the town, his tongue hanging out like a dog's. The flag, he thinks. The flag!

V

The commander runs through the town. Through the market square first, which the column of demonstrators has left almost bereft of citizens, then along the Burstah, always beside the march, stared at and smiled at, viewed with indifference and the subject of whispered comments. He hasn't run like this since he was a pup, his chest is heaving, his heart pounding. He can see very little through his dirty, fogged-up spectacles; he runs into people, bangs against them, and they jump, swear at him and stop when they see who he is.

As far as the eye can see, farmers, a strange march, without rhythm, without music as yet. Walking side by side, in lines of eight abreast, but each one walks singly, slow, heavy, as though trudging through his own ploughed lea.

They have no eyes for him. He's still at the rear of the march, in the middle of the march, on a level with people who have no idea what's just happened. Whoever happens to see him says at the most: 'Look at the four-eyed cop! Wonder what his hurry is! We can look after ourselves.'

Now he's getting near the front of the demonstration. He's had it in view for a long time now, unfurled in the wind and the movement of the march: black field with white plough and red sword. And the dull metal of the scythe above, kinked in two places, but still pointing up, a symbol of rebellion.

This scythe, he thinks, impossible, I couldn't let it pass, Gareis can't have meant that. Besides, there is a local police ordnance by which uncovered scythes may not be carried into a built-up area. I must look up the paragraph before I talk to Gareis. – There they are . . .

Through a gap in the crowd he sees the flag-carrier, and the bespectacled man next to him. Suddenly he seems to see one of them laughing to the other.

They've seen me. They're making fun of me. Because I didn't get the flag. You wait, you!

They haven't seen him this time, the pair at the head of the march. Henning literally has both hands full with his flag, which he is carrying without a bandolier. It presses against his chest, he can feel the wind tug at it, sometimes it swings away from him a little.

He looks up at it, sees the kinked scythe, and thinks: It looks even better now. After a fight. That wretched policeman! Thinks he can impound this flag, like it was a bowling-association banner or a KPD poster. He'll be pretty fed up, I reckon.

Padberg is busy with the speech he will give in the auction hall. He may well mention this abuse of police power in it, he thinks. It typifies the government of today. The Reds and the Nazis are given their heads, we farmers are placed under emergency law.

VI

Where the road to Grünhof intersects the Burstah there is a traffic post. The crossing is manned from nine in the morning until eight at night. The Burstah widens at this point. There is a small ornamental garden here, the Stolper Torplatz, with obligatory war memorial.

Normally the traffic cop and naked war hero are left to contemplate each other undisturbed. Today, Sergeant Hart is looking down the Burstah, at the approaching procession. A quarter of an hour previously, some twenty of his colleagues led by Superintendent Kallene came by; they are to occupy the railway station and the streets from the station to the auction hall, which is the industrial part of town.

Then, just five minutes ago, a cyclist raced up, sweating, and as he flew by he yelled: 'There's all sorts going on! The farmers and your mates are scrapping. I'm getting reinforcements!'

And he was gone. Hart tries to imagine what happened: Have the police started something, or did the farmers? Or was it just a worker, pulling his leg?

He wants to go and help, perhaps his mates are in a bad way. Who's on duty at the market? Mechanically he waves a few cars on, and is happy whenever he can stand in such a way that he has the Burstah in view.

There, a long way off still, he makes out an indistinct mass.

A man with a loden hat and a chamois brush on it comes marching up in a hurry. His steel-tipped top-boots click along the paving stones. He charges up to Hart.

'Sergeant, is this the way to the auction hall? – Thank you.

Right. I'll find my way. – Well, you'd best make yourself scarce like your colleagues.'

Ten paces on: 'Or else you'll get a pasting, like your colleagues.'

Twenty paces on, growling: 'From us farmers! Yeah, farmers.'

'Stop!' yells Hart. 'Stop right there! I order you!'

He is about to set off in pursuit of the man, but two cars come along, he waves his arms, and the next time he looks around, the man with the chamois brush has gone.

He didn't go up to the station, surely! Otherwise I'd still be able to see him. Oh, I hope I catch you another time! Those shitty farmers. Giving us a pasting, you see if you're not the ones who get pasted! Damned shitty farmers.

Another man comes running along, staggering, with the last of his strength, straight for him. To his great astonishment, Hart recognizes his superior, Frerksen.

'The reinforcements!' he pants. 'We need Kallene with the reinforcements. The farmers . . .'

He stands there, no use for anything at all.

'Yes, Commander, sir! I'm here on traffic duty. I think a cyclist has already been sent for reinforcements.'

'Get them!' yells Frerksen. His voice fails him. 'Run, Hart, run. The farmers . . . The flag . . .'

Sergeant Hart glances one last time at the pale, contorted face of his superior, and is already off at a run to the railway station. He wonders who has already been given a pasting today . . .

Frerksen stands there, on the traffic island on the Burstah, spreads his arms, signalling to the traffic. If only they come soon, he thinks. The farmers are coming closer. Two, three minutes . . .

A cyclist comes up the Burstah, from the market square. He brakes at the traffic island and dismounts. Frerksen recognizes him: it's Matthies, KPD official, and royal pain in the bum.

'Inspector,' he says amiably, 'Commander, rather. I wanted to bring you something. I found it. I'm bringing it to you . . .'

And he hands Frerksen his battered, bent, fouled, naked sabre.

Frerksen stares at it uncomprehendingly. He is standing on the traffic island. Already people are gathering, the farmers are coming.

In front of him is Matthies, nasty smirk on his face, holding out to him his dirtied sabre.

'Where shall I put it?' asks Frerksen timidly and confusedly. 'I don't have a scabbard.'

'Put it away,' he whispers. 'Put it away somewhere, right now. There, behind the base of the monument. Put it there . . .' And his eyes achingly follow the Communist, who, with ostentatious slowness, slopes the sabre over his shoulder like a rifle, grinning round at people in all directions, clambers over the low hedge, slowly and pleasurably sets his foot down in the geranium bed, walks on, treading the flowers to mush, before disappearing, with a mocking grin, behind the plinth, as though – with the policeman looking on – to relieve himself.

I can't take this any more, thinks Frerksen in despair. I can't take this any more. It's inhuman. More than I can stand. If only I'd left home just five minutes later. What's keeping the reinforcements?

VII

They're on their way.

A score of blues are jogging over from the railway station. In response to the first confusing bulletins, Superintendent Kallene assembled all the men that were on duty in the northern part of town.

But the farmers aren't far either. A hundred yards, eighty yards off, the column in rows of eight abreast. The black flag in the van (still with no music), they are advancing.

Superintendent Kallene makes his report, but Frerksen isn't listening. 'The farmers fell upon us, your colleagues have been beaten. Now the flag must be seized. It's been confiscated. You, Soldin, Meierfeld, Geier, are responsible for getting the flag. The others will help.'

Kallene surveys the short distance that separates them from the head of the procession. From the elevated traffic island, he jumps down on to the roadway. 'Right, men! Go!'

He raises his hands. Unarmed, he runs against the march, his men at his side, some already ahead of him. Some have taken the raised arm of their commander as a sign to draw their swords, and are struggling to run and – unusually – draw their sabres at the same time. Others have unhooked their truncheons from their belts and are swinging them menacingly. Menacing, too, are the shakos pulled down low over their brows, secured by a chin band.

Only the foremost of the farmers have seen the attack, and pause, and try to stop, but are pushed along from behind.

Henning abruptly slows his pace. And in a feeling of mockery and obstinacy he raises the flag a little higher, pressing his back against those coming up behind. While he stands firm, they push through the line.

The oncoming police see him melt away, the front line has closed over him already. Now he is behind the second, now the third row.

'The flag!' yells Frerksen. 'I want the flag!'

The first policeman to come up against the farmers is Geier. They are like a wall in front of him, a wall of threatening, indifferent, brooding, white and brown faces. Hands are raised against his upraised hands, sticks are raised; who can say whether for protection or assault.

'Make way!' he roars.

The flag is billowing just ten or twenty yards off. He must get it. Where are his colleagues? Never mind, the farmers are yielding, his rubber truncheon is smacking against their upraised hands. Somehow a way is cleared in front of him, a short, open passage that he penetrates. And once again the man in front of him yields, melts away to the side. He can move on, he is closing in on the flag.

From behind and to the side, something thumps against his shako, and then he is struck on the left shoulder.

All the more grimly he lashes out at those in front of him. They'll be taught to give in, those stupid farmers, those shits, those bastards, damn them! The flag . . .

He rams his left elbow hard into the belly of someone. The man crumples over, others melt away, and press themselves harder against their neighbours. With one bound, half stumbling, half falling, the sergeant is up with the flag, reeling, he grabs for the flagpole, for a moment he is chest to chest with the flag-bearer, and with a shout of 'Gimme that!' he rips the flag to himself.

Henning looks at him. His eyes burn. 'The flag is ours,' he says. And yanks it back.

Holding the pole with his left hand, Geier hits at Henning's hands with his rubber truncheon.

Henning doesn't let go.

Geier is about to hit him a second time, when a hand reaches from behind and holds his. A brief tussle, a piercing pain, and his half-dislocated wrist drops the truncheon.

In a dense knot of people, they are fighting for the flag. Henning and Geier, in a continual moving whirl of bodies, wrestling, falling, on the ground.

'Give them a taste of your sabre, Oskar!' Geier hears a shout above him. 'It's what the bastards deserve.'

There is the giant Soldin, and with him ratty little Meierfeld. With the flats of their swords they dole out thwacking blows on the backs, faces and hands of anyone within reach. The crowd recedes, a small ring is formed, and reeling Geier gets to his feet, giving a mighty jerk on the flag.

But on the other end of the pole hangs Henning, lying on the cobbles, but his white face and clenched jaws indicate: he's not about to let go.

'Let go, you!' yells Meierfeld, and hits the recumbent man with the flat of his sword.

At the other end Soldin and Geier have joined forces. Another great jerk pulls the flag fully six feet, and Henning, on the floor, with it. The sabre swipes his arm. His dark suit gapes open like a mouth, the white of the shirt – and now, slowly spreading, red, bright, flowing red.

With his hands clenched round the pole, Henning kicks out furiously against the swordsman.

Meierfeld raises his sabre again. 'Will you let go, bitch!' And he brings it down, on the hand of Henning, which is straight away just a purple stain.

And now Soldin and Geier let go of the flag, raise their swords, and bring them down. Henning has rolled over on to his side, covering with his body the hand that is still capable of holding, while blows rain down on the other.

The police rain down blows, breathless, pale with fury, and round this little arena spins the stream of farmers, pressing, marching on, more new witnesses all the time.

VIII

A man is running the long way from the Central Prison into the town. He was standing in front of the dead grey wall when it suddenly acquired a voice, a white face appeared, and cries for help rang out: they were killing Reimers, the henchmen of this government, the beadles of the Republic, God damn the lot of them!

Banz is running as if his life depended on it. In fact, it is some-one else's life. He has long since shaken off his farming friends. Where are they now?

It's not two or ten or even a hundred farmers he needs. As he runs along, he has a vision of thousands of farmers standing in front of the dead grey cement wall with its barred holes. And when these thousands open their mouths in a great cry, then it won't be a cry for help, a cry from weakness, but the gates will fall open, the walls will come crashing to the ground, and out will come the condemned of the Republic.

He runs – and there flits through his brain the recollection of the three margarine drums with dynamite in the locked barn at home. These drums have the force of ten thousand farmers, they open gates, change things in people's minds, turn functionaries into timid, parasitical cringers, truly prepare the way.

But now he is bringing the farmers. He will shout and tell them how they are being cheated and swindled, how Reimers is still doing his time here.

The market square is empty when he reaches it, panting. Banz sees right away: they're already on the march, the pavements are deserted, the chairs empty behind the windows of the beer joints.

He runs on, turns the bend on the Burstah, and sees the street filled with an endless, swarming crowd of people.

'What's going on?' he asks, breathlessly. 'Why have you stopped marching?'

'There's some hitch at the front.'

'There's supposed to be a shindig with the Communists.'

'Where's Rohwer? Where's Padberg? Where's Henning?'

'No idea, I expect somewhere near the front, though.'

Banz must find them. He thinks for a moment. The narrows of the Burstah are impassable. It's all choked with traffic and pedestrians. But there is a parallel street, which he reached through a gate, a garden, a courtyard and a further gate.

Now it is plain sailing. He grips his stick harder in his hand and runs: he'll settle the hash of that Communist rabble!

He turns into Grünhofer Strasse, reaches the Stolper Torplatz, and now sees the narrows of the Burstah from the opposite perspective, and looks at the head of the march.

He stands there motionless, forgetting to breathe.

The collision with the police has stopped the front of the demonstration, but the following ranks have spilled out laterally: the whole breadth of the street is filled with a seething mass of peasantry, as dense as a wall.

And in front of this wall, at intervals of six or ten feet, is a blue chain of police, beating down on the demonstrators with sticks and swords, trying to drive back the front line, which is itself continually being pressed forward by those following.

With upraised hands and sticks, the farmers try to shield themselves against the blows, try to sidle down along the walls, looking for passages through to Grünhofer Strasse, only to be repeatedly forced back by fresh blows, to receive yet more blows.

Banz gives a roar of rage. This is the State! This State as it really is, exactly as one had always imagined it to be.

Bloodhounds! he thinks. Bloodhounds. Clubbing helpless citizens like seals.

Banz walks on. On the side of the road, he's spotted a gigantic policeman, bringing the flat of his sword down on the heads of demonstrators, all the time repeating his pointless mantra: 'Clear the road!'

He's already very close to him, came up to him from behind, with his reversed stick like a cudgel in his fist. Suddenly it seems cowardly to him, to fell the man from behind, so instead he gives him a hard kick in the side of the shin.

The policeman spins round, looks at him furiously. 'Clear the road!' he bleats.

'"Clear the road!"' Banz mocks him back. 'You bloodhound! "Clear the road" . . .!'

And strikes him with the handle of the stick on the temple, causing the man to throw up both his arms, spin wildly round on his own axis, and fall crashing to the ground.

Oddly sobered, Banz looks down at him. He looks at the faces all round, he seems to see them as though through a veil, looking at him critically, reproachfully.

'Well, you know,' he mumbles, 'he shouldn't have been doing that either, with the sabre.'

And he creeps off in the direction of Auntie Lieschen's pub.

I'll stay out of things for a while, he thinks ruefully. I'll drink a glass of beer.

He lifts his foot to take a step. The noise and the turbulence are behind him.

Then something strikes him sharply, pierces his brain like a hot iron. Fiery sparks whirl, and he plummets headlong with a shattered skull.

IX

The Altholm post office is on the Burstah, hard by the Stolper Torplatz. It has rather a lofty lower-ground floor, and two outer staircases lead up to the counters in the upper-ground floor.

At the time of the battle, the staircase was packed with curious onlookers, surveying the scene and experiencing history in the making. In the counter room too there are many people crowded together, the windows on to the street have been thrown open, and they are looking out. Debating, excited, everyone is speaking at once, customers and post-office workers.

One of the members of the public is the rustic gentleman with the chamois-brush hat, which he has, incidentally, now taken off. The secret representative of the regional government in Stolpe has the best seat in the house, and is half leaning out of the window, and is thus able to see, diagonally and from above, something the others can't, namely the battle for the flag.

Which is now almost over. Henning, who has still refused to relinquish the shaft, has been dragged bodily across the cobbles and against the kerb, has been further beaten, till finally the multiple severed muscles in his hands and arms have given way.

Then they took the flag off him, and now Superintendent Kallene and a few constables and Inspector Hebel are standing on the pavement with their booty, ringed by the surf of the witless and helpless wash of farmers.

From the station comes a little bearded man in grey street clothes and a little suitcase in his hand. The man from Stolpe sees him, the little manikin amuses him, because he doesn't know what to do in the bustle, pushes in here, comes running out there, tries one avenue, and is brought to a stop.

The manikin keeps running into the jam-packed crowds, like an ant he indefatigably keeps trying to break through, but not succeeding, and now here he is in the proximity of the flag.

Detective Tunk follows the soft, broad-brimmed grey hat that is now suddenly steering confidently straight for the group. There is an area of clear space around the group, the farmers are standing silently and staring, and are being shoved away.

Into that clear space the little fellow now plunges, and is already taking off his hat and moving his lips – Tunk can almost hear him speak, a politely couched question in a squeaky voice. But no one pays him any regard, the officials are standing with their backs to the people, grouped around their booty.

Then the little bearded fellow takes heart, puts out a hand and tugs at an official's jacket from behind.

What happens next is like lightning striking.

The official, a policeman, whirls round as though stabbed.

There is a flash in his hand, white and shining. The sabre slices through the air, straight into the face of the little man.

For a moment Tunk thinks he can see a deep, gaping slash across the nose and both cheeks. Then the manikin lifts both hands to his face, his deep gurgling 'Oh' is louder than everything else, and is clearly audible as far away as the window of the post office. And the man tumbles forward and is lost in the commotion of bodies.

At the same time the officials and their flag withdraw further to the wall, and in the distance music is heard, a louder buzz goes through the ranks of marchers.

Tunk with his chamois brush backs into the crowd behind him. 'Out of my way!' he shouts, and fights his way through. 'Is this a post office or a theatre? Clear off. I need to telephone.'

The further depths of the counter hall are empty, everyone is packed against the windows. The detective hurries up to the nearest phone box. 'It's high time,' he murmurs.

The door closes behind him, he sets a coin aside and picks up the receiver. An operator comes on the line.

'372. And hurry. It's urgent.'

'Please pay!'

There's a ring, and Gareis's girl secretary picks up.

'Quick, I want the mayor! It's a matter of life and death!'

'The mayor is on holiday.'

'You silly goose! Don't give me that!' shouts the detective. 'Haven't I said it's a matter of life and death!?! Will you call the mayor, you silly bloody girl!'

'Just one moment, please! I'm calling the mayor right now,' he hears the voice, a little faintly.

'But get a move on, will you!'

The detective is grinning like an ape, receiver in hand, he suddenly starts doing knee-bends, madly quickly, up and down, faster and faster, wilder, while his heart is beating more rapidly and his lungs pant desperately for air.

And so, when the mayor comes on the line, sleek, sleep-drunk (and very annoyed), he is able to sound completely plausible as he gasps: 'Mayor! Comrade Gareis! The farmers are fighting with the police! The commander has been knocked to the ground, two watchmen are dead. I can see ten or a dozen farmers pulling out revolvers even as I speak. Rescue –'

His voice is gone. And while Gareis rants and raves on the other end, Tunk quietly lays down the receiver on the shelf, doesn't hang up, creeps quietly out of the booth, and gently shuts the door.

And he goes into the phone booth next door, and in his normal voice, asks for number 785.

Landlord Mendel in Grünhof answers.

'This is the police. I want to speak to Lieutenant Wrede right away. He's sitting in your lounge.'

And then: 'Well, Wrede . . . well, you know . . . best not use any names. Anyway, I've done it. Get your men ready. In five minutes Gareis will call you. Of course that'll be the first you've heard of anything.'

Calmly Detective Inspector Tunk walks out of the call booth. From the booth next door, from where he phoned just three minutes ago, a post official pops out and looks at him doubtfully.

'What's the matter?' Tunk asks him encouragingly.

'You wouldn't by any chance have just called from this box?' asks the official shyly.

'Me? Didn't you see which box I just came from?'

'Of course. I do beg your pardon. But did you happen to see someone using this box?'

'See? Yes, wait a minute. It was occupied when I happened along. I thought it might be empty. But there was a worker, yes, a worker in a blue jacket. He seemed terribly wrought up about something.'

'Worker? Blue jacket? Thank you. Thank you very much. I'll pass it along. Thank you.'

And with that the postal worker dives back into the box, and the detective disappears into the crowd.

X

The Unicorn Pharmacy doesn't have a very good reputation in Altholm. People would rather go to the Salomon or the Aquarius, even though it might be three times as far to get to.

That's because Heilborn the pharmacist indulges a sort of perverse opinionatedness next door to barminess. It doesn't occur to him to give people what they ask for, he sells them only what he thinks is right. If Frau Marbede wants Pyramidon for her headsplitting migraines, then he gives her an enema, 'so that you finally get the dirt flushed out of your system'. And he has an endearing way of sticking some French letters in with the purchases of young men and women. 'You can thank me later, when you don't have to come knocking for Gonosan and clap injections.'

Of late the Unicorn has been almost entirely deserted. Apothecary Heilborn has extended his mission to the doctors of Altholm: he exercises a right of veto on their prescriptions, strengthens and dilutes as he sees fit, and has even been taken to court.

He won't be able to hang on to his knackery, as vengeful Altholmers refer to his practice, for much longer. But until they finally do withdraw the privilege, he continues to walk around his shop, and whiles away the hours administering morphine to himself at ever-more potent concentrations. That keeps him nice and busy, because he insists that the needles for the syringes have to be disinfected, and then the long dreamy states are there . . .

Sometimes he has company. In the back office Frau Schabbelt sits with him for hours on end. A pairing made in heaven, one might think.

There they are, old, greasy, dirty, with unkempt hanks of grey hair, dirty fingernails, pale, yellow-grey, with trembling lips. Sometimes Frau Schabbelt lays her head on the table, and sleeps the sleep of the dead, after the heavy intoxicants that Heilborn mixes up for her. Sometimes his head slumps forward on to his chest, strings of drool run down on to his waistcoat and shirt: they both have severed their ties with Altholm; neither has any family, any friends; no familiar, detested bed; no burial plot, purchased prudently in advance and waiting, fenced off, in the graveyard.

He says to her: 'No, don't go just yet. You have some more of your poison, while I treat myself to a lovely four per cent solution.' He potters off into the pharmacy.

She stares out at the yard, the grey, rotting, packing straw, the ugly plywood chests, bristling with rusty nails.

After a while, she realizes that he hasn't returned and she starts calling for him: 'Herr Heilborn! Herr Heilborn!'

But she tires of that, and with what's left in the glass and the bottle, she tries to get one more taste in her mouth, and then she gets up, and sets off, lurching and reeling, supporting herself on table, chair, cupboard and wall, in the direction of the shop.

There she finds Heilborn, backed against the wall, listening out. There is nothing to be seen through the tall windows, but a wild, threatening murmur is audible.

'Ssh!' whispers Heilborn, and sets his finger on his lips. 'Ssh! Be very quiet! They want to find me to haul me off to the funny farm, but they won't find me.'

The woman listens too. 'Nonsense,' she manages to say. 'There's lots of people there. Something must have happened.'

She walks over to the door of the shop and opens it.

Just in front of the pharmacy windows is the group of officials with their captured flag. The masses are some way off, so Frau Schabbelt can see Henning lying in the gutter, bleeding and pale, with eyes shut.

Five steps further on is a little manikin sitting on the kerb, with his face in his hands and blood pouring out between his fingers.

People are milling around at a greater distance, because the police are still patrolling with weapons drawn, and from time to time calling out: 'Move along now! – Don't loiter! – Move along!'

Frau Schabbelt scuttles down the steps to the man lying injured. She bends down over him, she calls to him, in her brain something has gotten confused: she thinks it is her dead son in front of her.

'What happened, Herbert? What are you doing, lying there? You shouldn't lie there!'

She looks crossly at the pharmacist, who is trying to pull the little grey manikin upright. 'Come here, you. He doesn't matter. This is Herbert. Herbert is injured.'

Now some of the farmers take up courage, a few of them step forward, help the drunken woman to pick up Henning. She cradles his head.

'There,' she says eagerly, 'in there, in the pharmacy!'

They drag him up the steps. Two others lead the little fellow with the beard, whom the apothecary is propping up from behind.

The police commander strides through the mob. 'Stop!' he calls out. 'These men are under arrest. No one is permitted to speak to them. Stop, I say!'

The old woman turns round. Out of the grey face with its thousand wrinkles, the grey eyes shine forth.

'Go away, you nasty snot-nosed boy,' she says. 'Your father cheated the farmers, and as long as you live you'll only be another cheat like him!'

From the Stolpe Gate cheerful marching music rings out. The band has at last managed to reach the head of the procession, which has re-formed and is just setting out once more.

'Off! March! To the auction hall!' yells Padberg. 'Everything else will be sorted out later. Let's leave this spot!'

The bearers with the injured go through the door of the pharmacy.

7

The Government Clamps Down

The band at the head of the procession plays 'Fridericus Rex', then the 'Deutschlandlied' and then the song of the Jewish Republic we don't want.

The farmers trot along silently behind, first along the Burstah, past the railway station, and on down the leafy suburban streets, where among gardens and villas the big factories are located.

Police escort the procession left and right, ahead and behind. It's as though these thirty or forty policemen are leading these three or four thousand farmers to their cells.

Padberg, back at the head of the column, next to Count Bandekow, Rehder and Cousin Benthin, feels bitter. How ignominious it all is! he thinks. If we farmers had raised our hands, those few town soldiers would be lying in the Blosse by now. How the whole country will laugh at us! If the police had tried those tactics on the Red Front, or Hitler's people, or even the Reichsbanner, they'd have been swatted away! But we farmers aren't taken seriously!

'My God,' he says out loud. 'I wish I knew what I'm going to write about this in the paper tomorrow.'

'You should talk to your colleagues here,' says Bandekow cautiously.

'My colleagues . . .? If you write for the *Bauernschaft*, you don't have any colleagues. It's my personal headache, the others don't care, to them it's just material! Am I supposed to describe how we let three little policemen make off with our flag?! The ignominy of it.'

'People,' wails Cousin Benthin. 'How am I going to show my face in Altholm after this?'

'Couldn't you have tried to get the flag through?' asks Count

Bandekow. 'Or take it back to the bar? Why did you want a fight over it?'

'Wasn't I against the flag from the very start?' asks Padberg angrily. 'And now it's all my fault. By the way, I wasn't even there when it happened.'

'Where were you?' asks Rehder. 'I thought the agreement was you should be Henning's minder.'

'His minder! Who would have thought those pigs would mount such a wild assault! I was at the back, I was trying to find out what happened to Rohwer.'

'Of course,' says the count ironically. 'Conducting a few inquiries. At the critical moment. So as not to get in the way, hah?'

'I want to tell you something,' says Padberg agitated. 'Am I the leader? Or are Rohwer and Rehder? And you too, Count, where were you, if I might ask? Yes! Send strangers to the front, and let them save your bacon, eh?'

'Fellows!' says Cousin Benthin in bewilderment. 'Don't quarrel among yourselves. The count was with me, to bring up the band.'

'No,' says Rehder. 'The count's right. You had taken on Henning, you're the one to blame.'

'Me? Let me tell you something! Fuck this kangaroo court! Do you think it's up to me to wipe your bottoms? First, you publish letters from Reimers that stink to high heaven –'

'That letter was a fake!'

'I wrote the correction, *I* know what's what! – And then you get a demonstration going, not even knowing that your leader's long ago been stuck somewhere else . . .'

'Did you know that then?'

'And then you take that stupid ruddy flag with you, even though anyone can tell there'll be trouble –'

'You personally helped attach the scythe.'

'Then you let your marchers be beaten to a pulp, and the one who's to blame for everything is me. If you thnk I'm going to stand by and let you get away with it, you're fucking mistaken. You can all go and take a running jump, you bunch of amateurs. I'm out of this. I resign! I'm giving up the paper. I don't want anything more to do with you. God knows there's other things

to do in this Germany, things that are better run, with better prospects, where they don't stand for militia poking you in the face
with their stinking fingers. – Thank you and goodbye! Top of the
morning to you, gentlemen. I'm out of here. You can assemble
by yourselves in future, you bunch of bleeding arseholes!'

And Padberg, bulging with rage, pushes off to the right, on to
the pavement, away from the column.

'Stop!' says a policeman to him. 'Get back in the column. No
one is allowed to leave.'

'What?!' roars Padberg. 'I'm not allowed to leave. When I'm a
free citizen in this blessed Republic? Have I not paid my taxes? Is
this not a public thoroughfare? Will you kindly stand aside and
let me pass, sir!!'

'Go back,' says the militiaman. 'Those are orders, and I'm not
making any exceptions. Carry on.'

'Who gives these orders? Show me the fellow! – I want to get
to the railway station. I've got a train to catch. I'm press, for fuck's
sake! Here's my card! Will you now –'

'It's just for a moment. The two minutes to the auction hall.
Then everything'll be sorted out.'

'Come on, Padberg,' calls Rehder. 'We've got something we
want to tell you.'

And Padberg, beside himself: 'Did you hear that? We're under
escort here like a chain gang. It's humiliating . . .'

'Here's a gentleman,' says Rehder, 'who's seen the whole thing,
the fight over the flag. He's indignant about the police. He wants
to tell the farmers about it in the assembly . . .'

Padberg turns to the gentleman who is offering to relieve him
of his bitter address in the auction hall. He looks at the gentleman.

Suddenly his rage has evaporated and he grins mockingly.

'Oh, so the gentleman from the Political Section has seen something he objects to in the policing? Perhaps I should introduce you?
This is Detective Inspector Tunk from Stolpe. And here are Herr
Meier, Herr Schmidt, Herr Müller and, er, Herr Schulze. So you
thought it was over the top, did you? Well, that does you credit!'

'My name is Megger. From the area around Hanover. You
must be confusing me with someone else.'

'Oh no, I'm not confusing you with anyone. It's not possible to get you wrong, Detective Inspector.'

'I am engaged in the cause of the farmers!'

'Sure you are,' says Padberg. 'Only you're on the other side. – Get lost!' he suddenly screams in fury. 'You little snot! You spy, you, get away!'

'You've surely . . .' the other continues obdurately.

'You there, Padberg,' Rehder calls out in excitement, 'there's Gareis!'

The mayor of Altholm is driving past in an open car. At his side, talking agitatedly, is his pale police commander.

'Well, there they are together again, the Red king and queen,' comments Padberg.

Hooting and buzzing, the car makes its way past.

'They're hatching their next cuckoo's egg, those two darlings,' Padberg explains. 'Well, what's happened to our yeoman from Hanover?'

But the yeoman is nowhere to be seen.

II

Short of beating Mayor Gareis's brains out, you can do little to keep him quiet.

For a moment he sat in the chair beside the telephone. The farmers are drawing pistols on the police! What on earth is going on? It's not possible!

Already his very next thought is: Who's fouled up here?

And after that: Let's try to keep things from getting worse.

He calls the town hall guardroom. 'Who is it? – Hart? This is Gareis. Listen, will you tell me what's going on?'

'Herr Mayor, it's awful. They're just bringing in my colleague Soldin, badly hurt . . . The farmers . . .'

'Thank you,' says the mayor, and hangs up. 'Fräulein! Fräulein! Will you get me Piekbusch right away! And now pay attention: As soon as I hang up, put me through to Mendel's Inn in Grünhof. – And one other thing, I want your colleague to call the station watch in the meantime and have Frerksen or Kallene expect me in ten minutes. And then you try and chase up the identity of the man who just called me. You got all that? All right!

'Piekbusch? Are you there? – Good. Send the next person in the waiting room to my driver. I want the car outside my house in three minutes. – No fiddle-faddle, just do what I tell you. I'm waiting. – All right? Done? OK. Next, in the top-left drawer of my desk there's a yellow envelope from the district president, will you bring that over to the telephone . . .

'You got it? – Good. Now read it out to me. Read it! Hey, where've you got to?! What are you playing at, Fräulein? Bloody tomfoolery! – Who is it? Lieutenant Wrede?

'All right, Lieutenant, you set off with your men. In ten minutes at the playground. Don't do anything before I've spoken to you. – The secret orders? – Yes, I'm still reading them. – All right. Of course. On your way.

'Fräulein! Fräulein! – Damn, the car's honking outside. – All right then. The secret orders will just have to remain secret.'

He gets up with a groan, looks around once more. 'Oh well,' he sighs. 'Rügen tomorrow? We'll have to see about that.'

Slowly and massively he shoves his bulk through the doorway and wheezes down the steps. 'All right, Wertheim, to the station guard-post.'

The roads are deserted. The car shoots off.

'Stop!'

The fire ambulance is driving past, Gareis flags it down.

'Who've you got on board?'

'Two badly hurt farmers.'

'Hurt how?'

'Sabre blows to face and arms.'

'Any more casualties that you're aware of?'

'Another farmer. And a sergeant.'

'Badly injured?'

'The sergeant probably a concussion, according to Dr Zenker. The farmer has a sabre blow across the arm.'

'Any others?'

'Not so far as we know, no, Mayor.'

'No gunshot wounds?'

'None that we've heard of.'

'All right. On your way.'

Gareis wheezes back into the car, lowers his eyelids, starts twiddling his thumbs.

The people on the street are saying: 'Look, it's our mayor. He's too fat. He's sleeping again. It's a warm day, though.'

Gareis thinks: Three badly hurt farmers, one lightly hurt policeman. – The farmers clearly haven't been all that aggressive. – I should have let Wrede stay in Grünhof. Maybe I've made a mistake here.

When he walks into the guardroom, he sees his police commander sitting hunkered at a table at the back, his face in his hands in the half-light.

How now! he thinks.

And, beaming: 'Now, boys, talk to me. In order would be nice. You first, Kallene.'

But the commander leaps up. 'I'd like to report, sir, that we have the flag! The flag has been confiscated and is being taken back to HQ!'

'What flag would that be?'

'The farmers' flag. The black flag, with the scythe on it.'

'A scythe on it?'

'A scythe mounted on the pole. An emblem of civil disturbance. I confiscated it.'

'All right, Frerksen, talk to me. Chronological order, if you will.'

And Frerksen reports.

'The flag was dodgy, sir. The public were offended. The scythe was a possible hazard.'

He describes how he proceeded. The first time, he requested, the second time, he demanded. How he was pushed back, beaten, had his sabre taken from him.

'Was I to give in? Were the farmers to be allowed to hang on to it? I sent men to retrieve it. The farmers put up tough resistance. Soldin is badly hurt . . .'

'I know.'

*　*　*

'Now your turn, Superintendent. Did you get a sight of the flag? Before the fight, I mean.'

'Yes.'

'Did it strike you as provocative?'

'To be frank, I didn't pay it any attention. It was hanging down when I passed with my men, at Tucher's. You see so many flags these days . . .'

'Hmm. And what about you, Pinkus? What does the press have to say about the feeling in the streets?'

'The workers are indignant. What are the farmers doing here! They were so aggressive, those bomb-throwers! Comrade Gareis, I tell you, the proletariat won't stand for it. We're on the Left here in Altholm, this is no place for shows of strength from the radical Right –'

'All right. All right. Thank you. Well, now . . .' The fat man lapses into thought. The clock in the guardroom is loud: tick tock tick tock . . . That's how quiet it is.

They've made their bed, thinks the mayor. Now we'll all have to lie in it. Things can't stay as they are.

Unclear: What shall I investigate, to see if it was properly done? We all make mistakes. What happened, after all? An incident during a demonstration, a little kerfuffle. Happens every day in Berlin. If there's no outcry in the press, it'll all be forgotten in a week. But we've begun, so we have to go on. I can't whistle the militia back to barracks, more's the pity.

He asks: 'Where are the farmers now?'

'They'll just be moving into the auction hall. For their mass meeting. I'm giving the demonstration a police escort.'

'Very good. Very good.'

Tick tock tick tock, goes the clock.

They stare at me as if I were Father Christmas. Frerksen looks as pale and gormless as a stuck calf. When things are really so simple. We just have to keep going. Whoever stops has made a mistake already . . .

And aloud: 'I will break up the demonstration, seeing as it's become disorderly. We're sending the farmers home. Militiamen are even now arriving at the playground. – You, Kallene, are to

go there right away, liaise with Lieutenant Wrede, and seal off
the auction hall. We'll go there directly. Frerksen, you come with
me.'

III

The holding pen of the Association of Holstein Cattle-Breeders
is ringed by a tall brick wall. A wide gate is let into this wall, and
the police have taken up position by this gate, while the column
of farmers, band to the fore, marches in. At this gate, police violence stops. In the hall, and on the surrounding terrain, the farmers have rights, this is their place. The police stand singly or in
groups either side of the gate. The further the column moves in,
the more police there are.

The farmers walk in, some with lowered heads, others glowering at the police, and clutching their ashplants harder. News of
the clash and the confiscation of the flag has spread. All the farmers have seen the group of police standing round the captured
flag on the Burstah. There's talk of serious injuries, of deaths,
the name of Henning – until recently unknown is in everyone's
mouths.

A few times bad words reach the ears of the police. They hear
'bloodhounds', 'murderers' and 'killers', but on the whole silence
prevails.

The dark and gloomy auction hall is overfull straight away.
Here, in their own four walls, the farmers feel among their own.
A wave of noise crashes like surf, a Babel of voices.

Then the arc lights come on and cast their light on the assembly.

This is no room, this hall built for showing off cattle, more a
circus, with a sand arena in the middle, with ramps leading up
to either side, with galleries and little staircases, and a dais at the
front, where usually the livestock appraisers sit, or the auction-
eers.

It's to this dais, in front of which the Stahlhelm band has set up,
that the farmers now raise their eyes. For the moment, though,

it's still empty. In the room behind it stand a group of men, unable to decide on what to do next, unable to decide what slogan to give out, or what can be said about what has taken place.

They all talk at once, and once more they hurl reproaches at each other.

'I'm not going to open my mouth!' yells Padberg. 'What is there to say about this royal balls-up? It was poor in the inception, and poor in the execution. You want me to make it look nice? No thank you.'

'It's just a matter of telling the farmers about what happened,' says Count Bandekow. 'You're the man for that. It's no different to what you'll do in your paper tomorrow.'

'Talk about what happened here? Pour oil on the flames? Thanks! Does any one of you have the least idea what will happen when three thousand people hear about how we were assaulted, beaten and robbed? No thank you. I've already got one case for ringleadership behind me, that's enough for me.'

He turns to find himself facing a man with a little badger-brush hat on his head, listening attentively in the crush.

'God damn us to hell!' rages Padberg. 'Has no one got the balls to chuck the stoolie out? Feinbube, you have seniority here, can't you show this gentleman where to go?'

Agricultural Councillor Feinbube is a little abashed. 'Yes, really, you oughtn't to be here at all. You are from the police, aren't you? Would you mind following me, or have you got a special written assignment?'

'Stop being polite to him!' yells Padberg. 'Throw the little sh—'

'You referred to me as a "shit",' says the top-boots. 'The assembled company are witnesses.'

'I said "sh" and that's not an insult. And now, clear off, will you, you sh—, you sh—, sh—!'

'Well, let's go. An intention to cause offence is certainly present. Come along, Agricultural Councillor. I've heard enough. More than enough.'

The lanky Feinbube and the false farmer walk down a corridor, a flight of stairs, along another corridor.

'I can find my way from here,' says the interloper. 'Down the steps at the back, and then the long passage . . . I don't want to inconvenience you any more . . .'

'It's really no trouble,' quips Feinbube.

'Some fine premises here for husbandry. I imagine the ministry awarded a grant?'

'I thought you might know that,' says the councillor.

'Neither here nor there. – I wonder if this is an exit here? This door –'

'Stop!' shouts Feinbube. 'That's the door into the hall.'

But the man he was escorting has already slipped away. Feinbube thinks about pursuing him, but the hall is jam-packed, the detective has melted into the crowd, and when Feinbube tries to ask people if they saw him, all he gets is indignant calls to be quiet.

Up on the stage, a man is standing and speaking . . .

It's Cousin Benthin, old Moth-Head as they call him, who is orating. There he is with his blotchy scalp, a dirty jacket, a pair of twill trousers, and dirty boots on his feet. He is an old man, and the people are laughing at him because his young wife is expecting a baby which is certainly not his.

But he speaks.

He is the only one who dared to step out in front of three thousand farmers. He speaks slowly and with trouble, in short sentences, between which he stands there with eyes half closed, seeming to think or perhaps to have fallen asleep. But he is speaking at just the right speed for this listenership, which doesn't like haste.

'He shook,' he is just saying as Feinbube enters the hall, 'he shook my hand, and he said to me, "Let us both, as old Altholmers, shake hands on nothing bad happening here." And this is what happened.

'They beat a young man to a cripple. They beat others till they were bloodied. And why? Over a flag.

'Fellow farmers, I've lived in Altholm all my life. Even before the War Altholm was known as a Red town. Well, let them, I thought, everyone must know what's best for them . . .

'In the last few years I've seen my fair share of flags. Both Red and others . . .

'What the Communists liked to carry around with them was straw effigies. One of them was the Oberbürgermeister, and the other was our Field Marshal Hindenburg. They carried them around on a gallows.

'The flag we had was a black flag. And the reason it was black was because we're in mourning for our dear German fatherland. And there's a white plough on it, because we're farmers, and we till the land, and the plough is the best thing on God's earth. And then there was a red sword, because victory will only come if we fight . . .

'The ones that were carrying the gallows, they went around unmolested, but with us they took away our flag.

'Now, my friends, you may ask, why didn't we defend it? There are so many of us, and the police were so few, and we have enough strong-boned young farmers on our side.

'Farmers of Pomerania, I tell you we let them take our flag because we obey our government. We let them take everything we have.

'They took away our brother Reimers, and they led away Rohwer, and put him in the clink.

'And they take the cattle from our byres, and the horses from our stables. They confiscate our grain while it's still on the stalk, and they chase us out of our farms.

'Now, you ask, why do we stand for it? Have we no representatives? No parliamentarians? No members? A Chamber of Agriculture and a German Agricultural Council? Why do they not help us? Why don't they set up an outcry?

'Dear farmers, they do cry out. As long as they're here, among us. But then they go to Berlin. And when they come back, we don't recognize them. We are told we have to understand that things can't happen as we would wish. Taxes and more taxes – it has to be.

'And then we understand, and we accept . . .

'And when you ask me, I say: Dear countryfolk, you must pay taxes, and more taxes. You should be happy you are required to pay so much, and that they take away your animals and your farms . . .

'The less you have, the less will be required of you. And then, when you are left with nothing, then the dear government will look after you, as they looked after your parents who had put by a few thousand marks, and who now go to the benefits office, which has a high-sounding name for them: social claimants!

'You must pay your taxes until you're bled white, I tell you. Till you can't pay any more, and have no more marrow in your bones, and are half starved. Then you won't make any more trouble for the dear government in Berlin, then you'll be meek . . .

'And that's why the Altholm police were completely right when they took away your flag. Workers are allowed to have flags.

'But you, farmers, you're not allowed to have anything.

'All you can do is take your lumps from the administration, and bleed and bleed.'

He stands there, Cousin Benthin, and for the moment he seems unable to continue. He mops his brow. Behind him are the farmers' leaders with lowered heads, or peering out into the crowd, which is going wild . . .

And at that moment, the door to the left of the raised stage opens: Superintendent Kallene appears, with his Hindenburg figure, in a blue tunic with red lapels . . .

He crosses the stage and stops next to Cousin Benthin, where he raises his hands for quiet from the wild crowd.

At that moment, the hearts of the men on stage stand still.

Perhaps this policeman is just stupid, or then again he might be insanely brave.

At any rate . . .

Hundreds of ashplants are raised against him, the air is full of wild, furious threats, the first sticks are about to be hurled at the stage . . .

The conductor of the Stahlhelm band has seen a fair few wild gatherings in his time. At that instant he gives a signal with his baton, and the band launch into the 'Deutschlandlied'.

A quiver goes through the entire assembly. Suddenly the farmers are all on their feet, singing, they're wild with enthusiasm, they hurl it in the face of the policeman up there, the representative of the German government:

'Deutschland, Deutschland über alles . . .'

Superintendent Kallene stands there with head lowered, not looking at all. Perhaps he has no feeling for the contrast: the small, dirty, used-up-looking farmer beside him, with the ugly, chewed-looking head, and himself, two hundred pounds, well fed, rosy-cheeked, clean and presentable.

When the first verse is finished, there's a small pause. Kallene repeats his hushing movement, he wants to address them again, but the second verse sets in.

He waits again.

The same thing after the second verse.

After the third.

After the fourth, which is a repeat of the first, Superintendent Kallene slowly and leisurely walks off stage. He's giving up, they're not going to let him speak.

The farmers watch him go.

Now there's another silence. The band stop playing. The farmers are looking at Cousin Benthin, will he carry on speaking?

Once again, the left-hand door on the stage opens, but this time a farmer comes on, a large, well-built man, with his hat pulled low over his face.

He stops. From the shade of the hat-brim, the eyes scan the crowd below, as if they were something he hadn't expected. He carries on into the centre of the stage, with a strangely unsteady walk, as though he were drunk.

The farmers stare at him, hardly any of them have come across Banz from Stolpermünde-Abbau. They stare at the big, unsteady-looking man, a feeling of apprehension spreads in the hall, as though something were about to happen.

The man stops, just in front of Cousin Benthin. His lips move, but no one can hear anything.

And suddenly he throws his arms up in the air, rips the hat off his head, and hurls it into the crowd. His head is laid bare – nothing but a terrifying, gruesome mass of flesh and blood.

The farmers release a yell.

And, as if their yell had restored the power of speech to the man, he roars: 'Farmers! Farmers! This is what Altholm has to offer! Farmers! Farmers! These are the acts of the government!'

The crowd bays like a thousand wild animals in one.

The man releases a chilling scream, and falls down in a heap.

All the doors to the hall are flung open.

Militia and police force their way in, with swinging truncheons. They call out:

'Empty the hall!'

'The meeting is over!'

'Leave the hall quietly!'

IV

'So we're going?' says Stuff to Blöcker.

'Yes, we'd better,' agrees Blöcker. 'Who could stand to see more of this.'

The union of militia and town police have won a resounding victory over the farmers. They were chased out of the hall one by one, and made to stand still like dolls, and be checked for weapons. Their ashplants were taken off them. Then they were driven out on to the road again, made to form up in a new column, which was in turn broken up. They were made to walk down this road, then that one, were forced to retrace their steps two or three times, following the whim of some sergeant or other. They were told not to use the pavement, and they were instructed to make way for cars.

Stuff takes a look back. There is the mayor in his black suit, surrounded by uniforms. Police hurry officiously back and forth, and the last few farmers slink out of the exit, heads lowered and meek.

'The airs that Red sow gives himself!' groans Stuff. 'Look at that, Blöcker, the way the fellow from the pinko press is sucking up to him.'

And it's true, the reporter from the *Volkszeitung* in Stettin, the newspaper for the class-conscious proletariat, is bang on form. A beaming Pinkus dances attendance on a militia officer, tosses a few words to his mayoral colleague, and spins round, with outstretched finger at a farmer, honest indignation all over his face.

'Wretched cribber!' growls Stuff.

'Swine, the lot of them,' Blöcker concurs. 'Well, just wait till tomorrow!'

They are almost at the gate, the two representatives of Altholm's fourth estate, when a rapid stride is audible behind them. They turn round.

It's Commander Frerksen who is in pursuit. 'Gentlemen, excuse me! The mayor would like to invite you to attend a press conference he is giving tomorrow, at nine o'clock.'

'Oh, really?' says Blöcker.

'You need us for something, then?' asks Stuff nastily.

'I will be presenting an official report on the lamentable occurrences.'

'Lamentable for you!' mocks Stuff.

'I don't know what you mean, Stuff. My superiors in the local government and the police are completely behind me.'

'Well, I'm not,' says Stuff.

'You mustn't listen to partisan witnesses.'

'Yours aren't, I take it?'

'I take it,' the commander turns earnestly to Blöcker, 'that the *News* will, as ever, manage to find a way that is favourable to our town?'

Blöcker shifts his shoulders doubtfully.

'But, gentlemen,' the commander cries out in consternation, 'the police *had* to step in. The authority of the State was being mocked. The constitution was being held in contempt. The law was being trampled underfoot! Were the police to be bullied by these rebels? Without a fight?'

There is silence. Frerksen waits for an answer.

'Well, are you going?' asks Stuff. 'I've got no more time. Things to do.'

'Wait up, Stuff. I'll come too. Good evening to you, Commander.'

Frerksen calls after the pair of them: 'See you tomorrow morning, then. Nine o'clock. Press conference.'

They shamble down the street.

'Bah!' Stuff suddenly exclaims. 'Are we going into town now? Come on, Blöcker!'

They turn back, pass the entrance to the cattle yard again, a stretch of avenue, then through a gate in a hedge, across a pasture and along the edge of a cornfield. Through a meadow, to a stream.

'Let's sit down here!' says Stuff. 'Doesn't that feel good! Can you smell the good air!'

'This meadow must belong to Benthin. There used to be a line of poplars along the stream.'

'No, this is Grünhof,' Stuff corrects him. 'That stream is the boundary between Altholm and Grünhof. We're not on Altholm soil any more.'

'It wouldn't be a bad thing to stay away for good. What a lot of bother there's going to be!'

'Do you have a cigar?' asks Stuff. 'Thanks, I'll help myself for later. I'm going to have a little nap. I still feel a bit woozy.'

'I wonder at us sitting in the pub, with something like this going on. Now we've missed the whole commotion.'

'Oh, I've seen enough in the auction hall. I know the score. And as for the rest, there's no shortage of witnesses.'

'You cut Frerksen good and proper, you know.'

'And why the hell not? I heard he was responsible for the whole damn thing. I'm going to give it to him, the wretched shite.'

'Don't you want to wait for the press conference first?'

'Wait? What is there to wait for?' yells Stuff. 'For them to lie their way out of the responsibility? As I say, I've seen enough. I know. Beating defenceless farmers, you wait, chum! The *Chronicle*'s got your number.'

'Is that OK with Schabbelt?'

'Schabbelt? What's he have to do with it? – I'll tell you something, just between you and me, Blöcker: Schabbelt's sold up.'

Silence.

And Blöcker: 'Then I'll tell you something too, Stuff, in strictest confidence: Gebhardt's bought it.'

'What?!' Stuff gives a start. 'You know that? Then the whole place knows, and no one's telling me.'

'No one knows, except a couple of us from the editors' conference: Trautmann and Heinsius and me. And it's supposed to remain a secret.'

'I've had it, then. That's it, Blöcker, I'm finished. – Give me a push, and I'll fall over. – Why's it supposed to remain a secret?'

'Because it's bad for business if people know the competition isn't really competition.'

'I see. Between two stools. As ever. The dear old *Chronicle*. Does Gebhardt interfere much?'

'Him . . .? He doesn't care about anything! If it brings in readers, he doesn't care about apostrophes.'

'Great! Then he'll let me stick it to the Reds!'

'I think so. You've got a readership on the Right. Talk to him about it.'

'Tonight?'

'Yes, if you've got time to see him then? Eight o'clock. Back entrance, he doesn't want people seeing.'

'Oh, Blöcker, Blöcker, Blöcker!' groans Stuff. 'So that's why you treated me to a beer this morning! I might have guessed . . . And if you'd got to the point a little quicker, then we wouldn't have missed the show just now!'

'So. Is eight o'clock all right then?'

'Eight. Yes. Under cover of darkness. Back entrance. I'll keep it like that from now on. I can sleep for an hour and a half now. And I will, I tell you, Blöcker. I'm fed up with the world.'

He lies back down on the grass, pulls his hat over his face and goes to sleep. The water burbles and murmurs. Blöcker drifts back to town. To listen out.

V

It's evening. Almost eight.

Lots of people are still out and about in Altholm. They'd like to see something in print about the events they witnessed, along with a firm editorial line on them. That's why there's quite a little crush around the *News* building at the Stolpe Gate. But all they have on show in the display-box are the pictures from round the world, nothing else. The windows are dark too. Only the four windows of the machine room at the back are lit up, that's where the presses are preparing the next-day's paper.

Gebhardt is in his office, he can hear the whir of the machines. The curtains are drawn tight, and only the desk lamp is on, casting a pool of light on a page covered with figures.

Gebhardt is checking and rechecking his numbers. He goes over them again, he looks at receipts, he works out averages. The numbers are all he is interested in. This building, with its thirty employees, the only reason it exists is to make the numbers grow.

There's safety in numbers, so to speak. Big numbers mean more power. People still dare to not take him seriously, even though he's the wealthiest man in Altholm, but that's only because the numbers still aren't big enough.

There's a noise outside. Someone's fiddling with the door, and blundering around in the unlit corridor.

Gebhardt opens the door, shedding a little light in the corridor, and asks nervously: 'Is anyone there?'

'Yes, me. Stuff,' and Stuff looms out of the darkness.

'I was expecting you,' says Gebhardt, and puts out his hand.

For a brief flash, an astonished Stuff sees the bowed neck of his new bread-giver with its rough frizz of hair, sees as far down as the top vertebra on his neck, and thinks in bewilderment: Good God, he's really bowing to you!

Then Gebhardt asks him to sit down. 'Do you smoke? A cigar? This is a fairly light one. These are heavier. Whatever you like. Here's a light. No, thanks, I don't smoke myself.'

Stuff sits comfortably in front of the desk, in a low armchair, his cigar is drawing nicely. Behind the desk squats the newspaper king, looking at papers.

'I asked you to come and see me, Herr Stuff,' begins Gebhardt, toying with his pencil, 'because I have a few things to discuss with you. I take it Herr Schabbelt will have told you I've bought the *Chronicle*?'

'Actually, no.'

'I see. Odd. But you know I have anyway.'

'Yes, I heard about it.'

'I bought the *Chronicle* because the opposition of two moderate newspapers in Altholm is nonsensical. We must stand together against the Red front . . .'

'Yes. We must,' says Stuff, for the sake of saying something, because Gebhardt has left a pause.

'I wanted to ask you whether you were prepared to go on devoting your gifts to the *Chronicle* under my control?' And, quickly: 'Lest you misunderstand, I mean financial control, it wouldn't really affect you. You are free in editorial matters. We might occasionally discuss the positioning of the paper. But in general you will be completely free, you know the readership best, after all.'

'So I could write about today's disturbances as I felt I had to?'

'Disturbances? Oh yes, there were some clashes, weren't there? Involving the peasantry. Do you have an interest in peasants?'

'Oh, yes. Rather.'

'I mean, of course, a financial interest. Are there many farmers among the subscribers?'

'Not many.'

'Then why? Why would you attack the farmers?'

'I want to report on the scandalous methods of the police.'

'My dear Herr Stuff! A newspaper should never be on the outs with the police!'

'But it's just the top echelon of the police. Which is Socialist.'

'Yes, I know. But it's still the town police, isn't it? A town institution. Do you know, by the way, why the mayor went on holiday just now?'

'He always goes at this time of year. It's the anniversary of his wife's parents.'

'I see. So it's not that he's avoiding these clashes?'

'No. Not at all. He had no sense of them being about to happen.'

'All right. If you're sure . . .? So you think it was the Reds?'

'The whole thing was masterminded by the Reds. And we have local elections in autumn.'

'All right, Herr Stuff, go for them. But not too hard, well, you'll know. We in the *News* will probably take up a wait-and-see position, we have too many readers among the workers.'

'That's the main thing, is it?'

'No, no, not like that. But we have a lot anyway.'

They look at each other, each smiling amiably. Then Stuff

struggles out of his deep leather armchair, panting a little. 'Well, I'll go over and write my piece for the morning, then.'

'Yes? – And one last thing, Herr Stuff: Officially we have nothing to do with each other, for the moment. I want our association to remain secret. Absolutely secret.'

'If I need to talk to you –'

'– then you come and see me in the evening, like now. No telephone, please. Word gets out.'

'All right,' says Stuff, and, already at the door, reaches out his hand to his new boss.

'Right,' Gebhardt says. 'Oh, one more thing. We didn't talk about the question of your remuneration. How could we forget!' And he laughs, a little forced.

'My remuneration . . .?' Stuff says in surprise. 'Is there a question? I got five hundred from Schabbelt, and could write my own expenses claims.'

'My dear Herr Stuff!' Gebhardt smiles. 'You must understand that that's not on. That's what finished Schabbelt.'

'What? My salary did? That's ridiculous.'

'Not just your salary – please don't be agitated – but the out-of-control costs of the business. Five hundred marks plus expenses. No, that's absolutely out of the question.'

Stuff's mood has darkened. 'So what is in question?'

'Well, what shall I say? I'm really not a Jew, and I don't want to starve you. I'll go to the limit of what's bearable, and even over. I say three hundred.'

'Nonsense!' says Stuff. 'No chance.'

'My dear Herr Stuff. Of course I'm perfectly happy to let you serve out your notice. That would be the first of October.'

'I don't have a contract with you! I can quit right now.'

'There are so many literate young persons these days. Anyone can write. And most of the paper is correspondence anyway.'

'All right, let's cut to the chase,' says Stuff. 'What's your best offer?'

'I will go some way to meet you, Herr Stuff. My manager, Herr Trautmann, will be very unhappy with me, but I'm going to offer you three hundred and twenty!'

'Five hundred!' demands Stuff. 'Plus expenses.'

'You are no longer in the prime of youth,' says Gebhardt cautiously. 'And the *Chronicle* hasn't exactly flourished under your editorship.'

'People say,' Stuff utters rather dreamily, 'that your name, Herr Gebhardt, fits you rather well. Plays on "giving" and "hard" do rather suggest themselves.'

'Three hundred and thirty.'

'How would you like it, Herr Gebhardt, if I were to quit now? Your takeover of the *Chronicle* wouldn't be a secret any more.'

'That's practically blackmail!' yells Gebhardt. 'Do you expect me to buy your silence?'

'Excuse me,' says a sleek voice from the doorway. 'The camel seeks its path in the fog. I couldn't find anyone to announce me. Good evening, gentlemen.'

'Good evening, Mayor,' says Stuff.

VI

With a dignified smile, Gareis extends his plump hand to the two men, and Stuff makes the discovery that he's not the only person to whom his new boss performs his fifth-former's low bow. Again, he marvels at the thick black scrub on the man's neck.

'Fancy finding the enemy brothers under the same roof!' exclaims the mayor, and looks from the sheepishly furious publisher to the sullen Stuff. 'In the evening, we make our way . . . Perhaps a wider public would like to be informed . . .'

'It was a perfectly routine conversation,' says Gebhardt curtly.

'It was very loud, and to my mind not at all uninteresting. Well, never mind . . .' The mayor's face changes, turns serious. Under the pockets of fat are clever eyes. 'I've come at a good time, to find the representatives of the serious press conveniently closeted together. I seek you out to assure myself of your impartiality. You, Herr Stuff, struck my police commander today as potentially biased.'

'Biased? Not at all.'

'Well, call it what you like. You don't care for him. But, gentlemen, reflect on what you're doing before you do it. The police
stand fully behind their actions. They enjoy government backing. And they also have the support of the working class – and
Altholm is working class. So if you position yourselves against
the police, you line up against your own town – the Vaterstadt,
as you like to say in your pages – and hence against your own
interests.'

'It seems to me, Mayor, that you're overestimating the importance of today's developments. There'll be a local top story tomorrow, and two or three brief notes to follow, in six months there'll
be some court cases – and there's an end.'

'I don't agree,' Stuff contradicts his owner. 'The struggle is
only just beginning.'

'On what side will we find you, Herr Stuff?'

'I'm just a simple editor,' says Stuff.

'An editor, of course,' the mayor nods disapprovingly. And
turning to the owner: 'By the way, you did know that the magistracy has decided in its wisdom no longer to favour the *Chronicle*
with its official announcements?'

'No!' explodes Gebhardt. 'Schabbelt didn't mention that to me
when he sold up.'

And Stuff, two seconds too late: 'It wasn't the magistracy that
decided that!'

The mayor smiles, the man understands. He turns his attention to Gebhardt, and on the other side, in the dark, is Stuff. 'Well
now, Herr Gebhardt, your newspaper refers to itself as proud and
upstanding, and your readers are workers. I imagine you'll be
wanting to keep the town's interests at heart in the way you talk
to them?'

'The town's interests, yes, quite,' says Gebhardt cautiously.

'Which means . . . it's so easy just now to yield to a certain
populist . . . wildness. It's important sometimes to oppose the
tide of feeling. You will receive our official report tomorrow
morning. I recommend you stick to that.'

'We will certainly publish the report.'

'I am most unwilling,' the mayor says, 'to lean on you in any way. But this is a contentious matter. I hope, but I'm by no means certain, that I'll find you on my side. It's not the side of the SPD, the Red side, the side of officialdom – as you may have supposed. It's the side of law and order, of work and constructiveness. On the face of it, a simple enough choice . . .'

The gentlemen stare ahead. The mayor looks sorrowfully from one to the other.

Then he gets up, and says, in a different tone again: 'All right, gentlemen, goodnight, goodnight. – If people are agreed, as you are, on the principle, then they'll end up agreeing on money too.'

And already out in the corridor: 'Don't worry, Herr Stuff. I'll find my own way out without a light. Anyway, someone might see you. Goodnight!'

Stuff, to Gebhardt again: 'Jesus Christ, the son of a bitch! The son of a bitch!'

And Gebhardt, with a sour-sweet smile: 'A bit prickly, the Red gent, wouldn't you say?'

VII

Tredup had yelled and screamed from the prison windows till hands grabbed him from behind and pulled him down.

He had been taken out of his cell into the detention room, which was called either 'detention room' or 'padded cell', depending.

Every prison has two types of prison warden: those who moved Tredup really didn't exist any more, at least not according to the regulations of the Prussian Ministry of Justice.

They had seized him under the arms, and dragged him noisily along the corridors and up and down the stairs of the prison. They had contrived to do it in such a way as to produce maximum contact between his shin bones and the iron steps and railings. And at the end of the staircase, when there were just another ten or twelve steps to go, they had suddenly let the troublemaker go, and he had fallen over and over like a sack of potatoes till he struck the cement floor, where he lay still.

Then they had ordered him to get up, warned him not to play-act, pointed out to him the consequences of his refusal, and finally, when nothing else helped, they had dragged him into the padded cell, tossed him on to the pallet, taken away his braces so he didn't get any silly ideas, and left him on his own.

Tredup had lain there for hours, in and out of consciousness. Once upon a time he had been impatient, yes, but decently enough accommodated in his cell. And then the queer goatee'd warden had persuaded him to call out to the farmers, which would secure his prompt release. Then the whole building had gone crazy, and then they had done this to him . . . They had broken him . . . So this was what prisons were like . . .

Causing a disturbance, resistance to the power of the State, mutiny . . . Was there prison for that? Jail? How long for?

Where he is now is a kind of birdcage, only with absurdly thick iron bars, half dark and with bare walls that give off an icy chill. Only a wooden pallet, made fast to a concrete base, no blanket, no stool, nothing.

If I have to stay here a day and a night, he thinks, I'll go crazy.

A double bang on the door starts him up. A voice says something

'Yes, please?' he asks in confusion.

'D'yer need a shit!' came the yell from outside.

'What? – No. I don't.'

He can hear voices outside. Then keys jingle, a warden comes in, but he stands in the other part of the room, behind the bars.

'Are you sure you don't want to relieve yourself?' asks the warden kindly. And to the prisoner in blue, who has stepped in holding a bucket: 'That's the way you're supposed to ask. Not what you said.'

'Bastard,' grumbles the prisoner with an angry look. 'Turning the whole prison on its head.'

'That's nothing to do with you,' says the warden in clipped tone. 'So, what about it? Do you want to try? We won't be back till tomorrow morning. We're not allowed to leave you the bucket here, because you played up.'

'No, thanks. But if I could have a blanket? It's really cold in here.'

'Of course. You're entitled to two. Bögge, will you bring them?' And when the prisoner's gone: 'You've got this thing here on the wall. You just need to pull on it if you need to, at night.' More quietly: 'But only if it's really urgent. The night shift doesn't like to be inconvenienced. All right, here's your blankets.'

It's quiet in the cell. Slowly it gets dark. Tredup tries to think of his buried money, and then about how he wants to get away from here, into a different future. Would the nice warden let him out for five hundred marks?

Suddenly the ceiling light blazes on. The key jingles again. A fat man with a face like a bulldog steps in, followed by a warden, both in white coats.

'Is this the fellow who made all that racket, then?' asks the fat man. 'He's a play-actor, you can tell that a mile off. Give us your hand,' he gruffs. 'Through the bars!

'Pulse is regular, a bit of a flutter now, of course. Scared, are we? Gotta suffer the consequences? Worries?'

Again: 'Why did you yell out the window?'

'I don't know . . . I couldn't stand it any more . . .'

The doctor, mocking, to the hospital orderly: '"Couldn't stand it any more"! Wimp! Didn't like it, no? We straighten out kids like you in nothing flat. We have a bit of fun with you . . .'

And, much louder: 'We'll ream you out! Don't give me your bullshit about being sick! I'll get you stuck in a punishment cell! You'll stay there.'

To the warden, suddenly pefectly quietly: 'Look at this wretch. Turns the whole prison upside down. He's got tears in his eyes now. It's a disgrace. Calls himself a German! It makes me want to puke!'

The door clanks shut again. The light is switched off.

Tredup lies in the dark, his face in the blankets, a sob welling up in his throat that only his fear keeps from bursting out.

Is there no limit to what they can do to me? How will I ever be able to look another human being in the face? I can't stand it here, I want to go home, to the little room on the yard, to Elise and the children.

The way Hans put his little hand in mine, and grabbed hold

of my finger. He trusted me. Who will ever be able to trust me again? It's all finished.

Why did they have to take away my braces? I'd have to shred the blanket now.

He must have dropped off, because suddenly there's another man in the grey-green uniform at his bedside, shaking him.

'Hey, you! What's your name?'

'Tredup.'

'Come with me. You're going to see the governor. Hold it, carry your shoes, you can walk in your stockinged feet. You've made enough noise for one day. No need to wake the others.'

They walk quietly through the sleeping prison, with hundreds of doors, behind each one someone sleeping or waking.

The warden shuffles along behind him in his slippers. 'Up the steps,' he says quietly. 'Along the corridor.'

I wonder what's happening now, Tredup thinks in alarm. 'Am I being punished? Couldn't they have let me sleep?'

'We've arrived.'

The warden knocks on a door, a bright light behind it.

'Well, go on in. – Put your shoes on first.'

Behind a desk sits a large, clean-shaven man with a healthy complexion, a friendly expression and a bald, gleaming head. The room is very bright and clean. There are flowers . . .

Tredup feels old, tired to death and soiled beyond belief.

'I see. So you're Tredup.' The man looks at him for a very long time. 'Tell me, Herr Tredup, what got into you this afternoon?'

Tredup looks at the man for a moment. He's not like the others, he thinks. And aloud: 'Someone came into my cell, and told me there were farmers standing outside. And if I shouted for help, they would come and liberate me.'

Governor Greve studies him intently, and his bright face seems to dull a little. 'Were you asleep?' he asks. 'Did you dream?'

'I wasn't asleep. – Yes, I was, on second thoughts,' says Tredup. 'But it was a prison warden, a man with a little yellow goatee.'

'A man with a little goatee,' the governor repeats slowly. 'How old are you, Herr Tredup? – You're married, aren't you? – With children? – Two. And all healthy?'

'I wasn't dreaming,' insists Tredup. 'The man with the goatee came in and told me what to do.'

'All right, you weren't dreaming. But if someone walks in and tells you to do something, do you always do it, without thinking?'

Tredup stands there in silence.

'After all, you're in prison. You've been here for a few days? You've seen the walls and the locks and the wardens with their guns?'

Tredup is silent.

'Even if the fellow with the goatee beard really did talk to you about the farmers, what did you imagine happening? Did you think they would attack the prison and liberate you? How many farmers were standing under your window when you started shouting?'

'I couldn't see any. I just shouted.'

'You "just shouted". Without hope. Just because someone told you to?'

'He told me I'd be freed.'

'Yes, of course.' The man suddenly lowers his gaze. Picks up some papers. Then, in a different tone of voice: 'The reason I sent for you. The prosecutor's office has agreed to let you go.'

'Yes?' asks Tredup fearfully.

'Yes. The decree arrived tonight. And since prison seems not to agree with you, I thought I'd tell you right away.'

'And I can . . .?' asks Tredup, falteringly. 'When can I go?'

'Tomorrow morning. Tonight. Whenever you like.'

'Really? Even though I yelled?'

'Even though. Yes, I'm thinking your yelling won't have any terribly grave consequences.' The governor picks up a piece of paper, looks at it with raised eyebrows, crumples it up and throws it into the wastepaper basket. 'Do you want to go home right away?'

'If that's all right?'

'We'll manage. You'll be able to come back and collect your personal items tomorrow.'

'Thank you . . . thank you so much . . . I'll never forget,' whispers Tredup.

'I'll ring for the night warden,' says the governor. 'He'll show you out.'

A bell sounds quietly in the distance, followed by silence.

'Incidentally,' the governor says abruptly. 'Mayor Gareis came to visit you a couple of days ago.'

'Really?'

'I wasn't able to accommodate his wish, but maybe you'd like to go and call on him now? He seemed to take an interest in you. – Warden, will you take this man to release. Zenker will still be around. – Goodnight, Herr Tredup.'

And he holds out his hand to shake.

VIII

Night has fallen, a good, clear, moonless July night. Above the small, rather dispersed settlement of Altholm, a mile this way, a mile that, the sky is full of stars.

You can see them, the stars, twinkling up above, and Gareis, still on his constitutional with Political Adviser Stein, looks up at them. 'You must remember, Stein: follow the back axle of the Wain, and you find the Pole Star. And the three all together, that's Orion's Belt. You've always been a city boy, but my father took me in hand. We walked home across the country, from some slaughtering where he'd turned out to help. Being a barber in the country isn't much of a living.'

'Everything's asleep,' says the political adviser. 'And tomorrow the battle resumes.'

'Is that such a bad thing? It's good to have to fight.'

'Is it worth it?'

The mayor stops. He pushes his hat back, and in the dark, his huge bulk seems to loom over his slight friend the political adviser. 'Sometimes I wonder what you're even doing in the Party? Is it worth it . . .? Of course it's worth it.'

'Comrades can be just as pig-headed as anyone else.'

'Well . . .? Anyway, that's wrong. They are dissatisfied, and dissatisfaction is more valuable than contentment.'

'I think you'll stand alone in the coming fight.'

'Will I? I don't think you know the workers. The workers will understand that I am fighting for them.'

'For them? But it was just Frerksen making a hash of things.'

'No. No. I won't admit that. Not even to you. He was in the right.'

And suddenly, very animated: 'Stop! Look! See that! – It was a shooting star. Did you make a wish? Of course you missed it. I made a wish.'

The political adviser: 'What did you wish?'

'I'll tell you in a month. Or in six months.'

'But you will tell me?'

'Yes. I promise.'

Tredup, too, trotting home from prison, is looking up at the stars. But he's not interested in the constellations. He just wants to see the place where he buried his money, when he was walking home from Stolpe. Ideally, he would go there right now, in the middle of the night, and dig it up from under the pines near the sand dunes. And would leave Altholm, Pomerania and Germany, and go out into the world. Some part of it where he didn't know the language, didn't know the country, where no one will ever learn what happened to him . . .

But he has Elise and the children.

With an oppressed hunch, turning to check for pursuers, he creeps into his hot, smelly flat.

Stuff is walking with lowered head. If he sees the stars at all, it will be their reflections in the water, in the pond, along which he is walking on his way to the pub. But he's not thinking of them, he's thinking of his new boss, his new wage, cut by a hundred a month (they finally ended up splitting the difference, and he gave up his expenses). He thinks about the muzzle they've slapped on him. Not being allowed to bite any more! Being prevented from snapping at the Red rabble by his cowardly boss. It would have been the best sort of end to his life, to be able to fight the good fight in good faith, used up, cynical old press warhorse that he is.

But he's not allowed to. He has to be tame, as always. Maybe a little jab occasionally, but having to kowtow to the Red majority in the town assembly . . .

I'll get you just the same! I don't care what it costs me!

He blinks up at a window that is still lit up through the shrubbery. Hospital, he thinks. Still busy dying and multiplying as ever. Wonder what the point is . . .

The man lying under the blinking light doesn't have any notion of dying. Henning lies, woozy with morphine, in dreams. He's waving the flag again. It whooshes through the beautiful blue-gold day.

And suddenly there are a lot of men there, the room is crowded with their shadows. That's right, they're standing guard over him, they told him he was lying there as a police prisoner. No clothes in the ward, nothing but the hospital gown on his body.

But there's no hurry as yet. When I'm ready, I'll make a break for it, even from prison. They'll have to tell Gruen to keep an eye on Tredup. It would not be good if they found out I was involved in the bombing as well.

Gruen meanwhile is looking. He's prowling around the town dumps, looking, a confused male witch, for three things: a tin can, a cardboard box and a broken alarm clock. He's grinning like a loon, and the lick of beard on his chin is trembling and dancing.

Will you take it on your oath as a servant of the State?

Of course I'll take it on oath, Governor.

The remand prisoner Tredup is adamant that you told him to shout to the farmers. He's dreaming. I was down on C1, giving out water.

On my oath. Definitely! The way they like you to swear on that constitution of theirs, no God about it, constitution . . . whatever they call a constitution . . . There's the tin can.

In their matrimonial bed, Commander Frerksen is holding his wife.

'It was a terrible day, Annie. But I did right. I have everyone's support.'

'And Gareis? What did Gareis say?'

'Gareis doesn't count. Someone from the government, an agent, told me I put up a good show.'

'What about the injured? Are they badly hurt?'

'They're all under arrest. Why should anyone feel sorry for them, they're all troublemakers. – Is that you, Hans? What are you doing?'

'I need to go to the lavatory, Father.'

'Not in the middle of the night, you don't. You should control yourself. All right then, on you go. But be quiet about it.'

Thiel too is trying hard to be quiet, as he saws through the last of the bars in the cell window in the Stolpe detention centre. It's not hard to get the message if you come upon steel files in the smoked herring you get once a week. Only it took him rather a long time to do the sawing.

But tonight he's almost there. The blankets, ripped up and knotted together into a rope, are ready on his bed. And once he's on the farm, he'll be at liberty again. He's a long way from being sentenced for the bombing.

Cautiously he removes the sawn-off bars from the corner – just enough to permit him to wriggle through – and lays them on the bed. He ties the rope to the remaining stump of bar, and hoists himself into the opening.

He listens. His heart isn't beating as fast as he thought it would, and his grip is dry.

The night is dark. The streets are very quiet. Up above are the glinting stars.

Yes, I was a junior official, who knew about nothing but figures. Suddenly I've turned into something completely different, and that's fine too. But I'll give Henning grief for leaving me in the lurch like this. If those files weren't from him. – Let's go!

He grips the rope and abseils down into the dark.

Also in the dark is Padberg, in a dark entryway opposite the *Bauernschaft*'s editorial offices. He is spying on the windows of his office, which are similarly dark. Or seem so. But twice already he's caught the flash of a light, perhaps a torch, he's pretty sure.

The mole is rummaging around again. How did he get in? Surely not through the front door, or the back, which leaves . . .? Over the roof or up from the basement! In that case he must live on the block, maybe in one of the abutting buildings . . . Ooh, wait!

But he can't remember where his typesetters live. Hang on!

The fellow just missed a trick, a white beam brushed the ceiling, before vanishing.

He's fairly bold. Just as well I've got the copy for tomorrow in my pocket, otherwise something might have happened to it. I'm curious whether he'll steal the hundred-mark note. If he leaves it, that would certainly mean something.

Padberg shrugs his shoulders.

There's little point in hanging on here. If I unlock the door downstairs, he'll disappear. But tomorrow, matey, tomorrow night I'll be waiting under the desk for you.

There's another desk where a lot of work is secretly being done tonight. In the Altholm town hall, long since deserted, the door to the mayor's office opens.

A small shadow stands in the door frame for a moment, and listens. Then he creeps up to the desk, feels around it, and pulls out the top-left drawer. He gropes inside it. On the top is a piece of paper, foolscap. Thick paper folded in the middle, to fit into a long envelope. The hands continue to grope. There, under it, is the envelope, hastily ripped open, but the blind fingertips feel the wax that sealed it.

'The secret orders,' whispers the little man. 'I've got them. Now you wait, Comrade Gareis, now we've got you where we want you.'

Across the sleeping countryside a car drives slowly, jerkily, grinding. Sometimes when it stops, and Bandekow and Rehder talk about the route, they can clearly hear the surf breaking to the left.

When the car left that morning, there were five in it: Padberg, Henning, Rohwer, Rehder and Bandekow. Where are they now?

Henning beaten to a pulp and locked up, Rohwer arrested and in prison, Padberg gone off in a huff.

Only two remain, but they have with them a third man. He's lying in the back of the car, Farmer Banz, whom they managed to hide from the militia in the basement of the auction house. For the most part he lies there quietly, but sometimes he speaks, and then what he says argues how good it was that they didn't leave him in the hands of the police.

'We have to get the dynamite out of the barn . . . It's not safe to leave it there in its present condition.'

'I can take it,' offers Bandekow.

'Yes, perhaps. But not tonight. Tonight everything's jinxed.'

'Yes. So you say.'

In the beam of the headlights, the cottage turns up. 'I hope we can get your wife up without too much bother.'

'And I hope she's not too alarmed.'

But the woman isn't alarmed. 'Are you just coming to collect *it*, or are you bringing him back?'

'We've got him in the car, but . . .'

'Is he alive?'

'Yes. But he's hurt.'

'Can I put him to bed, or are the police after him?'

'The police don't know anything about him. Maybe later, but not now.'

'You take hold of his feet.'

She holds the hurt head in her firm hands. They lay him on the bed in the room.

'Can we help with anything? Do you need money?'

'Just go. I'll get by.'

'Best not send for a doctor.'

'A "doctor" . . .?' she repeats mockingly. 'I had all my children without a doctor. That little scratch? I'll wash it out with cattle urine. And compresses against the fever. In another week he'll be lifting potatoes.'

'But –'

'No, no, just go!'

A man is dawdling along the Burstah, where only one light in three seems to be on. There is almost no one left on the streets, and so our man has the whole of it to himself. He strolls along the middle of the road, hands buried in his pockets, whistling to himself.

The man stops at the traffic island on the Grünhofer crossing. He's not quite so blithe and indifferent as he tries to seem. He looks closely at the street and the buildings, the patch of grass, the park around the monument.

On a bench he spots a pair of lovers, in the shade of the bushes.

He hesitates for a moment, thinks, but then he goes up to the monument anyway.

They'll not see anything. They only have eyes for each other, if that.

This time, Matthies, the KPD official, walks circumspectly round the geranium bed, careful to tread only on the grass. Then he is in the shadow of the monument, behind the plinth. He reaches down and picks up the handle of the sabre.

As I thought! He has too much to do, poor Frerksen, and forgot all about his sabre.

He pulls it out of the ground and stows it carefully down one trouser leg. Then he secures the basket to his braces.

There. I'll get you home like that, no bother. And I'd like to see the look on your face, Comrade Frerksen, when we cart it around on our next jolly, with a placard: BLOODHOUND FRERKSEN.

Matthies slinks past the lovers. 'Can I have some too, girl?'

The lovers, a dark knot, make no sound. 'Go to it, my son. The world needs proles.'

He disappears round the corner, past the *News*. The lovers take each other more firmly, under the starry canopy.

PART II

The Townies

The Origin of the Boycott

I

The sky slowly brightens with approaching morning.

Behind the curtains, fluttered by the occasional puff of breeze, Max Tredup has been able to make out the darker shadow of the window-crosses all night. But now the darkness loses its edge and outlines merge. An early bird stirs outside and tweets once or twice, as if mistakenly, in the great pre-dawn silence.

Tredup lies there perfectly still. He looks towards the window and tries to find courage to meet the approaching day. How is he to encounter people? With what expressions will they look at him, the released remand prisoner? Will Stuff shake his hand? Will Schabbelt throw him out?

He tries to breathe regularly, so that Elise won't know he's awake. But she's probably asleep. His shoulder touches her shoulder, they are lying on their sides, back to back, he can feel her heaviness, her warmth.

If there is no other way, he will take the thousand marks and disappear with them. Find a job somewhere, in a newspaper advertising department or as a copy-writer. He will send Elise money. He can't stay in Altholm.

'Tell me about the thousand marks,' says Elise.

'What thousand marks?' he asks, in bewilderment.

So Elise was awake after all.

'Is it as much as that? Gareis told me.'

'Gareis doesn't know anything,' he stammers. 'I'm supposed to be given some money. But I have no idea of when, or if it's as much as a thousand marks.'

'Turn round and face me, Max. Look at me. No, I don't need to see you to know that you're lying to me.'

'Where would I have a thousand marks? You went through all my things when I was in prison.'

'I did and all. You've tucked it away somewhere. You're different now.'

'I'm not different at all.'

'What shall I give the children for their tea? The grocer's wife makes a face when I keep asking her to put it on the bill.'

'Maybe Wenk will give me an advance today.'

'Ten marks. And I'm thirty-two in debt already. Where are the thousand marks? Why don't you give them to me? You always used to give me any money you had!'

'I haven't got any. That's all there is to it.'

'Yes you do. What do you want? Do you want to leave us? What's going to happen when the new little one comes?'

'A new baby?' he asks angrily. 'First I've heard of it.'

'You know just as well as I do that you got me pregnant today.'

'I never. You're imagining it, because you're after my money.'

'Yes, you did and all. What's the point in you being careful for a year, and then you're away from me for a week, and you come back and you're crazy?'

'Should I not have been careful in the last year?'

'Don't talk rubbish. You should either be careful all the time or forget about it.'

'And if I really did get you pregnant,' he says, slowly, feeling his way forward, 'well, there's a woman on the Kleine Lastadie who can get rid of it.'

'How would you know that?' she asks. 'So I get to go to prison as well as you?'

'She knows her business, the woman, she does it with water and a syringe.'

'Who told you? Did they tell you about that in prison?'

'No. Not in prison.'

'Oh, so you knew it before? So is that why you weren't careful last night?'

'I'm getting up now,' says Tredup.

'You're staying put. You'll only wake the children, and I'll have their racket from five in the morning.'

'You've changed, Elise.'

'Of course I've changed if you have. Where did you put the money?'

'I don't have any.'

'What are you going to pay the woman with, then? She's bound to want fifty or a hundred marks.'

'Twenty-five.'

'So where will you get them from?'

'I'll borrow them.'

'Who's going to loan you twenty-five marks? No one!'

'Oh, I'll get them all right.'

'Who from? I just want to know who from?'

'Well, I expect Stuff would loan me them, for one.'

'I see, Stuff. Fatty Stuff!'

'Yes, Stuff. So?'

'Then was it Stuff who told you about the woman too?'

'No, it never! Someone else told me.'

'Who?'

'Not Stuff.'

'I always had a feeling that Henni was getting big when Stuff and her were going together,' says Frau Tredup. 'Then all at once, she was skinny as a pine tree again.'

'You women are good at imagining things like that.'

'But then Stuff will have to give you at least a hundred marks, otherwise he could be in a lot of trouble.'

'But I keep telling you,' yells Tredup, 'that it wasn't Stuff! You're mad, got it, mad, mad! You're always on about money. Thousand marks, a hundred marks. It doesn't stop: money, money, money!'

'You'll wake the children with your shouting, but you don't care. They don't hang on to *your* apron strings and wail because there's nothing to eat. Miss Lange told me she'll send Grete home the next time she turns up at school without underwear. The boys try to cop a look. Give me money to buy underwear for her.'

'Yeah, yeah. Money, money, money. You'll make me a proper son of a bitch. I'll get some out of the safe, then, shall I? I'll find a drunk to rob. I'll send Grete round to Manzow on Calvinstrasse, because he gets a kick out of little girls. I'll –'

She slaps him, but not hard.

'Get out!' she yells. 'Get out! Go to your office, go on the street, get out of my sight. He's got a thousand marks, and talks filth about his own daughter just so he can keep his money for himself. Get out!'

Tredup stands in the corner. He is staring at his wife, who is sitting upright in bed, looking at him with bosom heaving. He is standing there in his short vest, his skinny, hairy legs bare, rubbing his face with his hand where she smacked him.

Suddenly he smiles. 'That felt like the time they threw me down the stairs in jail,' he says. 'I guess I've just fallen down your stairs.'

'What are you babbling about?' she asks.

'Nothing. Make me some coffee. Or tea. Or flour and water. Whatever you've got in the house. I need to be at the *Chronicle* at six.'

'All right,' she says obediently. 'Frau Wandler will be up, and she'll loan me half a pound of coffee.'

II

At half past six Heinsius is already up and sitting in his office, the chief editor of the *News*, a patriotic man who loves his city, author of several novels about the stolid yeomanry of Pomerania.

He sits there – writing.

He really is. All night he hasn't slept, ever since he's realized that the *News* will have to take up an editorial position on the events, which means he will have to write something.

Last night, when Blöcker was blathering on about the peasants' struggle, the police's wild assaults, extraordinary scenes in the auction hall, militiamen swinging batons, a megalomaniac police tyrant – last night he had smiled and said: 'You're exaggerating, Blöcker. Clashes during marches – ten a penny. Happens one day, forgotten the next. A paragraph in local news, the official report, a mood piece of thirty lines, max, that's about the size of it.'

'But the people are angry.'

'What people? The farmers? What do we care about the farmers! The townsfolk – *they're* not mad. Them least of all. At the most, they'll be pleased to have experienced something.'

'Actually, the townsfolk *are* mad.'

'Go along now, Blöcker, go along. Today I'm running with the memoirs of a dancer who appeared before the Prince of Wales. That'll interest people. But goings-on in Altholm? Has Altholm ever made the front page? You're exaggerating, Blöcker.'

That was last night. Then there were various phone calls.

The scissors-and-paste man Heinsius hardly ever leaves the building. He asks others to stand in for him. He's the quiet man in the cell, the cryptic, unpredictable one. A local reporter has to be out and about, a chief editor is the shrine in the holy of holies.

People have got accustomed to phoning the shrine. That's the form he takes, a voice, giving laconic answers, evasive, promising nothing.

'Our deliberations are not yet at a point. In the interests of our town . . .'

People called. The first . . .

A woman, a silver-haired spinster, he knew her. Rarely had Heinsius heard such indignation on the telephone.

'They were on the rampage, I tell you! They were swinging their sticks like savages, bringing down their sabres pitilessly on imploring hands.'

'These hands, ma'am. Are you quite sure they weren't raised to strike? Forgive me, the huge responsibility that rests on us compels the question. We must be absolutely certain.'

'Stuff and nonsense! I tell you, I had to leave the balcony and run to my room. I was sick to my stomach.'

'Yes. Yes. The sensitive female psyche. Does you credit. We've heard tell of such happenings. Some of our fellows have witnessed similar things.'

More calls followed. But: Am I supposed to tangle with the police? If only I knew what view Stolpe took of things. Bah, the official report and a local-interest note will cover it.

Then – at this point Heinsius had already gone home – there was a phone call from his proprietor, Gebhardt: 'What are we doing?'

'Equivocate. Delay judgement. Allow the smoke to clear.'

'I've spoken to a dozen people . . .'

'People only understand what's happened when they've read about it in our pages. Till that time, nothing's happened.'

'Then what's happening in our pages tomorrow? We mustn't spoil things with Gareis.'

'No? All right. I'll write something. I'll have it ready by eight o'clock.'

He said it, he solved the difficulties, the boss is relieved. Oil on troubled waters.

And then he spent a sleepless night, writing, writing . . .

War and peace. Peace is preferable to war. Its emblem, the scythe, menacing when newly hammered and pointing heavenwards. Turn its crook down towards the earth, once again it is a symbol of work and peace.

The black flag. Piratical heritage. Battle and triumph of force. And then again, all things come from night. The white plough tilling the black earth, symbol of work and peace.

I'd better skip the red sword, methinks.

Something else on the troubled times, the hardship of the countryside, political strife – who will take it amiss? No one. That's the way. A column and a half, a leader, and I'll put my name to it.

Three hours later, still night, still formulating new ringing sentences: Or should I maybe not sign it? Maybe I'll be compromised by it?

Best thing is to wait for the Stettin morning papers. Then I'll get a pointer from them.

Now he sits there and writes. From time to time, he turns an ear to the corridor. He knows the quick, light-footed walk of the owner. He needs to get to him first, for sure, before that cunning Trautmann fills his ears full of something.

The morning papers brought no certainty either. The government keeps its counsel. The Right-wing papers go on about police brutality. The Democrats bide their time. The SPD praise the police.

Wait and see. Symbol of work and peace . . .

Here comes the boss.

'Good morning, Herr Gebhardt! Good morning. A king of a day. Perhaps too much so for the farmers, who need rain. On the other hand, the townies are happy. A couple of school outings scheduled for today.

'You look thoroughly well rested, if I may say so, Herr Geb-hardt. I, on the other hand, have been tossing and turning . . . Well, that's my chosen profession, a difficult, wearing, soul-searching profession. I've written something. A column. If you happened to have a moment . . .?'

'Read it to me . . .'

'I called it: "Black Flag – Black Day".'

'Could that not be taken as an attack on the farmers?'

'Oh, do you think so? That wasn't my intention at all! I'll . . . Well, let's just call it: "Black Day", that never goes amiss.'

'Quite right,' his boss praises him. 'Now on!'

Heinsius reads it out, clenches his fists, raises his eyes heaven-wards, shakes the paper.

Suddenly his boss interrupts him: 'We have a small ad from Mingel's millinery, which I'd like to put on the front page, if pos-sible. A charming illustration. A little girl in a mirror, trying on a new hat. Very respectable. You wouldn't mind, would you, if I put that alongside your article?'

Heinsius makes a face. 'On the front page? In the lead article?'

'There's a fifty per cent premium.'

'Well, in that case . . .' and he goes on reading.

Finally the boss opines: 'All right. I don't think anyone will feel got at by this. And with the official report to come. I think we're covered.'

'"Coverage" is my watchword.'

'I know. I know. And I've given Stuff licence to go after the police a little bit, that's appropriate for him and that paper.'

'Stuff is going after the police? No! I'm not playing. Then I'm going to tear up this article.' Heinsius is incensed. 'Am

I going to let him take the wind out of my sails? Of course people would rather read a scold than my responsible contemplations. A hundred extra copies of the *Chronicle* in pavement sales. No dice.'

'But I gave him my permission.'

'Then I'll call him and rescind it in your name. What did we buy the *Chronicle* for if it's to go on pinching our readers?'

'Perhaps you're right.'

'I'm certain I am. Tell Stuff he can pee all over the mayor some time, that'll please him.'

'All right. Call Stuff. But I don't want to hear any more about it!'

'I'll take care of everything, Herr Gebhardt!'

III

Someone very gently and carefully pulls open the door to the *Chronicle* offices and looks through the milky glass into dispatch.

Thank God, the girl isn't there yet, and Wenk isn't either, who would have chased him off to find advertising.

Tredup walks in with palpitating heart, looks round the familiar room once more – the address book isn't in its usual place – and then he quietly opens the door into the editorial office.

There's Stuff, fat and flowing, in shirtsleeves, writing. Writing with enthusiasm, squinnying through his half-off glasses, with pink cheeks.

When the door falls shut, he looks up from his paper. 'Well, well, well! Look who it isn't! Tredup is back. How come they allowed a bomb-thrower like you back into circulation! Well, I'm glad you're back, I really am. Wenk is such a dullard.'

They shake hands.

'Well, how did you get on in prison? Behind the so-called Swedish curtains? I have a vivid sense of it! It's supposed to be a sort of health farm these days, with football and lectures and psychotherapy. Is that right? You'll tell me all about it, won't you? I'm under a bit of pressure at the moment. The police have been fabulously stupid. Well, you've been a little bit stupid yourself. That's the thanks you get anyway. I don't suppose you'll be selling them any more photographs?'

'Not likely,' says Tredup, feeling mightily relieved by Stuff's kind reception.

'And the to-do with the farmers yesterday. Our Police Commander Frerksen. – What? You haven't heard? Here, read this! Read it, man! If you don't know about this, you haven't lived. You can correct the silly cow's typos while you're about it. I stick it to those pigs. I'm not meant to. Gebhardt says "take it easy", but –'

'Gebhardt . . .?'

'Of course, Gebhardt! Oh, God, you don't know that either, that the good ole *Chronicle* has as of yesterday joined the Gebhardt stable of papers? Schabbelt sold up? Ach, it's Rip Van Winkle time. The man from the Magic Mountain! Jesus, Tredup, how will you adjust? Read! No, listen!'

Stuff stops, puffing and sweating. He mops his brow. 'What a morning! It feels good to be alive again. They're all going to catch it from me.'

The phone rings.

'Yes, Mayor? – Well, I need the report in half an hour at the latest. My sense of things? Well, one thing is for sure: Frerksen is toast. – What's that? Oh, come on, not even you could deny that he's made a gigantic rickets of everything, Mayor. – Oh, you thought he performed well? I would keep my voice down if I were you, and not say that to anyone else, because in twenty-four hours you won't be able to keep him afloat any more. – He has the backing of the government? I wouldn't be so sure. Different water flows into the Blosse every day, and why wouldn't the government have reversed itself, as they like to say, in twenty-four hours? – Yes, as a matter of fact I do go after him in my piece, you're damned right I go after him, I give it to him, both barrels. – Why? Well, Mayor, I suggest you start by reading the *Chronicle* this lunchtime instead of the *News*. – No, that is not against our understanding. Just because you give us the municipal announcements doesn't make the entire town administration right down to the lowliest charwoman a journalistic no-go area. – No, I'm not planning on going to the press conference. I don't have the time, frankly, Mayor, I need to put my paper to bed, the type-setters are waiting. – Good day to you, Mayor. – Yes, in three hours. – No, I can't manage it at this time. Goodbye.'

Stuff snorts and gets to his feet. He spreads his arms and shakes his head. 'My God, that thick, lardy oil, that supposedly oh-so-disarming soft-soap. But I told him where to stick it, didn't I, Tredup? The *Chronicle* hasn't spoken in such tones to Mayor Gareis before. I tell you, he stood in the auction hall yesterday like Luther in Worms and allowed those blue gorillas of militia-men to lay into the farmers!'

Shyly Tredup observes: 'But Gareis isn't such a bad man. If Frerksen has made a rickets and he stands by him, surely that's just decent of him?'

Stuff explodes: 'Gareis and decent! That's politics, it's the Reds standing shoulder to shoulder against the farmers. He's ensnared you too, that's obvious; you should see what happens when you want something from him, he just won't want to know.'

'It's happened already.'

Stuff crows: 'You see! You see! . . . Oh, who is it now . . .? Hey, what is this . . .?'

IV

Two shapes danced past, in a wild commotion, but they were gone before Stuff and Tredup could get the windows open.

'Who on earth was that?' mutters Stuff.

There's din and commotion coming from the front room. Wood bashes against wood, chairs are upset, Heinze can be heard beginning to squeal, a gruff roar by way of reply – and through the opened door two gentlemen ride in on chairs.

In the lead is Agricultural Councillor Feinbube. Spiked on his stick is a hunting hat with a chamois beard, raised high like a banner. Behind him on a rocking horse is syndic Plosch, from the local Craftsmen's Association, his duelling scars well reddened with alcohol.

Feinbube gives his mount a kick that causes it to collapse. With outspread arms he careens towards Stuff.

'Come to my bosom, Stuff, you old porker, come to my arms. The hour is now at hand when you can make good all your sins. Join the Green Front. Stick it to the Reds . . . Come!'

'It is necessary to dishtinguish,' says the at-least-as-drunk Plosch, 'between the human being Shtuff, whom we love, and the journalist, who is a shwine. – You are too, don't contradict me, you're a shwine of vasht proportions. I ushed to be a journalist myshelf onshe.'

'We have been beaten,' crows Feinbube. 'The Reds have smacked our bottoms. But we celebrate it like a victory. That Frerksen –'

'Frerkshen ish a shwine too,' explains Plosch. 'A vasht shwine.'

'Frerksen is responsible for everything,' affirms Stuff. 'But have you heard what happened to his sabre?'

'The sabre on Frerksen,' lectures Feinbube with heavy tongue, 'looks like a sword on a Jew.'

'Ah, boys,' yelps Stuff, 'you're in for a treat. The farmers took his sabre off him outside Tucher's. And then he tossed the empty scabbard into Bimm's. Then suddenly the Commie Matthies brought his sabre after him. He was standing there with the shiny blade –'

'It was folly,' explains the heavy-tongued Plosch, 'to attack marchers with sabres in the first place. Where do the police get shabres from? Why have they been issued with truncheons? Write it down, Stuff!'

'I have already. Wait, I'll read you something.'

'Not read. I feel thirsty. Haven't you got any schnapps here? We were drinking all night with Padberg, and we missed you, Stuff, you tell the dirtiest jokes. Do you remember the one about the cook and the pair of trousers?'

'No, wait. I'm going to read to you. I want you to hear how I stick it to Gareis.'

'Ah, never mind Gareis, just stick it to Frerksen!'

'Him too. Now listen up!'

'Did you know we want to cancel the point-to-point in Altholm? The farmers are in no hurry to come back here.'

'There's a long time till then. Listen to my article!'

'Ach, you and your writing. You'll only betray us again. You were born a swine, Stuff, you live like a swine and you'll die a swine too. Where's the official report?'

'Not out yet. But in the auction hall –'

'I was there. I can tell you about it. There was this agent provocateur –'

The phone rings.

'Can't you turn off the phone, Stuff, you ape? It's just giving yourselves airs to stick a phone in here. You crib everything you write from the other papers anyway.'

'That's right, Feinbube. – Yes, right away? It'll be difficult. OK, I'm on my way. – No, not yet. – Please. – Yes, please don't give yourself airs. You're not my boss. – Yes, I said I was coming. Right away. This I want to see.'

And, in a sudden rage: 'Listen, mate, you can take a –!'

Stuff hangs up. He looks distractedly round the room.

'Who was that then?' inquires Plosch. 'Who's that mate of yours?'

'Oh, that was just larking. That was the fire service. I have to go there right away.'

'Not possible. You're going to read to us, like you promised.

'Where's the schnapps?'

'Tredup can read to you. Can't you, Tredup, you'll read to them?'

'Yes.'

'All right then, gents. I'll be back in ten or fifteen minutes.'

'Stuff!'

But Stuff is already gone.

V

It's very quiet in the office after Stuff has left it. The two drunks stand by the stove and stare silently at Tredup, who is sheepishly browsing through some papers.

'Shall I read to you?' he finally asks.

Agricultural Councillor Feinbube belches violently. 'Tell me, what did Stuff address you as a moment ago? I didn't quite catch your name?'

'Tredup,' whispers Tredup. 'Max Tredup.'

Feinbube takes a step forward. Unsteadily. He drills the tip of his cane into the lino, props himself on the handle with both hands, and leaning forward stares at the man behind the desk.

'Now then, Tredup,' he says slowly, and one senses his effort to fight his intoxication. 'Tredup. A widespread name here in Pomerania.'

He stares.

'Shall I read?' asks Tredup quietly.

'Would you,' asks Feinbube just as quietly, 'by any chance happen to be the bastard who sold the photos of Gramzow to the prosecution? Because that bastard was called Tredup.'

'Photos? No, I've never sold any photos.'

Feinbube turns round. 'Take a look at him, Plosch. Take a look at that guilty conscience. The liar! The coward!'

Suddenly turning back to Tredup, beside himself with rage: 'You swine! You Judas! What have you done with the thirty pieces of silver you got for betraying our Reimers to the knife? Give them here, you traitor!'

He staggers closer. And in front of him, with pale face and shaking knees, Tredup is trying to shrink ever deeper into the corner.

'Where are they?' asks the drunk stubbornly, half raising the cane. 'Where are they? Spent them on women? Or drunk them away? Where's the rope you mean to hang yourself from?'

'I don't know anything about any pictures,' says Tredup, with teeth chattering. 'I've got no money. I've got nothing.'

'Do you know what you've done, you swine? I could smash your rotten cockroach skull with my stick. What have you done with the money?'

'Please leave me alone,' begs Tredup. 'You can't just ... It's wrong ... Do you really want to kill me just like that?'

In the background, Plosch calls out: 'Leave him be, Feinbube. Don't get your hands dirty.'

'Kill you is exactly what I have in mind. Exactly.' And the long, sinewy hand feels for Tredup's collar and twists it in a tightening noose round his neck.

'It's your fault that Reimers wound up in jail . . .'

Tredup gurgles: 'I was in prison too . . . the bomb . . .'

The grip loosens. 'What was that about the bomb? Say it, you liar!'

Tredup, hurriedly: 'It was in the paper. That I'd been arrested for planting the bomb in Temborius's house. Tredup, remember?'

'He's right, Feinbube,' says Plosch. 'They arreshted someone called Tredup for the bomb.'

'Then why are you running around like a free man?'

'Because they let me go at half past nine last night.'

'What did they let you go for?'

'Because they had no evidence against me.'

'Did you plant the bomb, then? How did you make it?'

'They couldn't prove I did it.'

'Who did you plant the bomb with? What's the name of your accomplice?'

'They couldn't prove it was him either. He's going to be released too.'

Feinbube turns away from Tredup and stalks slowly towards the door.

'Come on, Plosch, let's get out of this pigsty. Everything here stinks.'

He turns to Tredup. 'You're lying, sunshine. But we'll rumble you. And then we'll split your rotten skull for you. All rotten. Putrid. Shit, crap, syphilitics, the lot of you!'

Suddenly he's yelling again: 'You're a bunch of syphilitics! Low-down, nasty syphilitics! But we've got injections to treat the likes of you, toxic, and your Stuff. We'll wash you away with the clap injection!'

He reels away, followed by Plosch. Tredup slumps forward on to the desk and shuts his eyes.

VI

For a while there's quiet in the office; it's as though Tredup's sleeping. Then a door opens, and then another. The barrier in dispatch creaks.

Tredup raises his head a little, blinks in the direction of the door. Who's coming to torment me now?

The person coming in is none other than Stuff, but an altered, greyed Stuff, pale, with swollen tear bags under his eyes. He sits down heavily on his chair and stares into space.

'Shot,' he finally says. 'Gone. Dead. Extinguished.'

He sniffs sadly.

'Where's the script, Tredup? Did they read it? Did they like it?'

'No, they didn't read it. They wanted to beat my brains out.'

'You're so lucky, Tredup. I wish someone would come and beat my brains out.'

He picks up the pages of copy and stares at them. He looks like an old man, grey, greasy, gone to seed.

He holds them in both hands and tears them across. Stares at the pieces, and drops them in the bin.

'There! So much for my attack. It's the beginning of the Gebhardt era. Softly, softly, mind you don't tread on anyone's feelings, even your foe's. I'm not allowed to any more, Tredup! I'm not allowed to go after the Reds.'

'Big deal,' says Tredup. 'What would be the good? It's just more bother.'

'The Gebhardt era, with the woolly-mammoth hair and the *thé dansant* bow. You're allowed to break wind, but only quietly. Though there's more of a stink.'

'I've only got one request, which is to be left in peace,' says Tredup. 'If Wenk sends me off to look for advertisers . . .'

'The official report!' groans Stuff. 'That's all I'm allowed to print. Oh, Tredup, the whitewash! Listen: "The flag was confiscated because scythes are not allowed to be openly carried in a built-up area." What do you think of that?'

Tredup doesn't think anything of it.

Stuff continues: '"The farmers attacked the police with cudgels." – What bullshit! If three thousand farmers attack twenty policemen there's not going to be many policemen left. And I'm not allowed to say anything.'

Tredup doesn't say anything either.

'"The meeting in the auction hall had to be broken up because the police had got wind of the fact that some farmers had pistols." – Why wasn't there so much as a single pop?'

'I really can't say,' says Tredup.

'And I have to print stuff like that with no comment! And the poor public reads it and doesn't think anything of it unless it gets it pre-digested. If I'd known that, I'd never have got into bed with Gebhardt. Feinbube and Plosch are right to want to spit at me.'

'Do I have to get into bed with Gebhardt as well? Will you put in a good word for me, Stuff?'

'He won't see me for another three years, I swear! I'm not going to see him for the next three years. – And I'm not allowed to write for him at all.'

He stares straight ahead in despair.

'If you agree to help me get a proper job and with a fixed salary,' Tredup begins slowly, 'then I'll find a way for you to go on kicking up a stink.'

'There is no way. He's slapped a ban on me: I'm not allowed to write.'

'Not you.'

Stuff stares. Then quickly: 'OK, I'll help you, Tredup. You'll be taken on. How much do you need?'

'It must be at least a hundred and fifty.'

'Crap. How are you going to live on a hundred and fifty with a wife and children? It would only mean doing more freelancing like with the photos. Two hundred, at least.'

'Will he pay two hundred?'

'I know a way. I won't go myself, I'll use an intermediary. I promise you you'll be taken on at two hundred a month.'

'Word of honour?'

'Word of honour.'

'OK – you're not allowed to write for the paper. But if you get a reader's letter, a subscriber's letter, then you have to print it, don't you? You can't alienate a subscriber, can you, least of all if they take out space in the paper too . . .?'

Stuff stares, stares straight through Tredup, it seems, at the wall behind him.

Suddenly he leaps up. There's colour in his cheeks and his eyes are shining.

'Who is he?'

'I'm in with Textil-Braun. I'll write one in his name and tell him later.'

'And what will you write?'

'Wait,' says Tredup. 'You have to kick up a fuss to make people restless. Feinbube and Plosch were yarning before. Give me a pen and paper, I'll write it now . . .'

Stuff jumps to it. With shining eyes he watches the awakened Tredup and says under his breath: 'Christ, Max, where there's skulduggery to be done, you're the best.'

Tredup writes and writes. Then he picks up the piece of paper and hands it to Stuff.

Who merely says: 'You read it. What human being can read that?'

And Tredup reads:

'*Cometh the hour.* All over town, I keep hearing heated commentaries on yesterday's goings-on in our town –'

'That's the right tone,' says Stuff. '"All over town", and then "in our town". Very nice.'

'Truly a black day in the annals of Altholm. But much more important than that is an answer to the question: How are the inhabitants of Altholm responding to the events of Bloody Monday? Are they happy that the farmers, who were guests of our town (their demonstration was officially sanctioned), were beaten down, or are they upset?

I am appalled: everywhere I hear that the farmers are in a mood to cancel the great point-to-point that is due to take place here in three weeks. That was always good for bringing six or seven thousand rural

visitors to our town. God save Altholm from a boycott by the farmers!
Therefore, business leaders, artisans, small entrepreneurs, give us an
opinion: are you supporters of Bloody Monday, or not?

One businessman on behalf of many.'

Stuff holds the sheet in his hands.

'With this single piece of paper you have washed away all your
sins, Tredup, my son. It's a bullseye.'

He races into the typesetting room.

2

The Boycott Becomes Real

I

From time to time, not too frequently, so that the effect is not diluted, Padberg's newspaper, the *Bauernschaft*, issues an appeal, a summons to a Farmers' Parliament.

In almost identical terms, the farmers are called upon to send 'envoys across the land to raise those who work the soil to come to a Parliament for such and such a cause'. Time and place are transmitted by the envoy to the trusted ear, 'to be kept secret from wife and child, townie and businessman, barkeeper and servant'.

No one knows who was responsible for the old-fashioned terms, though the institution itself is of recent date. But they caught on because the farmers were familiar with them from church; at the time country people still read their Bibles.

And the young fellows were happy enough to take their brushed and combed farmhorses out of the stable on a Sunday morning. Bareback, or on an old blanket, or on some ancient estate saddleware, they rode over the land, stopping at each farmhouse.

A halloo from a horn, or the crack of a whip. And earnestly they would invite the emerging 'honest yeoman or husbandman or ploughman, to come on Wednesday of this week to the gorse place hard by Lohstedt, where the ancient burial mounds are, to hold court there over all, be they high or low, who carried the blame for the tragic Monday at Altholm'.

It was Padberg who came up with the place for the Parliament. A salutary change from the dance halls of bars with fading paper chains, and the reek of beer and tobacco, the green boards of stages and bandstands, the memories of women and song!

There, where the spindly umbrella pines stand, where the

golden gorse sprouts, where the scattered blocks of an opened
Hun grave lurk among the dark masses of juniper – there, when
night falls (and the calendar marks a moon), and there is a little
wind, and five thousand farmers and a Parliament . . .

Padberg, having gone off in a huff, has read the morning
papers and been converted. The news has carried far beyond the
province, the Right-wing press stands solidly behind the farmers
and united in condemnation of the police.

And Padberg gets to work. He sees prospects for a cause that
had seemed lost, perhaps a humiliating cudgelling can be par-
layed into a glittering triumph.

While the envoys are riding across the land, he is sitting with
six farmers in Bandekow-Ausbau. He talks to them about the
coming struggle. The doubters and despairers are shown victory
just over the horizon.

'The farmers are in a ferment. Another two or three weeks,
and all that will be left will be the experience of defeat. At the
moment they can still feel the smart of the police nightsticks.
They will do everything to get their own back.'

The count asks: 'Get our own back? We will draw up a protest
resolution. The magistracy, the government, the minister will
just stick it in the bin, and everything will be as it was before.'

'We won't protest, we will act. Every individual farmer will
be given a task. But I'll wait till the Parliament before telling you
about that. No one is to know in advance. And the Parliament
will be ordered like this:

'On top of the biggest boulder we'll have the court of judge
and six honest lay jurymen. One will bring charges against
Altholm, another will defend it –'

'Who's going to defend Altholm?'

'Who but Benthin?'

'No, I'm not going to do that. Not after the way they've treated
me.'

'You'll do it, Cousin. Orders from the Farmers' League. Anyway, you're not really defending it, you're just pretending to.'

'I don't want to do that either, just pretend. I'd sooner really
defend it.'

'All right then! And then there will be a verdict, and you'll see the country rise up, and the Altholmers will cry out, and the government will be reduced to despair, and the revenue departments will knuckle under – and all without violence!'

'You're very optimistic,' says the count. 'I saw you before the demonstration. Things looked good for us then, but you were full of foreboding. Today they look awful, but you're full of good cheer.'

'Those who are brought down shall be raised up,' says Padberg.

'That's not how it goes,' Benthin butts in eagerly.

'That's how it goes with us,' says Padberg. 'Now!'

II

Rural Constable Zeddies-Haselhorst is married to a farmer's daughter, one of the Rohwer girls. And so it came about that by way of women's loose tongues he gets to hear of the time and place of the forthcoming Parliament.

The correct thing to do would have been to notify his sergeant in Stolpe, but to a man living in the country among farmers, what's correct is not always right.

If word gets out who spoke, he won't be able to stay living where he is, and his wife will fall out with her family. The government will send in the militia, and a couple of platoons will scatter the farmers – and Zeddies himself is a farmer's son, who once as a poor drummer-boy capitulated with the Stettin infantry.

So he keeps the promise he made to his wife and doesn't tell anyone. But as night draws in, he doesn't care to be in the garden, or the house, or the woodshed. The stumps he needs to split were never so tough, the *News* carries no news, and the slugs in the strawberries are no fun to look at for a man who spent his day bringing a runaway maid back to her employers, conducting a couple of searches of the premises of thieving farm-labourers, and turning out to support an official on a confiscation order. Can't he have a little joy in his life?

It gets quieter, and then completely quiet. In the cowsheds of his neighbours there is peace, the horses are all out in the pad-docks, the playing children are at home and in bed, even the birds are tucked up. From the meadows that he sees from his bedroom window a fine mist rises, the bright streak on the horizon gets ever darker and dimmer, and the vault of the sky deepens. The stars glint, he counts three shooting stars in five minutes, and as the first one meant 'yes', then the third will mean 'yes' as well.

He gets into some other clothes, without any rush, and listens out to hear what his wife is up to. He ascertains that she's soaking linens in the wash-house, so he goes down the steps in his jacket, round the garden to the woodshed, where he gets out his bicycle.

At the garden fence is his wife's pale face. 'Are you going out at this hour, Heinrich?'

'A swift half at the Krug.'

'You have to leave the bike in Lohstedt and cross Baumgarten's paddock. You remember?'

'Yes . . .'

'Behind that the meadows begin. You go straight across, to the wood.'

'Yes.'

'There you'll find a stream. You'll find it by night in the pas-tures too. Follow it upstream, it's not very deep in summer.'

'But I'll still wind up in the swamp.'

'Everyone says the swamp is deep, but we used to play there all the time when we were little. At the most you'll go in up to your knees, and it's not hard to pull your feet out.'

'People say . . .'

'That there are will-o'-the-wisps and drowned bodies. Baren-thin's father met his end there. But not because the swamp is deep, but because he was pissed. He was lying face down in the muck. All it would have taken would have been for him to lift his head, if he hadn't been so drunk.'

'And will I get all the way to the boulders?'

'To within ten or twenty yards of them. And there's plenty of reeds. But you have to be careful not to rustle.'

'Well, then, I'll go the way you told me.'

'Go on, then.'

He swings himself on to his bicycle and disappears into the gloaming.

He leaves the bicycle behind the school in Lohstedt. Tonight it's better that no one sees him, he can't go to the pub, no one is to know he's here. Lohstedt, incidentally, seems deserted.

Then he crosses the paddock, down to the meadows, through the dew-wet grass.

By the stream, he picks out a willow that's been exploded by frost, a crazy shape, identifiable from all the other trees at a hundred yards, even in moonlight, and that's where he packs his shoes and socks.

Then he rolls up his trouser legs and climbs into the stream. The bed is pure sand, and he makes good progress.

After a while, the water flows more slowly, the banks are flatter, the bottom a little boggy. The pines yield to willow scrub, reeds, thick hummocks of moss.

He makes slow progress here, his feet get bogged down in the mud.

From time to time he stops and wipes his brow. He looks up at the stars and checks his bearings.

Suddenly he stops. There's a smell of smoke. It can't be that the smoke is coming from the boulders already. Anyway, the wind is from the side, if anything.

Who's lit a fire in the swamp?

However much he wants to go to the assembly, his hunter's instincts have been aroused, and he quietly feels his way left.

Here the swamp evens out, fewer hummocks, more willow. The smoke is thicker, the ground drier. A dense bush, and at the top of it, the reddish gleam of a wood fire.

Constable Zeddies stops and stares. He can't go on. If there's someone hiding, every step he takes will warn them of his approach. And there is someone, by the fire, a small fire of sticks.

He remembers something from his boyhood, when he still used to read about Red Indians – Karl May books, and Sitting Bull and the Last of the Mohicans. He goes through his pockets, but all he can find are half a dozen bullets, which would be a waste. They are tightly controlled, and he has to account for each one.

But what can he find to throw in a swamp that offers nothing more solid than soft mud?

He takes a bullet and lobs it towards the fire. It makes a sound like someone rustling in the bushes twenty yards away.

He listens, but nothing stirs.

He throws a second bullet a couple of yards closer to the fire. All quiet.

Three is a waste. The fellow has a sound sleep – well, he'll just have to wake him and chance a beating, if he's a real tramp. But wait? He doesn't have much time, he has to get to the Parliament.

So he makes his way through the bushes as quietly as he can, but it still makes a sound like twenty men, enough to waken any sleeper.

But there is no sleeper when he gets there, to the small, round, cleared space. The fire is all but burned down. The man who set it must have been gone for at least half an hour.

But not completely.

He's coming back. Look at the nest he's made himself.

A woven mesh of willow twigs, two blankets spread on top, dry moss packed underneath, a good kip for a man these rainless summer nights.

And board too. On a flat stone beside the fire is a half-eaten ham. A box of condensed milk. A pile of clothes. A bicycle. More food, and there, hanging on a strap from a branch, a hunting rifle.

Zeddies thinks hard: Are there any break-ins he's read or heard about in the last few weeks? Where does this booty come from?

He really ought to go back right away, wake his colleague in Lohstedt, and try to apprehend the thief. But he can't do that either. How is Zeddies going to be able to explain his wandering around at night, in civvies, in his colleague's patch – without mentioning the Parliament?

The man'll still be there tomorrow, he decides. And once I've been to the Parliament, I'll know better what to say and what not.

He takes the rifle off the branch, cocks it, and strikes it hard several times on the flat stones. Then he tries it out, and grins with satisfaction. You won't be shooting me with that tomorrow.

He hangs the rifle up and goes on his way.

III

It's almost eleven as Zeddies finally nears his objective. The moon is high, but the going is harder and harder: here at the rim of the elevated heath is where swampy water and stream have their source.

Zeddies has heard voices in the distance for some time now. First there were incomprehensible scraps of sound flying past him out of the trees and bushes, then there was a sort of murmured, unbroken monotone, and now . . .

Twenty yards ahead of him is a broad thicket of willow, which he intends to use as a hiding place.

He gets there, pushes himself a long way inside it, and all but leaped straight back out again. The other man's hand clamped itself on his shoulder.

'Easy there, mate!'

He's a very young man, unshaven, his pallor exacerbated by the moonlight, dressed only in trousers and shirt.

'Easy, mate,' he says. 'It's the defence speaking now . . .'

The place offers a decent enough view, the two of them are standing maybe thirty yards from a large boulder at the edge of the swamp. Beyond the rock, the land starts to climb, with a couple of umbrella pines, the twisted splotches of juniper and an army of people, whose faces make one single, indistinguishable blur.

But on the front of the rock there are a couple of people standing; and at the rear, turning their backs to the listeners, a few farmers standing close together, he counts six of them, one of them has a full beard.

'Who is that?' he asks the man sharing his hiding-place.

And he replies: 'Count Bandekow.'

Sure he's the fellow who's sleeping rough, Zeddies thinks again. But he's not your normal tramp or journeyman. Well, he too seems to have his reason not to want to be seen by the farmers. For the moment, we're both secure and in the damp, whatever happens next.

Zeddies can't see the speaker for the defence, the jurors are in the way. He hears an old, high, squeaky voice, increasingly emphatic now in the peroration.

'Yes, my fellow countrymen, what the prosecutor said about Altholm was true enough. But what is Altholm? I too am Altholm. And Altholm means artisans and shopkeepers. Altholm is women and children. Altholm is doctors and bishops.

'I don't know what the judge and jury will decide in their wisdom about Altholm, but consider, my fellow farmers, that the guilty are few in number, and that there are many many people living in Altholm.

'There are only a handful that are guilty. On the marketplace, the man stood and shook my hand and said: "We're both from Altholm, and we'd hate to see injustice happening here."

'But the little people who cut felloes for wheel rims, who lay the fires in the parlour grates, who hammer the shoes for the horse, who sew the collar for the harness, who grind the rye, and sell the paints, who are kith and kin to us – spare them!

'Farmers, spare them!

'They beat us shamefully, they trampled us underfoot, but we will only beat those that beat us. Let the others go free!'

Silence. The jurymen stand up on their rock, the moon is swimming overhead, so steep that people's shadows are practically underfoot, a soft breeze momentarily rustles leaf and twig – then silence again.

The judge speaks: 'Accuser, you have the floor.'

And Padberg steps up, right to the edge of the rock, and he stares out over the assembled listeners.

'Peasants of Pomerania,' he says, 'who have come in the night-time, summoned to the due Parliament over the town of Altholm!

'There were three thousand of you there on that day. We were guests of the town, we had spoken to the mayor and to the police; the streets, marketplace and auction hall, all were given over to us. We were guests of Altholm.'

Padberg leans out on his rock, stares at the crowd, as though looking for one particular individual among them, one face in the mass.

Suddenly he shouts: 'Hey, oldster! Can you still feel the

militiaman's rubber truncheon? It was the first blow you felt since you were out of short trousers, that was Altholm conferring the blue badge of honour upon you!

'And you, agricultural college student! Wasn't that fun, when the town constables chased you out of the hall to the station, and then drove you out of the station into the outlying streets? They were staging a rabbit race with you. Wanted to let you know how the rabbits feel when your father hunts them. That's the type of education they give you in Altholm.

'And you there, peasant with six horses! Remember how they smacked you with the flat of their swords so hard that your wife sat up half the night, cooling the broken skin. The official report makes mention of two injured. Altholm! There were three thousand injured, three thousand immedicably injured!

'The defence lawyer agrees: yes, they dealt harshly with you that day – but who dealt harshly? One man. One ambitious individual, seeking to ride roughshod over the farmers. But the mass of the people is innocent. So he said.

'I, though, tell you this, farmers: the people are just as guilty. Who lined the pavements and watched? Did you happen to look up at the windows and see them all packed?

'Yes, yes, they couldn't have saved you, but could they not at least have gone away? Did they have to stand there watching? Did you hear so much as one person boo? We have the saying that "silence indicates consent".

'Well, Altholm consented!'

The speaker pauses. The farmers are still silent, Zeddies can only sense them from back where he is, but nevertheless a feeling went through them like the first puff of warm wind before a thunderstorm. The moon is so bright, and it is so dark, and it were better he had stayed at home and known nothing about all this. The young fellow next to him has his face in his hands and is half lying on the willow twigs – perhaps he's crying, perhaps he's asleep.

Padberg resumes:

'The speaker for the defence said there are workmen, there are relatives, there are people in those buildings in town who may not be to blame in any way, and we should spare them.

'Farmers! They are precisely the ones who are guilty! They are the ones you must punish! Not the police lackey, not the fat mayor, they are not the guilty ones, your relations are, your in-laws! The smith who shoes your horse, the carpenter who repairs your roof, they are the guilty ones!

'Gareis is a Red, and Frerksen is a Red – we've known that for years. And for years too, ever since the Revolution, since before the Revolution, since before the War, we've known what the Reds bring into our lives: Expropriation! Robbery! Theft! Drudgery! Immorality! Godlessness!

'But who gave those officials sway over us? Did they turn up one day and seize the mayor's chair by force?

'No, they were elected!

'Elected by your kith and kin, by your artisans, your shopkeepers! That's why they're all to blame!

'Did the poor townies not know what they were doing?

'They knew. But that's the townie for you: making deals with every Tom, Dick and Harry, always dickering, on terms with everyone.

'Therefore, farmers, show no mercy! Punish them hard, the Altholmers, bring them to their senses so that they chase away their officials. Then take the punishment from their shoulders.

'And so I urge you: farmers of Pomerania, find guilty the town of Altholm with all those who dwell in it, who go about their trade, with officials and workers, policemen and women. They are all guilty.'

The crowd is silent.

The judge steps forward. Count Bandekow stands at the front, with his high top-boots, the sweated sheepskin, the foot-muff. His hand slices the air.

Then he speaks: 'Peasants of Pomerania, all those of you who live from the soil, if you have heard, then say: "We have heard."'

A dull, murmurous groundswell goes up: 'We have heard.'

'Peasants of Pomerania, if you have found guilty the police of Altholm of the crimes of Bloody Monday, then say: "They are guilty."'

A dull groundswell: 'Guilty.'

'Peasants of Pomerania, if beyond that you have found guilty the town of Altholm with all who live in it, then say: "It is guilty!"'

And again: 'Guilty.'

The voices have become louder and louder, by now the peasants are yelling.

The judge cuts through the air again and silence slowly returns.

'Prosecutor, what is the penalty you demand for the town of Altholm?'

The judge steps back, the prosecutor steps forward.

Padberg takes a piece of paper from his pocket and unfolds it. Everyone can tell from the size of the paper: it is a newspaper.

'You have all heard: the murderer has no peace, he returns to the spot, today or tomorrow, his conscience will give him no rest.

'And if you hadn't found it guilty, the town of Altholm, then you would be able to read a confession of its guilt. It is plagued by a dirty conscience.

'It is written here in the Altholm *Chronicle*. I will read you two sentences:

'"I am appalled, everywhere I keep hearing that the farmers are not going to hold their riding tournament in Altholm."

'And again:

'"May God protect Altholm from the farmers' boycott!"

'Here, the guilty conscience has devised its own punishment. No God will come forward to protect it.

'Peasants of Pomerania, I demand that the countryside impose a boycott on the town of Altholm, until it has been punished for its wickedness, until it has chased away its politicians and is at one with us again.

'Let that be its punishment!'

Padberg steps back and a vast noise erupts. All speak, shout, murmur, threaten, shake their fists, argue, dispute, shout 'Hurrah!', shout 'Boo!'

The judge vainly waves his hands, no one will listen to him.

The young fellow in the bushes says: 'There are too many farmers here who earn their living from Altholm.'

And the rural constable: 'It will break up in disagreement, I know my farmers.'

A voice speaks up: 'But the farmers don't know you, whoever you are!'

And two iron hands grasp at the two of them.

Constable Zeddies-Haselhorst needs about five seconds to make up his mind. If the tall peasant with the thin lips and the cold eyes who has him in his grip succeeds in dragging him to the rock, three hundred – no, a thousand – peasants will know who he is, and he will be doomed.

And even if they let him go without breaking his bones, he will still be lost. What will he say to his superiors, his colleagues at work, his farming in-laws?

Five seconds – and the grip on his collar is iron. He has to free himself, and so he drives his knee up hard into the man's groin. The man gives a stifled groan – he's winded – and crumples over. But still holding the collar in his iron grip, which Zeddies is barely able to break.

Zeddies looks at the man sprawled in the swampy water, half starting to run, when the other fellow, the young man in shirt and trousers, starts yelling at the top of his voice: 'Farmers! Here! Traitor! Farmers, help!'

At that, Zeddies delays no longer, he jumps into the water, which splashes up around his face, and runs as fast as he can with heavy, club feet. He can hear heavy sticks coming down either side of him, and stones splashing the water.

Zeddies runs, but can hardly leave the spot. There ahead of him is the willow bush where he found the thief's nest. What an idiot I am for bending the lock on the rifle! How good it would be to have that in my possession now!

And he thinks about the young, unshaven burglar.

Suddenly he cracks it. I could slap myself for not realizing that half an hour ago: that man is Thiel, the young bomber, I saw his picture on the wanted list. He escaped from the detention cell in Stolpe. Now I must get back and report him.

Twenty paces further on: they don't seem to be pressing me too hard. Or will I not report seeing him? I may as well forget about him, the farmers have got him again.

He reaches the stream, whose bed is firmer underfoot.

IV

They raised the winded man on to the rock. There he sits, face in hands, still bent double with pain.

Thiel is right at the back, with Padberg, he was lucky to be spotted by someone who knew him, if he'd fallen into the hands of the farmers, he'd be in a deal of trouble.

Benthin leans over to the groaning man and talks to him. Then Bandekow, one of the jurymen, another, more.

Confused rumours buzz through the horde of waiting farmers. Their leader has been set free, only to be murdered here in the swamp. The fellow in the dirty shirt is the police spy who was supposed to do it. No, he's the one who saved his life. The son of a farmer from outside Stolpe. The flag-bearer Henning, who's broken out of prison.

Two jurymen help the winded man on to his feet, he puts his arms round their shoulders, they take him by the hips, so standing he faces his farmers.

'They have released me,' thus Franz Reimers slowly, 'from the prisons of the Republic. Why, I am unable to say. All I know is that they will come for me again, today, tomorrow, some time. And some of you with me.

'But they let me go at a good time. My wife, who sent me here, told me in a few words what is at stake tonight. So why wait, speak, deliberate? When you fall into the sea, do you start swimming or think about it first?'

Farmer Reimers pauses.

'The gentlemen in Berlin are playing a game of cat and mouse with us. And the administration in Stolpe and Altholm have to do what the minister with the Polish name wants done with German farmers. But cat and mouse is a game best played in the dark, and there's the odd cat that's found out the hard way that its mouse was actually a bulldog.

'You're wondering whether to ostracize the town of Altholm?' There is silence. The crowd waits in suspense.

Suddenly very loud: 'Doesn't the Bible say: "an eye for an eye, a tooth for a tooth"? Aren't children punished for the fourth or fifth generation for the sins of their fathers? Are you too cowardly to perform God's Will?'

He pushes away the arms that are supporting him. He stands there alone, a dark, slender form, his arms down by his sides. He speaks loudly:

'We, the peasants of Pomerania, do hereby ostracize the treacherous town of Altholm!

'No one is to dine or sup with an Altholmer, buy anything from him, receive any present from him, lend him anything. You are not to bid them the time of day, or speak an unnecessary word with them. Whoever has family in Altholm, tell them that from now on they are to keep away from land and farm until the boycott is over.

'Whoever was in the habit of going to the weekly market at Altholm, may continue. He may sell, but not buy. Whoever delivered eggs or butter or potatoes or poultry or wood to Altholm, should stay away from the town, because you are to set foot in no dwelling therein.

'See to it that your wives do as instructed by the Farmers' League, that they not buy anything in the shops of Altholm, nor purchase anything in the stores of the Jews.

'Whoever contravenes the rules of the boycott, in ways great or small, knowingly or unwittingly, he shall be as though he were from Altholm, with the despised people, no one shall speak to him, and none shall know him.'

The farmer stops. Padberg leans over to him and whispers something.

Reimers says: 'There was a spy among us, we know not who, but we shall find out. What the man has heard does not bother us, for tomorrow the whole land will know that we have ostracized Altholm. If we meet secretly and in the dark, it's merely lest the bailiffs of the Republic disperse us.'

With raised voice: 'Now go home, farmers!'

3

The Reconciliation Committee at Work

At the corner of Calvinstrasse and Propstenstrasse the garden of the wholesaler Manzow abuts on that of the haberdasher Meisel. Both men are on the town council. Manzow as council leader, even – the outcome of a deal with the SPD – while Meisel, a bundle of energy, remains Altholm's unofficial news bureau.

It's a fine July morning, not too hot, a cool breeze is coming in off the sea, taking the edge off the sun and stirring the leaves in the garden where Manzow is taking a stroll. He has just crawled out of bed, drunk a pot of black coffee, and is trying to get the taste of yesterday's booze-up out of his mouth with a lot of chaw.

Manzow has two nicknames in Altholm: the 'White Negro' and the 'Children's Friend'. White Negro on account of his features, the thick lips, low forehead and frizzy hair, and Children's Friend, because . . .

He's in the habit of peeking over the fences of the neighbouring gardens, even though he knows all the mothers have strictly told their little ones not to make peepee in the garden, or indeed anywhere else near Manzow's fence. It's not impossible that an adorable little creature of eight or nine might . . .

But it's his Party colleague Meisel, master of a four-storey emporium and a team of seventy rag-and-bone men, whom he sees.

'Morning, Franz.'

'Morning, Emil.'

'Did you stay up late last night?'

'Till five. There was a jumped-up policeman who tried to tell us that three was the curfew hour. I told him where to go.'

'Really?' Meisel is listening keenly.

'I wrote out a bye-law, saying that in my capacity as leader of the council I was delaying the curfew until six o'clock.'

'Wonder what Gareis will say to that?'

'Gareis? Nothing! Do you think he can afford to make trouble for me now that the boycott's begun and the point-to-point is off?'

'I went to the station earlier,' says Meisel, 'to get a shave. Punte says he's going to have to let three apprentices go. The farmers have stopped coming in for a shave or a trim.'

'Gareis ought to shave them himself – he probably remembers how from his old man.'

'I think Gareis has been soft-soaping the farmers for long enough.'

The men cackle, and a few birds are scared off.

'Krüger at the station says he's down two hectolitres on market days.'

'All the small businesses are complaining.'

'I'll tell you something,' says Manzow pompously. 'You know my business. I never had all that much custom from the town. But the pedlars used to come and buy from me: haberdashery, scents, soaps, braces, material, all their stock in fact.

'And now they're saying they can't buy from me any more. The farmers ask them: Where are you from? – Altholm. – Then you just go back to Altholm. – No one's buying.'

'Everyone from Altholm has a tale to tell. The travelling salesmen in oils and lubricants and machine parts – they're being chased off the farms. The farmers have got themselves a list of all the Altholm plates.'

'It's madness,' moans Manzow. 'Are we going to have a drink before the meeting, by the way?'

'Sure. – And Meckel, who runs the driving school, he says he's lost seventeen pupils from the country districts.'

'The agricultural college has no one at all registered for autumn.'

'Yes, and all the while that ridiculous Frerksen is running around in his uniform, more full of himself than ever.'

'Don't say that. Don't you know he went to Stolpermünde on

holiday? They managed to get rid of him inside a week, do you know how? Every morning there was fresh shit on his sandcastle, and their rooms were crawling with bugs.'

'Apparently his son said that when the demonstration was over he said all the farmers were criminals and deserved to be beaten to death . . .'

'Even Frerksen's own parents said Fritz shouldn't have gone after the farmers with sabres.'

'They've stopped talking to each other.'

'Gareis can't keep him any longer.'

'Well, we'll hear about that later today. You are coming, aren't you?'

'Absolutely.'

'And we'll have a little drink beforehand, so it's not so dull?'

'Tucher's all right with you?'

'I'd rather Lieschen's myself. Then we can get in a bit of filth as well.'

'Keen on the little girls again, are we?'

'Always. Always. Pluck the rose before it blows.'

'Wonderful. I must tell my missus that.'

The men go off into another round of cackles, and the birds get another fright.

II

At twelve noon in Mayor Gareis's big office some thirty gentlemen are assembled: the masters of the guilds, the representatives of the various retail associations, the manufacturers, the director of the Revenue Department, Revenue Councillor Berg, Heinsius and Pinkus from the fourth estate, a man of the cloth, Bishop Schwarz, a cinema owner, the entire magistracy and numerous town councillors.

The gentlemen are in animated conversation, everyone has some piece of frightful news to share. The press is busy taking notes.

Still no Gareis.

'What's keeping him?'

'He's still in negotiations about the horse tournament.'

'Golly, if that goes down the pan too! Six thousand farmers spending all of three days in Altholm!'

'Six thousand? Make that ten. Gareis has done some real damage.'

'Gareis? I blame Frerksen!'

Medical Councillor Dr Lienau – the Stahlhelm badge prominent on his lapel – leaps into action: 'Gareis? Frerksen? They're all one and the same, if you ask me. Pinko trash. What I want to know is where's Stuff, the only nationalist reporter here?'

Heinsius of the *News* knows. 'Stuff's not been invited.'

'What? Not invited! And you of the press stand for it? Where's your solidarity?'

'He wrote about police terror.'

'Well? And wasn't that what it was? Anyway, aren't you now working for the same boss?'

'Oh no. We're nothing to do with Herr Stuff. Completely separate editorially.'

'I can't believe our press representatives –'

'Ssh! Gareis!'

'Gareis!'

'Gareis!!'

He walks in, bigger than all of them, heavier than all of them. Greets a few people here and there. Almost while still moving, behind his chair, the chairback in his hand, he starts to speak: 'Gentlemen, please sit down.'

Scrapes of chair legs, whispers, a certain amount of toing and froing.

And Gareis is off: 'Gentlemen. Thank you for coming. A warm welcome to the distinguished representatives of commerce, trade and craft in our town, to the authorities, the church and, last but not least, the press.'

A voice growls: 'Where's Stuff?'

'Correct. There is no Stuff here. Would have had no business being here either, as he wasn't invited. – Today's subject is known to all of you: the farmers' boycott, and our measures against it.

'One other thing before we get going. The demonstration – "Bloody Monday" as the absent press representative so effectively and destructively dubbed it – remains off the agenda.

'We here, gentlemen, can't make up our minds whether mistakes were made. Every one of us is touched to some degree. The minister has called for a report. That's where the decision will be made.

'So I would ask you kindly to keep the events of Monday out of the discussion.'

Pause. Gareis begins afresh – really, he does.

'Gentlemen, we all know that the movement that goes by the name of the Bauernschaft imposed its boycott against our town as a protest against the behaviour of the Altholm police.

'I'll pass over the fact that this boycott is very premature and unjust in its application, setting aside the question of its justification. You might say that at this moment in time the farmers aren't able to be patient and just.

'And I'll just quickly make the point that this boycott affects only the innocent. If the police really are the guilty parties, I and those under me continue to draw their salaries. You are the ones to suffer.'

'Quite right!'

'The farmers' leaders can't have overlooked that. If they wanted to impose their boycott regardless, that seems to me to indicate that they are driven more by propaganda objectives than indignation about the 26th of July.

'And I can also let you into the secret that the farmers are by no means united behind this boycott. In confidence I tell you that there were animated scenes at their nocturnal meeting on the Lohstedt Heath. My source assures me that it was the intervention of Reimers at the eleventh hour that brought victory. It was not an idea that came from the farmers. My source –'

'Will you name names?!'

'You'd like that, wouldn't you, Medical Councillor? But I'm not in the business of betraying my sources.'

'I don't care for –'

'Nothing, Councillor. Here we play by my rules. You're free to go if you don't like what I'm telling you. –

'Now all that may be as it is, but we're saddled with the boy-cott. The town is full of wild rumours of the effectiveness of the boycott. Gentlemen, don't let yourselves be taken in. The boy-cott has very little effect –'

'Oho!'

'Tripe!'

'It's ruinous!'

'Absolutely!'

'– Altholm is an industrial town. Its purchasing power is vested in the proletariat. Surely you won't suppose the farmers have ever done much buying in Altholm? After they've finished mar-keting, maybe the good wife would buy some thread, and the man a glass of beer. Nothing of any consequence.

'Yes, the odd travelling salesman has been sent packing. But rest assured, the farmers wouldn't have bought anything off him anyway, farmers aren't flush before harvest-time. It's just a glori-ous excuse for the farmer to say: "You're from Altholm, so I'm not buying anything."

'But gentlemen, even if things were different, even if the boy-cott were catastrophic, we could still do nothing worse than talk it up. If we keep saying: "Boycott, what boycott? The boycott is just a rumour propagated by the *Bauernschaft* newspaper" – then, gentlemen, the boycott will be over inside a month.

'We need to combat ignorance in our own town. Of course we can't have merchant Schulze, who has had thirty pairs of trousers hanging in his shop that no one wants, going to merchant Schmidt and saying: "That farmers' boycott has cost me thirty pairs of trousers in sales." And we can't have continual agitation in the press, little disturbing news items, much less continual talk about police terror. In our moment of need we have to stand together.

'Here among us we have the editor Herr Heinsius, a loyal son to our town, and a passionate supporter of patriotic causes. I think he will today agree to wrap a cloak of silence around the events of the 26th of July. You shrug your shoulders, Herr Hein-sius, but I can see you will soon be nodding your head.'

Rehfelder barracks: 'Stuff! Editor Stuff!'

'Gentlemen, let's not worry our heads about Stuff. I think

you're underestimating the power and influence of Herr Heinsius here. If Herr Heinsius declares the moderate press will be
silent, then Herr Stuff will be silent with it. – And of course, Herr
Heinsius, I'm silent myself.

'Those were two things I wanted to put to you: deny the effect
of the boycott. Silence on the 26th of July.

'The third – well, I don't exactly want to impose a counter-
boycott on the farmers. I'm quite happy for them to continue to
come to market here. But if gentlemen here would tell their lady
wives to support our own local businesses in their purchases,
especially when it's a matter of farm produce . . . well, I'm sure
such a modest hint would have its effect too. We know who wears
the trousers where the men in this room are concerned . . .'

Grateful laughter.

'Gentlemen, all round me I see contented, mirthful faces. You
know some things may look black from a distance, but closer to
they're more like white. There's one thing you may be sure of,
the inconvenience the farmers are putting us to right now is tiny
compared to the advantages we enjoy on the other side.'

'Piffle!'

'I have started talks with a number of workers' associations.
They are almost universally of the view that Altholm should be,
so to speak, compensated for the losses occurring through the
farmers. The workers will hold their meetings in Altholm.

'All of that will bring footfall and increased custom to our town.
And, compared to that, the cancellation – or postponement – of
the equestrian event is really rather minor.

'I now throw open the floor.'

Mayor Gareis sits down abruptly and, with lowered eyelids,
awaits the storm that his last announcement is bound to provoke.

III

Political Adviser Stein, the dark, bespectacled little man, gets up
and nervously reads from a piece of paper: 'First to ask to speak
was Chairman Besen. I call upon Herr Besen to speak.'

Political Adviser Stein ducks back among the bobbing and
weaving heads. The chairman of the Guild of Landlords and
Publicans rises under his crown of white hair. 'Well, gentlemen,
what shall I say . . .?'

'If you don't know, don't bother!'

'What shall I say? As usual, Mayor Gareis has given us a super
little speech, and I think won over almost all of us. I came here
feeling pessimistic, Altholm is quite depressed at the moment,
and then the farmers' boycott on top of that, which is affecting
the hospitality industry very badly . . . But when I heard the proposals of the mayor, I thought: Yes, that will work . . .

'Yes, gentlemen, and then we hear offhand that the riding
competition has been cancelled. And we are comforted by some
vague promise of workers' meetings, well, who knows?

'I certainly don't want to upset the mayor and his Party. But
we publicans know what workers get through at such meetings,
and what farmers get through. And I have to say, Mayor, with
respect, you can bring all the labour organizations in the world to
Altholm and they won't make up for the one horse show.

'I would also like to stress that it was the *Chronicle* – for which the
mayor had so little good to say today – that first drew attention to
the boycott several days ago, and the possibility of the tournament
being cancelled. I went to see you that day, Mayor, and you told me
that wasn't true, the horse show was staying in Altholm. It seems it
wasn't the *Chronicle* that was unreliable, but yourself . . .

'So, gentlemen, we in the hospitality sector have held a sur-
vey on the losses we incur through missing out on the horse
show. We carefully checked the figures we were given, we made
adjustments, and even then we reached the horrendous number
of twenty-one thousand marks. Representatives of other sectors
will no doubt have their own submissions to make . . .

'In view of these facts, I'm inclined to think we shouldn't get
into a tussle with the farmers, and make no mistake about it,
what the mayor is proposing is a fight.

'Almost all of us are connected in some way to the countryside, and I suggest we make use of our connections. I suggest we
elect a committee to work on a reconciliation with the farmers,

and that this committee gets round the negotiating table with farmers' representatives at an early date.'

Chairman Besen has said his piece and Political Adviser Stein gives Medical Councillor Dr Lienau the floor.

'Gentleman, look at the mess we're in! The three of us, representatives of the Nationalist movement, have issued warning after warning, but has anyone listened to us? Of course not. They wanted compromises with the Reds, and now we're up the creek!

'We've just listened to the rather astonishing presumption of Mayor Gareis, who invites us here only to say, yes, I'm afraid the police have made a rickets of things, does anyone have an idea how to make them better again.

'I move that we assembled here deplore the recent police terror, and express profound regret to the farmers.'

'Merchant Braun has the floor.'

'Yes, gentlemen, I feel rather like Herr Besen. I too was pessimistic, then a little hopeful, and now I see everything in pretty bleak terms. The suggestion I want to make is combining the mayor's position with Herr Besen's. In other words, try to negate the boycott, and open immediate talks.'

'Bishop Schwarz.'

'Sirs! I represent no material interests. I assume too, that I have only been asked to listen. But as a representative of the Church, I would like to warn against setting out on the road that Mayor Gareis urges.

'We are supposed to say that the boycott is ineffectual, even though we hear on every side of the damage that it does. We are thus being asked, putting it bluntly, to lie. But, gentlemen, it has always been the case that in the long run honesty is the best policy.

'As a representative of the Church, I can only urge peace. Make your peace with the farmers. Gentlemen, Herr Besen's proposal is the right one: elect a committee, negotiate with the farmers. And do what Medical Councillor Lienau says as well: express your regret. You can do that without taking a position. Without getting into the whys and wherefores of the thing, it does remain humanly regrettable. Say as much. There's no disgrace to that, no need to feel ashamed.

'If you follow that path, you will be sure of the support of the Holy Church.'

'Editor-in-chief Heinsius, of the *News*.'

'Gentlemen, respected listeners! You all know how rarely I leave my editor's office. I trust to the electric spark to carry news of what's going on in the world into my little cubbyhole. Only when a man is quiet, away from the fuss and bother of opinions, is his ear acute enough to hear the pulse-beat of time.

'If I have departed from habit on this occasion, if I, as the representative of the greatest newspaper of our town, condescend to enter the arena of dispute and make so bold as to address you, then it's only because from the very outset we have followed the developments with great concern.

'Even when the demonstration was first bruited as a plan, we pricked up our ears and asked ourselves: Where will all this end?

'And then, when it actually happened, when the lamentable clashes took place, when the ghost of the boycott first appeared like a menacing shadow on the wall, and then became actuality, then, my dear sirs, then, with waxing concern, we asked ourselves: Where will all this end . . .?

'When the mayor spoke of the press stirring things up, he certainly can't have meant the *News*. The *News* is not a partisan paper, the *News* transcends party, the *News* is governed only by the consideration of what is in the best interests of our town.

'And then, when we examine these interests, when we submit to dispassionate scrutiny, as we must, then the question arises . . .

'I see here gentlemen from manufacturing, from trade, from finance. The clerisy is represented. Many councillors. The magistracy.

'But, gentlemen, the question arises: Where is Oberbürgermeister Niederdahl?!?

'Where is the leader of our community in the hour of danger? Councillor Röstel is standing in for him, good. But, gentlemen, there are situations where a stand-in is not good enough, where only the helmsman's hand is strong enough to wrench round the tiller.

'Gentlemen, where is our helmsman?'

'Homeowner Herr Gropius.'

'Gentlemen, I come to you on behalf of the private home-owning sector, and as the representative of the Reichswirtschafts-partei.

'Gentlemen, we raised our voice in warning when the construction of five new public conveniences was approved. Gentlemen, we warned you when the supplementary town taxes were raised by sixty-five per cent. Gentlemen, you know our watchword: cut expenditure, cut taxation. Gentlemen, even in this weighty hour, you find us where you always find us: with finger upraised in warning. Don't carry on down this ruinous road!

'Gentlemen, on behalf of private real-estate ownership, and of the Reich Economic Party, we as responsible citizens declare: We will vote against any measure that incurs new expenditure.

'Gentlemen, you have been warned!'

'Party Member Matthies!'

Straight away, a lively discussion sets in.

'Gentlemen! The class-conscious proletariat looks on with a mocking grin at the way the Social Democrats have once more fared. Those betrayers of the proletarian –'

'Stick to the subject.'

'"Comrade" Gareis asks me to stick to the subject. But right at the outset he has forbidden us to speak on the subject. Gentlemen, a veil of shame is to be draped over the deeds of our blood-thirsty police –'

'Get to the point! Or we'll have the next speaker.'

'Comrades! The proletariat is in no way surprised by events. Even now, hundreds of thousands of workers are languishing in tens of thousands of bourgeois jails, brought in under and at the hands of Social Democrats!'

'Next speaker!'

'When a hundred workers are clubbed down, Comrade Severing doesn't mention it.'

'You are not allowed to go on speaking. Next speaker.'

'But if a couple of farmers get a whack across their thick skulls, then there's hell to pay.'

'Would you like me to have you escorted outside, Matthies?'

'We in the KPD seem to exist under a different dispensation. We are not permitted to speak at this assembly, even when others can speak as much as they want to.'

'If you agree to speak on the subject, then you can speak.'

'I will speak on the subject. Comrades! The class-conscious proletariat wants none of your November Socialism! It's nothing but the handmaiden of the bourgeoisie, and the blood-dripping executioner of the disempowered worker.'

'Hoo! Hoo!'

'Long live the USSR!'

'Quiet!'

'Usher, will you escort the gentleman outside.'

Whistles. Laughter. Shouts. Catcalls.

Matthies, in the doorway: 'Long live the Soviet Republic! Long live the World Revolution!'

Exit.

Mayor Gareis rises to his feet.

'Gentlemen, I just want to answer some of the points that have been put to me.

'So far as the riding tournament is concerned, it's true that I told you, Herr Besen, that it would definitely take place in Altholm.

'Well, I was disappointed. I relied on a man's word of honour, and I will even give you his name: it is Count Pernath from Stroheim. When we laid out the course last year, when we built the spectator stands at great cost, the count promised me – we shook hands – that the tournament would take place in Altholm for at least the next five years.

'Yesterday, I received a letter from him, saying that in view of the changed circumstances, it would not be held in Altholm.

'I leave it to the gentlemen to judge the behaviour of this man of honour.'

'Faugh!'

'Yes, "faugh", indeed, Medical Councillor, and to Count Pernath. – As far as the "warning" in the *Chronicle*, that Chairman Besen referred to, I have it here in front of me. It is not an editorial passage, it is an anonymous reader's letter.

'This letter appeared at a time when the farmers were not

even thinking of a boycott. That, to me, is an instance of stirring things up, gentlemen. Of course, the conduct of the measured and praiseworthy *News* is beyond reproach.

'Herr Heinsius asked why Oberbürgermeister Neiderdahl is absent from our deliberations. All I can say by way of reply is that he is on holiday, being kept continually informed. He is prepared at a moment's notice to break off his holiday. He stressed that. I deemed it unnecessary.

'Gentlemen, as the tournament shows, our situation is that of a town surrounded by enemies. We may expect help from government, but I have no idea when. For now, there is nothing so needful as that we stand together and fight together.

'The suggestion has been made that we sit down and negotiate with the farmers. But, gentlemen, you won't sit down round a table with farmers, at best you will find yourselves opposite some so-called farmers' leaders, hoping to take advantage of the difficulties of others.'

'Disgraceful!'

'Yes, I find it disgraceful too. But that's how it is. – No weakness, gentlemen, don't negotiate. Oppose the stubborn Pomeranian farmers with the stubborn Pomeranian townies.

'Be united, gentlemen.

'Now I invite Political Adviser Stein to speak on a technical matter.'

The slim, dark-haired, nervous little fellow gets up.

'Respected gentlemen, as some of you may know, I am an official in the welfare department, which is responsible for physically and legally looking after the illegitimate children of the town.

'We have heard complaints about the losses accruing to the town from the cancellation of the tournament. Chairman Besen named a sum, a frightening sum: twenty-one thousand marks.

'Well, gentlemen, the town is to lose that much and more, because certainly other sectors will have figures of their own to match. But what, I ask myself, could possibly be gained by the cancellation of the tournament? I should like to make a small counter-reckoning, if you'll be patient with me for a few moments.'

Political Adviser Stein, grown a little self-assured, smiles round at the expectant faces.

'Yes, I'm wondering, couldn't the town draw some benefit perhaps from the fact that the tournament isn't being held? I'm not talking about direct costs that the town incurs, and that came to nine thousand marks last year. I have something else in mind.

'Gentlemen, imagine the farm lads coming into town for a week, give or take. They come with a little money in their pockets, and they have a bit to eat and drink, and they live it up a bit.

'Well, I'm sure you'll agree the town girls are better looking than the country girls. They take more trouble, are better turned-out, even a farm lad will see that.

'And when I come to look at the new arrivals some nine months later, I find confirmation of the extent to which the farm lads have managed to find favour with the town girls. This year, fourteen illegitimate children appeared on our books, all the product of last year's tournament.

'Well, gentlemen, you'll say that's not so bad, those are farm boys, they'll pay up. And then we approach the fathers – those of the farm boys, I mean – and they moan and groan, and it's all how expensive the boy is to feed and clothe, and that he doesn't earn any money. And now he'll have to go to winter school, and then he'll have to be put through agricultural college for a couple of years, and the help he gives on the farm really isn't worth mentioning, and certainly not worth pocket money.

'And in the end it's the town that's left, so to speak, holding the baby. Now I'll invite you to do some sums: fourteen children, first through infant care, then a children's home, then an apprenticeship or traineeship. A town can't raise a child for less than five thousand marks.

'That makes seventy thousand, the lot. Add in the running costs of the competition, seventy-nine thousand marks. That's quite a bit of damage to make up, if you ask me.'

Political Adviser Stein sits down, and his pallid little cheeks are flushed.

Gales of laughter.

Bishop Schwarz rises and agitatedly says: 'I object to the frivolous way this whole sorry subject has been broached by a representative of the State. If quarters where one might look for the setting of a good example judge moral questions in such a –'

'It wasn't judging!'

'What do you mean, "wasn't judging"? It was flippantly spoken of, and that amounts to the same thing. Unfortunately, the Church community all too rarely finds support from the town council in moral matters. The removal of bushes and benches in the old cemetery that were propitious for nocturnal indecency had to be done at Church expense. Gentlemen, please, on the very graves of the departed!'

Gareis stands up.

'What Political Adviser Stein had to say was a question of political economy, and nothing to do with morality.

'I don't think further debate will take us forward, so let me close our session today. I ask you, gentlemen, to vote on my proposals. Those in favour of the three positions I advanced, kindly raise their hands. –

'That's a minority. So you choose to decline my suggestions. I'm sorry I can be of no further assistance at the moment. – Herr Besen?'

'One moment, if you please, Herr Mayor. There is another proposal on the agenda, namely to enter into immediate negotiations with the Bauernschaft. Can we please vote on that?'

'By all means. You've heard me warn you against it.'

'Those who support negotiations, raise their hands. – That's a big majority. Thank you, gentlemen. It only remains for us to name the members of the committee, for which I would like to suggest the name 'Reconciliation Committee'. I would like to start by nominating Mayor Gareis.'

'I decline. And as for the rest of the nominations, would the gentlemen have the kindness to conduct them elsewhere, for instance in the Ratskeller. I'd rather not have a procedure of which I so thoroughly disapprove conducted in my rooms.'

Medical Councillor Dr Lienau remarks audibly: 'In other words: If things don't go the way Herr Gareis wants, you're out on your ear.'

'That's right, Medical Councillor, you're out on your ear. Good day, gentlemen.'

IV

A farmer emerges from Altholm Station and crosses the fore-court in the direction of the *Chronicle* building. The farmer, a large, heavy-built man, labours along with a stick. But he won't be put off by cars, and makes straight for the policeman who's controlling the traffic.

He comes to a stop in front of the official and looks at him stubbornly. 'Officer,' he says.

The policeman, supposing some directions are required from him, says: 'Yes?'

The farmer asks: 'Where do I leave him? Will you take him?'

'Him? Whom do you mean?'

'Who I mean? Him! My stick! I've heard it said we farmers have to hand in our sticks when we come to Altholm.'

'Get along with you! I won't have my leg pulled by the likes of you.'

'Where's my other stick?' asks the farmer, in a sudden temper. 'The one you took off me on Bloody Monday.'

He looks with cold fury at the irritated officer.

'Just move along, I said.'

'You take sticks away from invalids, eh? So they fall down on the pavement? Some heroes you are.'

The farmer stumps off towards the *Chronicle*, the officer crossly watching him.

Inside the *Chronicle*, Stuff and Tredup are arguing again.

'You're crazy, Max, with your crush on Gareis. He's the worst of the flaming lot.'

'No, it's just that he's not keen on you, because you keep

attacking him! Anyway, it's by no means certain that he wrote the article in the *Volkszeitung*.'

'Of course he wrote it. Accusing me of fabricating readers' letters! "Why shouldn't the editor of the *Chronicle* count among its readers?"'

'Come on, Stuff, it was hardly a bona fide letter, was it?'

'What business is it of his! Anyway, we were right. The boycott's up and running, and the tournament was cancelled. – Enter!'

The door opens to the dispatch office, which once again is deserted. There at the counter stands a large man, a farmer. Stuff walks over to him.

'Hello. What can I do for you?'

'I'm Farmer Kehding from Karolinenhorst. Are you the fellow that writes the newspaper?'

'That's me.'

'What's your name, then?'

'Stuff. Hermann Stuff.'

'Then you're the man I want. I thought I was at the *News* here.'

'No, no, this is the *Chronicle* all right.'

'Then I've come to the right place.'

Pause.

The man picks up his stick and lays it on the counter.

'This is the stick from the official report.'

'Oh yeah?' says Stuff.

'You printed it, didn't you! This is the stick in the report that was described as being three inches thick and a dangerous weapon.'

'And you got it back?'

'Nah! This is that stick's brother. – How much d'you reckon I weigh?'

Stuff has a guess: 'Sixteen stone?'

'Seventeen, not bad. And I suffer from gout. Can I walk with a little bamboo wand, then? Dangerous weapon – don't make me laugh.'

'You're right.'

'But you printed it.'

'I printed the official report. But I printed quite a few things besides.'

''Course you did. And now I want you to print something else. A letter. A reader's letter, signed with my full name. It's all written down here.'

It's an open letter to the Altholm administration, with the eight-day demand that the guilty Police Inspector Frerksen and the guilty Mayor Gareis be dismissed forthwith, otherwise the farmers will take their own measures. 'In the name of many farmers, Farmer Kehding-Karolinenhorst.'

Stuff stands there uncertainly. 'It's a bit sharp, isn't it?'

'Damn! Wasn't it a bit sharp of the militia to knock away my stick and leave a cripple to fall down on the pavement?'

Tredup appears at Stuff's shoulder and whispers something. 'This is perfect, don't you see? Then you can show Gareis and the *Volkszeitung* that your readers' letters are the real article.'

'Who's that, then?' asks farmer Kehding.

'He's a sort of secretary to me,' says Stuff.

The farmer looks from one of them to the other under his big bushy eyebrows. Suddenly he yells: 'Give me my paper back, you inky fingers! You're every bit as bad as what the other lot are.'

He stomps out of the dispatch office and slams the door.

Stuff squints in bewilderment through his glasses.

'That "secretary" of yours didn't seem to agree with him,' says Tredup.

'No, there's nothing the matter with him. He must have got wind of your photographs, Max.'

'My photographs, come off it –'

Textil-Braun walks in. 'Who was that maniac here a moment ago?'

Stuff is cautious. 'Him? Oh, just some farmer. We get quite a few of them these days.'

'Would you have five minutes for me, Herr Stuff? I've got news for you.'

'No, not really. But for you, 'course I do. Come on in. You too, Tredup, maybe there'll be a small ad in it for you.'

Textil-Braun sits down with dignity and looks rather full of himself. He's a little weasel of a man, currently far too taken up with his own importance to favour his friend Tredup with a look.

'What I have to inform you about, Herr Stuff, is that it's been decided that the press is to suspend all communications regarding the farmers' business.'

Stuff is so amazed that all he can say is 'I see'.

'Yes, the public are getting restless. And the public need to calm down a bit.'

'May I ask you, Herr Braun, who's decided what my paper's course of action is going to be?'

'Herr Stuff, we've known each other for a long time. I'm a loyal advertiser in your pages. You're not about to be offended?'

'I'd just like to know who's taking decisions for my paper. Is it Gareis?'

'No, that's just it. It's not Gareis. We went to see him, and he was all for taking the farmers on. But we didn't want that.'

'Of course not.'

'And then we formed the Reconciliation Committee, which is to bring about reconciliation between the town and the farmers, and we decided that for the time being we're going to have no more writing about the farmers. We want some peace and quiet.'

Stuff takes off his pince-nez and wipes it carefully with his handkerchief. Then he puts it on again and looks thoughtfully at his interlocutor, the busy little merchant.

'Herr Braun, is your hearing good?'

'I believe so,' says the textile man cagily.

'And you don't take me for a bloody fool?'

'Herr Stuff, please –'

'Yes or no!'

'No. Of course not. Herr Stuff –'

'Did you hear what I asked you a moment ago? Do you understand . . .? I want to know who "we" is. Not "we" formed a committee, "we" took the decision . . . That one part of "us" is the Franz Braun Textile Emporium, that's something that "we" here have hoisted in, but you're not a committee of one, are you . . .?'

'Herr Stuff, can't we deal with each other calmly? You make things so difficult for me. And at bottom, the fact is that you weren't invited, and the negotiations were confidential. I'm really not sure I can name names.'

'Really not sure? And you're foolish enough to think that in response to some titbit of yours I would revise the news section of my newpaper?'

'Yes, in a word, I am that foolish. If you want to talk like that! You will change your news section.'

Stuff is becoming increasingly friendly. Something of concern sounds in his voice. 'Really? Can you remember exactly which door you came in at?'

'You will change it, because others have promised on your behalf. Yes, I may as well tell you, your colleague Herr Heinsius has assured us of your discretion.'

Silence. A long silence.

'I see.'

Stuff gets up with a jerk and walks over to the window, turning his back on Tredup and Braun.

'I see.'

And Braun, sweetly appeasing: 'Ah, Herr Stuff, I am sorry . . . We know, now . . . Heinsius let us into the secret. I certainly won't hold it against you, what you said to me just now . . . I'll go on taking space . . .'

'I think you'd better go, Herr Braun,' says Tredup.

Braun hesitates. 'I'd still like a solemn and binding declaration from you.'

'Seeing as you've got it from Heinsius, why exactly do you need mine?'

Stuff turns round, red-faced. 'Throw him out, Max! Throw the worm out. Or I'm afraid I may end up hurting him.'

And Braun, measured, hat already on head: 'Thanks. I'll find my own way out, Herr Stuff. I don't know what's so special about you. I could have spilled the beans about the reader's letter that's in my name . . .'

He's talked himself out.

Stuff is gawping. Then: 'It's the funniest thing, how mean stunts you pull sometimes come back and bite you. Or they do me anyway. – Turn the radio on, for Christ's sake! Berlin on record. No, forget it, I'll make a phone call. Get out, you, I don't need an audience when they cut off my balls.'

In dispatch, Tredup beholds Miss Heinze.

'Hello there, Heinzelmann. Any idea where Wenk is?'

The lady declines. 'You'd best ask him that yourelf.'

Tredup performs the familiar drinking-from-a-bottle mime. 'This?'

'Could be.'

'You too look somehow begloomed.'

And Miss Clara Heinze, suddenly indignant: 'Well, why wouldn't I? When you go around doing such horrible things!'

'Me? Like what?'

'With the farmers, what do you think?'

'But, Clarabelle, what do the farmers have to do with you?'

'You think they don't? My beau was going to the agricultural college, and now he's having to stay home!'

'You poor thing! No, really, truly, you poor thing! But take comfort, there are plenty of fish in the sea, and townies are more generous with their money.'

'Money! As if I cared!'

'Golly, if it isn't true love that's touched her heart! But take comfort, a farmer would probably have got you pregnant.'

'Don't you worry yourself about that, I can look after myself. If I may say so, Herr Tredup, you've become a really horrible man since you got out of prison.'

Suddenly he's all confused. His flippancy is shot to hell. 'Do you think?' he asks worriedly.

'You were dirty-minded before. But you seemed to know that you can be in a bad way, and do lots of bad things, and remain somehow decent.'

'And now?' he asks.

'You know how you are. You saw me perfectly well the other night, when you were so drunk. And you with a woman like that. Yuck, Herr Tredup, when you've got such a sweet, pretty wife.'

'My dear girl –'

'I'm not your "dear girl". You say that to your wenches. To crooked Elli, that bitch!'

'I know for a fact that you –'

'Yes, I know, me too! If I'm supposed to be able to feed and clothe and house myself all on fifty marks a month, then it's no wonder that come the twentieth of the month or so I go and see a couple of gentlemen. It's too bad none of you has the gumption to go and tell Herr Gebhardt that that's what he's driving me to. And you compare me to a cow like Elli, who is a slattern who does it with everyone and checks herself into hospital every other month –'

Stuff calls: 'Tredup, come here, will you!'

Tredup casts a sidelong glance at Miss Heinze. 'We'll talk more –'

'You get lost. I've had enough.'

Stuff has flushed cheeks. 'Well, Tredup, I managed to get it out of Gebhardt. It seems they really did form a committee. They want reconciliation with the peasants. I tell you, they're in for a shock!'

'What about us?'

'Oh, we have to keep our traps shut. The boss told me so in no uncertain terms: until I get the all-clear I'm not allowed to carry anything at all.'

Tredup: 'And what if a bomb explodes at Gareis's . . .?'

Stuff stares at him. 'Did you just think of that as well? Yes, if, if. He can have it as far as I'm concerned.'

He mops his brow. 'Nonsense. The bombs are finished. There are no more bomb throwers. But something else: if we had the letter from that farmer, Kehding, now . . .'

'Yes?'

'I'd give fifty marks for it.'

'But why? You just said you're not allowed to run anything.'

'I'm going to spit in his beer for all that. Do you think I'd let that insect, Textil-Braun, walk all over me? What if Kehding gave it to us in the guise of an advertisement? The readers' letters have been banned, but surely we can't turn away advertisements?'

'No.'

Pause.

A little louder, Tredup says 'Yes.'

Another pause.

'What did you say? A hundred?'

'All right then.'

'Give me twenty up front.'

'All right. All right.' Stuff pulls the note from his wallet and

stares at it. Then he draws a cross on one corner of it. 'There you
are. Twenty. On account.'

Tredup grins cheekily. 'You don't need to sign it. You know
you'll get it back.'

Stuff ignores him. 'When the farmers go drinking, it's usually
in the back room at Auntie Lieschen's.'

Tredup says grumpily: 'I wish I knew why I have to keep tidy-
ing up after you.'

'Because you need money, my boy. Once you're rich, the
others can tidy up after you. – Watch yourself. You're not exactly
flavour of the month with the farmers.'

'Bye-bye, Comrade.'

Stuff stares after him. I must stop doing this. It's the last time.
Definitely the last time.

He twiddles with the radio buttons.

A hand taps him on the shoulder.

'There.'

Tredup lays farmer Kehding's open letter on the table. And
twenty marks with it. In two ten-mark notes.

'It's to be in the form of an advertisement. Quarter page. Thick
black edge. He didn't want to spend any more money than that.'

Stuff stares at the money and the paper. Then at Tredup, who
is pale.

And who murmurs: 'You can always claim you thought advertisements were OK.'

Stuff says slowly: 'How is it that the cowards are always the
brave ones. – Was it very hard?'

'I stood out in the yard for a couple of hours, you can see
through the window into the bog. Waited till he was drunk
enough. Then I held his head for him while he puked. The piece
of paper was in his pocket.'

'Did he recognize you?'

'I don't think so. Hope not.'

Stuff counts up money. 'Eighty. Is that right? Well done, my
lad. I'd like to go out on the town with you tonight. You look to
me as though you could do with some guidance. But I'll probably

go straight over to Auntie Lieschen's now and carry on drinking with the fellow. He mustn't remember anything tomorrow.'

'Are you taking the piece of paper with you?'

'Type it up and give it to the setters, there's a good fellow. Leave the place name off, there's plenty of Kehdings in the area, and he shouldn't have to bear too many consequences of this. In judicial terms it is a case of menaces.'

'Blackmail?'

'No, just menaces. It's less bad.'

'What do we care about him anyway. Let him go to prison!'

Stuff looks at Tredup. 'You need to talk to your wife some-time, Max. This is all no good. And I swear to you that this is the last bit of skulduggery you'll ever do for me.'

Tredup walks right up to Stuff. He whispers: 'I'll tell you some-thing. I think dirty work is the only thing I'm good for.'

He leaves quickly, and Stuff has to type up the open letter him-self.

V

Manzow has said: 'Of course we'll take the car. If the negoti-ations are successful, the town will foot the bill.'

Dr Hüppchen asks anxiously: 'And what if they don't?'

'If they don't! How can they fail! With Dr Hüppchen along for the ride.'

And Dr Hüppchen, puny, ascetic, gives an awkward but flat-tered giggle.

So there were six of them setting off at four o'clock to Stolpe in the large touring automobile: Manzow, Textil-Braun, Dr Lienau with Stahlhelm badge and duelling scars, Rag-Meisel, Dr Hüpp-chen and, finally, their driver and car-rental man, Toleis.

'I took Toleis,' Manzow explained, 'even if he does charge five pfennigs a mile extra. If the farmers try to beat us up, at least we'll have one experienced thug with us.'

Toleis has done time for assault and GBH – oh, six or eight times.

And Dr Hüppchen looked at Toleis admiringly and twittered

out in his little birdlike voice: 'You will show me your biceps later, as you promised?'

To which Toleis gruffed back: 'You're a pervy bastard, with all due respect, Doctor.'

The assembled company roared with laughter, Dr Hüppchen hiccupped, and the mood was excellent.

Dr Lienau sang barmaid rhymes into the fresh breeze, Manzow was talking smut with Textil-Braun, whom he rarely saw, and who knew jokes. Dr Hüppchen gazed at Toleis's bull neck, and Rag-Meisel heard it all and made mental notes for subsequent retellings.

On the way, they stopped for a swift half, which turned into a few slow pints, with Dr Hüppchen sitting some way away with his lemonade, with which he washed down a banana he pulled from his pocket. Dr Hüppchen was teetotal and a raw-food man.

Whoever was told about this invariably said: 'And it shows.'

Just before six, they pulled into Stolpe and parked in the market square.

It hadn't been easy to get in touch with the farmers. Manzow had tried in vain. In the end it was Lienau with his Stahlhelm connections, some Nazis had been involved as well, and instructions had come down – no one knew who from, or through whom – to come by car and wait in Stolpe Market.

They came and waited. It was taking its time.

'Shall we wet our whistles?' asked Manzow.

'No, better not. I'm sure the farmers will supply refreshments.'

'I hope you're right!'

'We'll end up meeting in some bar or other, I expect.'

And Manzow, alarmed: 'You mean it might be dry? Anything but that. I can't be doing with teetotal – forgive me, Doctor.'

'That's quite all right. I thrive on lemonade.'

'You don't exactly look thriving.'

A man or youth – he's a bit far away to tell – comes swinging across the market, with dirty top-boots, dirty grey jerkin, freckles and a short yellow fringe of hair.

He's coming straight for their car.

'Surely it's not him?'

'No, it'll be Padberg at least.'

The man stands next to the car, surveys its load, and says: 'You'll have to clear a space for me beside the driver, so I can give directions.'

'Are you the one, then?'

'I don't know.'

'Are you come to get us?'

'I'm to show you the way.'

'Where to?'

'I don't know.'

'Well, let's go, then. Meisel can sit at the back between us two fatties.'

'You sure you're the right man?'

The fringed simpleton has had enough and isn't answering that question any more.

'Is it a long way? You could at least tell us if it's far, so we know if we need to fill up.'

The man glances at the fuel gauge and says: 'That'll do.'

The reshuffle is complete, the guide sits down beside the driver, has him turn round, and they drive the way they came.

A few protests are mooted, but somehow the atmosphere has gone a little flat. That peasant at the front, that dirty pig, has rained on their parade.

Halfway between Stolpe and Altholm, there's a left turn along a field track.

'Thank God,' says Manzow. 'I thought they were taking us back to Altholm.'

Field track, then sand path. Then a logging rut uphill, then a left, then right at a fork.

'That's the way to the forest lodge.'

'It's never. The forest lodge is miles left of here.'

'Toleis, do you know where we are?'

Toleis merely lets out a grunt.

Manzow begs – his voice now sounds completely different – 'Won't you tell us where we're going, sir?'

The grey jerkin doesn't answer.

They emerge from the woods. A huge potato field, blue-green, as far as the eye can see, going up a slope.

The car slowly crunches over the sand.

Toleis turns round: 'There's a surcharge for roads like this!'

Manzow sighs. 'For God's sake, Toleis. Just take us somewhere we can get a drink.'

And Toleis: 'All I know is that we're somewhere between the Oder and the Vistula. But where . . .'

Another wood. A clearing. The blond fringe makes a sign to stop. Everyone sighs with relief. The blond gets out, stretches his legs, lights up a rollie.

The gentlemen stand a little awkwardly beside the car and look around. A recently made clearing, darkening forest all round, sinking sun. They've given up asking their guide questions, and talk among themselves. 'The farmers had better be coming.'

'Bastards they are to send us on this wild goose chase.'

'Ssh! There's something rustling.'

All look at the dark woods, but nothing emerges.

'Probably some animal.'

Toleis finally asks the farmer: 'Should I turn the engine off?'

'Yeah, go ahead.'

So it's here. They are relieved to be at their goal, however unpromising.

But the minutes tick by, ten, twenty, half an hour.

The gentlemen are by turns tense, bored, impatient, worried, done in.

Now Lienau tries his luck with the country boy.

'It's after eight. What's going on? Is this a wild goose chase, or what?'

'No,' says the farmer.

'What's going on, can you tell me? Why aren't they coming?'

'It's still too early. It needs to be dark.'

'Then why were we told to be here at six? Why are we being kept waiting?'

'We've been kept waiting since the 26th of July.'

'That, if I may say so . . .' Dr Lienau bursts out. 'That's a typical farmers' impertinence. That's bottomless disrespect. We are the leading citizens of Altholm, do you understand? We're not your navvies, all right? We –'

It's deepening dusk, and they all see the farmer get up with a jerk and head off in the direction of the dark forest.

In confusion they call out: 'What's going on?' – 'What are you doing?' – 'Please don't . . .!'

Dr Hüppchen rushes after him and lays his frail fingers on the farmer's arm. 'Please, sir, you weren't going to leave us all on our own, were you? The medical councillor meant no disrespect.'

'I'll only take youse if you quiet down.'

They have to get over the 'youse', because Toleis explains that he's lost his bearings. They pile back into the car, they chunter to themselves, a sort of dulled fatigue settles over their alcoholized brains.

All jump up when Toleis suddenly switches on the headlights. The motor hums, Toleis jumps on to his seat, the farmer sits down next to him.

The drive begins all over again.

But there is a tension in them all, the nervous expectation of something unpredictable.

Once, Dr Hüppchen whispers: 'This is so wonderfully dramatic,' but the others don't understand. To them it's just a mean trick. They try to see something of the scene as it slips by in the conical light of the beams, but it's all just trees, grain fields, potato fields, wood, the occasional unlit farmhouse squatting between grain barns.

Field and forest tracks. Never a road. Wild tracks, taken at terrific speed, Toleis pulls out all the stops. A clock strikes eleven, suddenly many more clocks. A set of chimes.

'Say, aren't those the chimes of Altholm?'

'No, there's some like that in Stolpe too. We must be right by the sea, can't you smell it?'

The guide turns to mutter something to Toleis.

Who starts swearing: 'God dammit no! Not that . . .'

It's a set of six frail planks across a rapidly flowing stream.

Hüppchen gives a little scream: 'Oh no! Please not!'

The car accelerates. Hüppchen is thrown back on to the seat with another little scream. They feel the planks give way, crack and splinter – and they're on a meadow. A few willows by a ditch. A pasture.

Then suddenly a stretch of road, proper paved road. And they stop behind the dark, windowless back wall of an immense-seeming building.

The farmer jumps out and holds open a door.

'Gentlemen, step inside.'

A dark door opens silently in the dark façade. They go inside, half numb from their ride, with stiff legs.

And as they walk in, for all of them the penny drops: 'My God, we're in Altholm! This is the auction room for Jersey cattle!'

One of them says audibly, through gritted teeth: 'Fucking farmers!'

VI

The enormous room is completely dark.

On the other side, on the platform, there are a couple of candles stood on a table. Two plain stearine candles on a couple of chipped enamel candlesticks.

The gentlemen grope towards the two flickering points of light. They bump into overturned benches, chairs, railings and pillars. They lose contact with each other, call out to one another in stage whispers that seem to come from all over, and finally all meet up again at the foot of the stage.

'Who's our spokesman?'

And Manzow: 'Me, of course.'

The door to the left of the stage opens and two men walk on. A tall, strongly built man a few of them can recognize: Franz Reimers, the leader of the Bauernschaft.

And another, in horn-rims. He too is familiar to a few: Padberg of the *Bauernschaft* newspaper.

Manzow starts speaking right away:

'Thank you, gentlemen, for keeping your word in the end. You've had your fun with us. Well, we don't mind that, so long as the end result is good.

'Well, gentlemen, what I suggest is this: We put an end to ceremony and the atmospheric lighting, and sit down somewhere, if you're agreed, where we can get a mug of beer and a shot of corn, and say what's on our minds. How about it?'

Every word of Manzow's was repeated by a slavish echo. Anyhow, it's dispiriting enough to be speaking at the feet of people towering above you on a stage. The friendliness sounded off, the mateyness forced.

Reimers the farmer says:

'The Altholm representatives wish to know under what conditions the farmers are prepared to forgive the humiliation done to them, and conclude peace with the town of Altholm.

'The conditions are these:

'One: The return of our flag, with all honour.

'Two: The immediate dismissal of the guilty parties Frerksen and Gareis.

'Three: Criminal proceedings and punishment of the police officers who assaulted farmers with naked weapons.

'Four: A lifelong and adequate pension for injured farmers.

'Five: A fine of ten thousand marks.

'If the representatives of Altholm here present are prepared to accept these conditions, I have drawn up a document which they can sign, as liable bondsmen.

'And no discussion.'

'But Herr Reimers,' calls Manzow, half indignant, half amused. 'We can't do that. The flag was seized by the prosecution office. How can we sack public officials? How can we predict the outcome of legal cases –?'

'Do you accept the conditions?'

'But how can we –?'

The candles on the stage are snuffed out. A door bangs. The gentlemen are left standing in the dark.

VII

It's after midnight when they finally find their way out of the hall, with matches and curses.

There are incidents: Medical Councillor Dr Lienau takes a

tumble, loses touch with the rest of the group, and is brought to light much later by a rescue expedition, with barked shins and swearing horribly. He claims bitterly that the hall is full of hidden farmers, who under cover of darkness were hitting him.

Then Dr Hüppchen's quiet squeal is heard, the sound of a slap, and Toleis's low voice gruffs: 'Doctor, you're a pervert!'

(How come Toleis is in the hall? He was meant to stay and watch the car.)

Finally the last of them emerge through the dark doorway, standing under the night sky, which has never seemed purer or clearer.

They stand there at a loss as to what to do, but Manzow declares: 'We can't break up like this. First we have to talk about what we'll tell the others. Anyway, I'm thirsty.'

'So am I.'

'Me too.'

'All of us are.'

'I suggest,' Manzow proclaims, 'Toleis drives us all to the Red Nook. There we can say what we have to say and remain undisturbed.'

'Oh dear, does it have to be such an off-colour place!' begs the doctor.

'If we go, then so can you,' says Manzow.

'Anyway, it's almost midnight, and no one will see us.'

A quarter of an hour later, they're at Minchen Wendehals's in the Red Nook, comfortably ensconced around a big corner table.

It's a pleasant nook they're sitting in, with cheerful wallpaper and agreeable low lighting, separated from the other bar by a curtain. The waitress is neither unsettlingly attractive nor simply too tarty, and they're over the initial surprise that – with the exception of Dr Hüppchen – she knows them all by their first names.

They're also agreed that they will order and pay collectively. Only they're not quite sure what that means in precise terms. But when the six pork knuckles arrive, with sauerkraut and mushy peas on the side, that doesn't seem to matter all that much.

The gentlemen tuck in. Beer and schnapps are also there in abundance.

Suddenly Textil-Braun emits a cry: 'I say, gentlemen, look . . .'

In their initial hunger, no one had paid any attention to Dr Hüppchen; now they're all staring in horror at his plate.

The vegetarian has scorned his meat, but the raw-food man has compromised to the extent that he ate his peas and his sauerkraut. But the teetotaller didn't want beer and schnapps, he secretly ordered himself some raspberry juice, and now – hideous to behold – he has poured some of it over his cabbage and mushy peas.

'What's the matter, gentlemen? It's delicious!'

And he raises a forkful to his mouth.

'Doctor!!!'

'Do me a favour, will you, and eat that somewhere we don't have to see it.'

'But just try –'

Manzow complains: 'I can feel my gorge rising, and my teeth are on edge.'

And Lienau: 'That's so warped. The French eat shit like that.'

Dr Hüppchen flushes: 'But you don't have to look! – Of course, if it does put you off . . .'

After all, the gentlemen are clients of his accountancy office, also he is syndic of the small-business group. So he swings his chair round, turns his back on the company, and eats with his plate on his knee.

All are relieved.

'Your mother must have been a strange woman!'

'I pity whoever marries you, Doctor!'

'Who's going to marry him?! Toleis, do you want to marry the doctor . . .?'

Because they've brought Toleis in with them, partly because they're not sure if they can find their way home in one or two hours by themselves, and partly to be sure of getting his silence.

That's really the most important thing, the silence, and no sooner is the table cleared, and the waitress sent away, than Manzow rises to his feet.

'Gentlemen! After today's ordeal, I know we're all longing for the pleasurable part of the evening . . . So I'll try and keep it short.

'The committee has, for the moment, let's say, failed in its task. No fault of ours. With the patience of saints we endured an undignified drive and contemptuous treatment in the auction hall.

'The demands we were finally confronted with, gentlemen, were so absurd that they couldn't even form the basis for any discussion.

'I suggest we go back to our mandant and give back our office.

I further suggest we tell Mayor Gareis that on reflection we agree with his idea of taking the fight to the farmers and opposing the boycott.'

An indignant Lienau calls out: 'What, and side with the Red bastard? Never!'

'Have you got any better ideas?'

But Lienau, stuck and scowling over the rim of his beer glass: 'Never!'

'We must also decide,' Textil-Braun chips in quietly, 'what to report on today's experiences. If what happened gets out, it can do us a lot of damage.'

And Meisel: 'I suggest all participants pledge themselves to silence.'

'I wouldn't give such a pledge,' declares Lienau. 'Stuff must get to hear about this.'

'What good would that do? Stuff's not allowed to publish anything, that's already settled.'

'Stuff published the open letter to the town, don't forget.'

'That was a piece of work! He'll live to regret it too, Stuff! The town is starting proceedings.'

'Come on, that was a small ad.'

'An ad – how can you be so naive!'

'Come on, one Stuff is worth ten thousand of those smarmy *News* types.'

'Haven't you heard that the *News* and the *Chronicle* are stable-mates and all?! I feel sorry for you.'

Manzow beseeches them: 'Gentlemen, please, we're not here to discuss Stuff!'

No one listens.

'Even if Gebhardt buys Stuff a hundred times over, the man won't be bought!'

'Don't say that so loud, there are probably people here who already own him.'

'All right, who? Gossip isn't the same thing as evidence!'

'Well, the Stahlhelm, for instance.'

'The Stahlhelm's never paid so much as a penny to Stuff.'

'No, they gave it to Schabbelt. When Hindenburg got elected.'

'That's a scurrilous lie. Our venerable president doesn't need –'

'And now Stuff's flirting with the Nazis.'

'With those green youths? I'm sorry, Herr Braun, but you really are a political novice!'

'Councillor!'

The storm, the fight even, seems unavoidable when Manzow upsets a couple of beer glasses. At the same time he calls out: 'Betty! Betty! Betty!'

And when the waitress appears: 'Look what I've gone and done. A fresh tablecloth please. And then, why don't you come and join us for a bit? And bring your friend, Berta, as well. And if you know of a couple more nice girls . . .?'

'I'll go and see, Franz,' says Betty. 'But you'll have to have wine, otherwise Frau Wendehals won't allow it. We can go and adjourn to the club room . . .'

Betty vanishes, and Manzow announces: 'In five minutes, the girls will be here. By then we have to have agreement.'

'Who said anything about girls?'

'Are you going to buy the wine? I can't afford luxuries like that.'

'Those nasty whores.'

'Hey! The term "whores" is inappropriate. These are all respectable girls who won't go with just anyone.'

Manzow rises. 'Can we have a vote, please? We resign our posts. Those in favour . . .?

'Damn. Three for, three against. Hang on, Toleis, you're the driver, who said you could vote? All right. Three for, two against. Carried. We resign.

'Two: We declare the negotiations a failure because of intransigence on the part of the farmers?

'Four in favour, one against. Toleis, put it away. You'll only confuse me.

'We accept Gareis's proposals? Two in favour, three against. Rejected, then. Even so, I'm going to go and talk to Gareis. If you're going to be such bloody idiots, I don't see why I should do what you want.'

'Why are we voting, then, if you're going to do what you want anyway?'

'Quiet! – Now I want everyone to pledge themselves to silence regarding all the details of today. All right? – Three in favour, two against. So we all pledge.'

'Why? I didn't give my word.'

'But, Councillor, you've been outvoted!'

'Does that make me have to give my word?'

Dr Hüppchen pipes up, 'Toleis should have got a vote too.'

'Listen, we're not starting all over again. Everyone is hereby committed to silence.'

'I'm going to tell Stuff anyway!'

'In that case,' Manzow says coolly, 'everyone will pay his own share of the costs of the expedition. I was going to put it on the municipal traffic public relations budget.'

'Even the girls?'

'Everything!'

'Hmm,' says the medical councillor. 'If that's not corruption. But all right. I'll keep quiet, if it matters so much to you.'

'You see! It just needs finessing, and a bit of common sense. And now let's go over to the club room. Don't want to keep the girls waiting now.'

VIII

Three hours later.

There is an oppressive heat in the club room, but the curtains are tightly drawn. Clouds of smoke hang under the ceiling.

On the leather sofa sits Manzow in trousers and shirt – no collar – discussing marriage with Toleis.

'You know, Toleis, if my old lady wanted something, I'd know it the day before. I'd sniff it out. I can smell it on her.'

Toleis nods solemnly. 'Yes, Herr Manzow, I've heard of that happening.'

Medical Councillor Dr Lienau has one hand buried in a girl's cleavage and is singing whatever comes into his head, in complete disregard of the gramophone, to whose music, Dr Hüppchen, the only sober man present, is dancing with another girl.

Textil-Braun, lucky man, has his arms round two girls. They are playing drinking games with him. He opens his mouth carefully, slurps, and babbles on: 'I'm not letting you!' and gets wine all over his chest.

Meisel is listening to what the waitress is telling him, about what her brother heard at the Labour Exchange, from the Communists.

'I tell you, chubby, they've got his sabre. They're just keeping it secret.'

'Gareis said the whole episode with the sabre was a lie.'

'Maybe they lied to him. I even know who's got it.'

'Ach!' yells Manzow. 'Don't keep going on about that sabre! We've all got one of our own! Or haven't we?' And he looks around provocatively.

There's something in the air. It must have been a cue, because they all look at each other, only Dr Hüppchen goes on dancing.

'Or is there anyone here who's not got a sabre?' bellows Manzow. 'I want to see the bastard!'

And Braun echoes: 'Bastard, come forward!'

And Meisel: 'Hey, psst! Doctor! Didn't you hear? You're to come forward.'

'What was that . . .?' asks the doctor. 'I'm afraid I missed that.'

Expectant silence.

'Hey, Doctor,' begins the Medical Councillor, 'I was wondering why you've got such a squeaky voice. Was it always squeaky?'

'You wouldn't exactly be an asset to the church choir either,' squeaks Dr Hüppchen, and goes on dancing.

'The bastard doesn't drink,' wails Manzow. 'What's the use of anything if the bastard doesn't drink? Someone here's not pulling his weight!' he complains.

And Lienau: 'Come on, fellow, let's get a drink down you. A proper one, mind!'

Pause.

All of a sudden the men are no longer interested in their girls, they are all fixed on the doctor, who is dancing with floppy limbs.

Betty brings in the cognac.

'There's no one in the lounge bar, you can make as much noise as you want.'

The beer glass full of cognac is hidden behind an array of glasses and bottles.

'Quiet!' yells the medical councillor. 'Turn that music down! Come over here, Doctor, we've got something to say to you!'

The doctor comes over expectantly.

'Let go your wench! What do you think you're doing with a woman?'

Suddenly the medical councillor bellows: 'Everyone stand! Dr Hüppchen, advance!'

He giggles sheepishly. 'I say, you're not going to shoot me, are you?'

'Dear Doctor!

'Esteemed comrades!

'It's now three years since Dr Hüppchen came to our beautiful town. When we saw the plate outside his door, accountant, we thought he won't be with us long!

'But Dr Hüppchen has stayed. He has become a citizen and a valued member of our community. That's why it's only fitting that we adopt him as a full member of our group and make an honest Altholmer of him.

'Do we want to do that, my fellow members?'

Shouts of applause.

'Are you willing, Dr Hüppchen?'

'Yes. Thank you very much –'

'I'm talking, thank you. Now kneel down. – Come on, man, I told you to kneel!'

'It's a bit dirty here, and this is my best suit –'

'Kneel down on the armchair if you must. That's actually better. – Now, Betty, if you'd kindly blindfold the good doctor.'

'Oh, not that! Please –'

'Oh, don't be a spoilsport. Every one of us went through this rite. I'm going to knight you in the Altholm fashion. Tie it tight, Betty. Can you see anything, Doctor?'

'Not a thing. Oh, please –'

'Doctor, before I knight you, you have to swear your oath of allegiance. Say after me: Ulam.'

'Ulam –'

'Much louder! Arrarat . . .'

'Arrarat.'

'Not like that. You have to open your mouth much wider. Again. Very wide. Ulam Arrarat . . .'

'Ulam Arra –'

Two men hold his head fast, the third slowly tips the cognac in a thick stream down his neck.

'Guh . . . uh . . . uh . . . help! Gentlemen, no, how can you . . .?'

He tears off the blindfold and stares round, seeing only hostile faces. Even the perpetually smirking Meisel looks cross.

'It's time you learned, Doctor! It's mean always being sober when everyone else is getting drunk. That's not solidarity or companionship.'

'I would never have . . . Gentlemen, my principles. It's cowardly . . .'

And suddenly he's smiling miserably. A bad approximation of a smile, a sorry-looking grimace.

'Of course. I understand. It doesn't matter. If force is applied, it doesn't count.'

He's smiling again.

Manzow pats him on the back. 'There, you see, my lad. We look after you too, we're going to get you a few new clients. Now, drink!'

Dr Hüppchen looks at him beseechingly. 'But I'm not permitted to –'

'Drink. That's an order, Doctor. There now. – And now, seeing as we're all drunk together, I want to suggest we make ourselves comfortable. Properly comfortable. What are we doing in full fig in this wretched heat? The girls look better without, too.'

And he starts slowly unbuttoning his trousers. 'What are you waiting for!'

'You're right!'

'Oh, Fatty Franz! You're so sweet!'

'Shirt off, Minna!'

'Cheer up, Doctor! It's all right!'

'Shame is in the eye of the beholder.'

'Will you look at that Betty, she's not wearing knickers!'

'Did you not notice that? What were you doing with yourself all evening?'

'Well, how about it, then, Doctor?'

He stands there in his shirtsleeves. 'I don't really feel all that warm,' he whispers.

'Come on, man, come on! No hanging about, no excuses. Look at Toleis! What an athlete, eh?'

Someone starts singing: 'Where'd you put my sabre? My sabre? My sabre? – In between your labia! Your labia! Your labia!'

A serious-looking Manzow walks up to the doctor. 'Now, Doctor, no more stalling. You don't want to spoil things do you? Everyone always participates with us.'

The doctor has sweat on his brow. He looks whey-faced.

One of the girls says: 'Oh, won't you let him go.'

The medical councillor slaps her down: 'Who asked you, cow?'

'I'm giving you your final warning, Doctor. You'll bear the consequences!'

'Come on, drink, Manny, it'll get your courage up.'

And the girl gives him another glass of cognac. Dr Hüppchen drinks.

Then he starts undoing his buttons and taking off his clothes. The others pretend not to look, and don't take their eyes off him.

Briefly he hesitates, then he pulls his shirt up over his head.

One of the girls squeals: 'Oh, it's adorable! Just like a baby's!'

A roar of laughter goes up.

The women squeal, the men whinny, rumble, roar.

And the chorus sets up: 'Where'd you put my sabre? My sabre? My sabre?'

Dr Hüppchen staggers, naked, into the door. Collapses. Lies there motionless.

The singing continues: 'In between your labia! Your labia! Your labia!'

4

The Townies Fight — Each Other

I

Mayor Gareis asks cautiously: 'Are you sure you haven't imagined any of this? Dreamed it up when you were drunk?'

Dr Hüppchen in the big leather armchair says keenly: 'Actually, I wasn't really drunk. I felt very clear-headed, and then suddenly I was gone.'

Gareis tips his head from side to side. 'It's a ticklish matter. It can be difficult afterwards to tell when you were sober and when you were drunk.'

'But they dressed me while I was unconscious. I'd never have dressed myself like that. My underpants were stuffed in my trouser pockets!'

'Yes. Still, Doctor, I think all these are things you are telling me privately, not in my capacity as head of the police.'

Dr Hüppchen looks at the mayor stubbornly. 'Police Commissioner –' he begins.

But Gareis is quick to interrupt him: 'You are a citizen of this town. You make your living here. Among just this class of merchants and business people. You think the main culprit is Manzow . . . ?'

'Yes, Manzow instigated everything.'

'Very well. Now you know that Manzow is a big wheel in this community. Don't get excited, Doctor. I'm just stating a fact. Rightly or wrongly, he is a big deal here.'

'And that's why he should go scot-free –?'

'Listen. I've heard all sorts of stories. The reason he's getting away scot-free isn't that – it's because you need him. Imagine: You bring a case against him. Imagine: It goes before a judge. What's to say the judge doesn't see the whole episode as a drunken spree?

All kinds of things take place on stag nights. And then the result: he's acquitted. At the most, people will laugh at him: old Manzow, what a card, he knows how to have fun, he's not uptight. Meanwhile, Dr Hüppchen is forced to move to a different town because he's lost his clientele.'

Hüppchen stares straight ahead. 'But it was so humiliating! So cruel! How can I bring myself to speak to the gentlemen now? I'm so ashamed.'

Almost gaily Gareis says: 'Of course you can talk to them. You haven't done anything humiliating, that was them. Why should you feel shame on their account?'

'I suppose you're right.'

'So you came to see me in a private capacity?'

'Yes. Right. Privately. Thank you, Mayor . . .'

'Now just one second!' The mayor waves the visitor down as he makes to stand up. 'Don't thank me yet, Doctor, because I'm about to give you a dressing-down. Because the one to blame for the whole thing is you.'

Dr Hüppchen is utterly bewildered. 'Me . . .?'

'You live among middle-class people, and it's among middle-class people that you want to make a living too. Then you too must be middle class like them. You don't drink, you don't smoke, you don't eat meat. You see, Doctor, that's not on. Not in Altholm. In Berlin or Leipzig possibly, but not in Altholm.

'Recently, at a dinner, someone said to me: "What bastard here is drinking lemonade?" The bastard was you, and from his perspective the man was completely justified.'

Dr Hüppchen draws a deep breath. 'My convictions . . .'

'I know, Doctor, I know. But we're not twenty for the whole of our lives, we want to earn money, we want to get ahead, we want to be something, achieve something. – Shall I tell you how I came to be elected mayor, with the votes of the Right?'

'All right . . .'

'It's because I'm so fat. Because I'm a fat pig. It sets people at ease. If I was ten times as diligent, but thin, they'd all be screaming: a Red fanatic! A bloodhound! – And I'll let you into another secret, namely why they're all against me now. It's because I go against the flow, because I won't sacrifice Frerksen. They don't understand that. They've had some trouble, and now they want their scapegoat. Someone has to be slaughtered. And because I won't allow him to be slaughtered, they're all now inveighing against me. That's the way it is.'

'Hmm. Perhaps you're right.'

'I know I'm right. And it may well come to pass that I'll wind up in the same boat as you, that they'll want to strip off my shirt as well, because I show myself to be different from them.'

The mayor puffs. Suddenly he smacks his hand down on the table. 'But it's all right to be different from them, dammit. It's all right to push back against them. Otherwise the world would make no sense. So I'm keeping Frerksen.'

Gareis laughs. 'Anyway, I have to keep him for the sake of the comrades. The prestige of the SPD is at stake. It's one of the funny things about life that you don't do the things you do because you like doing them or believe in them. No, there are often completely different reasons. Anyway, the ones to suffer right now are the middle classes, and the farmers are laughing. I expect they're making things up even now –'

Dr Hüppchen butts in: 'But the reconciliation was a flop! That's what made them all go and get drunk last night!'

And he blushes beetroot.

Gareis says reflectively: 'I was wondering all along about your strange company. So that was the Reconciliation Committee! And the farmers weren't playing?'

Dr Hüppchen: 'I spoke out of turn a moment ago. I gave my solemn vow to –'

And Gareis: 'Taken care of, Doctor! You haven't told me anything. And I'll have a word with Manzow one of these days, tell him to leave you alone.'

'Thank you, Mayor!'

'That's quite all right. Maybe I'll be coming to you with something one of these days. Good day to you, Doctor.'

II

Secretary Piekbusch comes to answer Gareis's bell.

'Next to see you is the man from the *Chronicle*.'

'Oh, Piekbusch,' the mayor says slowly, fixing his secretary with an intent look, 'The secret instructions haven't turned up yet, have they?'

'No. But I swear, Your Honour, that the second I put the telephone down, I laid them back in the drawer. I know that for an absolute fact.'

'And you can't remember what was in them either?'

'No, not a thing. I was so excited at the time . . .'

'If they said what I think they probably said, then it's really only the farmers who have any interest in them. – All right, send Herr Tredup in!'

Tredup walks in. In the doorway he begins to speak: 'I wanted to thank you, Mayor. I heard you came to visit me in prison –'

He breaks off. The mayor looms massive and tall behind his desk, not extending his hand in greeting, not offering him a chair. He says gruffly: 'That was in the past, Herr Tredup. But what vile things are you doing now on the *Chronicle*? Cutting deals with the farmers? Whipping up feeling against the town? Anyone who attacks his own friends from behind in a fight is both a coward and a traitor. Tell your friend Stuff I said so. And make a note of it yourself.'

'Mayor, please! It's nothing like that –'

But the Mayor will not be placated, he remains angry. 'Pah, nothing like that! Bogus readers' letters, just to whip up feeling. Talk of police terror and bloodlust. Sir, I've read your articles on police terror aloud to the entire police force. There, I told them, that's the *Chronicle*, your pals, your mates you go drinking with, make up your own minds. They really ought to know better, but instead they go wittering on about police bloodlust!'

'But Mayor, Stuff had to do it! When the whole press was against the police, Herr Gebhardt said . . . You know Herr Gebhardt is the new owner of the *Chronicle*?'

'Yes, I know. What did he say?'

'He sent Stuff on ahead. Your readers, he said, like that sort of thing. And that way we can give the Socialists a good smack. Come election time, some of that will stick.'

'Did you personally hear Gebhardt saying those things?'

'No, not personally. Stuff told me.'

'There's too much gossip about you, Tredup. You can't be everywhere at once. You've started drinking too. I would quit that if I were you. – Now sit down.'

They both sit.

Tredup says quietly and modestly: 'I've also joined the SPD, Herr Mayor. – My sympathies are with you. It's unfortunate I make my living on the other side.'

'I see! You've joined the SPD, have you? How wonderful. Maybe they can do something for you one day. – Now tell me about those readers' letters.'

'The readers' letters are genuine! Stuff didn't make those up! The latest one, the open letter, I got from a farmer who came round to give it to us.'

'Is it still there? Could you show it to me?'

'I don't know. Stuff will have it if it still exists.'

'And what was the name of the farmer?'

'Kehding, I think it was. Yes, Kehding.'

'And where was he from?'

Tredup hesitates. Then: 'I can't remember. I think perhaps it didn't say on the letter.'

'But he will have told you where he's from. You see, that's where you go wrong, all these half-measures and half-truths. It's no good.'

'But I really don't know the name of the place.'

'Well, get me the letter.'

'I'll try. If I can get it, I definitely will.'

'Just do it, all right?'

Pause. The mayor, with wrinkled brow, looks down at his feet.

'Ah well,' he finally says. 'In the end a newspaper man follows the numbers. If your readers like that sort of thing. And did they like it?'

Tredup says proudly: 'We sold thirty-five copies at the station.'

'I see. That's not so very many, is it?'

'We usually sell two!'

'Then it is a lot,' confirms the mayor. 'And the subscribers?'

'Oh God, the subscribers are used to it. They're all old people. It doesn't matter what we print, they're always going to like it.'

'Are they all old? We don't have seven thousand old people in Altholm.'

'Seven thousand? Do you believe it's seven thousand? We don't have seven thousand subscribers!'

'I don't believe anything. I just heard that the *Chronicle* goes fishing with a document that says they have seven thousand subscribers.'

'There is such a document,' Tredup agrees eagerly. 'I sometimes use it myself to try and hustle for advertisements. But it must be at least three years old. And we're losing sixty or eighty subscriptions a month.'

Gareis does some mental arithmetic. 'Then that would mean you only had around four thousand five hundred subscribers?'

'Yes. No. I don't think we even have that many. I once had a look at the books, when Wenk – who's our managing editor – was away on holiday. I couldn't see more than four thousand.'

'I see. Well. I suppose all newspapers play these games, some of them are subtle about it, some less so. Of course not the major newspapers, but the small and middle-sized ones. There's nothing to it really. Who was it who issued the confirmation? Was it a notary?'

'Yes, it was Herr Pepper on the marketplace. But back then everything was still legit. It was true at the time.'

'Ha. All right. Could you let me see the confirmation some time, Tredup?'

'Not easily. Honestly, Mayor, I'd love to, but Wenk keeps it in his safe, and the only way I can get my hands on it is if a new client appears on the scene with a sizeable contract.'

'Hindrances,' says the mayor uncharitably, 'all I get from you are hindrances and endless "if onlys". Sometimes you have to be swift and daring, take a risk.'

'I'm only too happy to try. Sometimes Wenk leaves the key in the safe when he goes out for a drink. But bringing it all the way to the town hall? Wouldn't it do if I brought a copy?'

'Copy! Copy! Well, all right, bring me a copy. But I want it today.'

'Today? How do I know if Wenk will go out for a drink today?' In haste: 'But I'll see, maybe it can be done.'

'Well, just you go and see. See you this evening. If I'm not here, you can leave it with my secretary, Piekbusch.'

'And you will think of me some time, Mayor, like you promised? If a job as a janitor should become vacant, or something? Now that I'm in the Party?'

'Good day, Herr Tredup. I will think of you some time. Quite. Good day.'

'Good day, Mayor. And thank you very much!'

III

Gareis beams all over his fat face when Manzow appears. 'My word, Franz, take a look at yourself. You look as yellow green as a forest in spring. Is it the drink that does that?'

'No, it's the anxiety,' replies Manzow crossly. 'Ever since your protégé Frerksen stirred up the pot, business has been awful.'

'It always is in summer,' says the mayor with equanimity. 'Only difference is this time you've got someone to hang the blame on . . . Honestly, though, Franz, you shouldn't drink so much. It doesn't agree with you.'

'Alcohol doesn't do me any harm.'

'If you were thin it might not! But with fatties like us, it always affects the heart. Every time I drink a pint, I worry.'

'It's every time I don't that worries me!'

But Gareis doesn't give up. 'Honestly, Franz, you look terrible. It doesn't agree with you. You should quit.'

'What, what?'

'Well, the elections are in six months' time. And the Red Nook isn't exactly a respectable joint.'

Manzow gloops at him, but only quickly. 'Damn the . . . Who was it this time . . .? No sooner does a man take a breath than the chief commissioner knows . . . I tell you, Mayor, you shouldn't use those whores as spies.'

'You're too wild, Franz. People gossip. Plus, who do you take with you? A driver, a young buck, for God's sake! People are bound to talk!'

For a brief moment, Manzow seems very small. 'God, I wasn't thinking. I was so furious. It all went wrong. But . . .' And already he's starting to recover himself. 'But you're one to puff yourself up. I only have to say Stettin.'

Gareis is unmoved. 'Stettin is Stettin, and Altholm is Altholm. – What made you so furious?'

'Business, my God! The pedlars aren't selling so much as a pair of bootlaces!'

'So you want to go and celebrate that with a chauffeur, a medical councillor and an accountant? Has your business really taken such a hit with the farmers?'

This time Manzow is left speechless a little bit longer. Finally: 'That's not something the girls have told you!'

Garcis basks a little. Gareis brags a little. 'Franz, I know everything. Here . . .' he taps his desk, 'is where all the threads meet. You only ever get to see a tiny piece. I see the whole thing.'

'Now who was it who blabbed this time . . .?' ponders the wholesaler.

'Incidentally,' remarks Gareis, 'how many sales do you think the *Chronicle* has?'

'The *Chronicle*? I can tell you that precisely. I buy space there, after all. Seven thousand.' Suspiciously: 'Why are you mentioning the *Chronicle*?'

'No reason. Just happened to come to mind.'

'Has Stuff been talking? But Stuff doesn't know anything. Stuff – Lienau, the medical councillor! That bastard wasn't going to give us his word of honour.'

'But what's it matter to you how I know. The main thing is, I know the reconciliation is a busted flush.'

'Rubbish! If Stuff carries a report of the farmers making

monkeys of us in the paper, then I'm done for, then I'm fucking toast.'

'You are! I'm surprised at your being so naive myself.'

'That's what made me so mad. But I thought, oh, farmers, how are they going to hurt me? And then they proceed to run me criss-cross-country for five hours till I land up back in the auction hall at home.'

Gareis laughs heartily.

'But you didn't know that already, did you, Mayor?'

'Of course I did. I only want you to understand how happy your fellow citizens will be to read about it.'

'Don't give me that! They would be just as happy to read about all sorts of other things, for instance you and Frerksen taking your hats.'

'Could be. Certain other things would equally displease them. What would you do if I saw to it that none of the Altholm papers reported that farrago of yours?'

'We'll play ball with you. We'll adopt your approach.'

'My Lord!' says the mayor. 'Aren't you the generous one! What other alternative do you have? One approach has failed, you can only try the other.'

'You see,' says Manzow tauntingly. 'You don't know everything, after all.'

'What don't I know?'

'You don't know about the telegrams, and you don't know about the committee setting out first thing tomorrow morning either.'

'My God, how earth-shattering is that! Tell me! Are you off to be conciliated again?'

'Oh, don't be such a tease, Mayor! If I break my solemn word of honour and tell you, will you at least see that it stays out of the newspapers?'

'The local Altholm ones, yes. I can't do anything about the others.'

'All right. That's a deal, is it? – This morning, when our people got wind of the fact that there was going to be no reconciliation, and the boycott was set to continue, they were all shit scared.

In order to calm them down, all the businesses sent a hail of telegrams to Temborius, to get him to intercede, speed up the inquiry, punish the guilty.

'And tomorrow a deputation is going out to see Temborius and to tell him just how bad the boycott is, because you go around everywhere saying it's ineffectual.'

'I see. And you're going with them?'

'Of course I am. I'm even going as spokesman.'

'And what did you come here for, now?'

'To tell you that we accept your recent proposals. We're with you: boycott and counter-boycott.'

The mayor was black as night and enraged as a bull. Manzow should have kept to polite replies, nothing more. He sends fearful, hurried, covert glances at the irate man, anxious to avoid his eye, dreading an outburst.

Which comes, but not as expected. In loud rollicking laughter, the mayor dispels the tension and fury.

'Oh, you bloody idiots!' he yells. 'You push-me-pull-yous! Accept my suggestions, and go to the president to demand my punishment! You veal calves! You morons!'

'Not your punishment,' says Manzow, apparently in earnest. 'The punishment of the guilty parties.'

'That's enough, Franz, now mercy, please. I've had all the humour I can take. So let's get this straight: You're fighting – until further notice – on my side? The effectiveness of the boycott is to be denied? The farmers will be boycotted when they come to market? Silence on the 26th of July?'

'Yes. All agreed and decided.'

'Good. Very good. All right, Franz. All that's left for me to say is good luck in Stolpe. I'm afraid I won't be able to make it. Have to be in Stettin, there's a meeting about the river. You can come and see me the day after and tell me all about it. Bye now.'

'Bye, Mayor.'

Gareis is left staring fatly into space. He has a feeling: This is all so stupid, so pathetic, so ignominious – it's not worth it. Why do I keep throwing myself so whole-heartedly into it? I must be just as stupid.

He has another feeling: This isn't going to turn out well. This isn't going to end well.

And third, he knows he has to do something. Carry on down the chosen road, seeing as he doesn't want to turn back, and, for example, sacrifice Frerksen. He has to ring the bell and send for Political Adviser Stein. Things need to be done fast, very fast.

It's not worth it. It's not going to turn out well. But I need to act.

He presses the bell. 'Get me Political Adviser Stein, if you will. And come in with him.'

When the two of them are there:

'Fellows, things are starting to happen. I have to go to Berlin right away to see the minister. They are inciting Temborius against us. So I incite the minister against them. Officially, I'm in Stettin to see about the Blosse. The car will take me to Stettin. I'll be back tomorrow evening.

'Stein, twist, weave, duck for all you're worth. Got it? And another thing: that snoop Tredup will be bringing in a letter, Piekbusch. Thank him. Make sure this one doesn't get lost. Ideally, keep it on your person.

'Now I hope to God I manage to catch the minister. Frerksen should try and keep out of sight, if he can, Stein. Be good, chaps! Don't do anything I wouldn't do!'

By the time he's in the corridor, he's already out of breath.

IV

'Hey, aren't you going to stop for lunch today?' Wenk asks Tredup, who's prowling around the *Chronicle* offices in a particularly aimless and distracted way.

'I'm waiting for Stuff. I need to talk to him about something.'

'Stuff is out at the jury-court today. He won't be back until four o'clock.'

'Then he'll call me. He knows I'm waiting for him,' Tredup lies, and prowls off again, through the editorial office into the typesetting room, to the machine room, where the rotation presses are just spitting out the latest edition of the *Chronicle*.

He fishes out a copy for himself and another one for Wenk, and turns up in dispatch.

'There. Hot off the press.'

But he is too agitated to read, and keeps asking Wenk about the paper: 'Hey, Wenk, what does it really say on our certification? Is it seven thousand or seven thousand two hundred?'

'Seven thousand one hundred and sixty. Why do you want to know?'

'Oh, the department-store geezer was thinking about putting out an insert, and needed to know the exact figure. You're sure about it, are you?'

'Seven thousand one hundred and sixty. Quite sure.'

Pause. Wenk reads assiduously. Tredup racks his brain. He squinnies at the safe, where the keys are hanging, where the certification is. Unattainable. And the mayor's waiting.

'It's a bit of a specious thing, that old certificate. Don't you think, Wenk? Borderline dishonest, really. Did Gebhardt say he wanted us to go on using it?'

'Yes, he did say that.'

'Was anyone actually there to hear him say it?'

'No.'

'And you think if it turns out that it was dishonest, and we're in a courtroom, you or I, you think he really will hold up his hand and say he gave us that instruction?'

'How's it ever going to get out? Anyway, we are pretty near seven thousand.'

'I'm not sure. The counter on the rotation machine has got a different number.'

'Nonsense. Anyway, that counter's been broken for six months.'

'What about paper? You can work out how many copies we print from the amount of paper we get through.'

'Who's going to calculate our paper use? I don't even do that. The machine master comes and says we're on the last roll, and I order more.'

'But with the inserts? Say we get some leaflet to put in with the paper, and they give us seven thousand two hundred copies – what do we do with the spares?'

'Then we have some cheap fuel for the lead stove. Now let me read my paper in peace, will you?'

'But that's a swindle!'

'Of course it is. Not that you've ever swindled anyone in your blameless life. So calm down.'

Silence. Tredup goes on his walkabout again, goes into the typesetting room, comes back, stops in front of Wenk again.

'Has anyone told you that the *Chronicle* is being wound up?'

'That's nonsense. I would know.'

'That we're all going to be out of a job?'

'Nonsense. Gebhardt would hardly have gone to the trouble of acquiring us if he wants to put us out of business.'

'He'll have got rid of one competitor.'

'If he lets the *Chronicle* go bust, then someone else will come along and start a new paper. Then he'll have got himself some fresh competition.'

'Do you think Gebhardt bought the paper on the basis of the certificate, or did he know the actual number of subscribers?'

'Why don't you ask him that yourself?' And Wenk turns a page.

'I don't think you've got the real certificate here at all. Ours is just an unsigned copy.'

Wenk slams his hand down on the table. 'Will you leave me alone with your bloody certificate?! I don't know what's got into you today!'

Tredup stomps off. That was a defeat. I'd better not start talking about it again.

He hangs around with the typesetters, and goes back again. When he's in the editorial office, he hears voices in dispatch. He stops and listens.

'Yes,' Wenk is just saying. 'Your husband is still here, Frau Tredup. He's in the typesetting room now. Please take him with you, he's a bloody nuisance today, he must have sat in some itching powder.'

'Is he like that here too? What's he doing here still? I thought he was off for lunch an hour ago.'

'Am I his keeper? He says he wants to wait for Stuff. But Stuff isn't going to be around any time before four.'

'Tell me honestly, Herr Wenk, do you think my husband has changed?'

Wenk is evasive. 'Maybe a bit nervous? Prison does that, they say.'

'Is he doing any work?'

'Well, Frau Tredup, you'd better ask Herr Gebhardt that. I don't dole out report cards here, it's the boss who does that.'

'I will go to him!' says the woman. 'They've wrecked my husband!'

'Who have?'

'Stuff, who started him on drinking and whoring. And the ones who gave him money, Frerksen and Gareis.'

'Was he really given money? By Frerksen and all? For what?'

'Of course he got money. But he won't give me any. He's got it hidden somewhere by the Baltic. He talks about it in his sleep.'

'What's Gebhardt got to do with it? I wouldn't tell him about anything, because Gebhardt will just throw your husband out.'

'He ought to throw Stuff out. Stuff is the worst. And I'll drive a wedge between them yet, so I swear. And I know how, too.'

'How?'

'Wouldn't you like to know. So you can go and tell your Herr Stuff about it –'

Tredup comes strolling out of the editorial office. 'Shall we have lunch, Elise?'

The woman looks at him cursorily, gives Wenk her hand: 'Goodbye, Herr Wenk.'

'Goodbye, Frau Tredup. I'm happy to see you haul him off.'

They walk off, Frau Tredup a step ahead. As they pass the narrow little lane that connects the Burstah and the Stolpe Road, Tredup says: 'Go left down here, it's quicker.'

The woman hesitates briefly, and turns left. She is in the lead. Between dark firewalls. The lane is narrow, just five or six feet.

Suddenly the woman feels herself grabbed from behind, spun round, and looks into a face pale with rage.

'Max!' she cries out.

Her husband doesn't speak. With one hand he presses her to

the wall, he draws back the other and hits her three, four times in the face, hard.

She stares at him. Peers out fearfully from under a sheet of hair that has fallen into her face.

He looks at her a moment, his fury starts to ebb. Then he quickly turns and runs back to the *Chronicle*.

Wenk looks up. 'Well, made a run for it?' he grins.

'Who does she think she is!' rages Tredup. 'New fashions. Picking me up for lunch. I'll teach her a lesson, I promise you, Wenk, my hand is itching.'

'If you think that's the best way to teach her?'

'Absolutely. – Does Krüger have Bavarian beer?'

'Why wouldn't he? He always used to have it.'

'Will you get us two pints? I'll buy.'

'Now, before lunch? My wife will smell it on me.'

'What does your wife care if a businessman treats her husband to a glass of beer? Are you to miss out on a client because your wife doesn't approve of beer in the morning?'

'You're right. I'll send Fritz.'

'Don't send him, go yourself. The typesetters talk enough as it is about our drinking.'

'Where's the money?'

'Here.'

'You know what? I'll telephone. Then Krüger can have them sent here.'

Tredup, standing right by the safe, hiding the key with his back: 'Yes, so we can spend another hour waiting. It's lunchtime, they'll all be rushed off their feet at Krüger's.'

'Well, I guess I'll have to go, then.'

'And not before time either! Surely you can make the short trip if I'm buying?'

'I said I'm going.'

No sooner has he gone than Tredup tears open the safe door. There are three little drawers inside, in addition to the files for accounts and cash.

In the first there are employee and sick-fund cards.

The second is full of all kinds of junk.

The third – thank God, there it is. But there isn't time to write it out. He sticks it in his pocket, he'll have to see later on how he can return it.

Tredup puts the keys back, stops them swinging, and walks up and down. He can feel the paper burning a hole in his pocket.

Then they drink their beer, and then along comes Miss Clara Heinze to relieve Wenk so that he can go off for lunch too.

Wenk locks the safe, and his desk, picks up his hat.

'Cheers, then!'

'Cheers.'

He stops one last time in the doorway. 'Will you be here when I get back, Tredup?'

'Yes. I'm waiting for Stuff. I'll be here.'

'Then I'll leave the safe keys here. There's a chance a messenger from the *News* will come with some money. Eight hundred. The receipt's in the file.'

'OK, then. Enjoy your lunch.'

'Cheers.'

Tredup sits down at his typewriter in the editorial office, pulls the certificate out of his pocket, and starts typing.

Surely there was some easier way of getting hold of it.

V

Thiel has found a hideaway in an attic at the premises of the *Bauernschaft*.

It's not even a room, more what they call a side-loft hereabouts, a cubbyhole under a slant roof, with a little pane of glass that can be swung open on an iron hinge. One corner is full of junk: broken typesetters' galleys, decrepit rolls, machine debris. Under the window, Padberg has left him a few rugs and a stack of review copies of new novels. 'So you don't get bored.'

Here, a width of boards from the toilet, Thiel spends his days. The cistern next door continually floods, and any illusions Thiel may have had about *Homo sapiens* have failed to withstand the sounds of moving bowels.

But he isn't allowed to move himself, no one in the building can even guess at his presence. At night, Padberg brings him food, drink, reading matter and smokes. He's not mean about it, he seems happy to foot the bill (or have the paper foot it) to keep his guest in a good humour, but he is implacable in his insistence that Thiel not leave the premises.

By day, Thiel is kept locked up, his door is padlocked shut. He could try to loosen the staples, some bit of mechanical debris could be used to fashion a lever. But after once getting out, and running into Padberg on the street, he is keen to avoid a second such encounter.

Padberg had quietly taken him by the arm and, chatting the while, had walked him back to the editorial offices. But no sooner was the door closed than a hail of blows descended on Thiel. He was thrashed, a pitiless beating, for as long as Padberg's strength – which was something to behold – lasted.

'You stupid boy, all I need is getting into trouble over you! I rescue an idiot from prison and end up taking his place! Take that! And that! And that! Get it!?'

Two days later, Padberg is all right again. He knows what young people are like, he doesn't hold grudges. And he doesn't tire of setting Thiel on the nocturnal visitor of his, Padberg's, desk. He wants Thiel to catch him.

But Thiel remains doubtful. 'If there was someone, he's not there any more, Herr Padberg. I'm on guard all night. There's no one.'

'You're on guard? That's just it, you're not. Last night you left the light on in my room, I was just passing by outside. You mustn't do that. I could see you standing there, you fool.'

'Me . . .? You think I . . .?'

They look at each other. Thiel doesn't need to go on. Padberg understands, and believes him.

'That means *he* was there again. My God, Thiel, something is going on. You have to catch him. You've got the truncheon, haven't you?'

The *Bauernschaft* office is in an ancient building on the Stolpe Road. Two floors, with a big sloping roof like the side of a hill. It used to have a long garden at the back. Then the building became a newspaper premises, and a typesetting works was put up in the garden, as wide as the original house, with an external staircase leading up to a bookbindery on the second floor. Further into the garden, they added a machine house, where the lead stove was placed, and the rotation press, and the stove to heat the matrixes. The machine house was connected to the cellars of the front house by a covered walkway, so that the newspaper bales could be rolled through to the back. And they added a third shed with packing tables for the delivery girls.

Then by and by the remains of the garden were filled in with staircases and little passageways. In the house proper, walls had been knocked through and others put up: it was a warren of a place, a fox-burrow, a labyrinth –

Thiel knows it now. In the evening, at night, when darkness has fallen in these August days, he sets off without a torch, without any light at all, with nothing for company but his rubber truncheon, the only weapon Padberg will let him have.

He used to be convinced there was no intruder, and that Padberg was imagining things. He has spent hours wandering restlessly through the complex, not least to tire himself out for the day ahead, and never found anyone.

But last night there was a light, Padberg saw it, and really saw it too, that was clear from his expression.

So there is someone else around, some other ghost haunts this place besides him, someone cleverer than he is, otherwise he would have seen him by now.

Thiel ponders. He has enough time to ponder, God knows. Now he remembers that Padberg said early on that he had seen the spy at work and how he was always gone as soon as Padberg set foot in the building.

Either he has someone looking out for him . . .

But that thought straight away confuses Thiel. The ancient building has too many entrances and exits. There would need to be ten lookouts, and even then there would remain the possibility of being surprised.

Or else there's some mechanism, some light or bell signal that warns the man. The whole building is full of wires, after all.

Then there's nothing for it but to hide in the editorial office himself, to hunker under the desk all night long.

But Padberg has already tried that himself.

So once again, Thiel prowls around aimlessly, through the dark corridors, up and down the unlit staircases, into the front rooms illuminated by the street lamps on the marketplace, into the typesetters' room, whose skylights catch a glimmer of the never-completely-dark August sky, into the garden, which to his eyes is almost bright.

One time, when he's about to take the stairs from the dispatch to the editorial rooms on the second floor, something happens: he opens the door on to the staircase in that insane, silent warren of a house, and he hears in the dim distance, very softly, a bell.

For a split second Thiel stands motionless.

Then he races up the stairs, tears open the door to the editorial office . . .

His truncheon is held aloft over his head . . .

But there's no one in the room. Along the walls are the broad bands of light from the street lamps. To Thiel's night-accustomed eyes the room is bright as day. And it's empty.

But the door let into the opposite wall is swinging! It's still swinging gently!!

Thiel knows: a moment ago there was someone in here. *He* was here.

He goes over to the desk.

The desk drawer is open. Empty. Stacked up on top of the desk are its contents: being gone through, half gone through.

Thiel puts them back in the drawer. He'll not be back tonight.

'Well, never mind, next time,' Padberg comforts him.

'Yeah. Or the hundredth time, but I'll catch him.' Padberg is happy.

'And where's the bell?'

'Genius, I tell you! How I had to look for it! Over the stove there's a cleaning vent in the chimney breast. That's where it is. It's pure chance that I happened to hear it at all.'

'You left it there, though?' asks Padberg, concerned.

'Of course! It'll still ring, but not for me any more. I switched it off. There's a switch there, so you can turn it off during the day.'

'All right then!' says Padberg. 'Happy hunting!'

'Cheers!' answers Thiel, and his stuffy loft doesn't seem so bad any more.

VI

When Max Tredup came home late that night – yet again – it wasn't from any bar or steamy embrace.

He had gone up late to the town hall; he knew the mayor often sat in his office deep into the night, just because he was too lazy to go home, as people said.

But the mayor wasn't there, the mayor had left. The mayor had left instructions to leave the letter with him, Secretary Piekbusch. Tredup wasn't ready for that, he had to ask the secretary for an envelope – a crested envelope with the Altholm arms on it – which he then addressed to Mayor Gareis and marked *personal*.

Then, as he was going, he watched as the secretary tore open the envelope.

After the fevered chase, there came lassitude, after the excitement of hope, the more familiar position of despondency. It was one thing slapping his wife around at lunchtime – he was desperate to get his hands on the safe keys, it was all in the heat of battle, he was following secret instructions from the mayor. But in the evening, following Piekbusch's contempt in the anteroom, the way home stretching out ahead of Tredup, the blows became what they were: a piece of wretched behaviour with consequences he was afraid of.

Tredup didn't go home.

He sat on a bench for a while, outside the town, in front of the playground. This was where the Circus Monte with its gypsy wagons had set up its little two-pole tent, from which night after night the oom-pah-pah music had sounded. Back then he hadn't been able to tell Elise everything; today . . .

He got up and went to the station. He bought a ticket for

Stolpe, or more accurately to Stolpermünde. He wanted to get the thousand marks – the nine hundred and ninety marks – and give them to Elise, and say, everything's all right now.

He wanted to clear the air with Stuff. He would go to Gebhardt and say: Such and such is what the mayor offered me if I betray you to him. I'm just telling you for your information.

Then, in Lohstedt, he got off and gave in his ticket.

It was still too soon. Too soon to give Elise the money, to cut off his last escape route. For now there were other ways to bring her round: a bit of tenderness, a bit of attention, staying at home for an evening or two, a bit of bad-mouthing Stuff. And then some surprise: a bunch of wildflowers. Yes, that was the right thing, it didn't cost him anything, and it also proved he hadn't been in a pub.

Later on, walking from Lohstedt to Altholm, through the deepening and quietening night, with the flowers in his hand and a breeze in his face, he grows milder. Something of the fear that always seems to occupy his heart dissolves. He tries to sing some of the songs he learned at school once, and they even come to him when bidden. Life's not so bad.

And, by golly, he has to bear it in mind that Elise is pregnant again. He must see that he gets the address from Stuff.

How long ago was it? Right after his release from prison, which puts it four weeks ago, five. Perhaps still too early for the operation, well, but he could talk to Elise about it tonight, no harm in giving her a little hope and courage.

Six miles from his beaten wife, a reconciliation seems easy enough. Once he's in the yard, though . . .

Well, he's standing in the dark, it's past midnight. The two windows to his room are open, the wind is tugging at the curtains, his wife still has a light on.

He creeps closer, to spy on her. She's bound to be sewing, darning something for him or the kids.

No, she's not sewing.

She's sitting by the cupboard, she has some paper in front of her, she's writing something. He has a good view of her face in the lamplight.

Oh, it's a good face. It's not for nothing that you spend years with one woman, have children together, sleep with her, and talk to her about money, or what to eat tomorrow, and if the film was good or bad.

It's the face for him.

His heart feels soft. He quickly walks in.

She hurriedly makes to push her writing away when she hears him. But then she remains seated, with her back to him, and she doesn't say anything when he says hello.

He feels a little shiver. It's close in the room, and in spite of the open windows, there isn't a good smell. He can't get the children into the habit of walking across the yard to the outhouse at night, they prefer to use the potty, and Elise refuses to back him up.

The cool, pure night air is a memory. Even so, he reaches over her shoulder, and drops the bouquet in front of her, on top of whatever she was writing.

She stares disbelievingly at the flowers, she doesn't seem to get it. Then she turns round and looks at him.

He is sober. He has definitely had nothing to drink.

She raises her head a little, her throat tautens, quietly she says: 'Thank you.'

Then, when she sees the change in his face, she remembers her writing. She makes a grab for it, but it's too late. He's already got it in his hands.

It was chance that his eye happened to light on the envelope with the address. It was another chance that the address was so big, so legible, written in a deliberately childlike hand, that he could read it at two paces by the light of the oil lamp.

But what sent his hand arrowing down at the letter was pure, deliberate malice.

She sees it's too late. He's already reading it. She stands up, and leans with her back to the wall. Her head is lowered, she doesn't even want to know what his face expresses while he reads.

Once, as he mutters: 'Oh, wonderful! Wonderful!' she says quietly: 'Think of the children, Max!'

And, a little later: 'I'd never have sent it, you know.'

But it's a pretty document that's fallen into his hands. His bouquet happened to lie right across that precipitate of poison and cruelty, a few cornflower petals have fallen there, he blows them furiously out of the crease in the paper.

'What in God's name . . .?' he begins. He is still more puzzled than angry.

'No. Don't,' she says hastily. 'Let's not talk about it tonight, Max. If you like, tomorrow. You brought me flowers. Let's try once more. I want to be the way I was before. Put it away now. I'll burn it. I swear I'll never write another one. You know I'd never have sent it anyway.'

He doesn't hear her. 'How can you?!' he says. 'So cruel. Do you know that that's blackmail, and you can go to prison for that? And Stuff would always have believed it was me. Everyone would have thought so. I'd have wound up in prison –'

'No, Max, please, not now –'

'I never said it was Stuff who got the girls to have abortions. You jumped to that conclusion yourself. It was somebody completely different who told me –'

'Please, give me the letter.'

'And do you know what the really low thing is? Not only would you have got Stuff and me involved in it, the girls would have suffered too. Because you wanted to extort five hundred marks from Stuff, they would have had to go to prison. Did that not occur to you?'

'I was so angry,' she murmurs. 'And I wouldn't have sent it. Even if Stuff deserves it.'

'He doesn't deserve it.'

She says quickly: 'He's a bad man. He gets you to drink and visit girls. And you've stopped working. Wenk says you've completely stopped going after advertisements.'

'You're lying. Wenk didn't say one word about that. I heard what you and he were saying this morning.'

'And the way Stuff is with his girlfriends is beastly. To think that you wanted to take me to the same woman, to get our baby . . .'

She shudders, and turns to look at her sleeping children.

'What else! Do you want another baby? Haven't we got both hands full with the two we've got?'

'But we have money now. We can perfectly well afford a third!'

'We have no money. The thousand marks that Gareis blabbed about seem to have gone to your head. But I don't have them, and you won't ever see them.'

'You're lying. You keep telling me such vile lies. It's just like the lie about Stuff. First you claim it wasn't him with the abortions, and then you tell me not to drag him and his girls into trouble. So you do have the money.'

'I've got nothing!' yells Tredup in a fury. 'You're so low! Always after money! You want to blackmail my best friend for five hundred marks, that's how low you are.'

'I don't want money at all. I don't want your thousand marks, and I don't want Stuff's horrible money either. But I know that until I have your thousand marks, I won't have you either. As long as you've got them, you'll think: I can always leave, and you don't give a shit about us.'

'That's woman's logic for you! You don't want my money, but you do.'

'That's right! And if you don't understand that, you don't understand logic.'

'And as for the five hundred from Stuff . . . Betraying my friend, getting innocent girls packed off to jail, yuck!' and he spits.

'Hey!' she cries, with eyes blazing. 'You watch it! I could tell you something.' She stops. 'No, I don't want to. I'm not going to talk about it any more.'

He mocks her: 'Because you don't know anything! But I tell you, if you ever write a letter like that again, if you ever mail one! That's grounds for divorce. I'll be out of here so fast. Any judge worth his salt will grant a divorce where the wife is so low.'

'Oh?' she says. 'Oh? And if the man is so low? If the man goes out and sells photographs and betrays poor farmers so that they wind up in prison, I suppose that's decent? And he doesn't even give the money to his wife, he drinks it up and spends it on girls. Decent, eh? And I was never, ever going to send my letter. You, if you remember, did sell your photographs.'

'That's completely different,' he says in confusion. 'A press photographer has to sell his pictures to any interested party.'

'Oh, it's different, is it?' she cries in a fury. 'I can't actually see the difference. But, of course, if it's you doing it, it's always different, isn't it? Do you know what you are? You're a traitor! You've already betrayed me. I've heard about how, when you're drunk, you tell them what I'm like in bed. And –'

'Enough,' he says dully. 'The children –'

But she's not hearing him now. 'And I want my letter back. I don't want you running around with it in your pocket, and some time when you're pissed again, telling everyone what a mean wife you've got. Give it to me.'

She reaches for it. He holds on to it.

Now she's really fighting for it. He holds both her wrists in one hand, and in the other he holds the letter. Suddenly she dives at him with her teeth, and with a cry he lets go of her wrists.

She reaches for the letter, but he hits out at her. They stumble through the room, bumping into furniture, the children are crying.

The letter, crumpled in his hand, no longer holds him back. He punches her three or four times with his closed fist. She screams and falls down.

The door opens. The greengrocer who owns the house, and one or two neighbours, appear.

'I'm not having any more of this, Herr Tredup. I've had enough. You're always coming home drunk and having rows. I want you out of here on the first.'

The woman stands up and walks over to the door. 'Get out of here. This is no business of yours. And we're not accepting your notice. The housing department gets to decide whether we stay here or go somewhere else. Isn't that right, Max?'

'Yes, Elise,' he says.

VII

District President Temborius gets up.

'Thank you for coming to see me, gentlemen. I found what you told me very distressing. It will be checked, and I can only ask you to bear with me until that time. Patience, patience and more patience. But I think I can fairly tell you now, without being indiscreet, that not only here, no, but in the highest places, eyes are being directed at Altholm, and that steps are being considered – grave steps.

'Again, thank you, and please be patient.'

Temborius bows. Next to him, leaping up, the two other members of the Stolpe government also bow: Government Councillor Schimmel and Chief Adviser Meier.

The representatives of the financial and business life of Altholm are a little dilatory, but even they manage the getting-to-their-feet-and-bowing in reasonable time. The whole table bows and sways like a rye field in a high wind.

Then the Altholm delegation take their departure.

The president watches them go, one hand on the desk, the other clutching a medallion on his watch-chain. Chief Adviser Meier is stacking files, and Government Councillor Schimmel is scanning book spines on a shelf.

The door closes, and all three relax.

'Well, that was that,' says the president, sitting down. 'I must say, I'm not surprised. Not at all. – But please, gentlemen, won't you stay a little longer?'

The other two sit down.

'We have concerns. Concerns,' says Temborius, and it's quite clear that he is not unhappy with the concerns that are pressing on him at this hour. 'The lower reaches of the administration make mistakes. Then the people come to us. And it's up to us to make things better. But I think I can see the way of atonement and conciliation.'

'Certainly,' remarks Government Councillor Schimmel, 'Gareis has made mistakes.'

'Gareis!' And after a pause, a little louder: 'Gareis! Chief Adviser, what did I tell Mayor Gareis when he came here before the demonstration? Tell me!'

'That he would need the militia,' Chief Adviser Meier hurriedly replies.

'Yes. I said that as well. But that's not what we're talking about just now. What did I say in this very room, Chief Adviser?'

Meier racks his brain. His boss has said quite a lot of things in his time, after all. 'That the farmers were aggressive.'

'Yes, dear Chief Adviser. I also said that. – But it's important to separate the essential from the inessential. What did I –? All right then. I said the demonstration must be banned. Did I not say that? Did I not call for that? Repeatedly? Using all the authority of my office?'

'Yes,' the adviser says hurriedly. 'You called for it again and again.'

'Exactly. I called for it again and again. And now that the car's lost its way, does the man come to me? Has he turned to me for help? No. The representatives of commerce come to me. He's back in Altholm, writing a report. Nothing else. And what a report, at that!'

The gentlemen stare into space. Their boss feels a need to talk, very well, let him.

'What is in the report? The boycott is a busted flush. Its effects are barely noticeable. – Well, gentlemen, you've heard the representatives of the town, have you not?'

The gentlemen confirm that they have.

'The boycott is catastrophic, ruinous, it's bringing the economy of the town to its knees, but no: a busted flush. – A cobbler might write such a report. It is in fact cobblers.'

Suddenly Temborius is smiling again. 'Well, I'll fix it. I'll even things out.'

Very warmly: 'Did you ever, Government Councillor, examine the legal side of the affair? How does the state prosecution office view the events?'

'There will almost certainly be charges brought against some of the farmers. The leaders will be made an example of. Juridically these are the possibilities: Damage to property. Insulting behaviour. Actual bodily harm. Breach of the peace. Causing an affray.'

'Well, that's quite a bit to be getting on with.' The president is far from dissatisfied. 'No laughing matter if you're a farmer. And you think convictions will be brought in?'

'I do. – I should also like to point out that according to my information, the parties of the Right may well be bringing parliamentary questions shortly in relation to the events of Altholm.'

'Correct. You are well informed, Schimmel. I too have my

ministerial sources. You know, gentlemen . . . And in view of these forthcoming questions, I'm actually in favour of proceeding with all speed, for once.

'The minister has not yet asked for the files. I am therefore still free to take decisions as I see fit. The minister's reactions are not completely predictable, because unfortunately Herr Gareis too has certain . . . Well, just let me say I don't completely understand the minister and his likes and dislikes. At least, we may be sure that he won't reverse any previously passed decisions of mine. Therefore . . .'

The gentlemen prick up their ears.

'We will . . .'

The historic significance of this moment is shiningly apparent in the face of the president. He holds a pencil upright in the air.

'We will once again adjust, correct, compensate, conciliate, rub out the errors of the lower layer of government. For that, we mustn't too closely identify ourselves with any position. We must be fair to everyone.

'The feelings of the peasantry, the feelings of the townspeople, the feelings of all Pomerania are running against the Altholm police. But we will give the police confirmation that they behaved correctly, we will lend our support to central authority, we will not stiffen the necks of the rebels.

'But . . .' He smiles subtly. 'We will slaughter a goat. Feast of reconciliation. Make a sacrifice. Purim, I believe your people call it, Chief Adviser?'

The adviser smiles in turn.

'This is what we will do. We say the police have acted correctly, but . . . There is a middle way. It's all possible nowadays. Administration has become such a refined art. I'm not thinking of Gareis, Gareis still has some strength. But maybe that over-assiduous gentleman, what was his name again . . .?'

'Frerksen?' volunteers Chief Adviser Meier.

He is praised. 'Correct! Well done!! Frerksen. Then, when we have soothed popular feeling by this sacrifice, then, gentlemen, we bring them to the table. Then, under my chairmanship, we will iron out some differences and effect conciliation.'

'With the farmers too?'

'By all means. We invite, first and foremost, the large agricultural associations, the representatives of the communities, the
interest groups. If, say, we include three of those peasants among
thirty others, rest assured they will follow the majority. We have
plenty of experience of that.

'Thank you for the moment, gentlemen. I must say, I feel
rather optimistic. Not a facile optimism, no, not at all, rather
an optimism based on mature experience. The storm has blown
over, lightning has struck, hail has come down.

'And at that moment we come along and put up a rainbow.

'Thank you, gentlemen.'

VIII

The morning sun shines brightly into the front room of
Stolpermünde-Abbau. It paints a broad band of light on the wall,
just under the ceiling. And that golden beam, in which there are
thousands of dust particles jigging and dancing, moves, slides
down the wall, till it settles, just as broad and beaming, on the
checkered coverlet.

Then it brushes the pillow.

The invalid becomes restless. He turns his head this way and
that, but the light is everywhere. So he opens his eyes, shuts them
quickly, opens them again.

Banz sits up.

It's a slow process, his bandaged head keeps wanting to return
to the pillows. In the end, though, the man is sitting upright and
looking out into the room.

He nods slowly when he sees where he is.

Then he listens. The house is very quiet, the buzzing of flies is the
only sound, hundreds and hundreds of flies. Again, the man nods.

And listens further. Listens out into the yard. But there too everything is quiet. Not the clank of a cow's chain, not a single footfall.

All quiet.

The man is set at ease. But there is one thing he still wants to

know. There is a calendar hanging beside the door. If his wife has
kept good order, it will have been kept up to date. Then he will
know what day it is today. But the calendar is hard to see from the
bed, Banz has to lean way out from the pillows. He blinks his eyes
hard, the type on the calendar is so blurry.

Then Banz loses his balance. His head strikes the side of the
bed and then a chair leg, and the man is left lying on the ground
at the foot of the bed. His head hurts, he fills a little sick, but
Banz is grinning with satisfaction: it's much cooler outside the
bed.

Now there is nothing for it but to wait for his wife to come. To
go by the sun, it must be about eleven, he shouldn't have more
than an hour to wait.

He still can't read the calendar. He will try later on to drag
himself closer to it, but not now, he is still too feeble. With astonishment, he realizes that he can feel flies walking around on his
hands. He must have been ill for a long time for his skin to have
become so soft.

He lies there a while, drifting in and out of consciousness. When
he wakes up again, the sunbeam is still at the head of the bed.

He listens, and maybe it was the sound that woke him up:
there's somebody out in the yard. He hears the footfall distinctly.
It's not familiar to him, no farmer's tread. There's something
hasty and stumbling in it. Not one he knows.

Well, he'll see soon enough who it is outside, if he stays alive
long enough. If the fellow wants something, he'll come in. Banz
almost completely shuts his eyes, and peeps at the door through
a crack in them.

Sure enough, here he comes. The metal bell at the top of the
door that rings when someone opens it sounds. The man is in
the hallway.

Of course he starts off by knocking on the door to the left. Strangers in the house always knock on the left, which is where the children sleep. Then there's a knock on the middle door. The kitchen.

Now he's knocking on the door to Banz's room, but Banz
doesn't dream of calling out 'Come in!' He's lying there on a plate
for a visitor, in his nightshirt on the ground, with his bandaged

head against the chair leg, apparently unconscious. He'll soon see what kind of fellow it is, if he comes in and sees all that mess.

The door opens, and a squinnying Banz sees it's someone in uniform, in a field-grey uniform. He tries to think what sort of uniform it is. Reichswehr? But that doesn't have the red epaulettes. Then he sees that the man doesn't have his sword-belt on. That means he's not here on official business.

Now Banz keeps his eyes clenched tight. Let's see if he's the sort of idiot who'll be taken in by his seeming unconsciousness.

The uniform, after standing in the doorway for a moment, walks into the middle of the room. He has a firm stride, as though to waken the sleeper, but Banz thinks: You tramp all you like. I can tell there's something not quite right about your gait.

The man stops, clears his throat, and says: 'Hey!'

Banz thinks: Well, 'hey' is something they all know how to say. Let's see what else you know.

Apparently the man at that instant has reached his limits. There is silence in the room. Only the buzzing and droning of flies.

Wonder what he'll do? thinks Banz, and he feels like blinking his eyes, but manages not to.

The man takes another couple of strides closer to Banz. Then away again. Then a chair is moved, and the man sits down.

Not so bad, thinks Banz. Just leaves me lying here. Well . . .

The man rustles in his pockets, Banz hears paper. Wonder if he's got a warrant? But those aren't executed by the Reichswehr.

A couple of unidentifiable sounds, then a match is struck – puff puff puff – and there's a glorious smell of cigars.

Son of a bitch, thinks Banz, and blinks his eyes. 'Are you awake now?' asks the man.

'Depends,' says Banz, opening his eyes wider. 'I don't exactly know you.'

'You can't know everyone,' says the uniformed one, who also sports a yellow goatee.

'You're right about that,' agrees the farmer.

Pause.

'What uniform is that, by the way?' asks Banz.

'That's a prison-warden uniform,' says the uniform.

'So you're in prison?' asks Banz.

'For life,' replies the man, and laughs. A whinnying laugh. Just like a goat.

Pause.

The man says extenuatingly: 'This is a Republic uniform, I know. Earlier, I used to be a naval officer. That was blue or white. In those uniforms we never starved. No, sir.'

'No,' says Banz.

Pause. The flies drone.

'Are you comfortable like that?' asks the man.

'You can leave me like this. It's not bad.'

'Must be cooler than it is in bed.'

'It is that, too.'

The man rustles in his pocket.

Wonder what's coming now? thinks Banz.

The man produces a piece of paper.

Is it that prison guards make their own arrests now? thinks Banz. They used to have militia to do that.

'Here,' says the man, and passes Banz a newspaper. It's been read many times, he can tell, the folds are crumbling, and the front part is quite grey.

It is a police announcement. The reward posted for information leading to the arrest of the Stolpe Bomber has been increased to ten thousand marks. The announcement comes complete with pictures. There is a margarine crate. An alarm clock. A tin can and some wires. All the things you need to make a proper bomb. And a detailed description of how it was put together. If you like, a recipe for home-made bombs. The police will have found some bits and pieces, and experts had reconstituted it. A good job.

'A good job,' says the man. 'If you like, a recipe for how to make bombs. I must say, I think it turned out pretty well.'

Banz prefers to shut his eyes again at this point. He knows nothing. He hears nothing.

The man continues to chatter away: 'I assembled all the stuff at the dump: boards and tin can and wires and battery and an alarm clock. With me, no one will be able to source the components.'

Banz is fast asleep.

'Then I studied clockmaking. My sergeant swore at me for taking his clock apart. But I learned a lot from it, and the one from the dump keeps good time. It'll go off whenever I want it to. To the minute.'

Banz is snoring by now.

'And the battery's easy enough to fix up. It's so stupid just to throw them away. All you need is acid, and the glue at the top, you can get that. Then you load it up. You should see the lovely spark it strikes when my alarm clock goes off.'

Banz is asleep.

'Now all I need is something to fill the can with. But it won't be that hard to find, what do you think?'

But Banz is asleep.

The uniform says: 'I've thought about who to take out first: Gareis or Frerksen. Frerksen was the first to cut loose, and sicked the police on to the farmers, but Henning did say: "The son of a bitch is Gareis."'

Banz blinks.

'Henning said: "If the high-ups aren't in the mood, Frerksen has his tail between his legs." It was Gareis who lured the peasants in. Henning says first he was all friendly, and allowed everything, just to get them demonstrating. So he gets some bodies to smash up, to make an example of them, because they don't pay their taxes, and that business with the oxen.'

Banz listens.

The man explains: 'Henning is still in hospital. And we have to stand guard outside the door. Because he's a prisoner. That's how I got to meet him.'

'Why is Henning in hospital?'

The goatee is all contempt. 'Don't you know? You really are a hick farmer! Don't know anything about anything. Because Henning refused to surrender the flag they beat him up so badly in Altholm they crippled him for life.'

'Right. I see,' says Banz. 'I think that was news to me.'

'Henning is a hero,' says Auxiliary Warden Gruen, proud to know such a hero. 'He got thirty-one sabre blows on his arms and hands. The farmers all swear by Henning. And even in Altholm they know that the flag-bearer is a hero.'

'A flag-bearer,' says Banz, 'stands and falls with his flag.'

'That's right,' says Gruen. 'That's why he's a hero.'

'So he is,' says Banz.

Pause.

'What about it, then?' asks the uniformed man. 'Do I break open the barn and get the stuff out? Or are you going to give me a key?'

Banz reflects. 'I don't know if it's still there,' he says finally.

'Of course it's still there. Where else is it going to be? The others don't want it, that's for sure.'

'The key's hanging in the kitchen. Beside the butter churn. Unless my wife has pocketed it.'

'All right,' says the man, and he goes out.

Banz hears him fossicking around outside, that same stumbling gait. When he hears it, he feels like saying to the man: Get lost, won't you? But he can't get up.

Then the barn door bangs open. He even hears the sound of the padlock.

Wonder if he'll find the chest? thinks Banz. If he comes back and says, Where are the chests? I'll lay him out.

The door rattles again. The keys jingle again. The stumbling gait approaches.

'I hung up the key by the butter churn. I'll be on my way. Shall I lift you back on to your bed?'

'Where're you carrying it?'

'I've got it loose in my pockets. It'll attract less attention that way. – Shall I pick you up and put you back to bed?'

'I'm fine as I am. Just go.'

'I'm going.'

'You do that.'

IX

It's a radiant morning, and every bit as radiant, as bright and as round as the glorious August sun, is Mayor Gareis, stepping into Political Adviser Stein's office in the ninth hour.

'Top of the morning to you, Political Adviser. How's it hanging?

By golly, how dark and grim and anxious you're looking! On a morning like this! Did you go for a stroll last night?'

He doesn't wait to hear the answer.

'I was out and about in Berlin, I tell you, what a city! The work there must be there! I'd love to be unleashed on Berlin!'

He stands there in trousers and waistcoat, swinging his great belly. He laughs.

'The fools here say I want to be Oberbürgermeister. My God, maybe I do a bit, just to annoy that administrative genius of a Niederdahl. But be stuck here in Altholm all my life . . .? I don't think so. A cosy home with roses growing in the garden, and the same squalid horse-trading every budget . . .? No thanks! It's Berlin for me!'

He drops heavily into an armchair, which quivers. 'Or Duisburg. Or Chemnitz. Or some dormitory town outside Berlin that I could get moving. But Altholm? Altholm? Where's the charm of Altholm?'

'It seems to me,' his adviser remarks drily, 'you can't have visited your office yet.'

'Nor have I, nor have I. And when I see your face, Steinchen, it makes me feel like skiving off and going to the country. What would you say to ordering the car and driving out to the seaside? Have a swim. Go and eat somewhere afterwards. There's surely going to be some restaurant somewhere where they don't know my face, and they'll feed us, in spite of the boycott. And then slowly drive home in the evening . . .'

'They've turned off all the lights here,' the adviser remarks enigmatically.

'Well, then, I'll turn them all on again, Steinchen, I will. So. I take it some nonsense or other happened the day I was gone. It's always the way, isn't it? All I need to do is pack my suitcase in the afternoon, and people will start braining each other in the marketplace.'

'I would go and have a look, Mayor.'

'If I know I'm going to step in dog shit, why be in such a hurry? Is it the farmers?'

Political Adviser Stein nods sorrowfully.

'You know, the business with the farmers doesn't interest me any more. I've really stopped caring about it. It's dealt with. Steinchen, I've been to see the minister. We talked it through, my God, there's a man, at last. I feel I can stomach the Party again, it's not just bickering and deals, but people who want to get things done. Never mind how. – No, the farmers' rumpus is over. The men of the Right will get their answer in Parliament, and it will be nice and clear, and they won't ask any more questions. Political Adviser, the minister is giving us his backing.'

'That's as may be, but the district president isn't.'

'Temborius? The foldaway file? The stodgy legal gateau, dusted with dust? What does it matter what he wants, if his boss has decided?'

'What if Temborius has got in there first?'

The fat man leans way back in his chair, shuts his eyes, and twiddles his thumbs.

'All right,' he says slowly, 'Political Adviser Stein, then we step in the shit with the full weight of our personality. What is it?'

'Temborius has written. To the magistracy. And to you. The one to you is on your desk. But the one to the magistracy is enough on its own. Full of misfavour.'

'Oh, I knew that.'

'Frerksen is relieved of his post.'

The fat man jumps out of his chair. 'Frerksen relieved? That's not possible. That's betrayal. That's the administration stabbing us in the back. The government kowtowing to the peasants. The government shopping their own police. That's not possible. He's not allowed to pre-empt the minister!'

'He's done it.'

'Quick, Adviser! Run! I need the letter. Go and get me my letter. Do you think there's still time? I want to show those pieces of work in Stolpe who has nerves, who can fight, who has the support of the workers . . . Run!'

The adviser is already back. He hands Gareis the letter.

He tears open the envelope, standing up. Gives it the once-over. Reads it a second time. Then lets it drop.

'And they expect a man to go on working. That administrative genius! He's wrecked my entire outfit here. He's strengthened the boycott. Woe is Altholm! The president has got it in for you.'

The fat man turns round, walks over to the window, stares out.

Comes back. 'Draw the curtains, will you? This August sun is unbearable. All right, Adviser, here, read it. President Temborius disapproves in the strongest terms. The demonstration should have been banned. If the police did anything, then it should have been in accordance with his secret instructions –' He breaks off.

'Those wretched disappeared secret instructions. If only I had the least idea of what was in them. I can hardly tell Temborius I've never seen them.'

He looks at the letter again. 'Commander Frerksen's approach deserves severe censure. Frerksen will be relieved of his duties by the executive until such time as the legal process has run its course, and is confined to indoor work forthwith.

'Final position reserved till the court case is over. Files on the case passed to the Minister of the Interior.'

Suddenly the big man grins all over his big moon face, and there isn't the least doubt: something has really cheered him up.

'Well, my dear Political Adviser, this really is what you call a defeat all down the line. Temborius was quicker on the draw. I was thinking how clever I was when I set out to see the minister.'

The storm is over, the fat man is thinking.

'First,' he says, 'I'll send Frerksen away on holiday. Call him, and have him come right away. He may as well be gone from here for the next four weeks. – Then I'll go round to the councillors and enjoin them all to keep quiet, on their oath. Do you think they won't give me an oath? Stein, this is no rehearsal any more, there's no quarter given nor asked, I'm going to kick them in the balls unless they do what I say.

'These letters from Temborius, these rulings – no one must know about them. It would do us too much damage. And since this is ultimately about the public purse, the councillors will keep quiet.'

There's a knock, and Commander Frerksen walks in.

'Tell me, Frerksen,' says Gareis, 'what's all the talk in town about your sabre? You do have your sabre, don't you?'

'Yes, Your Honour.' And he drops his hand on the hilt of his sabre, but blushes furiously.

'So what are people doing, talking about it? Was there a time you didn't have it?'

'Yes, Your Honour.'

'Don't be quite so martial with me, if you don't mind. I can't follow if you do. So, you lost your sabre once?'

'Yes, sir –'

'All right, all right. And when did you get it back?'

Silence.

'You can't even give me a martial answer to that. So you didn't get it back?'

Silence.

The mayor sits up straight. 'Is it really true then that the KPD official, Matthies, is in possession of your sabre, Commander? He has been heard to boast to that effect.'

'I don't know, Your Honour. He brought me my sabre when I didn't have a sheath for it. And then, later, I must have forgotten about it.'

'Tsk, tsk. So you forgot about your sabre. It's easily done, I suppose. The absent-minded professor and his umbrella. The commander and his sabre. One more thing: can you tell me why, in your eloquent reports on the demonstration, the losing of your sabre, the reunion with your sabre, the forgetting of your sabre, are all left unmentioned? – Yes, please! Your answer, Commander.'

But Frerksen says nothing.

'Would you explain to me, then, why it is that your son tells everyone at his school that you said the peasants were all criminals and should be stood against the wall and shot? No, no, please, Commander! No figures of speech. Your son said those words, his headmaster told me so in person.'

Frerksen stands there in silence.

'You're listening, Commander, you're not answering. Perhaps you want time to think about your answers? You shall have it. I want you to go home and consider yourself on leave. You're not to spend your holiday in Altholm. Initially, it will be for the next four weeks. Leave me your address. I'll let you know if it's to be extended at all beyond four weeks.

'That's all, Commander.'

The creature in blue uniform clicks its heels. Then, not before time, the door shuts after it.

The adviser, white-faced, says: 'My God, Mayor, Frerksen will never forgive you.'

'Forgive me . . .? One day he will thank me. Is it better to tell him the president has dismissed him? Firstly, he'd have gossiped about it. Secondly, his self-esteem would have been destroyed. Now he's in a fine old rage against me. That'll strengthen his spine. He's always been a bit of a pudding anyway, Frerksen, a soft and yielding pudding. It would be no bad thing if he got a bit brown and crisp.'

X

There is one person in Altholm who really suffers as a result of the events of the 26th of July, suffers night and day

It wasn't hard to guess how Altholm Gymnasium would position itself in relation to the events of the 26th of July: a flag-bearer hurrying along with his flag was far too compelling an image for young people to resist. And since Henning was a hero, it followed that his attackers were villains.

But who was the leader of the villains? Who was the unhappy individual who had drawn his sabre on the hero?

None other than Commander Frerksen.

He was the sinister power, the Nifling, the monster, he was Ephialtes, the bogeyman, the principal of darkness.

And it was unfortunate that such a man should nonetheless have a protector. What a wretch that protector must be, someone who evidently turned black into white, and white to black.

At the age of eleven, Hans Frerksen, the second-former (green cap, gold braid on azure ground), had to fight the fight for his father every day.

He fought it bravely, without a word about it at home.

It had begun quietly the day after the demonstration, with looks, whispers, gawping stares, and Coventry.

That night Hans had heard a conversation in his parents' bedroom, which was also his own bedroom. His weak bladder had woken him just in time to hear his father say that these peasants were villains and crooks, and deserved no sympathy.

He had smiled to himself at first when they stared at him, those boys were so thick. They didn't understand about anything. Their first instinct was always to blame the police, and later on, when they understood, they would see that the police had done everything right.

But this isolation went on a bit long, for a child anyway. In the yard at break, he was the object of stares. Big boys, even sixth-formers, asked to be brought to him, and then they would look at him and say, 'So that's who it is,' and walk away again. After break, when everyone pressed in through the narrow doorways, up the narrow staircases, there was a kind of air pocket round Hans Frerksen. No one likes to come too close.

It took an alarmingly long time for the truth to come out, and the worst of it was that even the teachers were not immune. It showed in all sorts of contradictory ways. Some asked him an unusual lot of questions, others purposely ignored him. But the way they quizzed him, and the way they ignored him, had this in common: the understanding that this is Frerksen, the son of that other Frerksen.

He was isolated, so he isolated himself further. He didn't want to have anything to do with any of them, he could bide his time, one day they would come to him, and he wouldn't know them. He would refuse to pardon them. He would be implacable and proud.

But then one day, Hans Frerksen changed his tactics. He felt so hollow inside, there was nothing left in him, his pride was exhausted. He went on to the attack. He pushed into the rings of the others, he interrupted them, he didn't care in the least when they walked off. He walked off after them.

He started talking about the peasants, those crooks, and at least then they started to listen to him. Even though they still didn't ask him any questions or take issue with him, they did at least listen, and then they went away and laughed sardonically.

There were nicknames for him now, and allusions were made. There was an awful lot about some sabre or other, he had no idea what that was about. Then they started stuffing issues of the *Bauernschaft* in his desk. The story of the sabre was told in that, there were great tirades about Red Frerksen, Bloody Frerksen, who liked nothing so much as bathing in peasants' blood.

Of course it was all a lie, but you couldn't ignore it, so you exaggerated just as those others exaggerated, and you talked about criminals who deserved to be put up against the wall.

What happened, happened. First he was asked to see his form master, and a few days later it was the headmaster.

Blah, blah. 'Did you say something about criminals who deserved to be stood up against the wall?'

'Yes,' says Hans Frerksen.

'How did you come to say such a thing? Did you hear it anywhere?'

'My father said it, and my father knows.'

'Boy, think about it. Your father can't possibly have said that.'

'Yes, he did. He said it.'

'But Frerksen. There were four thousand peasants in the town. You're old enough to know that they can't all be criminals. Do you think they should all be shot?'

'Yes.'

'But surely you've read that one of the people hurt was a dentist, someone who wasn't involved at all. He's not a criminal, is he?'

'Yes, he is.'

'But how? Think. A dentist on the way to help a patient?'

'It's wrong to participate in crowd events. My father says where there are crowds of people it's best to go away. If you stay in a crowd, you're responsible for what happens to you.'

'But it doesn't make you a criminal.'

'Yes,' says the boy.

The headmaster is getting impatient. 'No, it doesn't. And the peasants aren't criminals either.'

'Yes, they are,' avers Hans Frerksen.

'You just heard me say they're not. I'm your teacher. I know more than you do.'

'My father says they are criminals.' And, obstinately: 'They all deserve to be shot.'

'No!' yells the head. Then, more quietly: 'It's upsetting to hear this from you. I know your views will be different when you're older.'

'No!'

'I want you to keep quiet and listen. I said your views will be different –'

'No,' says the boy.

'Dammit, will you keep your mouth shut! I'm going to have to punish you. – I'm forbidding you, do you hear, to talk about these things with the other boys, at school or during break. Not one more word, all right?'

The boy looks at him stubbornly.

'Did you understand, I asked you.'

'But what if they start it! I can't allow them to talk against my own father.'

'Your father . . . All right, I'll have your teacher tell the form that the class is not to talk about it. Then you'll keep quiet, won't you?'

The boy looks at him.

'All right, Frerksen, you can go now.' He's by the door when the head calls out to him: 'When did your father say that about them being criminals?'

'At night, the night after the demonstration.'

'At night? Were you awake?'

'Yes.'

'Do you sleep in your parents' bedroom?'

'Yes.'

'Did he say it to you, or to your mother?'

'To Mum.'

'OK. Thanks. You can go.'

He went. But, actually, it was worse after than it had been before. Yes, there weren't so many references to it in his presence.

But, quite apart from the fact that they went on and on about it behind his back, they simply stopped talking to him altogether. He was ostracized, despised, and then he had shopped them and told tales. Like father like son, both villains.

It must have been ten times at least that Hans vowed to talk to his mother about it. But when he saw her, timid, shy, with red-rimmed eyes, he held back. He understood that she was in just such a bad way as he was. Her parents had stopped coming to the house, and other relatives had as well. Twice they had found excreta in the bag for the morning rolls hanging on the door, and the little cherry tree in the garden had been snapped one night.

Everyone had their load to bear, Gretel as well, even though girls are different, they talk and talk about everything until they no longer know where they are.

He comes home at lunchtime and hangs his cap on the hook. Drops his satchel on the chair in the hall.

Dad is already home. His sabre is in the coat-stand. The damned sabre! Of course everything they said about it was a lie. But Hans would still like to know where the old sabre is. This one is new, he spotted that right away.

Out of the dark behind the coat-stand his mother emerges. She is crying so much her cheeks are shiny with tears. 'Oh, Hans, Hans, what have you done! Daddy . . .'

The boy looks at her. 'Don't cry, Mum. I haven't done anything.'

'Don't lie to me, Hans. Whatever you do, don't lie. There, go in and see Daddy. I wish I could help you, my poor lad. Be brave, and don't tell lies.'

The boy goes into his father's room. His father is standing by the window, looking out.

'Hello, Daddy,' says the boy, trying very hard to be brave.

His father doesn't answer.

For a while they both stand there in silence, and Hans's heart beats with terribly fast, painful strokes. Then his father turns. The son looks at the father.

'Hans! What have you . . . No, come nearer. Stand in front of me and look at me. Tell the truth, boy. What did you say to your headmaster?'

'The other boys . . .'

'No, I'm not interested in that. No irrelevancies. What happened with Headmaster Negendank?'

'The headmaster asked me if I said the peasants were criminals who deserved to be shot.'

'And . . .?'

'I said yes. Then he asked me if the dentist is a criminal as well.'

'Yes, and . . .?'

'Then I said, he is one as well. If someone is in a crowd, whatever happens to him in the crowd is his fault.'

'And? Go on!'

'Then the headmaster said they aren't criminals. Then he told me not to say again that they were.'

'And . . .?'

'That's all. Then he sent me away.'

'Are you sure that's all?' asks the father. 'Didn't you tell the headmaster that you'd heard the thing about criminals and being shot from me?'

The boy looks at his father speculatively.

'Did you tell him that? Answer me! I want to know.'

'Yes,' says the boy quietly.

'May I ask how you come to spread such lies about me? What's going on? Who told you to say that?'

'No one.'

'Who said that? Did I say it?'

'Yes, Dad.'

'There!' The first blow strikes him. The blow administered by a strong man to the face of a child, without holding back. 'I'll teach you! I said that? When did I say that?'

The boy covers his face with his hands and doesn't speak. 'Take your hands down. Don't make such a fuss. When did I say that?'

'The night after. You said it to Mum.'

'There! There! There! I never said it! Never!'

'You did!' yells the boy.

'Never! You hear me: never! – Anne, come here.'

The mother comes in, pale, shaking, teary.

'There, look at this fellow, your son. He's wrecked my whole career with his criminal talk. That lying rascal claims I said to you the night after the demonstration that the peasants were all criminals who deserved to be shot. – Did I say that, Anne?'

The son looks at his mother, imploring and serious.

The mother looks at her son, then her husband.

'No,' she says, hesitantly, 'you didn't quite put it –'

'No! None of that! Just: did I say it or didn't I?'

'No,' says the mother.

'There you are! You wretched liar! Take that! That! That! Stay away, Anne. The rascal deserves it. Let go of my hand, Anne.'

'No, no. Not now, Franz. Not in the heat of anger. He was only wanting to stick up for you!'

'Thanks for the support. Thanks for the support of a liar. We're going straight to the headmaster, and I want you to tell him you told a lie. And there'll be trouble if you try and say anything else!'

He grips his son by the wrist. Drags him through the streets to the Gymnasium.

But the headmaster is at home.

Another schlepp. The livid, trembling man drags his son along.

The headmaster isn't available at the moment. The headmaster is having lunch.

I must see the headmaster.

'Here, Headmaster, I've brought you my son. I've only just heard what a shameless and barefaced lie he told you. Hans! I want you to beg the headmaster's pardon right away. Say: I have lied to you.'

The headmaster, napkin in hand, walks sheepishly back and forth. 'Commander, not like this. Not in the heat of the moment. Look at the boy. He has to be spared.'

'Bah, spared! I'm sorry, but who thought to spare me? – Say: Headmaster, I have told a lie.'

'I have told a lie.'

'My father didn't say anything about peasants being criminals.'

'My father didn't say anything about peasants being criminals.'

'They don't deserve to be shot.'

'They don't deserve to be shot.'

'All that was just a lie.'

'All that was just a lie.'

'There. – Of course the headmaster can't be expected to pardon you today.'

'No, no. I'm even of the view –'

'No. Don't be too soft. I would like to ask to have him be punished severely in school as well. Probably I'll send him to a different establishment. The Gymnasium is far too liberal for liars like him –'

'Commander, please won't you calm yourself. In the heat of the moment. And when there are so many things that can be said in such a matter. Liar . . . Liar . . . He's only a boy. Hans, will you go and wait next door for a minute.'

'No, he stays here. We have to go on to Mayor Gareis. I'm afraid he has a lie to confess to there. Hans, take your cap, we're going –'

'You can't be serious, Commander. Look at the boy. – As I thought! Collapsed in a heap! Yes, you feel ill? Lie down there till you feel better. – Darling, will you get the boy a glass of water? – Sir, it may be better if you visit the mayor by yourself. And then send the boy's mother round here to pick him up.

'Now, please leave. I really don't have any time for you right now, Commander. The boy is more important to me at the moment. Good day, Commander.'

In his muzzy, confused mind, the boy is thinking to himself: Daddy's a liar, Mummy's a liar, Daddy's a liar, Mummy's a liar.

Two days later in the *Chronicle*'s display case he reads that Police Commander Frerksen has been temporarily relieved of his duties for incorrectly applied police tactics.

But by then his father is already on holiday. Gone away.

XI

When Stuff wants to know something about detective work, he has to go and call on the gentlemen. They never come to him. The high-ups don't like it. There's always something faintly compromising about being seen walking into the *Chronicle*.

The one exception to this is Perduzke, the perennial deputy, who is still waiting for his promotion to come through, and who is incapable of wrecking things with the Reds for the simple reason that they're thoroughly wrecked already.

Emil has come to see his mate again. They put their heads together over the big desk and they reminisce about the days when there was still a whole infantry regiment based in Altholm. Then they rant about the times, the awfulness of the world, for which the Reds are largely to blame, and the apprentice typesetter is kept crossing the yard, for cigars and beer, or schnapps and beer.

Today, though, Perduzke won't cross the threshold, he pulls something white out of his pocket and opens it out.

'I'm here on official business, Herr Stuff.'

'Great. But you can still sit down. Or do you want to arrest me straight away?'

Perduzke grins. 'Oh, they wish! They've really had it up to here with you and your mischief-making. – The endless back and forth today at the town hall.'

'What back and forth was that?'

'It's as if you stirred up an ants' nest with a stick. There are so many rumours going around. There was a letter on Gareis's desk from the district president. And then, two hours later, Frerksen is going on holiday.'

'Emil! Oh, sweet, lovely Emil! Frerksen's going on holiday! Is being frogmarched off on holiday! The president gets involved. Police tactics not lawful.' In deep earnest: 'What did the letter say, Emil?'

'I don't know, I swear to God. I don't know.'

'Don't be a coward, Emil. I swear, I'll never betray you. Do you want a schnapps? Do you want a freshly tapped beer? Do you want three freshly tapped beers? Do you want seven cognacs! Name your price! What was in the letter?'

'I said I don't know. Also, you shouldn't jump to conclusions. How do you know there's any connection between the letter and the holiday?'

'Frerksen on holiday! That's the beginning of the end! I tell you, Emil, he won't be coming back. He's finished. And I'll find out every bit of what the letter said.'

'But anyway, I'm here on official business. You published an open letter in issue 171 of the *Chronicle*.'

'Yes? Did I? If you say so, Emil, then it'll be true.'

'The letter was signed "Kehding".'

'Kehding? There's lots of Kehdings in these parts. What did the letter say?'

Perduzke grins. 'Well, you'd better read it. Otherwise this'll take me too long.'

Stuff reads the letter with creased brow. 'I see. But I'm not responsible for this being printed. This isn't editorial matter, it's an advertisement. You can tell that from the thick black border.'

'Oh, so you weren't aware of the letter?'

Stuff is happy. 'I've nothing to do with advertising! I'm the editor, even a junior detective ought to understand that.'

'And who is to do with advertising?'

'Oh, I don't think there's anyone in particular. The secretary does it. Whoever happens to be around. If people bring them in early, and there's no one else available, I think even the cleaning woman has been known to take receipt of them.'

'No-o. Really? That I didn't know. Is that the way they do it in the *News* too?'

Stuff gestures grandly. 'In the *News*? That's the way it's done all over the world, in the biggest papers. Ads are like fly specks. They're not something you give your attention to.'

Perduzke fixes his eyes on the ornament on the stove. 'Then there's probably no point in my asking if the original manuscript of the advertisment still exists?'

'My dear Emil, I'm afraid that's completely hopeless!'

'They're not . . . kept anywhere, the originals, the manuscripts?'

'Kept?! Have you any idea what they look like once they've been set? They're black, I tell you, from the typesetters' paws, a Negro is snow-white by comparison.'

'And you wouldn't happen to remember where this Kehding, who seems to be a farmer, where he hailed from?'

'Where he hailed from? Hm, hard to say.' Stuff sighs. Goes over to the bookcase. 'Here's a copy of Niekammer's *Agricultural Estate Address Book for Pomerania*. I'm sure he's in here. You wouldn't happen to know his first name, would you now, Emil?'

Perduzke gulps. 'No, I'm afraid I don't, actually.'

'But, then, you'll know the place he comes from, Emil? With luck, the place might only have three or four Kehdings, and then it might be possible to track him down.'

'But it was *you*, fellow, who were supposed to tell me the place!'

'Ooh!' yelps Stuff. 'Sweetheart! Frerksen's on leave! Frerksen's got the chop. Frerksen is toast.' He sings it and beats out a rhythm to it on the desk. 'Are you finished officially, now, Emil?'

'So you're officially giving me the information that the original of the open letter no longer exists, and that you don't know where that Kehding is from?'

'Officially. What about him? Facing a charge?'

'Yes. From the town administration. For threatening behaviour.'

'Well, they ought to know. And you really don't know what it said in the president's letter? Unofficially, Emil?!'

'Unofficially, upon my honour, I don't!'

'Then I'll have to find it out some other way,' reckons Stuff. 'It must be possible.'

'Do you have any idea why Manzow always gets away with murder with little girls?' Perduzke asks.

'Aa-ah!' says Stuff, languidly. 'You've heard about that too. But that's an idea. Manzow is a big fellow, and a friend of the Fat Man.'

'I never said anything, mind,' says Perduzke.

'No, no, quite the contrary,' affirms Stuff. 'And now we're going for a swift half. And then I'm going to dig up the tomahawk and go on the warpath against Big Chief Manzow. How!'

'You are a great big kid, you know that?' observes Perduzke.

Stuff looks at him with melancholy, blinking eyes. 'Froth, Emil, froth. I wish I was.'

XII

Bang in the middle of the town, Manzow has his really lovely garden, with fruitful trees, flowers, lawns and bushes – and sometimes he goes for walks there, even though the chances of seeing children making peepee can be no more than one in ten thousand.

Stuff spots him a long way off, without being seen. That way, he can approach with caution, because he knows from experience how the big Manzow, for all his amiability, sometimes ducks away from him. It dates from the time when the *Chronicle* used to be the Stahlhelm organ in town. And Manzow was a liberal even then. Stuff was going after big businessmen (he wrecked the *Chronicle*'s advertising income), but they took it against him that he had dropped a few hints about the child-friendly Manzow. A harmless quirk. He wouldn't hurt a fly. Such an eccentric. And the children don't even know what it's about.

Stuff is very near by. He quickly takes a dozen steps, leans over the garden fence, and calls: 'Good morning, Herr Manzow. Lovely day, eh?'

'Do you think?' retorts Manzow. 'Good morning to you too, by the way. You must excuse me. Breakfast is over. Got to work.'

He's in a bit of a rush today, thinks Stuff. So it's true. There's some complicity.

And aloud: 'I have a question I'd like to ask you, Herr Manzow.'

'Oh, really? I'm afraid I haven't got the time.'

'I'm sure your business can get by without you for a minute or two,' pleads Stuff. 'And this is important to you.'

'I'm the best judge of what's important for me. Dealing with my customers is important.'

'And, in the meantime, you're being officially dealt with, Herr Manzow.'

'Don't bandy words with me. I've no interest in secrets.' But, even so, Manzow comes closer, and now leans on the fence from the other side. 'What do you want to know, Herr Stuff? My colleagues are all on holiday.'

'Know? Oh, nothing. I know everything. Even about a certain letter from the district president.' Stuff pauses, and is happy to note that he's scored a bullseye.

Manzow gulps. He really is gulping for air. 'It's just what I say!

It's just what I always say! No one can keep a secret. Now, how in all the world –?'

'Oh, I know even more than that, Herr Manzow. There's another letter, a reader's letter. Or more precisely a personal delivery.'

'No, tell me how you know that the district president wrote to Gareis . . .'

'A worker brought it in. A certain . . . Matz?'

Manzow seems to be smacking his lips. There is a bad taste.

'Yes, Matz. A very long reader's letter. Not a pretty one, Herr Manzow. People will wrinkle their noses when they get wind of it.'

'It's incredible what certain people will say. They are real blackmailers.'

'Did he want to blackmail you? He never said so.'

'Don't be an idiot,' growls Manzow. 'I didn't say so either.'

'Oh? No? I misunderstood you, then?'

'I don't know any worker by the name of Matz.'

'But what about little Lisa Matz? Between you and me, I've looked her up in the registry office. Turned twelve this April, Herr Manzow. Twelve years old!'

'Some girls are early developers. And anyway, nothing happened.'

'No, no. Of course not. Would we be standing here otherwise? Would you be standing here otherwise?'

'Herr Stuff,' says Manzow in a sudden fury, 'I don't care for your methods. I won't be roasted over a slow fire. You're after something. What are you after?'

'Maybe I just want to roast you over a slow fire, Herr Manzow,' growls Stuff.

'I'm not your plaything!' Manzow roars. 'Go to hell! Do what you want!'

He storms off back to the house.

Stuff watches him go, reaches into his pocket, fishes out a cigar, bites the end off and spits it out.

The back door slams shut.

Stuff gets his lighter out and slowly lights his cigar. Stands by the fence.

A maid comes running out of the house, a maid with stout red arms. Stuff rejoices silently to see the full bosom jounce up and down in the loose blouse.

The girl is blushing and confused. 'Herr Manzow says to say he doesn't want you leaning on his fence. The fence is newly dug and it'll get skewed, Herr Manzow says to say.'

'Thank you, my dear,' says Stuff, and flutters his lashes. 'Tell Herr Manzow from me, sweetheart, that I'm happy to stand here till the fence has fallen over.'

The maid manages a little smile, only a very little one, because she's not really supposed to, and she goes back into the house. This time Stuff is able to watch her bottom swinging from side to side under the blue cotton. It's an extensive bottom; in his enthusiasm for it Stuff props his other arm on the fence.

Five minutes pass. Stuff smokes.

The door opens and out comes Manzow. He walks smiling down to Stuff. 'I've thought about it, I'll give Matz a hundred marks and a job in the municipal gardens.'

'Good,' says Stuff, taking one arm off the fence.

'And you.' Manzow reaches into his pocket. 'I've got a copy of the president's letter here. Wasn't that what you were interested in?'

'If you hadn't been a Liberal, Herr Manzow,' says Stuff with sincerity, 'I think you could have been some man.'

He takes the other arm off the fence.

'Gareis got a letter too. It's said to be even harsher than this. But I've nothing to go on.'

'Fine. This one here will do me.'

'I don't want your word of honour, Herr Stuff. But see to it that you keep your lip buttoned. Otherwise I'll find myself in a lot of trouble.'

'I've never yet betrayed a source,' says Stuff proudly. 'At some point a man has to keep standards.'

'That's right,' says Manzow. 'I take a bath every morning myself. Good day to you.'

'Good day,' replies Stuff, and watches him go, at least as admiringly as he watched the cook's arse. He is a bastard all right, but what a bastard! A hundred-per-cent-driven-snow bastard.

He pushes off in the direction of the newspaper. Today the

Chronicle will show its competitors a clean pair of heels. Heinsius will burst! Oh, what the hell, he'll just cut and paste it anyway. I'm just a coolie for the worms on the *News*.

XIII

The publication of the president's letter in the *Chronicle* was like a bombshell.

The town was in a ferment, heads came together and flew apart. Gareis had to get his hand bandaged, he had smashed an ashtray in his fury.

It was in its way an exemplary letter, balanced and wise, distributing light and shade, giving unto each their just deserts, peasants and police.

For up in heaven Temborius thrones.

The government had been mild and gentle, in spite of its bad experiences it had allowed the peasants to protest.

The peasants had been wicked, they had packed a provocative banner with them, they had carried an open scythe through a built-up area (paragraph three of the police by-law from the year dot), had attacked the police, had held incendiary speeches, and in general had held little Father State in contempt.

The police had done right to proceed against them.

The police had *not* done right to proceed *in such a way* against them.

'There are doubts on the tactical execution of the police action. I therefore relieve Commander Frerksen of his executive power until the publication of the inquiry report into his role.'

Amen.

Raging, whooping, grinning, sobbing.

And Gareis, after the first outburst of rage, closeted in his office, brooding: Where did Stuff get that from? Who gave that letter to Stuff?

He sends for Tredup, but Tredup is ignorant, and quite genuinely so. Gareis can see that he would all too willingly have said if he'd known.

Nothing, no, but he will listen out, and try to discover.

But there's no need for Tredup to listen out, by that evening Gareis knows. Manzow didn't give anything away, Stuff kept mum, but all the same, by evening Gareis knows who gave the copy to Stuff.

It was Manzow's maid, the girl with the boobs, talking about what a nice fellow Stuff is. He winked and smiled at her. She was sure he would like to go out with her some time.

The man she does go out with, to whom she confides this, asks how she came to know Stuff.

Via Manzow. They had a terrific quarrel today, and she was sent to chase Stuff away from the garden fence.

Did he go?

No, the two men patched it up. Manzow went back out to see Stuff, and pretty soon they were talking again.

The man, the boyfriend, happens to be a comrade. An SPD member. When a comrade happens on some piece of information, he takes it to Pinkus, the reporter on the *Volkszeitung*. He pays fifty pfennigs for any item he can use.

This one he can't use, it's not printable, surely the comrade understands? Anyway, it might get the girl in trouble with her employer.

The comrade doesn't seem to be too bothered.

At any rate, Pinkus flies in to Gareis with the news. Gareis is a first-rate politician, he is so well connected. Pinkus doesn't intend to grow old as local-news reporter in Altholm.

Gareis listens, and Gareis puts two and two together.

For a moment, he wonders whether he should talk to the girl, but what he's heard already is quite enough. When he's alone again, he picks up the phone.

'Herr Manzow please. – This is Mayor Gareis. I'd like to speak to Herr Manzow in person. – Hello, is that you?'

Very softly: 'You gave Stuff the letter from the district president. Don't deny it. I heard it from him. You will know what you've done. I am calling a Party emergency meeting tonight. I will move that the SPD breaks off its pact with the Liberals. – Good evening, Manzow. – No, no, it's all right. Take care you don't get any more charges filed against you. My wastepaper basket is out of commission. – Evening. Evening. – Ach, don't talk rot. Bye.'

Three minutes later, the telephone goes in the editorial offices of the *Chronicle*.

'This is Manzow. I want to talk to Herr Stuff. – Stuff, is that you? You son of a bitch, you let Gareis know that I gave you the letter from the district president. You are the biggest bastard in the whole of Altholm. – Shut up. I don't care what you do. I'm going to sue you for blackmail, you yellow journalist! I will talk to Gebhardt, I will complain about you to him. From this day forth, you're finished in Altholm! You low-down bastard, you. – Shut up, I tell you. I'm not talking to you any more. Bye!'

Two minutes later, the phone goes at the *News*.

'This is Stuff. Get me Gebhardt, please. – Herr Gebhardt? – Yes, Herr Gebhardt, Manzow's just called me. Somebody or other told Gareis that Manzow was the source of the letter. – Yes, the letter in question. – No, I haven't mentioned it to anyone. – No, definitely not. – No, I have not blabbed. I haven't drunk a drop in ten days. – Trouble? I wouldn't make trouble for myself. – Exactly, I must have been spied on. There must be a spy in the office. – No, no, I'm sure the telephone's safe. But if you could call Gareis? Someone has to stop Manzow from creating too much havoc. – You know, havoc. Herr Gebhardt, there's havoc being created all the time. It's hard to know what he'll try and do. – Yes, I think that would be best. – Yes. Thank you. Good evening to you, Herr Gebhardt.'

Ten minutes later, the phone rings at Mayor Gareis's.

'Here's the *News*. Gebhardt. – Yes, in person. I've just seen what Stuff has got up to, Herr Gareis. I've been away. – No, I'm furious. Can we talk? – No, I have something else in mind. – Tomorrow morning at eleven? That will be fine. – I quite agree. Things need to calm down. Good evening, Herr Mayor.'

5

Another Creak

I

Thiel wasn't able to sleep by day in his garret. Even though he lay down naked on his pile of rugs in the corner, the sweat was breaking out of him in streams. And then there was the stench from the toilet next door, worse than ever.

He was shattered. This waiting around was exhausting. No one came, but he heard thousands, tens of thousands, every hour. They came through the sleeping, restless, creaking, unlit house, creeping here, creeping there, laughing with big white faces lit up by the street lamps, or lurking in corners, perfectly still, their faces in the shade.

These nights robbed him of his sleep. When he heard the flush next door, he felt tempted to get up, bang on the door, tear open the dormer window, yell out into the street: This is the Stolpe Bomber! Ten thousand marks for the first man up the stairs!

Late in the evening – the typesetting machines had stopped rattling and the building was getting quieter – he had suddenly fallen into a dead sleep.

Now he has the feeling of having been startled awake. He sits up and listens.

It's completely dark, and the building is quiet.

He strikes a match and looks at his watch: almost midnight.

He pulls on a pair of trousers, and on the chair by the door finds the plate of food left him by Padberg, and a bottle of Moselle.

So it seems Padberg has been by and not woken him, the wretch. Another twenty-four hours in which he won't get to speak to a soul.

Thiel eats hastily and keeps listening at intervals. The house seems alive, waiting for him with all its rooms, the machine rooms still filled with the movements of people who are permitted to live, whereas he wanders around like a ghost.

Then he feels his way down the steps into the garden.

First the garden, the air, the stars, the green. He's brought his Moselle with him, and drinks it there, on a spot of muddied lawn.

Then he gets up again – he will remember later that he felt particularly glad and alert and cheerful – and goes into the machine room. There in a lean-to are a couple of shower stalls. He gets under one of them and showers.

Now he feels great. He picks a hooked wire off a nail and teases open the drawer of a desk. That's where the master mechanic keeps all kinds of personal junk, including cigarettes, so he helps himself and lights up, even though he has some of his own.

Who cares if the master mechanic rants and raves a bit if there are some missing, they are all comrades here. Let them suspect one another, a little suspicion within the Party will keep the dialectic from going stale.

But actually it's not about cigarettes. That's not why he forced the lock. The master mechanic keeps a supply of dirty postcards as well. God knows what he does with them, sells them to his colleagues, or keeps them for his own delight if he's an unhappily married man.

At any rate, there's a fresh bunch of them tonight, as Thiel sees by the light of another match. Then he retires with them under a table, whose top catches the light from outside.

Half an hour later, he starts on his tour and goes through the garden, into the typesetters' room, to dispatch. He's no fierce guard dog tonight, he's relaxed, even humming to himself a little.

He opens the door from the landing to dispatch. The door that causes the little bell to go off in the chimney breast upstairs. And there it is, a very quiet, distant ringing.

It occurs to him that he slept through the evening and forgot to unhook the bell, as he usually does. He stands there frozen.

Upstairs he hears the sound of feet, quick male feet.

In that same instant he bounds up the unlit stairs as fast as he can. He's not thinking, he's just reflexively racing upstairs, to catch the spy. As he runs, he clutches his truncheon, to have it ready to swing.

The landing is pitch black. But there are yellowish glimmers through cracks in the door to the dispatch office. There are lights on inside.

His momentum doesn't let up. He opens the door. And the bright, quiet expanse of Padberg's office greets him. The five overhead lights are burning, the desk lamp is on, the curtains are drawn.

But there is no one there.

Thiel looks across to the other door. It's shut, and not swinging.

He drops his haste; quietly, on tiptoe, as though in the presence of someone he shouldn't disturb, he creeps into the room, towards the desk.

The middle drawer is open, and is empty. Whatever was in it is stacked on top of the desk, for inspection. Two piles of paper, one on the right already perused, with the white backs of the pages facing up, the other, on the left, still awaiting inspection, the written surface facing up.

Mechanically, Thiel reaches for the top page, picks it up, to scan it . . .

And a feeling of extreme danger comes over him, a wave of fear, his heart starts beating painfully, even though it feels terribly weak . . .

He is standing about a foot and a half in front of the curtains, which are now attracting his attention. From so close, he can see that the curtains aren't hanging straight down, there's a strange bulge in them, one might almost imagine there was someone standing behind them.

Thiel looks down at the ground. The curtains don't quite reach down to the floor. There is a little gap where they end. And in that gap is a pair of shoes, a pair of black, dusty man's shoes, with the toes pointing towards him.

Thiel starts to shake, everything is so ghostly. This unlit, rambling house, the night garden, the sleeping outbuildings, and in the midst of it all, like a room in a dream, a lit-up room, deathly silent.

A man in front of the curtains and two shoes peeking out from under them. The man's hand reaches for the curtains – they're a russet colour – but it's shaking so hard that he takes it back.

Thiel stares at the bulge in the curtain.

There is so much going on in him in those moments: happy childhood days, the clear and sober workspace in the Revenue Department, with the adding machine clattering away the whole time, an evening of skat with friends in a country inn, the faces of his three friends and card-playing partners, but above all Kalüb-be's foot seeming to hover over a brown-flecked moth on the dusty country road – and the foot being taken back.

Thiel quietly sets the truncheon down on the desk behind him. He grips his right wrist in his left hand, and moves it, still shaking, to the curtain.

His fingertips touch the material and his heart seems to turn over.

He takes the curtain and peels it slowly back from the face that comes into view, a white, wrinkled face, snow-white, with a tangle of dark hair above it. Dull eyes look at him.

Here is a man in the dark blue typesetter's tunic. Slowly it dawns on Thiel that he has seen him once before, in the days after the bombing when he was still at work for the *Bauernschaft*. A typesetter.

The two men look at each other, don't move their lips, only look at each other, the spy and the bomber.

The other man's look is dark and somehow murky . . . and slowly everything drifts into a sort of dream to Thiel. He's no longer sure if he's the one who's standing behind the curtain or the one drawing it aside. He stands there dimly, reaches into the dark, everything goes hazy . . .

Slowly – oh so slowly! – Thiel allows the curtain pleats to cover the face, he reaches for his rubber truncheon. Backing away, keeping his eye on the voluminous material, he leaves the room. At the door, he switches the light off. And then he climbs heavily and muzzily up to his garret.

Once in his garret he lies down on his rugs and tries to think. But everything is far too obscure. The thought keeps coming to him: I've been a coward. I should have smashed him in the face with the truncheon. I've been a coward.

And: If only I hadn't taken out the dirty postcards! I was feeble! A coward!

Suddenly he jumps up. He must have been asleep. But only for a second, he thinks.

Now he hears through the whole building the sound of a key being pushed into the lock on the front door, then someone unlocks the door, and comes up the stairs, and it's a familiar tread.

Well, well, he thinks. Well, well. Here's trouble.

But there isn't anything. He hears Padberg going into his study. Hears him fossicking around.

No trouble?

But the man must be there, the typesetter with the dark hair and the muddy eyes!

No trouble!

Is the typesetter not really there?

Slowly Thiel climbs down the stairs. He feels incredibly tired and has a bad taste in his mouth.

Padberg is sitting at his desk, smoking a cigar and stuffing papers into a briefcase. A suitcase is by the door.

'Evening, guard dog,' says Padberg in tip-top mood. 'You were so fast asleep earlier I couldn't face waking you.'

'Evening,' says Thiel.

'Listen,' Padberg resumes, 'I have to go to Berlin right away. They're thinking of getting up some sort of united front against the farmers. That dummy Temborius is bestirring himself. Maybe there'll be some work for you to do again soon.' And he mimes a throwing action with one hand.

'Are you going tonight?' asks Thiel.

'Yes. Right now. The car will be here any minute. I'm getting a ride to Stettin, and I'll catch the early train to Berlin.'

'I see,' says Thiel.

'I don't know when I'm coming back yet. It'll be difficult with your meals. I'm thinking your being here without me will be a bit of a problem. Best thing would be if you set off right away for

Bandekow-Ausbau and stayed with the count. You know the way, and the count knows you. Here's fifty marks for you, just in case. But you won't really need money.'

'No,' says Thiel. 'What about here?'

'Here? You mean, keeping an eye on the place? – There's the car already. I have to go. – No, don't worry about here. I've got all my important papers with me. – All right, I must go. Bye-bye, Thiel. Heil Bauernschaft!'

'Heil Bauernschaft!'

'Will you go now too!'

'OK,' says Thiel.

'Well, bye-bye again . . .'

II

In the meeting room at District President Temborius's there is a good atmosphere. Actually, a very good atmosphere.

At a long green table, representatives of the rural and urban population of the district of Stolpe are seated together, chatting. At a cross-table thrones the president with his staff. He's a different sort of president today, smiling affably, making little pleasantries, a good-humoured man, blessed with a light hand, who will resolve all difficulties.

He has succeeded in doing what seemed hopeless, in bringing people from town and country round a single table.

Admittedly, the city government of Altholm is somewhat weakly represented. Their noses, of course, are out of joint, and they have sent only Political Adviser Stein, in a passive, information-gathering capacity, because they are furious that the district president has shown himself more gracious and skilled than their Gareis.

Well, but the town is present all the same: crafts with its guild masters, small business in the form of the weighty Herr Manzow, manufacturing with its syndic.

The rural representatives are almost too many to be counted. There is the Agricultural Chamber, represented by an agricultural councillor, a couple of Agricultural College directors, two seed inspectors.

There is the Agricultural Union, with two board members.

The local farmers' co-operatives have sent five men.

There is the Water Meadow Cultivators, with two men.

Country schoolmasters are represented, the country clerisy, country hospitality.

Oh, Chief Adviser Meier can be extraordinarily efficient, identifying in the most remote corners organizations that one might invite. Who else would have tracked down the Union of Pomeranian Poultry-Breeders, or the Rural Housewives' Association? He did!

And his paper on the juridical and legal bases for the actions of the police on the 26th of July was an example of measured care and delicate formulation.

Almost better, almost more effective than the police-tactical reflections of Police Colonel Senkpiel.

He himself, Temborius, has taken on the domestic political origins and implications of that day, not unsuccessfully, it seems to him.

Everything aired in the most loyal, dispassionate way, no aggression, no vindictiveness. The stained-glass windows are open in the committee room, air and light flood in, in a way the whole world floods in, the people in the room seem to have the world in view. They would have willingly answered any questions, too, but everything had been so exhaustively treated that there were no questions.

Now a pause has been called. Before moving on to point two of the agenda, the resolution of the boycott, the gentlemen are given the opportunity to confer with one another, under guise of a break.

So the gentlemen hold a confab.

Here, for instance, is Manzow with Dr Hüppchen, and today Manzow is a completely different man to then. He has a tricky tax question, and would value the doctor's advice, but, no, of course he wouldn't dream of getting it here and for free, he knows that even accountants need to make a living, haha!, and so he will consult the doctor in the course of the next few days.

And – he allows it to be glimpsed – the syndic of the Retailers'
Association is getting on a bit . . . 'Well, something else for us to
talk about, dear Doctor!'

Inevitably, Dr Hüppchen thinks a little emotionally of Gareis,
whom he presumes to be behind these overtures. But in answer
to his question as to Gareis's whereabouts, he hears to his surprise the rather contemptuous: 'Fatty Gareis! He's long dead!'

'Dead . . .?'

'Well, didn't you read the letter from the district president? If
that's not dead . . .!'

The honorary master of the Bakers' Guild is standing with
Bishop Schwarz.

'This is all looking very auspicious, wouldn't you say, Your
Reverence?'

'Oh, yes. Peace always wins out in the end. I'm sure we'll come
to some sort of understanding.'

And Chief Adviser Meier has an astonishing experience – his
boss, District President Temborius, gives him a little pat on the
back.

'Well done, Meierchen. There, you see!'

Chief Adviser Meier isn't altogether sure what he ought to see,
but he smiles a gratified smile.

'Didn't I tell you once before that you'll do well in Prussian
administration? Why should all Jewish lawyers become barris-
ters? We can use some of you in administration.'

Adviser Meier stammers something.

'I say,' cries Temborius a little excitedly, 'what's that? Is that
yours? Did you sanction that?'

'No, I don't know. I have no idea –'

'Stamp it out! Stamp it out at once!'

At the door to the chamber stands a youth, an ordinary
common-or-garden youth of fourteen or fifteen years old, doling
out newspapers.

They are carefully thrice-folded newspapers, newspapers coyly
hiding their mastheads on the inside. But the adviser is full of
grim foreboding.

He plunges towards the fellow, trotting half the length of the committee room, calling out: 'Hey, you there! Who gave you permission to hand out newspapers here?'

The boy looks up. He's already given out most of his stock to the men at the meeting. The ones he still holds he tosses on to the ground, cries out a 'Heil Bauernschaft!' and leaves.

The adviser stoops to pick one up. He can't help it, the others are all looking, he opens out one of the parcels. And now it becomes apparent that it wasn't just to conceal the masthead that the papers were so carefully folded. On the front page, in the middle, thickly marked out in red pen, is something, an open letter. Meier sees the name 'Temborius', he reads on, he is shaking in his shoes. He's sweating.

Oh, everyone else has already read this wretched open letter, it's only his boss, District President Temborius, who stands there all alone, watching with furrowed brow.

He will call him any second.

Chief Adviser Meier walks with heavy tread to his boss. He can remember running around this building, a long time ago, a bomb was due to explode. To walk to his boss, to hold the news-paper under his nose, is harder.

He puts it down.

'What's going on? Reading the paper? Now?!'

Then Temborius's eye is caught too, and he reads.

Meier stands half a step behind, waiting. Once he hears him laugh aloud, mocking, sardonic, angry. 'Me, Jewish? I think I owe that to you, Meier.'

Then the district president smoothes out the sheet.

'If the gentlemen would kindly return to their seats, so that the meeting can continue.'

The gentlemen oblige him. Most of them conceal the paper shamefully in their pockets, only a few have the gall to spread it out on the table in front of them.

'Gentlemen! Respected company!

'Our positive and conciliatory meeting has been disrupted by a harsh discord. From some unqualified side, soon to be identified and severely punished, a newspaper has been distributed, a sheet . . . well, in a word, the *Bauernschaft*!

'I have seen it being held in many hands here, but to demonstrate the spirit which animates that group called the Bauernschaft, which sets its face against all State authority, to incriminate this spirit, which bears the sole responsibility for the events of the 26th of July, I propose to have this bit of mischief read aloud. – Chief Adviser, if you will!'

The adviser trembles. Shakily, he begins:

'Open Letter.

Brave Comrade Temborius,

You have invited us to a discussion of the events in Altholm. Your endeavour is to transmute a police scandal into the tepid wash of a discussion, in the hope that peace will return after a few high waves.

This Judaical method of taking an adversary and leeching him dry, whose outstanding exponent you are, is well known to us. Your blood qualifies you particularly well to expound this system. With their rubber truncheons your servitors have decorated wealth-creating taxpayers with the blue badge of the free Republic. Instead of punishing the guilty parties, you send them on recreation holidays. Sadly enough, not to Jericho or Jesusalem.

What are you even trying to do? You have no existence for us, you and your clique! The leeched-out and trampled people decline to sit down round one table with its enemies.

You, Herr Temborius, don't help us by negotiating but by taking yourself off, the sooner the better, and your administrative apparatus with you! The practical German people will be able to help themelves.

The Knights of the Rubber Truncheon and the Blue Bruise.

The Bauernschaft.'

Chief Adviser Meier has finished. Deathly silence.

Temborius gets to his feet again: 'Gentlemen, we have listened to what they had to say. We have listened, with probably more than a mite of disgust. I propose we carry on with our talks. We have now reached point two of the agenda for the day: the resolution of the boycott.

'Before the administration comes forward with its proposals,

I should like to ask whether there are any suggestions from the floor? – Yes, please, Herr . . . er, Agricultural Councillor Päplow!'

'Pardon me. I actually have no suggestions at the moment. But pursuant to the letter we have just heard, I should like to ask: Are there representatives of the farmers here among us?'

Temborius laughs a quiet, slightly irked laugh. 'But, gentlemen, you are all of you representatives of the countryside! I see in front of me at least twenty men who could with every right describe themselves as representative of the countryside.'

But Agricultural Councillor Päplow remains obdurate. 'Forgive me, President, those are two completely different things: farmers and countryside. The farmers in this sense are a movement. Are there representatives of the farmers here?'

He doesn't even ask the president, he looks around the company. All the heads are looking back at him, but none nods.

Agricultural Councillor Päplow gestures with his hands. 'Then, gentlemen, I don't see what we're doing here. I'm sorry, it wasn't us that imposed the boycott, and by the same token we're not the ones that can lift it either.'

'But, gentlemen! Esteemed gentlemen!' calls the district president. 'We're in danger of losing our way here. Of course you didn't impose the boycott, that was the work of people I don't want to have here. But you are prominent figures from the countryside and agriculture. You are important men. If you say: The boycott will end – then the countryside will listen to you. Then the boycott is over. That's what we want. A resolution against the boycott from prominent figures like yourselves.'

'I'm sorry,' says the agricultural councillor. 'I haven't been authorized to adopt any such position by my chamber. I am here purely to gather information.'

'So am I.'

'Me too.'

'Same with us.'

'I,' says a rough-hewn fellow, getting to his feet, 'am from the Bauernschaft –'

'Well, then!'

'Why not say so sooner?'

'So they are represented here.'

'– let me talk, people! I've been invited as chairman of the local farmers' union in Stolpe. That's why I'm here. But I'm also with the Bauernschaft. I sympathize with the movement, I mean, it speaks to me.

'I can only say that my local union doesn't give a damn about the goings-on between the Bauernschaft and the town of Altholm. We have nothing to say on the topic. Forgive me, President, if I'm unmannerly, but it's nothing to do with the president either. Let the Bauernschaft sort it out with the people of Altholm. If Gareis had been here . . . but as it is there's no one present who has a dog in this fight.

'That's what I have to say. Thanks.'

The president stands there stiffly.

'I should like to thank the previous speaker for apprising me of my duties. The only ones who can tell me what my duties are are my legally instituted superiors, the Ministry of the Interior, and my conscience. But I should like to ask the previous speaker a question. – Were you present in Altholm on the 26th of July?'

'Yes, I was there.'

'And did you take part in the meeting afterwards that was dissolved?'

'I did indeed, Herr President.'

'I see. – Well, what do you say to the letter that was just read out? Do you find yourself in agreement with it?'

'What to say, Herr President? I didn't write the letter now, did I? It's a bit sharp, I think. Having met you, Herr President, I can say I find you quite personable . . .'

'Thank you. I'm flattered.'

'Well, you *are*. Personable. But, Herr President, couldn't you see your way to doing what you ought to do? I don't know what that is, but all the books and files you have here . . .'

He looks around, a little uncertainly.

(Manzow whispers to Dr Hüppchen: 'You know, he's no fool! He's making a bit of a monkey of old Temborius.'

And Hüppchen, surprised: 'Do you think? I took him for naive.'

'No, there's only one person who's naive around here.')

'Yes, quite. I lost my thread: couldn't you leave us farmers to ourselves? You know, we're not murderers, we're not robbers, we're not rapists – can't the government leave us be? You have your fine stone palace here –'

'Thank you! No, really, thank you very much, sir! Perhaps you wouldn't mind sitting down now. Thank you. Telling me my business –'

'Well, then, I'll be going. You coming with me?'

Three get up to go with him, friends, colleagues from his committee. By the time they go through the door, there are eight of them, a dozen.

Stricken, the president watches them go. 'Well, I think we'd better pick up where we were . . . Was there something else, Councillor . . .?'

'Forgive me for interrupting once more, President. I didn't want to be like those farmers and leave without thanking you. We all here understand and honour your good intentions. But it's probably still too soon. We need to wait. There are still injured men lying in the hospital in Altholm. The farmer can still feel the blow that struck him. Perhaps it was right to strike him, even though your decision, Herr President, to suspend the police chief from duty, doesn't exactly speak for that.

'At any rate, it's too soon, Herr President, none of us who represent farming and the country round this table is entitled to say "yes" or "no". We can only view the chasm between town and country with deep regret. We hope that time and your efforts will one day manage to bridge it. But for now, it's still too soon.

'Herr President, call off these hopeless talks.'

The president says slowly: 'Gentlemen, I'm afraid I don't understand you. You turned up, the talks were going well, the atmosphere was encouraging. The negotiations bade fair to come to a constructive conclusion. Then this wild, ugly letter from the Bauernschaft, and suddenly everyone is panicking. What's it all about? Who are the Bauernschaft? You're running away from a ghost. For the sake of our province, pass the resolution – which, only half an hour ago, you would have passed easily – that the country organizations disapprove of the boycott, and all will be well.'

The agricultural councillor answers with head lowered: 'Very well. I'll be quite open with you. Half an hour ago, I might indeed have sided with the resolution. But when I read the Bauernschaft letter, I thought: What am I getting mixed up in? Is this any business of mine?

'Don't get obsessed with the ugly tone of the letter, which will have been composed by some journalist or other. Composed, yes, but thought and felt in the hearts of thousands of farmers. They're excited, they're offended, they're hurt. It's not a question of passing resolutions, but of passing time. And a very deft and careful touch.

'Herr District President, we hope you will have this touch. I hope you have the patience to go with it.'

Agricultural Councillor Päplow, a fat, white-haired gentleman with a veined drinker's nose, stands there a moment with lowered head. Then he walks out of the room. Three or four gentlemen follow him.

The district president smiles. It's a feeble smile. 'Gentlemen, as you see . . .'

He gestures. 'I would have liked to be of assistance to you, gentlemen of Altholm. But, for the time being, I'm afraid I see no possibility.'

Very quickly: 'The conversation is hereby at an end.'

III

Newspaper proprietor Gebhardt is received by Mayor Gareis, directly, without recourse to the outer office. He counts as an important visitor. He is an important visitor. Piekbusch is charged to intercept him in the corridor and lead him straight into the inner sanctum.

And the mayor is quite canny about it: he never allows his guest to become aware of the physical contrast between the two parties. It might after all upset or irritate the little magnate to confront someone so much bigger than himself. No, Gareis would rather risk seeming impolite, barely bobbing up out of his chair, briefly peering at the frizz-grown neck, and already both are comfortably installed.

'I'm happy,' Gareis says with a smile, 'to have some news for a newspaper man. Herr Oberbürgermeister Niederdahl is on his way back now.'

'Now?' repeats the magnate. 'When he left, if I am not mistaken, the talk was of a silver wedding.'

'Silver wedding is sometimes the waiting to see where the more powerful forces are lined up.'

'So that you can join them.'

The mayor confirms: 'So that you can join them.'

It's a start, an encouraging start. The two men meet in their antipathies, which is generally more important than where your sympathies are.

Gareis picks up the ball and runs with it. 'As of now, there's no saying which the more powerful forces are. I fear the conciliation meeting today at the president's will fail.'

'I'm more hopeful there myself.'

'Well, let's wait and see. Perhaps we won't have long to wait.' And he gestures at the telephone.

'And you, Mayor, aren't attending?'

'No. I am here.' And, to soften the impact: 'I wasn't directly invited.'

But Gebhardt is annoyed. 'At least Frerksen is finally out of a job.'

'Not so,' says Gareis. 'He is temporarily relieved of his command of the police executive, which is rather different.'

'His leave reminds me a bit of Niederdahl's leave.'

'Again, not so. I just sent him away for a while to make him a little less visible.'

'Well!'

'That's neither weakness nor an admission of guilt. But, my dear Herr Gebhardt, we're doing too much talking. What is the 26th of July? What is a boycott? Nothing at all. If no one mentions it, nothing at all. It's all talk, you see. It's not the farmers out in the sticks talking it up, it's you people here in town, you especially. My suggestion: Let's have an end to all the talk about the 26th of July. I will instruct the *Volkszeitung* not to have anything more about it. Not another word. Now you promise me the same with the *Chronicle* and the *News*.'

'The situation is so unpredictable.'

A pause.

The mayor starts again. 'You are doing the business of the Oberbürgermeister, you're opposing me. Let's be frank. You don't want him any more than I do. The only way you'll get rid of him is if you make me stronger. At the moment you're weakening me. What's the point of all the chit-chat about the 26th of July? It's criticism of me.'

'Of you! My dear Herr Gareis, who is criticizing you! Frerksen, yes, but you –'

'You're mistaken again. Frerksen is neither here nor there. This is about me. Carry on along your present path, and one day I hear you crying: Gareis must go!'

'Not possible.'

'Perhaps then you'll remember this hour. – But why do you persist? Is it only the pleasure of offering sensations to your readers? There are others, you know . . .'

'For instance?'

The mayor slowly says: 'One would have to talk about it. There is impeccably dramatic material. All I will say . . . no, I won't say anything just yet. I would like to hear you say you will forbear. Everything argues for it.'

Gebhardt is evasive. 'But, Herr Gareis, think of all the things that might happen. I can't promise –'

'No, you don't want to. That's a pity.'

The phone rings. Gareis picks up, says who he is, listens for a long time, and hangs up.

'A second piece of news for you,' he says, turning to Gebhardt. 'The conciliation meeting at the president's has broken up in chaos. The Bauernschaft has crudely insulted the president. The representatives of agriculture left the venue with loud protests.'

'That is . . . I really hadn't expected that. So for now all bets are off.' Gebhardt gets quickly to his feet. 'I must try and find out some more details. We had someone at that meeting. Maybe

Stuff will get it into the next issue. The *News* will certainly carry it. That's a bit of a sensation.'

He stands there, all set to go.

The mayor stands up as well. He is enormous. His bulk is unbelievable. He has no more thought of sparing his opposite number's feelings.

'It won't be a sensation. Because you won't be carrying the story. I say no.'

'Who would stop me?'

'I would, for example. Only me, Herr Gebhardt, the Red mayor. The pol. I want quiet, and I'm going to get it.'

Gebhardt says coolly: 'We'd better leave things right there. Crude threats may be the fashion in your Party, but –'

'Threats are good wherever and whenever common sense fails. Herr Gebhardt, you can't behave like a duck, setting off after the bait when a sensation is dangled under your beak. That's all right for Stuff. But you . . .'

'And for me too. How can I keep such news from my readers? My duties –'

'Stuff and nonsense!' says the mayor. 'Will you agree to keep the peace, let's say, until the cases come to court?'

'I wouldn't dream of it. Good day.'

'One moment. I can't let you go yet. I'm afraid the police want to question you. A charge has been laid against you.'

'A charge . . .?'

'Exactly. A criminal charge.'

Gebhardt considers. 'If my driver has made a rickets of something, then he's fired.'

'Not your driver. Sit down again. – This is a charge of deception.'

'Ridiculous!' But Gebhardt sits down anyway. 'You're playing a dangerous game here, Herr Gareis. It can cost you more than your office as mayor.'

'True. But I know my hand.' He pulls a thin file out of his desk.

'About two weeks ago, the cloth merchant Hempel went to the *Chronicle* to see about taking a fold-in leaflet. He spoke to your managing editor, Wenk. He wanted to know the size of the readership, in order to set up his printing order, and gauge the possible effect of advertising. He was quoted a figure of seven thousand one hundred and sixty.

'Hempel queried this number. He had heard tell of the *Chronicle*'s dwindling readership. Whenever he spoke to friends and customers, he heard of people who had stopped taking the *Chronicle*.'

'Surprising, really, that he didn't give up his plan.'

'Ah, you think so too?' The mayor smiles. 'There are eccentrics. People who spend their money without sense.'

'A quick question, Mayor. Herr Hempel is an ornament of the Reichsbanner?'

'An ornament. Yes, indeed. Even though questions should be left to me. – Well, Herr Hempel doubts, presses, finally Herr Wenk takes out of the safe a notarized certificate confirming the figure seven thousand one hundred and sixty. Hempel thinks: A notary, well, then everything's hotsy-totsy. He gives the order. The order is put through. A bill is made out. The bill is paid. Then Herr Hempel hears that the readership of the *Chronicle* is more of the order of three thousand nine hundred –'

'Ridiculous.'

'Isn't it just? With a readership like that, who would buy space, or commission leaflets? – So he heard the readership is about three thousand nine hundred, and that the other three thousand three hundred of his leaflets have been used to heat the stove. Herr Hempel feels damaged, and wants to press charges.'

Pause.

At this point Herr Gebhardt smiles. 'Dear Mayor, I'm surprised. Frankly, I'm very surprised. I really would no longer mind not carrying the story of the meeting breaking up in acrimony, I have a very nice new story for my front page.

'But first I would like to ask: Why aren't you questioning the managing editor of the *Chronicle*? And secondly, you know I only took over the paper a few weeks ago, and had reasons not to pay unduly close attention to my acquisition. How can you assume that I am familiar with this notarized form? And thirdly, granted it exists, what gives you the right to question its accuracy? Burning three thousand three hundred leaflets in a stove! I doubt your source will have counted them. The court will learn that there were more like two hundred.'

'Nice,' nods Gareis, 'very nice. But you underestimate me, Herr Gebhardt. Have you ever seen eel-fishers? Eels are slippery buggers. Hard to get hold of. You catch eels with a fork.'

Abruptly Gareis stands up. 'You catch them with a fork, Herr Gebhardt. I haven't yet told the whole story, and you have a very bad memory or a good deal of faith in the forgetfulness of your fellow men. Let me begin again:

'When Herr Hempel went home after seeing your managing editor, Wenk, he remembered that he had seen a notarized certificate, but that this certificate hadn't had a date on it. Or, more precisely, it may have had a date, but the date was handily covered by a thumb. The certificate could be ancient.

'Herr Hempel is an unusual man. He could have gone to Wenk and said: I didn't see the date, would you mind showing it to me! And then he could have cancelled his order if the date was a little on the old side. Herr Hempel, though, did something else. He decided to place a bigger order. So Herr Hempel didn't place his order with the *Chronicle*, Herr Hempel went to the *News*.

'There he met your business manager, Trautmann. He spoke to him much as he had spoken to Wenk, he asked for the readership of the *News*. He heard the figure fifteen thousand. If both papers . . .? Why both? There is only one! – But Herr Hempel showed his knowledge, and in the end Herr Trautmann conceded: all right, twenty-three thousand total, for both papers.

'All right. Now they started to negotiate. Hempel wanted a reduction if he leafletted both papers, Trautmann was tough, no reductions, you had stipulated that. Finally Trautmann agrees to ask you, Hempel comes with him.

'Perhaps now you remember, Herr Gebhardt, that this man came to see you with your business manager? Herr Hempel has declared on oath that he asked you: "For the *News* it's fifteen thousand?" – And you replied, "Yes." – "And seven thousand one hundred and sixty for the *Chronicle*?" – And you replied, "Yes." – "Won't twenty-two thousand suffice?" the cautious Herr Hempel asked.

– And you, Herr Gebhardt, replied: "No, it's around twenty-three thousand."

'Such is the sworn statement of Herr Hempel. And that's what I would call an eel-fork.'

'That's a put-up job! That's low!' yells a furious Gebhardt.

'It's certainly low,' says the mayor contentedly. 'A low blow hurts.'

Pause. Gebhardt gnaws his lips and stares ahead of him.

A rustling disturbs his thinking. Mayor Gareis is balancing the thin file over the wastepaper basket.

All the while he is whistling softly and absent-mindedly to himself. His whistle is juicy, the fat man is the embodiment of bonhomie.

Hurriedly Gebhardt thinks: I could live perfectly comfortably off my interest. And not have to deal with all these awful people.

The file is back on top of the desk.

Gebhardt says hastily: 'Yes. Yes. In God's name, yes.'

'In your name as well?'

'All right. Yes.'

'Until the court case?'

'Until the court case. – But then I get the other material you promised?'

'My dear Herr Gebhardt, that was in the event that you freely agreed. Now I will need to await developments. Everything is so – what was your word? – "unpredictable". And now no more readers' letters. No more open letters in the advertising section. Nothing.'

'Nothing.'

'I'm furious with myself,' says the mayor. 'You should think about that too. The news about the failure of the talks at Temborius's, that was my scoop for you.'

'You'll know why. – I'd like to take that file with me, Herr Gareis.'

Gareis laughs. 'I believe you. What a weapon that would be against me. – But I'll give you something else instead. Here.'

It's a document, more precisely, a manuscript copy. The manuscript copy of the notarized certificate.

'I'm astonished,' mutters Gebhardt. 'The thing is meant to be in the safe. Surely . . .'

'That's right. That's right. That's why I'm making a present of it to you.'

'Now will you tell me the name as well?'

'You'd like that, wouldn't you. Well, I'd say it's one of three: Stuff, Wenk, Tredup.'

'That's obvious. But you won't tell me who?'

'I'd sooner not. You'll work it out.'

The gentlemen part.

Later, the telephone rings at the *Chronicle*.

'Herr Tredup is to see Herr Gebhardt immediately.'

Tredup has a bad conscience. He's still pondering what this is going to be about.

The telephone rings a second time.

'If Herr Tredup could come and see Mayor Gareis right away. Right now.'

Tredup makes big round eyes.

IV

A simple thought process tells Tredup it's better on this occasion to leave his boss waiting, and see the mayor first. If it's about what he thinks it's about, then at least Gareis will tell him what Gebhardt knows.

But Gareis is very curt with him.

'You're a literate fellow, aren't you, Tredup?'

And when Tredup looks uncomprehending: 'I mean, you are able to write: "Herr Meier has once more vouchsafed his trained bass-baritone . . ." Or: "Herr Schulze, the psychologist and graphologist, has become the talk of the town, and no one should pass up this opportunity to visit . . ."? You can write things like that, can't you?'

'Yes, I think so.'

'Well, then, your hour and your appointment are at hand. Herr Gebhardt will send for you.'

'He already has.'

'What are you still doing here, then? To everything he says, just reply: "Stuff!" Promptly, or reluctantly, doesn't matter. The answer is always: Stuff. And then you're a made man.'

Tredup hesitates: 'I don't understand –'

'My God, and why should you? Did you understand what you were getting into when you sold the photos? Well, Herr Gebhardt has in his possession the copy of the notarized certificate –'

'How come –?'

'But talk and blather and witter on you can do? That's what you're all like. Hurry along. And remember: Stuff! Always Stuff! Stuff every time.'

But Tredup doesn't hurry. He stops for a long while on the bridge over the Blosse and watches the languid water. His mind is full of a thousand ideas, mainly trivial variations on the theme: What am I doing?

Once again he has half a mind to go out to the woods on the dunes, pull up his money, disappear off somewhere, but it's not time yet . . .

And he slinks off in the direction of the *News* building.

He's expected there, and Trautmann, his business manager, knows what it's about. He darts him a poisonous look. 'Took your time, didn't you? I can see why. The boss is pretty mad at you.'

He walks Tredup – like a prisoner – to the boss's office. In the passage, Editor Heinsius's head pops up.

'Nosy parker!' growls Trautmann.

But the boss says: 'Thank you, Trautmann. You can leave us alone now.'

Trautmann protests: 'Herr Gebhardt, can't I –?'

'No. Please, Herr Trautmann, will you leave?'

Trautmann growls: 'But he's bound to try and trick you,' and disappears. Tredup is left with the distinct feeling that Trautmann's stopped just behind the door, and is listening for all he's worth, and, looking at the boss, it's clear he has the same feeling.

All the more resolutely he begins: 'Herr Tredup, I took you on on Herr Stuff's recommendation, having no direct personal knowledge of you. You had no references. Well, your performance has been mediocre. The sale of advertising in the *Chronicle* is poor. It may be that times are hard, but I have the feeling a lot of the fault is yours. The *News* seems to be doing very much better.'

'The *News* has a print run of fifteen thousand.'

'And the *Chronicle*?'

'About seven thousand readers.'

The boss stops, half smiles, and remembers the eavesdropper outside.

'Only numbskulls fall for that. *Readers* and subscribers. There's a difference. You may as well claim that the *Chronicle* has fourteen thousand readers.'

'If I claimed that, not even the numbskulls would fall for it.'

'Ha. So what do you do if someone says: "Readers! I want the number of subscribers." What do you do?'

'I refer them to a notarized certificate.'

'And if they don't believe you?'

'Then I produce it.'

'Do you ever let it leave your hand?'

'Never.'

'Are you sure?'

'Quite sure.'

'And yet, it must somehow have fallen into others' hands. Today I was shown a manuscript copy circulating in the town. A complete copy, with date.'

Tredup doesn't look. Very indifferently he remarks: 'I know . . .'

'You know? So. You know. How do you know? Since when have you known?' The little magnate is agitated, really very angry. He takes a chance, and looks his employee indignantly in the face.

He says back: 'I thought you knew . . .'

'You thought . . . You thought what? What am I supposed to know? Out with it!'

Tredup says slowly and unwillingly: 'I thought you knew a preparatory meeting had taken place . . .'

'What meeting! Jesus Christ, can't you open your mouth? All you fellows have a way of putting me on the rack. Please say what it is you have to say.'

Tredup says: 'A new Right-wing paper is supposed to be being started. The business world is annoyed with your monopoly of advertising, and the two recent price hikes. Moreover, in the view of the political groups, the *Chronicle* has become unreliable. That's why a new paper is being launched.'

The boss, impatient: 'You're wasting my time. This is ancient history! I've heard it all before. Go on!'

Tredup, peeved: 'Well, anyway, there was a meeting and a discussion.'

'Well – and? Who was discussing what?'

'I'm not giving any names,' says Tredup tartly.

'What do you mean, "you're not giving any names"? Surely you'll give your employer some information?'

'I'm not giving any names.'

'My God, you go into all this detail, and you leave off the names! What's it all got to do with the certificate anyway?'

Tredup smiles a cunning smile. 'Six gentlemen took part in the discussions.' He waits, and when Gebhardt has become sufficiently impatient: 'The sixth distributed five copies.'

'Six . . .? Five . . .? Oh, I see, the sixth of them gave out five. Well . . . Why was Stuff so insistent that I take you on?'

The door opens a crack, and Trautmann's foxy face intrudes. 'Why don't you ask him what kept him just now? He was asked to come right away.'

The boss goes red, shouts: 'Herr Trautmann, please –!'

But the door is already shut.

Herr Gebhardt gulps, then he says: 'So where were you all this time, Herr Tredup? It was forty-five minutes since my call, and it only takes five.'

'I didn't think it was *that* urgent. I looked in on Meisel, to do with an advertisement.'

The door pops open. 'I'll give Meisel a call right away.'

The door shuts.

These offences against his majesty incline the boss to treat his suspect with greater leniency. 'Why won't you name the names, Herr Tredup? When you've told me so much?'

Tredup feels his heart thumping. The fox will be back any

moment. Will Meisel have let slip that he saw him this morning, and not just a moment ago?

He says: 'I'd really like to accommodate you, Herr Gebhardt.' His voice has a wheedling tone. 'But I don't even know the names for certain. People don't tell me everything either. And then afterwards, it becomes a big issue, and I'm out of a job.'

'Now, now,' says the proprietor soothingly, moved by so much desire to oblige in his employee. 'Surely I'd have something to say first. Was it a serious discussion? Not just castles in the air?'

'A bank manager was present,' explains Tredup.

'That can only . . . Well, we won't use names. And also?'

'A book publisher.'

'Well, well, so little Krauter's felt the sting of ambition? Let him see how easy it is to destroy a fortune with a newspaper. And then . . .?'

'Two business people. Retailers.'

'And . . .?'

'A wholesaler.'

'Well, we only have one here. And . . .?'

'I'd really rather not . . .'

'Oh, come along. If you've told me five, you'll tell me six.'

Tredup makes an effort. But it's difficult. Not so much the lying, as that it seems so crude. Gebhardt must realize what this whole farrago is about.

He says quietly: 'The sixth was a newspaper editor.'

'I've seen that coming for a long time,' says the boss proudly.

Through the door dives Trautmann's head. 'He really did go and see Meisel.'

'Come on in, Trautmann,' says the boss complacently. 'I'm learning a lot here. Well, I'll tell you later. At any rate, Herr Tredup is without stain.'

Trautmann squints doubtfully.

'Tell me, my dear Trautmann,' asks the boss, 'is there no way we can get out of our contract with Stuff?'

'I see! Well, now, indeed. Who always said so, Herr Gebhardt? Who always asked why we had to have a contract with Stuff? He'd never in a million years . . . Well, really, we . . . A way out? I don't think so. It's a sound contract.'

'We need to get rid of him. Someone who does deals with the other side has no place on my paper.'

'Newspaper people are all like that,' observes Trautmann sagely. 'That one,' pointing out the door, 'is just the same as well.'

The door flies open, and Heinsius's tousled head appears. 'What do you think you're doing, blackening my good name to the boss, Herr Trautmann!'

The door shuts, and the manager says tuttingly: 'Listening at doors . . .'

The boss looks irked. 'It has to stop. This snooping . . .'

Trautmann comforts him: 'All newspaper people do that. It's the way they are. That's their profession.'

And the boss: 'But you listen too, Herr Trautmann!'

Trautmann looks injured. 'Me? All I do is in the interests of the firm, keeping myself informed on occasions when you forget to call me in.' And, pityingly: 'Otherwise, there'd just be too much of a rickets being made.'

'Herr Trautmann, I will not have you cast aspersions!'

One of those poisonous scenes between boss and business manager is about to develop, in which Trautmann always comes out on top because he has tougher nerves.

Tredup intervenes: 'I know a way for you to get rid of Stuff.'

Both spin round. They've almost forgotten him in his corner.

'Without scandal?'

'Without compensation?'

'Without anything.'

'And how is that . . .?'

'I'll do it on my own. There's something I know about him.'

'And it won't come back on me?' the boss asks fearfully. 'I really don't want a scandal!'

'I'll do it all myself.'

'And what do you want in return?' asks Trautmann. 'You won't be doing it for nothing.'

'Yes. I couldn't offer you any money. The *Chronicle* is indebted as it is.'

'Not money.' Tredup hesitates, and then, slowly: 'I want Stuff's job.'

The boss exclaims: 'But that's completely out of the question!'

And Trautmann: 'Why so? I think he's useful.'

'Do you think?' Gebhardt asks. 'Well, perhaps it's worth considering.'

'I need a firm commitment,' says Tredup.

'We can give you that,' announces Trautmann.

'Is Herr Gebhardt agreed?'

'It's as Herr Trautmann says,' affirms the boss. But that's not quite enough for Tredup.

'This is certain, yes?' he asks hesitantly.

'Quite certain,' says Trautmann.

'I'm depending on it,' says Tredup.

'You can.'

'It'll take a couple of weeks, the business with Stuff.'

'That's your affair.'

'And of course he mustn't hear from you that you suspect anything.'

'He won't.'

The boss is already back at his desk, crunching numbers and statistics.

'All right then, goodbye,' says Tredup. 'And many thanks.'

'Goodbye,' say the other two.

Outside, Tredup thinks: I'm sure they want to screw me. But I know too much. The thing about the print run alone. – Well, time to saw off Stuff. – Maybe I'll end up doing nothing at all.

V

Banz has recovered to the degree that with the help of a stick he can walk out of his room, across the yard, and to a field where his wife and children are working.

He likes it when his wife goes out on the field as well, so that there's some supervision. He himself does the housework, a fairly minimal bit of sweeping, peeling potatoes, the cooking. He does it with long pauses, in which he props himself dizzily against the wall. Then he sees red, and everything spins in front of him.

After a while, it passes. And he hobbles on, out to work and to the field. I'm just about ready to retire, he mocks himself. An old man of forty-five. Well, you wait, you people of Altholm, till I can fix myself up with a lawyer.

Because by now Padberg and Bandekow have been to see him. Banz is no longer under suspicion. No one knows he has clubbed someone down, and he himself is careful not to mention it, not even to those two. He will sue the town of Altholm, and they will have to pay him damages, a pension. He was struck down from behind as he climbed the steps to a pub to drink a glass of beer. The inn people, who found him slumped on the steps, will be his witnesses.

Banz hobbles on. The children are mowing the oats, he has to see how far along they are.

Of course he can see from some way off that they haven't done half of what they would have done with him to set an example. Their idea of a swathe is a tiny arc, and the oats aren't exactly thick. And forever having breaks, and sharpening the blades, useless they are.

Three hundred yards off, he has a fit of rage, one of those fits that come over him so regularly these days. He starts shouting and yelling and waving his stick around.

Afterwards comes his giddy spell, and he can't get down quick enough, he half falls to the ground. And there he lies for a while, dozily, his brain refusing to work. The family are used to it, they won't come and help him up. Let him lie there. No wonder – what makes him really lose his rag is when they do come and help. Let them do their thing, the rabble, the bloody rabble.

Slowly he gets up. It's not so easy out here, where there's nothing to grab hold of. But in the end he does it, with the help of his stick.

Then he shambles on, swearing to himself, keeping his eyes on those pathetic mowers.

For a while he stands there with them, without a word, walks along beside them, right next to the scythes. They're mowing like the devil now, reaching out as far as they can in his direction. He'll have to look out for himself, the old geezer, stands around, does fuck all, just eats and scolds and does nothing the next day.

The old man walks along beside Franz, keeps pace with him. 'What's the matter with your scythe?' he asks. 'It's loose. You need to drive the wedge in.'

The boy mutters something under his breath, and carries on mowing.

'Show us your scythe!' the farmer orders him.

The boy gives back: 'Come on, I gotta keep up with the others.'

'Gimme your scythe!'

They all stop, and Franz steps out of line.

'You carry on,' says the farmer. 'Everyone move over one! – And you, women, stop standing around gawping!' In a sudden fury, he screams: 'You're not mowing anything, and half the oats are still not stacked! Get on with it! I'm keeping you on until the whole lot is stacked!'

Silently, mother and daughter go back to work.

The farmer tests the blade. 'This hasn't been whetted. Did you whet it last night?'

Franz looks furious.

'Did you whet it? Open your mouth.'

'Yes,' says the boy.

'No, you didn't. You're lying. Look at the rings round your eyes! What were you up to last night? Where do you go to rut?'

The boy is silent, the girls giggle, the lads smirk.

'Where do you go out to at night, I asked.'

'I don't go anywhere.'

'When did you last whet the scythe? Tuesday?'

'Last night.'

'You're lying, damn you! Fornicator! Where do you go? – Staying up all night with wenches, and hanging around all day like a fucked-out puppet – what do I feed you for?'

The boy glowers fiercely

'Where d'you get the money from? You must pay women, looking the way you do! They wouldn't fuck you for nothing, you ugly dwarf! Where d'you get the money?'

'Where am I supposed to get it from? Have we even got any?'

'You wait,' says the farmer. 'You'll be found out. Here's the scythe. Go to the rabbit field and start mowing there. You're no use here. – And I want you to finish the rabbit field tonight. If I see so much as a blade of grass, there'll be trouble!'

'That's not possible.'

'Did you hear what I said? Mow it! Mow it! I want it mowed clear!' shrieks the furious farmer, smashing his stick on the ground. 'Go! Let's prove you spend your nights shagging! Leave your sap in bed, when we need it out here. Off with you. Scram.'

'Go along, Franz,' says his mother.

'I can't do it all on my own,' says the boy hesitantly. The old man is now lying on the ground again, out of his mind. 'Let Minna come too, so she can pick up the swathes.'

'You go too, Minna,' says the mother.

They both head off towards the corner of the woods. The farmer, restored to consciousness, watches them go.

'Come here, woman.'

The woman comes.

'Squat down beside me.'

The woman does so.

'Is the money still there?' he whispers.

'All of it,' she says.

'You're lying,' he says angrily. 'There's fifteen marks missing. I went there this morning.'

'I took them for the pharmacy,' she says quickly.

'You're lying,' says the farmer. 'Franz took them.'

'Franz doesn't steal,' the woman insists.

'Yes he does. If I catch him near the hiding place, I'll beat his brains out.'

'Franz doesn't steal,' the woman insists.

'You're all liars, the lot of you,' says the farmer. 'But I'll pick myself up. Then you'll be in for a surprise. And those folks in Altholm will as well. You wait.'

He pulls himself up and hobbles back towards the yard.

VI

The permanent Deputy Inspector Perduzke has been assigned the interrogation of the remand prisoner Henning.

'I'm surprised they haven't given up,' he says, and makes to go.

'Aren't you taking any files with you?' asks his colleague, Inspector Bering.

'No, I'm not. – Where are the cigarettes?'

'There must be some in the cupboard. – Do you think he'll fall for it?'

'Gifts keep a friendship alive,' says Perduzke, crams a carton of a hundred into his pocket, and heads off.

At the hospital, he once again finds the man who's supposed to keep guard on Henning inside with him, instead of outside the door. For once, though, Perduzke doesn't tear him off a strip, he just says: 'Off you go, Gruen. I'm here on duty.'

'Just don't get any ideas,' says Gruen, his little blond goatee wagging crossly. 'There's all sorts of ways to serve the Republic.'

'There's a blonde nurse on the ward called Ellie,' says Henning with a kind smile to Gruen, 'I think you'd like her, and she's already getting on my nerves a bit. Damned pretty, though.'

'Women!' says Gruen contemptuously. 'Nothing but women on his mind! Some hero he is! A piece of meat, and all his thoughts are out the window.'

'Save it for Ellie,' says Perduzke, and pushes Gruen out the door. 'We don't need you here right now.'

Then they are alone, and Henning sits down on a chair in front of the window. He looks fit and healthy again, the only suggestion of the much-mooted cripple being that he carries his arm in a sling.

'Sit down, Perduzke. So you want to question me again?'

'I do. I've got to. Here's some cigarettes.' And he gruffly puts the carton on the table.

Henning looks at the pack. 'Seconds. Not for resale. – How is it that in every German city detectives always turn up with these terrible cigarettes?'

'Oh, so you've had dealings with detectives in every German city, have you? – Ah, leave it out, I don't know, the questioning hasn't begun yet. Why seconds? Well, I suppose the cigarette factories have to have somewhere to send their seconds. So they make them over to the police, so we have some bait for our hoodlums.'

'Thanks,' says Henning, 'but no thanks. I've got a whole cupboard full of fags.'

Perduzke pulls his notebook out of his pocket. 'We'll start the questioning, then, Henning.'

And Henning: 'The usual preliminaries first. I demand to be taken to the interrogating magistrate.'

'Take it up with your lawyer. – I have been assigned the duty of questioning you –'

Henning drones mechanically: 'I would like to protest that my initial questioning is being carried out by a policeman. I will only speak in front of a judge. I will not answer questions put to me by a policeman.'

'All right, done,' says Perduzke. 'Aren't you afraid you'll get bored, Henning?'

'Duty must never become boring, Perduzke,' Henning lectures him.

'Moving on to the interview proper,' says Perduzke, looking down at his notebook.

'I wish to point out that I won't answer any questions,' says Henning.

'Is Georg Henning your real name?' asks Perduzke, blinking over a black-rimmed pince-nez.

'My goodness,' says Henning happily, 'you've changed the record. At last it's not that dreary 26th of July any more. – I decline to answer.'

'Were you not previously known as Georg Hansen, Lieutenant Parsenow and First Lieutenant Hingst?'

'Well, well, well,' says Henning, his brow darkening a little, 'there's a thing. – I decline to answer.'

'Were you not active with the Hamburg unit in the Baltic area?'

'I decline to answer.'

'Did you not belong to the Ehrhardt Brigade?'

'I decline . . .'

'Did you not belong to the Horse Guards, and were you not on the staff of the Hotel Eden?'

'I decline . . .'

'Were you not involved in an attempt on the Reichswehr barracks in Gemünden?'

'I decline to answer the question.'

'How do you manage to support yourself?'

'I decline . . .'

'Can you name any farmers who have purchased machinery from you in the last six months?'

'I decline to answer.'

'Where were you at the time the farmers' flag was designed?'

'I decline . . .'

'Who provided you with materials that went into the making of the flag?'

Who? – What? – Where from? – Why? – When . . .?

'I decline . . . I decline . . . I decline . . .'

'Well, that's about it for today. Would you like to sign a statement to confirm that you have refused to answer questions?'

'I refuse to sign any papers.'

'We're finished, Herr Henning.'

'All right. All right. So the interrogation is over?'

'The interrogation is finished.'

'Well, we had all sorts today.'

'True. But only – stonewalling.'

'Stonewalling?'

'I don't think I'll come again.'

'So who will there be instead?'

'No one.'

'You mean . . .?'

'Just what you think.'

'But that's impossible!'

'All sorts of things are possible these days.'

'Say, when?'

'Another two or three days, maybe?'

'And: definitely?'

'Yes, inasmuch as a junior detective like me has any idea of these things: yes.'

'Well, I'll say farewell, then.'

'Farewell, Herr Henning.'

'Goodbye.'

'Yes. At the hearing.'

'So there will be a hearing?'

'Yes, of course. Why wouldn't there be a hearing?'

'Indeed. Why not? – But is it certain, Perduzke? Because other-wise . . . You know, the security in this place isn't especially tight.'

'You can depend on it, Herr Henning. Good day.'

'Good day. And send Gruen in to me.'

'What is it?' asks Gruen crossly.

'They're letting me go at the beginning of next week, my dear watchdog,' says Henning.

'Delay! Delay! Delay! If I was you, I wouldn't wait.'

'Of course I'm going to wait. Certainly now. A little wait now, while the temperature's going up everywhere, that's the best part of this whole nonsense.'

Gruen looks at him disapprovingly. 'I think you get a kick out of a bomb going off. The bastards there are on this earth!'

'Get out of here, you donkey!' roars Henning furiously.

VII

In the *Chronicle*'s dispatch office a man appears in a grey-green uniform, with a goatee.

Fräulein Heinze says: 'You must have come for the freesheets for the prisoners.'

'I want to talk to the editor.'

Heinze is uncertain. 'I don't think he's available right now.'

'Don't think. Ask him.'

The Fräulein gets up dismayed, gives her fingernails one last, longing look, and vanishes.

She returns. 'You can go through.'

She sits down. Gruen tries to find a way through the barrier, misses the little door, and vaults it with a loud crash instead.

Fräulein Heinze is indignant: 'Were you brought up in a barn!' – but Gruen is already in the office.

Stuff greets him: 'Well, what are you after, jailbird?'

'I need to ask you something, Stuff.'

'Ask away. We never starved in that uniform, eh?'

Gruen narrows his eyes and raises a very thin admonitory finger. 'Are you in on the conspiracy too?'

Stuff laughs. 'Are they playing with you again? Are they shooting for your blond curls, old jailbird? – Of course I'm in on the conspiracy. I'm sitting right at the sweet heart of it.'

Gruen shakes his head. 'They all want to do deals. All of them. Even Henning stinks. Ever since he's heard he's being freed, he's been delaying. Delay, I ask you. I'm not going to let them make a fool of me.'

Stuff pricks up his ears. 'Henning freed? You're crazy!'

'Other people are crazy. I've got my finger on the pulse. Back on July the 26th, I was the first to notice what was going off. If the peasants had done what I wanted them to do, and stormed the prison and sprung Reimers . . .'

Stuff says sorrowfully: 'You're raving again, Gruen. Reimers wasn't even in your jail at that point.'

Gruen says enigmatically: 'Reimers is still with us, but he's being hidden.'

'You're crazy. Reimers has been free for weeks now.'

'Reimers comes in lots of disguises.'

'You really should get your head examined, you know. I'm serious, Gruen.'

'Don't talk nonsense. Tell me instead why you didn't write about the meeting at the district president's? The *Bauernschaft* was full of it. None of the town papers carried a word about it.'

'Didn't suit me,' growls Stuff. 'Things need to cool down.'

'Cool down? They need to heat up. You see, you're in on the conspiracy as well.'

'Things can't always happen the way you wish they would,

Gruenie. I expect there's people you'd like to release from your Red hotel, and can't.'

'Not one. They're all common criminals, and the other ones are being tested. – Are you going to write about the meeting?'

'Oh, give over. No, I don't want to.'

'You've got to, Stuff. You mustn't betray the cause.'

'Listen, jailor man, just get it into your head: I can't. The high-ups, the politicians and whatnot, they've stuck their heads together, and the little fish have got to obey.'

'Why have you got to obey?'

'Because otherwise I'll be out of a job. And whoever takes my place will be worse.'

'Who comes after you is no concern of yours. You've got to write something.'

'I know more about this than you do, Gruen. Leave me be.'

'In on the conspiracy too,' says Gruen. 'In on the conspiracy. Henning, Stuff, everyone.'

'What's Henning got to do with it?'

'Enough. Same as you. But the lightning is in the cloud, and at the right moment it will strike.'

'Gruen, I'm telling you '

The door opens, and Tredup walks in.

He gives a start when he sees Gruen. The two of them scowl at each other.

'Who's that, Stuff?' Gruen asks quietly.

'Don't you two know each other? This is our advertising manager, Herr Tredup. – Auxiliary prison warden, Herr Gruen.'

'I do know him,' says Gruen quietly. 'He's the fake Reimers who shopped me to the prison governor.

'He's the madman at the prison I told you about, Stuff. The fellow got me in big trouble . . .

'You have people like that working for you, Stuff?' Gruen remarks. 'In that case the lightning has been hanging around in the cloud too long.' Suddenly he stretches out his skinny arms. 'It will destroy all of you . . .'

Suddenly he disappears. Fräulein Heinze is heard screaming outside. They both run out.

'What is it?'

'What's the matter?'

'Why did you scream like that?'

'That madman! He frightened me! He suddenly jumped over the barrier.'

'Yes, I think he really has lost it now,' says Stuff pensively. 'I'd better do something quickly to keep him from getting into trouble. Will you take on the cinema and the market news, Tredup?'

'What was the film?'

'Ach, the usual tosh. Just write: "Dina Mina displays her impish talents to full advantage." The cinema ad will give the details. Surely I can trust you to do that?'

'That's what they're all asking me now,' mutters Tredup crossly. 'Of course I'll display my impish talents to full advantage.'

VIII

As Stuff approaches the back of the hospital – he prefers side streets to main roads – he sees that the generally peaceful avenue has become a sort of *paseo* at this early-evening hour. Girls are wandering up and down in pairs, schoolboys are in evidence staring, and there are some older girls too, girls of twenty or twenty-one.

Stuff knows that from time immemorial the Burstah has been the main drag of Altholm. If its function has been taken over by the hospital road, there must be a reason for it. The reason is not far to seek: it is standing in an upper-ground-floor window of the hospital, smiling, calling down the odd word, blowing kisses. It is a beaming Henning, Henning the folk hero.

And however inclined Stuff might be to hold Henning in high regard ever since he lay on the cobbles bleeding from two dozen wounds, this seems to him to be overdoing it. Jerk, he thinks, as he goes on his way.

He had thought it would be difficult to get through to the remand prisoner. But this is the hour when supper is served at the hospital, the sisters are all far too busy to notice him, and he doesn't see a sentry.

Fine state of affairs, thinks Stuff. Bit of a miracle Henning is still around.

He knocks, waits for a moment, and goes in.

Henning is still parked by the window, waving to his admirers. On the table are the thick end of a dozen bouquets, white parcels of chocolate, packets of cigarettes galore, and, here and there, half unpacked and indifferently left lying around, samples of handiwork.

'Forget that nonsense, Henning,' says Stuff impatiently. 'I've got something important to talk to you about.'

'Nonsense? That's what you think. This is laying the groundwork for my forthcoming court appearance.'

And he continues to wave and smile out the window.

'Rubbish! Those deluded teenagers won't save you.'

'Maybe not, but they'll tell their fathers and brothers and uncles what a sweet, kind, natural boy I am. And those fathers and uncles and brothers will be witnesses at my trial, or even on the jury, or at least friends of others that are.'

'They'll send you down, you know that.'

'Not at all. With an atmosphere in the town like this. And half crippled as I am – that always plays well.'

'Can you really not move the arm in your sling?'

'Absolutely not. That arm is going to cost Altholm a packet in the months ahead.'

'Jerk,' and Stuff at last has managed to hit the correct tone. 'You're mad. You'll be lucky if you get off with one or two years behind bars. Getting off free and being paid damages – dream on.'

'We're not there yet.'

'No, thank God. Because before we are I need to know something, which is: What did you do with Gruen?'

'With Gruen? With that maniac Gruen? What good is he to anyone? He's the original overwound spring.'

'Get to the point, Henning. You've planted some idea or other in his head. The man's barking, you don't use him! He's got half a dozen kids or more, starved herring that he is. You don't get someone like that to do your work for you.'

Henning abruptly turns round, and slams the window shut. 'Who do I get to do my work for me? Who am I meant to be using? Stuff, what's got into you? If that idiot Gruen said something . . . then it was his own innate madness. If you know anything about me, Stuff, it's that I don't mind putting my foot in the dog shit. – But we can see right now.' Henning pulls the door open. 'Gruen, come here a minute, will you?'

'There was no sentry outside when I came by.'

'Liberal conditions, eh? But honestly, I haven't seen the guy for five or six hours. And he is meant to be on duty till eight p.m.'

'No, because he was visiting me. Gave me lots of stupid talk, accused me of not writing enough about the farmers –'

'He's got a point there.'

'Fat lot you know about it. – But he was threatening, saying we were all involved in some conspiracy to betray the cause. "The lightning is in the cloud, and at the right moment –"'

'Blathering imbecile.'

'It got me thinking. There are infectious jokes. Did he ever ask you – this is an idea of mine – how you connect an alarm clock to an electrical timed fuse? Or how much dynamite you need for a proper bomb?'

Henning stares.

Suddenly his face turns pinched, the nose yellow and pointy. He slams his hand down on the table.

'Oh, how can I be so stupid! Bloody idiot! Wretch! Those town troops should have beaten me to death, dammit!'

'Stop swearing. Tell me.'

'I can't remember now how we got on to it, but somehow he managed to get the address where the dynamite is stored out of me. Yes, that was it, he offered to help, and said there was no safer storage for it than prison. So we argued back and forth, and finally I ended up boasting how secure our hiding place was.'

Stuff groans and stares in disbelief. 'Henning! Henning! You're like an infant crapping its nappies! Can't be expected to keep anything back! Everything's got to come out!'

'Stuff, we've got to find him! It's all I need, with me about to be released, shenanigans like this.'

'But you can't get out of here!'

'What do you mean, "can't"? Don't you know some way I can get past those hysterical bitches on the street?'

'Yes, there is a way. We go through the boiler room and out the coal cellar. Leave a piece of paper saying you've gone out for a walk and are coming back later. They won't do anything then. They'll keep mum, seeing as it's their own sentry who's gone missing.'

An hour later, Stuff is ringing the bell at the prison gate. Henning is standing in the background – it's almost dark.

They've been all over town, talked to the wife, quizzed the kids, no one knew where Gruen was.

It turns out he is actually here.

'Doing a turn on the late shift. Standing in for a sick colleague. Happy to take over, can use a little extra cash.'

'Could we talk to him? Only for a moment.'

'Completely out of the question, Herr Stuff. Conversation in prison at nine at night! The director would be on the case first thing tomorrow. But why don't you wait for him to come off? He'll be out in a couple of hours.'

'Through this gate?'

'Yes. It's the only one! You ought to know that, Herr Stuff!'

'Would you happen to have noticed if he had a little case with him? Or a cardboard box?'

'Nope. Can't remember. Don't think so.'

'Well, goodnight to you, and thanks. Here, take another cigar.'

'Thanks. Do you want me to give him a message, Herr Stuff?'

'No. Nothing. Evening.'

'It all sounds perfectly OK, doesn't it? Why would he take on someone else's night shift to earn a little extra money if what he really wants to do is throw a bomb?'

'Everything's possible with Gruen. He walked off the job with you and took on another one here.'

'Anyway, I'll tell you this much, Stuff. We've got two hours –'

'One hour and fifty.'

'It's enough. In that time I have to get hold of a woman.'

'Aren't there enough nurses?'

'If you knew. The minute you want something, the sentry turns out to be a proper sentry. I could have made bombs to my heart's content, but a girl in my room, absolutely not. Pure jealousy.'

'All right then. How do you want her? Fat? Thin? Blonde? Brunette?'

'I don't care, Stuff. Just so long as it's a woman.'

IX

At nine o'clock there's a ring at Mayor Gareis's door. It's Political Adviser Stein, come to fetch his friend and master for a walk. They always go for walks together when it's dark, and almost always along a little-used path that meanders along between fields and meadows.

'You know, Adviser,' says Gareis. 'It's important not to show too much of oneself to people. The less they see of you, the greater your mystique. Take me: if they saw me walking, they would say: Christ, here's Fatty Gareis trying to lose a couple of pounds.'

They walk slowly up the suburban street, at the end of which the mayor lives. They turn up the path. The odd summerhouse and allotment, and then the advance guard sent out by agriculture against industry: potato fields.

'Potatoes,' muses the mayor. 'I prefer them to roses. Same family – did you know that? – potatoes. At home, whenever there wasn't anything proper to eat, we always had potatoes. We all filled up on potatoes.'

'A bit dull, don't you find, fields?'

'Do you? Not me.'

'Yes,' says the political adviser absent-mindedly. 'You know, the farmers have stopped supplying the town now. They only take their pigs and their potatoes as far as the town limits. – There, you bloody Altholmers, if you want it, come and get it. The boycott is getting more and more rough.'

'Adviser, would you mind not talking about the boycott, just for an hour. As if there was nothing else to do in the world. Unemployment's getting worse. Our town has the highest unemployment in the entire province. And my welfare budget has been exhausted for the past two months.'

'So what do you do?'

'I carry on spending. I'd like to see the accountant who would refuse me the money. And at least on that point, I've got the whole Party behind me.'

'Only on that point?'

'They don't consider me a proper Red any more. I'm too farmer-friendly for their liking. I think I'm meant to destroy them with fire and sword.'

'But if they're not going to support you, who are you going to look to in the coming struggle?'

'Myself. I always think in the end they'll realize they still need me. That I was right all along.'

'Yes, and Temborius's defeat will strengthen you.'

The mayor stops. 'That defeat is the worst thing that could have happened. Since learning about that, I've almost given up hope of an accommodation.'

'But why? They're all running back to you now.'

'Can I do anything final without the help of the government? It's the way it is, they're always going to want to put their oar in, otherwise it's no go. Henceforth, Temborius will chuck a spanner in the works whenever he can.

'He's such a confounded bureaucrat, his heart bleeds when things don't run smoothly. It really causes him pain.

'Well, and then he thought: All right, I'll be a trimmer, I'll meet you halfway, you'll see you had the wrong impression of me . . . You don't like Frerksen and Gareis? Fine, I'll give you their heads on a plate!

'He does it, and then he sends for them. The speed with which he does it, so soon after the sacrifice, you can tell, he couldn't wait for things to be smoothed over. Then he can go to Berlin and brag about peace with the farmers. Triumph of my diplomacy.

'And they go and spit in his face, they really hawked up some nasty phlegm. Believe me, the man sits in his office and weeps bloody tears, because for once in his life he acted against his principles and tried the humane route, and offered them his hand in peace. He's now breeding a real hatred in his bosom, and I promise you there's nothing worse than a hate-filled bureaucrat. If you can't count on anything else in the world, there's something you can build your house on.

'And he will make any future reconciliation impossible. He won't stop until the last farmer starves. He will happily sacrifice Altholm with its forty thousand inhabitants, he'll even sacrifice his own career. And he'll be the one who shatters all my good work.'

'You can build it up again wherever you go, Mayor.'

'But I'm not even entertaining the idea of going elsewhere. Maybe I can still win. I can point to farmer-friendly policies, all the things I've done things for them! The exhibition. The auction hall, which I financed. Or scraped together. The horse market at the equestrian show. And the training courses in winter. Well, one day when they've quietened down a bit they'll remember them all. And then there won't be a big palaver about reconciliation, then we'll just do something nice, which will help the farmers come into some money – and we'll all be friends again.'

'May I point out that you've been talking about the boycott for the past fifteen minutes?'

'I know. I'm no good at keeping to my own rules. But now we're going to walk briskly for the next half an hour. And I swear I'll be thinking of anything but the boycott.'

Silence follows, not just for the next half-hour but for fully an hour of walking.

Then the path goes through a small copse. There the mayor sits down and listens to the night wind in the branches.

'Isn't it good? What a wonderful institution the wind is. One should keep time for something like that. You can spend for ever thinking about stuff. There's something so . . . Did you ever think about how you recognize the different trees, Stein?'

'The leaves, maybe?'

'But in winter you can still tell which is an apple tree and which is a cherry.'

'I can't, I have to say. But presumably by the colour of the trunk, and the type of bark, and what have you.'

'And if you're two hundred yards away, could you tell then? No, it seems to me every type of tree has a particular angle of extension, so many degrees at which it puts out its branches. Or variations of different angles. I'm sure there are people who know such things. But unfortunately we never come across them, you and me.'

'I certainly can't help you.'

'Are you upset, Adviser? Don't be. – Shall we turn back?'

They approach the town once more, when suddenly a man emerges from the darkness. Little more than a shade. He asks politely after the time.

The luminous dial on the mayor's watch indicates half past eleven, and just as he says so, the clocks of the town all strike, some tinny, some clangorous, all seven of them.

The man thanks him and heads on out of town. Then he stops and calls out of the darkness: 'That was Mayor Gareis, wasn't it?'

The man is quite some way off, and Gareis calls back: 'At half past eleven at night, just plain Gareis will do. Leave the mayor in the town hall.'

The man seems to be even further away, but seems to have an unquenchable thirst for answers. 'Are you actually married?' he asks.

And the mayor echoes: 'Christ, man, would I be so fat if I wasn't?'

'Any kids?'

'No. Not as of now. Anything else?'

And honestly, the questioner – he's now at least fifty paces off – calls back: 'Why did you have the peasants beaten down?'

'They did that themselves,' comes the sibylline reply, and Gareis hears a cheeky, cackling laugh.

'He was a few sheets to the wind,' says the adviser reprovingly. 'I really don't understand you, Mayor.'

But the mayor doesn't reply.

'That was funny,' he says at last, 'and a little bit eerie. Well, I think I need a good night's sleep, nothing less will do me good.'

'Why eerie? It didn't seem eerie to me. Just aggressive.'

'Aggressive? If you say so. He seemed to me to be someone looking for extenuating circumstances.'

'You've lost me there.'

'I think . . . Let's go on. It doesn't matter. Anyway – there's no protection against it.'

'Against what?'

'Against being accosted by a drunk, I suppose.'

They walk on. They turn into the suburban street and find themselves outside the mayor's house. There are two men standing there, watching them.

Gareis recognizes one of them, but doesn't want to know him. He walks straight up to his front door, but the man addresses him.

'Excuse me, Mayor. Did you happen to run into a man with a little goatee beard? It's very important.'

The mayor replies coolly: 'I would have preferred not to have to talk to you for a while, Herr Stuff. Something about you doesn't smell right. But since it does seem to matter to you: on the footpath to Lohstedt, about five minutes ago, a man accosted us. It was dark, but from the sound of his voice he might have had a goatee.'

'Might I ask, Mayor, what he was after?'

'No, no more questions, Herr Stuff.' The mayor turns to Stein. 'Goodnight, Adviser –'

But Stuff won't be shaken off. 'Don't be vengeful, Mayor. I swear, tomorrow you can cut me dead as much as you like, but today please answer me: what was the man after?'

'You're a queer fish, Stuff,' says the mayor, not without a tinge of admiration. 'Too bad you're a newspaper man. – My adviser was of the view that the man was drunk, but that wasn't my feeling.'

Stuff presses. 'What did he ask you?'

'The time. Just as it was striking half past eleven. Whether I was the mayor. Whether I had children. Whether I was married.'

The adviser completes the list: 'Why you had the peasants beaten down.'

'Did you give him sensible answers?'

'Except for the final question, yes.'

'That was him, Henning. I tell you –'

'Henning . . .?' asks the mayor, acutely.

'Here he comes!' yells Henning. 'Run! Run!'

Out of the dark allotment path a man shoots past like a rocket. Over his head he is ready to hurl something that looks like a parcel.

Stuff barges the mayor in the back. 'Run! Run, Mayor! A bomb!'

And Stuff races off. Stein is already running. Henning has a twenty-yard start on both.

The four of them run down the barely built-up, deserted suburban street, the mayor bringing up the rear, already panting for breath. Behind him, fleet-footed, races the starved herring, madman Gruen, whirling the bomb over his head. In a shrill voice, he yells: 'The plot has been discovered! The traitors are assembled. All will be annihilated by the lightning from the cloud!'

The outcome of the race is hardly in doubt: every second Gruen is closing on the mayor.

He hears the light and rapid footfall, thinks: done for either way. It all depends on my being able to snatch the bomb away from him with my hands.

He turns with baffling swiftness, crashes into the arms of his pursuer, knocks him to the ground with the sheer bulk of him, falls down on top of him, feels him holding the case tightly in his hands, feels an absurd bite in his arm, yells: 'Stuff, come here! Stuff, help!'

And, quite astonished at himself, he hears himself call: 'Brave Stuff, help me!'

He wrestles with the other man for the bomb, which he is trying to smash down on the ground. The other is fighting tooth and nail, the mayor feels any moment . . .

Ten seconds, twenty seconds . . .

Then Stuff, slightly out of breath, but calm, is saying: 'Let the case go, Mayor, I've got it.'

And takes it from Gareis's hands, holds it to his ear. 'It's ticking,' says Stuff. 'So far everything's going well!'

The mayor struggles to his feet, looks at the man lying on the ground. 'Unconscious. Perverse idiot. Deranged, isn't he?'

'Totally.'

'Tell me, Stuff, what do you actually do with a bomb like that? The thing could go off any moment, could it not?'

'That's what I was just going to ask you, Mayor,' replies Stuff, and holds the little case at arm's length. 'What if we set it down in the meadow over there.'

'Why not? If it hasn't gone off before that?'

'That would be pointless, wouldn't it? I suggest I go at this point.'

'I suggest we both go together.'

'But that's really unnecessary,' says Stuff.

'Let me have my bit of fun,' says the mayor.

And they walk over to the meadow.

Unconscious, on the road, lies Gruen. Somewhere further on, rapidly approaching the centre of town, are Henning and Stein, both running hard.

X

It's the same night, the same hour, and Thiel is on his way from Bandekow-Ausbau to Stolpe. He too hears the clocks strike half past eleven, and he works out: Just after midnight I'll be back at the *Bauernschaft*.

He couldn't bear to stay on the farm.

A week ago, when Padberg left, and he went upstairs to his garret, he thought: Why do I have to play the guard dog? There's nothing of any interest left in the desk. And those days in the garret next to the toilet . . . no, no more. I'm going to the country.

Today he told Count Bandekow that he had a headache, and went off to bed at nine o'clock. At half past, he was taking his departure through the vegetable allotment.

He couldn't bear it.

There is the sprawling villa in town, with the unlit rooms, the corridors, the staircases, the halls, the garden, with the strange bell, with the desk and the mysterious typesetter. He wants to catch the man.

Thiel walks rhythmically and fast. It's a fine, moonless night. Hardly any pedestrians or cyclists any more, just the occasional car, throwing clouds of dust, or a motorbike clattering past.

The first houses on the outskirts. A gaslight comes to meet him, burning there stupidly by itself, lighting a patch of meadow, and some roadway. On the road is a perfectly round stone, a fieldstone the size of your fist, burnished smooth. Thiel kicks at it, and the stone rolls off a little way, unevenly, with seeming reluctance.

'All right then,' says Thiel, and he picks it up instead and puts it in his bag. As he does so, he has two pictures in his head: one, a memory of a Bible illustration, David with the sling in the fight with Goliath. And then he sees himself standing behind the door of the editorial suite of the *Bauernschaft*, with the light on inside. There's a man hunched over the desk. Thiel picks up the stone and hurls it through the crack in the door.

'All right,' he says impatiently, 'we'll do that.'

He arrives in the streets of Stolpe, silent and deserted here too. No more than the occasional lit-up window. Only the pubs are still open. Music comes out of one of them: radio or gramophone.

Suddenly, Thiel feels a yen for a glass of beer and a schnapps. What is he risking, if it comes down to it? Who knows who he is here in Stolpe? Not a soul! And he steps in.

The bar is almost deserted. A solitary customer is propping up the bar, a dark, stout man with a little beer belly. The barkeeper is chatting to him.

When Thiel orders, the two of them look at him. The beer belly has an unpleasant way of staring. Even so, Thiel keeps his position at the bar.

He takes the first swallow. The barman says: 'Here's health!'

'From the country?' asks the dark man.

'Yes,' says Thiel. And with a sheepish little laugh, he says: 'Why, do I look it?'

The man motions with his head at Thiel's shoes, which are thickly coated with dust.

'Of course,' laughs Thiel. 'Well, that wasn't so hard, was it?' And looks back at the other fellow's shoes. A vaguely uncomfortable feeling comes over him. The other fellow has black Oxfords.

Well, there's plenty like that in the world. Drink up and go.

'Teacher?' asks the man.

'What makes you say so?' asks Thiel, evasively.

'No, you're no teacher,' says the man, without going into any further explanations, and continues staring at Thiel.

He takes another gulp of beer, orders another double, and asks the barman for no good reason for directions to the station.

After he had stiltedly talked Thiel through something he'd long known, the dark-haired man threw in: 'There's no more trains tonight.'

'I know,' says Thiel. 'I just want to go to the left-luggage office.'

'That's shut as well,' says the man.

Dammit! thinks Thiel. Why did I come here! And he feels for his purse.

Of course it's in the bag that has the stone lying on top of it. As he pulls out the purse, the stone clatters out on to the floor.

Thiel and the fat man both stoop for it at once. Thiel is the quicker, and hastily and sheepishly stows the stone back in the bag.

'Do you collect stones, then?' asks the man.

'I'm building a house,' says Thiel in a tone that won't permit further questions. And to the barman: 'Pay, please!'

He pays and leaves. He has a feeling between his shoulder blades that they are both staring at him. Bloody yokels! Idiotic of me to ever go in there, he thinks again, and he steps out to make up for lost time.

He reaches the back wall of the *Bauernschaft*, pulls himself up over a plank, and finds himself standing in the garden.

All quiet and dark.

Shall I go to the machine plant first and filch a few cigarettes from the foreman?

But he doesn't feel up to it. The dark-haired fellow at the bar is preying on his mind.

Instead he climbs the outside staircase on the main building, and when he reaches the first floor he doesn't go inside, he scales the wall, using ledges and drainpipe, up to the second floor.

He's thought it all out. He's remembered the façade correctly. This way he won't get to the editorial office from the ground floor but from the second floor. If the man's in there, he won't be alerted: there's no warning bell set off from upstairs.

He's in luck. There's a window open on the second floor in the bookbinding plant, he swings himself in and stands in the silent room, waiting for his breathing to slow.

Nothing stirs in the sleeping building.

But Thiel knows the building isn't really asleep. He knows that today he will reach his objective.

He takes his shoes off and puts them down. Then, with infinite caution, he opens the door to the proof room and slides in.

He stands in the middle of the dark room. He rests his hip against a table, both hands are on a high desk.

He stands there, listening. The editorial office is directly below.

Everything is still, perfectly still.

And slowly out of the silence, a quiet sound rises to him, almost a no-sound, something terribly slight, carried on the wind.

Endlessly slowly, Thiel drops to his knees, and then presses his ear to the floor for a long time.

Far off, ghostly, he hears footfall, back and forth, below him.

The man is there.

While he gets to his feet again, he is thinking feverishly. First he needs to shut the window of the proof room to make sure there isn't a draught when he opens the door on to the corridor. The bookbindery door needs to be closed too. You never know, if the door downstairs is open, a draught might alert him.

He does everything, and opens the door on to the corridor. Yes, the door downstairs *is* open, he can hear the man walking about.

He feels mighty safe, thinks Thiel. You wait!

He feels his way to the top of the stairs. Of course he can't use the staircase, a single creak would wreck everything. But it's an old villa, the steps have a nice wide balustrade, and he slides down it, as he might have done as a boy, only braking all the time.

He is down in the passage, two steps from the door, which

is ajar. The way to the door takes for ever. He is irritated by his
heart booming, by his trembling limbs. He's by the door. He
pushes three fingers in the crack and slowly pulls it wide. He sees
a white face bending over the desk, in the beam of a torch . . .

The door gives a creak.

The face scoots out of the beam. Thiel sees an arm upraised.
He reaches into his bag.

The light goes out.

Thiel slings his stone. There's a messy sound. Someone
screams, roars: 'Aaah! Oooh!'

More feebly then: 'Oooh!'

Thiel takes a step into the dark, feels for the switch, the bright-
ness is painful.

The man in the blue typesetter's tunic is sprawled on the carpet in front of the desk.

The drawer is open. The desk is covered with pieces of paper.

Suddenly Thiel doesn't know what to do.

The man is motionless and bleeding.

What's it all about? What do I do now? What am I going to do
with this guy? I haven't thought past this moment.

A fine, tinny rasp sounds in the wall. Someone is downstairs,
someone else who has no lawful business here.

Slowly the footsteps come up the stairs.

Thiel could still flee, but he is fixated by the man on the carpet,
just starting to come round, opening his eyes, looking at Thiel.

Now the footsteps are very close.

Is it Padberg?

In the door stands the pot-bellied dark-haired man from the pub.
Behind him are a couple of policemen. He looks into the room.

Then: 'Detective Inspector Tunk. You're under arrest, Herr
Thiel. No fuss, or else . . .' And he half pulls a pistol out of his
coat pocket.

A relieved Thiel thinks: Thank God, now I'm out of this trouble.
Somehow everything is going to get sorted out. And aloud: 'I
suggest you start with this burglar here.'

'We'll begin with you, if you don't mind,' says the detective.
'Let's get you braceleted. Put your hands together.'

The cuffs snap shut.

'And what are you doing here?' the detective asks the typesetter.

'I was getting some manuscripts for Herr Padberg. And then
this guy turns up out of the dark and hurls a rock at me.'

The detective looks at the rock, lying harmlessly on the carpet.

'Nice houses you build yourself, Thiel. I can think of one you'll
be spending some time in.'

And to the typesetter: 'What was the manuscript you were
told to get Herr Padberg?'

'The one on the desk,' says the typesetter, pointing.

Suddenly Thiel is struck by something. The drawer was empty
when Padberg left. And now . . .

Oh, we're so stupid! he thinks. We kept thinking about things
being taken away, but not of incriminating material being introduced . . . poor Padberg!

The detective browses for a while. 'Nice. Very nice. A black day
for the Farmers' League, I'd say. Wouldn't you agree, Herr Thiel?'

'They're all damned lies,' says a furious Thiel. 'Padberg knew
he had a housebreaker. He cleared his desk when he went to Berlin. Whatever's here has been smuggled in by Commie forgers.'

'An interesting idea,' says Tunk. 'Nice. Cleared his desk, you
say? Well, plenty of time to talk about all that. Is Herr Padberg
at home?'

'He sent me here when he came back from Berlin tonight.'

'Sent. Came,' fusses the great political detective. 'Fetch would
have been better. Well, we'll go and fetch him. He won't slip
through our fingers. Let's give the great farmers' movement a bit
of a going-over, shall we, Herr Thiel?'

'Fetch away,' says Thiel angrily. 'We're not finished by a long
chalk.'

6

Gareis Triumphant

I

A quiet, oppressed bunch of people sits in the rooms of the *Bauernschaft* the following morning. Not in the editorial rooms, though, the detectives are still in there, turning the place upside down, reading, confiscating.

They are all up in the proof room, new faces, farmers brought in overnight by Cousin Benthin, whom Padberg managed to call just before he was arrested: Biedermann, Hanke, Büttner, Dettmann.

The old ones are all gone, the old ones are all in prison: starting with Thiel and Padberg, then Bandekow, Reimers, Rohwer and Rehder.

Down in the setting room the linotype machines are waiting to be fed, so that the newspaper can be made up. The whole country, alerted by the morning press, is waiting to see what the *Bauernschaft* is going to say.

And what does the *Bauernschaft* say?

Who is writing?

The man already writing away, covering page after page with swift pen, is Georg Henning.

Released with the adventurer's luck from police detention just as all the others are arrested, he takes the early-morning train to Stolpe, into the eye of the storm, and now he's sitting there writing.

Cousin Benthin is very depressed. 'What will the farmers say? Chucking bombs isn't our style. They shouldn't have done that. People will say: Gareis and Frerksen were right all along.'

'Nonsense!' Henning manages to interject. 'You shouldn't believe all that rubbish. Who chucked the bombs: Thiel and Gruen! Are they farmers?'

'But Padberg –?'

'Don't talk nonsense, Cousin Benthin. These are things you don't understand. First, Padberg isn't a farmer either, and second, he's completely innocent. He doesn't know anything. The Reds have laid a bad egg in his desk. Hear what I've written. Sub-headings that go off with a bang:

'"Embarrassment for the Police" – "Government Attempts to Muzzle Awkward Squad Farmers" – "Sacked Tax Official and Deranged Prison Warden are the Bombers" – "Red Gareis Runs for His Life" – "Appeal from Franz Reimers to the Farmers" –'

'What, you've got an appeal from Franz Reimers?'

'You bet I have – I've just written it.'

'But you can't do that!'

'Why the hell not! I know what Franz would say. It's just as if he had written it. That our movement is irreproachable, that of course we're not to blame if outsiders and madmen chuck bombs.'

'Right,' say the farmers.

'That's exactly how it is,' they say.

'We're opposed to violence. We condemn all acts of violence. We won't besmirch our cause.'

'That's good.'

'Franz is right.'

'And the more the government persecutes us, the more firmly we stick together. The bloody day in Altholm is unforgotten. The boycott continues.'

'That's good. Right.'

'It's exactly the way Franz would have put it.'

'Get it out in print, it'll allay fears in the country.'

'Yes, the peasants are angry. Why do these other people keep getting involved in our business?'

'We ought to do everything ourselves. Not use any outsiders.'

Büttner, a little fat man with white-blond hair and a round bullet-head, says: 'The thing about the boycott . . . It'll be tricky. It's already starting to crumble. There are some . . .'

They all turn to look at him.

He comes over all embarrassed. 'I don't want to shop anyone.

But Bartels round our way has bought a grandfather clock in Altholm.'

'Someone near us has delivered eggs to Altholm. He took them into Frau Manzow's house.'

'Langewiesche bought his potash in Altholm.'

'Stop!' yells Henning. 'I'm writing that the edict against traitors is to be stepped up. You farmers, I'm making you responsible for putting it into effect!'

'What can we do?'

'How do we go about that?'

'I'll tell you. Tell your sons and your lads to think up punishments for those that break the boycott. They'll enjoy thinking of ways that will make life hell for others.'

'Not the lads. They're impertinent enough as it is.'

'All right, not the lads, then. But ask your sons. And talk to your wives. They're sure to come up with something.'

'You've got a point.'

'And you have to be sharp as tacks. A blackballed farmer in every third village, lots of talk about it, lots of telling everyone what he did and what happened to him – and all that bomb nonsense will be forgotten. Everyone will rally round again.'

'You're right.'

'I think you've got a point.'

'I have an idea what to do with Kantor.'

'All right then, get to it! I have to go to typesetting.'

On the corridor, Cousin Benthin stops him for a word.

'What is it now, Cousin Benthin?'

The old man looks at him mournfully. 'What about you? How can you? You've got your hands dirty as well.'

Henning laughs. 'Me, Cousin Benthin? – Nothing ever happens to the likes of me, you can see that for yourself.'

'But what if Thiel blabs?'

'Even if Thiel betrays everyone else, he'll not betray me. Back before everything began, I swore to him that if he gives me away, I'll cut him into little tiny pieces. There's no prison in the world where he's safe from me. – And he knows that, Cousin Benthin, he knows it!'

'But the police? Surely they'll find out.'

'Oh, Cousin Benthin! They're not much good at finding things out. Anyway, ever since the episode with the flag, I've been a hero. They won't dare go near me. They're all on the Right anyway, the cops. They like their heroes as much as the next man.'

'To listen to you, Henning, it seems like you must always be right about everything. But I know you're not, and no amount of talking is going to change that. Ever since I met you, I've slept badly. And I don't really have much relish for life. – Henning, Georg, I want you to promise me you're a decent man.'

'Cousin Benthin, as I hope to go to heaven, I promise you I'm a decent man.'

'Then that's all right then, son. You go on and do your work.'

II

The joint session of the Town Council and the magistracy is over. Oberbürgermeister Niederdahl has just closed it.

The first man out, the Oberbürgermeister having barely fin ished speaking, is Blöcker of the *News*. He is in a hurry to get to his choir meeting.

Normally Stuff is hard on his heels.

This time, though, he is still seated, stunned by what he has heard. Vainly he tries to shape it into a report for tomorrow's paper. The vehemence of Gareis's attack, the incredible humili- ation of the Right-wing parties, the undeniable disgrace of all the Centre Party representatives, have left his head reeling.

Little Pinkus from the *Volkszeitung*, that SPD poodle, smiles a slimy smile at him. 'Rough – eh, Stuff?'

Stuff yells at him, pounding his fist on the table: 'Will you shut up, you wretched copyist!'

The little fellow ducks his head.

Gareis steps in between them. 'Gentlemen, please. – Pinkus, enough. – Herr Stuff, if I could have a word with you . . . ?'

And when Stuff stares at him in a fury: 'Brave Stuff . . .'

Stuff accompanies him silently through the mob of representatives and magistrates. Then along several corridors and flights of steps to Gareis's office.

Already after ten paces he has forgotten the man beside him and their exchange. He's back with his plans for the Nationalist appeal, which he had up and running when Gebhardt condemned him to silence.

The Nationalists are only weakly represented in Altholm's government: a dozen veterans' organizations, the respectable middle classes, the Stahlhelm and all the stout housewives between them couldn't manage to return more than three representatives.

But three is enough to launch a question, which is precisely what Stuff dinned into Medical Councillor Lienau. 'All the bourgeois, the Volkspartei, the Democrats, the Centre and the KPD are just waiting for it. Do it.'

Well, he prevailed over Lienau. Stuff won, and a short question was drawn up: 'What does the administration propose to do to restore normal relations between town and country?'

Then, the night before the question was due, there were the arrests. The whole situation was transformed. Stuff had been compelled to report on the attack on Gareis, the bomb that had gone off harmlessly in a meadow, the mysterious attack on a typesetter in the editorial office of the *Bauernschaft*, the arrests of the farmers' leaders.

He implored Lienau to retract the question.

The Stahlhelm man had refused. 'Retract it? Are you kidding? When the call is to go over the top, we go over the top. We don't care about the strength of the enemy. Why should I care if Gareis has suddenly become popular!'

But then the indomitable hero didn't appear: minor, though necessary, surgery made his participation in the meeting impossible at the eleventh hour.

Two Nationalists were left to justify the question: Notary Pepper and the butcher and cattleman Storm, member of several veterans' associations.

The question was left to the butcher to ask.

Halting and uncertain, he read it off a piece of paper, probably in Lienau's illegible doctor's scrawl. He broke up every sentence, breathed at the commas and overrode the full stops.

The delegates, depending on Party allegiance, listened to his stumbling performance hugging themselves with joy or with a sense of acute embarrassment.

But they were all united in heaving a sigh of relief when he was finally done.

Mayor Gareis rises to reply instantly. He offers no defence. He reads a sentence just published in the *News*: "'If, as appears to be the case, the farmers are not a million miles from the bomb attempts, that certainly sheds a different light on the 26th of July and the tactics of the police.'"

'There you have it, gentlemen. Facts bear out a case. They have borne out mine. All of you sitting here, down to the rather abject reader of the question just a moment ago, all of you are convinced in your heart of hearts that I am right.

'But why? Not because I behaved correctly, but because a bomb happens to have been thrown. And today I am doubly right, ten times more right, because the intended victim of the bomb was me.

'But ladies, gentlemen, tomorrow may bring fresh news. Tomorrow it may turn out that a pair of chancers threw the bomb. Tomorrow some more confused individual from circles politically sympathetic to me may have the idea of throwing a bomb into the house of the farmers' leader Reimers – and straight away I'll be in the wrong again.

'No, thank you, then, gentlemen! Do you want me to tell why I have done such and such, and not done this and that? You want me to provide justifications?

'Surely you see that justifications are irrelevant, and reasons footling, and that quite other things are involved.'

He stands there magnificently, an irate elephant, an incensed schoolmaster over a mob of bewildered imps.

'Thank you! *Thank* you!

'I decline to fish my justifications from the failed throw of some benighted individual.

'You, Herr Storm, asked me, asked the administration, what we propose to do to bring about the restoration of more normal relations.

'This is my reply: I propose to wait. You may not find that satisfactory. I find it entirely satisfactory. It's all one can expect from a man who wants to set his house in order. I shall wait.

'More will doubtless happen before peace has been concluded between town and country. I will be ten times in the wrong. I shall wait.

'I would urge you to do what I myself propose to do: To keep my counsel and wait.'

He sits abruptly.

He sits there perfectly still on his big stiff leather chair, hands folded across his belly, his fat face either smiling or not.

He has shown them his teeth.

'Thank you, gentlemen . . . *Thank* you . . .'

They sit there, not breathing.

Then a slight commotion comes over the chamber. On the stage someone laughs.

The Oberbürgermeister stands up. He asks in a whisper whether the point raised in the question is going to be discussed further. Three votes would be required.

The Oberbürgermeister sits down again.

The two Nats get to their feet. They request further discussion. Naturally.

They look around for a third supporter. Everyone looks around. Won't all the bourgeois members stand up as one? A third man!

Stuff too stares around feverishly. It can't be. They're a man short, they only need one! Those bourgeois . . .

Certainly, there are some who would like to rise. But the one in the leather chair, who seems already to have nodded off again, he is not an opponent at fencing, he is a wild bull who knows no rules.

The Oberbürgermeister waits a very long time. For a very long time Notary Pepper and Butcher Storm are left to stand on their own.

Then Oberbürgermeister Niederdahl gets up and announces that the motion has been declined and the session is over.

III

Stuff, with death in his heart, stands in Gareis's office. Gareis leaves him to dangle. He bundles files on to the desk, he looks across at the man by the window staring sightlessly into the September evening. Gareis starts to read.

Stuff sighs gustily.

And Gareis: 'Why sigh, Herr Stuff? They're just human beings.'

'Yes,' scowls Stuff, 'human beings.'

'Dear Herr Stuff, you shouldn't overestimate the importance of this hour. For the moment I'm on top again. Another week or month, and I could be at the bottom again.'

Stuff says crudely: 'You don't even believe that, you've won.'

'Not for long,' says the mayor.

'It was humiliating!' groans Stuff.

'It was poor stage management,' says Gareis comfortingly. 'Who would entrust a job like that to a master butcher? And who wouldn't think to assure themselves of at least one vote from the other camp first?'

'So your stage management worked better.'

'Not really. No one was put under pressure.'

Silence. A long silence.

As though able to read Stuff's mind, Gareis says: 'I too have thought a lot about leaving Altholm these past few weeks. Not just Altholm either, but all forms of local government. Anyone who wants to do real work gets so fed up with the constraints of politics.'

'I'll show you something,' says Stuff suddenly. 'Read this.'

It's a typed letter, unsigned, with the Stettin dateline. The esteemed Herr Stuff is informed by a girlfriend that people have been made aware of his faults. These faults have been listed in brackets, and include: inducement to commit perjury, inducement to commit an abortion, procuring an abortion. The

respected Herr Stuff is advised therefore to move the sphere of
his activities away from Altholm. A grace period of four weeks
has been granted him, otherwise . . . and so on and so forth.

'Who?' asks Gareis. 'Is it really a woman?'

'Could be, though I don't really think it is. It makes no difference.'

'No,' says the mayor, returning the letter. 'No.' And suddenly:
'Why don't you go to the *Bauernschaft*? That's the place for you.
And there are vacancies after the arrests.'

'Am I supposed to be a coward and run away?'

'Sometimes it can be the right thing to do, to be a coward and
run away.'

'Well, I'm not going to do it,' says Stuff. 'I want to stay here at
least until the trial. – Anyway, Gebhardt wouldn't let me go.'

'As far as that's concerned . . .' says the mayor slowly, and then
stops.

Stuff looks at him a long time. Their eyes meet.

Finally Stuff says: 'I see. Well, in that case, I have the feeling
I've just been terribly naive. Perhaps you're better acquainted
with the hand that wrote this letter. Perhaps . . .'

'Enough!' says the mayor. 'Enough!'

Stuff stops.

'It wasn't for any of this,' the mayor begins in an altered tone,
'that I called you up. Yesterday I called out to you at a moment
of extreme danger. And I did so in words that now, today, sound
a little unusual. You remember, don't you. – Now I don't want to
live in a state of constant skirmishing with the man who came
to my aid.

'But your position, and mine, both of us here in Altholm, are
incompatible. I am prepared to leave Altholm. If you would prefer it that you go, then I will be glad to be of assistance. It doesn't
have to be Stolpe and the *Bauernschaft*. I know people in Berlin
and the length and breadth of the Reich. It wouldn't have to be
an SPD paper, Herr Stuff. You could remain among those who
share your views.

'What do you think?'

It's almost dark in the room. 'What I did for you last night,

Mayor, has nothing to do with you. I would have come without those – as you say – "unusual words". For anyone.

'But I'll give you a truth for a truth. I lied to you once. Here in this very room, you asked me if I had anything personal against you. I said no.

'That was a lie, Herr Gareis, I must tell you so quite frankly: I can't stand you. You are disgusting to me. You are disgusting to me as a representative of the class whom I take to be the ruination of Germany. I don't care how serious you are about your work and your good intentions: you are simply incompetent.

'You are a politician, and will always be a politician. Your plans, your good intentions, are decided and corrupted by a party that has declared war on all the other classes.

'An hour ago, I saw you spit in your opponents' faces. You were arrogant. You showed no mercy to that poor tongue-tied butcher, and you despised the lot of them.

'Are you really any better than them?

'I can't do anything for you. I can't even make way for you.

'But all these are not reasons. I want to tell you that I grew up here in Altholm. Back then there was a barracks here, with a whole infantry regiment. When there were parades in the street, I ran along beside them, a little boy in bare feet. I cut school and missed meals to be there. Later on, I served here.

'You broke all that. Your Party has made Germany into something small. You duped the men in the trenches.

'It's in my blood. It's in my nerve endings. Each time I see you, each time I hear your voice, I feel it: the politician. The big, fat, gorged politician.

'I felt it last night, even last night when you were sprawled out on the ground, my first thought was: The politician.

'That's all there is to say, Mayor, I can't stand you.'

Mayor Gareis tried to interrupt him once or twice. Then he let him speak.

Now he stands up and turns the switch. The light breaks into the dark room.

He extends his hand to the other man: 'All right, Stuff, farewell.'

'All right then, Mayor. – Maybe we will manage to convert you one of these days?'

'I'm afraid that won't be possible. – Good evening to you, Herr Stuff.'

'Good evening, Mayor.'

IV

Farmer Bartels is a perfectly ordinary farmer. He is just like the other farmers in Poseritz, just like their fathers and forefathers before them, and presumably their sons and grandsons will turn out just the same as well.

But for the farmers in his village, he is something else, namely a traitor.

A terribly rustic attribute has been his downfall: he is a shade mean. Mean when it comes to spending money on other people.

What brought him low was this:

His wife is a born Merkel, and the Merkels live in Altholm. Two of his wife's brothers have a clock business on the market-place in Altholm.

It had been arranged for a long time that Bartels was going to give his wife a grandfather clock for her birthday. She had long wanted a dark oak box with a bright brass face and a sonorous gong. His brothers-in-law were going to let him have the clock for its factory price, which was sixty marks less than the store price.

The birthday approached, and Bartels wasn't sure what to do. He wasn't the type to blunder ignorantly and stupidly into misfortune, he thought about everything in advance, he spent nights awake thinking. He knew the boycott had been called, he himself had been present on the heath at Lohstedt, but sixty marks give or take . . .

One night in bed, he starts talking about it with his wife: 'I'm lying here thinking whether I wouldn't be better advised to buy that clock in Stolpe . . .'

'In Stolpe?' she asks in puzzlement. 'They don't have clocks like that in Stolpe.'

'Or in Stettin, then.'

'They don't have them in Stettin either, not like the one that Hans and Gerhard have in Altholm.'

'But it's a factory make, and they don't just make them for your brothers.'

She shifts the area of debate. 'And you want to spend an extra eighty marks on it?'

'Sixty. Yes, that's what's bothering me.'

'Stettin is much further to go as well.'

'Maybe they could send the clock?'

'Then you'd end up paying the railway something. And packaging. Otherwise, you just wrap it up in a couple of horse-blankets.'

'I can't take the buggy into Altholm.'

'Come on, they don't have spies by the side of the road.'

'Couldn't you wait for the clock? It would only be a month or two.'

'Then what do I get on my birthday instead?'

'Just wait, I suggest.'

'And not get anything on my birthday?'

'Listen to me!'

'My brothers might be able to send it somewhere else?'

In the end, her birthday comes, and the clock is there. The farmer didn't go to Altholm to pick it up, but to Stolpe. The clockmakers had it taken to Stolpe in their car and left it there. The clock was bought in Stolpe.

They weren't supposed to talk about the clock. It stands there in the parlour. Now, in summer, with harvest approaching, no one much comes to visit. Neighbours who come by stay in the kitchen or the milking parlour or the garden. Exchange a word or two of gossip, on the quick.

But the clock strikes, and the farmers' wives hear it.

'Have you got a new clock? It has such a pretty chime.'

'My husband bought it for me in Stolpe. It was a birthday present.'

'In Stolpe? Did you fall out with your brothers, then?'

'No, not at all. But for the boycott.'

'I wouldn't have done that myself. What are your brothers going to think? Blood's thicker than water. Where did you get it?'

'I can't tell you that. My husband got it.'

'Didn't he give you a receipt for it? Clocks like that come with a guarantee, so for three years you can get them repaired free of charge.'

'I expect my husband's got it in a drawer somewhere.'

'Do you think? Couldn't you look?'

'Now? When my hands are full of earth?'

'No, not now. It's just that we were thinking of getting a clock. But if you can't . . .'

'Not at the moment.'

They come asking a second time, a third time, a tenth time. The clock has such a lovely tone, like an organ, so full and smooth. Wouldn't they just love to have one like it.

After a while they stop asking, they know what happened.

Not just from Frau Bartels's short answers, no, they suddenly know that the Merkel boys drove to Stolpe in the car and left the clock in the Posthorn.

Now they know, and still nothing happens. Bartels heaves a sigh of relief.

The weights are up, but the clock has stopped. It won't chime and it doesn't tick.

On Sunday, the farmer opens the clock case to have a look. Everything looks shiny and clean. On one big flywheel a drop of oil has been squeezed out, he wipes it absently with his fingers. The oil is grainy, it is so full of sand it crunches.

The farmer gets it. He feels a little frisson of chill. The clock will have to stay as it is, there is no prospect of getting it fixed.

The way Bartels is, he would rather have double or tenfold certainty. That evening he goes to the Krug. There's not many farmers in the bar, while the dance floor is packed. Farmers don't tend to like the carry-on of young folk. But there are maybe six or eight in attendance.

They don't reply to his greeting, but stand up, leave their beer half drunk, and walk out.

There's a stand-in at the bar, who serves him a glass of beer.

The barman joins them, he gives Bartels a furious look, and throws his glass out of the window on to the cobbles outside.

The farmer looks furious too. But he keeps his mouth shut and goes to watch the dancing.

The music is going. It's still early, the clientele is mostly farm-hands and farm-maids. The farmers' children won't be along till later. The ones who are there don't know him that well, don't care either way, they look at him, they ignore him, they dance past him.

He is certain the barman hasn't been in, nor the stand-in waiter either. But the music suddenly stops. There is an empty space around him, getting wider and wider. The young people go over to the windows, to the doors, he is standing there all alone.

Then suddenly the electric light goes off; he feels his way out on to the village street: the whole of the Krug is in the dark.

It's the beginning, he thinks. They're under duress. Things will be back to normal in a week.

But in the morning his wife wakes him up. 'Go out to the hands. None of them are up yet. The cows are in pain, they need to be milked.'

The farmhands are in their room. But it's not a matter of waking them because they're already up. They want to be handed their papers.

He refuses and goes to milk the cows himself.

At nine, he's just finished milking, the hands turn up with the militiaman. He is given a talking-to, and told he is not allowed to withhold their papers. If they run away from him, he can bring charges against them in a work tribunal, but now he has to let them leave.

When he gives them their papers, the two maids are standing by. Half an hour later, he and his wife have the farm all to themselves.

It's not such a small farm as that: he has four horses, twenty-two cows, not to mention calves, pigs and poultry. The grain is ripe on the stalk.

It's more than any two people can cope with.

He silently puts the horses to and takes the milk to the dairy.

'Take your milk. We don't need it here.'

'But this is a co-op dairy and I'm a member.'

'Look at your contract. You have to have the milk delivered by eight o'clock. It's almost noon. Take your milk home.'

He does so. He pours the milk in the pig troughs, that way he won't have to think about mixing their feed.

The farmer's wife goes around in tears, once she says quietly to him: 'Go and see Büttner. He found out about Stolpe.'

'That bastard? Never.'

That afternoon he goes.

The conditions he is offered are outrageous: a thousand marks penalty payable to the Bauernschaft, public burning of the clock, and, worst of all, he has to beg pardon of everyone in the village publicly.

Publicly, in front of everyone: women, children, farmhands, maids.

You can't let too many people know what happens to those who make deals with Altholm.

'It's just a clock. And I really did buy it before the boycott.'

'Exactly, otherwise it would be costing you three thousand now.'

'I don't mind asking forgiveness of the farmers, but in front of the women . . .'

'In front of the women.'

He walks out, he will never agree to that.

In his yard, there is an uneasy feeling, the animals are tugging at their chains, they can feel things are amiss.

The pump for water for the animals – the pump won't draw. He takes it apart. The pump leather is missing. This morning it was still there. The pump won't draw.

He could cut himself a new leather, he has a tanned cowhide put by for bootsoles, maybe it would work for a day or two. He gets the hide and starts cutting.

Then he throws down his knife and the hide. Goes inside, puts the clock on a dog cart and tows it through the village in front of Büttner's house.

The villagers stand in front of their houses and stare. The children stop playing and stare.

That evening, in front of the war memorial on the village square, he repeats the sentences that Büttner says:

'I have betrayed the farmers in Poseritz, and I have betrayed the farmers in the whole country.

'I am deeply sorry.

'I regret my wickedness, I see my sin, and will atone for it, without compulsion or anger.

'Whoever is my neighbour's enemy is my enemy. I must not sit down with him at one table, I must not have dealings with him, I must not exchange words with him.

'I am heartily sorry I have breached this.

'I beg forgiveness from all the farmers in Poseritz, with their wives, their parents, their children, their hands and their maids. I sincerely beg you all to forgive me . . .'

The wind blows in the poplar trees above the memorial. The flames of the fire that is consuming the ill-fated grandfather clock cast their flickering light over the assembled people, a village community of three hundred souls, a single cell in the great body of the Bauernschaft.

Farmer Bartels stands there, looking pale, one hand behind his back, the other stretched out to District Headman Büttner, who is not yet ready to accept it.

Behind Büttner stands Henning, who is thinking: This will do the trick. This would gladden Franz's heart. This is exactly his style. And it will be incredibly effective in the countryside.

In his breast pocket, he can feel the crinkle of the fifty-mark note, the first instalment of the fine.

Finally Büttner gives Bartels his hand. 'And in full view of the community, do you promise us that you are without hatred, without rancour, without resentment? '

'I promise.'

'That you have come to us freely and voluntarily, having seen your own wickedness?'

'Yes.'

'In that case I forgive you on behalf of the assembled farming community. What was, is no more. No one is to remind you of it or offend you on account of it.'

By the time Farmer Bartels gets home, the hands are already in the cowshed, the light is on, they're spreading straw for the night.

He lies down to sleep. He feels it's all been a bad dream.

V

Stuff and Tredup are sitting facing each other in the editorial office.

Stuff has just given his latest manuscript to the boy to be set, and is digging around in his desk for something.

Tredup is logging imaginary visits to clients in the card index system, all with the same comment, 'Declined.'

For some time Stuff has not spoken to Tredup, and generally carried on as though he didn't exist.

He breaks wind, mutters, 'Better out than in!' and rustles his paper again.

It's stupidly warm in the room, a few flies buzz around, and now there's a bad smell too. Tredup wonders whether he ought to go out looking for ads, in a sort of *pro forma* way. He could sit by the playground and read.

Stuff loudly and distinctly says: 'Shit!' and with such venom that Tredup in spite of himself looks up.

Stuff looks him in the eye, then looks down at a letter he has opened out in front of him. Tredup needs only a cursory glance, he knows the letter.

He masters himself, and goes back to jotting notes on the index cards.

But Stuff is really in a filthy mood today. He is incredibly provocative, and at the top of his voice he starts reading the anonymous letter:

'Stettin, 6 September.

Dear Herr Stuff,

It seems both my friendly warnings have gone unnoticed by you. You have taken no steps to leave Altholm. So that you know that I am in possession of all the details: the woman's name is Timm, and she lives in Stettin on the Kleine Lastadie, a back building, up one flight of steps. The girl's name is Henni Engel, and at the time she was in service to Dr Falk. If you haven't left Altholm by the 15th of October, I'm taking the details to the public prosecutor.

Final warning from a well-intentioned lady friend.'

Stuff finishes reading, and is blowing hard.

'Shit!' he says again.

Tredup badly doesn't want to look up, but he does anyway. Stuff is looking straight at him and grunts in his face.

'Shit!' he says for the third time. 'Yes, I mean you, Tredup, don't look so gormless.'

Tredup has the feeling he ought to show some reaction – indignation would be good – but he can't muster more than a feeble 'Ridiculous'.

Completely unimpressed, Stuff goes on: 'Do you think you can just carry on like this, sonny boy? First the photographs, and then a bit of treachery here, another bit of treachery there? Do you think I don't know how often you run along to the town hall?

'Do you think you can do it all with impunity?'

Stuff expectorates, leans further back, and holds Tredup in his grip.

'Say, sunshine, don't you sometimes feel that famous spot on the back of your head that felt so vulnerable three months back? No? I would feel it if I were you, I'd damned well feel it.'

Stuff folds the letter up leisurely and puts it back in his pocket. Suddenly he starts laughing loudly. 'Absurd creature! Because he's spent a fortnight in jail, he thinks he's a big gangster and can dabble in blackmail. You want your bottom smacking, sonny boy!'

He cumbrously gets to his feet, and is abruptly furious: 'I swear, Tredup, if you have the gall to type one more of those lousy letters of yours on my typewriter, I'm going to knock your block off –'

Tredup stammers in bewilderment: 'I don't know what you're talking about. I don't understand you. You surely can't think . . .?'

Stuff isn't even listening. He's grabbed his hat off the hook and is looking with displeasure at his feet in their clapped-out shoes.

'They smell. Like stinky cheese. Really must give them a wash one day,' he mumbles.

Then he snaps out of it. 'Do you have a message for your wife, Tredup? Because I'm on my way to see her now.'

And he's gone.

Tredup is left on his own, seething with helpless anger.

Stuff, that bastard, isn't taking those letters seriously. He reads them out loud, as though he knew for a fact that they were from Tredup. And this last one Tredup was so hopeful of. The trouble it took (and money too) to get the names and addresses. And Stuff just laughs.

Well, if Stuff thinks this isn't serious, he's making a bad mistake. If all else fails, he, Tredup, will take matters to the prosecutor. Then Stuff would get his comeuppance all right.

He is racked by the question of whether Stuff actually has gone to see Elise. After a couple of minutes he gets up and goes home.

What if Stuff is actually telling his wife everything!

He doesn't get as far as the parlour, he doesn't even set foot in the yard.

At the other side of the yard, he parks himself behind a lilac bush.

The parlour window is open, and inside there is Stuff, sitting on the bed, chatting to Elise.

The two of them are talking together perfectly calmly. Mainly it seems to be Stuff who's doing the talking. He'll be giving Tredup a paint job. And Elise is nodding in agreement, a couple of times she launches into long, urgent speeches.

Tredup keeps an eye out to see if Stuff pulls out the letter, but it doesn't happen, at least not while he's standing looking. Perhaps it happened before he arrived.

Then the conversation appears to end. Stuff gets up, and they both go over to the window to look out. Tredup disappears completely behind his lilac bush.

When he peeps out again, the coast is clear. Stuff is gone, and Elise is sprinkling water over the ironing on the kitchen table.

She answers his greeting with a proper, hearty 'Hello!'

'Is supper soon?' he asks, walking back and forth in the parlour.

'In half an hour. When the children are back.'

She doesn't even ask him why he's back early himself.

He walks up and down, and spots a sodden cigar end in the ashtray.

'Whose is this?' he asks, picking up the cigar end.

'Herr Stuff, of course. You know that.'

'I know that? How do I know that? Is Herr Stuff such a regular visitor here, then?'

'Because you were standing behind the lilac bush,' she says.

'Me? What do you mean?' he stammers, and goes red. The woman is alarming. What in all the world did Stuff tell her?

And now she suddenly does something completely unexpected: she drops her work, goes over to him, and presses her cheek against his.

It hasn't happened in weeks and weeks.

He keeps very still. Her hair tickles his temples.

'Let's be friends again,' she says quietly. 'Shall we be, like the way we were before?'

He is completely bamboozled. (What was it Stuff said to her?) But his hand wangles its way into hers.

'Herr Stuff isn't a bad person,' she says abruptly

'Oh? Do you reckon?' he asks. He is really floundering.

'He explained everything to me. That you're still in shock from your time in prison. That we need to be gentle with you. I was so stupid. Please forgive me, Max.'

'That's all a load of nonsense,' he says mouthily, and tries to break away. 'I'm perfectly healthy.'

'Of course you are,' she says sweetly, and looks at him.

'Was that why Stuff was here, to fill you full of that nonsense?'

'But he told me that you were becoming editor of the paper on the 1st of October. That that's a certainty. Didn't you arrange that between yourselves?'

'Yes. Yes,' says Tredup vaguely. 'We arranged that.'

And inside: So the letters did have an effect! Nasty of him, to try and frighten me like that. He must be really shitting himself if he's leaving on the 1st without a struggle.

But he can't quite convince himself that Stuff is leaving out of fear. He didn't look exactly frightened half an hour ago.

He asks: 'Did he really say that? For definite?'

'It's definite, he says, because he starts in his new job on the 1st. Only we're not allowed to tell anyone else about it.'

'No, no, of course not,' says Tredup. He tries to feel happy, he's won after all, but what was Stuff's question again: Do you feel that spot on the back of your head?

He can feel it again.

Stuff is trying to lead him into a trap.

'Did he not say where he was going?'

'No. So he didn't tell you either?'

'No.'

'And then you'll be certain to bring home at least a hundred marks more. You see how right we were to keep little Bootsy on board?'

'Yes,' he says, 'yes.'

'Come on, give me a kiss, Max.'

She puckers up for a kiss.

He kisses her and thinks: Trap. Trap. I need to be much more careful.

VI

One bright and sunny September evening, Commander Frerksen sets foot in his boss's office for the first time in a while.

Mayor Gareis is sitting behind his desk, roly-poly as ever. He waves a greeting with his short, fat-fingered hand and grins.

'Why, there you are, Frerksen. Forgive me for summoning you back telegraphically. It seemed to me you'd been away for long enough. Was it pleasant in the Black Forest?'

Frerksen bows: 'Yes, Mayor.'

'Chance to get away from all this filth here, what? Become a new person. You've got a tan, and a new jut to your jaw – or was that there before? Well, anyway, it's time you were back at work. And I can do with a little holiday myself.'

Frerksen smiles gallantly.

'Do you remember how on the 26th of July I was all set to go

on holiday? I'd packed my bags. Now it's September. At last, summer is over.'

'Is the mayor still proposing to go to Rügen?'

'Oh Lord, no! What would I do there? I'd rather go back home,
look at the old villages, wallow in a little sentimentality. – Well,
while you were gone, things got a little aerated. They're quieter
and cleaner now. But there's one piece of news still to come,
which I want the town to have. It'll be circulated to the press
tomorrow. Here,' and Gareis hands him a piece of paper.

Police Commander Frerksen has returned from holiday today, and
taken over the reins of the police administration, having been restored
to executive duties by fiat of the Minister of the Interior. The proceedings started against him have been suspended.

'Well, so what do you say?'

'This is very – pleasant,' murmurs the commander.

'Stop that, Frerksen! Kindly be happy! This is our victory. Your
victory, above all. Have you any notion of how upset the gentleman in Stolpe will be today! A couple of weeks ago he made
you walk the plank. Well, I've been a bit buoy myself, and the
result was that the minister moved the cold pot back on to the
hot plate. You have cause to be happy.'

'Yes, Mayor.'

'I see,' the mayor said in a change of voice, 'that you want to
be childish about this, Herr Frerksen. The commander likes a
good sulk.'

'Mayor, please –'

'Don't plead. As you will have been reading the Altholm
papers, you should have understood that in the hour of your
leaving I made a lot out of the sabre episode, so as to save you
from the very much sharper disapproval of the district president.
You seem not to have understood, and prefer to sulk.

'You can be cross with me for as long and as much as you
want. I don't care. I would only warn you against taking steps
in a spirit of irritation, or starting negotiations – we understand
each other.'

'I would like to assure the mayor that I am not sulking.'

'Don't give me that. I expect you're regretting it now. The jut of the jaw was a temporary illusion. – We have to be able to work together, Frerksen, for a long time to come, and I am the only person here who will have you. Who has an interest in keeping you. If you'd rather believe others, go ahead. Only I would have hoped you might have learned from your experiences.'

The commander's face is flushed. He whispers: 'I am not cross at all. I never was.'

'Don't say anything. You didn't shake my hand. You didn't sit down, the way you always used to. You kept very quiet. You were stiff as a board. In a word: you were sulking. But let's leave that now. You will have time until the beginning of October to understand our relationship, undistracted by my actually being here; I won't be back till the trial begins. Good evening, Commander.'

'Good evening, Mayor.'

VII

'Pickbusch,' says Gareis to his secretary, 'while I'm gone, I'd like you to keep my office locked. I only want it cleaned with you there, present, understood?'

'Yes, sir.'

'You will turn everything upside down. Clear out my desk. Sometimes a paper can get stuck in the back of a drawer. Look through every folder that's been in my office these past months, until you find the secret orders.'

'I've already done all that.'

'Then do it again, more thoroughly. People don't steal files here, do they?'

'Those farmers –'

'Pish, farmers don't go stealing files. No farmer could get it into his head that a piece of scribbled-on paper can be worth more than a piece of blank paper. So find those orders.'

Piekbusch shrugs his shoulders.

'Find them! Find them!! – There, and now goodbye.'

'And the Ober?'

'I'll tell him,' whispers the roly-poly mayor, rolling his eyes, 'where he can go.'

Strange, because of late he's been sticking to him like glue.

Niederdahl is a mild, shuffling individual, a little yellow in every sense, it's his nerves. He smiles mildly, he only whispers, his ideal is to manage the affairs of the town without anyone even noticing.

Thus far, next to the active, booming Gareis, he has only managed to achieve the latter end – that of being unnoticed – the management part is so far eluding him.

Gareis gives brief summary reports on the state of things across the board. The Ober listens in silence, confines himself to occasional cross-questions: 'There is a file on that, isn't there?' – 'There is a mark on a file somewhere, isn't there?' – which Gareis usually bats aside with a lordly 'I would assume so.'

'So far as the police administration goes,' Gareis continues, 'it will be conducted as usual in my absence by Councillor Röstel. There are no new developments. Commander Frerksen is abreast of everything.'

'Frerksen is no longer on holiday?' whispers Niederdahl.

'He'll be taking up the reins again tomorrow morning,' smiles a blithe Gareis.

'Wouldn't it have been in the interest of general tranquillity to have left him on holiday until the trial is over?'

'It was in the interests of the good name of police administration to have him reappear.'

'But he can't shoulder any executive duties.'

'He can. The minister of the interior has rescinded the order of the president.'

The Oberbürgermeister looks at his mayor. Even the whites of his eyes are yellow.

Suddenly Niederdahl squawks into action. His little white hands with their thick blue veins emerge from spotless cuffs and pound on the table.

'The files! The files!' he screams. 'I want to see the records!

The paperwork! Why was I not shown the files?'

'There is no file as yet,' says Gareis lethargically. 'I obtained instructions from the ministry by telephone today. Written instructions will come by post tomorrow.'

'Telephone! That's not a process. All instructions go first to the office manager. Then to me. – And only then to you, Herr Gareis! – *And only then to you!*'

'But I was called to the phone, not the office manager.'

'Telephone doesn't count. There's no such thing. It could have been a hoax call. Have you notified Frerksen already?'

'I have.'

'That's not possible. That's a violation. What's going on? What methods are these? What about the president?'

'I expect he'll have to suck it up,' says Gareis coolly, eyeing his victim.

'Your way of doing business is isolating us. Altholm is isolated. What is a minister? Here today and gone tomorrow. Do you propose to base local politics on ministerial decisions? Stolpe, Stolpe is where our interests are.'

Gareis quips back: 'Would you like me to inform the minister of your caveat?'

The Oberbürgermeister is abruptly silent. He unfolds a white handkerchief and mops his face. When he surfaces again: 'Forgive me, dear colleague! You understand, my nerves, my gall bladder. I'm a sick man. The worries –'

'You just leave the worries to me. I've got a broad back.'

'Yes. True. You're healthy. Enviable. – And you say the minister's instructions will come tomorrow?'

'Definitely.'

'That's bound to put a few backs up in Stolpe! We could have employed Frerksen on administrative affairs. We could have made him office manager.'

'He's a good policeman, remember.'

'But the alienation produced by his appointment. We need someone to carry the can.'

'Not this time. – I'm giving a short bulletin on his reinstatement to the press.'

'Must you? Wouldn't it be enough if people just saw him back in uniform?'

'His decommissioning was in the papers, so the papers will have to report on his recommissioning.'

'But not before the instructions have come through, surely?'

'All right then, I'll have it embargoed by the press until the day after tomorrow.'

'I'd like it better if I could inform the press myself at the right time.'

'As soon as the time is right.'

'Of course. As soon as the time is right.'

VIII

The mayor asks his secretary: 'Piekbusch, don't you have a cousin or something who drives to Stolpe every evening?'

'Yes I do. The electrician, Maaks.'

'Will you get him to post three letters in Stolpe tonight?'

'Fine.'

'You remember the communiqué you typed for the press regarding Frerksen?'

'Yes, of course.'

'The Ober was a bit sticky about it. He'd rather notify the press himself. But once I'm gone, there's no knowing when he'll get around to it.'

'I see the point.'

'Will you type up three of those communiqués, on unheaded paper. A bit differently, like so:

'"As we have heard from well-informed sources", and so on and so on. Three unmarked envelopes, to each of our three daily papers. No sender.'

'Of course. I'll do that.' Pause. 'Where do I take the postage from? It's not official business.'

'If you won't then I suppose I'll have to fork out myself. How much?'

'Forty-five pfennigs.'

'There. – After the election, though, I'm going to take care to have a slush fund set up. It's an absolute necessity for ministers – ministers and anyone in active life.'

The following morning, Oberbürgermeister Niederdahl gives the district president a call.

'Yes, the ministerial confirmation has arrived just now.'

'We have yet to hear from Berlin. I find it all . . . Well, Herr Niederdahl, these are our friends, that's where the cultivation of authority gets you nowadays.'

'President, you should have seen Gareis. He was oozing self-satisfaction.'

'Well, in the end, even the minister's decision means little. The court's verdict, that's what will really matter.'

'But what if the court finds against the police and for the farmers?'

'You would think. But it could as well be against the farmers and also against the police.'

'Yes. Yes. There'll be a way. – And the communiqué?'

'What communiqué? Oh, you mean about Frerksen? Bin it. We're not about to go and shout it out from the rooftops!'

'I'd just suggest, President, that the other party may have taken steps –'

'Steps? What steps?'

'Well, having the press informed by back channels.'

'Give the editors a call. They'll do you that little favour, Herr Niederdahl.'

'Bound to. Of course. How not?'

'This is Oberbürgermeister Niederdahl's office on the line. The Oberbürgermeister would like to speak to Herr Stuff. – Ah! In person? One moment, I'll connect you.'

'Yes, my dear Stuff. Good morning. As a gifted newshound, you will surely have heard that our controversial commander has been seen back in uniform today. – Have you not? As I thought. – Correct. A decision taken at ministerial level, but not yet a binding one, the last word will be spoken by the courts in October. – No, no, admittedly. A certain party, I don't need to identify it any further, of course has an interest in getting the minister's decision bruited about. – No, no, that's not in our interests at all. – No, we, and still less you, have no interest in it at all. – Well, I'll be counting on you, then. You won't cover it. Your colleague on the *News* has already agreed as well. Thanks again. Good morning, Herr Stuff!'

Stuff keeps the receiver in his hand a moment longer. Then, with a broad smile, he sets it down on the cradle.

So you gave them your word, did you, Heinsius? Wagging your tail again, like a good dog? Yes, yes, no, no. Niederdahl, you're a good man, but you're too plodding, too plodding by half.

'Fritz!' he booms out.

The apprentice setter appears.

'Fritz, take the item on Frerksen out of the local section. The organ concert review moves up one spot. Tell them in there, I'm doing a whole column on Frerksen. I'll have it ready for you in ten minutes.'

It'll all have to be in the running headline, thinks Stuff. Because, basically, that's all I know.

What about:

SERIOUS DIFFERENCE OF OPINION BETWEEN MINISTRY AND DISTRICT PRESIDENT . . .?

A bit watery.

Or:

POLICE COMMANDER FRERKSEN, DISMISSED BY TEMBORIUS, RE-INSTATED BY THE MINISTER . . .

Too long, much too long. Come on, Stuff, three words.

I'll go and get a drink.

In the cognac he found a title:

MINISTER ENDORSES POLICE TERROR.

And a subtitle:

FARMERS DEPRIVED OF CIVIL RIGHTS.

Stuff grins.

'Listen, Fräulein Heinze, if anyone calls this afternoon, I've gone away. In fact, I'm on holiday. I won't be available for the whole of next year.'

* * *

Herr Gebhardt asks grimly: 'How far along are you, Herr Tredup?'

'Stuff is certain to go by the 1st of October.'

'That's what you tell me. He hasn't given his notice.'

'It's definite. Perhaps he's trying to get you to sack him.'

'I won't do him the favour. And have the man on my payroll for another six months?'

'If you ask me,' says Herr Heinsius, 'today's piece is justification for instant dismissal.'

'And the whole town learns that my employees do what they freaking like? No, thank you. – Are you quite sure, now, Herr Tredup?'

'Quite sure.'

'What makes you so sure? If you can tell us. What have you done? What sort of pressure have you brought to bear on Stuff?'

'I'd really rather not . . . He is definitely going.'

'My employees keep secrets from me. Of course. Very nice. Very nice . . . That's all for today, Herr Tredup.'

Stuff is sitting in the snug at Tucher's, drinking.

A man walks in, the train-driver Thienelt. 'You shouldn't have done that, Stuff.'

'Done what?'

'Today's article. Everything was so nice and peaceful.'

'Since when does the Stahlhelm stand for peace?'

'Yes, but you have to have periods of quiet sometimes. Business is so poor, Stuff.'

'Well, next time you can have quiet.'

Textil-Braun comes in. 'So there you are, Stuff. I am here to convey to you the disapproval of the retailers of Altholm. It's time you kept quiet.'

'I'm perfectly quiet. Me and my beer.'

'Everything was nice and peaceful, you must pay some regard to business.'

'I do. I do. I leave all my wages in various bars.'

Braun, poisonously: 'It's impossible to talk to you seriously, Herr Stuff. But it'll show in the subscription figures, you mark my words.'

The waiter says to Stuff: 'They're all upset with you about your article. I thought your article was fine.'

'How fine? I thought it was crap.'

'I thought it was fine when I read it.'

'Franz, I'm not going to give you another penny in tips. You really don't need to come crawling to me.'

'No, no, Herr Stuff. I'm not. I won't. I really thought it was pretty good. People had half forgotten about the boycott. And suddenly it's everywhere again: the farmers, the farmers.'

'Well – so?'

'If people talk about it, it means they're getting angry about it, Herr Stuff.'

'And why shouldn't they bloody well get angry? I get angry every day.'

'You're used to it, Herr Stuff. But you should see how much schnapps is sold here each day. Whenever people are angry about something, they start drinking more schnapps than beer.'

'I drink a schnapps with every beer myself. Sometimes two.'

'But that's just what I was saying, Herr Stuff, you're used to it. But the people aren't used to it. They want their peace and quiet.'

'All right, Franz. And now I'd like some myself too.'

'Very well, Herr Stuff. Another schnapps? Coming up!'

'I seem,' says Stuff complacently, 'to have damaged the psyche of the whole of Altholm!'

PART III
Judgement Day

Stuff Moves On

I

The 30th of September is a fine blue-and-gold autumn day with a crisp lustre in the air. It's also a Monday, a working day like any other.

The 1st of October, *eo ipso*, will be a Tuesday, and on this Tuesday the case against Henning and associates will begin, for breach of the peace, insulting behaviour, actual bodily harm, damage to property, aggravated assault . . .

Moreover, the 1st of October is, as it is every year, moving day, people moving house, employees changing jobs.

For fully a week now Max Tredup has been in a condition of wild excitement. Herr Gebhardt has summoned him twice, to inquire what was happening in relation to Stuff's promised departure. Tredup assured him he was going.

Gebhardt, though, doesn't believe him; Tredup, bullish, insists; Gebhardt on the first occasion sceptical, and on the second he lost his rag.

Tredup is not so unshakeably convinced as all that: Stuff gives no signs either way.

Tredup has been following Stuff everywhere these past few days. Stuff acts as though nothing's up. Tredup stands guard outside half a dozen bars, Stuff drinks away the nights. Tredup runs to Stuff's landlady, Stuff hasn't given notice.

Do I go to the public prosecutor and press charges after all . . .?

But he told Elise he was going!

Didn't he . . .?

Tredup sits at one desk, Stuff sits at the other. They look at one another, or, rather, Tredup sneaks numerous swift, sly looks at Stuff, while Stuff is unaware of Tredup's existence.

It's the afternoon of the 30th of September, a fine autumnal afternoon.

Stuff is trimming his nails.

Then he looks at his watch, sighs, and starts digging around for something in his desk.

Could it be that he's packing!?

Stuff has unearthed a pristine notepad and put it in his pocket. He stuffs the rest of the mess back into the drawer.

In no particular direction, Stuff says: 'Tonight you'll be going to the Nazis.'

Hopefully, Tredup says: 'Yes?' and then, tenderly: 'How come? Don't you have the time?'

But he's had his lot, because Stuff is already halfway out of the room.

Tredup jumps up, chases after him, lays his hand on Stuff's shoulder, and whispers imploringly: 'Man, you're driving me crazy!'

Carefully, with finger and thumb, Stuff removes the offending hand and lets it drop. Serenely he whistles in the advertising manager's face.

'Stuff, don't go on tormenting me! Please tell me if you're going or not.'

'Yes,' says Stuff, 'I'm going – to court. And right now.'

'Stuff . . .!'

Whistles.

'You told my wife you were going on the 1st of October.'

'Fool!' says Stuff deafeningly. 'More fool you! October 1940!' And he exits whistling and slamming doors, leaving one rather crushed Tredup in his wake.

II

After Stuff has dealt with Tredup, he doesn't go to court at all, but to Auntie Lieschen's. He sits there the whole afternoon in a state of pleasant excitement, drinking a lot, and feeling like a boy skipping school. In the end he gets up and walks over to the

News. It's already dark there when he arrives. He gropes his way into the corridor, a little light from the typesetting room strikes a doorknob, causing it to shine. Stuff turns it, and the door opens. Stuff is in Herr Gebhardt's room. First of all he draws the curtains, then he switches on the lights.

Stuff sits down at his boss's desk, stretches his legs, and thinks.

'Heigh-ho,' he sighs. 'Oh well. I will have to say goodbye to him, I suppose.'

He tries the telephone and gets put through.

'Number ninety-six, Fräulein,' he says.

'Herr Gebhardt? – Ah, Herr Gebhardt! This is Stuff here. – Yes, Stuff. – Herr Gebhardt, I just happened to be passing the *News*, when I saw a light on in your room. I go in, total disorder, desk wide open. – No, I haven't informed the police, I wasn't sure if that was what you wanted. – Will you be coming yourself? Right away? – Yes, I'll stay here and hold the fort. I can try and set things to rights, a little – Oh? I'm not to touch anything? No, no, not if you don't want me to, of course not. – No, I won't read anything, how could I? I don't read! Left to myself, I never read, Herr Gebhardt . . . Oh, he's hung up. Shame.'

Stuff snoops sadly. Finds a clean sheet of paper, writes on it in red, in enormous letters:

'BYE-EE, PAPA GEBHARDT. STUFF MOVES ON.'

Puts it down on top of the empty desk. Takes another look at the scene, draws over the red with a blue pencil. Takes another look. He plucks a white aster and a red aster from a vase and lays them either side of the paper.

'That's better,' murmurs Stuff to himself. 'Nothing like a bit of class.'

He leaves the premises with the light still burning clear and bright. Stuff potters on down to the station, downs three lagers and six schnapps, and piles on to the last train to Stolpe.

'Bye-bye, Altholm,' he says. 'See you tomorrow.'

III

The Nazis always hold their gatherings at Tucher's on the market, and that's where Tredup bends his steps a little before eight o'clock.

It's the first political meeting he's attended, hitherto Stuff has seen fit to send him only to the cinema or the market. Slowly Tredup walks through the dark streets, he wonders if it had any significance, Stuff sending him to the Nazis, or if it was just his bone-idleness.

Anyway, tomorrow is the 1st of October, the day by which Stuff was supposed to be gone, and the day the trial begins. If nothing happens tomorrow, the charge will have to be made out and sent to the public prosecutor.

Or will he try sending Stuff one more threatening letter?

Trying and tormenting, these thoughts always on the same topic, till Tredup emerges from the darkness of Propstenstrasse on to the marketplace. The buzz of a large crowd, shouting, wild oratory from a hoarse, yelling male voice. – Tredup jumps up in the air and races towards the far end of the marketplace and Tucher's.

A dense crowd impedes his progress, the entire square is full of people, curious Altholmers. But the police are keeping the road clear, and it's one of these policemen that Tredup makes for. 'Officer! Tredup from the *Chronicle* here. Can I go through? I'm standing in for Herr Stuff.'

He is allowed to go on another twenty steps, at the end of which he has to say his piece to the next policeman, and is allowed to go on again.

Under the light of the arc lamps there is a vast crowd, half of Altholm seems to be here, pressed together and listening to the yelling. Tredup can see one or two red flags waving.

A voice in the crowd calls out to him: 'Oi, you! Tredup!'

It's his landlord, the greengrocer from the Stolpe Road.

'Yes, what is it? I'm busy. I'm here for the paper.'

'Then mind you give the police what for! It's a disgrace! It's a scandal!'

'What's a disgrace? What's going on here anyway?'

'I don't know any more than you do. But the Communists are being allowed to hold their incendiary speeches on the market-place –'

'I see. – Well, sir, thanks, I've got to be going on –'

'Mind you give it to those policemen!' booms after him.

Bystanders, catching the conversation, hum in agreement.

Another twenty steps, another policeman, and Tredup is getting close to Tucher's. Here the pavement has been cleared too, it's well lit and deserted in the light of the lamps outside the bar. In the middle of the street is a bunch of police, Tredup makes out Frerksen and some detectives in civvies. He spots Deputy Inspector Perduzke.

At the entrance to Tucher's are a couple of youths in Hitler uniforms, with the swastika armbands round their biceps. They look pale, with red slashes across their faces, a trickle of blood on the forehead of one of them. He wipes at it with a handkerchief.

Right opposite, the whole marketplace under the trees is full of Communists. Secretary General Matthies is standing on an upturned market cart, haranguing the crowd.

'What's going on? What happened?' Tredup charges up to one of the two National Socialists.

'Who are you?' the man replies dismissively.

'Tredup from the *Chronicle*. I'm here for the press. Herr Stuff couldn't make it tonight –'

At the name of Stuff both the faces brighten. 'Ah, if Herr Stuff had've been here, he would've stuck it to the police! It's a disgrace –!'

'What's a disgrace? Everyone's saying it's a disgrace, but what is exactly –?'

'Listen: our meeting was set for eight o'clock. At quarter to, there were just about a score of us present. Suddenly the Communists turn up, three hundred of them with fanfare. Stop outside the bar. Their leader, Matthies, says something –'

'"Smash the Nazis!" is what he shouted,' says the second National Socialist.

'They all come charging down the corridor to the door of

the hall. A sudden swarm of them, I tell you. Me and my mate here, we're standing by the door, taking entry money. "Twenty-five pfennigs," I say to the first man up. He smashes his fist up through the plate and sends all the money flying. I give him an upper cut. Next thing I know, there are about ten of them on top of me. By the time I get to my feet, the whole horde of them are all over our bar –'

'Pretty much the same thing happened to me –'

'And? What happened then?'

'All our people in the hall were knocked about. One or two were able to run out the back and call for help. Then the police arrived. As they went in the front door, the Communists left by the back, and then they stopped under the trees, and they're holding their meeting there now.'

The speaker gulps: 'So much for police protection!' he spits out in a fury.

'What about you? Are you holding your meeting inside?' asks Tredup.

'How are we supposed to hold a meeting now? You can see how the police are keeping people away! Anyway, the mayor's banned our meeting.'

'Really? Banned it?'

'Get your head around that! Those scum are allowed to talk outside. Nothing happens to them. But us –'

'Hang on a minute,' says Tredup eagerly. 'I'm going to take this up with the mayor . . . You have to have your meeting . . .'

Tredup scoots over to Deputy Inspector Perduzke. 'Herr Perduzke, can you tell me where the mayor is?'

'Where do you think he is? He'll be at the town hall guardroom. Taking his ease, while we take the humiliation.'

'How do you mean?'

'"How do you mean"? Stuff wouldn't be asking "how do you mean"! It's obvious. Matthies the troublemaker, who ought to be taken in right away for theft and assault, stands there speechifying, and we are put out on patrol to make sure no one disturbs him.'

'But what's it all for? Herr Perduzke, I don't understand it –'

'I believe you. Why don't you ask your friend Frerksen. He's having a high old time, strutting about like a stork in lettuce.'

Tredup dashes up to Frerksen. 'Commander, could you explain to me . . . I'm here for the *Chronicle*, in lieu of Herr Stuff. I don't understand . . .'

Commander Frerksen politely touches two fingers to the brim of his cap. 'Good evening, Herr Tredup. Here for the *Chronicle*, are you? That's good. In that case we can hope for balanced reporting . . .

'The situation is pretty straightforward. Over there – the National Socialists, and here – the Communists. The police in between, keeping them apart, avoiding clashes.'

'But the Communists raided the others, so I heard?'

'That's been rumoured. It's not quite the moment for a full investigation.'

'But the Nazi meeting has been banned?'

'Only for the time being. Perhaps for another fifteen minutes. The fact of the matter is: our strength is too weak, Herr Tredup. I have thirty men here with me. What am I going to do with them? The militia's expected from Stolpe at any moment. Then we can disband the Communists and allow the Nazi meeting to go ahead.' He looks sweetly at Tredup.

Tredup is vanquished. 'That seems perfectly right to me. Of course you and thirty men can't just –'

'Out of the question.'

'And could you tell me where I might find the mayor? Perhaps he has some instructions for me?'

'The mayor is in the town hall guardroom,' Frerksen says curtly.

'Don't you think I ought to see him too?'

'Oh, why ever not?' says Frerksen coolly. 'On your way. And, now, if you'll excuse me.'

And the commander resumes his march down the middle of the road, just exactly halfway between the warring parties.

In the town hall the only light on is a single yellowish bulb in the landing.

Tredup feels his way to the door he knows to be marked with a sign: POLICE GUARDROOM. NO ENTRY.

He knocks once, but no one answers.

He knocks a second time; again, silence.

Cautiously he opens the door.

Inside, it feels just as dim and dusty and deserted. But Gareis is there. Sitting on a table, his feet on one of the police daybeds, in a grey loden coat, his hat pulled down over his eyes.

In front of him is a worker, talking away rapidly and vehemently.

Gareis raises his head and glances at Tredup. 'Well, well, Herr Tredup, to what do I owe the pleasure? – I'm busy.' And already somewhere else: 'Please understand, Comrade, what am I supposed to do? I can't go after the Communists with just a handful of men.'

The worker is angry. 'The Party will hold it against you, Comrade Gareis, the feeling against you from the grass roots is growing stronger all the time. It's not on, allowing the Soviet sympathizers to hold their meeting on the marketplace, under our protection.'

'Our protection . . . Our strength is insufficient. As soon as the militia turns up, they'll be dispersed.'

'You laid into three thousand farmers with just three men. And now your strength is suddenly insufficient. No comrade will accept that.'

'Everyone with an ounce of sense will understand it perfectly well. Do you want us to follow the 26th of July with a 30th of September?'

'Will you at least have Matthies arrested today?'

'We have to listen to a couple of KPD people. Not everything the Nazis say is driven snow.'

'You always think of the others, Comrade Gareis, never of the Party.'

'I think of the others *and* the Party,' says Gareis.

'That's just it! That's just it! You want to please everyone.'

'I want to do things right. That's why I need to think of both sides.'

'But still the Nazi meeting stays banned?'

'No. No.' And once again, with a lot of emphasis: 'No. As soon as the militia arrives, the meeting is permitted.'

'Comrade Gareis –'

'Well now, Herr Tredup, what brings you here?'

'I wanted to ask you . . . I'm here on behalf of Herr Stuff . . . If you had any instructions for me?'

'Herr Stuff?' asks the worker – his name is Geier – looking angry. 'Not the fellow on the *Chronicle*?'

'Allow me: Herr Tredup from the *Chronicle* – Council Member Geier.'

'And you let him listen?!'

'He's one of us. He's in the Party. It's a good thing that he's heard us now.'

'Good. Well, I'm just not quite sure . . . Herr Mayor, the people are saying the police should step in –'

'You hear that!' says Geier.

'Step in with what?' asks the mayor, but just then the telephone goes.

He listens, speaks, thanks. 'The militia will be here in two minutes. They're just entering Altholm now. Will you excuse me . . . ?'

All three of them leave together.

As they step out on to the top of the town hall stairs, they can already hear the sounds of horns and cars.

The crowd has grown even larger, it stretches as far as they can see, a seething swarm under the arc lights.

The cars seem to be very near.

'From *that* side?' Gareis suddenly exclaims. 'From *that* side?! Dammit, those aren't militiamen, those are Nazis!'

Three motorbikes surge past, each bearing two men in Nazi uniform.

They slow down outside the town hall and, hooting incessantly, push their way through the parting crowd.

They are followed by lorry after lorry, each full of fifty or sixty Nazis. The swastika banner waves over each truck.

The young thugs stand there upright, proud, gazing out over the people . . .

'If the militia doesn't come right now,' says Gareis, 'we're looking at a battlefield with casualties in three minutes.'

The speaker outside Tucher's has ended with a loud appeal. A cheer echoes it. Another voice barks out an order.

And like a torrent the mass of Communists pour on to the empty road outside Tucher's. The handful of police are knocked aside, swept away by the crowd. Roars and cheers – 'Long live!' – 'Down with!' – 'Heil Hitler!' – red flags, swastika flags, blare of brass.

Gareis has gripped Tredup's arm. He clutches on to it. 'Militia!' he pleads. 'Militia, please!'

But the fanfares organize themselves into a marching tune, and a triumphant song rings out.

The Communists are arrayed in rows of four, red flags fluttering overhead, they begin their march . . .

The Nazis jump down off the trucks. There too, commands ring out, there too men form up into ranks, they stand outside Tucher's, four rows deep, facing the Communists . . .

'Here come the militia!' cries a relieved Gareis.

They must have left their vehicles a little further away. They approach in two long files, push themselves between the Nazis and the Communists, the Communists and the onlookers, separating the foes . . .

And now the KPD starts to march.

The fanfares blare, the whistles shrill; towards the town hall, past the steps they march.

They withdraw in good order, with laughing, triumphant faces. *They* have had their meeting.

'What's that?' calls Tredup, pointing to a dummy in the procession, swaying between two flags.

It's a straw doll in a blue uniform with shiny buttons, with a cap on its round straw head, and horn-rimmed glasses on its turnip nose.

'Frerksen,' says Councillor Geier. 'Our dear Comrade Frerksen . . .'

There's no doubt about it, everyone gets it, because in its raised broomstick arm, the figure proudly carries the celebrated sabre aloft.

'Frerksen as a Communist scarecrow,' says Geier. 'Casts a

wonderful light on our Party, wouldn't you say, Comrade Gareis?'

'Look!' says Gareis.

Six or eight militiamen suddenly appear next to the front of the march. With their rubber truncheons they wade in, towards the core of the procession, where the straw man is teetering along.

And teeters no more. From the steps it is clearly visible: he suddenly collapses, dropped, under the feet of the marchers, who kick him aside, trip over him, knock him out of the marching line.

Only the sabre . . .

With its point towards the night sky, and its blade repeatedly catching the lamplight, it is passed from hand to hand in the march. Wherever the militia go in to try to take it, even think they have it in their grip . . . it suddenly appears ten steps away, winking, mocking, threatening . . .

And now a figure pops up alongside the march, sweating, with rumpled uniform, skewed cap, crooked spectacles: none other than Commander Frerksen.

'The idiot!' scolds Gareis. 'When he should be keeping a low profile. Dunderheaded idiot! – Frerksen, come here!' he yells.

But Frerksen continues to wobble after his sabre. It sparkles in front of him, disappears, shines again, a little further off . . .

The music changes its theme. Suddenly everyone is singing, shouting, laughing and squealing. 'Where d'you put my sabre? My sabre? My sabre? . . .'

The procession disappears round the corner, and with it the commander.

'I'm afraid he's going to do himself a mischief tonight,' says Tredup, with a shudder.

IV

The train from Altholm pulls into Stolpe a little before ten o'clock.

Tired from so much drink, Stuff has had a little zizz. Now he's standing rather crossly on the platform, wondering where he can find Henning. He may know Altholm like the back of his hand, but it's all he knows, he's been to Stolpe maybe a dozen times in the course of his life.

Well, I suppose I'll try the *Bauernschaft* first. I'm a bit of a donkey to have set out just like that.

First, he needs a little refreshment, though, and when the waiter in the station buffet has served him his third treble, the foundation has just about been laid for a request for information.

'Henning? No, no one of that name here.'

'The man who works on the *Bauernschaft*, you know, Padberg's paper?'

'We know Padberg all right, but he's –'

'Disappeared,' Stuff volunteers. 'Bye-byes. That's not new.'

'Now there's a young man filling in for him –' the waiter recalls.

'My! Yes! Wonderful!' cries Stuff. 'That's the man I'm looking for. That's Henning.'

'I see, so that's Henning? I never knew. Young fellow, blond, blue eyes? Usually goes around in a track suit?'

'Yes. That's right. That's him. And does he ever come here?'

'No, he definitely does not come here.'

'Where does he go, then?'

'I couldn't tell you. I just wait tables here. But he seems to be a one for the ladies. I only ever seem to see him in female company.'

'And where do you take a lady here?'

'To a café, sir, to one of the cafés.'

'How many are there?'

'Well, there's the Café Koopmann, for starters.'

'Where's that?'

'On the marketplace.'

'Aha. I know the marketplace. Go on.'

'Well, but you don't take a lady to the Café Koopmann. Frau Koopmann won't have that.'

'Oh, Christ,' groans Stuff. 'Then can you tell me where you take a lady in this town?'

'To the Fichte or the Grand.'

'Where are they? Are they hard to find?'

'Well, if you don't know your way around here –'

'No, I don't! Is there a taxi service?'

'Yes.'

'Here at the station?'

'Yes.'

'Then I want –'

'But not today,' explains the waiter. 'It's reserved for the entire day.'

'Who for?'

'For Lawyer Streiter.'

'Well, then, I suppose I can't have it.' Stuff sighs resignedly. 'Then I'll have to try and find all these cafés by myself.'

'It's not so easy in the dark,' says the waiter. 'Would the gentleman like another beer?'

'No, I'd best be going. But you can bring me a double schnapps.'

The waiter brings it.

'Would I be right in thinking,' he begins, 'that you're going to those cafés to look for that gentleman?'

'Yes,' says Stuff.

'But he's not in any of the cafés.'

'No? So where is he? Can you tell me?'

The waiter seems offended. 'He'll be at the Hotel Crown, with Lawyer Streiter.'

'And you wait till now to tell me that?'

'How was I to know you were looking for the gentleman!'

'But that's what I said.'

'I thought you were looking for a girl to go out with. When they're looking for a girl, gentlemen often have this roundabout way of asking.'

'Nonsense. Anyway. But Herr Streiter is in the taxi, somewhere far away?'

'The lawyer and Herr Henning are already back.'

'Thank God for that. And where is the Hotel Crown?'

'Just across the street, sir. You can't miss it.'

V

The Crown seems to be functioning as the impromptu farmers'
headquarters, all the tables are jam-packed, and the air is thick
with shouting and talking.

Stuff blinks his way through the tobacco fug, and then slowly
and inquiringly makes his way through the bar.

At a small table in a corner, Henning is sitting with a gentleman who is definitely no farmer. The lawyer, thinks Stuff. I'll call
him legal councillor, that always goes over well.

And he lays his hand on Henning's shoulder.

'Evening, Henning, evening, Legal Councillor. Editor Stuff at
your disposal. Mind if I join you?' Stuff sits down expansively. 'So,
here I am, my son.'

'So I see,' says Henning. And, by way of a little explanation:
'Herr Stuff is with the *Chronicle* in Altholm, Legal Councillor.'

'Guessed right!' thinks Stuff aloud. And then: '*Was. Was* with
the *Chronicle.*'

'What do you mean, "was"? Have you quit?'

'What do you think? Who else is going to handle this thing for
the *Bauernschaft*, if not yours truly?'

'Herr Stuff! We've got a substitute in place. It would have been
a great thing to land you, but I really had no notion that you
might be available. Surely a letter or a phone call wouldn't have
been too much to ask for?'

'Whatever for? Surely you don't want some inexperienced
trainee who doesn't know anything about anything to cover the
trial for you?'

'He's not inexperienced at all. We got him from Berlin, and
he's been round the block.'

'Sure! But what does he know about farmers. I'll do the court
report. Let the young fellow do local and regional news, that's
really poor in the *Bauernschaft*.'

'But what's it going to cost!' exclaims Henning.

'Expensive! Of course it's expensive. I cost six hundred a month,
and I'll agree a contract with you for five years,' says Stuff agreeably.

'You've got a screw loose,' says Henning. 'Why would we go and do that?'

'Of course you're going to do that. You'll count yourselves lucky too,' says Stuff.

'There's something to be said for having the court reports done by someone local,' Streiter chips in.

'All right, my boy, so everything's rosy. Over the next few days we'll draw up this contract with the *Bauernschaft* people. For tonight, your verbal agreement's good enough.'

Henning reflects. Finally: 'All right. Write the court reports. We'll talk later.'

'Fine,' says Stuff with equanimity. 'In three weeks you'll be licking your fingers for me. I'm in no rush. – And as for the court case, will you go along with it, or are you about to do a bunk?'

The question was a little unexpected. The lawyer winces, and Henning doesn't say anything.

'Well, then I'll tell you, Henning,' Stuff says. 'You stay here. It's better for the others in the box with you, and you're not risking anything.'

'That's what you say,' says Henning.

'That's what I know. Seeing as an ex-Stahlhelm assistant judge gave me a peek into your files.'

The lawyer gets up with a jolt. 'Will the gentlemen excuse me a moment. The toilets are that way, I presume?' He disappears. The two men look at each other.

'Now, Stuff, no bullshit,' says Henning, 'what does it actually say in my files?'

'That you're a good, pure, truthful boy,' beams Stuff. 'Apple of your mother's eye. That the fly hasn't been born yet that you could do anything mean to.'

'On the level?'

'On the level: there's nothing incriminating in your files from previous life or convictions. Not even any bombs.'

'And why would there be at that, Stuff?' says Henning with sudden exuberance.

'Where would you be if you didn't have your old piss-artist Stuff,' he replies, doubtfully.

VI

Tredup is doing lots of overtime.

It's way past eleven, and he's still hunkered in the editorial office, writing his piece on the evening's doings.

For the police? Against the police? For the police! Against the police!

If there was a flower to hand, he would happily unpetal it.

The best course, finally, is a sort of middle way: the ones who are right are the Nazis, who are fine figures of chaps. Moreover, their cashbox has been nicked, and they've had a few bloody noses. They have every right to a little popular sympathy.

Whereas the ones who are absolutely in the wrong are the Communists, who are always so noisy, and stare aggressively at people, and go parading a stolen sabre and are forever bearing witness to something you don't want to know about, as if they were so many early Christians.

And the police are maybe half right. Admittedly, they should have been there sooner. But they weren't really to know that the KPD were planning an ambush. Second, they should have made their presence felt a bit more, but the fact is they really were too weak. And third, the thing with the sabre should never have happened, but maybe it really couldn't be found anywhere before.

So all in all it was a black day in the history of Altholm, not quite as bad as the 26th of July, but jolly nearly.

When he's finally finished, the telephone goes. Almost midnight.

Tredup answers, '*Chronicle.*'

'Yes, this is Gebhardt here. – What are you still doing in the office? You've probably got an appointment with Herr Stuff? – What's that? Well, you do know Herr Stuff has finished today, you've only been telling me so for the past six weeks. – Oh, you don't? Why do my employees always take me for a fool? – No, that's all right, Herr Tredup, I know, I know. – Well, I suppose I have to take the plunge. Starting tomorrow you'll be writing the court reports for the *Chronicle*. Don't worry about the local news, we can supply you. – But I repeat: this is a try-out. An experiment. It depends how well you do. – We had a different arrangement? We had no arrangement, let me tell you! We only ever talked about taking you on on a suck-it-and-see basis. And now that Herr Stuff has left in such poor style . . . – Salary? Salary increase? I'd like to see you earn it first! I don't even know whether you can write. It's not easy to earn money. Nothing easier than making demands, but it's my money. – No, no discussion, don't bother! Ten a penny. Good evening, Herr Tredup!'

Tredup gawps. He gawps just exactly as his predecessor Stuff used to gawp in this same seat.

2

Three Happy Days

I

The following morning, Tredup is in a genial mood. He has had some sleep, and no longer has Gebhardt's whining, wheedling voice in his ear; Tredup has hope, Tredup has a little joy.

Squeezing his Elise, he even speaks up for his boss, because he doesn't want to be without hope.

'In the end, I'm bound to say he's right. He doesn't know the first thing about me. He's got no idea about whether I can write or not. Wait till he sees that I'm as good as Stuff, and maybe better . . .

'I'm off to a good start. That was luck . . . The piece about the trouble yesterday, I tell you, Elise, that was really good.

'I made it very dramatic, and showed that it was pure chance that the 30th of September didn't turn out as another 26th of July.

'And now a run of court reports every day. I'm going to slog my guts out. I'm going to write good reports. I'm really going to describe what goes on in that courtroom. I need Wenk to give me an accreditation as a reporter, the court ushers don't know me.

'And then, on one of the next few days, if everything pans out, I'll take you along too.

'The defendant and the judges and the prosecution and defence lawyers, you won't have seen anything like that, and stuff like that is bound to interest you, isn't that right, Elise?'

'Yes,' she says, 'I'd like that. If you're not embarrassed to be seen with me. Because it shows already. I always put on weight so early.'

'That doesn't matter. It's not a shame to be pregnant if you're married. Maybe it's even a good thing. Maybe Gebhardt will be around and see it, and slip me a little extra in my wage packet.'

'I don't want that,' she says, 'I don't want him to see. I can't stand Gebhardt.'

'Why? Gebhardt's all right, he'll probably bump up my wages himself, once I've gone to see him ten times. I'm not ashamed. I'll keep asking.'

'I really don't like him. Ever since he told the Heinze girl he won't pay her any more, what she's getting is already more than enough, ever since I heard that I don't care for the man. He should be ashamed of himself! The girl needs to live too.'

'Lord, Elise, all bosses are that way. They don't understand the first thing about getting by on an income. They read in the paper that an unemployed man and his family have twelve marks forty to get them through the week. And then they think, if that's enough for a whole family, then it's plenty for a single girl with no dependants.'

'That's right. I should like to see him try. Let him and his wife and children – if he's got any – let him try and get by on what we get by on.'

'A week's not the point, Elise. Anyone can do it for a week. The awful thing is to live like that the whole time, without any prospect of things getting better, that's the awful thing. And we'll never be able to teach Gebhardt that. We'll get some money, never you worry. We'll get there, Elise. Three months ago, I was only on commission, and today I get a fixed wage, and I'm an editor.'

'And the thousand marks –' Elise begins.

But he doesn't want to know. 'And I tell you, we'll get up now, and have some coffee. And then I'll run along to the Baltic Cinema and look at the stills. They said they'd supply me with all the local news, but I'd still rather do some of my own legwork and writing.

'I'm going to go along to the weekly market as well. It's too early to do the actual market report, but I'd like to write a mood piece about what it's like when the carts come in and the stalls are set up, and Hänsel from the market police goes around, giving everyone their places. And a couple of traders almost come to blows about where they're put.

'People like to read things like that. I want to make it a good paper.'

He lies there with eyes open, dreaming, distracted, all over the place. Elise wants to peg him back to the thousand marks, but then she feels sorry for him. He's as happy as a sandboy, and she doesn't want to spoil it.

'Then I'll get up and make us some coffee,' she says, and tries to escape from his embrace.

'You do that. I've got to go. Oh, Elise, Elise!' He squeezes her tighter and tighter, and shakes her. 'Elise, I'm a newspaper editor! Aren't you pleased?! I'm an editor, I am!'

II

Militiamen are deployed outside the large Marbede School sports hall. Curious onlookers throng the street.

It's already a quarter past nine as Tredup approaches at a great lick. He's running late but hopes he can still snaffle a decent place at the press desk.

He runs up to the nearest militiaman. 'Tredup, editor at the *Chronicle*. Here's my press pass. Has it started yet? Have I missed anything? Why are there so many militia here? I presume they stayed over from last night?'

'Can I refer you to Lieutenant Wrede, please.'

Tredup makes the acquaintance of Lieutenant Wrede. No, it hasn't begun yet. – No, there are fifty policemen, as requested by the court. – No, of course in consultation with the police administration. – Yes, they'll be staying here for the duration of the trial. – Accommodation has been found for them in hotels. – Yes, he would like to ask the editor kindly not to mention that.

Tredup wrinkles his brow.

It would only make for more talk about waste and luxury, when the simple fact was that there were no other billets available in Altholm.

Tredup promises not to publish. And reserves the right to reverse himself just the same. Fifty policemen staying in hotels? The expense must be horrendous!

Tredup hurriedly enters the sports hall.

By removing the gym equipment, a reasonable meeting room has been created. Of course the regular courthouse would have been much too small, and they were reluctant to use the dance hall of a bar or pub. Still, there's an odd atmosphere, the judge's table, and behind it climbing frames with ropes – the ropes admittedly tied up – but it still looks ominous.

Tredup finds the press desk directly opposite the place for the defendant, and scouts around for an empty chair. There are already a dozen gentlemen present, and many other places are reserved for one name or another.

So those are the big cheeses from Berlin, whispering together. They know each other. Tredup doesn't know anyone. There are none of the local Altholm scribes as yet. If only Blöcker was here, or at least Pinkus from the *Volkszeitung*, with whom he might exchange a few words, explain the capacity in which he was here.

Suddenly the doors are thrown open at the back, and the public are admitted. And through the other door, escorted by court police, are two of the defendants: Padberg and Farmer Rohwer. Tredup looks out for the only face familiar to him, Henning, who once came to see him over the photographs, but he's not there yet.

Then the door opens on the right-hand side, a little man comes in rather uncertainly, looks about him, one of the ushers says something to him. The little man takes five paces, and then jumps back again. He does not look good: across half his face, and the bridge of his nose, is a bright red broad scar. And the nose itself, greyish, pale, looks like a shapeless potato.

The usher takes the little man by the arm and leads him to where the defendants are. He sits down right at the end. He looks around timorously, and then buries his face in his hands.

From chit-chat among the press, Tredup gathers that the man is a dentist from Stolpe, against whom, rather bafflingly, charges have been brought. (Which is supposed to be an outrage.)

Then the fourth chair among the defendants is taken: Henning has arrived, his arm in a black sling. In the gallery, people stand up to see him, all craning their necks. One press man, two seats

from Tredup, starts to sketch him, as though this is the star everyone has been waiting for.

And Henning carries it off. He greets the other accused, shakes
hands with them, even introduces himself to the dentist, and the
two of them have a little conversation, Henning smiles.

Tredup is taking eager notes.

A voice brays next to him. 'What's this, then, that dreadful rag
the *Chronicle* represented by two scribblers?'

Pinkus from the *Volkszeitung* has taken the seat next to Tredup.

'Why two?' asks Tredup irritatedly. 'I'm representing the
Chronicle.'

Pinkus grins. 'What about Stuff? What's he doing?'

'Stuff? How do I know?' But he's silenced straight away.

Stuff is sitting diagonally across from him, and looking straight
at him through his rather dirty pince-nez. Tredup says a sheepish
hello, Stuff majestically inclines his head.

While everyone stands, because the court are now filing in,
Tredup doesn't know what to make of it. What's Stuff doing
here? Has he patched things up with Gebhardt? Or is he just here
in some private capacity? Is everyone toying with him? Is he never
going to live in peace or have any joy in his life?

While the names and details of the defendants are being established, and the opening statements are read out, Tredup falls
to pondering. From time to time he manages to write down a
couple of sentences.

Why go to such trouble? It's not going to work for him.

The questioning of the defendants goes on for ever. The judge
has a kindly way of speaking to them. He addresses them as 'Herr',
and doesn't hurry them. And he is utterly precise in the way he
tries to establish every step of each of the defendants in the course
of the march. Behind him is a large blackboard, on which each
house on the market and the Burstah has been marked.

'Where were you standing then? – Were you already in front
of Bimm's? You know, the shop . . .'

The prosecutor is silent. The defence offers occasional amplifi-
cation, say for the tongue-tied Rohwer.

It isn't until the farmers' flag is brought in that the trial and

courtroom come to life. It has been taken apart, and now there is
a group clustered round the judge's table: Henning and Padberg
are screwing the scythe on to the flag, and the judge is looking on
with interest. The prosecutor and his deputy are watching from
a couple of paces away, the defence lawyer is by Henning's side.

Padberg raises the flag.

The soiled cloth droops miserably along the pole, while the
scythe, thrice dented and bent in the fight, looks sorry for itself.

'Would you like to show the court, Herr Henning, how you
carried the flag? Oh, of course, your arm. I'm so sorry. Perhaps,
Herr Padberg, if you'd be so kind?'

But Padberg is clumsy. He is small and dumpy and has certainly never carried a flag in his life. It wobbles around in his
hands, lurches forward, the judge and usher just barely prevent it
from crashing down on top of them.

Impatiently, Henning slips his arm out of his sling. He takes
the flag from Padberg, and holds it out in front of his chest. Then
he suddenly raises it aloft.

Something carries him away, he raises it higher and higher, lets
it fall to one side, catches it in his other hand, the banner unfurls:
black field, white plough, red sword.

It beats and clatters, blows to the right, blows to the left.

In the public gallery a few shouts are heard: 'Heil Bauernschaft!'

The defence lawyer steps in. 'Your arm, Herr Henning!' he
reminds him. Suddenly Henning's arm drops, his face grimaces
in pain, with difficulty he holds the flag aloft in his other hand,
until Padberg and Rohwer relieve him of it altogether.

It's over.

But Tredup's hand is flying across the paper.

'"Crippled" Henning is the Flag-Waver. – Defence Counsel
Comes to his Aid. – Flag Works Miraculous Cure of Bad Arm.'

That's the sort of stuff that would surely gladden the heart of
Mayor Gareis. Actually, all the defendants are perfectly pleasant
types, Henning in particular is really very nice, but a writer for a
paper can't pass up on detail like that. It's just what people like
to read.

The usher tiptoes along behind the press desk, whispering the word: '*Chronicle*' – '*Chronicle*' – '*Chronicle*' . . . Alarmed, Tredup spins round. 'Yes. What is it?'

'You're to step outside a moment.'

He's been called away. Stuff has won out. Back to selling advertising space, after once getting to sit at the press desk in this courtroom.

Tredup scoops up his papers and slinks out of the hall. One last look round at everything he'll never see again: the judge's table with the jurors, the little corner table where Councillor Röstel sits, representing the government in Stolpe, Chief Adviser Meier, Padberg is just talking.

Exile from paradise.

The door shut after him.

But outside in the anteroom, there's only Fritz the trainee in his blue tunic. 'The manuscript, please, Herr Tredup, it's almost noon.'

Tredup sighs with relief, assembles his pages in order.

'You know, Stuff is here too,' he says, trying to sound casual about it.

'He looked in on us this morning too. To say goodbye. He's now with the *Bauernschaft*,' Fritz reports.

'Yeah, with the old *Bauernschaft*, eh,' says Tredup, and looks out of the window where things seem to be brightening outside. 'What's the weather like?' he asks.

'It's clearing, Herr Tredup.'

'It's clearing, ha,' he says, and he strides confidently back in through the door, past the policeman, into the courtroom.

III

The final defendant to be questioned late in the afternoon is the dentist Franz Czibulla from Stolpe. The little bearded man steps up in front of the judge's table with trembling limbs, repeatedly hiding his wrecked face in his hands.

The judge asks: 'You are bringing a charge against the town of Altholm?'

'Yes, Your Honour, I was so badly beaten up! I need to be among people, to earn my living. How can I show myself to people as I am?' Once again, his hand reaches up to cover his face.

'So, you were coming from the station . . .?' the judge begins.

'Yes, I was coming from the station. I was on my way to my patient Hess in Propstenstrasse, I had made him a set of dentures. Herr Hess often can't get away, so I come to him instead.'

'We will be hearing from Herr Hess later,' says the judge. 'So, you were proceeding along the Burstah? Were there a lot of people?'

'No. To begin with, not at all. It was deserted and terribly quiet. It struck me as unusual.'

'So that struck you?'

'Yes. How quiet it is, I was thinking. And then I looked in at the shopfronts, and again: Altholm is very quiet today.'

'You didn't stop to think why that might be?'

'No. If I'd known what was going to happen to me, then I would have thought about it. But how can you know that?'

'Did you not know that a demonstration of farmers had been slated to take place in Altholm? It was in all the papers.'

'Maybe I read about it. But I'm certain I didn't think about it.'

'So you are no farmers' supporter? Most of your patients are country-dwellers.'

'I'm a businessman, Your Honour.'

'You are said to have expressed your approval of the Bauernschaft movement, though.'

'I'm a businessman, Your Honour; when I'm with a farmer, I agree with what he says, and when I'm with a Socialist, I say yes to him.'

'So your reason for coming to Altholm was not to demonstrate?'

'I came for Herr Hess's teeth.'

'As you walked on along the Burstah, what did you see?'

'There was a sudden crowd of people, and policemen standing everywhere.'

'And you didn't stop at that point?'

'I had an appointment with Herr Hess. Herr Hess likes me to be punctual.'

'Well, perhaps you would tell the court what you saw then? Were the farmers hitting the police, or were the police hitting the farmers? What was happening?'

'There was no hitting going on at all at that stage. People were pushing here and there, and the police kept calling out, "Make way, make way . . ." And when I'd gone another ten paces or so, there was the gentleman lying bleeding on the road.'

The judge explains: 'Herr Henning, you mean.'

'Yes, I know it was Herr Henning. I know him.'

The prosecuting counsel gets to his feet. 'Would you ask the defendant how he comes to be acquainted with Herr Henning?'

The judge: 'I'd rather have questions later. But very well: how did you come to be acquainted with the defendant?'

'Really only since this morning, but I saw him in hospital a couple of times.'

'Did the defendant not speak with his co-accused Henning while they were in hospital?'

Henning jumps up in agitation. 'Prosecutor, if your face had been as badly beaten as Herr Czibulla's, even you wouldn't feel like talking much!'

'Your Honour, would you kindly ask the defendant Henning to moderate his language. The defendant Henning –'

'Herr Henning, that's no way to talk. If everyone kept jumping to their feet and complaining when they didn't agree with something . . . You understand, don't you? Well, next time' – he smiles – 'curb yourself. – Has your question been answered to your satisfaction?'

'Not at all. Kindly ask the defendant if he was in communication with the defendant Henning in any way in hospital. There is such a thing as non-verbal communication too.'

'Your Honour, I really had other priorities than the gentleman. I saw him two or three times when he went to the bathroom and my door happened to be open on to the corridor.'

'Very well. – Then you saw Herr Henning lying on the cobbles? Was he alone or was anyone with him?'

'He was lying there all alone. I was very upset that there was no one helping him.'

'I see. Very upset, were you? Did that cause you to feel bitter about the police?'

'I didn't know at the time that the police had knocked him down.'

'But you could see that his wounds had been inflicted by sabre blows? Who would have a sabre other than a policeman?'

'It didn't occur to me then. I was trying to make my way through when I saw the man lying there, and that upset me. But I didn't stop and think about it. I had to get to Herr Hess.'

'What made you go to the group with the flag? That surely wasn't the direct way to Propstenstrasse?'

'The direct way was blocked. I couldn't get through. There was some space round the group with the flag.'

'Was your attention caught by the flag?'

'I never even saw it.'

'A big flag like that! Have another look at it, over in the corner. You could hardly have overlooked it.'

'Your Honour, there was so much to see on every side, I really didn't notice the flag.'

'All right then. You really didn't notice the flag. What prompted you to make straight for the policemen? I take it you could see they were policemen?'

'Yes, a couple of them were in uniform.'

'So what were you about then as you went up to them?'

'I don't really know . . . Your Honour, I wanted to ask some questions, how to get through, what was going on . . . I don't really know, I just wanted to get to the police. I felt very nervous.'

The judge: 'I see.' Hesitating, once more: 'I see. Well now, Herr Czibulla, it seems to me this last point isn't completely clear. You say you wanted to ask what was going on. Did you think the policemen had time to give you an answer?'

'Yes . . . no . . . Oh, I'm not sure.'

'You had noticed how much commotion there was. Was there not a lot of shouting and yelling around you?'

'Yes, there was a bit of yelling, but I couldn't work out what was happening.'

'So you thought the constables might put you in the picture? With a badly injured man lying on the cobbles?'

'Yes, because I wanted to know –'

'And then you also wanted to know how to make your way through the crowd? Wouldn't it have been simpler, I put it to you, if you had just turned back?'

'But then I wouldn't have seen Herr Hess!'

'You could have gone via Grünhofer Strasse.'

'I didn't think of that.'

'And you wanted to ask how to get through. But there was the crowd, two thousand strong. And you told us how the policemen kept calling out, "Clear the road." – Did the road get cleared at all?'

'No, there were too many people.'

'So how could the police help you if that was the case? You must have had some idea?'

'No . . . I no longer remember . . . I just wanted to ask what was happening.'

'That won't quite do, Herr Czibulla. You were very upset. You had seen a man bleeding on the cobbles. The police were standing with their backs to you. Was it not your plan to smack one of the policemen over the head?'

'Your Honour, as I stand here . . . I'm a dentist, what have I to do with such things?'

'Well, *that* gentleman sells farm machinery, it wasn't much to do with him either, if you want to put it like that, and still he was lying there on the cobbles.'

'I can't explain it,' whispers the little fellow, 'but I wanted to ask a question. The constables were standing there –' He breaks off and looks around helplessly.

The defence counsel gets to his feet. 'It seems to me that Herr Czibulla has given a perfectly plausible and sufficient account here. He was upset, concerned, nervous, a man was lying on the cobbles evidently in a bad way. Herr Czibulla was apprehensive. He heard people yelling all around him, people were agitated.

'In such a situation, a man with a timid disposition looks for shelter and protection. There were the constables. What could be more obvious than going over to them. That's what the police are there for. He didn't think twice about it, it was an impulse. Perhaps he really did say to himself, ask them how you'll get through and what's going on. But the main thing was finding some protection.'

The judge asks: 'Was it the case, Herr Czibulla, as your counsel Herr Streiter just speculated, that you felt yourself in need of protection, and sought out the protection of those constables?'

The little man whispered anxiously: 'I don't know . . . I just wanted to get to Herr Hess . . .'

'Well, let's leave that for now. – What happened next? Wait, one moment. Were you carrying anything when you approached the policemen?'

'Was I carrying anything? My briefcase.'

'Yes, in one hand. Which was it? Your left or your right?'

'My left. No, my right. Oh, I can't remember.'

'Then what were you carrying in your other hand?'

'In my other hand? Nothing.'

'Herr Czibulla, carefully consider your replies. What were you carrying in your other hand?'

'Nothing, Your Honour. Definitely nothing.'

'Weren't you holding a stick in your other hand?'

'A stick? I don't walk with a stick!'

'Or an umbrella?'

'Your Honour, I haven't had an umbrella for twenty-five years. Ever since I lost mine in the first year of my marriage, I haven't wanted to buy another one.'

Laughter in the gallery.

The usher runs down the aisle. 'No laughter! – No laughter! – Laughter is not –'

The judge: 'Thank you, Herr . . . Thank you, thank you, all right. – Herr Czibulla, I should warn you that we have a witness coming up who says you had a stick or umbrella in your hand.'

'Your Honour, that's just not possible. I never take a stick or umbrella. Ask my wife, ask any of my friends or relatives, no one has ever seen me with a stick.'

'The witness will claim that you rammed Police Sergeant Meier-feld in the small of the back with a stick or umbrella handle.'

'But how can he make such a claim! I plucked at his coat, Your Honour, like this, with finger and thumb.'

'Herr Meierfeld also stated that he felt a violent blow.'

'Your Honour, I said, "Excuse me, Constable," three or four times, and then I plucked at his coat. No harder than a mouse would pluck.'

'Well, you must have done it quite hard, because otherwise the officer wouldn't have felt such a shock.'

'As I say, no more than a mouse, Your Honour, very gently. And then he spun round and struck me with his sabre.'

IV

On the morning of the second day of the trial, the first witness was Police Commander Frerksen.

There is almost no one in the hall who doesn't know him, but all crane their necks when he walks in. At the back, some even rise to their feet. He walks up to the judge's table, slender and pale, leaning forward a little, shako and gloves in one hand, the handle of his sabre in the other.

'The bastard looks like he's been practising in a mirror,' growls Stuff. 'He's never managed that before, holding his sabre just like an officer.'

So he hasn't shot himself after all, thinks Tredup. I don't know how he does it, the sabre and everything, and only yesterday he was chasing up the street after it . . .

To begin with, Frerksen speaks terribly softly, only gradually does his voice become louder.

No sooner has he given his details than the defence counsel rises. 'I move that this witness not be allowed to proceed to the oath. The defence is of the view that this witness has exceeded his rights. A disciplinary process was already up against him.'

The prosecution disagrees: 'The disciplinary process has been suspended. In the view of the prosecution, there is no reason not to proceed with the swearing-in.'

And the judge: 'The court will retire to consider.'

Everyone streams out into the little square outside, where you are allowed to smoke. Frerksen remains standing in front of the judge's table for a moment, but everyone is looking at him. So he joins the throng pushing through the narrow little door, disappears from the general curiosity, and finds himself side by side with Henning.

It was a look in the eye of the other that made Frerksen aware of him. A glowering look of cold fire.

In the minds of both of them is the scene where the one gloved hand reached for the flagpole, while the other raised it triumphantly up up up.

And then the whole film to the point where Henning was carried into the pharmacy, and Frerksen came running up and called: 'Don't touch him! He's under arrest.'

They look at each other, pressed together, shoulder to shoulder in the human current. They just look at each other.

Then Frerksen presses to the right, by force he takes his eyes off the other man, looks to the side, so as not to have to lower his gaze.

Henning lights a cigarette.

Frerksen finds Political Adviser Stein together with Tredup. Stein has bought Tredup.

'I don't think,' Stein is just saying to Tredup, 'that we have to stand for any more of that from the *Chronicle*. The report on the Nazi meeting was distorted and sensationalized. As if the Nazis were so many baa-lambs. You tell that to your Herr Stuff!'

'But why?' stammers Tredup. 'It was all absolutely correct. The Communists had ambushed the Nazis! And the police were too weak to do anything about it.'

'A "Black Day"!' lisps the adviser. 'A "30th of September to follow the 26th of July". What a presentation! What actually happened? Nothing! But the police come in for it again. We know your Herr Stuff.'

'The police? But the mayor himself said . . .'

'Bah! If you want to be made privy to our press releases, then you don't kick us every time you get a chance. Simple as that. Herr Stuff ought to know.'

'I keep hearing the name "Stuff",' says the commander. 'But Herr Stuff isn't actually with the *Chronicle* any more, is he?'

'Oh?' inquires Stein, apparently quite astounded. 'So who was it who wrote that garbage?'

Frerksen motions with his head, and now Stein comes over all embarrassed. 'Oh, Herr Tredup, I'm so sorry! If only I'd known! But the mayor will be surprised at you, writing that way.'

'I gave an objective presentation of the facts,' says Tredup doughtily.

'Well, you won't make a lot of friends with those sorts of objective presentations. – Well, Frerksen, will you be sworn in or won't you!'

'I'll be sworn in later. It's a lot of tripe that I'm supposed to have made myself punishable.'

'Of course it is. You'll see the witnesses they bring in for you. The Reichsbanner and the SPD, the whole of the working class is squarely behind you.'

Frerksen changes hue.

A hundred yards away, outside the school gates, the same theme is being discussed. Gareis has thrown his fluffy grey loden coat over his tails, and is pacing back and forth, flanked by Councillor Geier and Party Secretary Nothmann.

'I wish I knew, Mayor,' says Nothmann, 'where you get your confidence from. This whole trial could turn into a calamity for us.'

'Wait for the witnesses. Yesterday it was the defendants, that counts for nothing. Of course all those fools feel pity for a cute lad like Henning. What a golden boy!'

'The witnesses are in the balance,' says Geier. 'They'll feel the atmosphere too. And that avuncular judge is a wretch. We know, we know.'

'What do we know?' asks Gareis irritably.

'For instance, that the judge, unlike the other gentlemen, doesn't come in every morning by train from Stolpe, no, he's staying with his brother-in-law, Thilse, the factory owner. Judge and factory owner – do you think people like that are going to be against the farmers! They'll stick together, mark my words! But

I'll tip the wink to Pinkus, so he can bring it out in the *Volkszeitung.*'

'Oh, please don't do that!' cries the mayor in consternation. 'Why shouldn't the man stay with his brother-in-law? That's not enough to make him biased.'

'You're slipping, Mayor,' says Nothmann. 'Standards. You used to be different. Of course that has to go in the paper. The worker who comes to give evidence must know what sort of man is asking him questions. That he's a friend of exploiters.'

'If Pinkus prints that,' says Gareis emphatically, 'then I'll wallop him so hard he won't know what hit him.' More mildly: 'How can you be such idiots as to mess this up for me? Oh, I know, it's not your fault.'

'You, Comrade Gareis,' says Geier, offended, 'you always think you're so clever, but we have yet to see you achieve much for the Party. We're forever having to go back to the membership, to explain, and justify, and ask for patience. Why don't you steer a course that the working man understands, not these subtleties that end up as neither fish nor fowl.'

'If the farmers go down, then you'll find out I was right all along.'

'If. And if they don't?'

'Yes?'

'Then, Comrade Gareis, you can pack your bags. We can't afford this sort of unideological slackness.'

'No,' says Gareis. 'No. So I've noticed.'

An uncomfortable silence descends.

Pinkus is seen waddling across the street. He is almost breaking into a trot, that's how much of a hurry he's in.

'I'm coming straight from Party HQ, Mayor,' he pants. 'You'll never guess what I've got.'

'Well, why don't you go and tell me, then.'

'A registered letter has arrived. From Frerksen –'

'What does he want? Why is he writing to us?'

'He's resigning from the Party,' squawks Pinkus.

The four men all stare at each other.

'Your witnesses, Gareis . . .' mocks Geier.

The mayor takes a deep breath. 'Mneh. Never mind!' And, emphatically: 'I promise you, I won't be packing my bags for a long time yet. I don't care who thinks he can take me down. I'm staying.'

He runs off.

'Today,' Nothmann says to Geier and Pinkus.

V

In the meantime, Frerksen is back in front of the judge's table.

He is speaking even more quietly, more hesitantly, more mildly. Perhaps it's the mortifying sense that his swearing-in has been declined by the court, perhaps it's the after-effects of Henning's glare . . .

At any rate, Tredup notes that this witness, this prize prosecution witness, has actually seen nothing, knows nothing, recognizes no one.

'So you had the sense that your meeting with Herr Benthin was being undermined? That you were deliberately being sent to the wrong pubs?'

'Yes, I'm not certain of that. If I said so in earlier interviews, it's possible I could have been mistaken. It was just a feeling I had.'

The judge asks: 'What led you to confiscate the flag?'

'I heard shouts of disapproval. It worried me. I thought it was a provocation.'

'Do you remember who shouted?'

'I don't remember.'

'Did you have the impression, as you were confiscating the flag, that Herr Henning offered you much in the way of resistance.'

The witness, haltingly: 'Resistance? No. Not really.'

'You said earlier that Herr Padberg had pushed you away from the flag?'

'No, I wouldn't be able to say that any more. I'm not sure if it was Herr Padberg or someone else.'

'You received a blow, though?'

'Yes. A hard blow.'

'And by whom?'

'I don't know. I'm not familiar with their names.'

A pitiful sight, a man twisting and writhing, anxious not to incriminate anyone, and to please everyone.

'Well,' says Tredup with a hint of glee to Pinkus, who is just returning, 'your prize witness isn't up to much.'

'Prize witness? What are we to do with Frerksen?'

'Frerksen's in the Party.'

'Frerksen . . .? Golly, whoever gave you that idea. Frerksen isn't SPD.'

'Really? That's news to me.'

'Do you think we'd want people like that in the Party?'

'So he's been thrown out?'

'No, no, of course not. But it's interesting you should say that.'

Meanwhile, Padberg has stood up in the little group of defendants. 'Commander, I have a question for you: were you in control of your nerves on the 26th of July?'

Frerksen looks at him tensely. The ingratiating smile round his mouth twists into something else. 'Yes, I was. – Allow me a question back, Herr Padberg, are you not an alcoholic?'

'No.'

'Have you never been booked into a drying-out clinic?'

'That's a vile slander.'

The judge intervenes: 'Gentlemen, please, what's the point? We're trying to sort this out in a sensible way. All right, Herr Frerksen . . .'

But the atmosphere gets worse and worse. It's clearly visible at the press desk. Pinkus writes nothing at all, because this is no good to him. And Stuff is scribbling away like crazy.

But during the break, Frerksen goes up to Tredup. The commander is so alone in this mob of people, no one wants to have anything to do with him.

From the group around Stuff he can clearly hear the voice of his old adversary: 'Frerksen? Done for! He'll be out on his ear in a month at the most.'

Now he goes up to Tredup, with a cautious, timid smile on his face. 'Well, Herr Tredup, can I ask you what people are thinking? What's the view on my evidence?'

Even Tredup sees no grounds to be merciful. 'Too weak. Flip-flops, Commander. – "Couldn't remember" – "Didn't recognize" – If a man does something like that, he has to stand by it.'

And he turns round.

Manzow is holding forth to his own circle: 'Frerksen was always a wet rag, but that's not such a bad thing for Gareis. It makes it easy to see who's responsible for dog's breakfasts in the past.'

'Say,' says Meisel unpleasantly, 'you're not about to go over to Gareis again, are you? That's not on, boy. Gareis is toast.'

'Go over to Gareis?' protests Manzow. 'Hardly. But surely you'll let me say what happened. It was Frerksen who cocked everything up.'

'And now Gareis is paying for it. That's always the way of it. As if we minded.'

VI

Behind the defence counsel is a little table at which two gentle-men are seated. One of them is Councillor Röstel, who is follow-ing proceedings as a representative of Altholm. When the dentist Czibulla was questioned, Röstel was writing avidly, because Czi-bulla is bringing a suit against Altholm.

And the second gentleman at the table is Chief Adviser Meier. He sits there looking faintly stricken, as though trying to hide behind his pince-nez. So far, by some miracle, things are going – touch wood – rather nicely, he'll be able to send an optimistic report back to his boss in Stolpe. So long as Gareis doesn't make a mess of things . . .

Meier would have liked to have a quiet word with Gareis first, he had the sense that back home, in that dark, dingy, lightless room, they would have quite liked to make things up with the man . . . But how could he take such responsibility upon himself? A word before a trial like that could be wildly misunderstood . . .

Influencing witnesses. It's safer to wait, in the end. Gareis will be sensible . . .

It's a little before eleven that Gareis makes his appearance. He is quite calm as he steps before the judge. His posture is good.

'Arrogant son of a bitch!' growls Stuff. 'Wearing tails, he's having a laugh!'

During the swearing-in of the witness, Gareis is obliged to interrupt the judge.

'Not the religious formula, please,' he interrupts loudly, and the judge quickly apologizes.

Then Gareis gives evidence.

He had not been opposed to the demonstration. It hadn't been until he had seen a letter in the press from the farmers' leader Franz Reimers, calling for protests outside the prison, that he had lost his sympathy. He had then agreed with Farmer Benthin that Benthin with some of the other farmers' leaders should come to him just before the demonstration. Unfortunately, Benthin hadn't kept his end of the agreement.

He himself had gone home at noon to pack for his holiday.

As the witness speaks, the black robe of the defence counsel inches forward slowly and unstoppably. The man keeps his yellowish skull lowered, his hands in the folds of his robe.

Were it not for the dark shadow moving towards the witness, everything would be in order. For Gareis's cool speech spreads clarity and calm. Now the counsel raises his right hand in the direction of the judge.

'I request leave to ask the witness a few questions at this stage, which may perhaps cast a new light on his evidence.'

The judge makes an obliging gesture.

The counsel looks down at the ground. Nor does he raise his eyes when he asks: 'Your Honour. Was there not a discussion with representatives of the government on the day before the demonstration?'

'There was.'

'Did Commander Frerksen not participate at this meeting?'

'Herr Frerksen was present at it, yes.'

The defence counsel speaks very slowly: 'Was it not said on the government side that this farmers' movement posed a greater threat than the KPD, and that it was therefore necessary to clamp down on it with unusual severity?'

Gareis has switched fronts: he no longer addresses himself to the judge's table, he stands and faces the counsel. Legal Councillor Streiter inclines his head a little to look up at the giant in front of him. Gareis replies just as slowly, and with utter calm: 'The talks with the government went on for perhaps an hour or two. I don't recall individual phrases verbatim. I don't think that the words you used were said.

'As far as substance is concerned, it's fair to say that there was a gulf between my views and those of the government. A gulf that still exists today. The government sought a complete ban of the demonstration. As far as I was concerned, there were neither legal means nor any political justification for doing so. I declined the ban.'

Chief Adviser Meier, at his table at the back, groans: 'I knew it. Now the pot is broken. Oh, boss, boss!'

The counsel asks: 'Would a third person present have been able to understand from the words of the government delegates present that the government sought an unusually severe response to the farmers?'

Gareis hesitates, but only for moment. His eye wanders to the spot in the gallery where the commander has sat down.

Only for a moment. Then, just as calmly, he answers: 'That was indeed the impression. I should add that I was out of the room for maybe a quarter of an hour. During that time, I spoke to Farmer Benthin. Of course I don't know what Commander Frerksen may have talked about with the government representatives during those fifteen minutes. When I returned, though, he was under the distinct impression that the government desired a sharp approach. I left him under no doubt that my own preferences were different.'

'He's hung Frerksen out to dry!' shouts a jubilant Stuff from the press desk.

'My understanding is,' the counsel says, 'that Commander Frerksen had the impression that the government wanted an exceptionally tough approach to the farmers. Whether Herr Frerksen later acted in accordance with the wishes of his direct superior, or those of the government' – the lawyer hesitates – 'that is something we can determine only by the nature of his conduct during the demonstration.'

Pause.

'Are you done with your questions, Legal Councillor?' asks the judge.

'No,' says the counsel. 'No, not quite yet.'

Another pause.

He's not a bad impresario, this defence man. He knows how to use a pause to raise expectations. The whole room is waiting with bated breath.

'Your Worship,' the defence counsel begins again, 'did you receive any other expression of government policy – other than what was said at that meeting?'

Gareis closes his eyes for a moment. Then, hesitantly: 'I don't remember. There were so many conversations . . .'

The defence counsel takes his time. He has folded his hands behind his back and is trying to see the tips of his shoes under his robe.

'No,' he says, 'I'm not talking about any verbal understandings. Let me jog your memory. Did you not receive a letter from the government, a set of secret orders, conveyed to you by a militia officer?'

Gareis looks straight in front of him.

'Yes,' he says slowly. And then again: 'Yes.'

'And what was contained in those secret orders?'

Gareis is still looking straight ahead. He doesn't answer.

'Let me rephrase my question,' says the counsel. 'Did these secret orders not contain instructions to proceed against the farmers with all conceivable rigour?'

Long silence.

Very long silence.

'Now, Your Worship, please answer the question.'

Gareis recovers his self-possession. He turns towards the judge's table: 'Is the question allowed?'

A thousand little creases play around the judge's eyes. He gestures as if in regret. 'Actually, yes.' And after a pause: 'But you must know how much you are permitted to divulge of government policy.'

Gareis thinks about it. 'I am of the view that I am not permitted to divulge this. These were, after all, secret orders.'

The counsel contradicts him: 'I am of the opposite view.'

And the judge: 'That's easily enough resolved. We have a representative of the government here with us.' Turning to the little table at the back: 'Chief Adviser . . .?'

And the adviser, eagerly: 'I'll check back right away.'

He's already halfway out of the court.

'Half an hour break,' announces the judge.

VII

Tredup rushes to the typesetting room. It's almost noon, but this sensation has to make it into the *Chronicle* today. He's not going to flub this.

He wrote his piece during the hearing, now he works on the running titles. They write themselves.

The heading, right across the front page:

SENSATIONAL DEVELOPMENT IN FARMERS' TRIAL.

The second headline:

MAYOR GAREIS REFUSES TO ANSWER QUESTIONS.

Charging through the dispatch office, Tredup calls out to Wenk: 'Come into the typesetting room, quick. A big story. An extra two hundred street sales, I reckon. But it's still got to be typeset.'

Hurriedly, he tells the story.

The maker-up is grumpy, but he feeds the manuscript into a machine.

Wenk, meanwhile, rather astonished: 'I'm amazed you're so keen, Tredup! I had you down for an admirer of Gareis?'

Tredup stops for a moment, then: 'What does that have to do with anything? I write it the way it is. How can he be upset if what I write is the truth?'

'I only hope you're not fooling yourself. It's good for us anyway. Anyone who sees the headlines is going to stop and buy the paper.'

'I've got to get back to the court. Will you do me a favour, Wenk, and read the corrections, make sure there's no slips?'

'I suppose so. Hope the whole thing isn't rubbish.'

'Nah. Today we'll pip the *News*. Today I'll make my name with Gebhardt.'

When Chief Adviser Meier left the courtroom, he had every intention of calling his boss, District President Temborius. But where do you make such a call from? It's an important and highly confidential conversation. He knows his master, knows he'll have to report in minute detail on the way Gareis commented on the differences with the government, and endeared himself to the farmers.

Is it possible even to conduct such a conversation over the telephone? People can listen in every step of the way. No, Chief Adviser Meier decides he will have to go back to Stolpe in person. But he can only do that if he's first checked with the judge, got his agreeement that he can leave his post this afternoon, that no important witnesses will be called. Well, everything goes smoothly with the judge, he sees no obstacle.

'Let's question the mayor tomorrow or the day after. If you get a positive reply. No, this afternoon I'll just question a few small fry, unimportant witnesses. You can go with your mind at ease.'

But Chief Adviser Meier did not go with his mind at ease. He sits in his second-class compartment and racks his brain how to tell his boss that Gareis has exposed the government on every point, up to but not including the secret orders.

He really was in a quandary. Well, perhaps the orders were strong stuff. Temborius hatched them in concert with Colonel Senkpiel. So, one would have thought that was meat and drink to Gareis. I really don't understand . . .

'I'm a long way from giving up,' Gareis declares to Political Adviser Stein. They are hurrying towards the town hall. 'Why *secret* orders? Temborius will know why he called them that. He'll never allow me to speak about them.'

'I'm not so sure . . .' says Adviser Stein.

'That first instant I thought I'd had it. The judge is a decent man. The thing about clearing permission to speak was the only salvation.'

'Salvation?' says Stein doubtfully. 'Don't you have the feeling that this whole business with the secret orders is getting a touch mystical?'

'You mean, it's rigged? I think so. The bloody things disappear, no one knows the first thing about them, but at the right moment Streiter comes up with them. Very good, by the way, Streiter, the prosecution is looking a bit tired.'

'I wasn't that impressed. Anyone can shoot with pistols like that.'

'But not everyone has pistols like that. Now it's just a matter of whether the little angel Temborius will piss on the touch-pan or not.'

'I don't get you.'

'You don't know that expression, little kidney-Stein? There's a church somewhere that has a beautiful painting of the sacrifice of Isaac. Medieval. Isaac is tied on to a woodpile. Abraham stands there with a huge cavalry-pistol, about to pull the trigger. But up in a cloud there's the little angel, pissing down on the touch-pan. And one of those scrolls unwinds with the legend: "O Abraham, your shot will misse, while the angel himself doth pisse."'

And the mayor croons to himself: 'O Streiter, Streiter, your shot will misse, for Temborius himself doth pisse.'

'I certainly envy you your peace of mind!' says the adviser.

Secretary Piekbusch steps out to meet them. 'Herr Mayor, there's just been a call from the court: you don't need to go back for questioning today. The consultation with Stolpe is going to take a little longer. They'll call for you when they want you.'

'What did I tell you?' crows the mayor. 'Temborius is peeing. It's no bad thing if he lets a little grass grow over the story. Then today's scene will be as good as forgotten.'

He stares into space. 'But let's put the time to good use!

Piekbusch, we're going to look now! All three of us are going to look.'

'And what are we looking for?'

'The secret orders . . .'

Piekbusch rolls his eyes. 'Where have we still got to look, Mayor?'

'All over. All over. All over. And tomorrow they'll be on my desk.'

Wenk is happy. The big headlines have done their job. Two hundred and ten extra copies of the *Chronicle* have been sold.

It's never happened before. The man from the station bookstore had to send over four times for additional copies.

'Really, Max, you ought to go out tomorrow morning before the court sits next, to get in a few advertisements, I'm sure you'd find some takers right now.'

But Tredup doesn't like to be spoken to like that. 'You've got to be barking. I'm to go off hunting ads, when I'm the editor?'

'Well, who else is going to do it? They're not going to come here and order them.'

'Did Stuff go after ads? No, he did not. You'll just have to take on someone else.'

'You try telling the boss that! Anyway, Gebhardt never said anything to me about you being the editor.'

'Because it's self-evident, that's why. A child knows the editor doesn't go hunting for ads. What would people think?'

'They know it's what you've always done.'

'Well, now they know that I write court reports. Anyway, I'm far too busy.'

'It's six o'clock now. You could easily pull in three or four ads by seven.'

'It's six o'clock now, and I'm going home. All right, Wenk. Don't get too jealous. Gebhardt bumped me up another hundred and fifty too!'

With that Tredup is out the door, and laughing to himself all the way home for the way he stuck it to Wenk. Even if the bit about the hundred and fifty isn't yet true, it's bound to be true by the 1st of November.

He tells the story to Elise and the kids. They're sitting round the table, and he relates the whole trial. He shows where they all sit, the judge and the jurors, the prosecutors and the defence counsel.

'This is where Gareis was standing, and he kept turning more and more till he was directly facing the prosecutor. He's some fellow, I tell you! Very calm, but a fox. "What was in the secret orders, Mayor?" – And Gareis is reduced to a stammer: "I refuse to give evidence." He was really in trouble.'

'Papa,' calls Hans. 'Papa. In the *Volkszeitung* it says the mayor is only waiting for leave from the government to give the evidence.'

'That comes to the same thing, Hans. That's what I wrote too.'

But nevertheless, an uncomfortable feeling comes over Tredup. Right away: 'I've got a ticket for you too, Elise. For tomorrow. I scrounged one off the usher.'

'But I can't go in the morning, Max.'

'Well, then you'll just have to go in the afternoon. It's just a pity because tomorrow morning Mayor Gareis will probably be on the stand again. It'll be a sensation.'

Gareis already knows that he won't be on the stand tomorrow.

But he has been requested to keep himself available.

And the mayor says that he is firstly always contactable at the town hall, and would also like a word with the judge tomorrow.

The gentlemen agree on a lunchtime meeting.

Gareis, on the face of it, has more time to look, but he's not looking any more, and he doesn't make Stein and Piekbusch look either.

'The business with the secret orders is so much hokum,' he says grumpily, slumped in his armchair. 'It's already clear that Temborius isn't going to go any further down that road.'

'What if the minister agrees, though?'

'If Temborius is taking it so hard, then the minister isn't going to say yes.'

'I'm not so sure –'

'Oh, Stein, stop bleating, will you? I've had it up to here with your bleating. The whole of Altholm does nothing but bleat! But that prick Tredup is going to catch it from me for that shameless report of his.'

For the tenth time the mayor casts his eyes over the newspaper, where he has already been to work with red and blue crayons.

'You wait, my boy,' he says. 'Just you wait. I was probably the only soul in Altholm you hadn't betrayed yet. But wait, because tomorrow you'll find out what it means to betray Gareis.'

'Tredup is a prick, all right,' says Stein calmly. 'You should never have got involved with him.'

'If I'm going to restrict my dealings to gentlemen,' says the mayor, 'then I couldn't be in politics. But just because I am, it doesn't mean I'll let any old dog piss on my leg.'

3

The End of Tredup

After lunch the next day, Tredup takes his spouse by the arm, and they go along to court. They're in plenty of time. Tredup had thought Elise would be walking much more heavily by now, but in actual fact her walk is quick and light-footed as a girl's.

So they go for a walk in the park. They don't often go out together, and it's a fine day. The October sun means well, the sky is a deep blue, the trees look terrific in their gaudy finery.

They walk up and down, for a while they talk about the kids. Then Tredup makes plans for everything they're going to do once he's on three hundred and fifty marks. Maybe Hans will be sent to a grammar school, he has a good brain. But above all, they need to establish a reserve for bad times

'Fifty marks in the savings bank every month. Then we don't need to be so worried the next time Gebhardt gets a bee in his bonnet. And we should treat ourselves to a radio.'

Elise laughs. 'All those plans, from just three hundred and fifty marks, Max! But remember you need a suit for yourself, and some new shoes.'

Tredup is umm-ing and er-ing. It hurts him in his heart. Now that things are going well, he has to be good.

'Elise,' he manages to blurt. 'Elise!'

'Yes, Max?' she says, and looks at him.

There's silence for a moment, and the two of them just look at each other.

'Elise . . .' he begins again, and he gets stuck again.

But she's understood him already. 'I've always known, Max. There's no need to say any more.'

Suddenly he's mad keen. 'Elise, it's not that I wanted to be bad.

It's just I was so frightened of the future. I thought we would just fritter away the thousand marks, and have nothing left for when things get really bad. Oh, that's not quite it either ... I don't remember what I was thinking ... I just couldn't –'

'It's all right, Max. It's all right. Calm yourself.' She strokes his hand again and again. 'You've told me now. It's all right.'

And he, keen as anything: 'As soon as I have some time, as soon as the case is over, I'll go and get it for you. You're to have it all. It's nine hundred and ninety marks. Imagine!'

'We'll put it in the bank. And then we'll maybe see about getting a nice shop, ideally not here, but in Stargard or Gollnow or Neustettin.'

'But I can't leave here if I'm the editor.'

'But maybe you'll give that up if we have a nice business to run instead? You know, Max, I don't think it agrees with you. Don't be cross with me.'

'What do you mean, "it doesn't agree with me"? Oh, Elise, that was only when I was running around selling advertising. Now –'

'Max, the mayor!' she exclaims.

Suddenly Gareis and Stein have appeared from behind some shrubbery and are making straight for them.

Tredup barely has time to pull off his hat. But a mere two feet away, Gareis walks straight past them, talking away to Stein as though he doesn't see them.

'My God, what's got into the mayor?' says Elise. 'It was almost frightening the way he seemed to look right through you, Max!'

'What do you think's the matter with him?' says Tredup. 'He's hacked off about my article.'

'That'll blow over. This afternoon I'll flatter him a bit, and then the sun will shine again.'

But Tredup is very pale. He shivers.

II

Tredup has got his wife a good seat in the third row, and on the aisle, so that she can dash out if she feels sick. Then he sits down

at the press desk and fiddles around with his papers. He's showing off a bit, but there are so many people watching, it would be
almost unnatural if he wasn't.

Gradually the usual business sets in again: the usher carries
in stacks of files, two policemen bring in the defendants, the
defence counsel runs in, only to run out again.

Tredup and Elise exchange glances from time to time. He sig-
nals every new development to her with his eyes. And then they
smile.

The judge appears, as ever, without warning, along with the
associates and the jurors. The defence follows. All are upstanding. Then the two prosecutors rush in, and after them the doors
are closed.

The judge says quickly, and with an expression of some displeasure: 'Before we resume proceedings, Mayor Gareis would
like to make a personal statement.'

Tredup's heart starts to race.

The mayor approaches from the door, dark and massive, he
stops in front of the judge's table, but half facing the press desk.

Tredup lowers his head. Something unstoppable is coming
towards him.

'I have . . .' begins the mayor. He is holding a half-folded newspaper in his hand, which he is scowling at . . . 'I have requested
the opportunity to make a personal statement. In a local daily
newspaper, let me spell that out for you, in the *Pomeranian Chronicle for Altholm and Environs*, a report has been printed on yesterday's proceedings, specifically on my testimony, against which I
am moved to protest.

'Here are headlines the full width of the page: 'SENSATIONAL
DEVELOPMENT IN FARMERS' TRIAL – MAYOR GAREIS REFUSES TO
ANSWER QUESTIONS . . .!

'Let me remind you that I did not refuse to answer questions.
There is a difference of opinion as to what I am permitted by the
government to say. Once this point has been cleared, then I will
either give evidence or not, according to the instructions of the
government. Refusal to answer is a flat-out lie.'

Tredup sees the fat, white face with the angry, glinting eyes looking straight at him. To the side he catches the judge shake his lowered head.

'Since there was no refusal to answer questions, there is no sensational development either. The second lie.

'I would like to protest against this dishonest and unscrupulous style of reporting. Of course I have no complaints against the other gentlemen of the press. Their work is meticulous and conscientious, and I hold it in high regard.

'But all the more do I seek protection against the wild scribblings of an outsider. I ask that the court afford me some protection against it.'

Gareis looks at the judge, whose head is still lowered while he writes something. The mayor makes a bow, and leaves the court.

'Ooh, that must have hurt!' says Pinkus from the *Volkszeitung*. 'Biff! Bang! Wallop! Rather you than me!'

The court experiences some commotion. While Gareis was speaking, everyone sat glued to their chairs. Now they shuffle about.

Tredup can distinctly feel them taking their eyes off him, now they are looking at one another, holding whispered conversations: 'Yes, it's the pale, thin one. He's the one he was talking about.'

But still Tredup doesn't dare look up, he feels this is the end for him. First the disgrace over the photographs, then the arrest for the bombing, now this – he won't recover from this.

Finally he does look up, he has to. He meets his wife's eyes, and Elise is smiling. She is smiling at him with her eyes, giving him courage, promising not to abandon him. She has, as he once said, turned up all the lights in her eyes, and the whole Christmas tree is ablaze.

Tredup looks down. He feels wretched. He would ten times prefer it over Elise's supportive look if Stuff said across the table: Don't get your knickers in a twist about it. Your turn today, mine tomorrow. Just grin and bear it.

But Stuff is writing away like there's no tomorrow.

III

Right at the back of the gallery is where Herr Heinsius – the great Heinsius of the *News* – is seated. Heinsius is here incognito, Blöcker is manning the press desk and writing the report.

Heinsius doesn't want to be spotted, so he has pulled his broad-brimmed hat way down over his eyes and put up his collar. He sits there hunched between Altholm's citizens, listening to what they say to each other, hearing the voice of the people, and form-ing his own opinion accordingly.

Tredup is one of those people who just have no luck. Heinsius, who is present just twice during the twelve days of the farmers' trial, happens to catch Gareis's attack on the *Chronicle*.

Heinsius can't get out of the court quickly enough, this time there is no reason to wait for vox populi to make up his mind for him.

While he hurries along the streets to the *News*, he keeps repeat-ing to himself: Untruthful, unscrupulous reporting. Scribbles of an outsider.

His fury increases, because of course the other two clinched Tre-dup's hire without consulting him. He'll show Trautmann and Geb-hardt, he'll bring it home to them what folly they do when left to themselves. Presenting him with a fait accompli like that: Guess what, Tredup will be doing Stuff's old job for the time being.

And this when Heinsius has a nephew, a nice, literate young man. He always scored 'A's in essay-writing at school. Wild scrib-blings of an outsider. They'll have to acknowledge their mistake.

He doesn't bother to knock, the normally obsequious Heinsius barges into his boss's office. 'Herr Gebhardt! Has no one called you yet? Haven't you heard? Just as well you're here too, Herr Trautmann! I've run so fast, I'm quite out of breath!'

They both stare at him in astonishment.

'What on earth is the matter, Heinsius?' growls Trautmann.

And the boss: 'What is it this time?'

'Well, the best thing is probably to shut the *Chronicle* down right away. I don't know what you paid Herr Schabbelt for it, no one tells me these sorts of things. But it's money down the pan, Herr Gebhardt, money down the pan.'

Gebhardt has stood up, puts the press guide down on the left, puts it down on the right. 'Herr Heinsius, if you could bear to tell me, in consecutive sentences . . .'

Heinsius is very surprised: 'Didn't Herr Tredup tell you, then . . .? That's what you get when you put outsiders in such posts. I don't often find myself in agreement with Gareis, but I have to agree with him on this, when he calls Tredup an unscrupulous, sensation-hungry outsider. In a public court of law, Herr Gebhardt! With the whole of Altholm in attendance! In front of the judge and counsel! Within hearing of the entire German press corps! Mendacious, skewed scribbling!'

Trautmann says ill-humouredly: 'Let him chatter away, Herr Gebhardt. If we don't listen, he'll get to the point in about five minutes.'

But Gebhardt, very agitated: 'Tredup seems to have put his foot in it again. Hiring the fellow was your idea, Herr Trautmann!'

'My idea! Don't come the raw prawn with me, Herr Gebhardt! Not you! Who made the deal with Stuff? Who then wanted to be rid of Stuff at any price? You make your bed, you lie in it. Anyway, we only *promised* Tredup that he'd get Stuff's job. I wouldn't have given it to him, Herr Gebhardt, not me!'

'Where is the issue of the *Chronicle* in question? May I see it, please, Herr Heinsius.'

'If I can give you some advice,' says Heinsius, suavely after Trautmann's grumpiness. 'I would send a boy to the court and have Tredup sent for. Let some of the shame drain from people's faces.'

'I still don't even know what's going on,' growls the boss.

'But I just told you. Gareis publicly in court protested against Tredup's scribbling. Inaccurate, unscrupulous and untruthful.'

'So we heard. And who writes for the *Chronicle* if we turn Tredup loose?'

'They could run Blöcker's report, couldn't they?'

'I suppose so. All right. Send someone.'

When Heinsius is outside, Trautmann says: 'Why do we have

to do what Heinsius wants? Gareis is forever coming down on someone or other, it really doesn't count.'

'It's a good way of losing Tredup,' says the boss, conciliatorily.

'If you say so. But I'll tell you this, Herr Gebhardt, if Heinsius is trying to give his nephew a leg-up, young Marquardt, that's not a good idea. The fink is only twenty-two and lives in bars.' In a whisper: 'And they say he's got syphilis too –'

Heinsius is back.

'Now show me what Herr Gareis was complaining about. Remember, he's not as important as all that. – All right. SEN-SATIONAL DEVELOPMENT – REFUSES TO ANSWER QUESTIONS. Is that everything? And what did Blöcker write? Pass me the *News*. MAYOR GAREIS REFUSED TO ANSWER SEVERAL QUESTIONS.' Gebhardt looks up. 'Well, Heinsius, I mean to say, what's the difference?'

Heinsius is a little taken aback. 'But we didn't give it the big wahoo! Tredup's headline goes right across the page, with us it's no more than the column's width. Tredup has everything in bold, we have small caps. And anyway . . .' his voice sounds tetchy, 'it's success that justifies itself. Gareis explicitly said we had fair and objective reporting, when he laid into Tredup. That sticks. Most people don't compare newspapers when they read them.'

The boss growls: 'Well, I've sent for Tredup at your insistence, what if he puts up a struggle?'

'But, Herr Gebhardt, how can he? You just tell him what Gareis told him . . .'

'Bah,' says Trautmann. 'Heinsius, I think you've gone and made a muck of things again. You're as tightly strung as an old maid. You're forever making trouble for the boss, and the only one who can straighten things out around here is me.'

Turning to the boss: 'Leave it to me, Herr Gebhardt, I'll take care of him –'

'But I'd like to be the one who –'

'No, don't bother, Herr Gebhardt. You're not made for this sort of thing. You're too soft. You're like a child. The instant someone has tears in their eyes, you're dipping your hand in your pocket and slipping him another five marks. I'll take care of it . . .'

'Well, all right then . . .'

IV

A quiet knock.

Now Tredup is standing in the doorway, looking at the three gentlemen. He's hurried, and is panting. The decision can't come soon enough. Even though he's frightened.

'Well, hello, Tredup.' Trautmann is the only one to reply to his quiet greeting, and looks at him hard. 'You know what you're here for. Your guilty conscience driving you on, eh?'

Pause. The boss stands at his desk, staring into space. Heinsius tries to make out the name of the artist on a picture on the wall. Only Trautmann is paying any attention to Tredup. He even manages to lay his arm avuncularly round the sinner's shoulder.

'Well, Tredup, your time as editorial nibs is up, I guess we all know that. Take comfort, Kaiser Friedrich only lasted ninety-nine days, and it wasn't even his fault. You're young, you've got time, I'd recommend you move somewhere else. You've made too much trouble for yourself here.'

Silence. Tredup stares. Tredup's lips are trembling.

Finally he comes out with: 'What if I were to go back to selling space . . . ? Would you consider taking me back as advertising manager . . . ? Herr Gebhardt . . . ?'

But Trautmann's not having it. 'You know yourself that that's not on, Tredup. First there's the chit-chat about the photos, and then there's the time in chokey. All right, you were innocent, but something always sticks. People don't like that sort of thing. And now this. I've always stuck up for you around here, Tredup, you know, it was me who told the boss to give you a try-out in place of Stuff. You were there yourself. So if I tell you it's no good and you'd better piss off out of here, then I think you should piss off out of here . . .'

Tredup gulps. He moves his shoulders, a little. Then, *piano*, he says: 'My pay . . .'

Here Trautmann loses his temper. 'Your pay? Today's the third, that makes two and a half days. You're on two hundred a month. Say twenty-five working days, that's eight marks a day. I make that twenty marks, all told. – What if we demand damages? Have you any idea how much you've hurt the *Chronicle*? No, Tredup, it doesn't do to get cheeky. You should just be happy that Herr Gebhardt's a merciful employer. Some other bosses I could name would take you to the cleaners. You've got money left from the sale of the photographs, apparently. What if we had your assets frozen . . .?'

Tredup stands there a moment with face down and arms drooping. Then, perfectly quietly and unexpectedly, he says: 'Goodbye,' and turns and leaves.

The three gentlemen unfreeze.

The boss says quickly and emotionally: 'Trautmann, go after him. Give him a hundred marks.' Then after a pause: 'Fifty marks.'

Trautmann says cosily: 'Pish! Why throw away good money? It's not as though we've got it to burn. But that's you all over, Herr Gebhardt, as soon as someone squeezes out a tear or two, you go all soft. Tredup will make his way. Weeds are tough.'

V

As Tredup leaves through the door of the *News*, Elise is waiting on the street. She takes him by the arm, glances up at his face, and just says: 'Let's go, Max.'

They turn on to the Burstah, walking along in silence, and then they go down the Stolpe Road. They walk slowly, he's looking ahead, she's quiet.

Only, she's slipped his hand under her arm, and is holding it in hers, stroking it quickly and encouragingly. They walk slowly along, it's clear that she is expecting.

Then Elise knocks open the gate with her foot, they cross the yard, mechanically he lets go of her arm, reaches for the key in his pocket, and opens the door. He heads straight for the table, and sits down just exactly as he is, in hat and coat, and stares into space.

She says: 'Hans is still at gym class. And Grete will be at her friend's, their thoughts are just beginning to turn to Christmas.'

He doesn't say anything.

She says: 'The best thing is if we move to Stargard. My sister Anna's there. And my parents aren't far either. Let them do their bit to help. All those years we never came to them for anything.'

'Those farmers!' he says angrily. 'Those farmers will fall over themselves to help us.'

'Then we'll try and find a business we can run. I'm not so much in favour of cigars, it seems to me people smoke less when money's tight. I think some kind of food shop.'

'With our shekels!' he mocks.

'All right, so we'll start small. The wholesalers will give us a bit of credit. I'm sure we'll make a go of it. We just need to make a start.'

'No. No. No!' he shouts. 'I'm not making another start. I've made a hundred starts, and the only thing that's happened is I'm deeper in. I've hoped so many times, and tried, and nothing's worked. Nothing we try is going to work, Elise. There's no sense in making the effort.'

She strokes his hair. 'Of course you're sad now. And it's mean of them, of all of them, to abandon you now, when you've gone out of your way to be helpful.

'But you shouldn't exaggerate either, Max. The children are growing up, Grete helps me a lot, and Hans is a sensible boy as well. They've enjoyed a good childhood, both of them. You made it possible, Max.'

'No, Elise, you did –'

'Max, it was you! Think of other families where the father is on the booze or chases after women, and beats the children or terrorizes them. You've always been nice to them, and helped them with their homework, and you build toys for them. Do you remember how you ran everywhere when Hans wanted fishes for his aquarium, and you ended up being given those four tiddlers? No other father would have done that. None. And that's in the evenings when you're exhausted!'

He listens to her. His eyes come flickering to life.

'And it's not true that we're not getting anywhere either. We've managed to get quite a bit of clothing and linens in these last months. I don't think we've ever had so many socks and stockings in our married life! And I've got three hundred marks hidden in the house, and there are the nine hundred and ninety of yours.'

'You see, isn't it good I didn't bring them sooner?'

'And I'm thinking you ought to go and get the money today. And tomorrow you're on the first train to Stargard. I'll give you a letter to take to Anna, you can stay with her. And she'll feed you as well. That won't cost anything, and we can make it up to her later.

'And then you'll look around for an unfurnished room for us, if there was a bit of garden with it that would be nice. Then tomorrow evening you write me a card with our new address on it, and I pack, and in three days we'll all be together again, in Stargard.'

'Yes,' he says. 'Yes.'

'And you'll see how pleasant the people are in Stargard. They're so different to those buttoned-up Altholmers.' She laughs. 'One day you'll meet "Heaven-Forefend-Franz". You'll die laughing. Well, I'll tell you stories about him –'

'Elise,' he says keenly, 'if I'm to get to Stolpermünde tonight to fetch the money, I'm going to have to catch the ten past four train. I'll have to run to the station.'

'All right, Max, off you go then.'

'Oh, Elise,' he says, and stops. 'To be away from all the squalor and the lies. To be an honest man again. Not to have a bad conscience.'

'All right, Max, you'd better hurry.'

'Yes, I have to go.'

'When will you be back?'

'Ten fifteen. I'll be here at half past.'

'All right, Sonny.'

'Bye-bye, Missie.'

She watches him jogging down the length of the Stolpe Road. She watches him till he's gone round the corner.

VI

The witnesses due for questioning in court that afternoon include a series of Altholm's finest.

But the defence counsel asks that a witness known to him, Farmer Banz from Stolpermünde-Abbau, be questioned out of turn. The man had been badly injured in the course of the demonstration, was still far from well, and couldn't be expected to undertake two separate trips to court.

The prosecutor offers strong resistance: 'The witness Banz is wholly unknown to the prosecution. In none of the statements taken at the demonstration was any mention made of any badly injured Farmer Banz. So far as the prosecution knows, there is no decision of the court even to have this witness from wherever he is. I move that the fellow be left out of account.'

The defence counsel explains that the reason nothing had been heard of him was precisely that he had been lying injured in his remote Abbau. He asks that he be called, because he had important testimony to offer.

The prosecutor asks that the judge make a ruling.

The court withdraws, and after three minutes the decision is announced that the witness is to be heard.

The door opens, and Farmer Banz from Stolpermünde-Abbau enters.

He is a large, dry man, always a little hasty. Now he plunges towards the judge's table in such agitation that he stumbles several times. He drags a stick after him, in his left hand he is holding a paper bag. No sooner has he arrived in front of the judge's table than he hurriedly begins to speak: 'Your Honour, let me tell you –'

The other motions with his hand. 'One moment. One moment. You'll be able to tell us everything in a moment. First we just need to know who you are. Your name is Banz?'

Growly: 'Yes. Banz.'

'First name?'

'Albin.'

'Your age, Herr Banz?'

'Forty-seven.'

'Married?'

'Yes.'

'With children?'

'Nine.'

'Your farm is said to be exceedingly remote?'

'No one comes out there from one year's end to the next. All I have is gulls and bunnies.'

'I must now swear you in, Herr Banz. You must swear that what you say is true. The sacredness of the oath you swear . . . Prosecutor, yes, what is it?'

'The prosecution is opposed to the swearing-in of this witness. As we have just heard from the defence, the witness claims to have been hurt by the police. If that were true, then there is the urgent suspicion that the witness has committed a criminal act, in the course of which he may have received his alleged injuries. We therefore move that the witness not speak under oath.'

The defence counsel has already moved nearer to the judge's table. 'There is not the least reason not to question the witness. He received his injuries while purchasing a glass of beer – not a punishable act in our view.'

The judge smiles benignly. 'So far as I'm concerned, we could always swear in the witness after his evidence is concluded. Would the gentlemen be agreeable to that?'

They have withdrawn to their respective tables. In the middle is Banz, looking from one to the other, trying to grasp what is happening.

'Now, Herr Banz, could you tell us what happened in Altholm that Monday. Are you comfortable standing, by the way, or would you like a chair?'

'I'll stand, Your Honour. I would never sit down in Altholm! – So, I was coming from the station –'

'One moment. What were you doing in Altholm in the first place? Had you heard or read about the demonstration?'

'Someone told me about it.'

'Who told you about it?'

'I can't remember. Everyone was talking about it.'

'But you were telling us how terribly isolated your farm is, and how no one ever comes there?'

Banz stands still for a moment. Then he flushes pink. He leans forward, props his hands on the judge's table, and shouts: 'Your Honour! Your Honour! What are you doing to me! Your Honour, you're driving me mad! I want my rights! I want my rights! I want my rights!'

He rips open the bag and produces a shapeless, slimy something or other. He drops it on the judge's table.

'That's my hat, Your Honour! That's my hat that was on my head! They smashed it into my head, it's supped full of my blood, it's supped full of the fact that I've become a sick man. That's Altholm for you, Your Honour! That's the hospitality of Altholm! When I saw the fat police pigs sitting outside just now, I saw red, Your Honour. And you're asking me, Your Honour, who it was told me about the demonstration. Is that justice? Is that my rights, Your Honour? I want my rights . . .'

He is foaming at the mouth. Two court ushers have run up, the defence lawyer and the prosecutor have moved nearer. The gallery is on tiptoe.

The judge waves them all away. Gathering up his robes, he walks round the table to the maniac and pushes him down on to a chair. To an usher: 'A glass of water, please.'

'No, Your Honour, thanks all the same. I'll not drink anything here in Altholm. I'd sooner die than drink anything here.'

The judge looks at him alertly. 'Were you always so temperamental, Herr Banz?'

'Before the demonstration, Your Honour, I was the calmest man on earth.'

'Yes, Prosecutor, you have a question?'

'The witness referred to "fat police pigs" a moment ago. I move that such and similar expressions not be allowed to stand from the witness.'

For the first time the judge is truly agitated. 'I will not stand for your interference with the way I manage my court, Prosecutor! Yes?'

'In that case we have no option but to bring charges. We reserve the right to charge the witness for insulting a public official.'

'Please yourself!' And, more conciliatory already: 'The witnesses should be allowed to talk in whichever way is natural to them. – Now then, Herr Banz, if you're ready, tell us what happened to you. You were coming from the station. What time was that?'

'You wanted to know who told me about it. I went to Stolpe to the Revenue. Everyone was talking about it on the train there. And in the Revenue and the Krug as well.'

'And you wanted to participate? Did you know who Franz Reimers was?'

'Of course I did, Your Honour, every child knows who Franz Reimers is.'

'All right. – So you travelled to Altholm.'

'It's almost five miles from mine to the nearest station, Your Honour, and in the morning the cattle want their feed. So I was on the one o'clock train. I was at Altholm station just after three. I asked someone, not a policeman, if the farmers had been through yet. There weren't any police around. No, he says, the farmers haven't been through yet. Then I walked down the Burstah. And when I got to the square where the naked man is –'

'The war memorial,' says the judge, half under his breath.

Irked, Banz repeats: 'That's what I said, the naked feller. Then I saw what there was, Your Honour, and it was incredible, it's beyond anything I could describe. The way the police were setting about the farmers is something your five senses couldn't deal with.'

Banz is now talking calmly and respectfully, his words are coming out slowly and carefully. The judge looks at him attentively.

'All right, and then?'

'And then suddenly one of the blues comes dashing up to me, and yells: "You bastards, break it up!" And I reply: "We're no bastards, you know, but you have to obey the authorities. I'm going to get myself a pint of beer." And I turn round and I'm on my way to the Krug, and I'm standing on the steps to the Krug, when I get a blow across the skull. I've been bedridden eight weeks, and you can see me for what I am today. I used to be a strong man, Your Honour.'

A pause. A lengthy pause.

'Now, Herr Banz, I have some further questions for you. You're calm now, aren't you?'

'I'm calm, Your Honour. It comes over me from time to time. But after, I'm as meek as a lamb.'

'All right, Herr Banz, when you were walking down the Burstah and first saw the fighting, how far do you think you were from it?'

'How far? Well, it could have been a hundred, two hundred yards.'

'At any rate, you were standing by the war monument. By the "naked man". And did you walk on?'

'Yes I did, Your Honour.'

'Why? If you see people fighting, isn't it better to go the other way? Or did you want to come to anyone's assistance?'

'No, Your Honour. Not at all. I wanted to get a view of what was going on. There were always people in the way.'

'So how near did you get? Ten yards, five yards, three yards?'

'Not that near, Your Honour. But it could have been about ten yards.'

'How were the police fighting? I –'

'It was horrible, Your Honour. Simply horrible.'

'I mean: were they standing with their backs to you, or facing you?'

Banz hesitates. Then: 'Some were like this, and some were like that.'

'But the demonstration was just then facing you. They had come from the other way. So really the police should have had their backs to you.'

'And that's how it was with most of them.'

'But not all?'

'Not all, Your Honour.'

A momentary pause. The judge is thinking.

'Were you standing alone, Herr Banz, or were you with others?'

'I was on my own, Your Honour.'

'Were others standing very near you?'

'I couldn't say, Your Honour. Not very near.'

'Why do you think a policeman went up to you when the demonstrators were standing on the other side?'

'I couldn't say, Your Honour. I don't know what made the man walk up to me in particular.'

'So you couldn't say. – You told us earlier, Herr Banz, that the policeman called out to you: "You bastards, get out of the road!" What made him say "bastards"?'

'I can't say why the man referred to us as bastards, Your Honour.'

'No, no, I mean, you were standing on your own. Why did he say "bastards"? He should just have said "bastard".'

'I don't know why he said it, Your Honour. It's just what he said.'

'So you can't think why he said it?'

'No, I can't, Your Honour. But he said it all right.'

Again the judge stops for thought.

'What did the policeman look like who shouted those words to you?' he asks finally.

Banz reflects. 'He was a little guy. Scrawny little guy . . . There wasn't much of him.'

'But you'd recognize him again, wouldn't you?'

'I couldn't say, Your Honour. My memory's not what it used to be.'

The judge thinks again. Then he goes back behind the table and says a few words to his deputy, Bierla. Bierla leaves the court.

Banz watches him go nervously.

The judge asks him: 'You had a stick with you, did you not, Herr Banz?'

'Yes, I had a walking stick.'

'Could it be that you threatened anyone with your walking stick?'

'Your Honour, please! As if!'

'Or perhaps you just gripped it a little more tightly. You must have been tense –'

The door of the hall opens. Led by Deputy Bierla, some twenty policemen walk into the room. They stand in two rows flanking the judge's table.

'I would like,' explains the judge, 'to clear up the present case of Banz, which strikes me as somewhat mysterious, and of obvious relevance to the assessment of the police action. As quickly as possible. These are the Altholm constables who are due to appear as witnesses this afternoon. If Herr Banz doesn't find his man among those present, then we'll summon the others tomorrow. – Usher, light please.'

Suddenly the gym hall is radiantly bright. With white face, propped on his stick, Banz stands in front of the two rows of policemen. Once he glances quickly round behind him, but not to his defence counsel, rather to that corner where Councillor Röstel is sitting all alone, seeing as Chief Adviser Meier isn't back from Stolpe yet.

The judge comes out from behind his table again.

'Now, Herr Banz, let's walk along the row together. Look at each gentleman in turn. The one you're looking for may not be among them at all. Not all the police are here present. I will exchange a few words with each of them, so that you hear their voices as well –'

'Your Honour, I've seen them all, you can send them away, my one isn't present.'

'Your Honour!' shouts the giant Soldin from the second row. 'Your Honour! That's him! That's the man who knocked me down with the handle of his stick. Stop . . .!'

The judge has been sent tumbling into the row of policemen. Banz has leaped back, and is running towards the table where Councillor Röstel is. The councillor steps out to meet him, but gets a blow from Banz's stick. Behind the table is a door that leads to the schoolyard. Banz tears it open, crosses the yard, into the school building (there are militiamen at the front gate) . . . The whole room is in confusion, all are pressing towards the doors, witnesses rush away. The prosecutor yells: 'The defendant! Constables, keep an eye on the defendant!'

There is pandemonium.

VII

For one moment, Banz stands on the wide school stairs, catching his breath back. The steps look tempting, but Banz knows that's a trap. In ten or fifteen seconds, they'll be combing the building for him.

A little set of steps to the side leads down into the basement, and Banz runs down them. They end at an iron door, open, luckily. And still better, with the key in the lock. Banz takes it out, goes through the door into the dark basement, and locks it from the inside.

He leaves the key in the lock.

The dark passage leads straight on, with many doors off to either side. Banz walks straight along, towards a core of warmth he can feel ahead of him. Then he finds himself standing in the boiler room. Under both large boilers there is fire. The water hums. Of course, they're already heating, to keep the gym warm. Next door is the coal cellar, and on the other side planked off from the wood store is a sort of closet with a chopping block and an axe hanging on the wall.

And not just that. Here are washbasins, jug and soap, a piece of mirror is up on the wall, and from a hook hang the blue overalls of the heating man, begrimed with coal dust.

Banz takes off his jacket and waistcoat, he pulls the baggy blue ones over his own, and puts on the jacket. Then he goes through his pockets, puts everything in them bar watch, penknife and money with the clothes, and bundles them up.

Ideally he would consign it to the flames, but he's upset about the jacket, which is almost new.

So he stuffs the whole thing down the back of the coals. Maybe he'll be back here one day, or else someone will find it who can use it. There's no need to go far for dirt in a coal cellar, so Banz rubs his face and hands, takes another look at himself in the mirror, grabs a coal scuttle, and cautiously opens the window.

It's all below pavement level, at the top of the light-vent is a grille that isn't secured.

The hardest thing is to climb on to the pavement without being noticed. Once he's out, he's three parts safe.

But getting out discreetly seems impossible. Feet tramp almost incessantly overhead. Banz gets bored waiting, so he walks back down the pasage – he can hear them working on the iron door – looks inside the various side rooms, and eventually finds the bicycle cellar.

Here he has what he wants: a door that leads out, a set of steps up into a little patch of grass and flowers, and best of all: a solitary bicycle. It must be the janitor's.

Banz leaves the coal scuttle, but takes the bicycle, quickly unlocks the door, pushes it up the incline to the street, and as soon as he's on the pavement, he hops on to the saddle.

There are enough people running around, Banz sees militiamen and constables wherever he looks, but they must all be struck with blindness. They have a vision of Banz as he stood before the judge's table, and don't even see this blue-clad collier.

In short order, Banz is on the Stolpe Road. He knows that he can't use his disguise and bicycle much longer. They'll soon notice there's some gear missing, and in another fifteen minutes all the rural cops for miles around will know, and they'll send cars and motorbikes to hunt him. He can't cycle much more anyway, his flight from the hall took it out of him, his whole sick body is packing up, he has moments where he feels so dizzy he can hardly keep hold of the handlebars. Five minutes later he parks the bike behind a bush and sits down next to it. He's only a little way out of Altholm, just after Grünhof, but he can't go on. Let the bastards catch him! He'll take his knife and make an end, big deal.

He drops off behind the bush.

Not much later, and he comes to, chilled from lying on the ground. But he feels stronger, no longer thinking in terms of quitting. He thinks what farmers he knows hereabouts, but the only one who comes to mind is Cousin Benthin. It's very doubtful whether he'd do anything to help, he's really just a big girl's blouse. Anyway, it would mean turning back to Altholm, and he doesn't think he could face that.

The street he can see through the sparse foliage is far from busy. It might be four in the afternoon, give or take. He's been on the run for just an hour and a half. They won't be looking for him here, they'll be at the station in Stolpermünde, or waiting for him at his farm. Well, let them wait!

A lorry trundles past doing an even forty. Packed to the gills with empty fish crates. It's one of the lorries that ply from the herring fishing communities on the coast to Stettin.

Perhaps the Stolpermünde lorry will be along some time?

It's the time the lorries are coming back from the fish market. Banz lets a whole string of them go by, because he doesn't know the drivers. Then he realizes he's been an idiot because for him a driver he doesn't know is better than one he does.

Banz thoughtfully pricks his back tyre with his knife, the air whistles when he pulls it out. Then he stands by the side of the road with his bike.

When the next fish lorry comes by, he waves energetically, and when the driver shows no sign of slowing down – they all want to be home by six – he steps out into the middle of the road. The man brakes so hard that the lorry veers sharply towards the verge, and the whole pile of crates lurches.

The driver, a man in his thirties, starts swearing at him: 'You silly bugger, what do you think you're playing at! If you finished up under my wheels, that'd be no more than you deserve!'

'You can give me a lift to Stolpe,' says Banz calmly. 'As you can see, I've got a flat.'

'What do I care about your goddamn tyres?' the man curses. 'You can walk, so far as I'm concerned.'

'There's five marks in it for you!' says Banz, still careful to stand directly in front of the truck.

'I've had offers like that before,' the man curses. 'We get to Stolpe, and you turn your pockets out: Sorry, mate, got no money.'

'Here,' says Banz, holding up a silver fiver. And he explains: 'You see, my little boy's got shingles, and I have to go see the wise women.'

The man growls to himself. 'Where're we going to put your mount? You can see I'm full up.'

'Throw it on top.'

'You do it. And give us the fiver.'

'Only if I can sit in front.'

'What is it with you?' says the driver, once the lorry is clattering along the road. 'Do you really believe in those women? I thought it was only silly farmers do that.'

'It's not faith,' says Banz. 'I've seen it happen with my own eyes.'

'Funny,' says the driver. 'I've never seen anything like that. It must take care to avoid me.'

'They once blew away my shingles,' says Banz. 'They sit at your bedside, there has to be three of them present, and they take turns blowing in your face.'

'I almost wouldn't mind shingles, just to have it happen to me!'

'I wouldn't say that if I were you.'

'And what are you doing, you going to fetch them home?'

'No, I'm not. That would be much too expensive. I'm going to give them a photo of my little lad, for them to blow on this evening, and tomorrow the shingles will be gone.'

'You could have mailed it, couldn't you? Saved yourself five marks.'

'Yes, and have them only blow for half an hour. No, I'm going to sit there and time them. They have to do it for two hours, or else the shingles will be back.'

'Country living, eh,' remarks the driver. 'I'm from Stettin myself. They don't know about rubbish like that there.'

'No. You've got a health system. At least you know who's killing you.'

'You're right,' says the driver appreciatively. 'Those panel doctors are no good. I had a swollen hand once . . .'

And in half an hour they're in Stolpe.

'Where d'you want me to drop you?' asks the driver.

'Which way are you going? Out to Fiddichow? Then you can drop me in Horst. Those women live in Horst.'

'All right then.'

In Horst, Banz clambers out of the lorry. 'If you want, we could have a drink together?'

'No, thanks. You've had enough expenditure.'

And the lorry disappears.

Banz has a three-hour walk ahead of him from Horst to Stolpermünde-Abbau. But he's not thinking of going straight to the farm, he just wants to get his money out of its hiding place under the pines. Then he'll go on, either across to Denmark or along into Holstein. The farmers' movement there is said to be pretty active. He certainly won't let them nab him.

He walks easily into the evening. He pushes his bicycle for quite some way, then he realizes it's no good to him any more and he chucks it in a ditch. But in the next beech copse he finds a suitable sapling, a couple of inches around, and cuts it. Now he has a stick again, and walking is easier.

He's been walking off the road for a long time already, sticking to the edges of fields and footpaths, sometimes going for a quarter of an hour at a time over glebe land. But the direction is right, and even when there's a night sky you can sense which way the sea is. By the time Banz first hears the sound of the waves, it's already quite dark. He's not quite sure where he is, but he senses that he needs to bear left. This is where the heathland abuts on the strip of coastal pine trees, and he keeps walking along the edge of the wood. He often stumbles over roots and stones as he gropes his way forward, and his fury at the Altholmers surges up in him again. It's their fault, their doing, that he has to tap around out here like a mole.

Suddenly he sees a light behind a corner of the wood, and it's his house. He's been stumbling across his own potato patch for the past fifteen minutes and not known it.

The light must have some significance. Either the cops are there, or his wife has left it on as a sign to him that she's ready. Why else would a light be on at this hour? But he has no plan to go inside, maybe he will later on. Because he's hungry.

Slowly he pushes into the pines. He walks very cautiously, careful not to snap a single twig. They can surely imagine that he won't go barging into his own house, they must have set up spies in every corner of the woods.

He takes a hundred paces. And another hundred. And a third. Then he stops and listens out.

Something is wrong somewhere, he can sense that. Something is cracking, rootling, snuffling.

He has another twenty paces, perhaps twenty-two, to the hiding place.

He stands and twists off one of his boots, and then the other. He knots the laces together and hangs the boots over his shoulder.

Now he walks on quietly, step by step, holding his breath. It's dark, yes, but the trees are still darker than the air between them. The pine-needle-covered ground is blacker still, but it has grey-white patches, where the rabbits have scuffed yellow sand out of their burrows.

He stands by a tree and looks. He knows the tree he is leaning against.

It's four steps to the hiding place.

The ground is dark, but there, where the hiding place is, is a big patch of turned-over sand. He knows that.

And this patch – standing there still, he can see it – is sometimes there, and sometimes not. Something bulky and black is moving across it. Cracking, grubbing, snuffling, rootling.

Like a bolt of lightning it comes to him: the police have already called. So they know for a fact that he won't be back, and so that bastard Franz, the first opportunity he has, he hasn't even fed the cattle first, has come to steal . . . and root up . . .

The night isn't so black. A whole fireworks display rattles off in front of him, everything is whirling and dancing, and at intervals there is the night sky again, before it is cloven by a blinding light . . .

Ah, ah . . .

For a moment it's better. He's upright, and the dizziness slowly leaves his brain, and the trunk comes to rest behind his shoulder.

But then the thoughts are boring into his skull again, like ants swarming in the grey matter, and he sees Franz, the cunt-struck punter, snaring the girls with his father's money, he sees the plump featherbeds and the plump, white limbs. He's banging away, and his old man gets nabbed and hauled off to chokey, because the son is a lecher.

There's the red mist again, it lights a forest fire, cuts with knives, and drills with awls.

Banz leans right back. In his hand he is carrying a stout, strong stick, a length of beech.

Ah, ah . . .

He takes two or three strides. Long, swift strides. The toad squatting on the ground spins round. But there is the blow, dealt with the length of the whole stick, and the lever of the arm. And now listen to the gurgling scream: 'Wooaahh!'

And then Banz has to sit himself down again. He hunkers on the ground beside his victim, and beside himself.

VIII

It's still night. A cool night, without stars, moonless. Near by, a light breeze in the pines and over his left shoulder the endless surge of the waves. There must be low rain clouds in the sky, he can feel the pressure.

Banz is back, and he knows what's happened as well

But it ll be a lesson for Franz not to sneak his father's money for the maids, he'll not try that again.

He's been lying there long enough now.

The farmer puts out his hand in an arc until it encounters cloth, he crouches down very close to the fellow.

His fingers, like clever, inquiring beasts, travel along the cloth. They encounter flesh, a hand.

And they leap back: the hand is cold and stiff.

With a bound, the farmer is crouched over the man. Is he dead? It was only a little blow with a stick. A man's skull can survive much worse blows!

But when he holds the hands in his, he knows two things: he is dead, irrevocably dead. And: he's not Franz either. This is a soft, long hand, and Franz has stubby, rough paws. This – it dawns on him – is the true owner of the money.

The farmer moves his head from side to side. He is sitting next to someone he has never seen, whom he has killed. It gets worse.

'There's some that have no luck in this life,' says Banz. But he means himself.

Half an hour later, he sees his wife, who is circling the house at a distance.

'Are they still there?' he asks.

'Gone for two hours now.'

'Really gone?'

'Franz crept after them for a whole hour.'

'Franz! – How many of them were there?'

'Four.'

'And all four have left?'

'All four.'

'Are the children sleeping?'

'All sleeping.'

'Bring food, drink, clothes and underclothes, my hat and coat and . . .' – he hesitates – 'a stick. Plus a pickaxe and shovel. A lantern.'

'Don't you want to go inside and eat?'

'No, I won't go in the house again.'

'Banz!'

'Get a move on, before it gets light.'

He stands and waits. The poplars he hears were planted by his father. The wind is coming from the direction of the farm, there's a smell of manure. This winter he was going to build a manure pit, so that the rain didn't keep washing away the precious nitrates. Won't happen now. The fence needs a couple of new posts, and he wouldn't have minded planting one or two more trees in the orchard. Won't happen.

He picks up some of the stuff, and they walk off into the woods. Don't speak.

Only when they're under the trees does he tell her: 'Don't be scared. There's a body.'

'A body?'

'I beat his brains out. Didn't mean to. He was over the money.'

'Who is it?'

'I don't know. I'll take a look with the stable lantern.'

'Why did you do it?'

'He was over the money. I thought it was Franz. I was angry.'

'Ah,' she says. 'Ah. You've been angry for thirty years. For forty years.'

'I know,' he says.

They walk in silence a ways. Then she asks: 'Where will you go?'

'I don't know. Have to think about it.'

'What will become of the farm?'

'The farm is yours!' he says furiously. 'Yours and yours alone. Chase the kids away when you've had enough of them. It's yours. We planted it.' More quietly: 'Perhaps I'll have you come later.' He stops, and drops his load.

'All right,' he says. 'No further. You get some tree branches and rocks together. He's got to go deep into the earth, on account of the rabbits. Then I'll pack the branches and stones on top.'

He checks to see her start looking. Then he lights the lantern, takes the pickaxe and shovel, and sets to work.

An hour later, it's all done. He sits with her at the edge of the wood, and eats.

Silence. Once, he asks: 'Do you want any of the money?'

'No,' she says. 'Not.'

A while later: 'You ought to get the Jersey cow bred. She'll not give milk until the springtime.'

'All right,' she says. 'I will.'

A while later, she quietly asks: 'Who was he?'

And he, quieter still: 'I don't know. A youngish fellow.'

'God,' she says.

'You'll have to clean the pickaxe and shovel so that it doesn't show that they've been used of late. And go out more often than you usually do, and check there's no animals turning up the ground.'

'Yes,' she says.

He stands up. 'I'd best be going.'

She stands in front of him.

He says it again: 'I'd best be going.'

She says nothing.

He turns slowly and walks off in the direction of the sea. Suddenly she cries as loud as she can: 'Banz! Oh Banz!'

He turns to look. Five paces away.

In the dark she sees him slowly, thoughtfully, nod. 'Yes,' he says sadly. 'Yes.' And then after a while: 'That's the way of it. Yes.'

He continues to walk towards the sea.

IX

At a quarter past ten that night, there is a knock on the Tredups' door.

Frau Tredup has been writing the letter to her sister, and glances up at the clock. Max has been quick.

But then it's not Max, it's Stuff standing outside. 'Is your husband home, Frau Tredup?'

'No, Herr Stuff, but he ought to be back any moment.'

'Do you mind if I wait for him here?'

'Come on in, if it's not too messy for you.'

Stuff sits down a little awkwardly, looks at his cigar, looks at the sleeping children, and puts his cigar away.

'Smoke if you like, Herr Stuff. The children are used to it. My husband smokes too.'

'No, no, I'd better not. – How is your husband?'

'Well, he was a bit depressed first, but since we took the decision to move away, he's cheered up.'

'Are you moving away?' Stuff jumps. 'Surely not on account of Gareis? I tell you, Frau Tredup, your husband will come up smelling of roses. Tomorrow the entire press desk will present a protest letter against the low attack from Gareis. Everyone signed it,' says Stuff, and grins. 'Only the *Volkszeitung* refused to join in. And of course the *News*.'

'That's nice of you, Herr Stuff, very nice. And Max will certainly feel better for it. But it's too late. Herr Gebhardt sacked Max on the spot.'

'But that can't be! That's outrageous. Tredup doesn't have to stand for that. Sacked? With no severance?'

'No severance pay.'

'You must protest, Frau Tredup. Shout it from the rooftops!'

'No, we're not going to protest, Herr Stuff. And in actual fact, I'm quite glad it's happened this way.'

'Great! That too!'

'It means Max leaving Altholm. The place didn't agree with him, Herr Stuff.'

'Well, Frau Tredup, I think you have a point there. If you hang around with pigs too much, you end up becoming one yourself.'

'God, Herr Stuff, it's a different matter with you. You're a grown man. It doesn't matter if you do something like that from time to time. But Max is just a boy, and he gets himself soiled from top to toe once he starts playing with dirt.'

'You're a good woman,' says Stuff approvingly. 'You're the salt of the earth.'

'Well, that's as may be, Herr Stuff. But who knows what you'll say tomorrow.'

'Same thing.'

'It's after half past, he ought to be here any minute.'

'Where is he anyway, so late?'

'He went to Stolpe.'

'To Stolpe? At dead of night?'

'And beyond. I'll tell you where he went, Herr Stuff: he's gone to get the money.'

'The money?'

'Yes, the money.'

'Where has he got it?'

'As if I knew. He said something about Stolpermünde.'

'In the dunes, eh? Not bad.'

After a while: 'Sorry for speaking out of turn, Frau Tredup, but if I was you, I think I would have gone with him.'

'Why should I have gone with him?'

'Well, if he got the push this afternoon. You know how impulsive he is.'

'No, he was fine when he went this afternoon.'

'Until he runs into someone who has a go at him, and he won't dare show his face here.'

'Oh, Herr Stuff!'

'I'm a hopeless ass,' says Stuff slowly. 'An idiot. Of course everything I said was nonsense.'

'He really ought to be here by now. It's a quarter to eleven.'

'Perhaps he missed the train. It's pitch black outside. Perhaps he's got to look for it somewhere.'

The woman pleads: 'Wait a while longer, won't you?'

'Happily, Frau Tredup. I'm not missing anything.'

'Shall I get you a beer? You're used to it of an evening, Herr Stuff.'

'No thanks. No beer. I'm getting too fat as it is.'

'There's a train just before one o'clock. We could perhaps meet it at the station?'

'No thanks. Don't be upset with me. I'm not leaving here. I have a feeling I ought to wait for him here.'

'Then of course we'll wait for him here.'

At half past one.

'It looks like he didn't come with that train either. Why don't you go home now, Herr Stuff?'

'And you?'

'I'll wait.'

'Then I'll keep you company. The milk train is at ten past six.'

'But you need to sleep, Herr Stuff.'

'I'll be fine on your sofa. You go to bed.'

'Herr Stuff!'

Uncompromisingly: 'I'm keeping you company.'

At three, the oil lamp goes out after a brief flicker. Frau Tredup puts it outside, and looks at Stuff, snoring on the sofa.

And she sits down again to wait.

At half past six, Stuff yawns and stretches.

In sudden alarm: 'My God, half past six? Has he not come yet?'

The woman: 'No, he hasn't. And I know he won't come now. He's taken the money and left us. It's what he always wanted.'

'No, Frau Tredup. I think he'll have spent the night in Stolpe. He'll be along in the course of the morning.'

'No,' says the woman. 'He's not coming any more. He's left us.'

'You mustn't think that. As soon as the trial is over for today, I'll go to Stolpe and Stolpermünde and make inquiries. – But by then he'll be back.'

'He's not coming back,' says the woman.

4

Gareis's Head on the Block

I

On the 4th of October it rains. It's a proper autumn day. The wind tugs at the trees, chases sodden leaves through the streets, and chucks rain at the windows. Gareis stands at the window, hands crossed behind his back, and looks out.

He is nibbling at his lower lip.

His outer office is full, but he doesn't want to see anyone. What are they all after? A job, a grant, an order, somewhere to live.

Three hundred and sixty-four days a year he runs around fulfilling innumerable personal requests, steering a course that will keep the ship going forward, that will benefit the town.

Today he doesn't feel like it.

He's waiting for a call from Berlin. He's waiting for Pinkus. He's waiting for Stein. The call doesn't come. Pinkus doesn't come. Even Stein is taking his time.

The trial is already in its fourth day. They're laying into the police from morning till night. The police are pretty hacked off about it. Poor, noble peasants, poor, noble townspeople, wicked, wicked police . . .

What's it for? What's the point? Where will it get anyone?

If they were going to shut the police down, or prove the police are deleterious, are unnecessary, that would be some point. But this?

Gareis stands in front of his desk. 'Widow Holm's petition for half a ton of coal briquets.'

People are cold.

'Petition from the invalid Mengs to the Welfare Department for two hundredweight of potatoes.'

They are hungry.

They want a gas lamp. Space on the municipal noticeboard is up for lease. Funds need to be secured for the completion of the new hospital. A bus line to Stolpe has to be put out to tender. Post or rail contracts secured for Meckerle's factory otherwise facing bankruptcy (with three hundred and fifty jobs).

There were things to do, things to buy. The town needed looking after.

And there they were sequestered together, three hundred souls, for nine hours a day in the gym hall, threshing straw. They would move their tongues in their mouths until something was brought about that no amount of labour could uncreate in ten years.

The mayor pushes the bell, one, two, three times.

Piekbusch appears.

'Tell me, Piekbusch, is something the matter? You've looked so puffy these past days.'

'Puffy, Your Worship?'

'A bit like a window that can't be opened. – This wouldn't be a case for fleas, would it?'

'Fleas, sir?'

'To put in your ear, man.'

'Not me, Your Worship!'

Gareis looks long at his secretary.

Who is equal to it.

'So: no fleas here,' Gareis says grumpily. 'Where's Stein?'

'He's probably still in court.'

'Can you call him? I want him. Right away.'

'Yes, Your Worship.'

'Hold on! – What's keeping the call from Berlin?'

'I've given them a gee-up twice already.'

'What's keeping it, I asked you?'

The secretary shrugs.

'Stop! Why do you keep running away from me, Piekbusch? – Why is Pinkus not here?'

The secretary hesitates.

'Well? Out with it!'

'Pinkus is in court.'

'Why doesn't he come when I send for him?'

'Pinkus says to say he has no time.'

It comes out sounding rather graceless, and this time the secretary avoids the eye of his boss.

Who whistles. A long-drawn-out whistle.

'Well, well, well! So old Pinkus has no time for us.'

Very quickly: 'Wait, stay where you are, Piekbusch. Stay where you are. Don't move!'

The mayor goes to the phone, his eyes on his secretary.

He picks up: 'Is that the Central Exchange? – This is Mayor Gareis. – Give me long distance.'

Piekbusch says: 'Your Worship –'

'You shut your trap! And stay where you are! I'll teach the pack of you –

'Long distance? – Supervision, please! – Yes, Supervision. – Ah, excuse me, Fräulein, my secretary asked for an urgent call to Berlin thirty or even forty minutes ago, to the Prussian Ministry of the Interior. – Why has the call not been put through? – Yes, please check, I'll wait . . .'

Threateningly into the corner: 'You keep very quiet, Piekbusch! If you kick up, I'll throw the phone book at you!'

'Your Worship, I –'

'Silence –!

'Yes, Fräulein? – No record of a call? Not possible! There must be a mistake on your end. – No mistake? One moment, Piekbusch, she says there is no mistake . . .?'

'Your Worship, may I –?'

'Nincompoop! – Very good, Fräulein, the fault is ours. My secretary has bodged it. – Yes, please, if you would. Prussian Ministry of the Interior. And, Fräulein, urgent. – Yes indeed. Urgent. To me, Mayor Gareis, in person. Thank you.'

He puts the receiver back. Stretches.

Slowly and massively he walks, menacing elephant, towards the pallid Piekbusch, crouching there in the corner.

'Your Worship,' he begins, oddly fluently, eloquent with fear: 'You will not hit me, you will not threaten me, Mayor. You know very well what Party discipline is. I couldn't. I was ordered to.'

'You were ordered! Who ordered you?'

'You know I have said more to you than I am allowed to. When you're gone, it won't be easy for me to get a job, and I don't want to be unemployed.'

'When I'm gone, eh – is it come to that? You're mistaken, Piekbusch, you're all mistaken. Just tell me one thing, Piekbusch . . .' The Mayor ponders. 'Those secret orders, was that on instruction from the Party as well?'

He looks narrowly at his secretary.

'No, Your Worship, as I live and breathe! They're just lost. I don't know anything about them. Let me be struck down on the spot, Mayor, if –'

The telephone rings.

The mayor says gently: 'Piekbusch, go and get Stein for me right away. And, please, do it. Otherwise I'll break every bone in your body.'

The telephone rings madly. The mayor picks up the receiver. Piekbusch goes.

II

The slight figure of Political Adviser Stein slips in through the side door of Gareis's office.

Gareis comes smiling to meet him. 'Well, Steinlein? You trust yourself to come, in spite of all the interdictions?'

'Interdictions?'

'Don't pretend with me. I know what's going on. And you're not worried what the Party will do?'

'What do you mean?'

'Do you really not know? Were you frozen out of the plot? Are you such a hopeless case? – Maybe you are. The Party seems to have imposed a kind of ban on me, censored me, blackballed me, call it what you will. No one is permitted to deal with me any longer.'

'Surely not! Mayor, that's not possible –'

'Everything is possible, if you're unsuccessful. – But I'm not yet – unsuccessful. – Were you over there?'

'Yes.'

'Is Chief Adviser Meier back?'

'As of this morning he's been seated at his little chair again.'

'And . . .?'

'Nothing. He didn't want to say anything. He said he didn't know anything. The government decision has been conveyed to the judge in a sealed envelope.'

'That's so Stolpe! That's Temborius all over! Secretive to the last. Well, I can tell you what's in the sealed envelope –'

'Really?'

'No comment.'

'Really, Mayor? That would make me so happy!'

'I am happy. If the business with the secret orders was a trap, then it snapped shut before I got anywhere near it. They're the mugs now.'

'Are you really sure?'

'I've just spoken to Berlin. The minister wasn't in yet. But Government Councillor Schuster told me the decision had been taken: thus far and no further. They are displeased with the progress of the trial. Berlin doesn't want the police to be in the soup. They want the whole peasant business cleared up. The secret orders will remain just that.'

'But Schuster's supposed to be a friend of Temborius?'

'Precisely! I always said Temborius would be against it. So: no evidence!'

'Thank God! What would you have done . . .?'

'Mneh,' says the mayor, beaming, 'I would have wriggled out of it one way or another, but this is ideal.'

'This is ideal. But then I don't understand why the Party –'

'They're barking up the wrong tree. The courtroom atmosphere has got to them. Bloodthirsty police. Whetted sabres. The bloodhound Frerksen. – No good Party heart is equal to that.'

'You mentioned Frerksen. He turned up again today.'

'I'm no longer interested in Frerksen.'

'He asked for a chance to explain himself. He turned up with about seventeen by-laws in his hand. He justified the confiscation of the flag, the attack on the demonstration. Police by-laws from year such-and-such: One: Carrying naked scythes through the town is forbidden. Two: No sticks are permitted at demonstrations. Three: The procession organizers have failed to register the demonstration properly. Four: The procession used more than half the roadway, which is unlawful. Five to seventeen: Similar transgressions.'

'Was it very effective?'

'Absolutely – for Streiter. He asked him: "At the moment you had the flag seized, Commander, were you aware of all these by-laws?"'

'And Frerksen: "Not explicitly."'

'Streiter: "But their gist?"'

'"Yes, most of them. More or less."'

'Then Streiter: "In view of your phenomenal memory for detail, I am surprised that you, Commander, had forgotten the important stipulation that demonstrations are to be protected by the police under all circumstances."'

'Frerksen was floored.'

'I can imagine. Do you have any sense of whose catspaw he is at the moment?'

The adviser reflects. He purses his lips, whistles a snatch of something. Stops. Then: 'Irritating. The song has two verses, one about the lowlands, the other about the highlands.'

He looks expectantly at his boss.

'You mean to say?' he asks in surprise.

'Well, the highlands must get their act together sometime. But –'

The telephone rings. Gareis picks it up, listens.

'Well, Adviser, I'm being asked to appear. Will you come?'

And, when they are out on the street: 'It would be a strange sort of botched feeling if I didn't know how come and why. If I go through with my testimony, step on a few toes, and then plonk myself between Meier and Röstel, and listen to the rest of it. Even if it takes another month, my brain still craves new proof that people really are that stupid.'

'Thank God you telephoned Berlin!'

'You can say that again: thank God!'

III

At the door of the court, Gareis and Stein part. Stein slips into the public gallery, while Gareis is kept waiting. Another witness is just being questioned. Stein listens, slightly bored. It's always the same story: don't they ever tire of it all!

Then the judge announces: 'We will now conclude the questioning of Mayor Gareis,' and all heads turn alertly towards the door.

The usher standing in the corridor is heard to call the name, and Gareis appears. For a brief moment he stops on the threshold and surveys the court.

There he is. Mayor Gareis, police boss of Altholm, and also head of department for Welfare, Housing, and Town Development. A big man. He strides slowly and with dignity to the judge's table, stops directly in front of the judge, and inclines his head to him. A greeting from a potentate, polite, warm, but still seeming to say: You know, I'm not really that happy with the way you've conducted this case.

The gallery (with Stein) sees him from behind. A vast black back topped off with a massive well-shaped head. His left profile has been offered to the defendants, the defence and the government table, his right to the prosecution and the press.

The judge returns the greeting with head and hand. Then he speaks a few sincere words: 'We are sorry, Your Worship, to have kept you away from these proceedings for so long, when, as Commissioner of Police, you would surely like to have attended. But the decision from Stolpe on the matter of your permission to speak has only reached the court this morning. At ten o'clock this morning, to be precise. I had you called straight away.'

Gareis inclines his head and waits in impeccable calm.

'You were sworn in, Mayor, on the occasion of your first questioning here. Your oath holds still.

'The issue of the degree of your freedom to speak arose from several questions put to you by the defence. On the morning of the demonstration, you were served with some secret orders by the district president, only to be opened as and when you made use of the militia.

'You made use of the militia, you opened the orders –'

'Had them opened, in point of fact.'

Pause, smile: 'What did these secret orders contain?'

Gareis says slowly: 'I beg your pardon?!'

'Yes. The government's decision. You are given full permission to give evidence. On any matter put to you. Including the secret orders. Absolutely.'

For the first time, Stein sees his lord and master lose his composure. The mayor stands there, he looks this way and that, he shifts from one foot to the other. Finally, in a quiet and strangely confused-sounding voice, he says: 'I don't understand. The government . . . No, there must be some mistake . . . Would you mind . . .?'

The expressions of those faces raised to him become tense, pinched, impatient. The defence counsel, leaning back in his seat a moment ago, has got to his feet and is coming silently closer, a step at a time. The two prosecution lawyers have put their heads together and are whispering animatedly. In the gallery you could have heard a pin drop.

'By all means . . .' says the judge, and passes the letter to the mayor. 'See for yourself . . . The decision of the government . . .'

Gareis reaches for it quickly, and then reads it painfully slowly and for a painfully long time.

He lowers his hand.

With slightly firmer voice, he says: 'As I supposed. There must be an error. This morning I heard from the minister that I may not give evidence on the matter. Now I really don't know . . .'

The judge: 'But here it is in writing, Your Honour . . .?'

The judge looks towards the government's table, where Chief Adviser Meier slowly and reluctantly gets to his feet, slowly approaches . . .

Meanwhile, the defence counsel, now standing right next to the witness, says: 'I beg the court to set aside the concerns of the witness. We have here a clear, unambiguous determination from the government in Stolpe. The witness works for the Stolpe government, they are his legal superiors. Their decision is absolute.'

The judge says: 'Perhaps Chief Adviser Meier, who brought the permission from Stolpe, could tell us something about the process by which it was arrived at?'

The defence demurs: 'In terms of the juridical process, the permission is completely . . .'

'But if the adviser is in a position to enlighten us . . .'

The adviser: 'I don't know who in the ministry will have given Mayor Gareis the minister's decision. I may say that the permission to speak was not issued without detailed consultations with the minister.'

'The minister wishes the evidence to be brought forth freely.'

All step back a little, Gareis stands alone.

The judge says: 'And who was it who gave you the decision, Mayor? Would you be able to say?'

The mayor murmurs: 'It was given me over the telephone.'

'On the minister's express say-so?'

'No, not exactly.'

The judge: 'Well, Your Honour, then things look pretty clear to me. The government's decision permits of no other interpretation. I must ask you to set aside your doubts and give evidence.'

The mayor stands there full of tormenting unease. He looks across to the door a couple of times. The defence counsel remarks ironically: 'Mayor Gareis has made us extraordinarily curious about these secret orders. Such unwonted hesitation on his part –'

And Gareis, in a sudden fury: 'Councillor Streiter is perhaps in a better position to know the reasons for my hesitation than anyone else in this room.'

To which the counsel: 'If you mean by these words to insinuate that I know the contents of the secret orders, then I reject that.'

The judge takes a hand: 'Gentlemen, please! – Herr Mayor, if you would be so kind as to carry on with your evidence, you had the secret orders opened . . .?'

'Yes,' says the mayor absent-mindedly. 'Yes.'

He is standing quite alone. The others have stepped away from him. The light dribbling through the windows is grey; the mob of onlookers recedes into the grey distance at the back of the hall.

The great figure of the witness, troubled just a moment ago, composes itself. 'Yes,' says Gareis once more.

He turns towards the gallery, he is looking for a face. His eye meets Stein's, the two look at each other. The mayor raises his hand.

Then he turns to the judge. His voice is clear, his speech uninhibited, as he says: 'I was in my flat, busy with preparations for my holiday. The telephone rang. A man who addressed me as "Comrade" told me that there had been bloody clashes between the farmers and the police. The farmers were rampaging through town, armed with pistols. First I called the town hall guardroom –'

'One moment, please,' says the judge. 'Who called you?'

'I don't know. I tried to establish the identity right away. I was told by someone at the post office that a worker in blue working clothes had called. This worker proved impossible to trace.'

'And that was the first report you had of any clashes?'

'That's right.'

'A somewhat exaggerated report, it would appear.'

'Very much so.'

'And on the basis of that you took your decisions?'

'Not only that. The town hall guardroom confirmed to me that some clashes had taken place.'

'And you have no suspicion who the mystery caller was?'

'No.'

'What did you do next?'

'After a policeman confirmed to me that there had been some violence, I called my office and told my secretary to have my car pick me up at home. I had already told the telephone switchboard to connect me with the militia commanding officer in Grünhof immediately after the first call. When my secretary had ordered the car, I instructed him to open the secret orders from the government, which were on my desk, and read them out to me over the telephone. My secretary opened the envelope. But then the conversation was accidentally interrupted without him getting a chance to read a word of it to me, and I was put through to the militia in Grünhof. I ordered their officer, Lieutenant Wrede, to have his men advance to the proximity of the auction hall and await further orders from me in person.'

'So, if I understand you correctly, you deployed the militia before you knew the contents of the secret orders?'

'That's right.'

'Then what did you do? Call your secretary back?'

'No. The car was waiting outside, I thought there was a pitched battle being waged, I drove directly to the station, to question Commander Frerksen.'

'So when did you finally clap eyes on the secret orders?'

The mayor says: '*I have never seen the secret orders.*'

'What?!'

A ripple of surprise runs through the gallery.

'I have not seen them to this day.'

'Mayor!'

'Never. Not a line. Not a word.'

'Mayor, I remind you of the oath you have sworn.'

The mayor says curtly: 'No one is more aware of that than I am.'

The judge collects himself, shakes his bell, to silence the murmurs that are becoming louder and more intrusive by the second.

'But then you were at least made acquainted with the contents of the secret orders?'

Gareis says: 'To this day I have not the least idea of what they contain.'

The noise erupts. Almost everyone is standing. The members of the press have forgotten to write. Prosecution and defence counsels are standing next to the witness. Chief Adviser Meier at the government table keeps taking his monocle out, rubbing it clean, and screwing it back in with shaking hands.

The judge calls out: 'I want complete quiet, please. Otherwise I have no option but to have the court cleared. Ushers, militiamen, the gallery must sit down. Gentlemen of the press, your desk is there . . .'

Calm gradually returns.

The judge: 'Your Honour, would you expand a little on your statements? They are so astonishing . . .' His polite voice sounds needling, even surly. 'Perhaps you would suggest witnesses to what you've . . .?'

The mayor has become prefectly calm. 'I drove to the station, and heard reports from the superintendent and commander. Then I went on to the auction hall. Things were pretty wild. I had no more thought of the secret orders. Nor did Lieutenant Wrede remind me of them.

'That day I didn't return to my office. Similarly, over the next few days, there was so much to do that I didn't think of the envelope. By the time I remembered it, it had disappeared. I had people looking for it for weeks, but it didn't turn up. My secretary, Piekbusch, assures me that he returned it to my in tray. It disappeared from my in tray. Perhaps it was mislaid in some file, perhaps it simply – disappeared. I asked my secretary several times, he has read the orders, but is unable to remember a single thing in them. – That's really all I have to say.'

Silence. A long, unhappy silence.

'Mayor,' the judge begins slowly and cautiously. 'You will understand that your remarks today have given rise to a profound – well, let's just say, profound surprise. I must ask you why you didn't tell us what you've just now told us, two days ago. Why take refuge behind that permission-seeking?'

'No one,' the mayor says slowly, 'enjoys confessing to errors of omission or commission. I genuinely believed the government would not favour the making public of its secret orders. That they would save me from publicly admitting my mistake.'

'Effectively,' says the judge, 'you have gambled at the court's time and expense.'

The mayor makes no reply.

'You have,' the judge continues, 'falsely given the impression that these secret orders were of especial importance, and may have contained specific instructions with regard to the peasants.'

'That may yet be the case.'

The judge says sharply: 'That is a conjecture, Herr Mayor. We don't wish to hear conjectures from you, but facts. Among the obligations of your oath are the promises not to pass over anything and not to add anything. The court will have to consider whether you are not in violation of your oath.'

The mayor gently inclines his head.

'For the time being, we're finished with you. But I would like you to keep yourself available for further questioning if called upon.'

'You can get me in my office at any time.'

'That will do.'

The mayor is about to move away when Legal Councillor Streiter says: 'One word, if I may, Your Honour. The witness insinuated that *I* might be apprised of the reason for his unusual reluctance to talk about the secret orders. Would you kindly ask the witness what he meant by those words?'

The judge: 'Your Worship, would you say . . .?'

And Gareis: 'If I said something of the sort, which I don't remember doing, then please put it down to my agitation. I meant nothing by it. It was intended purely as self-defence.'

And the defence counsel, with all the asperity of which he was capable: 'Would Your Honour point out to the witness the quite inadmissible nature of such insinuatory behaviour. I reserve the right to bring charges against the witness.'

Gareis lowers his head.

The prosecuting counsel gets to his feet: 'We too announce that we are considering bringing charges against the witness.'

Silence. Gareis looks for Stein, but when he finds him, he sees his friend has lowered his gaze.

'That will be all for now, Witness,' says the judge.

IV

Mayor Gareis walks out into the hallway.

There are witnesses waiting to be called, a couple of policemen, the cloakroom attendant. All stare at him. Then, with an eagerness that's half concern, the attendant helps him into his coat.

So that's how they'll look at me from here on in in Altholm. Sheepish and eager.

But only a few steps later, he corrects himself: No, only for the first few days. Then they'll become impertinent. Where there's carrion, there are crows.

He heads for the Burstah.

Tredup must have felt a bit like this when I tore him off. Poor wretch. If you have power and can look after yourself, you forget how defenceless a little man can feel when he's being kicked. Poor wretch.

The mayor lengthens his stride. The wind pushes rain into his face. He jams his hat low down on his brow, but when he turns on to the Burstah, he doesn't head for his office, he goes the other way, away from the town hall, up towards the station.

He passes a cigar shop, turns round, and quickly goes in. 'Five Brazilians at twenty pfennigs, please. Yes, they'll do. Some real coffin-nails.'

'"Coffin-nails", very good, Your Worship.' The shopkeeper bows and sniggers.

You won't be laughing at my pleasantries and bowing tomorrow, matey, thinks the Mayor. And, aloud: 'Plus a directory, please!'

He looks up an address and goes on his way. He turns down the Stolpe Road. He stops outside number 72. Eyes the house. The greengrocer in his shop unenthusiastically gives the information that the Tredups live round the back, on the yard side. Gareis makes his way there and knocks on the door.

A voice calls: 'Come in!'

The room he enters is a paupers' room, the one where these people do all their living. Gareis takes it in at a single glance. Everything is here: the kids' toys, the plates, the tub, the sewing machine, fourteen books, a bicycle, a sack of potatoes and the beds.

The woman was lying on one of them, and has got up now and silently eyes the visitor from the door on the opposite side of the room.

Even the mayor is struck by how much the woman has changed

from when he saw her just a couple of months ago: the lank hair falls into the pale, wrinkled face. The lower part of her face is so pronounced, the teeth seem to have lengthened behind the thin bloodless lips.

'You look very pale, Frau Tredup,' he calls. 'Are you all right?'

The woman eyes him.

'Yes,' says the mayor, 'I'd like to talk to your husband, if I can? 'There's something I have to say to him.'

The woman doesn't answer.

The mayor is patient. Then he asks her: 'Is your husband not home?'

The woman still doesn't answer. She stares at him, blankly, unblinkingly.

'It's perfectly natural,' says the mayor, 'for you to be angry with me, Frau Tredup. Your husband will have told you – well, that's why I've come. We are not always in charge of our nervous systems. I was unfair, and I've come to tell you so, in person.'

The woman looks at him expectantly.

'I'll do whatever I can to help him. I heard he lost his job. I'm sorry about that. I'll gladly . . .'

But the woman says nothing.

The mayor is a little discouraged. 'You know, you ought to give me a chance to talk to your husband. If you don't want to forgive me, that's your affair. But maybe your husband . . .'

The woman walks slowly towards him, across the whole breadth of the room. She walks lightly, almost on tiptoe, as though not to disturb something, something sleeping as it might be. She stops in front of the mayor – who looks at her attentively – stops and whispers: 'I'm waiting . . .'

The mayor isn't afraid, but he feels uncomfortable. 'Yes?' he asks.

'He's still not back,' says the woman.

'Did he go somewhere?' the mayor whispers back – it seems to be catching.

'I've been waiting since yesterday evening.'

'And he hasn't come back?'

'No. And he won't come back either.'

The mayor looks at the woman appraisingly. 'How long is it since you've slept, Frau Tredup?' he asks. And when she doesn't say anything, he takes her arm and leads her to the bed.

She follows him unresistingly, her face twisting like that of a child about to cry. He picks her up and lays her down on the bed. He pulls a blanket over her.

'Now, go to sleep, Frau Tredup,' says Gareis. 'He'll be back.'

She moves her lips, as though to contradict him, but she's already asleep.

The mayor watches her for a few moments, then he tiptoes out of the room.

V

Gareis steps out on to the street again. The visit has done nothing to cheer him up. Tredup disappeared – well, people have been known to disappear over such things.

He'll be back, he says to himself.

He'll not be back, says the dull voice of the woman.

The mayor, lost in thought, has followed the Stolpe Road out of town. He crosses the railway line. To the right of him are the large, ugly, smoky hangars of the rail-repair workshops, to his left the equally ugly railwaymen's cottages of the Reichsbahn. Then the fields begin, rain-sodden, neglected fields.

And then the town seems to start again, only it's not Altholm any more, it's Grünhof.

'MENDEL'S INN. TWO INDOOR BOWLING ALLEYS. A BIG SHOOTING RANGE.'

This is where the militia were waiting. Well, well. Hmm. I could always think about something else for a change.

In front of him is the bus stop. A bus has just drawn in, on its way into town. Six or seven people were standing waiting for it, including someone in uniform. But they don't climb aboard; on the contrary, a couple of people get off.

Voices are raised.

Gareis speeds up.

The people are in a heated exchange, the uniform, now inside the bus, answers aggressively and rudely. The mayor recognizes Police Superintendent Kallene.

The bus is about to drive off, accompanied by the abuse of those left behind, when Gareis appears and waves to the driver to stop.

'What's going on here?'

A moment's silence.

Then ten voices shout all at once: 'It's awful, Your Worship!'

'I won't be thrown off the bus.'

'I've paid my fare.'

'Sitting down here himself, what a way to behave.'

'That's the police all over. Of course we've got no flaming rights.'

'All right,' says the mayor. 'What's going on, Superintendent?'

'The bus is licensed to carry twenty passengers. I take a count, and find there are twenty-three on board. I duly put three of them out and gave the driver a ticket.'

'And sat himself down too!'

'Not as though he weighs anything. The police are lighter than air, didn't you know?'

'Don't talk rot, Superintendent! Get off the bus! We'll discuss this. I can't do anything for the rest of you. Twenty is the legal limit, and legal limits can't be exceeded in my presence.'

'That's all right, Mayor,' says a worker. 'I was just angry with the copper for sitting himself down and turfing off the rest of us.'

'On your way, driver,' says Gareis, and walks on.

The incident did him a bit of good. There's always things need doing in this world, he thinks. I'm not completely washed up just yet. Disappear? Pah, not while there's so much work to be done! Wouldn't dream of it. I got a good kicking. It was overdue.

But I was silly too. I earned it, really. Next time I'll take more care.

Poor Tredup, you were never up to much. Always the back roads, the alleyways, never the bright lights. You'd have tripped over anyone's leg, it happened to be mine. Poor wife.

It's raining fairly hard, and the wind doesn't drop the other side of Grünhof. But now the fields are quite presentable, ploughed

and ready for the winter sowing. Some farmers are out ploughing in spite of the rain. Gareis steps out.

VI

In the courtroom, the defence has applied as a matter of urgency
to have the contents of the secret orders made known.

'This matters to us because we see these secret orders as a
link in the chain of exceptional measures undertaken against
the farmers by the government. We already know that, in the
government's view, the Bauernschaft was especially dangerous,
and that Commander Frerksen took a harsh approach to be
official policy. We may have District President Temborius called
as a witness.'

Chief Adviser Meier stares with horror.

'For the time being we ask the government's representative
here present to comment on the secret orders.'

But Meier won't even go up to the judge's table. He waves
away at a distance: 'I am not authorized to appear as a witness.
I have no permission from the government to speak. Besides, I
actually have no idea what may have been in the secret orders.'

The judge says: 'Is that really important to you, Legal Councillor? Given that the secret orders were apparently never even
read.'

'It is exceedingly important to us. It's important as a picture of
the government's attitude. Moreover, it may have been commu-
nicated to the militia by another channel, which might explain
the merciless procedure adopted in the auction hall. We ask that
Lieutenant Wrede be called to the box.'

His appearance is agreed. A militia officer present indicates
that Wrede is in Altholm, and perhaps even in the public gallery.

And lo, Lieutenant Wrede gets to his feet and walks up to the
judge's table.

The judge says, smiling: 'Lieutenant, have you been following
today's proceedings?'

The lieutenant bows.

'So you know that the contents of these secret orders seem to slip away as soon as we think we have them within our grasp. May I ask you before swearing you in whether you know the contents of the orders?'

'Yes, sir.'

'Then I will swear you in. – Yes, Prosecutor?'

'I would like to ask the witness whether he thinks he is allowed to give evidence without the approval of his superiors.'

A ripple of impatience goes through the gallery. The judge folds his hands in a gesture of infinite patience.

The lieutenant rasps back: 'I have no concerns.'

The prosecutor insists: 'Your responsibility, Lieutenant –'

The lieutenant interrupts him decisively: 'No concerns whatever!'

The judge sighs with relief. 'The religious form of words, or . . .?'

'Yes, please.'

The oath is sworn.

'Well, now, Lieutenant, tell us in your own words what you know of these secret orders.'

'Secret orders – that's just words. Military expression. Only signifies that the orders are for police eyes only.

'Of course I don't remember them word for word. The gist was two hundred men to be placed at the disposal of Herr Gareis, further reserves to be made available at a given place and time, and the use to which they were to be put defined.'

'That part interests us the most.'

'Well, they probably said the militia could only be used if the town police were not enough. That in the event of serious fighting, especially the use of firearms, headquarters had to be contacted.'

'And beyond that?'

'Beyond that? Nothing. I think that was the lot.'

The defence counsel gets to his feet. 'A question to the witness, if you please. – Lieutenant, do you recall any stipulation in the order to the effect that the militia should be especially rough or aggressive with the farmers?'

The lieutenant does not disguise his contempt. 'No. Not a sausage.'

'Would the witness give me a precise answer?'

'No, there was nothing like that.'

'You remember that clearly?'

'No possible error.'

'Who issued the orders?'

'I can't say for sure. But I would assume Colonel Senkpiel.'

'In Stolpe?'

'Of course.'

'Perhaps the witness will forgive my ignorance. – Anyway, the defence should like to reserve the calling of Colonel Senkpiel.'

'And with that,' says the judge with smiling certainty, 'we can put these secret orders to bed. – Thank you, Lieutenant.'

VII

It's already dark, it's past eight in the evening, when Gareis next sees the inside of his office.

He remembered at intervals that he had promised to keep himself available for the court, but sod that. A day spent walking cross-country in wind and rain, and his battle-lust has returned, his don't-carishness is with him again.

I've been unlucky, well, my luck will change.

When he stopped at a village inn in the afternoon (in Dülmen), and ordered something to eat, when he saw them gawping at him, and coming to him with their stupid lies, that they didn't have anything, were right out of eggs, ham, potatoes, you name it, then he had pounded on the table with the roar of a bull, reduced the landlord in his corner behind the bar to a quivering jelly, and chased the old woman into the kitchen.

He was served a farm breakfast of prodigious dimensions.

They wouldn't take his money, but there was a collection tin on the counter for shipwreck victims where he threw his obol – including beer, he thought two marks a fair price – and the landlord looked as if shipwrecked men could expect no breakfast from him.

When he left the inn, word of his being there had spread: for a farming village on a rainy day in October, the street was unusually animated. He looked out for a familiar physiognomy, but he had no luck in Dülmen. So he walked through them; where they were clustered thickly he distinctly said, 'And a good day to you' – he looked directly at them, coughing or clearing his throat deafeningly.

Three villages on, or maybe four, he spotted a peasant he recognized. He couldn't remember the name, but he remembered the case very well through which he had come to meet the man.

A sow with her litter of piglets had been awarded a prize at the show in Altholm, and the prize was two hundredweight of lime marl, donated by the factory. But then the factory had made a fuss about the delivery, and Gareis had taken them to court. It was a date to which Stein probably went, at any rate the mayor did not know the outcome.

Now he wobbles up to the farmer, who is standing there with three others.

'Well, cousin, and did the lime marl finally get here?'

'Just the other week,' says the farmer. 'It's a disgrace that it took so long.'

'That's just how the manufacturers are with us too,' says the mayor. 'But we remain the cleverer, because we tricked them.'

'You probably mean you're cleverer. We farmers are on the bad side of any bargain.'

'How so? Is the marl no good?'

'Nothing the matter with the marl, but you Altholm people . . .'

'My dear chap,' says the mayor, 'don't you read the paper . . .?'

'If I've got a moment to spare . . .'

'No moment like the present. So you read the *Bauernschaft*. You're reading about the trial that's in progress. What do you make of it?'

'Well, Mayor, we're the ones who got clobbered and are going to be punished again, while your man Frerksen, who made a pig's breakfast of everything, is going scot-free.'

'Christian! And whatever your other name is –'

'Bruhn,' says the farmer.

'Well, Bruhn, you must have made an idiot of yourself one time or another. Ploughed too wet, or harvested too soon?'

'I have, Mayor.'

'Then you got your smack in the face. The soil all clods, or the rye grown out. Eh?'

'Many's the time, Mayor.'

'And your neighbour here, what's his name? Harms? Harms has done his share of stupid things too –'

'You're certainly right about that.'

'And he's still got his fields to come out lovely, and his rye drier than yours.'

Harms protests: 'No, Mayor, that would be –'

But the others: 'No, he's right. You may celebrate Easter at Whitsun, but by the time Christmas comes around, you're in shape.'

'You see,' says the mayor. 'Sometimes a man has luck with him, and sometimes he doesn't. Frerksen did his ploughing in the wet, and he's on top of the world, and you, you did everything the proper way, and you're in the shit.'

The farmers look at him quietly, their elephant.

'And because you believe in Almighty God – or so you tell your reverend, even though I know you for a bunch of heathens – because you have your God, you comfort yourselves with the idea that He will punish Frerksen and that wicked Babylon of Altholm, on Judgement Day, if not before. But what I don't understand is you selling your eggs and your butter for less, because of the sins of officials and politicians.'

'Mayor,' says a large, glowering farmer. 'I don't think for a second you're on our side. You're a bastard, like every other Red. But you're the kind of bastard we can talk to. If it's worth it to you, come over for a grog one evening, and we'll talk the whole thing over.'

'I'll take you up on that,' says the mayor.

'But don't bring anyone else. Come alone. So long as,' the farmer stops and grins, 'you're not afeared of us.'

'I'm quaking,' says the mayor, and shakes all his flab.

'I'll pass the word round the villages. You can go and take a look yourself, and we can talk about what we stand to lose, and what you stand to lose.'

'Boy oh boy,' says the mayor, 'you've got chutzpah. Won't Reimers object?'

'I'm District Headman Menken,' says the farmer, 'and I know how many stones I can carry up to the loft, and how many's too much for me. Reimers has been in it for too long, he has no idea of the way people feel out here, or how smug the company at the Bauernschaft has become. We'll talk with you, Mayor, and if we say "yes" to something, then that means "yes".'

'Boys,' says the mayor, and his belly swings from side to side with happiness, 'will you come and take a grog on me in the Krug? What's the use standing around in the rain, I'm happy to have heard a sensible farmer's word after all the argy-bargy these past months.'

'Let's go lift one, then.'

It turned into several. And then as he trudged home in the dark, the mayor thought: Me and step down? Me and chuck my job? I'm going to hang on to it with tooth and claw.

Other people have done far worse things: Manzow, Niederdahl, Frerksen, the lot of them. I'll stick it out, for three weeks there'll be a load of claptrap, and then they'll be over it, and we'll get down to it, and by Christmas the boycott will be history.

VIII

At eight o'clock, then, the mayor lets himself into his office.

Of course the place is dark, at this time of day there's no one in the town hall.

But he wants to see if there was anything in the mail. And maybe Piekbusch will have left a note on his desk that he was wanted in court. Then he'll go along to the judge, tonight, to the house of the industrialist Thilse, and apologize to him.

On the great oaken slab of his desk there is one single, solitary letter. One letter.

As Gareis rips the envelope open, his nerves start to tingle. He was standing, now he sits down.

It's an official communication:

Stolpe, 25th July.

To the Police Commissioner of Altholm, Mayor Gareis.

Private and confidential.

As of 9 a.m. tomorrow, two hundred State policemen under the command of Lieutenant Wrede will be placed at your disposal, with the stipulation that . . .

The secret orders! The lost orders.

Mayor Gareis reads no further. He crumples the letter on his desk, storms over to the door, roars like a wild man into the dark outer office, into the corridor: 'Piekbusch! Piekbusch!'

Then he stops to think.

He tramps back to his desk, slumps into his chair, shattered.

The secret orders . . .

His testimony today, in the soup up to his head and ears, and here it is: the vital document.

Gareis tries to light a cigar, but his hands are shaking, the matches snap, the thing chars but won't burn.

With jaw grinding, he chomps about on it, reaches for the orders again with his shaking hand, reads them.

Secret orders – it's a laugh. What a wildly deluded fool he was, not to have guessed that this was nothing but a piece of administrative bumf, an idiotic military bureaucracy as usual giving itself airs.

'. . . and attention is hereby drawn to the circumstance that in the event of firearms being used, approval from high command here must be sought . . .'

So there you are! In the event of blah, approval from blech . . . And I thought it was something important. Special measures! Why did it never occur to me that they will have their special measures, but not give them to me in writing?

After a pause, grinding his jaw with rage:

And I stood in front of them like an idiot, and told them just what an idiot I was! I made a monkey of myself. I was pathetic. I was embarrassed as a thirteen-year-old with a man staring at her breasts – Oh Gareis, Gareis, Gareis, doesn't it make you sick!

He gets up again, paces up and down, glowers at the walls in his rage. Then hunger for a human being to tell it all to drives him out into the corridor, he yanks open Political Adviser Stein's door and yells: 'Stein! Adviser! God!'

Silence. No sound.

He turns back. And, standing in the corridor, sees a light go on in the staircase, and hears voices approaching.

With one bound, he is back in his office, squinting through a crack in the door.

Three figures are approaching.

He carefully shuts the door. Jumps on to his chair in two or three strides. Stuffs the orders, plus envelope, into his pocket. Picks up his outsize pencil, has paper in front of him. Three or four open books grouped around him.

When they knock, he says, 'Enter!' calm as you like.

Even the cigar lights now.

IX

The three visitors are dear old comrades of his: there is Town Councillor Geier, Party Secretary Nothmann and finally the local bigwig from Stettin, Reichstag Member Koffka.

They walk in very quietly, and the expressions on their faces are less victorious than they might have been expected to be.

'Nice of you to come all this way,' remarks Gareis appreciatively, 'just to put an old donkey out to grass. Fine by me. Shall we have a beer at Tucher's?'

He sees them shudder at the suggestion of being seen with him in a bar, and grins.

'No, Comrade Gareis,' says Member Koffka, 'we don't feel like beer, and we don't feel like sitting in a bar with you either. But you can offer us a cigar if you like.'

The mayor does so, and says casually: 'You look in the pink, Koffka. All that talking shop in Berlin must agree with you.'

'Oh, Comrade Gareis,' says the MP dismally, 'you soon put paid to that occasional bit of health. I sat in your pretty gym hall this morning, and saw you in front of the bench, you cut some figure, I must say, Gareis!'

'Do you think?' says the mayor, indifferently. 'Of course you've never mislaid a letter in your life, Koffka, and then stood there and pretended you'd answered it long ago?'

'This isn't about me and what I've done and not done,' says an irked Koffka. 'This is about what you've done. And you've made a royal balls-up, Gareis, that would be true to say, and you've brought disgrace upon the entire Party.'

'I reckon,' says the mayor, looking pensively at the tip of his cigar, 'that this is my office. Which gives me the right to turf anyone out on their ear, and bodily, if they come here and make a nuisance of themselves.'

'That you may, Gareis,' says the other as calmly. 'You're physically and mentally completely up to it. The only question is whether that would help anything along. After all, you came within a hair's breadth of perjuring yourself today, and it's up to the three of us whether we want to pursue a charge of perjury against you, when we see the corner of those secret orders peeking out of your pocket.'

Gareis has himself under control, but not so much that he doesn't make an angry grab for his jacket pocket. He stuffs the letter back down, thinks again, pulls it out, and lays it on the table. He looks at the three men provocatively.

'Of course,' says Koffka, 'you can bang on the table and knock our heads together all you like, but you can't kill the three of us. I'm not even certain that a charge is forthcoming. But you would have to tell the court a mighty odd and implausible story if they have you back and all of a sudden you know the mystery orders.

'It seems to me that would be trying their patience too far. Public prosecutors don't like fairy tales, and your story would sound very like one.'

'So what do you want?' the mayor asks grimly.

'We want you to step down, Comrade Gareis. No noise and no fuss. Right now in our presence you write out your tender of resignation to the Town Council. That's what we want, Comrade Gareis.'

'I'm not going to resign, you can charge me if you want, but I won't resign. I'm not leaving Altholm! Not like that.'

'So how do you propose to go? In handcuffs?!'

The mayor laughs furiously. 'You think you're so clever. You think you've got me cornered. But I've got witnesses for what I said in court. Piekbusch can be summoned, Stein can be summoned. I'm in the clear.'

'It's not my sense that Piekbusch will be a favourable witness for you.'

The mayor cuts up nasty. 'I've known Piekbusch for years. Piekbusch is loyal.'

The three of them laugh, discordantly, each in his own way, it's not a good sound.

'Let's not pursue that theme any more,' says Koffka. 'In fact, let's not argue at all. Be sensible, Gareis, think about your situation for five minutes calmly, and then tell us we're right. Then we'll listen to you.'

The mayor looks at the three of them. There is something rather hopeless in his expression. Then he gets up and starts walking to and fro.

The visitors sit and smoke.

Suddenly the mayor stops. 'Koffka,' he says, 'old comrade, listen to me. I've done something stupid. I always thought it would somehow pan out. It didn't. But there are thousands of things that don't work out, and just for that you can't send someone out into the desert.

'You won't get someone like me again. Think about everything I've done in the past six years for the town and the Party. What was Altholm when I got here? A pigsty. Today, ask around the province, people come from the length and breadth of the Reich, because Altholm is a social model.

'Think of our old people's home with the big farm attached, and the school for re-educating unemployed industrial workers for agriculture. Think of our infant nursery. The children's home. The hostel for unmarried men. The trainee home. Think of the fact that there is no borstal in Altholm, that we keep the children and make human beings of them.

'Think of the swimming baths, the football stadium, the brand-new fire station. Think of the fact that, with all these things, the town's debts have hardly grown, that I've managed to scrape together the money, mark by mark, hundreds of thousands.

'Who else can do that? It'll all come to an end if you take me down. Suddenly all those institutions will cost money, they'll be closed, downsized, I know how it goes. Then the children will be farmed out to orphanages across the province, or fostered with drunken fathers and slovenly mothers, where they only care about the extra money they bring in. Can you answer for that, Koffka?'

'To hear you talking, Comrade Gareis, is to remember why we went on supporting you as long as we did, and covered your back. But it's no good, Gareis. It's over. We can't do it any more.

'The local elections are coming up. If you stay in office, the Party will see its share of the vote down by half.'

'More. Two-thirds,' grunts Geier.

'Quite possibly. You have no idea, Gareis, how unpopular you are among the comrades. You're big and strong, you talk to people on a one-to-one basis, and you talk their heads off. And because an individual says yes to you, you think he actually means it.

'Then they walk away, and behind your back they scream no no no, and they call you Mussolini.

'Which is fine as long as you're successful. But it fails the instant they see you weakened. Have you seen the papers today?'

'No. Not yet. I'm not interested really.'

'Well, there was really no need for us to come and take the trouble of seeing you. You're toast. You're dead meat. You took yourself off. All we want is for you to go without a fuss and a scandal. So be a sensible fellow, and write a letter of resignation.'

'Let me tell you something, Koffka,' says the mayor. 'You're a bit down just now. You're not feeling on top of things. I understand, I didn't feel on top of things this morning either. Then I went for a long walk in the countryside, to clear my head. I got talking to some farmers.

'They're going to talk to me, Koffka. I am the only man who can get the town out of this wretched boycott. They offered me talks. What's going to happen to Altholm if the boycott carries on through the winter?

'Give me another six months. Then I'll show you what I've done. Then we can sit down together again, and if you still want me to go, I'll clear off without a word.'

'You see,' says the MP, nodding to his cohorts, 'that's Gareis for you. One moment the farmers' lawyer clocks him one in court, gets him in trouble, and here he is now, cheerfully thinking about starting talks with those self-same farmers.

'Spontaneous individualists. Don't you love them? Probably doesn't even occur to Gareis to consult the Party.

'But I tell you, we don't give a shit about the farmers. What do we care about their boycott. No skin off the workers' noses! Or do workers own the businesses where the farmers have stopped buying?! You're doing the bidding of the middle class, of the farmers, next thing you know you'll be organizing night marches for the Stahlhelm and swastika processions for Hitler. And you wonder that the Party is unhappy with you!'

'You're an arsehole,' Gareis says crudely, but not unhappily. 'Even your thick Party skull must have hoisted in that when the bourgeoisie are having a bad time, the workers' life isn't a bed of roses either.'

'What do you say we wind this up now, Gareis? There's no point. You write your resignation letter. I hereby ask to be released from my duties. Right now.'

'No,' says Gareis firmly.

Koffka tenses. 'Then tomorrow morning your exclusion from the Party will be made known in every Party organ.

'We will take steps to see that the business with the secret orders is followed up.

'The SPD caucus in the council will demand your release from the municipal service.

'Then the government will institute disciplinary proceedings against you.

'Then you're completely washed up.

'Then you'll never get a decent job again as long as you live.'

The many percussive 'then's sound in Gareis's ears like hammer blows destroying his life's work.

He jumps to his feet and cries out in despair: 'But there's

nothing else I want to do anyway! I'm completely useless! What else am I supposed to do!'

'I have been asked,' says the MP Koffka, 'as soon as you have signed your resignation letter, to present you with your appointment as mayor of Breda.'

'What's Breda?' says the mayor suspiciously. 'Never heard of it.'

'Breda is a town on the Ruhr. Twenty-one thousand inhabitants. All coal-miners. Work. Work. Work. Nothing has ever been done for them.'

'And who is the Oberbürgermeister?' asks Gareis.

'You fall upstairs. You're number one and number two and number three. All you. The council is SPD and KPD and a few Centrists who don't matter. You'll be able to get to work there.'

The mayor looks worried. 'Show me it in writing, will you?'

'After you've signed.'

Gareis paces up and down. Then he sighs deeply, sits down at his desk, and starts writing. He carefully blots the page and passes it to Koffka.

'Address the envelope, Gareis. I'll take care of it myself tomorrow, so you don't have to trouble yourself.'

'There you are. And now the appointment.'

'Here. Tomorrow or the day after it will appear in the Party newspapers. Of course we're all backing you. In the course of the next few days, you'll be given a torchlight parade by the Party. As a farewell. Everything will be done properly.'

'Fine, great,' says the mayor. 'But now I'd be glad if you'd get the fuck out of here. I've looked at your mugs for long enough.'

'Evening, Comrade,' they say.

'Oh, crap,' he replies.

X

When they're gone, Gareis remains motionless in his chair. He's thinking, picturing the town where he's put in six years of work.

Buildings he's put up pass in review. He sees the dormitory in the infant nursery, with the sixty children in their sleepsuits, and their faces that look so human but at the same time so alarmingly alien.

He remembers how a doctor once told him: 'You know this is all a waste of time, Mayor. Inferior genetic material. Children of alcoholics, syphilitics, cripples, lunatics. In Sparta they would all have been brained, or put out on a hillside.'

He remembers being stuck with those words for months: 'all a waste of time, Mayor'.

He thinks of the five hundred faces in this town that he drove on to work of one kind or another, chased them up off their sofas, off their dream pillows.

He knows that if he leaves here, he will never be able to work like this again. Wherever he starts, he'll have left the work of his youth behind, and his illusions, and his energy. He won't be a young man any more, he'll be a man like any other.

The door creaks, he raises his head, and blinks out in tiredness.

His disciple is there, Political Adviser Stein. Black, pale, nervous.

'I wanted to say goodnight, Your Worship.'

Gareis ponders glumly. What does he want? Say goodnight? Why does he want to say goodnight?

And he remembers that this is Stein, who kept his head down in the courtroom and avoided his eye.

At the same time, he remembers that Comrade Koffka didn't mention Stein's name when he was talking about unreliable witnesses.

He darts a look at the other's shoes: they're covered in mud.

'Have you been out walking as well, Adviser?' he slowly asks.

'Yes. I came after you. But you were already gone.'

The mayor walks up to his late visitor. With one hand he bends the other's head back, so that his eyes are full in the light.

'Will you go with me, Stein, when I go?'

'You're not going to go!'

'Will you go with me?'

'Always.'

'Then goodnight, Stein,' says the mayor. 'Goodnight, Adviser.'

Witnesses and Expert Witnesses

I

Next to the sports hall is a small, cramped room: normally a cloakroom, study or marking room for teachers. Now it is the waiting room for witnesses. A dozen chairs have been packed in, and there they sit, townspeople and countryfolk, policemen and peasants, and wait, often for hours.

Because now, on the eighth day of the trial, the orderly progress of the whole has rather gone to pot. The defence counsel keeps making new applications, the prosecution lawyer has turned waspish and is fighting the feeling in the hall, the farmer-friendly feeling, with irony and sarcasm.

No session begins punctually, the court often sits for hours before opening, talking about this or that motion. The first day, the gentlemen of the press arrived at nine o'clock, the second day it was nine fifteen, now they go home to Stettin at night and only arrive on the ten o'clock train, and even then they're often early.

Stuff doesn't come from Stettin, he comes in from Stolpe. And now he's dawdling into court. He knows there's no rush, on the other side of the road is Chief Adviser Meier, deep in conversation with the chief prosecutor. And a little way ahead of him is Councillor Streiter with his client Henning.

Sometimes people stop and stare at them. Half the town seems to have visited the trial by now and knows them by sight, which means they have to stop and stare at them now.

'Lookee, there's Henning.'

'I ken. I ken. I was there the whole of the first day.'

Outside the school, Stuff runs into Sergeant Hart, and even though he's no longer interested in local news from Altholm, he still likes to stop and chew the fat with policemen. 'Well, Hart, my old soul, what are you still doing? Haven't you hung up your truncheon yet?'

Hart is hurt. 'If it was down to you, mate, we'd all be in the dock tomorrow for bloodlust.'

But Stuff knows the score. 'Did I ever write a word against you, Hart? As for some of your colleagues, you and I both know they're not exactly angels, there's no point in wasting words on that.'

Hart sighs. 'Lord knows. And I tell you, now that it's public knowledge that Gareis is going, Frerksen is getting more uppity the whole time. His rosters are bursting at the seams. He doesn't seem to care how many hours we're on our feet.'

'The fellow's got some neck, that's for sure.'

And Hart, eagerly: 'My words, those are my words exactly. And when he's made himself a laughing-stock and all. But that's the Right for you, kiss up and kick down.'

'Where are you on your way to, Hart?'

'To him, of course. He spends all day there, so he doesn't miss a single word of what anyone says about him.'

'He's actually working as unpaid secretary for the prosecution. Last night the legal councillor said: "I note that the commander is continually passing notes to the prosecutor."'

'And?'

'And he went red like he always does, and ran away, and was back in half an hour, writing notes again.'

They have got to the anteroom of the gym hall, and Hart looks around in the crush of new arrivals for Frerksen. Stuff finally looks in the witness room, but that is almost empty for now. A little man with chubby hands and a greedy white face is sitting there, and an elderly lady.

'Oh, excuse me, sir,' says the lady, 'I was asked to be here at nine o'clock. Is it not beginning yet?'

'They're not so precise with their time-keeping,' says Stuff consolingly, 'it might be noon, and it might be four, Fräulein Herbert.'

'Do you know me?'

'Of course I know you. Your father dusted my coat for me at school. I'll have a word with the usher.'

Stuff plunges away.

He's feeling a steadily increasing pressure on his shoulder: Hart has got his claws in him and is now jabbing him in the side.

'Are you mad?' asks Stuff indignantly. 'What have they done to you?'

'Who was that, mate, who was it?'

'That was Fräulein Herbert, the daughter of Herbert the primary schoolteacher. He's been dead these past five or six years. No, hang on, it was the year –'

'No. I meant the fellow –'

'What fellow?'

'The one who was sitting in there with the Herbert woman.'

Stuff stares pensively at Hart. 'I don't know him. Do you?'

'You bet I do. But not his name.

'What happened, I was on duty on the traffic island, five minutes before the fighting started, and this fellow comes up to me, asks me where the auction hall is, and he jeers at me, and says the farmers had beaten us up and we deserved to have our faces punched.'

'And why didn't you nab him?'

'I couldn't, could I? I was on traffic duty. But afterwards I felt mad I'd let the farmers get away with nothing, never mind us having our faces punched.'

'Say,' says Stuff slowly. 'I wouldn't let him get away with it. I'd have him.'

'If I only knew his name, or what he did.'

'A farmer?' suggests Stuff.

'No chance. Much too clean about the chops.'

'Then a manual worker.'

'Could be. You know, Stuff, when I give Frerksen my letter, I'll tell him to announce me as a witness.'

'Naah,' says Stuff slowly. 'Naah. I wouldn't do that if I were you. If you get that man, he'll only become a martyr or something. Tell you what, I'll take care of it for you.'

'You?' asks Hart doubtfully.

'Me. Yes, me. I'll see that you're brought on as a witness.

'Oh, I get you, you think because I'm on the side of the farmers?

Yes, but not for a piece of work like that! He's no farmer. He only harms the cause. He's a nasty man, and it'll be a pleasure for me to see him get his hide singed.'

'And you're not shitting me?'

'Hart, my old Dutch, why would I do that to you? Everything's on the level, OK?' And he pats the policeman on the back, rather moved by himself.

'Well, you know, Stuff, with you, you never know –'

'No. With me you always know. Namely that I'm always good for a schnapps and a beer for a thirsty soul. – Can you arrange to be waiting for me here at twelve?'

'Twelve? No. Maybe twelve thirty.'

'All right. Twelve thirty it is. Then I'll know who the man is, and you can do whatever you want to him.'

'All right. I'll be waiting for you here at half twelve.' And Hart sets off in search of Frerksen.

Stuff watches him go pensively with his sad blue eyes. Boy oh boy. Come tonight you'll wish you could smash my face in.

And he dashes off to find Councillor Streiter.

II

The judge says: 'Call witness Detective Inspector Tunk.'

A small, fat, whitish man enters the hall and stands in front of the judge's table.

Stuff observes to a colleague: 'I'm going to take this down. This is going to be interesting.'

'How so?'

'It'll bring you back to life.'

The judge half gabbles (this is after all the one hundred and twenty-third witness): 'Your name is Josef Tunk? Age forty-three years old? Are a detective working for the Political Section in Stolpe? Not related or connected to any of the defendants?'

Once these things have been duly established, still hurrying: 'You witnessed the events of the 26th of July? You wrote a detailed report on them that same evening? Will you tell us when you arrived from Stolpe, and what you saw when you got here?'

The witness clears his throat. He stands a little straighter. In an oddly squawking voice for one so round, he begins to speak:

'I took the nine o'clock train from Stolpe to Altholm. I had strict instructions from the government to confine myself to an observing role. I therefore did not liaise with the local police, but went straight from the station to various drinking establishments.

'They were all full of farmers. I saw that feeling was running very high.'

'One moment, please. Why "running very high"? Could you explain?'

'I just had the impression that the people were excited. It's an impression. An experienced detective picks up on these things in five minutes, or else he doesn't.'

'You don't recall any particular sayings?'

'No, there was a lot of swearing.'

'Who were they swearing at? The police? Mayor Gareis?'

'Just general swearing. The people were excited. You know?'

The witness speaks slowly and rather grindingly. Each word leaves his mouth with emphasis. He stands there, a heavyweight personality, perhaps thirteen stone live weight, an expert come to enlighten the court, fully aware of his worth.

'In the afternoon I was in the biggest pub, in Tucher's. The place was full to bursting. The atmosphere struck me as extraordinarily menacing. It was there that I saw the defendant Henning, who was working on the flag together with the defendant Padberg.

'I thought right away that I hadn't seen the last of him. I introduced myself to him, to ascertain his name.'

Councillor Streiter says: 'I'd like to ask the witness a question. – What was it about my client that convinced you at a glance that you hadn't seen the last of him?'

The witness changes his posture. He turns, looks the defence lawyer up and down, waits, then turns to the court, and asks: 'Is this question admissible?'

The judge motions with his hand. 'It is.'

'I could see it, because my experience as a detective told me it was so.'

'That's no explanation,' says the counsel. 'Kindly give me a precise answer: How could you tell you hadn't seen the last of Herr Henning?'

The detective says pityingly: 'An old detective acquires a sixth sense for these things. If he sees a man on the street, his sixth sense may tell him: That man is a criminal. That's the way it was with the defendant Henning.'

Henning leaps up in indignation. 'Your Honour, I crave your protection from the witness's insolence. The witness called me a "criminal".'

The prosecutor leaps up. 'I contend that this is not the case. The witness was speaking of a hypothetical case. I would like to remind the defendant that terms like "insolence" are actionable.'

It takes five minutes for the judge to restore calm to the proceedings.

Detective Inspector Tunk creaks on: 'The defendant would not give me his name. As I noted, he was warned not to by the defendant Padberg. Instead, Henning unfurled the flag, which was greeted with a wild shout of joy. I noted that the flag was extremely provocative and incendiary in its effect, and took the feeling of the farmers over the edge.'

The defence counsel asks: 'Would it be true to say that you found the flag provocative and dangerous while you were still in Tucher's?'

The detective condescendingly replies: 'That is what I just said.'

'May I ask you then, Detective Inspector, why you did not inform the police? So long as the flag was not on the street, it must have been a relatively straightforward matter to secure its confiscation.'

'As I said already, I was present as a special informant for the government. I was specifically instructed not to contact the local police.'

'So you preferred to allow a calamity to unfold? You preferred to countenance something that in your view was against the law?'

'I had my orders.'

'Thank you, Detective Inspector. I've heard enough.'

The official carries on with his evidence: 'When the flag-bearer appeared on the street with the flag, he provoked a storm of displeasure. People on the pavements, good, honest citizens, were outraged. My view that the flag would have a provocative effect was therefore borne out.

'The flag-bearer initially took up a place at the front of the column of people, but when he heard the storm of displeasure, he was frightened, and ran back into the pub.'

The judge remarks mildly: 'That must be an assumption on your part, that the defendant felt fear.'

'No assumption, Your Honour. I could tell from the discoloration on his face that he was afraid.'

The judge says: 'It has been recorded by witnesses that Herr Padberg told Herr Henning: "The scythe is loose," and that they retired to the pub to make it fast.'

'That's not true, Your Honour. He was afraid, I could see it in his face.'

'As I said, there are witnesses. The landlord of the pub has stated that the two men asked for a screwdriver to help them tighten the bolt.'

'They would only have done that to mask their retreat. They were frightened, Your Honour.'

'Then why, in your view, did they come out again with the flag?'

'Because lots more farmers had come out by that time. That gave them courage. The defendant Henning took up a position at the head of the column. From the other side of the street I could see Commander Frerksen approaching.'

The judge has his head propped on his hand. The associates are staring into the court, looking for acquaintances. The defence counsel is listening with a sceptical smile on his face. The prosecution is scribbling hasty notes.

Stuff groans: 'What a prize son of a bitch.'

Pinkus hisses back: 'Not what you want to hear, eh?'

Stuff eyes him through his pince-nez, and Pinkus ducks out of the way.

'Herr Frerksen was advancing calmly and confidently towards the defendant, and in a polite tone of voice said something to him that I was unable to hear. At that, the defendant Padberg leaped like a fiend at Herr Frerksen, grabbed him by the scruff with both hands, shook him, pushed him aside, and then the procession started to move.'

'This is new indeed,' says the judge. 'Thus far none of the witnesses has mentioned that Herr Frerksen was attacked at this stage of the proceedings. He himself has stated that he was pushed out of the way by the farmers as they set out on their march.'

Unmoved, the detective says: 'Herr Frerksen is mistaken. His memory is playing tricks on him. I am in the habit of making precise observations. My observations are reliable. – Then Herr Frerksen spoke with two police constables, and followed the train of people, which by then had moved on approximately sixty yards. When Herr Frerksen then appeared alongside the flag-bearer, he laid his hand on the flag.

'I could tell he was confiscating it. Straight away, the farmers raised their sticks, turned, and attacked Herr Frerksen, who drew his sabre. The defendant Henning wrested the sabre away from him, drove its point against the ground, and bent it. Then the defendant started punching the commander.'

Legal Councillor Streiter walks right up to the witness. 'Your account is manifestly unbelievable. Of numerous witnesses, not one has stated that Henning relinquished the flag even for a second. That is why he cannot have done those things that you are claiming on oath that he did.'

The witness replies with considerable calm: 'The observations of laypersons are meaningless. Laymen are incapable of distinguishing between legally significant and insignificant actions.

'I clearly saw Henning hand the flag to a farmer. The flag then went through another three or four pairs of hands. I find it very instructive that none of the witnesses has commented on this, though it happened in plain sight.'

The judge remarks mildly: 'I must point out, Detective Inspector, that Herr Henning thus far has not aspired to put a good face on anything. He has admitted everything that was claimed against him. Herr Henning, did you pass the flag on to anyone else?'

'I never let the flag leave my hands.'

Councillor Streiter says, not without asperity: 'It's fascinating to hear the evidence of the detective. I would like to say the following: I know the man who tore the sabre from the commander's grasp. I was told it in confidence. It was not Henning.'

The detective stands there unmoved. 'There are conscious deceptions and unconscious deceptions. I clearly saw the defendant Henning pass the flag to another, bend the sabre, and punch the commander.'

The prosecutor suggests: 'Herr Frerksen is in attendance. Perhaps he would like to comment?'

The commander approaches the judge's table. The judge says: 'You have already said in evidence that you are unable to recall individuals in the general turmoil. But perhaps you will be able to remember whether Herr Henning passed the flag to someone or not?'

The commander looks around hesitantly. He looks from one face to the next. Finally, hesitantly, he says: 'I can't make a definite statement either way. I suppose it's possible.'

'You see,' crows the detective, 'not even the commander will deny the possibility. If you think about it hard, Commander, you will surely also remember Henning grabbing you by the lapels and shaking you.'

'We object – that's leading the witness,' says the defence counsel.

And an alarmed Frerksen says: 'No, that's not what I want to say. I don't know. It could have been. But I don't want to say.'

Padberg has also made his way towards the little group, and is looking breathlessly from one to another. Now he says excitedly: 'Your Honour, I'm about to do something terribly stupid, but I can't stand to hear any more of this nonsense. I can't believe the twaddle this witness is coming up with.

'I, Detective Inspector, and no one else, wrested the sabre away from the commander. I did it from behind, I grabbed his wrist from behind and twisted it until he dropped the sabre on the cobbles. Wrest his sabre away from him! – Who would be so stupid as to grab the blade of a sword?'

General excitement. The defence counsel has thrown himself at Padberg and is chiding him. The detective stands there, completely unmoved.

The judge says: 'It does you credit, Herr Padberg, that you did not set your personal interests above other considerations. – I should like to ask you, Detective, to proceed carefully with your testimony, and in places where your memory is not quite clear, just to say: "I don't know."'

The detective says easily: 'Of course it may look for the moment as if I had been mistaken. Of course I am not mistaken. My portrayal of events is accurate. The self-accusation of Herr Padberg means nothing. He has secured himself a favourable opinion, whereas his friend would have been seriously incriminated by my testimony.'

The judge says rather animatedly: 'Detective Inspector, would you kindly leave the evaluation of individual testimony to the court. – Please carry on with your evidence. Will the defendants return to their places.'

Stuff grins along the desk at Pinkus: 'Grade A specimen, isn't he? This must be a proud moment for you.'

And Pinkus, quite astonished: 'You're surely not falling for Padberg's gambit, are you? It's one of the oldest in the book.'

The detective continues to give evidence. The court learns that he is the witness who spotted the dentist Czibulla with a stick or umbrella, though which he is not quite able to say. No possibility of error.

Czibulla jumps up: 'Your Honour, at my almost biblical age, do I look like the type who would attack large policemen with sticks?'

The judge, smiling, inclines his head from one side to the other. Then he asks Czibulla not to intervene in the hearing.

The detective continues to be full of rare perception. He gravely gives his deposition against Henning, against Padberg, against Czibulla, against Feinbube, against Banz, incriminating, incriminating, incriminating.

When he finally finishes, the whole court heaves a deep sigh of relief. Even Pinkus has written down nothing for the last half-hour.

The detective stands there, the prize witness, the expert whom nothing is able to shake.

The judge asks in a bored tone whether there were any questions for the witness, or whether he could let him go.

Then – to the general surprise – the defence counsel rises, and asks that the witness not be dismissed just yet, because further important testimony was coming for whose corroboration he would be needed. The witness is not allowed to go, but is told to find himself a seat in the gallery. In the front row. There he sits now, very self-conscious and very pleased with himself, just listening.

III

The next witness to take the stand is Fräulein Herbert, daughter of the deceased primary schoolteacher Paul Herbert. She is an energetic and forthright lady of fifty-seven. She swears the oath, in its religious form.

'Witness,' says the judge, 'you have applied in writing both to me and to the defence counsel, saying you had important evidence. Would you tell us please what you saw? You live at the corner of Stolpe Gate and Burstah, do you not?'

The witness was shuffling impatiently to and fro, now she calls out: 'Your Honour, I'm so indignant! I'm so indignant! I've been following the proceedings here in the newspapers. It's all wrong, Your Honour. It's all wrong.'

She stops to draw breath. The judge eyes her from below, with head inclined, undecided, the prosecutor is starting to harrumph again, the spectators in the public gallery are nudging each other and drawing attention to what everyone can see anyway.

'Old battleaxe,' mutters Stuff.

But the old battleaxe won't be put off, she knows what she's about.

'Your Honour, I was sitting on my balcony, doing some sewing. I had no evil thoughts in my head. And suddenly it was as though . . . no, Your Honour, if I live for another fifty years I'll still picture it . . .

'I read that what this is about is the police approach, and did they first ask that the flag-bearer give up his flag or hit him right away, and whether they used rubber truncheons or the flats of their sabres. I read that Herr Frerksen stood here and said he did everything properly by the book. I've known Herr Frerksen since he was a boy.'

She turns round and scans the gallery. In the front row she finds Frerksen and addresses him.

'Herr Frerksen, I know you for a quiet man, and I know you for a polite man. But what you did that afternoon is a scandal, there's no getting away from it, and you should be ashamed of yourself. You should be ashamed of yourself in all perpetuity –'

Frerksen has stood up, suffused in red, he begs the judge: 'Your Honour –'

Who says: 'Fräulein Herbert, you must address the court. Do not address your remarks to witnesses or the public. Would you now tell us quietly what it was you saw?'

'Yes, of course. I'll start right away. I just had to say that to him once, because he's a nice man the rest of the time, but what a bad man he was that afternoon. It's important to say it to someone's face, Your Honour, and not always behind their backs –'

'I understand. I understand,' he says placatingly.

'Fabulous woman,' comments Stuff. 'Ten of that sort and no farmers, and the police would be in the dock.'

'What sort of judge is he,' counters Pinkus, 'he just lets everyone do what they like.'

Fräulein Herbert begins again: 'I was sitting on my balcony, and that was when I saw Frerksen come charging up. I could see right away that something was wrong. Normally he's so kempt, but he looked as though he'd been dragged through a haystack. And he was running so furiously, anyone who didn't get ten yards out of his way he just charged into them, he was wildly inconsiderate.

'Then he stopped on the traffic island, and sent the policeman there away. By now I could see the farmers coming. And from the opposite side, there were suddenly policemen, at least forty of them.'

'Approximately twenty, we've been told.'

'Out of the question. Quite out of the question. At least forty, maybe fifty. And he addresses them, waving his hands in the air, and suddenly they all start running towards the peasants, Herr Frerksen in the lead. Some of them had rubber truncheons in their hands, and some of them had sabres, and a few were pulling the sabres out of their sheaths while they were running.'

'Do you remember if Herr Frerksen had a sabre in his hand?'

'Oh no, Your Honour, and you ought to know that. That was all over every paper, how it was found behind the monument. Herr Frerksen was just waving his arms around.

'And now, pay attention, Your Honour. I read all about the pro-ceedings in the papers, but they didn't have anything about what I'm about to tell you now. Where was Herr Frerksen when the attack started? His men were running faster and faster the closer they got to the farmers, and Herr Frerksen was running slower and slower. And when the police were getting going, and hitting at the farmers with their sabres, by that stage Herr Frerksen was ten paces behind his men. And the whole time he didn't get any nearer to the fighting.'

'But you said yourself, Witness, that he didn't have a weapon.'

'Then he should have borrowed one from one of his men,' Fräulein Herbert counters energetically. 'If you start something like that, you can't loiter in the rear, you have to join in. At least that's what I'd have done, Your Honour, take it from me.'

The judge looks at her, his face beaming with a sweet irony. 'And then what happened, if you will, Fräulein Herbert?'

'Then? Then the fighting started. You must have heard that described twenty times. But I'll tell you this, Your Honour, what they did to that young man,' she turns to look for him in the dock, spots Henning, and then beams: 'That's him. That's Herr Henning . . . What they did to him was horrible. He was lying on the ground, still holding on to his flag, and they were still laying into him. I thought: Are the people doing this men of Altholm? They're savages. They're pirates.'

She draws breath. Then, pointing to the collapsed-looking Czibulla: 'He caught it the worst. I saw him very well. He was running around like a headless chicken. I think the crowd utterly confused him.

'And the notion that he had a stick with him, or an umbrella, as you asked him the first day, that's simply not true. He was encumbered enough with his travelling bag. Look at him, Your Honour, if he had an umbrella, he would just leave it all over the place. His wife must be pleased just to have him get home safely, and remember his bag.'

The judge says a little labouredly: 'So you too are of the opinion that Herr Czibulla didn't assault the policeman?'

The witness is withering in her contempt: 'Of the opinion? Your Honour, that man and assaulting policemen? He'd be happy not to get hit himself. I read it in the *News*, about him plucking at the officer's coat, like a mouse. That's exactly right.

'And then he was dealt the most awful blow. That was the worst thing. When I saw his face, and the blood streaming down it, at that point I turned away, I couldn't watch any more. I went back in my room, and I felt so sick, please forgive me, I had to vomit.'

Silence.

Stuff is scribbling nineteen to the dozen. 'The voice of humanity and common sense,' he writes.

The judge says hastily: 'Are there any questions for the witness? If not –'

Then, despairingly, but reconciled to his role: 'All right, Councillor –'

'Fräulein Herbert, could you tell us, in this clash, would you say the police were the aggressors or the farmers?'

The witness is full of contempt: 'And you still ask me that after all I've told you? Of course it was the police that were attacking. They attacked like a mob of savages.'

Councillor Streiter smiles: '*I* know that very well. But there are still some in this court who question it.'

The judge: 'Prosecutor, your question.'

The prosecuting counsel begins quietly and innocuously: 'I'd like to ask the witness if her impression is that the whole bloody clash would have been avoided if the farmers had peacefully given up their flag?'

Councillor Streiter quickly intervenes: 'I object to the question, Your Honour. It's purely hypothetical, whereas my questioning was about the witness's actual impression of the scene unwinding before her eyes.'

The judge: 'The question is permitted.'

And the prosecutor: 'Would the judge pursue the question for me?'

The judge: 'All right, witness, do you think the bloody clash would have come about if the farmers had peacefully given up their flag?'

Before the witness can reply, the defence counsel cuts in again: 'I object to the question a second time, and ask for the court to take a position.'

The judge duly gets to his feet and leaves the court followed by his cohorts. A general conversation ensues.

Fräulein Herbert turns to the defendants' bench and shakes hands first with Henning, then Czibulla. The usher protests.

'*Magnifique!*' declares Stuff.

'She's no witness,' says Pinkus. 'She hasn't seen anything. Babbling on about blood. Completely hysterical.'

'Boy oh boy,' says Stuff. 'I'll tell her what you just said. Then she'll show you the meaning of the word "hysterical".'

'Please God, don't do that,' says Pinkus, and retreats.

The court returns and the judge announces: 'The prosecution's question will be allowed in the following form: Did the witness, in her observation of the police, take them for so heated that they would have struck, even given the withdrawal of the flag?'

Fräulein Herbert is about to reply when the prosecutor gets up and declares with a forced smile: 'We are not interested in putting our question in such a form, and withdraw it.'

'Then if there are no further questions to the witness? Fräulein Herbert, you are released. You can, though, if so inclined, take a seat in the gallery.'

Fräulein Herbert says, all too audibly: 'No thanks, I've had all I want,' and leaves the hall.

The judge: 'Usher, please call the next witness, Police Sergeant Hart.'

All duly seat themselves once more, police testimony tends to be neither illuminating nor popular.

IV

The judge says: 'The defence counsel has intimated that you wish to round off your testimony on a certain point.'

But the sergeant replies: 'The defence? That can't be.'

He looks suspiciously round at Stuff, but Stuff nods amiably back and blinks his eyes at him. The policeman concludes that Stuff must have pulled the wool over the defence's eyes, and he allows: 'All right then. Defence it is.'

The judge looks searchingly at the man, he senses there's something not right here; once again, as so often in this trial, someone is playing their cards very close to their chest, so he merely asks: 'What's this about, then?'

'When I was questioned a couple of days ago, I talked about how I was doing traffic duty on the Stolpe Tormarkt. And how a farmer came up to me, and provoked and taunted me to such a degree that I felt like laying about all the farmers. Well, I saw *that* farmer in the witness stand this morning.'

'A farmer?' asks the judge. 'You must be mistaken. We've had no farmer here this morning.'

'But I saw him sitting there, a fat, dark-haired man with a pasty face.'

The judge thinks for a moment. He can see the defence counsel on the point of jumping in, but he knows what's going on here. Nicely done, he thinks, Streiter is ten times as feisty as that dopey prosecutor. The sergeant has no idea. How did Streiter manage it?

But what he says aloud is: 'No, we haven't had any farmers giving evidence today. But perhaps you wouldn't mind turning round and surveying the people in the gallery. Perhaps your man is sitting there.'

While Police Sergeant Hart begins to look, the judge looks meaningly at one individual, who first turns his head away, then reaches into his pocket and pulls out a handkerchief and thoroughly and rather quietly polishes his nose.

None of which helps, because Hart goes straight up to him, and declares aloud (everyone is waiting with bated breath): 'This is he.'

'Are you sure?' asks the judge. 'This is the man who taunted, teased and provoked you?'

'No possible confusion, Your Honour,' says the sergeant. 'This is the man. Back then he was wearing top-boots and a green loden suit with tunic and a green hat with a chamois brush. The best corroboration is the way he was just trying to hide his face from me.'

'I was not trying to hide my face from him,' the man retorts roughly. 'I've got a cold, and when I have a cold, I have to blow my nose a lot. On the contrary, I'm grateful for the opportunity of completing my testimony.'

'Well, well,' says Hart, 'you talked a lot then, and you talk –'

The judge intervenes. 'The witness is to speak only when asked a question. Herr Hart, this gentleman is not a farmer at all, he is Detective Inspector Tunk from Stolpe.'

'Goddamn it . . .' the policeman bites his tongue, looks round at the press table, where Stuff, with his head down, is busy writing.

Hart turns back to the judge. 'Everything happened as I said. And if the gentleman is a detective, then I don't get it. He said to me, "*We* farmers gave you a thrashing – you'd better run, or else *we'll* smash your faces in . . ." I don't understand that, Your Honour, I just don't . . .'

The detective is quite calm. Imperturbable.

The judge asks: 'Is Herr Hart's account of your behaviour correct, in your view?'

'Entirely, Your Honour, entirely correct. I would only add that I was trying to nettle him even more than appears from his words.'

'And why is that? Wouldn't that strike you as a strange way of proceeding?'

'It seemed right to me, Your Honour. I acted after mature reflection. I had seen that the police numbers were tiny, and the farmers vastly outnumbered them. The farmers were aroused and pugnacious. The police were quiet and disinclined to take action.

'Moreover, I had seen the somewhat flaccid attitude of the commander, so it seemed to me that things needed gingering up.

'I was not allowed to liaise openly with the uniformed police. Therefore I chose this approach. I wanted to shake them up, make them a bit gung-ho, above all I wanted them not to be caught out by the farmers.

'What Herr Hart has said tells me that I succeeded.'

In the gallery, Herr Frerksen has got to his feet. Step by step he approaches the judge's table, now he says several times in quick succession: 'Your Honour! Your Honour!'

'Yes, Commander? Have you something else to contribute?'

His voice shaking with emotion, Frerksen says: 'The detective spoke of my flaccid attitude. I want to counter that by saying that in the auction hall, the detective explicitly congratulated me on my conduct. He said to me – and I quote his words verbatim – he said: "You put on a good show."'

'That's what I said, Your Honour,' says the unflappable detective. 'That's right. But you should have seen the man when he came running up to me – he knew me – and asked me what they would make of all this in Stolpe, and if he had performed well, and so on and so on. It was purely to calm him down that I said that, from the kindness of my heart.'

'Detective –' Frerksen begins.

But the judge takes a hand. 'This is without any interest for us. – Any more questions to the witness Tunk? You, Legal Councillor?'

'No, thank you. I'm finished with the witness.'

V

At the end of the testimony, the expert witness, retired Police Major Schadewald, enters the court.

He is a rotund gentleman with a shiny bowling-ball skull with three pigeon-egg-sized lumps on it.

The judge says: 'The expert witness is not here to offer any value judgements. He is here merely to tell the court how he would have solved the problem of taking a flag from a crowd of demonstrators. Three questions have been formulated for him . . .'

But first the judge paints the scene. He goes up to a blackboard.

'Here is the bar, Tucher's. Here is the demonstration route, across the marketplace, following the Burstah, past the Stolpe Gate, under the railway line, through the villa suburbs, approximately three thousand strong. You, Police Major, have some twenty men under your command, armed with nightsticks, sabre and revolver. All clear?'

Police Major Schadewald gives a distinct: 'Yes, sir.'

The judge: 'I'll ask my first question: Is it necessary and customary to follow a set plan if required to confiscate a flag?'

Major Schadewald gives a distinct: 'Yes, sir.'

Everyone listens hard, but nothing follows. The expert has given, in his view, a complete and satisfactory answer to the first question.

The judge: 'I proceed to question number two: Would the commander give detailed instructions for the execution of such a task?'

Major Schadewald gives a distinct: 'Yes, sir.'

And silence again. All are in despair. Good God, an expert who isn't in love with the sound of his own voice – is such a thing possible?

Then the judge puts the third question: 'What is the effect of a commander's calm or agitated demeanour, his precise or vague orders, on the group under his command?'

Expert witness Major Schadewald explains: 'The calmer the man in command, the calmer the men.'

And falls silent again.

The three questions are over.

The judge smiles, a little awkward, a little perplexed.

Then something occurs to him: 'Major, perhaps you'll allow me to put a supplemental question to my second. At what length and level of detail would you give instructions to your men? In fact, what orders would you give them?'

The expert opens his mouth to speak: 'First, I must know where I am going to take the flag back.

'Of course it would be at the narrowest part of the road, because that's where the demonstration can most easily be brought to a halt. So not under any circumstances the market-place, but' – he points to the board – 'the upper or lower Burstah.

'Then I would divide my men up into groups.

'Eight men would cordon off the road. They have to stop the march, but possibly allow the flag-bearer and possibly some of his friends to pass, thereby cutting them off from the body of demonstrators.

'Another group of five are the snatch squad. Two are given the order to take the flag-bearer by each arm if he refuses to sur-render the flag when I required him to. If the flag-bearer offers violence, they use their truncheons. No other weapon is appro-priate.

'The three other members of the squad intervene only if the flag-bearer's associates actively become involved.

'The rest of the men form a contingency reserve.

'I will have booked a car earlier, with which the flag, once con-fiscated, quickly disappears from sight of the demonstrators.

'As soon as I have the flag in my possession, I give orders to assemble. The cordon is withdrawn, and the march can con-tinue.'

That's it. The end. All shuffle in their seats.

Of course, that's all very well, and everyone realizes it, but nothing would have happened in that textbook fashion. The judge asks pensively: 'Is there always time for such detailed orders?'

And the expert: 'The marching route is long, almost an hour, which gives me the opportunity to pick my spot.'

'One more question: Would you and your men go to meet the march, or would you wait for them to come to you?'

And the expert: 'Wait. Wait, no doubt about it. Rather intervene late, but with precise instructions.'

The judge says: 'I have no further questions for the expert.'

Neither defence lawyer nor prosecutor makes a move. Retired Police Major Schadewald leaves the hall under the respectful gaze of many there.

6

The Judgment

I

The great day of closing speeches, and probably of the verdict, is come. The sports hall is packed to the rafters, there are even people standing in the passageways outside.

And more people turning up all the time.

'Nice and cosy here,' says the typesetter Linke of the *Bauernschaft* to Party Secretary Nothmann, once they have found a couple of seats in the third row.

'They've issued far too many tickets.'

'And to whom? To those fat bourgeois.'

'And they wonder that people don't believe in fair and unbiased judges any more. They can't even dole out tickets in an unpartisan way.'

'You're right, Comrade,' says Linke.

'Are they respectful to you when they question you?'

'I don't stand for any nonsense. The examining magistrate is another one. I told him Padberg sent me to collect his papers, and if he turns round and says he never sent me, then he's just lying, I said.'

'You're right. – Here we go. The prosecution first.'

'He won't bite the farmers either. We should have done something else . . .'

The prosecutor stands there with a sheaf of papers in his hand. He is a small, white-haired old gent, with a droopy, fraying beard. His pince-nez is hanging down likewise.

'None too fearsome,' says Medical Councillor Dr Lienau. 'They used to have really crisp lawyers put the fear of God into you. But not that one. Dear me, no.'

'You're right,' says the locomotive driver Thienelt, also kitted out with his Stahlhelm badge on his lapel. 'He looks – forgive me, I'm thinking of my bunnies back home – like a pregnant bunny rabbit. Mournful . . .'

'"Pregnant bunny rabbit", I like that. Remind me to write it down later . . .'

The prosecutor is already speaking. By way of economic consequences and party warfare he gets to this sentence, pronounced with emphasis: 'But politics does not cross this threshold.'

'He may say so now,' grunts Count Bandekow, 'but he took care to ask every witness on the peasant side what party he belonged to.'

'That's his living,' argues Farmer Henke-Karolinenhorst, 'he can't just stand there and give everyone five years.'

'He'd like that, I bet,' agrees Farmer Büttner.

But the prosecutor has already got to the evaluation of the testimony. 'Detective Inspector Tunk was violently attacked in the press, for observing things that none of the other witnesses had. But this witness did not observe merely *differently*, as a trained criminologist he observed *more precisely*. The prosecution follows the line of his testimony.'

'That's a disgrace,' says Police Sergeant Hart, 'that pig that did nothing but provoke me –'

'You pipe down,' says the perennial Deputy Inspector Emil Perduzke, 'the word of a detective in court is trusted by the prosecutors more than if it had come from God Himself.'

'The witness Tunk saw the defendant Henning take the commander's sabre, and trample on it to render it useless. Then he punched the commander . . .'

'Did Henning really do that?' a surprised Frau Frerksen asks her husband. 'You always told me it was Padberg, Fritz. He stared at you in such a mad way –'

'No names, Anna! For God's sake!' whispers Frerksen. 'My name will be mud –'

* * *

'No clash with State authority has so far been able to deflect the farmers from their course of implacable hostility against the administration. An exemplarily stiff punishment is what is required!' demands the prosecutor.

'Who'd have thunk it,' says Agricultural Councillor Feinbube. 'Now they're going to encourage our feelings for the Red Republic by giving out long spells in prison.'

'The defendants admittedly believed the approach of the police on the marketplace was unlawful. That must be seen as grounds for mitigation . . .'

'It won't be so bad,' says Cousin Benthin. 'Mark my words, he'll just demand a fine.'

'You can't mean that,' says Farmer Kehding-Karolinenhorst, 'when they gave me a week just for my open letter in the bloody *Chronicle*!'

'. . . but the ferocity, yes the sheer ferocity of the defendants in resisting is of course an exacerbating factor . . .'

'Henning should have had rubber heels fitted to his boots. Then he wouldn't have hurt the militia so much when he kicked them,' says syndic Plosch.

'Those lawyers! Those lawyers! The hair-fine distinctions they presume to make!' says the Reverend Thomas, shaking his head in dismay. 'I've heard tell of a case, Herr Plosch . . .'

'. . . the prosecution has no interest in a hefty punishment for the defendants, but . . .'

'This is going to come out dear,' says Trautmann, business manager of the *News*.

'How come?' asks Heinsius, now back in his corner.

'I know that as a man of business,' the tutor of the newspaper mogul Gebhardt opines. 'When I say, "I don't know why I bother about this or that deal", that's my way of saying I intend to make a spectacular profit.'

'The immoderate dislike of Police Commander Frerksen, an able and dutiful official, does not exactly show a spirit of contrition and remorse in the defendants.'

'It was me that bandaged Henning,' says Dr Zenker. 'I saw his arm. If anyone has anything to be remorseful about, then . . .'

'It's a poor lawyer,' says Prison Governor Greve with a gloomy smile, 'who can see both sides of an issue. I should know, I once stood where the prosecutor is now standing.'

'The fact that the police may have been the first to use force is immaterial. The police are allowed to use force.'

'Listen to that, so he can be cheeky as well,' says the weighty Manzow.

'Why in all the world did the accused not surrender their flag willingly? It was a minor matter.'

'I have to say,' opines the station barber Punte, 'if it was me carrying our association banner, and I was supposed to surrender it to that lackey Frerksen in front of all the lads, I think I'd have hit him over the head with it first.'

'Peace will only return once a verdict has been arrived at. Then the farmers will concede that they have been unfair in their boycott of the town of Altholm. There is no doubting the identity of the guilty party, neither in this courtroom nor outside it. In the final analysis, what caused this crime? Why did all this extraordinary misfortune happen? It was because someone wanted to honour a man who had already broken the law, and who was quite rightly in prison! Was this kind of thing in practice earlier?'

The defendant Henning calls out: 'Yes!'

The prosecutor looks at him angrily and disparagingly through his pince-nez. 'No, that was not the practice earlier.'

Henning protests by nodding his head.

The prosecutor has had enough. He gets to the tariffs.

'For the defendant Henning for riotous assembly and breach of the peace, for common assault with a dangerous weapon . . .'

'He must mean his rubber heels,' says Plosch.

'. . . fifteen months in prison . . .

'For the defendant Padberg for riotous assembly and breach of the peace, one year and two weeks . . .'

'For the defendant Rohwer for the same offences and common assault and damage to State property . . .'

'Didn't he tear a policeman's glove . . .?' remembers Stuff.

'. . . twelve months in prison.

'For the defendant Czibulla for riotous assembly and breach of the peace and common assault, twelve months.'

'They have to put Czibulla away,' says Councillor Röstel to Chief Adviser Meier, 'otherwise the town will be liable for damages and medical bills and a lifelong pension.'

'Ach, I'm sure they will,' Adviser Meier assures him, 'these punishments are so moderate, I think they'll just be nodded through.'

'Comrade, if that had been us,' says the KPD functionary Matthies, 'they would have thrown the book at us. We would have got long jail sentences.'

'Sure,' says the recently appointed municipal gardener – grace of Manzow – Matz. 'They won't lay a finger on them. But when it's unemployed workers . . .'

'Those demands are outrageous,' says Revenue Councillor Berg. 'If they'd wanted to, those farmers could have beaten the cops to a pulp.'

'And Henning is a cripple for life. And prison to follow. He's not come out of it too well.'

II

Two hours later, Streiter and Stuff go back to the Hotel Cap Arcona. Behind the pair of them marches Henning, flirting for all he's worth with his counsel's secretary.

The great Berlin lawyer is still glowing with zeal, with the adrenalin from his speech. 'And you really liked my speech, Herr Stuff? Was it really as good as that?'

'Extraordinary, Legal Councillor! Magnificent! The way you proved that even after the public were offended by the flag, it was still the police's duty not to seize it but to protect the flag-bearer, well, I thought that was –'

'Yes,' says the legal councillor self-complacently, 'the poor prosecutor. If he wants to come with precedents and verdicts in comparable cases, then he'll have to start getting up earlier. There's not many people in the whole profession who are so canny as I am.'

'It must take a prodigious memory,' says Stuff adoringly.

'Good God, yes. Of course. And diligence. Application. – And the way I gave it to them, the unwrapped scythe? Of course it hadn't occurred to any of those clowns that Henning had gone to the trouble of cutting off the edge with a pair of metal shears: effectively, it was no longer a scythe!'

'No, Legal Councillor. You couldn't see it from where you were sitting, but the expression on the prosecutor's face –'

'The poor fellow! Well, given that he's normally up against provincial lawyers, he doesn't need to exert himself very much –'

'There's only one drawback, Legal Councillor. If the verdict is pronounced this evening, then your lovely speech will be entirely wasted.'

'Why's that? How come, Herr Stuff?'

'Well, because the papers will only carry the judgment, and not your speech!'

'You're right. One ought to do something, then, to prevent the judgment from being spoken tonight.'

'What if you were to fall ill?'

'No, it doesn't look good. Henning, my lad, listen . . .'

But he needs to call him twice more before Henning will part from his new lady-friend.

Stuff asks: 'What are the chances of your having a nervous breakdown tonight? A proper one, that a doctor will confirm, and that I can report in the paper?'

'Tonight? Before the judgment? Oh, I don't think so. Anyway, we want to go out and have a drink tonight, whatever happens.'

'You could always drink in your room?'

'Oh no! Absolutely not! Today I've got to show myself to the people, lest they think I'm worried.'

A dark shadow has crept up alongside them and come to a stop. 'Excuse me, gentlemen, my name is Manzow, Democratic town councillor. Herr Stuff knows me.'

'That I do! I know you. Yes indeedy.'

'Gentlemen, I'm sorry to be waylaying you on the public street, but I'd like to have a word with you as soon as possible . . . The thing is this: I've tried to get into talks with the farmers about the boycott. They were unwilling at the time, and made monkeys of us.

'Now I'm making a second attempt. Before the verdict, so that you'll see our desire for peace is real. Couldn't we get together somewhere and sort it all out?'

'I believe it,' growls Henning. 'Your desire for peace is perfectly genuine, because you're afraid we'll be acquitted following the councillor's brilliant speech. Then the town will have to pay and pay and pay!'

'Excuse me, Councillor, for not yet having offered you my con-gratulations. I've never heard a speech like yours. I talk a lot myself, I have to, it's part of my job as a local leader . . .' Grunting sheep-ishly: 'The one-eyed man is king in the kingdom of the blind. But I've never heard anything like your closing plea, you know . . .'

Manzow becomes wilder and wilder in his enthusiasm.

'Tell me, gentlemen,' says the legal councillor, 'why not listen to what Herr Manzow has to say? It can't do any harm.'

'No, no. Absolutely not,' says Henning.

'Well then, Herr Manzow,' says the councillor, quite unmoved, 'we'll expect you in an hour at the Arcona. You'll probably find us in the back saloon. Who knows whether it'll come to anything, but . . .'

Manzow offers his profuse thanks and disappears.

'I wonder if that was right?' ponders Stuff. 'As soon as he catches a sniff of compromise he'll come over all insolent.'

'You won't catch me sitting down at a table with that fellow,' says Henning stubbornly.

'In that case I'll do it for you,' says the legal councillor, unmoved. 'I don't know what plans you had, but I want my fee. Why not get the Altholmers to foot the bill. That's much better than the farmers having another whip-round.'

'When you put it that way,' says Stuff.

'And now I'm going to call the court right away and ask that the verdict be put back to tomorrow. I have an important meeting. They won't mind taking the evening off. It could be midnight by the time they get around to the verdict.'

III

It's eleven in the morning. The sports hall is half lit by the wet, murky light of a rainy October day.

Even though the verdict is imminent, for the first time the court is almost empty. The town doesn't yet know it's coming, the Altholm papers don't hit the streets until the afternoon.

Stuff sits glumly at the press desk. His skull is clouded with alcohol.

Last night turned into one hell of a booze-up, and that wretch Manzow bought endless bottles of champagne, that girls' tipple, which gives you a head like a beehive if you mix it with beer and schnapps.

'I can feel every hair on my head,' he moans to Blöcker.

'I'm wondering what we're about to hear,' comes the reply. 'Henning looks a bit pale. I expect he's worried.'

'Worried?' says Stuff derisively. 'He's been puking his guts out since three. Boy, was he tanked.'

The court file in.

This time, the defendants don't sit, they await judgment standing up.

The judge covers his head with the cap and intones: 'In the name of the people, and of justice. The sentences are as follows:

'The defendant Georg Henning for resisting arrest in two instances, to three weeks' detention.

'The defendant Heino Padberg for resisting arrest in one instance, to two weeks' detention.

'The defendant Herbert Rohwer for resisting arrest and actual bodily harm, to two weeks' detention.

'The defendant Josef Czibulla is acquitted.

'The costs of those found guilty are payable by the defendants, otherwise by the State.'

The judge takes a breath, and a ripple goes through the courtroom. People look at each other. The defendants, the sentenced, stand quite still and look at the judge.

He begins with the reasoning behind the verdicts. In the friendly, fatherly tone he maintained throughout the trial, he says:

'Experience has taught one that it is difficult to reconstruct sequences of events like those of the 26th of July . . .

'The essential question is this: Were the Altholm police legally justified in their confiscation and removal of the flag?

'This court is persuaded that their conduct was unjustified in purely *objective* terms. The scythe was no scythe, nor was it a weapon, it was merely a symbol. The demonstrators had the right to carry the flag, the police had no right to take it away.

'On the other hand, this court believes that Frerksen thought he was subjectively in the right when he impounded the flag. He took the flag for a provocation, and thought he would not be able to prevent subsequent clashes. The flag caught him by surprise.

'Henning and Padberg both showed resistance at Tucher's pub, by holding on to the flag.

'The question whether there was a plan or conspiracy must be answered in the negative. On the contrary, both Padberg and Henning did all they could to calm the situation, and carry on with the march.

'Rohwer put up some resistance, and exceeded the bounds of self-defence.

'It has been shown that a number of countrypeople were involved in disorderly conduct around the war memorial, but that would have been significant only if the farmers had been the aggressors. The conduct of the police speaks against that. There is at least a suspicion that Frerksen was not equal to the situation, lost his head, and acted impulsively. He chose the worst possible place to stop the demonstration. He acted with his men without giving them any sort of instructions. The agitation of his officers is easy to understand. They had the benefit of no leadership when they ran to engage the marchers. They started laying about them immediately.

'It has been shown that while Henning was lying on the ground, he did kick out. But at that stage the police were not in the lawful performance of their duty. They had lost all discipline and were lashing out indiscriminately.'

(A big ripple through the hall.)

'The defendant Czibulla had to be acquitted because there was no proof that he approached the officer with any purpose other than to ask for information. The testimony of one witness that he had struck the officer with a stick or umbrella is opposed by the testimony of several other witnesses that he merely shyly tweaked at the jacket of the officer. The terrible blow he received is explainable only in terms of the uncontrolled agitation of the police.'

(Another ripple goes through the hall.)

'The defendants are entitled to mitigating circumstances. Nevertheless, custodial sentences were indicated, because their behaviour could have had dangerous consequences. What further speaks in their favour is that they believed themselves to be in the right. The flag was their emblem. And Henning allowed himself to be badly beaten for the sake of that emblem, which he took very seriously.

'The farmers kept their discipline throughout. Neither the police nor the peasants sought to provoke. Both, through no fault of their own, found themselves in a situation to which they were unequal.

'For reasons given above, the banner is to be returned.

'The condemned are given two years on probation.'

IV

'Congratulations,' Henning whispers to Padberg.

'You can talk,' he says. 'I'm on the hook for the bomb. You'd better flee soon.'

'Later today,' says Henning. 'I'm going to go abroad.'

'Heil Bauernschaft, Comrade.'
'Heil Bauernschaft.'

'Well, satisfied now?' Blöcker asks his mate Stuff.
'Satisfied. Satisfied,' he growls. 'It's another one of those on-the-one-hand, on-the-other-hand, faults-on-both-sides comprom-ise judgments. Objectively the police are in the wrong, but, hey, subjectively they're right. How do I sell a verdict like that to my farmers?'
'Would you rather they were banged up?'
'You bet I would! Put them away for years and years! That would be great propaganda. But something squishy and touchy-feely like this . . .'

'Well, thank you very much,' says Councillor Röstel. 'Now I can call in the dental practitioner Czibulla and ask him what sort of pension he wants from the town.'
'The money's not even the worst of it,' says Chief Adviser Meier. 'Think of my boss, Temborius! Three weeks in prison, and a police force lacking self-discipline. There'll be hell to pay.'
'The prosecution is bound to appeal.'
'And in six months we'll be chewing it over again. As if we enjoyed it!'

'Come on, Annie,' says Commander Frerksen. 'The people are staring.'
'Don't worry, Fritz, the judge said you were in the right. You were right to confiscate the flag.'
'Well, I'm not sure.'
'As for you having lost your head . . . He ought to try standing in front of three thousand farmers to see how he likes it. It's not very hard with the benefit of hindsight. You did very well.'
'Well, I'm not sure. All I want to know now is who my new boss is going to be.'

'I love it,' says Colonel Senkpiel to his Lieutenant Wrede, 'how clueless lawyers are about the damage they inflict on the police

when they have a go at them. It's just the town militia, and Frerksen's a twerp – he really blotted his copybook – but to say that
in front of the public. What's going to happen to our authority?'

'Three weeks and two weeks, what wouldn't you give for a
sentence like that?' says the official Matthies. 'I think, for pinching Frerksen's sabre, I'm going to go down for at least a year.'

'You will too. You will.'

The prosecutor: 'Typical.'

His deputy comforts him: 'It's not necessarily the last word,
this judgment.'

'No, no, of course not. But for the moment we've lost.'

'We should do something right away to show where we stand.'

'Such as?'

'We march straight to the police and confiscate the farmers'
flag all over again.'

'Nice. Very nice. – Chief Adviser Meier, one moment, please.
We intend to show what we think of this judgment, in other
words, to avoid future clashes, we're going to seize the farmers'
flag all over again!'

'Ah, a ray of sunshine,' Meier beams. 'That will delight the
president's heart. So there are still men.'

Epilogue:

Just Like at Circus Monte

I

A week after the verdict was pronounced, the *News* and the *Chronicle*, though not the *Volkszeitung*, carried the following full-page advertisement:

TOWARDS THE RESTORATION OF ECONOMIC PEACE WITH THE FARMERS' UNION!

After the verdict was pronounced in the trial of Farmers' Union leaders, and as there is agreement in principle, we have taken a step towards the end so dear to the hearts of all Altholmers: the promotion of economic peace. There is still one obstacle in our path, and that is the need to raise money to pay for the damages that have occurred. The undersigned therefore appeal to the population of Altholm with the request that they do whatever they can towards raising funds. Not until the promised sum has been raised will economic peace with the farmers' leaders be achieved, and the boycott ended. The committee asks that all participate, to the utmost of their ability.

People of Altholm, don't leave your town in the lurch!

The committee towards the restoration of economic peace. Town Council Leader Manzow. Medical Councillor Dr Lienau. Braun, trader. Dr Hüppchen, certified accountant. Council Member Meisel.

II

However willing Manzow the Children's Friend had found the representatives of the Farmers' Union to swill his champagne on that night before the verdict was handed down, the gentlemen remained unyielding in their demands. But what had seemed perfectly outrageous by candlelight on that chaotic night in the auction hall, today seemed somehow to be discussible.

'But ten thousand marks, gentlemen, that's mad.'

'Well, let's wait a little longer,' says Henning, 'it doesn't have to be now.'

'And what if you're sent down tomorrow?'

'Same deal. Do you think the farmers will drop the boycott if we're put behind bars?'

'I would like to remind you,' says the legal councillor, 'that apart from the payment of ten thousand marks, which is not nearly enough to pay the costs incurred at the trial, there are a whole number of injured farmers who need compensation. There is Henning, crippled for life, there are farmers who were struck with sticks, there is Banz –'

'Banz knocked down a policeman, for God's sake!'

'Well? It was in self-defence!'

'So what's your floor?'

'Thirty-five thousand. All in.'

'Mad.'

Henning drinks and repeats himself: 'Let's wait, then. Where's the rush?'

'Gentlemen, name me a figure . . .'

'One hundred and twenty-three thousand,' suggests Stuff.

'Won't you compromise at all?'

As the number of empty bottles rose, so the prospects of coming to an agreement improved. At four in the morning, a preliminary agreement is signed on a piece of hotel stationery:

One: Return of the flag with all honour, by a prominent citizen of the town.

'That doesn't mean you! Doesn't mean you!' burbles Stuff to Manzow intransigently.

Two: Payment of twenty-five thousand marks within the next fortnight.

'You come expensive, fellows. Cut-throats. But I'll manage it.'

III

It wasn't so easily managed, the expensive business.

Wherever Manzow asked: 'We'd like to do our bit. But the boycott has wiped us out, we're flat broke . . .'

'Maybe the Bakers' Guild . . .?'

'Maybe the retailers . . .?'

'Or the teachers? They're always idealists.'

At the end of six days, Manzow has scraped together just four hundred and sixty-five marks. Within another eight days, they need to have swollen to twenty-five thousand, otherwise the reputation of the great diplomatic conciliator is mud. And in two weeks there are the local elections.

It's dark, it's gloomy, there is no moon either in the calendar or in the sky, when Manzow slinks round to Mayor Gareis's flat.

Gareis doesn't seem at all annoyed. Gareis is perfectly friendly. Gareis even breaks out a bottle of wine.

Then, after Manzow has poured out his grievances: 'You're starting at the wrong end. You can have your reconciliation without it costing a penny. Go out into the country yourself and talk to the farmers. I'll give you the names of the sensible ones you can talk to.'

'Thanks a lot. For them to turf me out and beat me up! Give me the legal councillor and Henning any day!'

'Fine, if you've got twenty-five thousand marks.'

'I don't have a penny. I'm doing all the work.'

'You have to wonder, though, if the farmers will obey their leaders when they turn round and tell them: All right, the boycott's over.'

'Why wouldn't they? If they get the money? Just tell me how I get the money together . . .'

But if Gareis knows, he's not telling. He breaks out more wine, more brandy. He is in a wonderful mood. He talks about the town of Breda, where he's been appointed mayor, about his plans . . .

'You're the clever one again,' Manzow states. 'You clear off and leave us in the shit.'

Gareis says: 'Yes, that's right, I'm clearing off. And leaving you in it. How many times you'll be saying that over the next months and years. Gareis, he was clever, he made a mess, and he left us in it.'

'But isn't it true?' wails Manzow.

'If you weren't so stupid,' says Gareis, 'one could even feel sorry for you.'

IV

But the night visit to Gareis wasn't completely in vain. On his way home through the night, through the darkness, Manzow gets an inspired idea.

That's the way. – He calls the *Bauernschaft*.

'Could one of you come over so that we can discuss the transfer? – Yes, I think we need to make it a bit official. – Herr Stuff? That would be fine. – The money, yes, the money will be there. – Don't believe what the Reds write! Our citizens have once again displayed their generosity. – No, it wasn't at all easy, but *I* managed it. – I think we should do it quite soon. What about next week, three or four days before the local elections? – Saturday, the 17th of October? – Fine. Excellent. I'll expect Herr Stuff then.'

V

'Why are you so suspicious, Stuff?' says Manzow. 'If it wasn't evening now, and after closing time, I'd walk you to the bank right now and show you the twenty-five thousand.'

'I don't believe for one second that you've got together that money. I know my Altholmers! You've got something up your sleeve. You know what, let me talk to the treasurer or the bank manager.'

'Happily. We'll call in a moment. But first I have something I want confess to you –'

'Ah, here we go. I knew the cheese was off.'

'I banged away at Gebhardt. So of the twenty-five thousand, ten thousand are from his pocket.'

'Never.'

'If he can boast about it! I get Meisel to say that Oberbürger-meister Niederdahl had said: "Oh, Gebhardt, he would never contribute, he'll give you fifty marks, tops." Then he wrote out a thousand. – I looked at the number, and then I said: "Why don't you hang another nought on the back of that, Herr Gebhardt. You own a Rolls-Royce, for land sakes. A thousand doesn't sit well with that. Niederdahl will probably chip in a thousand him-self." Well, he groaned at me, but he put another nought on it.'

Stuff grins. 'As it's you telling me, Manzow, I believe you. The only thing that bugs me is that the guy goes to the Riviera, and he's already wondering how to get it back. I don't suppose any of his workforce will be able to look forward to a Christmas bonus.'

'So what we're planning on is this: ten a.m., meet outside Tuch-er's. Procession through the town to the auction hall. Handing over of the flag by Medical Councillor Dr Lienau. All the veterans' asso-ciations to be present. March back through the town, with flag and music. Festive lunch at various hostelries all over town.'

'What about the money?'

'You'll be given that in the auction hall as well.'

'Why not today or tomorrow?'

'Because we don't quite trust you either, Stuff. What if the farmers don't come through, what if they don't do what they're told –?'

'They'll come through.'

'– then I'll be humiliated. Three days before the elections. And I'll be liable for the money.'

'The farmers will come through.'

'Don't you be so suspicious. If I can't pay the money, then I'm the one who loses out. I'm finished in Altholm. I'll be uninsurable.'

'You're right,' says Stuff suddenly. 'You wouldn't be that stupid, Herr Manzow.'

'So now, I think, we should sit together and have a drink in anticipation of the reconciliation. The Arcona does a wonderful pheasant. With juniper berries and some delicious herbs, it's bliss, I tell you, with a sappy, heavy claret –'

'No, thanks all the same,' says Stuff. 'I need to go somewhere first. But I may pop by in a couple of hours' time.'

VI

Stuff walks slowly through the dark town.

Not really any better, he thinks. If anything, worse. Gareis was a swine, but he got things done. Manzow is a swine and he gets nothing done. Not an improvement from the Altholm point of view.

On the dimly lit Stolpe Road, Stuff sees a couple of fellows coming: Well, look who it isn't.

And aloud: 'Good evening, Your Worship.'

Gareis stops. 'And a good evening to you, Herr Stuff. Back in your old stamping grounds?'

'I've no choice. The story with the farmers –'

'Is this peace going to come about, do you think?'

'Yes, I think so. Next week.'

'The money's there?'

'What money?'

'I know, Herr Stuff. Still and all. The twenty-five thousand marks.'

'They're there.'

'Are you actually enjoying all this now, Herr Stuff?'

Stuff slowly raises his red-rimmed eyes to the mayor. 'Enjoying it? Christ no, Your Worship. But a man has to do something. Something other than drinking and womanizing.'

'And you get on with the farmers?'

'Farmers? What do I know about farmers? It's no different to the way things used to be here. Except that they meddle even more.'

'You really ought to come along with me, Herr Stuff,' says the mayor. 'A little industrial town, where nothing ever happens.'

'I'm too old and broken down,' says Stuff. 'I don't see the point of it, not of any of it. I just happen to have a thing against Reds. It's an instinct, I'll never change it. – When are you leaving us, Mayor?'

'Next Saturday.'

'Well, then, I'll bid you farewell.' Stuff gives the mayor his plump hand. 'I wish you all the luck, Mayor.'

'Thank you. And thank you again for that other time. – Good-bye.'

'Well, I doubt it. Evening, gents.'

'Good evening, Herr Stuff.'

VII

Stuff opens the garden gate at 72 Stolper Strasse.

As he walks across the yard, he sees that the windows are dark, even though it's not yet nine o'clock. He feels around in his pockets for some matches.

The door is open, and he walks in.

A voice asks: 'Who is it? Stay away. I don't want to see anyone.'

'Not even me?' says Stuff, striking a match and lighting the lamp.

The room looks terrible. Nothing has been done here for days. Wild, with tangled hair, the woman squats in front of the window. The children, still half dressed, are asleep. The bedding is black.

'Shame about the kids, really,' says Stuff, and lifts a bunch of stuff off the sofa, to make room for himself.

'To have them turn out the way their father did, you mean?' says the woman.

Stuff is patient. After a while he asks: 'Have you got any money left?'

'Don't know. Yes. There's money still. Over a hundred marks.'

'And what's to happen when they're spent?'

'How do I know? Something'll turn up.'

Another pause.

Then: 'So he didn't write?'

And she: 'He won't write.'

'Perhaps he's waiting to get established, so he can send you money?'

'He won't send me money. He'd rather keep it.'

Long silence. Then Stuff says determinedly: 'Now listen to me, Frau Tredup. I've got a three-room flat in Stolpe complete with gas, electricity, bath and all. Two rooms are all fixed up. The removal man will come for your things tomorrow.'

'I'm not going to leave here.'

Stuff continues, unimpressed: 'I'm taking the kids with me right now. I've already de-registered them at school this afternoon. If you want, you can keep house for me, if you don't you can stay here. But the stuff is going.'

'I'm staying here.'

'Wake up, Hans, Grete!' says Stuff. 'We're going to Stolpe. We're leaving.'

The children are awake and keen right away. Clumsily Stuff helps them dress and pack.

The woman sits by the window.

In a sudden bate, Stuff bangs on the table. 'The goddamned son of a bitch! Do you really think he's worth it?'

The woman doesn't budge.

Stuff sighs deeply. 'Well, come on, kids. Say bye-bye to your mother.' And suddenly he is all energy. 'All right, Frau Tredup, get going. Hat, coat. I'm not going to leave you here. The removal men don't need you. We're off!'

All this time, Manzow is sitting in the Hotel Cap Arcona.

That bastard, that bastard of a Stuff isn't coming! Perhaps he went to the bank manager? If he did, then I'm royally fucked.

VIII

The following morning, he knows he's not. He's looking forward to the coming elections with cautious optimism. He won't have to give a speech, but he will have the best propaganda you can have in the world: he will have brokered a peace with the peasants. The 17th is to be the day of conciliation.

On the morning of the 16th Manzow turns the material over to the press: the programme for the day, and what have you. And not even any undue emphasis on yours truly.

At noon on the 16th, Manzow visits Councillor Röstel. Röstel has taken over the Police Department from Mayor Gareis.

Manzow greets him most cordially.

'Well, you know what I'm here for?'

'No, not the foggiest.'

'Well, the farmers' demonstration tomorrow. The procession through the streets. I want to have it announced officially.'

'No idea. What is it?'

'You must have seen our appeal in the papers . . .?'

Manzow reports.

Councillor Röstel's brow darkens. 'Now? Right before the elections? Herr Manzow, what are you thinking of! That's quite out of the question!'

'Why "out of the question"?' Manzow is beaming.

'With every chance of further clashes! Who could authorize such a thing? The farmers and their flag through the streets! Absolutely not.'

'The court established that the flag is lawful and is entitled to police protection.'

'Whatever that means. – Anyway, the prosecution has impounded the flag again.'

'That doesn't matter. I've had a duplicate made. There isn't the least justification for banning it.'

Röstel is becoming more and more agitated. 'I can't believe you want a career in politics! Your plan is completely batty!'

'Why "batty"? Tomorrow the Communists will have their march, and the Reichsbanner, and we Democrats. Plus the party of publicans, the Reichswirtschaftspartei, is having a procession. And the Nazis. And you're saying the farmers should be left out?! Not possible!'

'You know very well what the difference is. There's nothing to discuss.'

'I asked the farmers. They'll be along at ten in the morning. And they will demonstrate, I assure you, Councillor.'

'The farmers will not demonstrate, I assure you, Council Leader.'

Manzow arrives in the editorial office just in time to inspire a fiery leader to the effect that even after so many sacrifices on the part of the population, the town administration of Altholm has set its face against peace. The newly installed Chief of Police Röstel etc., etc. The meritorious Council Leader Manzow was unable . . .

IX

On the evening of the 16th, Manzow is informed that the district president has banned the farmers' demonstration.

Everything's going swimmingly.

Manzow gets his people together, and at six o'clock the next morning he and the entire Reconciliation Committee set off for Stolpe.

The gentlemen are beside themselves. 'Unless the demonstration is allowed, the boycott will go on for all eternity, the farmers won't come another time.'

'And if it's not allowed, what do we do with the money?'

'Then everyone will get back what he paid in,' declares Manzow: 'Of course after our costs have been defrayed.'

At seven o'clock the car pulls up outside the president's villa.

His housekeeper, Klara Gehl, declares that it's impossible to disturb the president *now*. But the gentlemen are in a hurry. At ten o'clock the farmers will be in Altholm.

They are kept waiting outside for half an hour. At the end of that time a sweaty and unshaven Chief Adviser Meier appears. Summoned from bed, so that Herr Temborius will have a witness.

The conversation between the gentlemen is short.

Manzow: 'To our boundless astonishment, President, we heard that you cancelled the planned reconciliation with the farmers.'

Temborius, angrily: 'Yes, that's right. I wouldn't dream of permitting such madness. Bunch of criminals.'

Manzow: 'But all the other protests scheduled for today have been permitted. Is there one law for the farmers, and another for everybody else?'

Temborius: 'Public peace and safety are put at risk by the demonstration.'

Manzow: 'As the representative of the town of Altholm, I take full responsibility for any worker or bourgeois of Altholm who disrupts the demonstration.'

Temborius: 'And if some outsider should behave irresponsibly? No. No. Absolutely not.'

Manzow: 'Some outsider? The police have the power to block the approach roads.'

Temborius: 'I can't be doing with blocking public roads.'

Manzow: 'In that case the economic peace will have been shattered, and Altholm once more facing ruin.'

Temborius: 'National interests take precedence.'

Manzow: 'But the farmers are already on their way.'

Temborius: 'Militiamen will intercept them at the railway station, and see that they are promptly sent back from whence they came.'

Manzow: 'The government position is illegal.'

Temborius, odiously: 'Just leave that to me.'

Manzow: 'Good day.'

Temborius does not reply.

Outside, Dr Hüppchen says in surprise: 'You were really curt with him, Herr Manzow. The president might have been open to some form of compromise.'

'Him? Never. It'd look too much like weakness. Now it all depends on us getting a brilliant write-up in the papers emphasizing our excellent work. The Reconciliation Committee can't survive another defeat.'

'We can do that easily enough.'

'In that case we'll all look good tomorrow.'

'Why tomorrow?'

'Well, those of us on the list of candidates will anyway. Will you go to the farmers' reception at the station?'

'Is there any point? Maybe they'll just demand their money. Which they're not going to get *now*.'

Dr Hüppchen asks: 'Will the boycott continue now?'

'I don't think so. After the farmers have turned out for us once already? I think I've attained my objective.'

X

It's half past nine.

Gareis is taken to the station by Political Adviser Stein.

His wife has gone on ahead, his things have gone on ahead. Now his last and only loyal friend is taking him to the station.

As they walk along the very busy Burstah, a few greet the mayor, many see him and don't recognize him, and many more recognize him and don't see him.

'People are always saying,' says Gareis, 'that we politicians are disloyal. I have to say people give us a pretty good model – well, it'll be better in Breda.'

'Will it?'

'Of course it will. I've learned so much here. Next time I'll do it differently.'

'Differently how?'

'Just altogether. I think differently. I see everything differently. – You'll see. As soon as I park my feet under the desk, I'll bring you in.'

'That would be nice,' says the adviser. And after a while: 'Something I always meant to ask you, Mayor. Do you remember the evening of the demonstration day?'

'Unfortunately,' gruffs Gareis.

'Actually, I don't mean the evening so much as the night. We went for a walk. A shooting star fell.'

'Every chance. There are lots in July and August.'

'And you made a wish. You were going to tell me what it was for.'

'I made a wish, Steiny? Nonsense! I've never wished for anything in my life except work. Even without shooting stars. At the most, in certain extreme hours, for work to go smoothly. But one might as well wish for a perpetual motion engine.'

'You made a wish,' says the adviser stubbornly.

'Don't be silly. If I made a wish, then I've forgotten it. But of course I never made a wish. You will have made one.'

'That's funny,' says the adviser. 'You did make a wish. You wished for something very badly. And you'll never know whether your wish came true or not.'

'There's a mass of things I'll never know in my lifetime, Steiny,' says the mayor. 'It doesn't bother me very much. The things I do know bother me much more.'

They reach the station forecourt. A tidy and orderly forecourt. All the approach roads are occupied by militiamen. The station doors are cordoned off. Messengers dashing self-importantly hither and thither. On one traffic island, Colonel Senkpiel is enthroned among a cabinet of his officers. At his side, in impeccable posture, Commander Frerksen.

'What's going on here?' says the mayor as though electrified. 'I must catch some of this . . .'

And he marches up to the colonel.

'You'll miss your train,' calls the adviser.

'Good morning, Colonel. I may not be mayor any more, but I am interested in this kerfuffle that's going on here. What is going on?'

'Good morning, Mayor. You should be pleased you're leaving. The farmers want to hold another demonstration.'

'The reconciliation, yes,' says the mayor. 'Well . . .?'

'The government has banned the demonstration. We're looking after the reception and safe return of the farmers.'

The mayor stands there, looking pensive.

'Well, well,' he says finally. 'Ha. Well, excuse me, gents. Good morning.'

'Have a good trip!' the colonel calls after him. Frerksen, ignored, slides a finger up to the peak of his cap.

Silently, the mayor walks into the station, buys a ticket, passes through the platform barrier. He seems to have forgotten about his political adviser.

Who walks silently at his side.

There are militiamen on the stairs and on the platforms.

'When is the next train from Stolpe?' Gareis asks distractedly.

'Nine fifty-six.'

'And I leave at nine fifty-nine. I get on the same train after they've got off.'

On the platform are Manzow with a few other gentlemen. Dr Hüppchen waves discreetly. The others don't seem to see their one-time mayor.

The train pulls in. It's madly overcrowded. No sooner are the farmers, a couple of hundred of them, out of their compartments than the militia start in with their chant: 'Move along, please! Clear the platform! Move along, please!' Flanked by two rows of militia the completely bamboozled, baffled herd of farmers make their way towards the stairs. In their ranks, the mayor spots Stuff, Manzow, Dr Hüppchen, Meisel, the cursing medical councillor.

'You'd better hop on, Mayor,' his adviser reminds him.

They disappear.

'Yes. All right,' the mayor sighs.

Then, out of the compartment window: 'Of course it's right that the farmers don't demonstrate today of all days. But they're doing it for the wrong reasons again. All of them. Every one. Manzow. Temborius. The farmers. Not for the sake of the thing itself. There's always some nasty little ulterior motive.'

'I've just seen Stuff,' says the adviser. 'You know, six months ago, everyone was so mad at him, because he'd trashed a little circus. The performance was rubbish, but that wasn't why Stuff gave them a bad review, but because the circus director had failed to take out an ad in the paper.

'I was just reminded of that.'

'That's right,' says the mayor. 'That's just it. Spot on. And I too played my part in the Circus Monte, and I was just as bad as the others.'

'Not just as bad, Mayor, not just as bad.'

The train moves off.

'Yes. Oh yes. Just as bad.'

'But in Breda it will all be different, yes?'

'Let's hope so!' shouts Mayor Gareis, already ten yards along the platform. '*I* hope so very much.'

Notes

p. 19 *my blue cuckoo stamp*: Widely used jocular term for the government mark put on confiscated property, no doubt because the cuckoo usurps the nests of other birds. 'Zum Kuckuck!' or 'Geh zum Kuckuck!' are mild expletives in German.

p. 32 *their black-white-and-red banner*: From 1871 to 1918 and again from 1933 to 1945 – the periods when there was a German 'Reich' – black, white and red horizontal stripes were the colours on the flag; they were a heavy presence in Nazi iconography; during the Weimar Republic, they were used by anti-republican Monarchist and Nationalist elements to express anything from nostalgia to murderous hatred.

p. 57 *Bauernschaft*: Literally, farmers as a group or movement; Fallada's equivalent for the historic 'Landvolk' movement of the late 1920s in northern Germany, on whose leader Claus Heim the character of Reimers is based; italicized, it is the title of their newspaper.

p. 66 *the big S*: Syphilis?

p. 71 *the Kapp Putsch*: The Kapp Putsch was a 1920 coup attempt – from the anti-Versailles, Monarchist Right – to overthrow the nascent Weimar Republic. Perduzke's loyalty to the government – against his own personal politics, perhaps – entitles him, in his view, to a better job.

p. 112 *his 'Solingen assistant'*: Solingen is an industrial town in North Rhine Westphalia, known for the manufacture of high-quality steel; the UK counterpart is Sheffield. The handy 'assistant' would therefore be a pair of scissors.

p. 141 *Stahlhelm*: This veterans' organization, the 'league of front-line soldiers', was the largest of the numerous paramilitary groupings that sprang up after the defeat of the First World War and bedevilled the Weimar Republic throughout its brief existence. In 1930, it had as many as half a million members. Politically, it lined up with the National People's Party (DNVP) in the so-called 'Harzburger Front' of Right-wing opposition to the Republic. In 1934, it was assimilated by the Nazis into the SA (Sturm Abteilung (Storm Section), brown-shirted paramilitary force of the Nazi Party, established in 1921).

p. 143 *Basedow*: Or Graves' disease: symptoms include hyperthyroidism, ophthalmopathy and mental symptoms. Part of Fallada's descriptive arsenal (two characters in *Alone in Berlin* are also sufferers).

p. 173 *'Fridericus Rex'*: 'Fridericus Rex, unser König und Herr', 1837 setting by Carl Loewe (1796–1869) of words by Willibald Alexis, glorifying the (anti-French) campaigns of Frederick the Great;

p. 173 *the 'Deutschlandlied'*: ('Deutschland, Deutschland, über alles . . .'), Hoffmann von Fallersleben's (1798–1874) 1841 words to a melody of Joseph Haydn's which, ironically, was first composed as a birthday song for the Austrian Emperor Francis II, in 1797, and called the 'Gott erhalte'. It first became popular among German troops in the First World War. Once Austria ceased to be an empire, following the ousting of the Habsburgs in 1919, the anthem, so to speak, fell vacant. Its use as a German national anthem was conceded by the German President Friedrich Ebert in 1922 to Right-wing pressure (they were denied their flag, but given their song). The Nazis sang its territorially expansionist first stanza; the Federal Republic, after 1952, sang its abstract and idealistic third.

p. 173 *the song of the Jewish Republic we don't want*: This is the perfectly repellent ('grease the guillotine with the fat of Jews') SA adaptation of another nineteenth-century original. The refrain is: 'Blut muss fließen knüppelhageldick / und wir scheißen auf die Freiheit dieser Judenrepublik.'

p. 173 *Reichsbanner*: The 'Reichsbanner Schwarz-Rot-Gold' ('Black, Red, Gold Banner of the Reich') was a Social Democratic paramilitary force formed during the Weimar Republic in 1924.

p. 251 *Reichswirtschaftspartei*: *Recte*, the 'Reichspartei des deutschen Mittelstandes', the 'imperial party of the German middle classes', generally known as the 'Wirtschaftspartei' (WP) the 'economic party'.

p. 310 *Reichswehr*: The so-called provisional German army – when, under the terms of the Treaty of Versailles, it wasn't supposed to have a real one. Unusually for a Weimar institution, this 'army in denial' stayed out of politics. Banz will have been impressed by its small, elite character, but revolted by its loyalty and lack of anti-State ideology.

p. 390 *Centre Party*: An actual party – see the election result tables in the Appendix.

p. 391 *Volkspartei*: The so-called people's party, yet another nationalist, right-of-centre outfit, in this fissile and volatile period. Later incorporated – like all those (the Communists, the Socialists) that weren't banned – into the Nazi Party.

p. 471 *Kaiser Friedrich only lasted ninety-nine days*: This is Friedrich III (1831–88), the son of Wilhelm I, under whose long reign Germany was unified in 1871. Friedrich married the daughter of Queen Victoria (also Victoria), and was succeeded by Wilhelm II, who took Germany into the First World War. There are photographs of father and son, both in kilts, at Balmoral. He died of cancer of the larynx; the saying 'lerne zu leiden ohne zu klagen' – 'suffer in silence' – is attributed to him.

p. 500 *a snatch of something*: Fallada liked his songs. This is the 1836 song – to a folk melody – by the organ-builder Gottlieb Weigle (1810–82), 'Drunten im Unterland', hymning the Neckar valley. 'Down in the lowlands, things are nice as can be / whins in the highlands, vines in the lowlands / down in the lowlands, that's the place for me.' Stein seems to be warning his boss that things can't continue to go well for ever.

Appendix

German Parties and Elections in the Late Weimar Period

A Small Circus makes great play with political parties of the period. It seems almost surprising that, with so many characters in political office and at various levels of government, and so many scenes of politicking, deal-making and demonstration-tending-to-riot, it has no actual election in it; perhaps because it wouldn't have added much in terms either of disorder or direction: things – in the book, as in reality – wouldn't have become greatly better, or much worse. Weimar politics were distinguished by the number of parties, the virulence of their hatreds – especially internecine hatreds: the ones with most in common often the worst (the historic rift between the Socialist SPD and the Communists (KPD) is only the best known) – and the instability of the resulting coalition governments. One reason post-1945 Germany has its 5 per cent threshold of representation is to avoid any repetition of the Weimar-style fissuring of politics. Here are two tabulated sets of election results, the one from 1928, the year before the events Fallada based his novel on, and one from 1930, the year before it was published. The continual weakness of the centre is apparent, as is the way the Nazis (NSDAP) drew strength from conservative and nationalist ('völkisch') parties. In January 1933, they went on to become the biggest party, and took over the government (the so-called 'Machtergreifung'), although they never secured a majority in a fair democratic election. The names towards the bottom of each list, with their small-to-insignificant representations, emblematize both the seething, wriggling drama and the deep mistakenness of the events Fallada describes: the idea of radicalizing the countryside, and harnessing it to a single, rural, conservative, nationalist party.

German Federal Election Results in 1928

Social Democratic Party of Germany (SPD)	29.8%
German National People's Party (DNVP)	14.3%
Centre Party (Z)	12.1%
Communist Party of Germany (KPD)	10.6%
German People's Party (DVP)	8.7%
German Democratic Party (DDP)	4.8%
Reich Party of the German Middle Class (WP)	4.5%
Bavarian People's Party (BVP)	3.1%
National Socialist German Workers Party (NSDAP)	2.6%
Christian-National Peasants' and Farmers' Party (CNBL)	1.9%
Right-Wing People's Party	1.6%
German Farmers' Party (DBP)	1.6%
Agricultural League	0.7%
German-Hanoverian Party (DHP)	0.6%
Sächsische Landvolk	0.4%
Other	2.7%
Total	100.0%

German Federal Election Results in 1930

Social Democratic Party of Germany (SPD)	24.5%
National Socialist German Workers Party (NSDAP)	18.3%
Communist Party of Germany (KPD)	13.1%
Centre Party (Z)	11.8%
German National People's Party (DNVP)	7.0%
German People's Party (DVP)	4.5%
Reich Party of the German Middle Class (WP)	3.9%
German Democratic Party (DDP)	3.8%
Christian-National Peasants' and Farmers' Party	3.1%
Bavarian People's Party (BVP)	3.0%
Christian Social People's Service (CSVD)	2.5%
German Farmers' Party (DBP)	1.0%
Conservative People's Party (KVP)	0.8%
Right-Wing People's Party	0.8%
Agricultural League	0.6%
German-Hanoverian Party (DHP)	0.4%
Other	0.9%
Total	100.0%

* Statistisches Reichsamt (Hrsg.): Statistics of the German Reich.

Acknowledgements

The translator wishes to thank the Goethe Institute and the Alfred Toepfer Stiftung for a residency at Siggen in Holstein (Fallada country!) where the translation was completed, and to record a personal debt to the late Frau Birte Toepfer, an embodiment of gallantry and grace: I barely knew her, but I miss her.

It was a delight to work with Sarah Coward again, who edited the manuscript with sweetness and reason.